TO MARRY AND SUSPECT

Ellen Anthony

LN Books Limited

The characters and events portrayed in this book are fictitious. Any similarity to real persons, living or dead, is coincidental and not intended by the author.

First published in 2013
Revised 2023
Copyright © 2013 Ellen Anthony
All rights reserved.

Published by LN Books Limited
4500 Cannon Avenue #63
Klamath Falls, OR 97603

Paperback ISBN-13: 978-1-948168-11-3

*For Gracee Andel who keeps me young
and for Carey who listens to my
brainstorms.*

Table of Contents

Prologue

"How the hell did my brother end up dead in police custody?" Wilson Kucera thundered.

The lawyer in front of him visibly quaked, his hands clenching on his briefcase. He had not been invited to sit down.

"Well?" Wilson demanded. "Speak up. Was it murder? Can I get the sons of bitches?"

"No sir," the lawyer said. "Suicide. Maybe accidental but they're saying suicide."

Wilson shot a look at Mark Baxter, his vice president of special affairs, and responded. "My brother didn't have the guts for suicide. Give me details."

His tone was almost level, his only irritation showing now in the clipped words. The lawyer looked relieved but shouldn't have been. Others knew he was more dangerous when controlled and Wilson made a habit of controlling himself, his people, and his company.

"No one was in his cell," the lawyer said. "I've seen the footage. He took Bliss and laid down to sleep and died. They're still working on the autopsy. They've never seen anything like it."

"I bet they haven't," Wilson muttered. He considered having the autopsy halted but rejected it as too hard. Chances are they wouldn't find what they were looking for anyway. Even his own chemists had trouble detecting the inert compound that reacted with Bliss. How the hell had Ed gotten it?

"Ed didn't have the guts for suicide," Wilson repeated. "I want to know who saw him besides you and what cops were there. Someone slipped him some poison. That had to be it."

"Yes sir." The lawyer said.

"Did he leave anything?" Wilson demanded.

"Yes sir—a confession. I immediately moved to suppress it. It's sealed."

"A confession?" Wilson's lips tightened. "To what? He was up to his eyeballs in NOTHING."

"I haven't been able to read it, sir. No one except the officer who responded to the alarm has even glimpsed it. I had to suppress immediately to keep it that way." The lawyer looked shaken. "What do you want me to do?"

Wilson glanced at Baxter then thought. Chances are the confession had nothing to do with him or his affairs but he didn't know that for certain. It would also look odd if this half-assed lawyer backtracked and allowed it to be read without a hell of a fight—and he needed time to find out what his brother had been up to.

"Let it play out," Wilson said. "If the judge allows that confession, I want it in my hands in the same hour. You got that?"

"Yes sir," the lawyer replied. "Am I to mention your name?"

"Hell, no," Wilson said, his words clipped and angry. "You work for my brother. If he's not alive, you work for his widow. You aren't on my payroll."

"Yes sir." The lawyer bowed his head, unable to meet his eyes.

"Get out."

Wilson waited till the door was firmly closed before turning on Baxter. "What was he charged with again?"

"The murders of Jake West, Michael West, and Elizabeth West," Baxter said. "Elizabeth West was the problem."

"I remember now," Wilson said. "I want you out there personally. Find out who killed my brother and get answers."

"Yes sir," Baxter replied, his expression wooden.

"I want him cleared," Wilson said. "My brother was an idealistic fool but he was my brother."

Chapter 1 - Saturday, 30 Oct 2179

Jasper Stone studied himself critically in the mirror, his nerves on edge as he checked his midnight blue shirt and the four-pointed star he wore. Maybe he should have worn a tux after all but he knew it was far too late to change. The blue shirt with its white jacket and matching blue pants were striking enough. Was his hair okay? Of course it was. He eyed his dark brown hair and brows with a critical eye, wishing this day was over.

"You look fine," David West said then brushed some imaginary lint off his jacket. "Like that Sensor Man character you insist on being."

Jasper looked at him. His new in-law was dressed the opposite of him in a blue suit with white shirt. "Hadn't you better get moving before the women throw a fit?"

"I'm almost ready," David said. He ran a quick comb through his thinning hair. "I don't think I've ever done double duty at a wedding. Did anyone ever tell you your best man is also your protector according to the old traditions? I thought I was just going to give my niece away."

"Well, you've been trying to give her away for months. It's about time you did it in public."

"Right," David said. "Just remember I don't want her back. No more bullets." David smiled and opened the door in time to let Lori Brown in.

Jasper wondered why his old partner was here with him instead of with his bride until he saw the tiny box in her hand. "You got it?"

"Yes, just in time," Lori said. She poked her bouquet at the nearest man and opened the box to show him. Inside was a flat round image of the two most important women in his life.

"Perfect," Jasper said and reached in his pocket for his tweezers. "Be right back." Taking the image into the small bathroom, he carefully put a paper towel over the sink drain. Taking the star locket off his chest he turned it over to expose the picture of his first wife. It took just a few seconds to pry off the cover and remove the photo but he did it with care. The last thing he wanted to do was lose the microchip stored beneath it.

The picture of Carol had been a sore point with his wife-to-be. She'd wanted to replace it with one of her but hadn't dared ask. Lori had hit on the perfect solution. The next time Jewel turned this locket over she would see herself. Carol was still there in the background and she was smiling at Jewel. His precious Jewel with her chestnut hair was in the foreground and smiling at him. The two of them had never met in life but he knew Carol would thoroughly approve of his new wife. He hoped he could make her as happy as Carol had been.

The sliver of microchip didn't wobble as he replaced the picture. He hadn't lost it–his one concern on replacing the picture. It was far too important to his life and he couldn't entrust this locket to anyone else's care. He hoped he'd never have to tell Jewel about his DEA credentials or his work for them as a deep cover agent.

"Jazz, they need you," he heard through the closed door.

"Time, huh? Tell them I got nerves," Jasper said to his publisher but he hurried anyway, getting the cover securely on and the locket back around his neck. He'd have to scan it later but he knew the chip was still there. Slipping the old picture of Carol in the tiny gift box, he put it in the lock box with his com unit. Maybe he'd give the old picture to his daughter with a locket of her own.

"Lori left?" He glanced around the room but only Milt Anderson and his other college buddy, Troy Campbell, were there.

"She flew out of here pretty quick," Troy said. "What did she bring?"

Jasper flipped his locket and held it for them to see.

"Nice," Troy said. "That should keep you out of the doghouse."

"Maybe," Jasper said and flipped it back. "Let's get this done."

* * *

The wedding march began to play when he took his place by the altar and he was suddenly struck by the size of the cathedral, the crowd, and what was about to happen. Swallowing nervously, he steadied himself. God, maybe he shouldn't have insisted Jewel do this. It was overwhelming.

The Plains Cathedral was packed with people, most of whom he barely knew. Besides the reporters discreetly filming the wedding event of the year, there were family, friends, business acquaintances, West Foundation people and a bunch of movie stars he'd never met. Scattered through their number were also members of Reach Out, a charity he had a keen professional interest in. That didn't matter right now. What mattered were the women coming up the aisle toward him.

He forced himself to focus on his grown-up daughter. Lovely in white with red trim, Melody flashed him a shy smile as she stepped carefully down the aisle as Jewel's maid of honor.

After her came Lori Brown in a similar dress then Elinor West as Jewel's matron of honor. Her other aunt, the actress Jessica West, had chosen not to take her place in the line although she was listed in the program. Jasper could appreciate her reasoning. This was Jewel's day and the reporters were apt to forget that when Jessica West appeared.

Last came his precious Jewel on the arm of her uncle. She was radiant in white, the only red being the carnelian and red jasper necklace trimming her bodice. That had been his contribution to her finery and it looked wonderful but not as fine as the throat it adorned. God, she was beautiful. He knew every inch of that luscious girl but today she was truly his. He'd better not miss his lines.

Receiving Jewel from her uncle, he was aware of David West slipping into his place as his best man—his other role in this wedding—but after that his attention was solely on his bride and the preacher and the traditional vows they recited. Once they were pronounced man and wife, he casually flipped the locket and saw his wife's eyes widen then she was in his arms.

"Public, Jewel," he muttered against her hungry lips as she tried to make the kiss last. DAMN, SHE'S HOT. He firmly set her back on her feet and turned her to face the gathered guests.

"You're mine," she whispered, her blue eyes dancing. "Forever and ever."

"Don't I know it," he replied and raised her hand to his thin lips. Giving it a long kiss, his brown eyes held hers. It was all for the photographers but he meant every word he said. Jewel West was his forever more.

* * *

"You are one sexy man, Jazz Stone," Jessica West said as she showed him where to stand for the photographers. "When that hand kiss hits the news, you're going to start a whole new fashion."

Jasper took it in stride, knowing Jessica West didn't really envy Jewel or him. Her beau was discreetly out of range of the photographers but he was here.

"Jewel, that jasper necklace really makes that dress," Jessica said. "It's just enough color to draw attention to what you have."

"Thanks, Aunt Jessica," Jewel said with a sideways look at Jasper. "It's real red jasper you know," she said in a voice loud enough to be heard. "For my husband." She turned to him and bobbled on her heels.

Jasper caught her. "You can lose the heels now."

"Help me," she said and he obediently knelt to remove one heel and heard the predictable whir of cameras.

Were they going to be at this all day? Jasper held the pose and he supposed it looked like he was helping her get her shoe on. He was beginning to ache for a quiet room with just Jewel for company.

It had to be done. His new persona as a star musician invited all this publicity—and he really was Sensor Man. Even if he wasn't, the story of the cop marrying the girl who saved his life would probably get him as much attention in the world of bored readers. Since they couldn't fight it, he'd done his best to control it.

Other poses were suggested by their photographer and family crowded around in the now quiet church, the guests having moved on to the reception hall. Almost everyone was there. Sasha West would be digitally added to a couple of special shots just for her. She was still more than a month from Mars and would never be on Earth again. Her parents were here though and would see she got the vid.

"No more stone face, Jazz," Jessica said. "We need a really good animated smile. Jewel, perk him up."

Jasper eyed his bride suspiciously, wondering exactly how far she'd go in this public room. His lips twitched as she leaned closer but he fought the urge to smile. Make her work for it.

Jewel looked up at him with those beautiful blue eyes and her lips parted to show even white teeth. "I've got just the thing," she said and pulled his head closer to whisper in his ear. "Let's do this again tomorrow."

Jasper's look of horror wasn't feigned and the photographers caught it. Damn her. He did the only thing he could and swept her off her feet in one long and passionate kiss, one arm around her waist and the other crushing her veil against the back of her head. He held the pose till his back ached then carefully set her back on her feet.

"Never again," he fiercely whispered. God, he hoped they hadn't caught what she said. No, of course, they hadn't. Well, he was sure Jewel wouldn't tell them her little joke. He'd discovered his wife had a talent for handling journalists and actually enjoyed playing with them. How long ago had she thought up that line? He'd probably never know.

"Thank you, Mr. Stone and Mrs. Stone," Rex Allen called from the pool of reporters and he led the exodus of actual journalists out of the cathedral. Finally it was mostly family.

"Now for those special shots," Jessica was saying. "Where's our stand-in? Oh, there you are." She smoothly ushered the model in her matron of honor gown into position with the rest of the wedding party. "Don't worry about facial expression, dear. Your face will be edited out."

Sasha's parents, Ivan and Molly, took their places with Jasper and his bride and their stand-in daughter. They made it look good even though they'd only met the model that morning. Her height, weight, and coloring were the same as their missing daughter's.

Jasper gave the model a warm look then Jewel embraced her for another quick shot. Hopefully, these would help Sasha get over her disappointment at not being here.

"No business with the bouquet," Jessica said, turning down the photographer's suggestion that the model hold it. "No, that would not be appropriate." Her voice had an edge to it and Jasper knew why. Damn.

"I think we're done," Jessica suddenly said. "Thank you, Miss Griffin, for standing in. You did a wonderful job."

"My pleasure," the model said. "I'll just change if you're done with me."

"I'll help you," Molly Kowalski said. "That dress isn't easy to get out of." She followed her stand-in daughter to the changing room.

David had taken over speaking to the photographer, letting Jessica have her own private moment with her beau.

"The bouquet business got her," Jewel quietly said to him. "I didn't expect that either."

"None of us did," Jasper said and hugged his wife. Sasha was a widow, not a wife, and her husband was also missing from this family affair. No one had suggested a stand-in for the missing Jake or for Uncle Mike or Grandmother Elizabeth. They were all dead and the grief was far too fresh yet for flippancy. No, Sasha was alive and on her way to Mars. Including her was for her comfort. The others were gone.

Jasper buried his face in his wife's hair, dimly aware it smelled like apples. Three murders, three members of the West family gone but he had met Jewel when all odds were against it and she'd chosen him as her protector and her mate. Hell, she'd chased him till he finally said yes. Now she was legally his and there was no way her uncle would ever get her back. He married for keeps.

Chapter 2 - 31 Oct 2179

Cold. Jasper sipped his coffee and studied the snowy silhouette of Laramie Peak. The morning was that dull iron gray that foretold bad weather and he was thankful he wouldn't have to deal with it. Unless he chose to go out, he'd stay warm inside the city.

The orchards that stretched out from horizon to horizon had sprouted color and that he found fascinating. He'd seen pictures of fall foliage and even walked under autumn trees a few times but he had never seen the trees as they started to change. The closest tree had a branch here and there with yellow leaves but the rest of the tree was still green. No doubt today's cold weather would change that.

Damn, he liked this view. He'd spent most of his career, eighteen years of it, living in a windowless apartment in the city's underground and hadn't even known what he was missing. Now after just three months, he'd developed a habit of having his morning coffee right here where he could see Laramie Peak.

Most of all, he liked the peace the scene gave him. He couldn't hear the birdsong from outside without help but he'd discovered Jewel's family had installed microphones to pipe that in. There were also air vents to bring in the crisp outside air on autumn mornings. He didn't normally like being cold but he did like the way Jewel snuggled up to him when the bedroom was chilly.

His lips curled upwards as he remembered this morning. Last night they'd been too tired to celebrate their legal union but Jewel had ambushed him at the crack of dawn—not that he hadn't enjoyed it. His cheeks reddened and he laughed. That girl had an appetite and she was anything but passive in her lovemaking. Once she had him in her clutches, she gave it her all. It had been disconcerting at first but now he enjoyed her honest lust for him and was glad he'd been blessed with enough to satisfy her.

Half tempted to call her back upstairs for a repeat performance, he resisted. There was company coming and Jewel was whipping up something in the kitchen. Maybe later.

The reception had been fairly short for them. Following Jessica's guidance, they had stayed for two hours and accepted the good wishes of their guests. There'd been no gifts to unwrap since they'd made it known they would appreciate all gifts to go to Reach Out, Jewel's favorite charity but there had been people to meet and be polite to. Jasper had fielded four suggestions he give a public concert by referring them to his publisher. He never did live performances and Milt knew it.

When the two hours were done, he and Jewel and the other family members had left the reception for a private dinner at the Grand. Along the way he'd made his planned escape with Jewel and they'd come home. The photographers waiting at the Grand wouldn't be rewarded with him. Their dinner had been home cooked and much better than even the excellent service of the Grand.

Here they were private. The ownership of the West mansion had always been shielded behind corporate records so neither his nor Jewel's name appeared on the property records. It doubled the taxes on the house but was well worth it for the privacy it afforded. Reporters and his fans couldn't easily locate where they lived.

Where was Lori? He frowned as he glanced at the clock. Eight-thirty. If Jameson wanted to make the ten o'clock train, they'd better get here. Almost on the heels of that thought, he heard a soft chime and the voice of his security system said "Detective Brown is at the door, sir. She is expected? She's not alone."

"Let her in," Jasper said. "Both of them. Silent record mode."

"Yes sir." Butler responded.

Jasper knew this was a semi-social visit and there was no need to record it but he was still checking the improvements on his new security system. Butler could silently record any activity in the house as well as lock and unlock doors and notify him of arrivals. That last was the most important since the West mansion encompassed three floors and had such good acoustics that noise didn't travel from floor to floor.

This third floor was mostly his. His music studio was here but Jewel's pool table and the master suite shared the floor. His wife, he smiled when he thought the word, had long ago taken over the second floor. She spent almost as much time on the third floor now but the second floor with its four bedrooms, sitting room and playroom, had been hers for most of her life. The first floor, which opened into the city proper, contained the kitchen, the maid's room and bath, the dining room, a more formal living room, and a couple of rooms that had long since been regulated to storage.

It was far too much house for just the two of them but Jasper knew it wouldn't be just the two of them for long. His wife was determined to make it three just as soon as she could—not that he had any objections. Now that the knot was properly tied, he'd be even more cooperative.

"Company," he muttered and steered his thoughts away from his marital obligations just as they stepped off the stairs.

"Jewel is busy baking something that smells delicious," Lori Brown said. "A quiche? I think we have a few before she comes up."

"Good," Jasper said. "Let's get down to business then."

The Denver PD detective had worked with him briefly on the Executioner case. Like Jasper, he was near forty and looked fit but there the resemblance ended. Where Jasper was only lightly tanned and boasted thick brown hair, Jameson had the deep tan of a man who spent too much time above ground. It was to be expected since Denver was still half old town and Jameson's duties tied him to the old town. There was simply more crime there and more need for a homicide detective.

"It's good to see you again," Jasper said, quickly shaking hands. "And I'm glad you made it to the wedding."

"It was nice to see something good come out of that mess," Jameson said. "Nice house."

"One of the motives for the murders," Jasper said and motioned toward the glass door that gave such a wonderful view of the Peak. "Uncontrolled access to the city. No inspection station."

"Right," Jameson said. Like Jasper he knew how much smugglers would be willing to risk for such a prize, especially in a city like Plains where uncontrolled entrances were rare. "You haven't fixed that?"

"Better locks, cameras, and access limited to family and a few select friends," Jasper said. "We're actually testing new security systems with it."

"Good idea," Jameson said. "Well, we'd better get down to business before," he nodded toward the stairs. "It's old business but very strange."

"Oh?"

"Detective Brown told me you have a copy of that last visit to Kucera before he committed suicide. Can I get one? It's disappeared out of the police net."

"Disappeared?" Jasper asked, surprised. "How could that happen?"

"Hell if I know," Jameson said. "Kucera's lawyer asked to see it and it was gone. When we checked the logs for who had seen Kucera, the visitation log had been altered too. There's no record of that last visit. I know it happened and the detention officer knows it, but there's no official record."

"Did you give the name to Kucera's lawyer?" Jasper asked, intrigued. "Has this ever happened before?" He knew electronic storage wasn't infallible but the police net was supposed to be secure. For something this important to go missing was unheard of.

"It's never happened before and, no, I didn't give him his name. With a breach this big, it's better not to tell anybody what you know-and Wilson Kucera might have made it happen," Jameson said.

"But you're telling us," Jasper said.

"I gave Brown that record. If I want it back, I have to."

"But you need my copy," Jasper said, his frown deepening. "Lori, what's going on?"

"It's not in our police net either," Lori Brown replied. "I checked a couple of days ago and so did the captain. Our net techs have gone through backups looking for it but it's been gone more than three months."

"So I have the only copy?" Jasper thought that was interesting. "Hold on."

Going into the master suite, he opened the hinged painting that covered the wall safe and put his hand on the glossy black surface. Tapping out a pattern with his fingertips, he waited for the safe to acknowledge him. The delay was infinitesimal before the screen went green and he could open it. Ignoring the stack of paper money, he picked up a tray of flashers and pulled out the one he needed.

"If there's a possibility the net is compromised, I'd better copy it here," he said on returning to the main room. Ignoring the vid panel, he crossed to his computerized music equipment. He knew that was secure. It took him only a moment to stick a blank flasher in the copy slot. Ten seconds later, the file was copied and he popped it out.

"Sure that's the one?" Jameson asked. "Can you shut down internet here?"

"Butler, isolate vid screen three from system," Jasper said then had a thought. "Is Jewel listening?"

"Yes sir," Butler responded.

Jasper tried not to sound irritated at his wife's curiosity. "Police business, Jewel. Shut it down."

Without waiting for a response, he turned to blank the windows only to find Lori had beat him to it. They'd done this enough times in the past three months that she knew the routine.

"Butler, block all communication from this floor," Jasper said. "Report when secure."

"Secure, sir."

Jewel hadn't liked it when he insisted that her uncle's creation have overrides even she couldn't break but she'd helped him do it anyway. He'd agreed she could do the same to block him out on the second floor.

Finally satisfied all was secure, he placed Jameson's copy of the flasher in the vid slot and pulled up the file. An instant later they were watching the vid tape of Kucera's last visitor before he died.

The bearded form of Professor Andrew Nugent was just entering the cell and it was clear Kucera knew him but there was no overture of friendship. They stood well apart.

Edward Kucera had lost his professional polish, his street clothes having been changed for the orange coveralls all prisoners wore. His profile was haggard as he greeted his visitor.

"Drew? Why you?" he demanded then cleared his throat. "Why did you come?" His hand made a quick motion and the professor turned toward the camera.

"Is it on?" the professor asked.

"Probably," Kucera said. "I'm on suicide watch." He barked laughter. "Fools."

"I see," the professor said. "Well, you should be. I just found out you'd been arrested. What the hell were you doing? The West family..."

"What are you talking about?" Kucera quickly interrupted. "Jake was my client. I would have to be insane to have anything to do with his murder. He was worth too damned much to me—you know how hard I worked to get him that sponsorship."

The professor peered at him, his hand stroking his bearded chin. "Well, in 23 hours it'll be over. The judge waits."

"23?" Kucera froze, his face visibly pale. "23 hours?"

"That's what I'm told," Drew said without moving. "23 hours. You have an appointment."

"Why you?" Kucera was sitting on his bunk now, his back to the camera. "Why you?"

"My book," Drew said and his face was grim. "You know how I hate scandal but you used me and my book. I was questioned." He stood implacable. "I can't forgive that."

"It wasn't me," Kucera said. "I swear it wasn't."

"Then who?" the professor asked, his hesitation almost unnoticeable. "Give me a name."

"I can't," Kucera said.

"No, you can't," the professor repeated. "23 hours."

"Elaine will stand by you," the professor said. "She doesn't know."

Kucera cleared his throat. "Drew, I'm not guilty. You have to know that. Mike, Elizabeth..."

"I don't know what to believe," the professor said. "Jake named you. They'll find out and they must not know."

"Damn you," Kucera said in a voice so low that the microphone nearly didn't pick it up.

The professor either didn't hear or ignored it. "I'll look after Barry. He's got a head for history."

There was a long pause where neither spoke then Kucera stood up. "Thank you for coming. I'll think of you every time I pick up a book."

"Do that." The professor turned and called out to the guard. An instant later he was gone and Kucera was back on his bunk, his head in his hands.

Jasper studied that scene again, still struck by the bluntly delivered order to suicide. That's clearly what it was but why? Ed Kucera had written his own confession before doing it so it wasn't to cover up his crimes. What did he know? And how was the professor tied in?

"We haven't pulled the professor into an interrogation room," Brown was saying. "We've left him alone so far because we're hoping he'll lead us deeper into the blissex organization. There's clearly something there."

Jameson reset the vid and watched the interview again. "Did you catch Kucera denying that about a book? What book?"

"That was a decoy," Jasper said. "We got a tip that a package the professor was receiving had blissex in it. While we were watching the package, the blissex was actually coming in by another route. We know how it was done now but not who diverted us to the professor. If it wasn't Kucera, we may never know who."

"So what was in the package?" Jameson asked.

"Just a book," Jasper said. "A kid's picture book about a monkey."

"Curious George," Brown said, supplying the name. "It's a pretty pricey collector's item. The professor was not happy to have it stolen from out in front of him."

"If he was willing to deliver an order to suicide, he must have hated it and him," Jameson said. "What I can't figure out why this vid disappeared so completely. Our net is supposed to be impervious."

"What about Kucera's confession?" Jasper asked. "Is that still in evidence?"

"Apparently," Jameson said. "The lawyer has all but lost in his move to suppress it. There's supposed to be a decision this week."

Jasper thought that curious. The confession could damn not only Kucera but others and it still existed. The vid of the professor didn't. Why was one more important than the other? Anyone who could hack the police net should have been able to get rid of both unless....

"Is that confession still only on paper?" Jasper asked. "Locked up in the DA's safe?"

"As far as I know," Jameson said. "It was sealed ten minutes after it was found and the detention officer who found it signed the seal. If he read it first, he's kept quiet about it. The only thing I know is it's a confession. There were some other papers too, that were sealed with it. The only thing they didn't seal was a short letter to his wife."

"Any details on that?" Jasper asked.

"He just apologized for being a fool and said she was right," Jameson said. "They pulled her in for an interview but her lawyer stopped it."

"The FBI is digging into this too. They'd like to find a link between the West murders and Wilson Kucera. It's their opinion that Ed Kucera was not the mastermind. I agree with that since I know his reputation. He was a fairly decent lawyer and spread money around in some unusual places but there's never been even a hint of anything dirty."

"Yet Jake named him as the mastermind in his confession," Jasper said with a hint of steel. "I don't think Jake West would have lied about that hours before he was murdered." His wife's cousin had paid the price for his own involvement in the conspiracy—murdered by the hitman.

"That's right," Jameson said. "I've never seen that vid. Could I have a copy of it too?"

Jasper retraced his steps to his safe. When he returned, he heard the old-fashioned dinner bell on the stairs ring. It wasn't tied in to Butler.

"Yes, Jewel?" He flipped on the old intercom they hadn't pulled out.

"The quiche is done and you'd better come down here now if you want some. Tell Mr. Jameson there's a spot for him at the table." Jewel tried not to sound exasperated at being left out.

"Give me five," Jasper said, "then we're done."

Her mutter was, fortunately for him, not too clear. Jewel had a good share of curiosity and he hated to exclude her but she still had an nightmares about those she'd lost. He didn't want to worry her about Jake.

Copying Jake's confession took little time and they didn't view it all the way. Unlike the Kucera tape, this one hadn't disappeared. He'd held on to copies of it and Jake's murder for future reference since he now had a family connection and an old-fashioned desire to see justice done.

He'd let Jake's father and Jewel see the confession to settle their doubts but Jake's murder was far too unsettling. It might get viewed at the hit man's trial—if Samuel Starling ever came to trial—but he hoped it wouldn't be when David and Jewel were there. They didn't need that memory. He didn't even want it.

"Done?" he asked his guests.

"Done, I think," Jameson agreed. "What is quiche?"

Jasper smiled. "A delicious egg creation," he said. "You'll like it." And he led the way downstairs.

Chapter 3 - Friday, 5 Nov 2179

The music of a single violin tugged at him, persuading him to join in so Jasper did, waiting for just the right moment in the melody to add the far off call of a trumpet dimmed by distance. Yes, that was right. He repeated the call twice more then hit save and his music console remembered it. The violin continued but now it was joined by others and a cello as the tempo increased. Now the trumpet again–

An angry buzzing broke his concentration and Jasper snarled. "HOLD, damn it." He silenced his console and swung around and out of his chair. "Butler, who is it?"

"Sir?" The automated servant sounded perplexed.

"Ignore," Jasper said as he realized it was his com unit, not the Butler who had buzzed him. He forgot to turn the damned thing off. Finding it on the pool table, he answered. "What is it?"

There was a long silence then his partner answered. "It's eleven am. You weren't still in..."

"No, damn it," Jasper said then forced himself to be calmer. "I was composing. Sorry."

"Then I won't call back later," Brown said. "This is going to make you grumpy anyway."

Jasper stiffened, wondering what had developed then threw the call on to the big vid screen. "Okay, what happened?"

Lori Brown looked like she could walk into the room the image was so clear but she was seated at a conference table with Captain Reynolds. Jasper was uncomfortably aware the captain had heard his temper and vowed to remember his com unit next time.

"Captain," Jasper said, "Sorry."

His captain waved it away. "We thought you should know about this."

Lori took a deep breath and started. "We can't place Kucera in Plains on the Thursday of the funeral."

Jasper blinked. "What?"

"His lawyer produced his appointment calendar, affidavits from people Kucera was with and even some surveillance footage. Kucera was in a meeting with the board of Metro Hospital on that Thursday at two pm. He was in Plains on Saturday, July tenth, and left on Sunday but that was the last time he was here."

"You're kidding." Jasper knew they weren't. "Our transit records?"

"They confirm," Brown said.

"Any chance they were altered?" Jasper asked, remembering the missing surveillance footage.

"No, they weren't altered," Captain Reynolds said. "We can't put Edward Kucera in Plains."

"We still have a witness," Jasper said, wondering how this could have happened and knowing Lori would have tried every avenue already. "Willis Frazier. Didn't the judge give him the sewage farm again?"

"We're looking for him," Brown said. "We'll need the cell vid for a blind test."

"I'll bring a copy," Jasper said. "Let me know when and where. I want to sit on that interview."

"We thought you would," Captain Reynolds said. "Where's your wife?"

"I kicked her out," Jasper said. "Seriously, she went shopping with a couple of friends. She knew I was working today."

"Next time tell me," Lori said. "This would have kept until we found Frazier."

"Let's see if he can identify Starling too," Jasper said. "Do we have a vid where he says more? I only have the one line in the vid on Jake's murder." He didn't know if the hit man had broken his silence. It had been three months but the hit man had kept quiet during the first weeks.

"We have one," Reynolds said. "It's not admissible as evidence but we have one."

Jasper nodded. He didn't care if it was admissible. They could worry about that if it came to trial. Right now he just wanted to know if Frazier had told the truth.

After the call ended, he strolled down the stairs to refill his coffee decanter at the first floor kitchen. Frazier was just a snatcher, a petty thief, who had traded him an overheard conversation to get some charges dropped. Everything he repeated then had dove-tailed into what they already knew and given them slightly more information—not a lot but enough to know that Starling was a hired killer and he was definitely in Plains on the day of the funerals. They had assumed it was a meeting between Starling and Kucera. It had to be.

Damn it. Jasper rubbed his hand through his hair. Were they going to have to go back to watching over their shoulders for any threat? Kucera was dead, one Starling was in jail and the other dead—who did that leave? There'd been no attempt on Jewel, him, or David since.

The professor? Jasper considered that, suddenly aware that if Starling had gotten to the funeral on time, the professor—who was definitely there—could have too. Could Drew Nugent be the villain after all? He definitely had given Kucera an order to suicide but Jasper hadn't believed he was a killer. The man did have a real distaste for being questioned and scandals. Did he have something else to hide? He was going to have to find out.

This should all be settled by Kucera's confession. Damn, he wished they'd release that. Once that was entered into evidence, they could put this all behind them—unless Kucera wasn't the man at the Catholic church.

Well, there was no point in going back to work. Brown could call back with news Frazier had been located or Jewel could return and they both had to be at a Reach Out event this evening. That and his need to get his new album completed had kept them in the city. Of course, they hadn't decided on where to take their honeymoon. The places Jewel wanted to go were outside and it was too cold or too hot for most of them. He would have been happy just having his wife to himself in a first class hotel but Jewel had nixed that idea. They'd put it off for now.

He hoped they'd find Frazier soon. Remembering how every one of his suspects in that last case had died before questioning, he wondered if Frazier would join them.

* * *

Three hours later he was relieved to be sitting in the interrogation room across from the informant. Frazier looked a little bit better than the last time, calmer and a bit more self-assured. Jasper wondered if it was because he wasn't charged this time or because he knew he had something to trade.

"Thank you for coming in," Jasper said and didn't get the smirk he'd expected.

Frazier just nodded and looked uneasily at Brown. "I heard you got that Executioner fellow, Lieutenant—and you got shot."

"Yes," Jasper said. "I'm better now but I'm not a lieutenant any more. Detective Brown just asked me back because you know me. This is her case."

"Yeah, whatever." Frazier shrugged that off. "I haven't done anything since last time. I've been working in the sewage farms. Got hired to stay a month ago."

"Good for you," Jasper said. "Do you like those paychecks?" The snatcher had gone straight? Now that surprised him. It shouldn't though. He knew the man had a son and he'd practically begged him to get out of some drug charges last time because he didn't want to be transported and lose his family.

"Yeah," Frazier said. "I'm out of subby housing."

"I'm glad to hear it," Jasper said. "This is just about that tip you gave me. I need you to identify a couple of voices we have on vid. Maybe they'll be who you overheard and maybe not."

"Right," Frazier said. "Can we get it done? I'm due on shift in a couple of hours."

Jasper's eyebrow shot up but he nodded. Behind him he heard Brown speak to the technician. They couldn't allow Frazier to actually see the vid so it was being played in the tech booth and the vocals broadcast in here. The conversation between Kucera and the Professor was played first.

Frazier listened intently to what was said but didn't say anything until the tape was done. His eyes widened at one point but he waited for the end.

"He knows one of them," the technician said in Jasper's ear. "I got a reading."

"So was that one of the men from the confessionals?" Jasper asked.

"No sir," Frazier said. "Was that what I thought it was? Some sort of order?"

"Yes," Jasper said. "You didn't recognize either voice?" He knew the man was lying. He had to be. Ed Kucera was on that tape.

"Not from the church," Frazier said. "That's what you wanted, right?"

"But you recognized one of them?" Jasper asked.

"Yeah but not from the church. The guy giving the orders, I know him. Hell, you should know him too. That's the professor."

"You know him?" Jasper's eyes sharpened. "How?"

"Well, it was his book I stole," Frazier said. "And I've heard him on the subby channel. He teaches history."

"On the subby channel?" Jasper was stunned. "You're sure?"

"Hell, I'm sure," Frazier said with a grin. "Don't you ever watch vids? They jam history down our gullets every night on the subby channel. We're getting educated."

"But the professor has a program?" Jasper felt stupid. He knew the man believed passionately in history and was a major donor to Reach Out but a vid program?

"Yeah," Frazier said. "He's one of the better ones to listen to. He makes it interesting."

"Kucera?" The technician prompted and brought Jasper up short.

"Can you identify the other voice?" Jasper asked. "Yes or no?"

"Hear it again?" Frazier asked. He sat through the whole tape again but shook his head. "No, I know the professor. The other voice I don't."

"Was either at the church?" Jasper asked but his hopes were sinking. Not Kucera. Who the hell was it?

"No sir."

"Play the second tape," Jasper said to the technician. A moment later it began and Jasper listened incredulously to Samuel Starling.

"O, God, give him peace. Give me his sins and just take my brother to your care. I...he was my lamb. I was the shepherd. Let him have peace."

Praying! The damned assassin was praying. Jasper's eyes shot to Brown's but she didn't look at him. She knew this was inadmissible. She'd told him it was. Hadn't they got anything else out of the guy?

The tape wasn't long but it was painful to listen to and degenerated into sobs at the end. The cold Samuel Starling praying for his brother–the one who tried to kill Jewel and had killed a Cheyenne police detective. When it was done, Jasper cleared his throat.

"Yeah, I know him," Frazier said in a quiet voice. "That's the guy who killed the old woman. He was at the church."

"You're sure?" Jasper asked.

"Yeah, I'm sure," Frazier said. "I thought he was dead."

"There were two of them," Jasper said. "The brother died. This one is still awaiting trial."

"What about the other guy?" Frazier said. "The one giving the orders? Not the professor but the one at the church." His voice was sharper now. "Is he still around?"

"We don't know," Jasper said. "If you can't say he was the other man in the first tape, he might be. We thought we had him." Finally he acknowledged the truth to himself. It wasn't Kucera. Why the hell did he kill himself then? And what was in his confession? "We'll need you to ID Starling. An affidavit will do until it comes to trial."

"No," Frazier said.

"No?" Jasper was surprised.

"Nothing doin', lieutenant. If the other guy is still out there and he sees my name on paper, he'll shut me up. You get him before you ask me for anything," Frazier said with unexpected steel. "I'm not going to be anyone's target. I have a family."

"You're the only one who can place Starling in Plains," Jasper said.

"Nothing doing," Frazier repeated. "I want that on the record," he shouted at the tech booth. "I am not a bloody informant!" There was palpable fear in his voice.

Jasper stared at him, shocked that Frazier had just turned down his informant pay. The old Frazier would have wheeled and dealed and tried to get the pay without committing himself. This guy was different. Had a steady job made the difference or was it that threat he could have lost his family?

"You're not," Brown smoothly said, moving from the observer post to stand just feet away from Frazier. "And you're right, Mr. Frazier. This is all useless until we get the other one. We thought we had him. You proved us wrong."

"So you'll get him now?" Frazier looked uncertain.

"Yes, we'll get him," Brown said. "When we do, can we call you back in for another ID?"

Frazier considered then nodded. "Yeah, I want the bastard caught. The word is out that this was all about blissex and it scares the shit out of me. If you don't have him and that guy is the boss, I can't let anyone know I heard him. He takes whole families out."

"You think it was the boss?" Brown asked, incredulous.

Jasper left off thinking about Kucera at the words. If it was the local boss, they'd just got higher up the organization than he'd ever had. "What have you heard, Willis?" He deliberately used the snatcher's first name.

"I still got some contacts," Frazier said. "Not many because I haven't been hanging out. There's been chatter about a new pipeline and they want more delivery boys. I ain't doing it again after last time but they're hiring subbies. The chatter died down when the Executioner was caught but its back and they say that a VIP is here to make sure it goes right."

A VIP? Jasper caught his breath. Someone even higher up in the Blissex organization? Damn. They could get more than locals if they play this right.

"Willis, that bit of gossip just helped us a lot," Jasper said. "Are you sure you don't want informant's pay? We can hold it till it's safe."

Frazier stopped in the act of shaking his head. "You can hold it?"

"Yes," Jasper said. "You'll be assigned a blind number and only I, the technician in there, and Brown will know that's your number. To claim it, you'll just have to repeat the number in your own voice to unlock the file."

"Really?" Frazier looked incredulous. "Can't be a long number. I'm no good at them."

"Five digits," Jasper said. "Pick your own number then we'll change it a bit."

"I got a four digit one," Frazier said. "1929."

"Good," Jasper said. "Any part of that number tied to you?"

"No, it's a date when everything went to hell," Frazier said. "Are you sure my name won't be in some police file?"

"No, it won't. Informant's names and numbers are stored on paper in a safe. You have to know what safe and who has access to get there and I didn't even know that when I was with the department. In the system, you'll be informant 19299. Can you remember to repeat the last digit?"

"Yeah," Frazier said.

Brown stepped up with her police com unit. "Informant 19299 lock code," she said. "Just repeat the numbers please-one nine two nine nine."

Frazier did with a bemused look then waited till Brown moved the com unit away. "That's it?"

Brown said, "That's it. Technician, this interview is to be sealed under 19299. Got that?"

"Yes, Detective. Interview of Informant 19299. Shall I go through and bleep his name?"

"Yes, do that please."

"One moment," Jasper said. "Keep it rolling. Informant 19299, you're aware that I am not working for the department but have simply been asked to help conduct this interview as a courtesy?"

"That's right," Frazier said. "She's the official one." He nodded toward Brown. "A lot better looking than you too." He quipped with some of his old humor. "No offense."

Brown laughed.

"No offense," Jasper said. "End of interview."

"Got it, lieutenant. Good to see you again," the technician said as a parting shot.

"Frazier, I'm glad you turned yourself around," Jasper said. "How do you like that regular paycheck?"

"It's good," Frazier said, his smile fading. "And I'm not going back to the old life. That business with the blissex made me see what I was risking. I had a long talk with God while I was waiting on the judge."

"I've had a few of those myself," Jasper said. "We might need you one more time if we identify that guy in the church. Otherwise, just the affidavit. Brown will help you with that."

"Okay," Frazier said. "I'll see you around, Sensor Man."

Jasper smiled. "Yes, you will." Jasper recalled last time they'd met Frazier thought it had all been some huge joke and the real Sensor Man was laughing his head off somewhere. There were times when he wished it had been. Not today though.

"I have to get home," Jasper said to his old partner. "Talk about this tomorrow?"

She nodded and he left.

Chapter 4 - The Auction

"What is it?" Jasper raised one eyebrow as he regarded the wooden cabinet Jewel was admiring then looked at the auction program he'd brought up on his com unit. Item 133. Reading the description, he grinned. "You aren't going to bid on an antique toilet?"

"Oh, that's what it is?" Jewel lifted the lid and quickly set it down again after seeing the chamber pot inside. She retreated to his side with a grin. "You never know what will show up at a charity auction."

"I know," Jasper said. "It's a good thing they reveal all in the program."

Looking around, he saw the ballroom was slowly filling up with Reach Out members for this major fundraiser. They had a good setting for it. The Grand's ballroom was one of the largest and most elegant in the city. Tables were set with nice china but tonight the lights were turned up so people could see the items they were silently bidding on.

"So are you going to bid on the commode?" Jasper asked as Jewel brought out her own com unit. "If you win, where will you put it?"

"I'll give it to Uncle David," Jewel said, "and not tell him what it is." She gave him a wicked grin. "And you can't tell him."

"I won't breathe a word," Jasper said. She had a quirky sense of humor but so did her uncle—and he owed him one for not telling him about the pool table. Following Jewel down the line of auction items, he dismissed most of them. There was a diamond and ruby necklace that caught his eye but seeing Jewel didn't even give it a second glance, he walked on. A pair of maracas did catch Jewel's attention and she shook one to listen to the sound.

"Rattles or instruments?" she asked.

"Maracas," Jasper said. "From old Mexico. Let's see what it says." He turned to his com unit. "Age unknown. They might be a lucky draw item."

"Maybe," Jewel said. "Or maybe they're just what they seem."

"Could be," Jasper said but he entered a bid of fifty dollars anyway. He would probably get outbid and that was fine. If he did get them, he'd work them into his music. He was always looking for new and interesting sounds to add to his synthesizer system.

Jewel had told him about the lucky draw items before they arrived. Because some of the items were so odd and low value, charity auctions often turned a few of the lowest value items into Lucky Draws. If you won one of those, you got a thousand dollars and a special mention in the next program. The catch was you could buy a low value item thinking it was a lucky draw but discover you'd just bought a set of maracas instead.

His eye caught on a dome shaped vase with a pair of padded bamboo sticks stuck in it and he frowned, thinking the sticks looked more like drumsticks than flowers. Curious what it was, he checked his com unit and smiled. A lotus drum. Well, he'd never heard of that kind but it did look like a drum. It was obvious the auction organizers didn't know exactly what it was. They'd stuck the drum sticks in it so it looked like a vase. It was a pretty metal vase for all that with its black starfield finish but definitely wouldn't hold water with the various cuts in its surface. He itched to try it.

Taking the drum sticks out, he turned the drum right side up and stopped. A compass rose? His hand ran over the eight-pointed star in the middle top of the drum and he grinned. It was almost the same as the one on his locket. Now he had to try this!

Tapping his fingers on the various parts, he listened to the nice clear tones. They were metallic in nature but the drum was perfectly tuned. Nice.

"Hold this, Jewel," he said, handing his com unit to her. Picking up the drum sticks, he tapped the surfaces and the tones rang out crystal clear. Very good tone. He played a few more notes. Yeah, he could use this.

Laying down the sticks, he was surprised by sporadic applause from those nearest him. He grinned and waved it away before taking his com unit back to enter his bid. He saw there were six new bids in the last two minutes with the largest over five hundred dollars. He doubled it and knew he'd have to keep a sharp eye on that one. It was the only thing he'd seen here that he wanted.

The next small table they didn't linger at because it was a loose semi-circle of Japanese gods done in rare ebony wood. Jasper noted the item number and looked it up but didn't bid. He just wanted to see if anyone else was bidding on Jewel's contribution to the event. The set had two bids, neither one of them high for figures more than three hundred years old.

The set of Japanese gods wasn't complete. When it had been the appraised value had exceeded twenty-five thousand dollars. He hoped it would fetch a decent price but doubted it would. Few people would know anything about them and those who did would know how slim their chances were of replacing the missing figure. Fukurokuju, the tall-headed god of longevity, had been used to club Jewel's grandmother and was still missing. Jewel couldn't stand looking at the set so she had donated it.

Eyeing some antique books, Jasper deliberated then entered a decent bid for an illustrated child's book on the first moon landing. That was really ancient history to him but he'd learned recently that children's picture books were the most precious collectible for book collectors. Since he wanted to get closer to the professor, that book might be the key. His interest in books was legendary and he'd spent more than two thousand dollars for one just this year.

Paper books used to be common, he knew but that was long past. When the digital age arrived, the paper industry had faltered then ground to a halt. In less than forty years, ebooks had become the norm and paper books had turned into special order items. Third world countries had continued with paper books longer but even they had switched over as their smallest towns got computerized. Now every community of more than a hundred people had access to world news and education and paper books had become collectibles.

If the professor were here, he would bid on the books. Jasper intended to make it interesting and, if he won the children's book, he'd find a reason to sell it to the professor. He was curious what it said about the first moon landing though. By its publishing date, it had been written shortly after the first set of landings. The author hadn't known it would be another sixty-eight years before the new space age put another man on the moon. A whole lifetime passed with little progress in space. It took an asteroid to force the space program into a priority. Even then it had stopped and started several times before they finally got a successful colony on Mars. Two hundred years later, it looked like they'd finally gotten it right.

Seeing Jewel was done looking at items, he guided her toward a dinner table not far from his drum, He wanted to keep an eye on that but both the book table and Jewel's toilet cabinet were also visible from where they sat. Another couple, one Jewel knew, hesitantly asked to join them.

"Meredith and Galen Lowe," Jewel softly said. "Meredith worked with me and Galen sometimes worked with Uncle Mike."

"Good," Jasper said. "Please join us. We can watch who else bids on the toilet."

Meredith laughed so Jasper knew she'd checked that item out. Her husband looked confused until she pointed to the wooden cabinet.

"Is that what that is?" He grinned. "And here I thought it was a stereo."

Jasper nodded. "That would have been more interesting to me but it's not. Jewel would like to give it to her uncle."

"Tell the world why don't you?" Jewel gave him a mock scowl. "I just want to see his face when he figures out what it is."

"Minx," Jasper said. He fell back on that word a lot when Jewel was plotting–and she did a lot of it.

She gave him a look that brought laughter from Meredith and had her husband smiling.

"Newlyweds," he said. "Maybe we should leave you two alone."

"Don't," Jasper said. "Please, she'll behave if you're here. Won't you, Jewel?" He gave his wife a stern look but couldn't keep from smiling.

"I would really like to catch up on the news. Since I left the school, I haven't been out much," she told Meredith. "I miss the kids."

"They miss you too," Meredith quickly said then explained to Jasper. "I'm in administration at the same school. We met briefly when you visited."

Jasper studied her then remembered the woman who had passed him on to the principal. "Yes, I remember now. Assistant Principal?"

"Nothing that grand," she said. "I track academic achievement."

"Good enough," Jasper said. "You help spot the ones who need advance classes."

"Yes," she said with a smile. "And those who need more help."

"It's an important job," Jasper said. "It was someone like you who decided I needed to go into the high math curriculum. My daughter too." That had kept him in school when he'd been too bored to go on. The high math curriculum was an accelerated program for gifted students that focused primarily on math and engineering skills and kept literature and history classes to the legal minimum. His education had been totally steered toward engineering until he got to college and discovered music.

"High math?" Meredith looked curious. "Now a musician?"

"He's got a lot of skills," Jewel said. "He's even been helping me with Butler."

Galen suddenly looked interested. "The latest model? I wondered if that had died with..." he looked uncomfortable.

"With Uncle Mike?" Jewel asked, her tone brittle. "No, I wouldn't let that go. Since I needed something to do, I finished him. I'm also doing research and development for them. Since I'm part owner of the company already, I need to stay involved."

"I think Mike would like that," Galen said. "I'm surprised though you didn't just inherit the whole thing."

"That never happens," she said. "We use the three part plan." When he looked lost, she expanded. "Every company the family helps found has a three part ownership agreement. One third belongs to the West Foundation for the initial financing. They do some oversight to keep the company honest too. One third belongs to the family member who started it—Uncle Mike made me co-owner of his shares weeks before he died so I own them now. The last third is put into shares that the company employees have a stake in. That keeps them working hard for the company. We don't encourage public trading any more. I think Lunarex was the last company we had that went public."

Even Jasper sat up at that. "So how much does your family own of Lunarex?" He knew they had a chunk of it but was still finding out where the West family stood in the variety of businesses they had.

"We don't," Jewel said. "The Foundation has thirty-five percent. The founder's share got sold somewhere along the line—I think my great-grandfather did it. There was something about getting the public more interested in lunar mining by giving them a stake in it."

"I can see that," Galen said as if she just hadn't dropped a bombshell into the conversation. "I think I'll buy more shares of Lunarex now that I know who holds the biggest block."

"I said too much, right?" Jewel looked at her husband and sighed. "Ok, no more financial talk." She pulled the auction listings up and entered another bid. "Let's hope they serve the food soon. I'm starved."

"On that I agree," Meredith said. "Jasper, can I call you that? I really like what you played on that vase thing. Are you bidding on it?"

"Yes ma'am," Jasper said. "You can call me Jasper or Jazz. I answer to either one. Just no more lieutenant."

"Of course," she said with a look at her husband. "It's a shame you had to leave the force."

"Necessary," he said with a twisted grin. "It's simply not possible to be a sensa artist and a cop. Too many conflicts."

"So are you completely off the force?" Galen asked.

Jasper looked at him, suddenly aware he could be fishing. Why? "Yes. I still have friends on the force but I'm locked out."

Jewel looked at him with a puzzled expression but didn't say anything. Damn, he might have to quit telling her it was police business to keep her from coming upstairs or tell her he was still working on the family case. She didn't need to know it was tied to Blissex or Reach Out.

"So did you work on inspection systems too?" Jasper asked to divert attention. "I understand that's what Mike was working on."

"Yes," Galen answered. "We tried to improve them so they could scan cargo faster and in more detail. I think we've reached capacity though with the current system. If we push them too fast, pictures get blurred and detail lost. We tried solving the problem by alternating the hardware so they fired in sequence but the bugs haven't been worked out."

"Interesting," Jasper said, filing that away in his mind. He might have to cultivate a friendship with Galen. It still wasn't certain why Mike had been killed or whether it was connected with his job rather than his family. "Where does that project stand with Mike gone?"

"That one's dead," Galen said. "We had Seeker prototypes but can't get any more so it's been shelved. We're shorthanded right now and the budget got cut too–the usual bureaucratic nonsense."

"That I remember," Jasper said. "Have you ever tried to do a five man job with two and a half people?"

Galen chuckled. "Been there. If you ask for the half that thinks, you invariably got the wrong half."

"A half?" Jewel asked.

"Part-timer," Jasper said. "Worthless usually."

She turned back to her conversation with Meredith, only pausing when their salads were brought.

Jasper eyed the tables where the auction items were and his attention was drawn to a tall man in a very expensive suit. He looked to be in his fifties and his bearing was almost military in nature as he stopped by the drum Jasper coveted. His hand tapped the drum then his ice blue eyes met Jasper's. There was no hesitation, no seeking him out, the man knew exactly where he was.

Jasper tensed, not liking the look of those eyes. As the man turned away, he caught a glimpse of a small metal disk on one ear lobe. It was unusually plain but not a simple ring. Curious.

"Who is that?" he asked Galen and nodded toward the man just leaving the drum. "I've not met him before."

"Him?" Galen waited till the man turned. "That's Baxter. He comes to the auctions and other big events. He's from Chicago."

Jasper watched the man stop at the table where Jewel's Japanese figures were displayed. When he took out his com unit, Jasper pulled his out too, and found the item listing for the figurines. Sure enough a new bid appeared and it was considerably higher than the last leader. Tapping on it, he got the man's auction id. MB82.

He knew bidder's identities were supposed to be secret but once he checked his own he guessed their system. JS15 could only mean Jasper Stone and the fifteen probably meant he was the fifteenth to arrive. Pulling up the commode item, he confirmed that. Jewel still used her maiden name and her id was JW14.

Going back to the drum listing, he saw he'd been outbid four times, the last one being MB82 and the previous one being his wife. He entered a new bid then looked at his wife. "You don't need to bid on the drum. I'm getting it."

Jewel stopped, fork in mid-air and looked at him in surprise as he waved his com unit at her. "You broke the code?"

"Child's play," he said. "You figure it out."

That set them all to checking their com units. Galen Lowe snorted and laid his down first. "It's a good thing they aren't responsible for security. A second grader could do better."

"You're bidding on that ruby?" Meredith asked then realized she shouldn't know. "Well, thank you, dear."

"All the secrets are out," Galen said to Jasper. "I wonder how many husbands are bidding against their wives?"

"Probably all of them," Jasper said as the women continued to mess with their com units. "I'm sure we'll get a report soon."

He limited his scanning to just the five items he was interested in. The book had a fairly high bid from AN72 and he knew that had to be the professor. Discovering he could tap the bidder ID and get a list of his other active bids, he felt certain he was right.

On impulse, he entered a bid on the Japanese figures and waited to see what would happen. Within moments MB82 had outbid him. Checking his drum, he found he'd been outbid there too, and corrected that. The maracas hadn't attracted any attention though.

"When do they close the bidding?" Meredith asked as their entrees were brought around. "Is it lowest items first again?"

"No, they changed it this year," Jewel said. "They'll take the items over ten thousand off the list first and announce how many lucky draws are left. That's at 8:30. At nine, they'll take off those over five thousand and count the lucky draws again. The rest they close at ten."

"We can be home by midnight," Galen said. "I like that."

"Only if we skip the dancing and dessert," Meredith said. "And I want the Baked Alaska."

"Do they really expect items to go over ten thousand?" Jasper asked. "Other than that ruby necklace no one seems to want?" He'd seen the current top bid was already at eighteen thousand.

"Why aren't you bidding on that?" Meredith asked. "For Jewel?"

"Me?" Jasper was surprised. "When Jewel didn't even glance at it?"

"It's not jasper," Jewel flatly announced. "And Jasper is my favorite Stone."

Galen sputtered his drink at her bald statement and Jasper felt himself going red. Meredith laughed.

"If you say one more word," he said, absolutely certain she'd saved that line this time.

"What?" Jewel asked, all innocent now but her blue eyes were merry. "You want me to wear rubies now?"

That he knew better than to answer because he'd just get in deeper. Bending over his plate, he hid a grin. So she liked to wear him? Well, he'd test that again tonight.

Chapter 5 - Baxter

As Jewel predicted about a dozen items of the hundred fifty reached the ten thousand mark and were closed at 8:30. None of them were lucky draws and the ruby necklace cost someone twenty-two thousand dollars. It wasn't the Lowes.

It was probably worth that much but Jasper was glad Jewel hadn't taken a liking to it. He preferred to know the actual value before spending so much on jewelry. Aware that man-made stones often exceeded the beauty of the natural ones but had less value, he was cautious.

His drum was another matter. It was getting close to five thousand but he'd done a discreet check on the internet to find out what the value actually was. There weren't any currently listed for sale but the antiquarian encyclopedia had told him the drums were no longer being made and hadn't been for eighty years. Similar drums, none of them having the beauty of the one he was bidding on, sold for upwards of three thousand dollars and they weren't in production either.

It was curious that musicians hadn't kept them in production. They were light weight, required no power, and the one he tried had beautiful tone. Determined to get it, he entered a bid that would take it over five thousand. A few moments later, Baxter bid against him.

He raised his bid to six thousand then checked the listings for the Japanese figurines. Baxter had consistently bid that up. He entered a bid for six thousand to see if he would get the message.

The book he was interested in was still well under three thousand. It probably wouldn't close at nine. The commode would. Jewel was bidding against someone with the initials KR who seemed determined to get it. Well, his wife had her own money and he knew better than to suggest six thousand and fifty dollars was too much to pay for a joke.

There hadn't been any other bids yet on the maracas. Chances are no one would bother with them till after the most expensive items had sold and they started seeking out the lucky draws.

He could see Baxter frowning at him, his com unit still in hand. So he'd noticed the figurine bid. Jasper checked his drum, waiting for another bid on it but the minutes ticked by and it didn't come. Guessing he'd wait until the last seconds, he jumped up his bid in the last ten seconds by another five hundred and one. The auction closed with no further bidding and he relaxed.

Checking the figurines, he saw that Baxter had used the same strategy and gotten the set for seven thousand two hundred and one. Well, they both got what they wanted.

"I lost it," Jewel muttered but she didn't seem too upset. "KR took it up to seven thousand and I know it's not worth that much." She set her com unit down and looked at him. "But I like the drum better anyway. It's pretty and practical."

"And it's mine," Jasper said. "Third floor, not the living room."

"But it would look so good with roses in it," Jewel said. "Of course, I'd have to patch those leaks."

"And your pool table would look great as firewood," Jasper said and she laughed. "Let's claim my prize. Did you know that Baxter got your figurines? He'll take them to Chicago and you'll never see them again."

"Fine with me," she said, her smile fading. "I'm glad to be rid of them."

"I know," he said, his smile gone too, as he held her close. "I did make sure he paid a good price."

"Because he wanted your drum?" she asked with a bit of a smile. "Good. I never liked him."

"What do you know about him?" Jasper lightly asked.

"Not much," Jewel said. "He tried to flirt with me once and it gave me shivers. Uncle Mike warned him off after that."

Not a very satisfactory answer but Jasper didn't care just now. Claiming his drum, he caressed it with a gentle touch and was rewarded by the faintest of tones. God, he wanted to get out of here and see exactly what this little gem could do.

"I'm jealous," Jewel said.

"Jealous?" Jasper asked.

"Yeah, you're only supposed to look at me like that," Jewel said in a low, sultry voice.

He grinned at her. "I can't take this to bed," he said in an equally low tone. "And playing you will always be more fun."

His wife blushed, her cheeks turning scarlet. His smile broadened as he saw the effect his words and the memory of how he played her wipe away any jealousy. "Do you want to leave now?" He suggested as he felt his own readiness. "Who cares about maracas and books?"

Reluctantly, she shook her head. "No, we'd better mingle," she said. "But later," she planted a quick kiss on his lips and tapped his drum, sending out a low note that caused people to turn and look at them.

"Witch," Jasper said. "You tempt me but won't let me play."

She laughed, not bothering to find out whether he meant her or the drum.

Jasper offered her his arm and they set out to mingle.

There were a lot of notables at this Reach Out event, Jasper decided, and not all local. He recognized the city attorney, Rick Gordon, quickly and counted all five district mayors and the actual mayor in short order. Plains was so big it had been cut into five districts and twenty-three sections a long time ago. He'd served most of his career in the first district with his home office first in section three then section five. Through loan-outs, he'd been temporarily assigned to a dozen sections but five had been home until he resigned.

Professor Nugent was here. Seeing him talking to that Baxter fellow, he walked on. It was by sheer accident he found himself face to face with the city attorney.

"Sensor Man, I think," Rick Gordon said with a small smile. "How's the career?"

"Doing well, Mr. Gordon, and please call me Jazz," Jasper said, aware of his new status. "And I'm working on a new album."

"Good," Mr. Gordon said. "And it's Rick."

"Right," Jasper said, taking the invitation in stride. "Do you have any tips on climbing Laramie Peak?" He couldn't think of anything else that didn't skirt dangerously close to his DEA role but he remembered Gordon had climbed the peak before.

Gordon laughed. "Don't do it in this weather," he advised. "Wait till summer."

"Stupid question," Jasper said. "Sorry, I was reaching."

"Not any more stupid than what I was going to ask," Gordon said. "And it was did your wife buy that pretty vase and tell you to take care of it?"

Jasper smiled. "No, it's a drum. You didn't hear?"

"No, I didn't." Gordon looked intently at it as Jasper set it down on the nearest table. "Pretty though."

Jasper flexed his hands on the drumsticks and gave the drum a few taps, this time seeking out the scale embedded in it. A few more taps and he had it and started playing a simple melody. He could see Gordon's face as he followed the tune, his eyes keen and his whole pose intent on what he was doing. Good. He liked a good listener.

Finishing the melody, he reluctantly picked the drum up again. Later. He'd get to know this beauty later.

"And now I see why you carry it around," Gordon said and there was no hint of jest in his voice. "I heard you were good but—did you just buy that?"

"Yes," Jasper said. "And my wife is already jealous. Any good finds for you?"

"Not yet," he said. "I'm after lucky draws now. Those are more within my budget."

"Smart move," Jasper said, comfortable now. "This was the only thing that really tempted me—this and a book."

"A book?" Gordon's smile broadened. "Then you must be bidding against Drew."

"Drew?" Jasper repeated the name, not certain he wanted to reveal his interest in the man.

"Professor Andrew Nugent," Gordon said but his smile had faded. "Let's not play games, Mr. Stone," he said in a low voice. "You know him."

Jasper nodded. "Yes sir."

"Drew's decent," Gordon said, his voice still quiet. "Tread carefully with him."

"Yes sir," Jasper responded, wondering just why the city attorney was warning him off. Well, he would leave the book bid alone. That was easy enough to do. He wondered if Mr. Gordon knew he was Kucera's last visitor?

"The one bidding against me for this was a Mr. Baxter," he said, cradling the drum in the crook of his arm. "Have you met him?"

Gordon didn't blink. "Yes, that's Mark Baxter of Wilson Chemicals," he said. "One of Wilson Kucera's top men. Interesting man. He was here last July too."

Last July? Jasper caught the hint. Interesting, huh? Ok, he was just going to get interested in Mark Baxter. "He must come to a lot of Reach Out events."

"A few," Gordon said. "I know I saw him in July."

"Thank you, sir," Jasper said in a low voice. "And it's good to meet you."

"It's good to meet you too," Gordon said in a louder voice. "I love the way you play that drum." With a parting nod, he moved on to some other couple he knew.

Jasper didn't have time to sort it out. As soon as Gordon moved on, Jewel rejoined him and he was back to walking along the range of tables to see what could possibly be a lucky draw. Jewel was certain his maracas were one but could three pages of twentieth century stamps be another? He eyed the sheets of state stamps, all of them nineteen cent stamps, and thought about it then checked the bids. They were already up to four hundred dollars.

"I think I'll stick with the maracas," Jasper told her. "I know I can use them. Are you a stamp collector?"

"No."

"Your Uncle David?" Jasper hazarded a guess.

"No, not even him," she said. "Ok, no stamps."

"Then let's look at books," he said, spying the professor near the one he had bid on. "Wait, Drew's there."

"Yes, he is," Jewel said but tightened her grip on his arm. "I'm not going to avoid him forever."

Wishing she had one more time, Jasper steered them toward the professor's bearded figure.

"Mr. Stone," the professor acknowledged. "Have you become a bibliophile?"

So he'd broken the code too. "I was interested in reading this one," Jasper said. "But it's gotten too rich for me. I won't be placing any more bids."

The tension seemed to ebb out of the professor's lined face and he managed a smile. "Maybe next time," he said. "If you want to read it some time, just give me a call. I'm sure we can arrange something."

"Very generous," Jasper said. "And how have you been doing?" He still hadn't acknowledged Jewel on his arm.

As if he'd become aware of his lapse, the professor turned toward her. "Very well. Mrs. Stone, how have you been doing?"

Jewel's cheeks went a bit pink but she smiled and glanced up at Jasper. "Very well, Drew. I'm quite happy."

"Then you made a good choice," the professor said and he said it without any rancour. "I wish you long life."

"Thank you," Jewel said then released her Jasper's arm. "Oh, there's Elaine Kucera," she said. "I really must talk to her. Grandma would want me to." She abandoned them.

"Just make her happy," the professor said as he watched Jewel walk away. "She has a generous spirit."

"I know," Jasper said then quickly added. "Did you want to see Mrs. Kucera too?"

The professor turned a blank face to him.

"Sorry, I thought you knew them," Jasper said. "Especially Ed."

"We were friends for a while," the professor said. "That ended months ago."

"Sorry, I thought you visited him in jail," Jasper said as the professor turned away. "Maybe I was mistaken?"

"You are certainly mistaken," the professor said in a clipped voice then his ringed hand pushed his coat sleeve up and Jasper caught a glimpse of a jammer bracelet. "And I thought you had left the force, lieutenant." He said the last loudly enough to be heard then quickly lowered his voice. "If you want to talk to me about books, call me. Otherwise, leave it to the police."

He turned away, bumping into Baxter as he did then excused himself and walked on.

Baxter met his eyes then he too walked away. Jasper knew he'd heard but there was no help for that now. Hopefully, Gordon hadn't heard. He knew the city attorney would think little of him if he discovered he'd so quickly ignored his warning.

He'd always respected Gordon's decisions but he'd never been warned off before from a legitimate lead. Well, now he'd either blown it or the professor might make a slip. It was odd that he'd so quickly denied seeing Kucera in jail—and that vid had disappeared from official records. Could Gordon have had something to do with that? Could Gordon be tied in somehow? No, he was seeing shadows. The city attorney was the Plains city attorney, not Denver's, and it was pretty well known he hated blissex. Jasper wasn't positive but he half-remembered hearing something about a blissex loss in his family. Damn, his memory was going. He needed some time to sort this all out.

Why did the Professor wear a jammer to social functions? They were useless against room recorders but could jam com units in range and recording. Did he think Jasper was recording him? If so, he'd been a little late.

"Coming up on ten," Jewel said and took his arm. "And you haven't danced with me yet. If you want to get out of here and play," her eyes twinkled, "you'd better put down that drum and dance."

"I can dance with both of you," Jasper said and led her out on to the floor to prove it. Shoving thoughts of the professor to the back of his mind, Jasper concentrated on his wife.

Chapter 6 - Saturday, 6 Nov 2179

The kitchen of the West House was well appointed and cheery, designed by a woman who loved to cook. The yellow and chrome table would have looked out of place in another kitchen but here it added a touch of home. Yellow checked napkins and potholders lent more color to the white countertops and walnut cabinets. It lacked a window but there was a small vid screen where above ground homes had windows and it was framed with white curtains. Elizabeth West had done a wonderful job of making her kitchen feel like one from two hundred years ago.

Jasper could almost feel her presence as he set his breakfast dishes in the sink and poured himself another cup of coffee. It was soothing to be cooking here and he felt sure his wife's grandmother would approve of him and his cooking skills—not that he could compete with a woman who had taught cooking in her younger days.

Jewel had asked him once if he wanted to redecorate the kitchen but he saw no reason to. It was a touch of the familiar for Jewel and, if she was comfortable with it, he was too. He hadn't even bothered to change the vid screen from its cycle of horses in a pasture. So long as he didn't have to deal with real horses, he was fine with that.

Today was Linda's day off so he'd left Jewel sleeping and fixed his own breakfast. She was still abed but he thought she'd be slow to move today. He'd played her pretty well last night.

Now he'd have plenty of time for his new drum. As soon as Jewel was up and fed, he'd go back upstairs to his work. Right now he was content to be in the kitchen. He'd retrieved his new com unit from the safe and he was going to check out Mark Baxter.

"Butler."

"Yes sir," his automated servant replied.

"Is Jewel out of bed?"

"No sir."

"Notify me when Jewel is out of bed," Jasper said.

"Notify you when Jewel is out of bed," Butler replied. "Yes sir. Order noted. Anything else, sir?"

"No butler. That's all." Jasper was more familiar now with the order routines. It had taken some time and some adjusting before he could communicate with the thing without cursing its stupidity. He wasn't sure even now whether Jewel had corrected it or him but they got along better. He still preferred the typed order format and put Butler in silent mode whenever he could.

Butler was better than a paid servant though. He liked Linda and appreciated the company she gave to Jewel as she did the housework automations couldn't but Butler didn't demand his attention or interrupt his composing. It also answered the door and allowed him to remotely check who was there before letting them in. It couldn't make decent coffee though and deliver it upstairs. One of these days he was going to install a proper coffee system on the third floor and a bigger refrigerator too. He just hadn't gotten around to it yet.

Sitting down again at the kitchen table, he laid his old com unit down beside his place and set it to notepad mode. The new one he typed in his secure code then repeated his key phrase to unlock the hidden DEA access. Through it he could access the Plains police net or those in Denver and Cheyenne. If he requested broader access, he could get it but those three cities had been all he needed for now. His access would be noted, he knew but it wouldn't register as him. It would show up as DEA-C1832VB. If someone made an inquiry of the DEA to find out who he was, they would simply report it as a valid number. Since he was only using the usual logged reports, he needed no warrants for this.

"Entry log: Mark Baxter. Time frame January 1, 2179 to November 6, 2179," he typed in then followed it with "Exit log: Mark Baxter. Time frame January 1, 2179 to November 6, 2179." After entering that entry in the Plains database, he did the same with Denver and Cheyenne.

Who else? After some thought, he made the same requests for Professor Andrew Nugent, Samuel Starling, and.... what was his brother's name? John Starling.

Knowing it would take a while for those requests to finish processing, he sat back and thought. Mark Baxter worked for Wilson Chemicals. He wondered what his public profile would say.

Wilson Chemicals was the only licensed producer of Bliss, the top recreational drug. Non-habit forming, it worked by stimulating the pleasure centers of the brain. Unlike older drugs, it wore off completely in four hours and didn't affect performance after that. The mild legal dose was also harmless. People could still function under its influence but they were also easy to mug so most people used it only in the privacy of their homes.

Jasper didn't use it himself and he had made sure his grown daughter wouldn't be tempted to fall into the habit. Since he'd lost his only brother to an overdose of the illegally high dose form of Bliss—called Blissex—he'd dedicated his life to getting rid of Blissex and shutting down the illegal producer of it. So far he hadn't gotten anywhere but he'd been restricted to what he could do in Plains. Now as a DEA agent more information was available to him.

Looking up the corporate information page, he found Wilson Kucera first and found himself looking at the brother of the man who had been behind the deaths in the West family. Wilson Kucera was older than his brother and looked more decisive. His chin was firmer and his wide smile showed perfect white teeth. His hair was nicely thick and his tan indicated he had plenty of time to indulge in outdoor activities or solar baths. It was an ideal portrait for the perfect executive. He'd kept sole ownership of the company he had founded thirty years ago.

His brother had only been five years younger but hadn't matured as well. Jasper had seen him in some advertising as well as the cell vid and he simply didn't have the vitality and charm of his older brother. He knew from experience that often happened with younger brothers, although

Jason had been more charming than him and better looking too. His mother had said once that Jace would get by on his looks but he would get further with his brains.

He shouldn't think about Jace. He'd been dead for over twenty years. His father had been gone almost as long. His mother was still living but Jasper rarely heard from her. He'd sent her a wedding announcement, of course, and enough cash to see her safely to Plains but he hadn't heard anything back. He hadn't really expected to.

Baxter. He needed info on Baxter. Scrolling through the list of Wilson executives, he found him listed as Mark A. Baxter. Twenty-five years with the company, he was an Executive Vice President. Studying his picture, Jasper ignored the fake smile to study those ice blue eyes. They weren't smiling. The head was turned just enough that he could see that same damned earring. It still looked to be plain. He wished he'd gotten a better look at it last night.

Experience had taught him that women changed jewelry as often as they did clothes but men rarely wore the same thing twice unless it meant something to them. The star locket he wore was just one example. As Sensor Man, he'd made it his symbol, wearing it on his album cover and several publicity photos. That and his new wedding ring were the only pieces of jewelry he wore.

That earring might give him a clue as to what Baxter believed in. Come to think of it, the professor also wore rings. He'd seen them—two on his right hand. One had been small, unusually thin for a man's ring but he couldn't remember anything beyond that. Curious now, he left Baxter's portrait to look up the professor at Plains University.

His wasn't difficult to find either. A quick check of the faculty and then the history department gave him the man's official portrait. The professor looked to be about twenty years younger, his beard darker but he had the same spectacles. His right hand was loosely folded in front of him and one ring—a Masonic one—was clearly visible. A Mason? That surprised him. In his —perience, any—e who had earned that ring was law-abiding and unlikely to ever come to police attention. Was that why the professor had resented being questioned about the West murders? And could that be why Mr. Gordon had warned him off? Was he a Mason too? He'd have to find out.

"Coffee," Jewel moaned over the intercom and broke his concentration.

Jasper grinned, guessing she was still in bed if Butler hadn't told him she was up. "Move your lazy bones and I'll send some up in the dumb waiter."

"But I'm sore, damn it," Jewel said. "Bring it to me."

"And jump your bones again? Be right up," Jasper said.

"Don't you dare," Jewel said but her voice lacked conviction. "I just want to stay here."

"Breakfast in bed. Omelet for dessert?" he asked with a wicked smile and turned on the vid screen so he could see his love tangled up in the covers. The bedroom vid screen gave him an excellent view of the bed, something he usually hated but right now Jewel was stretching like a cat and he could see those luscious breasts touched by autumn sunlight from their windows.

Sorely tempted to do as he threatened, he just watched as his wife coyly smiled at him and completed her stretches, managing to lose more of the blanket in the process. He felt himself harden and knew it was a mistake to watch this. The minx would lure him back to bed.

"That's it. I'm coming up. If I find you in that bed, you're mine," Jasper said and half rose from his chair.

Jewel laughed and scurried from the bed, her indolence gone.

"Jewel is up," Butler announced. "You wanted to be notified."

"Thank you butler," Jasper said and sat back down. She's not the only one who's up. With an effort, he turned back to his work. He could hear the shower running through the vid screen and impatiently turned it off. He had to think about something other than Jewel.

God, he was as horny as a man half his age. Jewel was no teen either but she was making up for years of not having a man. He knew she'd had at least one fling in her college days and Mike had sent the boy packing because she'd told him. That didn't bother him. After all, he'd had a couple before he married Carol. It was just he couldn't concentrate when Jewel stretched like that and she had so many other ways of teasing him. He was enjoying it but it had been three months now and there were no signs he'd worn her out.

Well, he wouldn't be doing it today. When he got done with this, he wanted to really test that drum then get back to his composing. Hopefully, Jewel would curl up somewhere out of his way. He doubted she'd feel like going out after their hijinxes last night.

Seeing the entry reports were still not available, he turned to the stove and began fixing his wife's breakfast.

* * *

A homey silence filled the kitchen while Jewel ate and he studied the first of the reports he'd requested. Baxter had been in and out of Plains four times between January and June then had spent nearly three weeks here in late June and July with occasional exits. He'd been back in Plains for three days. What could hold an executive from Chicago in Plains for that long? They weren't a vacation spot–and he'd exited the city for a little over an hour each day through one of the above ground exits. Well, he could have gone walking. July was a hot month but the mornings were cool enough for casual walking. There was even a fitness trail above ground which he hadn't known about until Jewel showed him.

Baxter hadn't gone far when he left Plains during that period. He'd spent several nights in Denver but none of them consecutive. There was no clue to where he stayed, just the transit records showing he'd taken the train from Plains to Denver and back again. There was nothing in Cheyenne at all. He couldn't tie him to Jake's murder yet.

Making quick notes on his notepad, he saw Jewel watching him. "Police business," he said and knew she was going to ask since he obviously hadn't told the truth last night.

"I thought you said you were locked out?" Jewel said.

"I am," Jasper said. "This is old business. I left the force so suddenly there were incomplete cases. I'm consulting with Brown on those-that's why she has to physically come over instead of just calling me."

He saved his notes and turned the notepad off then flipped the new one to a blank screen and locked it. It would continue to receive the reports and save them but Jewel couldn't poke her pretty nose in.

"After three months?" Jewel asked. "There must have been a lot of cases."

"No, just two," Jasper said. "But sometimes you get new information. I've been working on one of those for years. So has Brown. I couldn't just leave it all for her."

"True," Jewel said. "And I shouldn't be nosy."

"You shouldn't," Jasper agreed then poured a last cup of coffee. "Got another puzzle for you. Do you think you can get our Butler to send the smell of coffee up to the bedroom?"

He was joking and she knew it but seemed to think about it.

"It would be far easier to put a coffee maker in the bedroom and remotely control it with him," she said. "That's child's play. I'd just have to install the right outlet so he could control it or one of those coffee makers you can turn on with your com unit. You'd still have to get out of bed to get the coffee."

"Well, you'll have to get up sometime," Jasper said. "What would you like to do today?"

Jewel met his eyes with a wicked smile.

His eyebrow raised and he waited. If she said it, he would.

She giggled and shook her head before she got serious. "I need a rest and you want to play with your new toy. How about the gym tonight?"

"Good idea," he said, relieved she'd backed down. "If you feel up to it."

"I will." She cradled her cup in her hands. "I talked to Meredith last night too. How would you feel if I took on some tutoring?"

Jasper was surprised. "Students?"

"Yes," she said. "I don't have to be outside for that. In fact, I can have them come here and we'll use the dining room. It will give me something to do."

"Great idea," Jasper said and meant it. He knew Jewel didn't need the money but she did need something to occupy her. "What subjects would you tutor?"

"English and history," she said. "I could do math but I get too impatient when they can't grasp it. I had enough troubles with English myself that I'm better at teaching it."

"I think it's a great idea. Why don't you call her and set it up?" Jasper said, relieved. "And didn't you say you wanted to get involved with that next Reach Out event too?"

"Yes, it's not for three months though. That can wait." Jewel fairly beamed that he'd approved.

Why the hell wouldn't he? Jasper wondered if she really thought he was against her working. She had money but that wasn't enough to give her purpose. She was married to him but he couldn't keep her busy all day. No, she needed work. So did he. They just hadn't discussed it before with the wedding ahead of them and his new album work.

"Jewel, I think it's a great idea," he said again. "I know how much you miss the kids. If there's any other opportunity out there you want to take, just tell me. I am not against wives working if they want to. That's medieval."

Her smile got wistful. "I thought you'd say that," she said, "but I wanted to be sure. Tutoring isn't worth a fight."

"No fights," he said. "While you tutor, I'll cook."

She smiled but he was serious. If she had students at the right hour, he'd get his chance to cook. Speaking of which, he remembered the dishes. He started to clear the table but Jewel stopped him.

"Let me do them. You need to work," she said in a soft tone.

They were both on their feet now and he pressed her against him then gave her a soft kiss. "You spoil me," he said and, scooping up his two com units, started for the stairs.

Chapter 7 - Nugent

Listening intently to his just completed drum solo, Jasper smiled faintly at the clear tones of the lotus drum. Very good. He could weave other instruments around that. Remembering the faint trumpet he'd used for his last composition, he considered it. Maybe but he felt something like a woodwind would work better. Warmer tones. Maybe an oboe. Yes, he'd see what he could do with that. When he got the oboe part down, he'd have to mesh the two. He still wasn't sure where he was going with this composition but that was okay. It would develop its own voice.

Jewel was curled up on the couch with a reader in hand but looked up as he shut down his equipment. He wasn't surprised to see she had come up in the middle of his playing. She'd learned to do it quietly and he wasn't really aware of anything but his music most of the time—one of the big reasons he would never do public performances. He knew he didn't stay aware of his audience and really didn't want people seeing how deeply he got lost in his music. Jewel understood that and had from the first time he'd played for her. Carol had known it too. He was blessed to have two such women in his life.

"Done?" she asked as the power light went off. "It was wonderful."

"I'm glad you liked the raw tune," he said. "Wait until the next step."

"I can't wait," she said with a smile. "But you barely touched your lunch. I think a good supper is in order."

Reminded, Jasper glanced at the tray Jewel had sat beside his console. A half eaten sandwich was still there but nothing else. What had she given him? He couldn't recall.

"I ate the chips," he said, hazarding a guess.

"Carrot sticks," Jewel said. "And a beef sandwich and two glasses of ice water."

"No coffee?" He was surprised.

"You didn't taste anything so why bother?" She shrugged then smiled. "I had to see if you'd notice."

"Then I guess you'll feed me lots of carrots and water when I'm not looking," Jasper said with a smile. Hell, he didn't care what he ate when he was working. There were times when he ate nothing at all. "I'm hungry now."

She twisted around and got her feet on the floor just as her com unit chimed. Fishing for it in the couch pillows, she looked at the number and answered.

"Yes, he's here. No, he's not busy. Let me throw it on the vid." Aiming her com unit at the big vid panel, she transferred the call and Jasper found himself looking at Lori Brown. Instantly Jasper knew something was up and Lori didn't want Jewel to hear.

"We need you, Jazz. There's a body and everything is just blitzed. You'd better come."

Jasper stiffened at the key word she'd thrown in.

"Corey Morales is here and he's asked for you," she said. "He found the body."

"Who is it?" Jasper demanded, his thoughts going immediately to Mel. "Not female?"

"No," Lori said, hesitated, then added. "It's the professor."

Jewel's gasp was echoed by his own incredulous "Who?"

"The professor. Please, Jazz." Her eyes shifted to Jewel and back to him. "For Corey."

"Right," Jasper said. "I'm coming. What's the address?"

"Section Two, Sawyer Street, Number 42," Lori said. "Maybe Jewel can call Mel and tell her Corey is all right?"

"Got it," Jasper said then turned to his wife. "Can you call Mel and tell her to come over here? I'll bring Corey home with me."

"Yes," Jewel said, her face pale. "Drew, I, oh, god." She looked ready to cry.

Damn, he hated leaving her like this.

"I'll send a squad car," Lori said. "It will be at parking in ten minutes."

"Thanks," Jasper said. "I'll be there."

Lori broke the connection and Jasper was finally free to hold his wife. "Jewel, let me go find out what happened. Maybe it was an accident. Call Mel and ask her to come over. Be sure you tell her nothing has happened to me or she'll panic."

"Right," Jewel said. "It's just, it's Drew." She looked up at him with liquid blue eyes, her lower lip quivering.

"I have to go," he said. "Call Mel."

He grabbed both com units and headed down the stairs. What the hell had happened? Why did Corey find him? He knew without asking it was no accident. Lori wouldn't have used blitz in her message if it didn't require him—and the professor was his chief lead.

By the time he reached the car park, he'd remembered to turn his com units back on and saw messages he'd missed on both of them all from Brown. She must have been desperate to call Jewel's number.

He listened as he waited for the squad car, his face getting grimmer. The professor had missed a class and Corey had gone over to check on him. Jasper wasn't curious how he'd got in. He'd find that out later. Right now he just needed to get there and find out what happened.

Why hadn't he reported that conversation to the captain this morning? If they had pulled the professor in for questioning about the Kucera visit, they'd at least know what he knew or he'd be sitting in jail waiting for his lawyer.

Damn, he'd been preoccupied. He called up the exit reports again and checked the one for Nugent. Yes, he'd left Plains on the day Kucera died. He'd been gone for two days, in fact. Where had he gone?

Checking the Denver records, he drew a blank and swore. It was only when he checked the transit records that he found proof Nugent had been in Denver but not the Denver underground. Hell, that didn't matter. The central jail facility wasn't in the underground. He'd been there. Jameson said there was no record of the professor being there but he had that tape. Useless. If the man was dead, they'd never get any answers.

The squad car arrived and he shut down his secure com unit and tucked it in his jacket pocket then hung his usual unit on his belt. He didn't know the officer driving the car so he sat quietly while the officer concentrated on the traffic.

The underground express lane was crowded at this hour with shift changers so it was slower going than usual. Even with a siren, it took time to weave through two miles of traffic.

He knew the alternate route on level three was even more crowded with bikes and trams. This was just a bad time to try to move in the city.

He hoped Corey was stronger than he looked. His daughter's boyfriend was a cellist and a student. Jasper liked his manners but this? He didn't know enough about him. Well, now he'd find out.

Sawyer Street was new to him. It was part of the University campus and reserved for senior faculty members so crime was pretty rare here. The wide street was dotted with bushes and vehicle traffic was permitted so the squad car delivered him to the door. One look at the news team that had arrived before him and he braced himself.

"It's Sensor Man," someone said and just like that cameras were pointed at him and away from the door of the professor's house.

"Lieutenant, why are you here?" A reporter asked.

"I was a friend of the professor's," he said. "That's all. Nothing official. I'm no longer on the force."

The reporter looked ready to challenge that but he just looked at her. "TV3?"

"Yes sir, Grace Rogers," she said, flashing him a tight smile before stepping back. "Thank you." She turned back to her camera and continued her report. "This is Grace Rogers reporting from the Plains University campus where Professor Andrew Nugent has just been found dead. Police have not released a statement but..."

Jasper walked on into the house, glad she hadn't pushed him. TV3 had already lost one reporter for doing something blatantly illegal to his old house. He hated to have to use legal muscle again.

The officer at the door let him through without challenge, just directing him on in. This house had two floors neither above ground. There was no body in the main living area but Corey was there.

The teenager looked relieved to see him, his brown face cracking into a strained smile as Jasper offered him his hand and gave him a quick hug.

"I'm sorry, sir," he said. "I couldn't think who else I wanted to see. My parents don't..."

"It's ok," Jasper said. "You did right. Detective Brown said you found him?"

"Yes sir." Corey took a deep breath before continuing. "I'm his teaching assistant. There's an afternoon class on Saturdays. When he didn't come in to teach, I tried calling. It wasn't like him to miss. He never missed." He dashed a hand across his face. "I, I had authorization to come in. He was in his office."

"That's enough," Jasper said. "You did right. Let me just see him."

"He's this way, Mr. Stone," a voice said and Jasper recognized his one-time temporary partner Detective Sanders. Had Brown asked for him?

"I'll be right back, Corey. Just sit and listen to the officer," Jasper said and followed Sanders to the office.

The room he walked into was extremely tidy and lined with bookcases, about two thirds of them full with plastic boxed books. There were more books on the desk, most of them unboxed, and old-fashioned paper notepads. What drew his attention though was the figure of Professor Nugent, his head tilted back and sightless eyes staring at something none of them could see. He was sitting in his office chair but not behind his desk. The chair had been pulled out into the middle of the room and the professor's hands were tied to its arms. His bearded face bore bruises that weren't there last night and he was very dead.

Jasper stared at him in shock, at first unable to comprehend it. Torture? Had he died of heart failure or something else? Remembering how Drew Nugent had hated scandal, his jaw tightened. If word of this got out, it would be all over the papers. On the heels of that, he thought how Corey must feel. Professor Nugent had been respected on campus. No matter what else he was, he was a damned good teacher.

The forensics team was already working on him, taking pictures of his position and the bruises. Jasper crouched next to the chair and studied the knots but they told him little. They looked to be regular square knots. The ropes weren't even ropes but electrical cord.

Seeing there was a floor lamp nearby, he moved over there and found the cord had been cut off. Whoever had done this had known he could do that. Professional? Probably. Certainly not a student.

"Jazz," Lori Brown said, motioning to him, "I've just finished checking. There's no household cameras here and no security system-at least not in this room. We don't have vid."

"Damn," Jasper said. "Did you see that lamp cord?"

"Yes. It's the same cord on both hands. They just split it." She studied the body. "Damn it, Jazz, he was our lead. How did they find out?" she asked in a low voice. "Only the three of us knew about him."

"And Jameson," Jasper said. "And I'm not sure of it but I think Rick Gordon knew."

"The city attorney?" Lori looked shocked. "How?"

"I don't know," Jasper said. "But there's something...." Crossing back to the body, he peered at his right hand and saw not one but two rings on it. Taking out his secure com unit, he photographed the hand then gestured for the technician to do the same. When that was done, the technician fitted a paper bag around his hand.

That was standard procedure. If the professor had scratched one of his attackers, there could be DNA evidence underneath his fingernails. He couldn't see the professor doing that though. No, he was far too dignified to put up much of a fight.

He looked at the picture on his com unit. One ring was Masonic. He couldn't tell the degree but it was definitely Masonic. The other ring was worn on his pinkie and seemed to be a signet but the band was oddly thin for a man's ring and the emblem was an eye. Could that be Masonic too? He seemed to remember a pyramid with an eye on it but there was no pyramid here. The symbol and even the ring was discreet as if it wasn't meant to be noticed.

Could it be the same symbol Baxter wore on his earring? He wasn't sure but his gut told him no. Any organization that welcomed Professor Nugent probably wouldn't welcome the likes of Baxter.

"What's this?" Jasper asked and poked a short rubber hose lying beside the chair.

"It's a tourniquet strap. They injected him with something," the technician said. "Hello, Lieutenant."

Jasper looked up and saw it was another he'd worked with. "Pedro," he said. "I'm glad you're on it. Is there any chance you've seen this before?"

"No sir," Pedro Kruger responded. "From his facial expression, it looks like he blissed out but bliss is rarely injected."

Jasper leaned closer, catching a whiff of death odor. How long had he been dead? Not since last night because he'd changed clothes. The tailored suit he'd worn to the Reach Out event had been changed for one of his usual tweed ones.

The professor's eyes were wide and his bearded mouth sagged open. His spectacles were gone and he wondered if they'd fallen off. It was unsettling to look into those sightless eyes he'd known in life and he had to force himself to keep his detachment. He was just another victim. "You're right but I have seen something like this in a text. You might want to check for reactions to Penatel or Penseek."

"Truth serums?" Kruger just nodded. "Yeah, that might do it. They both have bliss in them. And it looks like he was being questioned."

Jasper silently agreed. There was little blood and only facial bruising that he could see. Other bruising might show up in the autopsy though. So had someone else got interested in what the professor knew? Or did they want to shut him up because of him? He hoped to God that wasn't it. The professor didn't deserve this.

Remembering Gordon's warning and Baxter's interest in their conversation, he knew he had two possible routes of investigation, no, two new investigations. Damn it, he had to stay focused. "How many do you think?" Jasper asked Brown. "One or more?"

"More," she said. "At least two and possibly three. We're pulling the vid feeds from the cameras outside. There's a back door to this house but there was a chair against it so I don't think it was used."

"You might want to ask Corey what he knows about the back door," Jasper said. "Send me a copy of the autopsy?"

"Of course," Lori said.

"One thing I want you to see," Jasper said. "Come here." Removing the paper bag from the right hand, he indicated the eye ring. "Pedro, can you get another picture of this for the records?" He asked the technician.

"What is it?" Brown asked.

"I don't know," Jasper said as Pedro complied. "But it's odd and obviously meant something to the Professor. He wasn't one to wear excessive jewelry."

"The other one's Masonic," Pedro said. "The pinkie ring looks like it has the symbol of the Eye."

"What's that?" Jasper asked.

"There are lots of eye symbols," Pedro said. "This one isn't the Eye of Horus or the Eye of Providence but it might be related. If you look up secret societies, you might find it somewhere. I used to read that stuff."

"I'm glad you do," Jasper said. "Now Brown has a starting point." He'd almost said I.

"Yes, thanks, Pedro."

"I'd better get back to Jewel," Jasper said. "She was upset when I left. It was a good idea having her call Mel, by the way."

"We couldn't have her coming here."

"I know," Jasper said. "Is Corey under suspicion?" He looked to Sanders for the answer.

"Not yet," Sanders said. "He was pretty shook when I got here and he called it within three minutes of entry. I've checked the lock and got that. Before him only the professor opened it and that was from the inside."

Sanders' tone was brisk and professional, giving no hint of what he thought. Jasper frowned but remembered Sanders had met the professor at one of their previous interviews. It could be his way of dealing with it. "So he let them in?"

"It looks like he did," Sanders said.

Jasper frowned then motioned Brown to join him in a corner, further away from Sanders and the technician. "We might be back where we started," he said. "There is one thing." He quickly told her about being warned off the Professor by Gordon and his subsequent conversation.

"He denied being there?" Brown asked, her brown eyes wide. "When we had him on vid?"

"But that record has mostly disappeared," Jasper reminded her. "He might have thought it was gone for good."

"It could have been," Brown said, looking around. "I'll see the records of this one get copied to flashers and bring you one. Just in case."

"Thanks. I've got a copy of the rings. That pinkie ring looks interesting." He paused to think then shook his head. "No, I'd better collect Corey and get home. With the press out there, I don't dare stay too long."

"Right. Take care of him. He's a good kid," Brown said. "We'll finish up here."

Chapter 8 - Corey

Corey didn't talk much on the way back to Lily Street. Jasper couldn't see him because he'd had no choice but to put him in the back seat of the squad car but he would be better able to talk to him in Lily Street. The boy knew his house and would relax more there. He was glad the door logger cleared the boy of suspicion. Corey might have a brief questioning for the records but that would be it. Dealing with the memory of what he had seen would be harder.

He'd been caught on camera. Jasper frowned at that, knowing his fellow students would be after the boy to tell what he had seen. That could be a problem. If they wanted to preserve the professor's reputation, he'd better not tell them. He'd see what he could do.

Why the hell was he so concerned about the professor's reputation? Jasper found it hard to reconcile that with the suspicion Nugent had been involved but what the hell was he involved in? Someone had set him up as a blissex smuggler but he'd been an unwitting decoy. Then he'd been sort of engaged to Jewel except Jewel had already rejected him. Lastly, he'd turned up in Kucera's cell and gave him that order to suicide. That was the only concrete proof he had the professor was involved in something and he couldn't even say it was blissex.

On the other hand, the man had the respect of Rick Gordon and was well liked by his students—even his daughter. He spoon-fed history to subbies with his own vid program and—what had Frazier said? He made it interesting. He was finding it hard to reconcile everything else he knew about the man with that visit to Kucera and this.

What did he know that others wanted to know? Jasper knew that was the big question. It probably had something to do with that visit to Kucera— that visit that had disappeared from police records. Remembering the jammer he'd glimpsed on the professor's wrist, he frowned again. He had to tell Brown about that. It needed to be found.

"Here we are," the officer driving the squad car said and Jasper realized they were back where they started. "Take care, Sensor Man." He smiled but stayed in the car as Jasper let Corey out.

"Thanks for the ride," Jasper said. "Come on, son."

Corey looked startled at that then smiled uncertainly. "Thanks."

"I think I'm acting as your dad in this case," Jasper said as they walked up the stairs to street level. "I'll try to be a good one."

Corey nodded but didn't meet his eyes. "What will happen?"

"Let's wait till we get inside," Jasper said. "Mel is probably here too. I had Jewel ask her over."

The door to Lily Street opened before they could touch it and both women were waiting. Jasper pushed them back inside and they stopped in the living room.

His daughter, her auburn hair tied back in a ponytail, was the calmer of the two but she looked as pale as his wife. She'd been one of the professor's students. Had she ever told the professor who she was? Probably not. And since she used her mother's name, it wouldn't have been obvious.

Why hadn't he ever asked the professor what he thought of his daughter? He rubbed his eyes, realizing he'd lost that opportunity forever.

The others were waiting. He had to say something.

"Professor Nugent is dead," he said then looked at Jewel. "I'm not sure whether it was an accident or murder but I think it was an accident."

Corey muttered something under his breath.

"I know it didn't look like an accident, Corey. He was being questioned and they injected him with something–probably a truth serum. In any case, he had a reaction and died. I don't think they meant to kill him."

"He was beaten," Corey said. "Tied up to that...chair."

"Yes, he was beaten," Jasper said as the women recoiled from the news. "And restrained. I don't know what they were after but it's obvious the professor didn't give it to them. That's why they used a truth serum. I'd like to know how they botched it."

"Hell, if they had truth serum, they didn't need to beat him," Jasper said. "That's amateur and counterproductive. They left evidence of assault." Even as he said it, he felt a chill of realization. They didn't intend to leave the professor alive. He'd resisted them because he probably knew that. Who had wanted him dead?

He needed to think. Hell, he needed to pull this all together. Fall back on routine, he thought. Looking up, he saw Jewel. "I need coffee."

She left to get some.

"Corey needs some too," he said to his daughter. No sooner had she turned to go than he motioned for Corey to sit down. Taking out his secure com, he set it to record and laid it down. "Butler, record this room."

"Yes sir. Record living room," Butler responded. "Recording on."

Corey looked at him in surprise and Jasper smiled. "Jewel's toy. We're still testing him out on record functions. It's not official."

"Oh," he said. "Am I in trouble?" He looked worried.

"Not at all," Jasper said. "I spoke to Detective Sanders and he said you called it in very quickly and the door logger confirmed that. What you can expect is to be called in for an official interview in an interrogation room. They'll sit you in a chair which reads your vitals. It's all wired in so you won't really notice it. After that they'll ask you how long you worked for the professor, what you saw, and stuff like that. I'm going to ask you the same type of questions right now so you'll know what to expect. Got that?"

"Yes." Corey looked a little less worried.

"Now why were you so worried about calling your parents?" Jasper asked. "Where do they live?"

"They live in Arizona," Corey said, taking the second question first. "And they are really strict traditionalists. I came to Plains University to get away. If they hear I got into trouble, they'll try to get me home."

"You aren't in trouble," Jasper said. "Are you dependent on them for funding?"

Corey nodded and Jasper understood. He'd managed to get away from his family but still needed their money.

"Have you checked into scholarships?" Jasper asked.

"Yes sir. That's how I got the TA job. Professor Nugent knew about it and I was getting paid. Now," he said. "Well, I guess that's over too."

"Don't be too hasty in thinking doors are closed," Jasper said. He accepted a cup of coffee from Jewel and looked up. "Love, we're going to need supper. Can you order something in?"

She took the hint and motioned Mel to follow her.

With the women out of the way, he continued. "We'll talk about that later but I think we'll find a way to keep you in school."

"Thank you, sir." Corey looked relieved.

"You will have to call your parents though," Jasper said. "There was a network reporter there and I'm sure she got both of us on vid. She identified me and she'll have your name too. It's better you call them."

Corey looked unhappy but finally nodded. "Yeah, I'll think about it."

"We'll do it later," Jasper said, suddenly wondering what kind of home life he'd had. He was a decent kid but had he gotten that way because of his parents or in spite of them?

"So how long did you work for the professor?" Jasper asked. "And how many hours?"

"I started this semester," he said. "I helped set up classes and took attendance. Since I've already taken all but three of his classes and aced them, he had me set up as a tutor for the freshmen and sophomore classes. I worked about ten hours a week for him and picked up another ten tutoring. I was hoping to make enough to pay for next semester with a scholarship I have."

"Good plan," Jasper approved. "So what was today's routine?"

Corey thought. "Well, it's Saturday so there's only one class. I had to be there by twelve thirty to set up. There were his notes, his map of the Americas, and the 20th century map.Then I had to make sure the vid was up and running and key the proper program in. It's all routine but takes about twenty minutes to do. Once class started, I would take attendance so he didn't have to. If there was a test, I helped monitor but he didn't have one scheduled today."

"So what happened today?" Jasper asked. "From twelve thirty."

Corey hesitated. "Well, I set up and the students got there but he didn't. At ten after one, I called his house to see if he was running late. I left a voice message but he didn't call back. I thought maybe he'd left for class. At twenty after I called his com unit and got no answer back. That's when I thought something might be seriously wrong. He never does that."

"So?"

"I called the office and they told me to dismiss the class at one thirty and they would try calling him. I did that, checked back with the office then went to his house."

"And you had an entry code of your own?" Jasper prompted.

"Yes. Occasionally he'd forget something he needed for class and I would run for it," Corey said with a quick grin. "Part of the job."

Jasper nodded. "Was there anything odd about the front door when you got there?"

Corey looked blank then shook his head. "No sir."

"So you went in and what?" Jasper asked.

"I called his name first," Corey said. "When I didn't get an answer, I looked in the kitchen then went straight to his office. As soon as I saw him, I called the police."

"Did you touch him?" Jasper asked.

"On the neck," Corey said. "You can feel a pulse better there but I..." He bit his lip.

Jasper waited, feeling keen sympathy for him.

"No pulse," he said. "It was like touching dead meat. I knew he was gone."

Jasper heard a muffled sob behind him and knew the women were listening. He had to keep his focus on Corey.

"The back door," he said when Corey started to rise. He waved him back down. "The back door. There was a chair against it. Was that normal?"

"Yes sir," Corey seemed surprised. "I think the lock was broken and Professor Nugent hadn't bothered to get it fixed. He just kept the chair there. I never moved it."

Now that was odd, Jasper thought. He would have expected Nugent to be more careful of his security. A chair never replaced a good lock.

"So you never used that door?" Jasper asked.

"No sir. I think it just went into a maintenance corridor anyway. Most back doors do in this town."

"True," Jasper said. "Does that mean you're farm bred?"

"Yes sir," Corey smiled. "Our back doors go outside."

"I've heard," Jasper responded. "So does mine."

Corey smiled, his even white teeth adding color to his face. Jasper guessed from his coloring that he had just about every race in him. That was ok. So did Brown. Like her, Corey had gotten the better end of the deal with a straight nose not too big for his face and a fine color that never betrayed a lack of sunlight. He wondered briefly what his children would look like if he married Mel then put that thought aside. It was too early to wonder about that.

Had he missed anything? He didn't think so. Corey was unlikely to be questioned even this much. He'd handle it fine.

"I think we're done," Jasper said. "But there's something else I want to warn you about. When you go back to school, others will ask you what you saw. If you want to guard the professor's reputation, don't tell them any details. You found him in his office and he was dead."

"It's not a lie. I can even say he was in his chair."

"That's right," Jasper said. "No more detail than that except in an official police interview. Professor Nugent would want it that way."

"Yeah," Corey said. "He hated scandals."

"Yes, he did." Jasper studied him then remembered Mel. He looked up to see both women watching him. "Mel, will you remember that?"

"Yes, Dad." She hesitated. "Will you find his killer?"

"I can't officially," Jasper said. "I'm not on the force. I will work with Brown if I can to get this solved. You can't tell anyone that though. They'd expel me from Plains if they knew."

"I'd like to see them try," Jewel said, a flash of anger in her voice. "They should never have let you go. These things wouldn't be happening if..." She stopped, her voice cracking.

"Be sensible, Jewel. I couldn't have stopped this even if I was on the force." He rose to his feet. "There are other good people in the police force. The most I can do is be available when someone wants me. Unofficially. I'm not on the force and I have no intention of going back."

Chapter 9 - Questions

After a cyclist delivered their dinner, they sat down to baked potatoes, hamburgers, and green beans Jewel had whipped up to fill out the menu. At first the two kids just picked at their meal but they were college students and soon recovered.

After the dishes were done, Jasper led them up to the studio and encouraged them to experiment with his new drum while he thought. A quick message to Lori about the jammer bracelet got him Pedro Kruger's personal com unit number. The lab tech was a good pathologist and had worked with them in the past. Since they were dealing with Section 2 again, it was natural they requested him.

Why had Sanders been there? Jasper remembered that Sanders was Section 3, not Section 2, and he wasn't senior enough to get preference on loan outs. Brown was now the most senior homicide detective in their district with his separation. That meant she'd get assigned to any unusual or high-profile cases just like he had been. He did a quick check and found out Sanders had transferred to Section 2. He didn't think Lori had requested him. He wasn't experienced enough to partner her.

It was standard procedure for each district to have two or three really experienced people in homicide who would then get loaned out to other sections in their district when needed. They'd be partnered with a not-so-experienced local to give them more training. Most homicide cases were easy ones—family members—but occasionally there'd be a stumper or a high-profile murder. The West case had been a high profile and Jasper's orders had been simple: Keep their entry house tied up and give the family their due—They were, aft– all, a founding family. He hadn't expected the murders to multiply and he certainly hadn't planned on marrying into the family. He'd known going in it would be his last case for the city but it had turned out to be the biggest of his career.

Well, Lori Brown was now the senior homicide detective in District 1. The second ranked was Tom Black in Section 4. Jasper had worked with him on occasion and he was good. There wasn't a number three at the moment but Sanders wasn't likely to make it. He was still too new to homicide.

It wasn't his concern. Jasper walked down to the quieter second floor and called Pedro Kruger. It was promptly answered.

"Kruger here," the technician said. "Autopsy report is not complete, lieutenant. We came up with something in toxicology."

"You knew I would ask, huh?" Jasper said with a smile. "Let me guess. Was it a truth serum that had bliss as a component?"

"You got it in one," Kruger said. "But there's another chemical in his system we haven't identified. There's enough built up in his tissues that it looks like it wasn't a single dose but taken over time. I'm heading back over to his house now to see if I can locate any medicines he was taking."

"You're not waiting until morning?" Jasper asked.

"No sir. Brown got me thinking about that missing record and it made me nervous. The faster we are with this the better. I've got everything on flashers, by the way, as well as in the system. Brown says you're to have copies?"

"Yes," Jasper said. "But keep it quiet. I'm consulting but it's unofficial."

"Right. Well, I'm glad you are," Kruger said. "Detective Sanders is good but he's still out of his depth."

"Do you know why he transferred?" Jasper asked.

"No sir." Kruger's answer was a little too quick. "He still lives in Section 3."

Jasper frowned but let it go. There were other things he wanted to talk about. "Was the professor wearing a jammer bracelet when you took him in? I know he was wearing one last night at the Reach Out event."

"No sir," Kruger said. "Should I look for one?"

"Yes. It would probably be in his bedroom," Jasper said. "If not, his office."

"Interesting he should have one," Kruger said. "Was he a paranoid?"

Jasper paused then decided he didn't know. "I'm not sure. I do know he hated scandal. I would appreciate no public statements on how he was found until we know more–possibly not even then."

"Does your student know that?" Kruger asked.

"Yes. His name is Corey Morales and he's a good kid. We've already discussed it and he will simply say he found him in his office in his chair. Most people will assume he had a heart attack while grading papers."

"Good plan," Kruger said. "Ok, I'll keep to that line if anyone unofficial noses in. By the way, I think this was an accidental homicide but they planned to kill him anyway."

"My conclusion too." Jasper said. "If they just wanted to deep question him, they wouldn't have beat him. I know that memories can be blocked under deep questioning. Except for the time factor, they could have kept him from knowing they did it."

"And the injection site," Kruger said. "And the drugs leave traces in the system for days."

Jasper hesitated then asked. "Another area of interest?"

"Yes," Kruger said. "It was unlikely I'd ever stumble across that kind of thing in Plains but it happens. I like to know what's possible and how to detect it."

"I think you're wasted on Plains," Jasper said. "This city doesn't offer much in the way of conspiracy."

"I used to think so too," Kruger admitted. "But then I met you. Thanks."

Jasper laughed. "You're welcome."

"I'm at the house," Kruger said. "No reporters. Talk to you later."

"Later," Jasper said and broke the connection. Now Kruger he almost understood and he definitely appreciated. When the forensic technician had first asked to be assigned to his team, he'd wondered if the man was trying to jump ranks but had been assured he wasn't. Since then the technician had worked hard and uncovered odd bits that led to important conclusions–like identifying the passion flower poison that had been used on Mike. Maybe he'd identify what was used on the professor too.

Damn. He dialed his number back and Kruger answered immediately. "Forgot something," Jasper said. "Can you get the autopsy results for Ed Kucera? He died from a reaction to Bliss."

"That's in the works, lieutenant," Kruger said. "I got a preliminary weeks ago but not the toxicology results. I put in a request for that a couple of hours ago under the related causes of death clause."

"Why did they deny it the first time?" Jasper asked.

"Out of our jurisdiction," Kruger said and snorted. "We should have done the same to them on Mike West but we didn't."

"No, we didn't," Jasper said. "Thanks for being on top of things."

"Any time."

"Happy hunting," Jasper said and broke the connection.

Out of their jurisdiction? What did Jameson know about that? He'd been cooperative with Jasper but the Cheyenne Police Department hadn't once they'd known who Jake West was. He hadn't expected legal nonsense from Denver as well. He'd have to call Jameson in the morning and see what he could find out. The Denver detective owed him one.

"Coming down," his daughter's voice called from the stairs and he looked up in time to see her and Corey descending.

"What's this?" Jasper asked, seeing they were smiling.

"We've been ordered to study," Mel said. "Now I know you married a school teacher."

"She has her priorities straight," Jasper said with a smile. "When are your classes tomorrow?"

"Tomorrow is Sunday, Dad," Mel said. "No classes but we'll be gone around nine."

"She convinced both of you to stay?" Jasper asked.

"Yeah, she said pick our own rooms and camp," Mel said with a gleam in her eye. "I'm going to stay in her old bedroom. It's neater than mine."

Jasper smiled. "Yes, you can find the bed. Did they teach you how to pick up at that school?"

She gave him a pained expression and he laughed, guessing that topic was off limits around Corey. Well, he knew what his daughter's room usually looked like. If it was clean, he'd wonder where his real daughter went.

"What room did you pick?" he asked Corey.

"Just the guest room," Corey said. "Big bed and all." His eyes fell and Jasper tried not to grin. He'd been guilty of that kind of slip himself.

"Yes, you can spread out," he said. "Hit the books, kids. I'll just go get the coffee pot."

"Oh, Dad, Jewel says no more coffee tonight," Mel quickly said. "She said. I would NEVER say that."

Jasper stopped, knowing Jewel was right but being told so through his daughter put him off. "And here I thought she was wore out," Jasper finally said with an interested look up the stairs that had his daughter blushing. "Good night, kids."

He nearly laughed as he took the stairs a little quicker than usual. God, it was fun messing with their minds. Not that he couldn't but that wasn't what this was about. Jewel knew he was restless after too much coffee. He just didn't need his daughter brought into it.

Finding Jewel curled up on the couch staring into the flames of their fireplace vid, he stopped and all thoughts of coffee fled his mind. She'd been the hostess today, distracting the kids even though Drew Nugent meant a lot more to her but now they were gone and it was just them–her and the husband she'd chosen over Nugent. Was she regretting that? Probably not but it was still hard on her.

He sat down beside her and pulled her close. She sighed and rested Her head on his shoulder but neither of them spoke for a long time.

"Are they going to stay down there?" Jewel finally asked.

"Yes," Jasper said. "They might raid the kitchen but they won't be up here again tonight."

"That's okay," Jewel said and snuggled closer. "I am just so... sad." Her words were slow and halting. "Scared too."

He turned her face toward him and looked into those deep blue eyes. They were swimming with unshed tears. "This has nothing to do with your family," he firmly said. "And I'll find out who did it."

"I couldn't marry him," Jewel said with a sob. "He was so old."

"I know, love," Jasper said and just held her while sobs wracked her body. "And he understood. He was your uncle's friend and he just felt he could protect you. That was all."

"He said he loved me," Jewel replied. "I..."

"He didn't love you like I do," Jasper said. "Maybe like a daughter or a bright student but he didn't love you as a wife."

The sharpness of his tone made her look up and he knew he'd been too harsh but damn it, he'd asked the man. And he could see there was no chemistry between them. Drew had been fatherly, not sexual, when he looked at Jewel.

"Not like you," Jewel said with a sniff.

"Not at all like me." Jasper was blunt. "You knew that or you wouldn't have cut him off before you even met me. He wasn't interested in anything except protecting you when Mike was gone."

"But he would have," Jewel said.

"He would have," Jasper said. "He was a good friend and you need to remember that but he didn't really want a wife. And, you," he touched her nose, "would have demanded too much of him."

That got a laugh. "I, I couldn't."

"Then you would have been frustrated and unhappy and you would have made his life hell," Jasper said. "I could see you burning his books if you got unhappy enough. Be glad you said no. He probably was in the end."

She sniffed again but she was no longer crying. "I wouldn't burn books."

"No but you threaten to turn my drum into a vase," Jasper said. "If you got unhappy enough, you would. Jewel, I was a cop. I've seen what frustrated women can do. I've seen them destroy their hubby's toys before. I've even been to a couple of murders. He was better off without you."

"You!" She finally flared up. "You man."

Jasper grinned but he really wasn't joking. Had Drew been in any sense relieved that Jewel had refused to marry him? He should have been. The stoic history professor would have found himself in hell. He would have had to force Jewel into his mold to survive and eventually she would have exploded and took him with her. No, he had saved the professor then. He just wished he could be certain he hadn't killed him now.

"Now I can handle you," Jasper said, "even if you do wear me out. You are one hell of a lover."

Her irritation faded and she kissed him, a long tender kiss that let him know she felt it too. All kidding aside, they were made for each other. There was a chemistry, a flame, he'd felt only once before and it had never been this intense. If Carol had been a flame, Jewel was a bonfire. He didn't love Carol any the less but he was thankful he hadn't known Jewel when Carol was here.

When the kiss ended, he raised his hand to block her. "Not tonight," he said.

She sighed and relaxed back into his arms. "You're right."

"Did Corey call his parents?" Jasper asked. "It's getting late and he needs to do that."

"He did," Jewel said. "They were shocked like he said they would be but not eager for him to drop out of school. I couldn't tell if they were as bad as Mel said they were. Maybe because I was there, they were just nice folks."

"Possibly," Jasper said. "I'll see what I can do about keeping him in school. He's a good kid."

"As long as you don't become a grandpa before I'm a mother," she said with a trace of wickedness. "I want my turn."

"You'll get it, precious Jewel," he said. "But not tonight. Did you call David?"

She shook her head. "I couldn't."

"Your uncle will be calling here when he sees the news," Jasper said but she wouldn't meet his eyes. "Ok, I'll do it. Why don't you get ready for bed?"

Slipping out of his arms, she disappeared into the bedroom.

Nine o'clock. Not too late for normal people. Aware David was also a newlywed, he hated to call him this late. Well, it had to be done. He would just like to avoid another weeping woman.

The call with David was brief and not as bad as he expected. After assuring him Jewel was well and had a healthy appetite, he got down to it. David's frown deepened as he listened but he mostly just listened to the police style report Jasper gave.

"I'm sorry it had to be Drew," David finally said. "You're sure this had nothing to do with our murders?"

"Nothing," Jasper said. "I interviewed the professor myself and he was clean. There is a connection to Kucera's death though."

"There is?" David's frown returned. "How?"

"The professor was his last visitor before he died. What's more curious is his name and the vid record completely disappeared from police records after. I knew it and Brown knew it here and maybe three people in Denver."

"That's not possible," David said. "Or it shouldn't be. Who the hell could do that?"

"No one I know of could do it without a court order," Jasper said. "But it was done. That suggests Drew Nugent had secrets we knew nothing about. I think his death today was tied to those, not your family."

"Sounds it," David said. "Are they bringing you back in?"

"I'm consulting," Jasper said. "Quietly."

"Let me know what develops," David said. "I'll tell Elinor. The official story is he passed away in his office?"

"Yes."

"I'll stick with that," David said. "I don't want her worried right now."

"Neither do I," Jasper said. "Good luck on the baby."

"Thanks," David said. "I'm glad I don't have to actually do it. Doctors can be awfully proddy."

Jasper smiled. "So can I."

David laughed and cut the connection.

Jasper glanced at the calendar and saw they were still five or six days away from Elinor's big day. Having set aside ova nearly twelve years ago, she was being implanted with her first baby. From what he understood, that included some hormone shots and a lot of tears, some sperm from David, and a doctor's visit. Not nearly as much fun as what he and Jewel were doing. If it worked, his wife would have a new cousin in about nine months. He wasn't hopeful he could get his job done by then but he was trying. Just not tonight.

Chapter 10 - Sunday, 7 Nov 2179

Buzzing sounded in his ear, dragging him out of sleep. Jasper swatted at his com unit, missed, and grabbed it again. Pushing the answer button out of long habit, he half-growled a hello.

"Got something!" Kruger's cheery voice broke the morning silence and Jasper's eyes popped open. Before he could hit privacy mode, Kruger continued. "Found the pills, lieutenant. Just like you said, they react with bliss. The professor had a big bottle of them in his bathroom."

Jasper's hand got back to the com unit and he switched it to privacy and put it to his ear. Jewel, hopefully, was still asleep.

"Labeled?" he asked.

"Not the right label," Kruger said. "It was an old prescription bottle—about four years old. The pills were the wrong color so I took the bottle back to the lab. We've got a dead rat. It took the drug and no effect. When it got bliss too, it curled up and died. Brain death before the heart stopped."

"That fits with what we know about Kucera's death," Jasper said. "He was dead before the cell sensors knew it."

"Exactly," Kruger said. "Pretty cool drug. It seems totally inert until it interacts with bliss. I've got two other rats with it in their system. I want to see how long one dose is effective so I'll test one tomorrow."

"Good idea," Jasper said. "How much do you think the professor had?"

"He might have taken one each day to get to the level he was," Kruger said. "It was really detectable. Kucera had been in custody for six days and it still killed him. I wonder if his widow knows whether he took them daily?"

"She's not talking to police," Jasper said. "She wouldn't even talk to Jewel last time she saw her." He hadn't been surprised at that. Jewel had told him Elaine Kucera was being escorted by her lawyer at the Reach Out event. They had only managed to exchange condolences before the lawyer steered her away.

"I really need the toxicology on Kucera," Kruger said. "I can't tie them together without it."

"I'll call Jameson," Jasper responded. "Any chance this drug is registered?"

"No, it's not," Kruger said. "The pills are machine made with no marks. They probably didn't come into the city through legal channels."

"That doesn't surprise me," Jasper said. "What do they look like?"

"Yellow like low dose aspirin," Kruger said. "Same yellow but no marks. Same size too."

"Hold on," Jasper said. "The same color and size?"

"Yes," Kruger said. "If they'd been in an aspirin bottle with a seal, they could have made it in."

"Thanks," Jasper said and swung his feet to the floor. "What pharmacist did the professor use?"

"The prescription bottle is old, lieutenant."

"I know but people like the professor have regular habits. He might have got them at his regular pharmacy." Jasper knew he was reaching but it was something he could do. No, he couldn't. Damn. He couldn't just walk in, flash his badge and ask to see the pharmacy records for the professor. Brown would have to do it–or Sanders.

"Never mind," Jasper said. "Copy your report to Sanders and ask him to follow up on it. If the professor didn't buy any low dose aspirin there in the past year, we'll know he got it from another source."

"Do you think they'd actually ring it up as aspirin?" Kruger asked.

"I've seen stranger things," Jasper said. "There's usually another high-priced item on the same ticket when they do that except they never take the item."

"I'll copy my report to Sanders and Brown," Kruger said.

"Did you find a jammer?" Jasper asked.

"No sir," Kruger answered. "Lots of interesting books though. I wish I'd had time to look at them."

"I know what you mean," Jasper said. "I suspect someone will have to go through each book for clues."

"I volunteer," Kruger promptly said.

"I'll pass that on," Jasper said. "Just get me that autopsy first."

"It'll be complete before noon," Kruger replied. "Unless we get another case, I'll be free then."

"Be careful with statements like that," Jasper said. "No more multiples."

"Right. Got to go."

Kruger broke the connection before he could respond, leaving Jasper eyeing the com unit in his hand. He set it down then swatted his wife's behind. "Move it, Jewel."

"Ow," she promptly said with no trace of sleepiness.

"You heard enough, witch." Jasper made his way to the bathroom. "Next time remember to snore."

"Just for that, I'm going to use my own shower," Jewel announced and grabbed her robe to head for the second floor bathroom she had staked out as her own.

"Kids," Jasper said.

"It's almost nine. They had plans." Jewel's voice was receding beyond the rush of water.

Jasper grinned. It would serve her right if they overslept and caught her in that sheer robe. She had nothing on beneath. Well, he liked to see her strutting around in that thing. Corey might be shocked but he didn't care. Chances are the boy was gone anyway.

The pharmacy lead was probably a waste of time. What he needed to know about was who the professor rubbed shoulders with outside of Reach Out and the university–and the Masonic lodge. He had nearly forgotten that.

He wasn't a Mason. Did he know any cops who were? He couldn't think of any. That was something else to follow up on.

Wondering if Rick Gordon would be any use, he stepped into the shower.

* * *

"In obituaries, noted Professor Andrew Nugent passed away yesterday at his home here in Plains. Professor Nugent was a professor at Plains University and head of the history department. He also was the star of "History Lives," the lecture series on the STV1, and a well-known champion of Reach Out. Services will be held at the Cathedral but the date has not yet been set."

Jasper listened to the obituary, hoping that was it but the anchors cut to vid of the professor's house with its police lock. There was a crowd of students there and he wasn't too surprised to see Corey among them.

"Professor Nugent was extremely popular on campus for his fascinating lectures on history and his no tolerance policy toward bliss. He was also known for helping promising students in financial difficulty. The campus and even the city will miss him."

"Will his series continue on STV1?" the other anchor asked.

"We've been told it will," the first one said. "And rerun. It's far too popular for them to drop it."

Jasper raised an eyebrow. That popular? He glanced at Jewel as she joined him and took the cup of coffee she offered.

"Why is there a police seal on the door?" the second anchor asked. "Didn't he die of natural causes?"

The first anchor was ready with the answer. "The professor was a well-known book collector. Since he had no family living here, the police put the seal on to protect his collection. It will be gone once the books are inventoried and moved to a secure location."

"Yes, I heard the professor was a book collector," the second anchor said but he didn't go into the details of that strange book theft. "Again, Professor Andrew Nugent passed away at his home yesterday and services will be scheduled at a later date."

Jasper waited till the next story began but there was no footage of him at the scene and no pictures singling out Corey. There was nothing from that hectic scene yesterday and the police seal had been explained away. He'd never seen such restraint before.

"Now we know where Corey is," Jewel said. "I can't blame him."

"A vigil," Jasper said. "I hadn't realized how much a difference Drew made." He took a swallow of coffee to ease the tension in his throat. Students didn't gather like that for just any teacher. That was one hell of a tribute to the man.

Damn it, he knew there was more to Drew Nugent than just a popular teacher. He'd seen that vid of him ordering Kucera—and Kucera had been surprised it was him. There were clearly others Kucera knew so there had been some sort of organization. He doubted it had died with the professor.

He shouldn't have dismissed the man as Jewel's rejected suitor. He should have got to know him. He'd let his personal feelings—his personal life—get in the way.

That house—he was going to have to get in there with enough time to do a really thorough search. He'd have to get Brown's help. Those students at the door would have to go.

They were just finishing a late breakfast when Brown called. Jasper took his com unit to private mode right away to keep Jewel from hearing.

"Jazz here," he said.

"Morning," Brown answered. "Jazz, is Jewel home?"

He glanced at his wife and said "Yes, let me move."

"No, just keep her there," Brown said. "The confession has been released and it concerns her and you."

"Damn, I'd forgotten about that," Jasper said. "Right, we'll be here."

"I'll be there in a few," Brown said. "And an FBI agent is coming with me."

"FBI?" Jasper frowned, suddenly not liking the tone of her voice. Was she warning him? Before he could ask, she broke the connection. He looked at the com unit suspiciously. What was she trying to tell him?

"Jewel, forget the dishes," he said. "Linda will do them. We need coffee and cups upstairs."

"Ok," Jewel said. "How many?"

"Brown and one more," Jasper said. "Send them up in the waiter." He headed up the stairs, still uneasy about the tone of Brown's voice. He wanted to see that confession but there was something about the way she asked after Jewel.

"Butler."

"Here, sir."

"Record everything on this floor until I cancel the order. Confirm," Jasper said.

"Record everything on this floor until you cancel," Butler responded. "Start now?"

"Start now."

"Starting."

Jasper turned as Jewel arrived on the stairs and gave her a quick hug then joined her in setting up the small table with the coffee service.

"What's got you on edge?" Jewel asked when he stepped back to survey the room.

"Kucera's confession has been released. Brown is bringing it over," Jasper said.

"Couldn't she just copy it to you?" Jewel asked then said "Oh, no, of course not. You're supposed to be locked out."

Jasper looked sharply at her. "Yes, I am locked out."

Jewel nodded. "Yes, you are."

Damn her, she was entirely too observant. "Pedro called me. You will forget what you heard, love."

"That's who that was?" Jewel asked. "Yes sir. I didn't hear that much anyway."

"Just enough to be dangerous," Jasper said. "Look, that was about the professor. If you want me to solve his murder, you'd better not comment or eavesdrop again."

"Sir, Detective Brown is here. Is she expected?" Butler's voice broke in before Jewel could answer.

"Yes, let her in. Butler, silent mode," Jasper said.

"Yes sir, silent mode." The butler's canned voice cut off as it executed the order.

"I'll behave," Jewel quickly said, "but let me stay."

"This time," Jasper said and turned to face the stairs.

Lori Brown looked unhappy as she stepped off the stairs, almost grim. Her brown eyes met his in a pleading expression and Jasper knew this wasn't good. What the hell was going on?

He didn't know the FBI agent who followed her but he suddenly wished it was someone he knew. The man wore a plain black suit a little better quality than the standard suit city detectives wore. He'd already pulled out his badge and displayed it prominently on his breast pocket. This was clearly official.

"Let's see it," Jasper said without preamble. "I've been waiting for this."

Brown stuck a flasher in his vid screen's console and keyed up the pictures of the handwritten confession.

Jasper scanned it, skipping the official header to focus on the meat of it.

I confess I was a fool but I had nothing to do with murder. Why would I kill my richest client? Jake West was going to Mars and I was going to represent him here on Earth. When he turned thirty he was going to the richest client in my business. I didn't kill him or order him killed.

Mike West was a good friend. I didn't order his death either.

Elizabeth West was a charming lady and a friend to my wife. She was past eighty and had taken the walk once already. Why would anyone waste time or money killing her? I certainly didn't.

I admit to some contact with the man you've called Starling. I knew him simply as Smith. He was introduced to me and I introduced him to Jake—as a favor for a friend.

Somehow I've been framed for these murders but none of them, particularly Jake's, benefited me. There are only two people they would have helped. Elizabeth's granddaughter stood to inherit everything just like Jake. You may dismiss her as just a schoolteacher but she's a West and easily the cleverest of them. She and the man she intends to marry should be questioned thoroughly. He's almost as clever as she is—not quite for I know his true role.

I'm done. Clear my name.

--Edward Kucera

Jasper stared at the confession, momentarily struck dumb. Jewel? His Jewel? He glanced at her and saw she'd gone white. No, it made no sense. And how could Kucera know his true role?

"I never even met Kucera," Jasper flatly stated. "There's no way he could know my true role in anything."

"Never, lieutenant?" The FBI agent asked. "No contact?"

Jasper thought back. "I tried to get an interview with him during the West murders but he refused to cooperate. Vid call only. He never met me."

"Drew," Jewel said and Jasper stiffened. "He's talking about Drew." Her eyes flew to his. "And now Drew is dead. They were friends. Drew and Uncle Mike introduced him to Jake."

"Drew didn't kill himself," Jasper said, "and you sure as hell didn't do it. You were here with me."

"Who is this Drew?" the FBI agent asked. "And now he's dead?"

"Professor Andrew Nugent," Brown smoothly inserted. "He was found yesterday. The man was beaten then killed. My estimate is that it took over two hours with the time of death actually being around noon yesterday. There were at least two men involved."

"I'm sorry, Jewel," she added. "I can't tell you it was quick."

"Poor Drew," Jewel said, her voice cracking. "All he wanted was his books."

Jasper's mind was working fast. He knew where this had to lead. Jewel would have to go in for questioning and this time it wouldn't be a simple interrogation with truth sensors. They would drug her and take her down to where she couldn't lie—and he couldn't be there. Damn Kucera! What he wrote made so much sense, down to the timing of the murders. Once Jake was off planet, he couldn't be touched. It had to happen before he left but how the hell did Jake get talked into helping? Why did he point his finger at Kucera? Could his wife actually be devious enough to plan this and then marry him to keep him from finding out? She was the only one there when Mike died. He'd dismissed that before because she was so clearly shocked to find him dead.

How the hell had Starling known when Jake's body was going to be viewed? He shot a look at his wife. He'd been there when they came out of the building. He'd been there in disguise and ready to take David out. He hadn't gone for Jewel, just David.

Damn Kucera and his confession. He'd loved her. No, he still loved her. They were just going to have to get through this mess.

"Jewel, you'll have to come down to Denver for questioning," Brown gently said. "The judge has ordered it. Jasper will come later."

"Questioning?" Jewel looked dazed. "Not here?"

"No, it has to be in Denver," Brown said. "The FBI has jurisdiction. Let's pack you an overnight bag. You can call your uncle on the way. He'll arrange for a lawyer."

"A lawyer?" Jewel stopped, an edge coming into her voice. "You can't honestly believe that I killed—"

"No, of course not," Brown quickly said. "But we have to clear this up."

"Jasper?" Jewel breathed his name.

Jasper shook himself then turned to his wife. "You have to go," he said. "I'll be there by morning. Lori, are you escorting her?"

"Yes, it's set," Brown said with a warning look at the FBI agent. "Until she has a lawyer, I'll stand by. The Captain can tell you more–call him."

"Right." Jasper caught his wife's hand and walked a few steps away with her. "Trust Lori. They'll just question you. Unless you have something to hide, you'll be back here tomorrow."

"You don't believe them?" Jewel asked then drew back when he didn't answer. "How could you?" Her eyes started to tear up and her cheeks reddened.

"I don't know what to believe, Jewel," he said, his heart heavy. "Let's get this settled."

"I don't believe you would just toss me to the lions," she said, her words low and angry. "I love you, Jazz Stone!"

All he could do was watch as she stomped into the bedroom to gather her things. Lori followed and he sat down heavily.

The FBI agent kept his distance but his eyes showed some sympathy. He didn't move closer though.

Damn him, Jasper thought. How were they supposed to get out of this mess? Did Kucera know what a can of worms he was opening with that confession? Had he planned this to get revenge?

No, there was something deeper here. He'd known all along that it made no sense for Kucera to kill Jake-or involve him in his grandmother's death. The timing of the whole thing also stank.

If the motive had been to make Jake the sole survivor of the West clan, it could have waited–should have waited–until Jake was off planet and couldn't be implicated. But if the goal was to make Jewel the sole survivor, the timing was rushed but necessary. They had to get Jake before he entered quarantine.

Jewel, why? If it wasn't you, did Drew plan it? If he had, who had killed him? Thank God, Jewel had been here yesterday.

Chapter 11 - Shutdown

Jasper sat blankly staring at nothing while he tried to think but his thoughts kept returning to Jewel being accused and wondering if he could be wrong. He knew he wasn't but it made so much sense, he couldn't dismiss it. He turned it over and over in his mind trying to find something—anything—that would clear her and there was so much that wouldn't. The only thing he could be sure of is she didn't kill her grandmother. Not only had Jake—dmitted to clubbing her but Jewel had been with her class and she had eighteen kids plus teachers and the school's own logger doors to verify she was there. She couldn't have done that one and he knew it.

She had no alibi for Mike's death. God, could she have killed the uncle who helped raise her? No, he wouldn't believe that yet. He'd seen her fall apart when they found him.

Could she and Jake have planned this together? He was just starting down that path when his com unit buzzed and brought him back to reality. Thinking it might be Brown, he thumbed it on.

"Stone, where are you?" his captain thundered. "Didn't you get my message?"

"Message?" Jasper answered, his mind still distracted. "What message?"

"I needed you here at the professor's half an hour ago," the captain said in clipped tones. "We've got an hour, maybe two, before they shut this down."

"Who?" Jasper's mind cleared.

"Jazz, forget your damned wife for a minute," the captain said, his tone no milder. "Kucera as good as named the professor. The answer is here, damn it."

Abruptly Jasper's mind cleared. "You're right. I'm on my way. Who's shutting it down?"

"Never mind who. Just get your butt over here. I've got Hunter with me but I need more eyes we can trust."

"Got one, I think," Jasper said. "Be there as soon as I can."

Thumbing through his numbers, he called Pedro and the lab tech's voice promptly answered. "Pedro, we need you back at the professor's house."

"Oh, hi, bro. No, I can't make lunch today. Something's come up at the lab," the technician said, his voice cheerful.

Damn. "Are they taking it all?"

"That's right," he said. "Not today. Can I call you back later?"

"Yes," Jasper said. "Message received." He disconnected and concentrated on reaching the professor's house in time to do some good.

It took him nearly twenty minutes in the Sunday traffic but he got there on a city-owned bicycle he grabbed off a rental rack. At the door he had to wait for someone to let him in because he didn't have the lock codes.

Precious minutes lost. The students were gone and he was thankful for that.

Ed Hunter let him in, still in his regular blue uniform. He didn't ask questions but just led him to the study.

"Go over his desk, Jazz. I'm working on these shelves and Hunter has the other wall," his captain said as he took a book out of its plastic case and briefly shook it. A bookmark fell to the floor but nothing else, so he reboxed it and moved on.

"Who's pulling the plug?" Jasper asked again as he picked up an unboxed book and checked it for bookmarks.

"I can't say because I don't know," the captain said. "I got the word it was coming down and got over here. I couldn't use Brown. Ed, here, is a good man."

Jasper nodded, reaching for a third book then paused at the title. *Secret Societies* by Peter Mason. Realizing this could be a major clue, he opened it and started scanning the contents. Some words were underlined and there were a couple of penciled comments in the margins but there was nothing he could puzzle out quickly. He set it aside and continued his search.

"I'm bringing Ed in on the blissex case," the captain said as he continued checking books. "And he'll be a detective as soon as the paperwork gets through."

"Good." Jasper smiled at Ed but didn't stop in his search. It was unusual for the captain to call anyone by their first name so Ed Hunter must have impressed him quickly. It had taken him a lot longer to get that courtesy.

Jasper hesitated over a blank notepad, peering at it closely. "I think I have something," he said. Taking out his secure com unit, he took a picture of it then told his detection program to enhance. The words last written on the pad came into view as the software measured imperfections in the image and darkened them.

"What the hell?" Jasper read the note in disbelief.

"What is it?" his captain quickly came to his side to read it. "To T. S. J. Stone is asking questions about last visit to Denver. Are you sure all vids are gone? -Prof. N."

"T. S? Who the hell is T. S?" the captain asked. "Put that on this flasher." He handed him a pink flasher.

"I can't think of one," Jasper said, "but there's someone else." He tapped out the name on his notepad and showed it to the captain. His eyes went wide at what he read but he nodded. He'd gotten the message.

"Curious if he's involved," the captain said. "Delete that. So the professor knew you were asking questions and knew who killed the vids. Jazz, are you sure he's not a fed?"

Jasper looked at him in shock. Nugent a federal agent? Like him? No, there was no way he could be DEA but he could work for another branch. It was just so unlikely he couldn't grasp it. Who would want a history professor?

"I don't know," he said and saw Ed turn to look at him. "Is there any way we can find out?"

"Well, I think it's the feds shutting down this investigation," his captain said. "And I think only the feds could pull and destroy official surveillance vids. We might have to assume he was and call it a dead end."

"Does that mean you're a fed?" Ed Hunter asked. "Is that why you're here now?"

Jasper hesitated then knew he'd have to bring him in. Well, if the captain trusted him, he'd have to take the chance. He'd be partnering Brown, after all, and it would be damned awkward to exclude him when he needed to meet with her. Adjusting his secure unit, he thumbed in his code to bring up the special functions. Turning it to scan, he pressed the back of his locket to the unit.

The unit froze up briefly then his DEA credentials showed on the screen, complete with his badge and real name. His code name was not referenced. He showed the unit's screen to Ed Hunter and he whistled. A moment later Jasper was wiping the screen.

"Good to know," Ed said. "Do I call you Jazz?"

"Yes, we just became friends," Jasper said with a glance at his captain. "You're the fourth to know." It was then he noticed the ring on Ed's hand–a Masonic ring. "You're a Mason?"

"Yes," Ed glanced at his ring then back to him. "Twenty years."

"Nugent was a Mason," he told his captain. "It may be important. Maybe not."

"Yes, I knew Nugent was," Ed said. "There's already talk about the rites. What does that have to do with this?"

"Maybe nothing," Jasper said, "but he wore a second ring." He found it on his com unit. "Here, what can you tell me about this?" He pointed to the second, smaller ring.

"That's not Masonic," Ed said. "It looks almost like ours but we have a triangle and rays. This is just the eye."

"Symbol for another group?" Captain Reynolds asked. "Related?"

"I don't know," Jasper said and fumbled for the book on secret societies. "But there's this. It's marked up. I don't think the professor would keep a vandalized book unless there was a darn good reason."

"Good point. Let's just see if we can keep that from getting away with the rest." His captain took the book and slipped it into a thin brief case. "I'm going to break a whole bunch of regulations by telling you two to forget you saw this book for 48 hours. It'll be back here by then."

"Yes sir," Jasper promptly replied. "You might leave it in his nightstand when it's returned."

"Good thought. Ed? Do you have a problem with this?" His captain looked at him.

"I should but I really hate having our hands tied," Ed Hunter said. "I don't think this has to do with blissex but it's something big. No, I'll keep quiet. Who gets the scans?"

His captain hesitated then turned to Jasper.

"Sir, multiple copies might be best," he said. "And I know someone in the department that knows about secret societies. He also warned me they're already at the labs taking evidence from this case. Pedro Kruger, forensic technician, Section 2."

"I'll consider it," the captain said. "What did he have that they wanted?"

"He didn't say specifically but he came over last night and uncovered the pills that react with bliss. He gave me a report this morning on them—and they look like low dose aspirin with no makers' marks."

"Reacts with bliss?" Ed Hunter asked. "I've never heard of that."

"We have two confirmed deaths from bliss reactions," Jasper said. "Ed Kucera and Drew Nugent. There's bliss in most truth serums so Nugent got it that way. Kucera got regular bliss from a jail guard."

"Wait a moment," his captain said with a frown. "Kucera hadn't been questioned under truth serums–his lawyer had blocked it. If he had been, is there a possibility the truth serum would kill him anyway?"

Jasper looked at him, suddenly putting that together. "He'd been in custody for six days," he said. "Maybe the pills would wear off soon. If they were meant to be taken daily, they'd eventually seep out of his system. They gave him an order to suicide to prevent that from happening."

That suddenly made sense. "Kruger said the professor had measurable levels of whatever it was in his system. We haven't been able to get the Kucera autopsy report."

"Who gave him the order to suicide?" Ed Hunter asked. "How?"

"Professor Nugent. He was the last visitor Ed Kucera had."

Hunter looked stunned. "Him?"

"Him," Jasper confirmed. "If you need to see it, there's a vid of his visit–a vid that has disappeared from official police records."

"Yeah, I heard about a disappearing vid but not what was on it." Hunter looked grim. "Ok, I want to get to the bottom of this now. It's too damned odd for the Drew Nugent I knew."

"We'll get to it," the captain said. His com unit chimed twice then shut up. "Trouble," the captain said. "They're probably on their way. Clean it up and let's get out."

When his unit chimed again, just twice, the captain looked surprised then answered. "Reynolds here." His frown deepened and he let out an explosive "Shit!"

"Forget that," he barked at them and headed toward the door, com unit in hand. Jasper grabbed his briefcase and followed, Hunter on his heels. "I want a scramble and I want it now! Get every officer, on or off duty, into that train station–sections four, five, six, seven, and eight. Those bastards are not to get away!"

Jasper kept pace, his mind going fast. A scramble? That was a major alert. Something big had happened, maybe a bomb.

"Then call him! Tell the commissioner we have two officers down and this can't wait." The captain was blunt. When they reached the squad car, he motioned for Hunter to drive. "Shut the maintenance doors to those sections. We've got to trap them before they get her away."

Get her away? Jasper felt a chill creep up his spine. Two officers? The train station? When the captain turned to him, he knew. His heart thumped then turned to ice when the captain said "It's Jewel."

He didn't remember the rest of the drive to the train station. Jewel—someone had taken Jewel. His gut wrenched and his eyes burned but he had no time for that. Some bastard had taken Jewel. Anger melted the ice and his fists clenched. His jaw tightened and he just wanted out of the squad car. He wanted to find them and—Lori! What the hell had happened to Lori?

By the time they reached the station, he'd heard enough of the captain's one-sided conversation to know Lori Brown was down and possibly dead. His partner. Jewel was missing.

There were already a dozen squad cars when they arrived and two ambulances. A uniformed transit officer met the captain and began talking at once.

"Four men, sir. We have one—the FBI agent shot him before he went down. Our officer is down and they took a woman. They had a delivery car but they didn't stay with it. It was abandoned three blocks away. We're focusing our search on that area."

"Condition of the officers?" the captain snapped.

"One's dead—they slashed her throat. The other is still breathing. He was shot."

Jasper followed the captain, not even slowing when they passed the covered body of Lori Brown. Lori. Tears stung his eyes but he blinked them back. He had to find Jewel. His Jewel. He couldn't do anything for Brown but get her killers.

A train, one of the locals, thundered past on the far track and no one could hear. When it was gone, the captain asked "Any chance they got on a train?"

"No sir," the transit officer said. "The officers were headed for the VIP car when they were attacked. Other passengers saw it and called us. They saw them leave the platform through a freight door. Two men followed and saw the delivery van."

"Jasper, does your wife's com unit have a GPS?" The captain turned toward him. "What's the code?"

Jasper fumbled for his and dug it out. "12543894756 alpha tango."

"Write it down," the captain said. "I want that out on search."

Jasper knew that hope was vague but he clung to it. The GPS, if it wasn't blocked by something, would give them physical location but not the level. The city had six levels—six possible locations—a single GPS reading could be.

Lacking paper, he pressed search on his own unit first. It was his wife's com unit. He had the necessary permissions to locate her. When someone thrust paper and pen at him, he copied the number out and waited an impossibly long time for the program to tell him unit not found.

"It's blocked," he told the captain. "The inspection sensors—"

"I'm already on it," his captain said and continued to fire off orders to a steady stream of officers arriving from the surrounding sections. Jasper watched, helpless, until he saw an opportunity. Seeing the captain was putting them in groups of three, he started sorting them out for him.

He didn't know when the rough office was set up but he was suddenly in there and helping to mark down the results of reports officers called in. There were other vehicles moving in the maintenance corridors and he snarled an order himself to shut them all down but lacked the authorization codes.

"Damn it, nothing should be moving!" His voice carried through the rough office and it was suddenly quiet.

"What is he doing here?"

He turned to see the police commissioner and city attorney both there and knew he'd blown it but didn't care. Someone repeated his order to stop traffic with the proper codes.

"Jazz, sit down and don't try to run things," a female voice said but it was too late.

The police commissioner pointed to an officer. "Trank him."

He barely felt the trank shot. Jewel. He had to find Jewel. He felt himself sag then it went black.

Chapter 12 - Kidnapped

Low voices tugged at him, bringing him back from a nether region where he was chasing through endless corridors, looking for Carol. She was taking the walk. She was leaving him. No, she'd gone. He was looking for Jewel.

An aching void filled him. His eyes stung as memories surged back and he blinked them open to dim light. He flung out his hand to catch something, anything, and hit cloth clad muscle. A wordless sound of surprise told him it was someone.

"He's awake. Damn it, Jazz, that hurt." David West was leaning over him, one hand rubbing his leg. "Don't hit the wall. It won't give."

He blinked, his eyes finally adjusting to the light, and he sat up with an effort. The medical cot he lay on wasn't meant for easy rising. "Where am I?" he asked then stopped as the sound of a train filled the small room.

"When did you get here?" His head pounded and refused to clear as he looked up at David West. "Did they find her?" He braced himself for the worst.

"No but there's hope," David said. "Look at this."

A piece of paper was thrust into his hands. Carefully printed words swam before his eyes. "Call off the search or Mrs. Stone dies. Tell Stone to go home and wait for instructions. No more police."

"When? How long was I out?" Rage filled him that they'd done that to him but it was dull. He couldn't think. What the hell had they given him?

"You've been out seven hours," David said, his face grim. "They found that about four hours ago and did what it said. No more search–at least nothing visible. Every inspection sensor in this area of the city is still looking for her. They found her com unit with that note."

"And they called you?" Jasper felt stupid. Of course they had. God, he couldn't think.

"As soon as you hit the floor, I think," David said. "They had to show me you were there to convince me it was real and Jewel was kidnapped. I came on the next train. Elinor's at home."

"Sorry," Jasper said.

"For what?" David responded. "For not knowing two cops weren't enough to protect her? Hell, I would have done the same thing." He scrubbed his face then grabbed his hand. "Come on, let's get you up."

"What the hell did they give me?" Jasper asked, finding it hard to find his feet. "Where's everyone?"

"No more police," David said. "They took it seriously. Your captain stayed till I got here and gave me the details but the rest were gone. They didn't tell me what they dropped you with–maybe a trank?"

"I've been tranked," Jasper said. "This is a lot worse. I can't feel a damned thing. Jewel–"

"We'll get Jewel back," David firmly said. Putting a shoulder under his arm, he turned him around so Jasper could see the cot jammed into a corner behind a desk. It was a tight space littered with papers and discarded coffee cups.

"I need coffee," Jasper said.

"You always need coffee," David said. "Let's get you home."

It took the long ride home for Jasper to find his wits. Jewel. She was alive. They'd said that. His eyes burned as he thought of finding her lifeless body in some dark corner of the city. Taking a deep breath, he tried to shove that image away.

God, he'd doubted her. His precious Jewel was gone and he'd doubted her. The last thing he said—how could he do that to her? He had to get her back. He had to tell her he loved her. Burying his face in his hands, he felt the tears come and was helpless to stop it.

"At parking," David gruffly said. "When you're ready."

Jasper grunted and forced himself to pull it together. God, he felt weak. Could he even make it up the stairs. There was an elevator but it was half a block away.

"Pedro, take his other arm," someone was saying as Jasper struggled out of the car. "No, Mr. West, you just lead the way."

Jasper looked up and abruptly recognized Ed Hunter and the forensics technician, both in civilian clothes. He didn't know where they'd come from but he was glad of their help as they steadied him on the stairs and hustled him into the house.

"Let's keep him down here," David said. "Butler?"

There was no answer. Jasper raised his voice and said "Butler, silent mode off."

"Yes sir," Butler's voice echoed through the quiet house. "Stop recording?"

Damn it, he'd forgotten to stop it before. "Yes, stop recording and save." Jasper nearly lost it again. Lori was gone. Jewel missing. All he had was that damned recording.

He managed to make his own way to the couch but he wanted to be in the kitchen—Jewel's kitchen.

"He needs coffee first," David said. "Then maybe he can think. That must have been some powerful stuff."

"It was," Pedro said. "Not enough to drop an elephant but it's strong. Lieutenant, they gave you a dose of Sleeper after the trank. It'll wear off by morning but you're going to feel like hell."

"Thanks," Jasper said. "Any help for it?"

"Water, vitamin B, and your usual poison," Kruger said. "Alcohol will make it worse. Keep the coffee down to two cups."

"Thanks," Jasper said again and took the glass of ice water someone handed him. He chugged it down. "I think I'll stay down here."

"Good idea," David said. "Pot's on. You guys had better leave. Thanks for the help."

"Right," Ed Hunter said. "Wait a minute." He pulled two com units out of his pockets and laid them down beside Jasper. "I didn't know which was which so I kept them both for you—and there's this." He fished out the locket and carefully put it back around Jasper's neck. "The captain said hold it so I did."

"Thanks," Jasper said, his eyes burning again. He hadn't missed the damn locket. Jewel, he needed Jewel.

"Pedro?" Jasper mustered up the energy to ask before they left. "What'd they get?"

The forensics technician hesitated.

"It's ok."

"They got the pills, the rats, the samples, and took the professor's body too—and his belongings. We lost the rings," Pedro said in a rush then grinned. "But I've still got five pills. There were a lot in that bottle so I took them out and tucked them away last night. I'll wait a few days and test them again."

"The autopsy report?" Jasper asked, trying to focus.

Pedro produced a flasher and put it on top of his com unit. "I made eight copies. They got three of them. I can keep producing them but the original is tucked away in a public locker only I know about."

"Good," Jasper said. "I'll see you get a copy of that missing vid."

"I don't think I'll get Kucera's autopsy," Kruger said. "The professor's is all we have to work with."

"I know," Jasper said and tried to fit that in to his pounding head. "I can't think anymore. You did good."

He tried to focus. Something more he had to say. "Ed, you too. Is Lori really dead?"

"Yes," Hunter said. "She tried, Jazz. They were just too fast. I've seen the surveillance vid and—she tried."

Jasper nodded, unable to speak. His partner. His wife. Damn, he was useless. He managed to wave them away. It was a long time before he could raise his head and look at David.

"Coffee now, I think," David West rose to his feet and went to the kitchen. "I'm making some chicken soup. It's not as good as Mother's but it will help."

He handed him a cup of just warm coffee. "Elinor will come if she's needed. I didn't want her here tonight. I've also called the Foundation."

Jasper nodded. Finding his voice, he asked "Mel?"

"I've called her," David said. "I told her you were drugged up and she couldn't do anything tonight. She's not at her place. Corey and some of his friends took her and her roommate in for protection."

"Good," Jasper said. He hadn't even thought to protect his daughter.

"At least they gave you a cot," David said. "When I saw you in that vid, it looked liked they just propped you in a corner. If I could have made that train move faster, I would have."

"It's ok," Jasper said then cleared his throat. "All we can do is wait."

Chapter 13 - Monday, 8 Nov 2179

Somehow he made it through the night. He took the first-floor bedroom and David, after testing Butler to make sure it would notify him if Jasper needed help, took his usual bedroom on the second floor.

There were no messages.

It took both cups of coffee to give him the energy to climb the stairs and take a shower. Aware he was dehydrated, Jasper stayed in there a long time, only coming out when he recalled he couldn't answer his com unit from in there. Neither unit left his side. He filled the time by transferring the rest of his files to his secure com unit. That was now a priority.

It hurt like hell deleting Lori's number from his unit. They'd been partners for eight years. She'd seen him through the worst of Carol's illness and helped him through the grieving and now she was gone. He couldn't force himself to watch her last moments. He needed Jewel back safe in his arms before he could face that.

David was talking to the West Foundation, arranging for millions to be available if they needed it. Jewel's income till she turned thirty was limited to a hundred thousand per year but after that she'd have access to sixty million. The West Foundation as a whole though was worth billions—something they rarely talked about. There was a chance, a slim one, that the kidnapers wanted money.

If they wanted money, he'd pay it. Only fools would think they could move millions of dollars around without being caught but he'd pay it. Jewel was worth more than he had—more than the West Foundation had. He just wanted her back.

He called his own broker and made arrangements for a large sum in cash.

David settled in a chair across from him. "Better?"

Jasper nodded. "Headache is a dull throb now. What did they say?"

"I'm transferring thirty million to your account here in Plains," David said. "You'll need it here. They'd be fools to ask for more than that."

"I agree," Jasper said. "And you'll get it back."

"I don't care about that," David said, frowning. "But I want you two out of Plains—your daughter too. Promise me you'll get Jewel out as soon as you get her back."

Jasper nodded. "We'll go. I'm just not sure where yet."

"Denver?" David asked then shook his head. "No, Jewel would hate it and the Tower is no place for her. The Foundation complex in Houston is no better and they'd look for her there. I could call the Sullivans."

"I haven't met them yet," Jasper said. "Not really. I know they were at the wedding but.." He waved that away.

"Then let's talk to Ivan," David said. "That might be better anyway. It's Minnesota and it's winter and no one in their right mind would go there."

Jasper's lips twitched but he didn't feel much like smiling. "I'd live in a barn if it would help," he said. "And I've never touched a cow."

"You might like it, city boy," David said. "Let me call him."

"Have you seen that confession?" Jasper abruptly asked.

David eyed him. "Yes, I have and it's garbage. You should know that."

"I should have," Jasper said. "But I let them take her for questioning. That's why she was catching that train."

"You couldn't know and you had every reason to trust Lori Brown. Don't knock yourself out over that."

Jasper heard his words but they didn't sink in. He should have been there.

"I don't know if Ed Kucera was guilty but I know my niece is not," David said. "And if Jake said Kucera was behind it, he had to be involved somehow. My son wouldn't lie about something like that—not when his life was at stake."

Jasper found himself agreeing with that. How could Jake have named Kucera without Kucera being involved? Who had hired the hitmen if not Kucera?

"I'm going to have to talk to Samuel Starling," Jasper said.

"Good luck on that," David responded. "But I'm ahead of you. My lawyer has petitioned for Starling to be deep questioned about his employer. Since his testimony can clear Jewel or condemn her, it should get accepted. He's applied for euthanasia, by the way," he added. "It's been denied until his trial is done and sentencing completed."

"That doesn't surprise me," Jasper said. The right to euthanasia was in the U.S. Constitution now and had been for more than a century but it could be delayed in criminal cases. Once sentencing was done, it could be administered within hours but not before. Criminals could refuse it though few did. It was better to die than be locked up for years in the bare cell blocks that had survived the restructuring of the prison system in the mid 21st century—and no one guilty of premeditated murder got less than a life sentence.

"Let me call Ivan," David said. "I need to fill him in anyway."

Jasper nodded, knowing he couldn't handle that. He knew without asking that Sasha wouldn't be told. She was still between Earth and Mars and couldn't do anything but worry about it. Jake's widow would only be told about happy things on Earth. This couldn't concern her.

If they were going to leave, there were things that had to be done. While he waited for that goddamned message, he'd see to them—and contact Carlson. His superior at DEA would know what he needed now and get it to him. He might also know about those little yellow pills. Yes, that would occupy him while he waited.

The news coverage was too painful to listen to. It had barely started when Jasper turned it off, unable to relive those moments again. Nine days. They'd been married just nine days. He was going to make those kidnappers pay.

It was evening when the call came. Jasper found himself looking at his wife in a recorded message. She was in a dark room—a maintenance room of some sort–with a light focused on her. Her chestnut hair was tangled and her blue eyes were red from crying but she was alive and he loved her.

"Jazz, I'm alive. They haven't hurt me much but they killed Lori. I'm so sorry," she said, tears welling up in her eyes and her breath caught. A male voice said something and she hurriedly continued. "They want you to go to Lori's funeral. There will be a message there. Please go for both of us."

The message ended with that and Jasper swore. David replayed it and captured it on his com unit then forwarded it to his wife. Jasper watched it with sharp eyes over and over but there was nothing in that room that could tell him where in the city she was being held. It was a maintenance room like hundreds of others. He tried placing the male voice and even isolated it with his equipment but there wasn't enough there and he couldn't forward it to the Plains police for identification. He needed more.

Well, he wouldn't miss Lori's funeral anyway. They would see Sensor Man there and he would collect their damned message.

Chapter 14 - Funeral

The Cathedral Square of Plains was packed, the mall outside its doors unusually crowded for this hour of the day and Jasper was thankful he'd listened to David West and agreed to a hired car. On normal days all but trolleys were barred from this mall but today there was a steady stream of high-priced private vehicles and hired cars slowly wending their way through the trolley way to deliver passengers to the cathedral. A parking lot had been marked off for the private ones and chauffeurs kept a watchful eye on the pedestrians eyeing the cars.

He was amazed at the turnout, knowing the cathedral couldn't handle them all but people were there. There were plenty of blue uniforms and black-suited detectives but it was the number of ordinary people who brought him out of his apathy. He hadn't known Brown was so popular—or was it him? That thought brought it all crashing down on him again and he hastily put on his sunglasses.

Damn, there were reporters too. Couldn't they let him have any peace? His hands clenched and he had to force his anger down. Lori was dead. This wasn't about him. This was about a wonderful woman and a good cop who had given her life in the course of her duty.

"It's for Lori," David said at his side. "Every cop is here for her."

Jasper knew that was true. "The reporters."

"Ignore them," David said. "Let me get out first."

Jasper nodded. David left with a word to the driver and Jasper stayed in the car until David himself opened the door. The irony of the situation wasn't quite lost on him. How long had it been since he'd played bodyguard to David? Damn it, he just wanted to be here for Lori—and his wife.

"Here's Sensor Man," someone said the instant he stood up outside the car and Jasper braced himself for the onslaught of reporters. It didn't come. There were blue uniforms lining the steps of the cathedral and his path was clear. Without looking to right or left, he climbed the steps and reached the safety of the church.

"Jasper, this way," Ed Hunter said as he stepped through the door. "They want you up front. Lori's ex has requested it."

Jasper nodded. "David comes too."

"Yes sir." Hunter didn't blink an eye. "And the captain."

Jasper wasn't used to that kind of consideration from George Padilla but maybe it was his son's doing. Lori's son—the one she'd given up all rights to—was fifteen now and could have developed a mind of his own. He didn't know. The last time he'd seen him the boy had been a carbon copy of his abusive father. At least they were here.

"Why are all the people out there?" he asked Hunter as they walked down the aisle.

"The surveillance vid got leaked. It showed up on the subby channel first, then the news channels. Everyone in this town knows how Lori fought and about your wife. We couldn't stop it," Hunter said. "Illegal as hell but–" Hunter let his words trail off as Jasper bowed his head. "I'm sorry, Jazz."

"I haven't seen it," Jazz said.

"You don't want to," Hunter said. "Not until your wife is safe–maybe not even then."

Jasper nodded then turned his attention to the young man sitting in the pew. Thad Padilla was a well-grown 15-year-old with short-cropped hair and a black tattoo bracing his left eye. His tanned skin was two shades lighter than his mother's creamy brown color and his nose was wider but the rest showed his genetic link to Lori Brown. He was as tall as his dad now.

"Mr. Stone," Thad said with uncommon courtesy as he shook his hand. "I'm sorry about your wife."

"She's alive," Jasper said. "I'm sorry your mother isn't."

"She was a hero," George Padilla said. "A hero cop," he repeated and his eyes showed his pride. "Lori always was the best."

Jasper just nodded. He expected nothing less from this man. He fought down other memories and introduced them to David West before they sat down again. He didn't want to talk. He just wanted to get this over with.

Captain Reynolds joined them, his wife curiously absent. He knew David was showing him the brief message they'd gotten the night before.

The light of the cathedral was muted today by the gloomy sky outside. The stained glass windows that thrust up into the sun were still beautiful but it was like they were veiled in mourning. Was it raining above ground? He didn't know. He'd spent hours of waiting staring at Laramie Peak but he couldn't recall anything about it. The trees he'd admired just days ago had turned brown and gold. That was all he remembered.

There was a picture of Lori Brown in her formal blues decorating the altar, sitting next to the crematory urn she already occupied. Tears stung his eyes as he realized he hadn't been able to say goodbye. He'd been home waiting for that damned message. On impulse, he got up and rested his hand on the urn, wishing he could clasp her hand one more time and say goodbye.

The murmur of voices died down and he felt hundreds of eyes on him. Damn them. He was there for Detective Lori Brown. He returned to his seat and prayed for the service to begin.

David's hand clasped his then let go and he knew he had his support and sympathy. That mattered more to him than all these eyes. God, he'd been lucky to join the West family. Jewel was his life now but he couldn't help but respect David West and his unconditional acceptance of him. He knew David would do anything he could to help even if it skirted the law. He put family first. He was going to too.

The service was beautiful with the eulogy being given by Captain Reynolds. The police commissioner also spoke to the assembled officers but he expected that. It was the slide show that nearly did him in. There were pictures of Thad and George Padilla and Lori's parents–both dead now but the later pictures were all of her career in Plains. Pictures of him with her–of Carol and Mel with a laughing Lori–and lastly of Lori on his wedding day were too close to the bone. Thirteen days ago. He'd been married thirteen days. Was he going to be a widower tomorrow?

Jewel. He had to get Jewel back. The tears he shed were for her and he was ashamed.

After the service the cathedral slowly emptied out as officers had to return to duty. Some of them might have wanted to extend condolences to him but he stayed in the pew, unable to face them.

It was too soon. He couldn't honestly mourn Lori and let her go until he had Jewel back. It was too much for any man. He had to hold it together. Wiping his eyes, he took a deep breath. He owed it to Lori to get Jewel back. That's what she would want him to do. That's what he had to do.

"Got it together?" David asked and he realized his new kinsman was still by his side. The Padillas were gone.

"Yes, thanks." Jasper sniffed to clear his nose. "I kept thinking about–"

"I know." David's answer was grim. "Let's make sure it's never Jewel up there."

"I want to get those bastards," David said, his tone hard. "I found out the slasher was a true black–darker than any mixed blood American. That's all they have on him."

"Stealth mask or tattoos?" Jasper asked.

"Tattoos." It was Captain Reynolds who answered, finally visible as David rose to his feet. "He probably had them off in minutes. One was a glow job and those are always temporary."

Jasper nodded. They weren't illegal but most tattoo artists knew how the police felt about them. Of course, the man might have applied it himself.

"West says there hasn't been a ransom demand yet," Captain Reynolds said. "If they don't give you one soon, it's not money."

"I know," Jasper said. "It might be blissex." He was bitter, remembering just why the West house was valuable to drug smugglers. Did they want to use it and him to get drugs into the city? Three months ago he would have applauded that because he would get closer to the center of the blissex trade but he hadn't thought they'd take Jewel.

"We'll stay out of it until you get her back," Captain Reynolds said. "When you give the word, we'll nab the whole lot."

"No," Jasper said.

"No?" His captain's jaw clenched. "Spill it, Stone."

"They'll have insurance," Jasper said. "You know they will. If they return her, they'll know I won't call you. There will be something to keep me quiet. I can't risk Jewel's life for one shipment of Blissex."

"Then what do you suggest we do?" Reynolds asked, his voice dangerously quiet.

"Back off this time," Jasper said. "Let me get Jewel out. Once that's done, I'll make sure you get every shipment that goes through the house. This will be the only time they get through."

Reynolds looked annoyed but David stepped in as they had planned. "It might be really helpful to add new portable cameras along any route from Lily Street and see where the shipment goes and how it goes," he said. "They might give away a lot more that will be useful in the future. Stealth cameras not hooked into the city's system would be too new for them to know their locations. Pull them out the day after and download the data."

The captain looked thoughtful. "That might work. We'll set up the city systems to monitor as usual but new cameras–are you offering some?"

"The Trifecta Vid cam can store up to 38 hours of usable data," David said. "And there will be a shipment of a hundred on tonight's express compliments of the West Foundation. They're totally self contained with storage and internal power source."

"A hundred?" Reynolds was stunned. "Camouflaged?"

"Maintenance gray, no lights." David said. "Filter over the lens so it looks like a solid surface. The techs assure me they look just like another junction box."

"I've heard of them," Reynolds said. "And I've got an idea of the price. Thank you."

"They should never have touched my niece," David said in clipped tones and walked away.

Reynolds turned back to Jasper. "I'll keep those off of city inventory," he said. "Once they know we've got the best stealth camera on the market, they'll compensate."

"Have we got a deal then?" Jasper asked. "This time no interference?"

Reynolds studied him then nodded. "It's a small price to pay for what you offer. Good luck, Blitzen."

He rose and walked away.

Jasper waited until he was well gone before he got to his own feet. The cathedral was nearly empty now. Some people, those who didn't have to rush back to duty, had gone into the reception hall but he had no intention of joining them. He needed to find that damned message and get out of here. Now that Reynolds had agreed to pass up the biggest opportunity he'd ever had to nab a blissex shipment, he could concentrate on Jewel.

David met him halfway down the aisle. "Here it is," he said. "Just as we thought, it was left in the basket of cards." He handed him what looked like a card with Jazz Stone carefully printed in block letters on the envelope.

Jasper opened it, hoping it wasn't just a card directed to the partner of the deceased instead of her son. There was a picture inside of Jewel holding a sign that said "I love you. 11-10-2179" and he knew it was real. Together they read it.

"West goes home. No cameras. No police. Tomorrow night, upper door. If you want her back alive, be alone."

"You called it right," David said. "No money. They must have a huge shipment."

"The biggest probably," Jasper said. "They've got the whole department out of this one. They can risk it." He wondered how big it would be. In a normal month anywhere from a thousand to five thousand chews got into Plains. More than double that, he decided. "If they bring in too much though, the price will drop. When the packaging changes in January, they'll be stuck with it."

One thing Wilson Chemicals had agreed to when the blissex problem first developed was packaging and color changes for bliss so the illegal blissex could be identified. The foil backing on the bliss tabs changed color every three months and was date stamped for the month of use. The color of the bliss tabs was supposed to change every six months. Both changes were closely guarded secrets but the producers of blissex had proved adaptable. By the twelfth of every month new blissex tabs in the proper color and the proper packaging were showing up in the sensa dens. If anyone still had the old blissex, they didn't use them in public where they could be confiscated.

No, the color change of the packaging should stop them from bringing in more than five thousand chews. He hoped.

"I'll leave on tonight's train," David said. "And get things set up in Denver."

Jasper nodded. Now he had to face the crowd once more—and without the police barricade. Putting his sunglasses back on, he stepped out on the cathedral's porch and waited, nearly alone, while David called their driver. He heard the whir of cameras but no one actually approached him. He didn't have trouble picturing what they saw. Dressed all in black with the only color being the star locket on his chest and the white envelope in his hand, he must be the perfect picture of the mourner. Going in he had felt like it but now he was all too aware of the work ahead. He needed to be ready. He needed to save Jewel.

Chapter 15 - Friday, 12 Nov 2179

Jasper looked around the third floor again. Was everything done? Linda. Did he send off her severance pay? Yes. He didn't want the maid returning to the house in the next six months. If they returned after that, he'd see about getting her back. He doubted they would.

When they returned from the funeral yesterday a package had been waiting from Carlson, laid flat just outside the upper door. Everything he'd requested and some he hadn't thought of had been in there and he'd spent the night learning to use it.

David had left on the evening train after giving his captain a brief introduction to the technician escorting the stealth cameras. The plan had been for the technician to brief the ten officers—all trusted men—in their placement. Tomorrow they'd retrieve them and the technician would process their information. None of it was happening through the police labs. This time there would be no leaks.

He'd known for a long time there were leaks in the police force—one of the reasons he'd chosen to go to DEA and why the people who knew about it were so few. Now his effectiveness in DEA would be limited too. He had to get Jewel away from here. He couldn't protect her and still work for DEA. He should have known that wouldn't work when he married her.

It looked like he would be contributing something though. This house would be bait. He wouldn't allow Jewel to be here but maybe the drug smugglers would be stupid enough to use the house. He'd have to see. He'd set it up as best he could but now it would have to wait.

Wait. He was tired of waiting. Everything was done. He'd even walked in the garden one last time. The autumn days were really chill but he needed to check the outside camera. As he suspected, the lens filter was already coated with a tarry black substance. He didn't bother to fix it.

Was Jewel outside somewhere? He knew now that her abductors had put her in an insulated packing crate to whisk her away and it had given false readings to the inspection scanners. The crate had been found three hours later near a hydroponics farm and two levels up from subby housing in Section 18. He didn't know whether she was in the city or not but she should be returned tonight through that upper door.

"There is someone at the door," Butler said.

"Which door?" he asked.

"The front door, sir."

"Show me." Jasper stared incredulously at Detective Sanders. He was even in his uniform suit. What the hell?

"What do you want, Sanders?" he said over the speaker beside the door. "I was told no contact with police."

"I want to talk to you," he said. "I want to know why the hell you shut down the professor's case." His voice was angry and he said it loud enough that anyone could hear.

Was he drunk? Jasper fumed as he pounded down the stairs. Accusing him of shutting down an investigation? He was insane. Knowing he could get Jewel killed, he opened the door and grabbed the detective by the neck of his jacket and threw him against the wall.

"Get out of here!"

"That's assaulting an officer," Sanders said, one hand wiping at his face. "I could arrest you."

"You could get my wife killed, idiot!" Jasper flung at him. "I was told no police and here you come in uniform to accuse me of something I couldn't do if I tried. Get out of here—go sober up—then I suggest you get busy and find out who did shut down that investigation."

A glimmer of reason came back into his face. "You didn't?"

"I didn't. Someone named T. S. did. That's the only clue I got. Use it and leave me alone."

Jasper didn't wait for an answer but slammed the door.

Idiot! He should report him. His hand was going to the com unit at his belt before he remembered. No contact. He swore. Had anyone seen him come here? What would they think of him throwing that ass out? If anyone thought he'd work with a drunken second -detective, they were insane.

Suddenly he knew why Sanders had transferred to Section 2. Jasper had moved into Section 3. He'd only had the one case with him but it had been big and Sanders' career might have gotten a boost but then he'd brought Brown over. Instead of giving him the experience and training he had every right to expect, he'd sunk him.

To make it worse, Sanders had moved over to Section 2 and the first important murder had brought Brown in—and she had brought him in. Sanders had been thrown into the background again. Now Brown was gone and he was out and Sanders had that case to himself except there was no case. It had been shut down.

Damn it, the man was too green to know it wasn't his fault.

Jasper wanted the professor's murder solved but he wanted Jewel too. Drew Nugent was no longer important. He had to have Jewel.

He stood there a long time until his alarm went off and he knew the last preparations had to be made. He had to eat. He had to give Butler his last instructions. He had to be ready.

* * *

The autumn darkness had fallen outside and still no Jewel. Watching the clock he'd set on the pool table was fruitless. He'd dimmed the lights in this upper room so he'd have a clear view outside but maybe they were waiting to see if he was alone. What the hell did they want him to do?

Reluctantly, he turned the lights up to show the room, just keeping those over the pool table off. He could still see some detail outside but not a lot. If the moon had risen, it shed little light tonight. His drum was still out. Bringing it over to the pool table, he played a few notes and waited. Not even the clear tones of his new toy could hold his attention now.

A dark figure appeared silhouetted at the door against the autumn Starlight. Jasper laid down his drumsticks as the figure knocked. He could see two more but he couldn't tell if one of them was Jewel. What if they didn't bring her? What if he'd thought wrong?

No, he wouldn't believe that. Lackeys. Yeah, these must be the lackeys. He put his thumb on the door and it unlocked. Swinging it open, he wasn't surprised when the first one grabbed him, twisted his arm behind his back and used him as a shield.

"Where's my wife?" he demanded. "What are you doing?" He could feel the snick of a handcuff as it clicked around his wrist.

All of them were wearing black full head masks, the kind illegal in the city, and heavy coats against the autumn cold. Jasper filed that away. They must have been outside for a while. The cold was starting to penetrate the room too, and he shivered. He wasn't dressed for it.

The other two pushed past them, guns at the ready. Guns? Jasper had little time to think as one returned from the master suite. "It's clear."

"Check the other floors. Don't forget the storerooms." The lackey behind him ordered and Jasper felt the cold muzzle of a gun in his back. "Now, Sensor Man, we know about the safe. You're going to open it."

He swore and could almost feel the man's amusement as he marched him across the room to the master suite.

"Your wife was real helpful. She said you keep flashers, lots of them, in that fancy safe. You're going to give them up."

Jasper found they'd left his right hand free but there was little he could do. Jewel wasn't here so he had to cooperate. There were two men there now and it was the second who grabbed his right hand and forced it on to the surface of the safe. It flashed yellow.

"Do the combination," the lackey growled. "Now."

Jasper did the rapid, almost imperceptible finger tap and the safe flashed green. He was pulled back and forcibly sat on the bed. He didn't resist but anger rose in him. They were taking his music-his unpublished music–and he couldn't do anything to change that. His face twisted into bitterness as the second lackey riffled the safe.

"Money-thousands of it, cash cards, gee, we hit the mother lode," the second lackey was saying.

"What else?" Bossy demanded.

"Flashers and a com unit," second said. "Just like the bitch said."

"Clean it out. The boss wants the flashers and com unit."

"Right." Second casually walked over to the bed, grabbed a pillow, and stripped off the pillow case. Dumping money and cash cards into it, he carried the tray of flashers and com unit cradled in one arm. "Can I go for jewels too?"

"Hell, no," Bossy said. "Too traceable. And if they're not in the safe, they aren't worth crap."

"Those flashers are my music," Jasper said. "Just my music."

"Uh-huh," Bossy said. "You'll just have to write more. These belong to the boss now."

He waved his gun at him. "Get up. Back into the living room."

Jasper didn't argue. So Bossy wasn't the boss. He wasn't surprised. The boss would have Jewel and she wasn't here.

He hesitated at the door and promptly felt the cold muzzle in his back. "Don't think it," Bossy said. "I wouldn't have a problem plugging you. If the Boss gives the word, I'll do it and smile. You cooperate and he might not let me. You and that pretty wife of yours might just live."

"You wouldn't kill her?" Jasper ground out.

"If you're dead, she's no use to us. You give me any trouble, I might just make you watch her die." His cold voice made Jasper's blood run cold. This guy was a pro—and he wasn't local. He could hear a New York accent under that mask.

He didn't resist further but let himself be prodded into the studio. At a word from Bossy, the couch was muscled closer to the fake fireplace. Before he was told to sit, Second patted him down and removed his slim wallet and his other com unit. Once he was seated at the end of the couch Second yanked his arm up and cuffed it to one of the pillars supporting the mantle then yanked to make sure the pillar was secure.

Jasper knew they were and didn't struggle. He fought a strong urge to kick as Second put shackles on his ankles. He couldn't move. Fuming, he waited for what would happen next. He'd caught a glimpse of a fifth man walking around the pool table with something in his hand. Cold winter air was filling the room now and he shivered. Why didn't they close the damned door?

"No active cameras," Fifth said. "It's safe on this floor."

"Right. Check out the others. Tell Joey to guard the front door and Karl to get back up here."

So Fifth was Tech, Jasper thought. Joey and Karl were lackeys three and four. Bossy was getting careless.

"Boss, it's secure. You can bring her in."

"She can't walk. Send someone out to help me."

"Right," Bossy said. "Help him," he said to Second. When the man hesitated, he said, "Stone isn't going anywhere. Help the Boss."

"Yes sir."

Jasper didn't let his eyes wander from Bossy. He watched the man straighten the tray of flashers Second had put on the table. When he reached out to pick up a com unit, there was a patch of skin exposed between glove and sleeve-black skin. Was this the slasher who killed Brown? Determined not to show what he knew, he just watched as Bossy picked up the second com unit to find it locked too.

"Think you're smart hiding a second com unit, huh? Your pretty wife knew all about it. She said you were consulting on the professor's murder too. Stupid pillow talk."

"Why did you kill him?"

"Shut up." Bossy turned toward the door, his attention on the two men entering. "Here's the Boss."

Jasper didn't get up. He couldn't do more than crane his head to look as a limp Jewel was carried in. Her hair was covered with a tight black cap and she wore black trousers and coat. His heart thumped. Was she okay?

Her head was tilted back over the guy's arm and she looked as still as death. It was only the care they used in placing her on the couch that reassured him. His right arm pulled her closer and he felt for the pulse in her neck. His fingers quivered as he felt the nice steady heartbeat. She was alive.

"No active cameras?" A hard voice asked and Jasper looked up into the ice blue eyes of the Boss. Unlike the others, he wore a stealth mask and a black cap similar to Jewel's. When his head turned, Jasper caught the glint of gold and his blood turned cold. Mark Baxter.

Chapter 16 - Baxter

Mark Baxter was the Boss? An executive vice president for Wilson Chemicals was running the blissex trade? Holy hell. Jasper looked away, afraid Baxter would guess he knew who he was. If he even suspected Jasper knew, they'd both be dead.

His mind flipped over what he knew about blissex and he nearly groaned. There was no outlaw company making blissex–at least not without Baxter's knowledge. Was Wilson Kucera into it too? Probably.

He couldn't let any of this show. He didn't know this man. He was the asshole that had stolen Jewel that's all. He concentrated on Jewel, patting her unresponsive cheek and calling her name. "Jewel, love, wake up."

Baxter laughed. "That won't do you any good for another three hours, Sensor Man. She's got a good dose of Sleeper in her."

"Sleeper?" Jasper asked, vividly recalling his recent experience. "One dose?"

"Just one," Baxter said. "It's the one sedative that doesn't have bliss. Remember that because bliss can kill her."

Jasper froze then his eyes met Baxter's. "What do you mean?"

"You know what I mean." Baxter's voice was cold. "You've seen the results. Little Miss Jewel told us the professor had it. Hell, I saw him die and I know it was blister. What I want you to tell me is how he got it–and who gave it to Ed Kucera."

"The professor didn't tell you?" Jasper asked, playing for time. "You don't know?"

"If I knew, would I be kidnapping your wife?" Baxter leaned closer but stayed just out of his reach. "Would I be using truth serum on her? Tell me what you know now."

"What do you want to know?"

"Don't play games with me," Baxter snapped then turned to his lackeys. "Get the trolleys. I'll deal with Stone."

His men started out the door.

"X, have you got that door overridden yet?" Baxter asked. "It's freezing in here."

Jasper shivered again. Dimly he was aware the furnace had kicked on but it didn't help much. How long had it been? Was Butler recording? He'd programmed in a delay so Butler would start fifteen minutes after the door was opened.

God, he shouldn't have been so smart. If Baxter asked the Tech to check for recorders again Butler would get busted. He had to have that record though. No one would believe a vice president of Wilson Chemicals was running blissex without it.

"Tell me what you know about the professor," Baxter said. "Now."

"I don't know anything about the professor except he was the last visitor Kucera had," Jasper said. "He was engaged to Jewel so I questioned him about the West murders. He passed. If he hadn't visited Kucera, I would have had no interest in him."

"Why do you know he was there and the cops don't?" Baxter demanded. "Ed's lawyer said he had a last visitor too but he couldn't find out who it was."

"That I don't know," Jasper said. "Police records are supposed to be inviolate but his visit got erased. It didn't happen right away though. I saw the vid." Taking a deep breath, he played his card. "I have it."

He had Baxter's full attention now. "What does 23 hours mean to you?"

"23 hours?" Baxter responded. "What is it supposed to mean other than 23 hours?"

Damn. Well, he'd already guessed Baxter knew as little about the professor as he did. Was this really why Jewel was kidnapped or did he believe that damned confession? Was there really blissex here?

"There's a flasher in my vid screen drive," he said. "File name Kucera. See it for yourself."

Baxter studied him, tugged once on his upraised arm then left. Jasper waited till he heard Ed Kucera's voice then bent over Jewel again. He got the tight black cap off and his jaw tightened. They'd cut her chestnut hair and dyed most of it black. One strip down the side was a rainbow of red and green.

She was still unresponsive. Her breathing was even though and he could tell she was just asleep. How long before it would wear off? He had to get her out of here.

"That won't do any good," a voice said and Jasper found himself looking up into brown eyes behind a black mask. The skin around those eyes was light and Jasper made a mental note of that. "They gave her Sleeper a little over an hour ago," he said. "You've got three or four before it wears off."

"What else did they give her?" Jasper asked, guessing this was Tech or X. His hunch proved correct when the man picked up a flasher and examined it.

"Trade," he said. "They'll want me to break into these. What passwords?"

Jasper considered holding that back but any good tech could do that. Jewel could have. She just hadn't been that nosy. "Just one. Sonnet."

"Sonnet? Pretty weak." The tech snorted. "And the com units?"

"Figure that out yourself," Jasper said. "What did they give her?"

"The truth serum was Penseek," he said. "That was days ago. It's out of her system now. There's another drug I don't know much about. Timed release. Keep her away from bliss." He put the flasher down and picked up a com unit. "Got to work on this."

He left and Jasper wondered if the man thought he was a fool. It was clear they were going to add tracking software to his com unit. They had done it already to Jewel's. He'd checked it himself when the police returned it to him.

Well, if they were adding tracking software, they must plan to keep them alive. He couldn't count on that though. What had they found out from Jewel? She didn't know about his DEA status. She did know he was consulting with the department. Had she told them about Corey or Mel? If they had asked the right questions, yes. That was the key to using truth serums. People didn't just babble. They answered questions and you had to ask the right questions. A simple tell me order was useless. Even if you could prompt someone to respond to such an order, you were likely to hear about their childhood instead of more recent experiences.

Aware that his DEA credentials were in the locket around his neck, he decided he'd better stay cooperative. Baxter was back.

"That was all you had?" Baxter demanded. There were lines above those ice blue eyes. "Was he a fed? I know Kucera wasn't."

"I think so," Jasper said. "It would explain it, wouldn't it? How do you know Ed wasn't?"

"Ed didn't have the guts," Baxter said. "You guys were barking up the wrong tree."

"Were we? My wife sure as hell didn't do it," Jasper said, his hand tightening on Jewel's shoulder. She was oblivious.

"No, she didn't," Baxter said. "Ed thought so but she didn't. Your wife is just what she seems but you're not, Sensor Man. You've been working with the police."

"You expected something else?" Jasper said, glaring back. His jaw tightened and he knew he had to be very careful.

"It's going to stop," Baxter said. "No more police. You're going to tell them to leave you alone. You've got your wife back and that's the end of it. No cooperation. No contact. No old friends on the force. You'll stay here and compose your little tunes. Got that?"

Jasper nodded once, his jaw tight.

"No, I don't think you've got it," Baxter said, his voice cold. "Let me put it this way. If you don't do exactly as I tell you, your wife will die. I've got this little button, you see. If you don't do as I tell you, something is going to go very wrong with her. No police."

Jasper swallowed hard, his eyes never leaving Baxter. The bastard had just laid it on the line and his chest tightened. "What else?"

"You're going to tell West to back off and keep his nose out of the Kucera case."

"Okay. What else?" Like hell David would take orders from him.

"Blister," Baxter said. "You're going to find out where the professor got it. That's classified stuff."

"You just told me no police contacts," Jasper said. "How do you expect me to do that?"

"You'll find a way, Sensor Man," Baxter said. "The drug name is Blister. Your wife said you found it in the professor's home and in his blood. Find out where he got it."

"Who makes it?" Jasper asked.

"You can find that out too," Baxter's teeth were bared but his smile was half-hidden behind the stealth mask. It wasn't full face but covered his nose, cheeks, and part of his mouth. Jasper knew no cameras could see past the appliances to make an ID. The masks were expensive though. He wouldn't waste them on his lackeys.

"Keep her away from doctors if you want her to live," Baxter said. "One dose of bliss and it's over. If they mess with my insurance, it's over. If you don't do what you're told, it's over."

Jasper's fist clenched then he forced his fingers to uncurl.

Baxter saw and laughed. "Relax. You do what I want you to and she'll still live a long life. I want you to live too. I want you right here so we can use this house. You won't tell anyone and you won't do anything. You just play your music and be a good husband."

"Boss, we need another hand," someone said. "These stairs."

Baxter left them and Jasper thought fast. He couldn't take her to doctors? What had he done to her? Clearly he'd done more than put trackers on her. A transmitter? Had Carlson been right? He stroked Jewel's too short hair and tried to think.

Tech came back before Baxter did, laying down the first com unit and picking up the other. Tucking that into his pocket and picking up the tray of flashers, he took them away. Jasper craned his neck to see what he was doing and saw a trolley near the doors. One of the men came up the stairs and dumped coats into it. A mask fell to the floor and he picked it up and tossed it in too.

Apparently most of the men would be leaving via the front door into the city. Would they be stupid enough to carry guns with them? There were inspection sensors throughout the city that would alert on the shape of a handgun. Police weapons had a special pass embedded in theirs which sensors recognized as authorized but normally not even police carried handguns in Plains. They were armed with tranks and shock grenades.

Would it have saved Lori if she'd had a handgun? No, the slasher had used a knife. He wondered what kind it was since it had gotten past inspection scanners.

Baxter climbed the stairs again to stand in front of him. Squatting beside the couch, he checked Jewel's eyes then looked at him. "She'll be out till long after we're gone," he said.

He held up a key then laid it on the far corner of the coffee table. "When she can move, she can unlock you then I suggest you get her to bed. She's going to be woozy. Vitamin B and water will help get her going tomorrow."

"I know the effects," Jasper said.

"Yeah, you would," Baxter replied. "All that cop training. Just don't get cute on me. If you do, you won't get me. I'll still be out there and I'll kill your wife and her uncle and anyone else important to you. What happened to your partner will be nothing." His voice was cold. "You be here. You do what you're told."

Jasper's teeth clenched but he forced himself to nod. He had to look cooperative but he wanted this bastard. How the hell had he hidden what he was?

"Ready, Boss." The one he'd called Bossy said from the stairs. Jasper looked that way and caught a glimpse of a bald head blacker than any he'd yet seen. It was almost ebony. The man didn't come further up the stairs to where he could see more.

"Then go ahead and move out," Baxter said. "Stick to our route. Keep your com unit on so I can hear if you get intercepted."

"Yes sir." The black head disappeared.

"This is a dry run," Baxter told him with a grim smile. "No blissex. We're going to see how cooperative the police are going to be. We've already moved in enough blissex to take care of our clients. Our next shipment won't be for weeks."

Jasper ground his teeth. "So you'll move it through my house?"

"Sometimes," Baxter said. "We've got other channels. When we want to come through here, we'll just do it. No warning. You'd better be here."

Jasper nodded. So his house wouldn't be used often.

Baxter left him again, walking back toward the pool table. Jasper heard him messing with the balls then tapping on his drum. Would he take it? He almost wanted him to. It would be easier to prove Baxter was the one here if he had that drum in his possession.

Time passed slowly. Baxter didn't bother to talk to him again. God, it was still cold in here. He shivered and fingered Jewel's coat, wishing he had one of his own. It wasn't an expensive coat but typical of those who had to be outside. He was sure they didn't sell them in Plains. Maintenance people had city issued coats and few others ventured outside when the temperatures fell below freezing. He knew he didn't own anything this warm.

"Time to go," Baxter said. He picked up the thin wallet still on the table and thumbed through it. "I'll just take your ident card in case you get ideas about leaving. It will take you a week or two to get a replacement. There's a cash card to see you through," he tossed a fifty dollar card on the table then pulled on thick gloves over the thin ones he'd worn the entire evening. "You look cold, Sensor Man."

He went into the bedroom and Jasper held his breath until he came out again with the folded blanket from the foot of the bed. Did he have time enough to look around? He didn't think so.

With fake solicitude, Baxter tucked the blanket in around him and even lifted Jewel's head to rest on his blanketed lap. His gloved hand traced Jewel's jaw and Jasper bit off a curse.

Baxter laughed. "She's all yours, Sensor Man. I've had her long enough." With that, he motioned to his last lackey to precede him out the door.

Jasper tilted his head back and took a deep breath, unable to believe they were still alive. He waited, half expecting someone to come back but nothing happened. With difficulty, he half turned toward the room and surveyed it. The drum had been moved to a side table but it was still there. There were balls on the damned pool table and Jewel's cue was propped up against one side. Did they leave cameras? He didn't know. It was impossible to tell whether they had plugged cameras in downstairs. Hell, he had time enough to plant a stealth camera in the bedroom too. There were ones that plugged directly into a wall socket and used the house's own power to transmit images. He couldn't assume they hadn't done that.

There was nothing he could do just now. His arm ached and he shifted to a more comfortable position. Flexing his hand inside the cuff, he tried to keep it from going numb. It was cold. Deciding there was nothing he could do about it, he pulled the blanket closer and rested his right hand on Jewel's hair. All he could do was wait.

Chapter 17 - Returned

A faint stirring under his hand woke him from the light doze he'd fallen into. Jasper patted automatically then snapped awake. Jewel.

His left arm was numb and his neck ached but he'd felt her stir. He shifted a little and looked down at his wife.

"Jewel?" He stroked that godawful hair. She mumbled something and his heart thumped. "Jewel, time to wake up." How long had it been?

Forced to be still and wait, he'd finally drifted off to sleep. He rubbed his eyes as best he could with one hand then cleared his throat before rubbing her back again. "Jewel, love, wake up."

She stirred again then moaned. A sob finally escaped her and she crawled, still mostly asleep, against his side and clung to his neck, wracking sobs escaping her.

He patted her awkwardly, wishing he could hold her. Unintelligible words poured out and all he could do was let her cry. Remembering his own waking from that drug, he wished he wasn't so useless. He couldn't give her coffee or even water. All he could do was hold her and let her know he was here.

Desperate to get her awake and functioning, he finally lifted her chin and looked into her swimming blue eyes. They were still unfocused and dazed looking, her lips quivering.

Covering her lips with his, he willed her to have strength. His thin lips were tender, teasing on her full ones and he kept his hold on her chin when she tried to draw back, forcing her to stay with him. She was slow to respond but finally he could feel her cool wet lips warm under his. He willed her to kiss him back. He wanted the lusty Jewel who would take her turn but she wasn't there.

When he finally ended the kiss, there was more awareness in her eyes. Her eyes brimmed over with tears and she clung to him.

"Lori," she gasped. "I'm sorry, I, Jazz...."

"It's okay. You're safe," he said, his words catching in his throat. "Jewel, I need you. You've got to help me." He could feel the words penetrate. She didn't quit crying but she drew back to look at him. "I'm cuffed. My arm is ready to fall off. You need to get the key."

Now that he acknowledged it, his arm did feel ready to fall off. It had gone numb long ago. He didn't know how long a man's arm could take being raised and motionless but his had just about had it. Damn it, he needed that hand. Anger boiled up in him.

"Jewel, look at me." He hadn't gotten through to her yet. "You need to get the key."

Her eyes sharpened. "Where is it?" She looked around then reached for his raised arm.

He gasped as pain shot through him and she drew back. "On the table," he said. "The corner."

Somehow, drugged as she still was, Jewel found the key. It took her longer to get it in the lock. There was a lot of fumbling but he gritted his teeth and told her to keep trying. Finally he could feel the cuff release and he could lower his arm. God, it hurt. Pain stabbed through it as the blood returned but he forced himself to flex his fingers and bend his arm. Jewel was crying again but this time it was for him.

"Can you get us some water?" He managed to say, aware his throat was dry too. "From the bathroom. Don't go downstairs."

Shakily she got up then sat down again.

"Not yet, doll," he said. "Just sit for a while. Give me the key."

She did and he got his feet free. His feet weren't bad. Standing up, he made his way to the bathroom and filled the small water cups they kept there. It was harder getting them back to her with his bad arm but he managed. She drank hers and looked hopefully for more.

"In the bathroom," he said. "Let's get you there."

She still wore that damned coat. Suddenly detesting it, he made her take it off and leave it on the couch. Underneath her blouse was the same she'd been kidnapped in but the black trousers weren't hers.

Together they got back to the bathroom and he helped her to the stool then fetched cup after cup of cold water. Drinking almost as much himself, he knew he'd have to make her move soon. How long had they been immobile? Checking the bedside clock, he groaned. It was past midnight. She'd been out more than four hours? He hadn't much time.

He still forced himself to check the plug-ins in the bedroom for stealth cameras, found one and tossed it out in his studio. No spying in here. Finally convinced it was safe, he pulled a briefcase out of the closet and opened it, pulling out his secure com unit. Awkwardly, he typed in a text message and left the unit on his bed.

Jewel was kicking off those trousers when he returned.

"That's it," he said. "Everything off. Shower first." He turned on the water then helped her undress. God, he wished he could unwrap her properly but his damned arm. At least he could move it and he didn't think he'd lose any function.

Gathering her clothes together, he dumped them with the coat in the other room. He didn't have time to check them for tracers. Her first.

Shedding his clothes on the bedroom floor, he moved back into the bathroom to find his wife already in the oversized shower. Good. Maybe that hair dye would come out. There were things he needed under the sink. Reaching behind the cleaning supplies, he brought out some of the tools Carlson had lent him but it was only the scissors he took into the shower.

Jewel was crying again under the stream of water. Pulling her to him, he held her close and let her cry. Aware time was ticking by, he finally reached for the shampoo. "Love, let's get you cleaned up," he murmured and worked the shampoo in, his long slender fingers massaging her scalp and running through her hair. The black dye discolored the shampoo and he had hopes it would come out entirely.

Jewel relaxed against him, her sobs ceasing under his skillful hands. He rinsed her then shampooed her again before he found it. There. His fingers found a slightly angular lump in her hair. It was close to her scalp as he knew it would be. Grabbing hold of it with one hand, he clipped it out with the scissors then carefully set it where it wouldn't wash down the drain. A tracer. He knew there had to be one.

Running his hands through her hair again, he smiled down at her uplifted face. "That dye is going to come out, Jewel, but that colored streak." He ran his fingers through it. "I can cut it or leave it."

"Cut it," she said in a fierce whisper. "I hate it."

He cut it out. It went close to her scalp but he didn't care. Her hair would grow back and she'd be just as lovely as before. His chest tightened but he forced himself to keep his voice soothing. "All gone."

Laying the scissors aside, he turned to the task of getting his wife clean. This time there was no sex play. He scrubbed her back, checking it as he did so for any marks of abuse then soaped her firm buttocks. She half turned to glare at him reproachfully when his hands strayed. He just smiled and turned her back around. Her long legs were gorgeous, smooth to the touch and unmarked.

Turning her around, he let her soap him while he did her arms, pausing at what looked like a healing cut on her left one. That was new. "When did you get this?" he asked.

Jewel looked blank then her eyes welled up again. Damn.

He pulled her close to his soapy chest and kissed her tears away. "Love, I'm here. We'll get through this." He felt himself harden and cursed it. Now was not the time.

She felt it too, and giggled through her sobs.

He had to get her out of this. He knew it was the aftermath of the drug and what had happened but he needed her alert as soon as possible. Deliberately he pulled her closer, pushing her hips against his, and let her feel his staff rubbing against her mound. Her eyes widened and she raised herself on tiptoe to give him better access. God, he wanted her but not like this. He had to finish what he was doing.

Her hands clutched him around the neck and her breath was coming faster. Her sobs had faded and a flush of eagerness lit her pale cheeks.

Pulling away from her, he grabbed the handheld shower and quickly rinsed them both off. Leaving the water running, he led her to the bed and pushed her down on the coverlet. She was still slick with water.

Her white breasts poked up, their peaks upright and her hair, shorter than ever before, made a nimbus around her face. Parting her ivory legs, she raised her hips invitingly then moaned as his slender fingers found her clit and combed through her soft wet hair.

He played her. Ignoring his own throbbing need, he gave all his attention to teasing her, stroking her lips and making short teasing jabs against the flower of her need, each time probing a little more and sending her deeper into ecstasy. His hands found the second angular tracer quickly but he kept on. When he finally pulled it free of the hairs it was attached to, Jewel didn't do more than gasp at the brief pain.

She was so ready, her back arching to welcome him, her legs spread invitingly. He rested his head against her and she bucked then pushed against him and he was in. Laughing, she threw her head back as he pumped. Her cries urged him on and he felt the urgency of release but fought it, waiting for her. When her cry came, he let go and was wracked with spasms as his seed shot into his precious, precious Jewel.

Laying on her, he breathed in her clean scent and nuzzled her neck. He should move but right now a gentle lassitude filled him and he just wanted to stay right here in her arms. Knowing he had nearly lost her, could still lose her, he just wanted to stay in this moment.

She seemed just as content to stay there. Feeling her hands combing through his short hair, he was happy as he hadn't been for days. Raising himself up on his elbows, he studied her face and saw her eyes were almost clear. She squirmed and he moaned "not again, witch."

She giggled as he withdrew. Helping her to her feet, he studied her face, wondering if she'd really broken the grip of the drug.

"The shower's still on," she said uncertainly.

"You haven't finished washing me," he said and led her back to the bathroom. Closing the door, he picked up a plastic slate and showed her the words he'd already written on it.

"Don't react. They bugged the house and maybe you. Let me check."

Her smile faded but she gave him a tight nod. God, she was beautiful.

Picking up the flat paddle he'd left by the shower, he ran it slowly over her front and back. The tell-tale on the handle changed to red and he looked at the display. It had been a forlorn hope that she wasn't but he had to be sure. Now he knew what the insurance was and what frequency it used. Knowing the detector would keep that in memory, he laid it down and took Jewel back into the shower.

She cried again but it was different as he soaped her up one more time and rinsed her off then tended to his own body. This time it wasn't tears of grief but anger. He understood that. He was pretty sure she hadn't been conscious when they stuck it in her but it still made him madder than hell–and he thanked God Carlson had given him the right equipment. He hated to think what could have happened if he'd tried to take her away from Plains without it.

Pulling her close again, he bent his mouth close to her ear. "Remember what they've heard–you and me making love. They'll never have that."

She snuggled close to him. "What are we going to do?' she said in breathless tones.

"Leave," he said. "Tonight. When we turn off the shower they can hear. I want you to sound like you're getting ready for bed but get dressed. I have to see to a couple of things."

She nodded, her eyes never leaving his.

"If you fall asleep, I'll wake you when it's time," he said. "Don't worry."

"I won't."

Turning off the shower, he grabbed a towel and wrapped it around her then took a second to scrub at her hair. "Finally clean," he growled and she managed a laugh. "And now it's bed for you."

"Going to join me?" she said and he groaned. She laughed and he grabbed a towel to wrap around his own hips then followed her out to the bedroom.

"Pajamas tonight, love," he said. "I need coffee."

"You always need coffee," Jewel responded. "You won't sleep."

"I'll sleep," he said, his voice tight. "I'll sleep with you here."

She paused, her hands already working to fasten her bra stilled, and she looked at him with eyes haunted by their time apart. A sob escaped her but she shook her head and went back to dressing.

Damn, he had to say it. They had to play their parts. Opening the bedroom door, he closed it behind him. He didn't know how many cameras they had planted but he was going to give them a show. Discarding his towel at the stairs, he walked down to the first floor nude except for the locket on his chest. Glad there were no windows down here, he started the coffee pot then rummaged around in the refrigerator for something to eat. Halfway through his task, he had two more cameras spotted and knew they were seeing him in all his glory. He hoped they were as horny as hell.

Two sandwiches, some cheese sticks, and coffee was all he could think of. Pouring the coffee into his insulated carafe, he snagged their supper, two cups, and a notepad he'd need.

What was the time? Half past one. They had to be ready at three.

Turning out the house lights as he climbed the stairs, he tried to think if he'd missed anything. Thank God, Jewel was thinking clearly again. He wondered briefly if anyone else had ever solved that problem with sex and laughed, his voice echoing on the stairs.

Normally modest when he came to the windowed third floor, he turned toward that blasted door and stood there, letting anyone who watched see his naked manhood. He'd rub it in their face. Jewel was home and in just hours, he'd have her away from here.

"Sandwiches?" Jewel said when he nudged the bedroom door open. "I just brushed my teeth."

"You can do it again," he said. "How long is it since they fed you?"

Jewel looked blank. "Hours, I guess."

"Eat," Jasper said, putting the sandwiches and the notepad beside her. Turning back to the room terminal, he turned on music–his music–loud enough to drown out casual noises then went to his briefcase and pulled out a flasher. Sticking it in the vid screen terminal, he typed rapid commands on his com unit. Butler picked them up and stopped recording then shuttled everything he had recorded that night to his flasher. A second copy appeared on his com unit. Jasper didn't bother to watch it now but put the flasher back in his briefcase.

Jewel watched it all but her few words were about how hungry she was. Jasper picked up half of his sandwich and pushed the other toward her then poured himself a cup of coffee.

Jewel was smiling and he looked at her suspiciously.

"What?"

Her mouth full, she just pointed at him and shook her head.

He looked down, saw he was still bare but did his best to look obtuse. "What, love?"

She swallowed her sandwich and said, "You make me wear pajamas then stand there buck naked? I've half a mind to..."

"Don't even think it." Going to his dresser, he pulled on black briefs and t shirt then put on a black pants and shirt. He pulled out the jacket he would wear over it and started checking its pockets.

Jewel watched him then left the bed to change again. When she was done, she wore a short black skirt with black leggings beneath. Her blouse was a deep purple. Tucking a white and black scarf into her pocket, she turned to him for his approval.

"I like that nightgown," he said. "I think I'll like taking it off even more."

"Not tonight," she said, no trace of humor now.

"You should sleep," he said "I'm beat too. You first."

She obediently went into the bathroom and busied herself brushing her teeth. He sat down and wrote furiously, trying to get in everything she needed to know. When she came out of the bathroom, he went in and Jewel read the pad while settling into bed.

There were still things he had to do. After turning on the water, he checked the paddle he'd used and found the frequency listing it had stored. The jammers were there under the sink. Fishing them out, he set them to block the frequency. They'd protect Jewel if they worked right. He couldn't put them on her though until they were ready to leave. Finding the decoy transmitter, he set it to the same frequency. He'd turn it on only after he knew Jewel was protected. With luck, they would think that she—and he—were still sound asleep in their bed for long after they had gone.

It was risky but he knew surveillance was always the most careless on the first night and the most vulnerable hour was between three and four am. Even though people lived mostly underground now, their bodies still kept the same clock and drowsiness always hit between three and four in the morning. By four thirty it would be kicked so they had to leave on time.

When he came out again, Jewel was ready. Her hair was combed into some semblance of order and she held the notepad up with a simple sign reading "I'm safe" and the date and time. Jasper took her picture with his com unit and sent it off to David.

"Are you going to turn off the music?" Jewel asked as he made his last preparation and turned on the nightlight they would need.

"Not unless it bothers you," he said. "I like to sleep with it on."

"Can you put on Sleepwalking?" Jewel asked. "I like that one."

"You got it," Jasper said and changed it as planned. After that Jewel lay down on the bed and he joined her. "Sleep," he said and put his silent alarm in one ear. He noted the time was just past two. There was time for a catnap while the three-hour repetitive strains of Sleepwalking put their captors to sleep. He smiled at his wife and clasped her hand. She lay on her side and timidly smiled back then resolutely closed her eyes.

Composed to help Carol sleep when she was suffering from Hades Syndrome, now Jasper was using his tune to escape. His mind followed the tune until he too fell into a light doze.

Chapter 18 - Saturday, 13 Nov 2179

Cold. Jasper shivered then tried to put it out of his mind, as he walked firmly along the cement path, his hand around Jewel's. His other hand held his briefcase. Jewel didn't carry much more. Her free arm was wrapped around his drum, which she had grabbed on the way out the door, its drumsticks clutched in her hand.

It wasn't too dark to see the cement and he was glad—and worried—that the moon had risen. It looked full and gilded the tops of trees with silver. Above them Laramie Peak was clearly visible in the moonlight and breathtaking in its beauty.

He wondered if they would ever see it again like this but shoved the thought away. Safety. They needed safety. He eyed the shadows around them, the darkness under the trees, and wondered if he had outsmarted Baxter.

"He's there," he said to Jewel as he caught a single flash of light from the parking lot. He quickened his steps, eager to get there. Jewel matched his pace, her black clad legs visible against the lighter path.

He hadn't thought about the paths being lighter when he'd chosen black. He hadn't thought about the moon rising, although it made it easier to find his way. Never having been outside this late, he thought it would be pitch black but it wasn't. Stars blazed overhead and the moon made it light enough to see or be seen. He just hoped Baxter's men were truly asleep. If they still had the audio on in his house, they should be.

"Ray?" he asked as they got closer to the source of the light. He couldn't see him among the shadows of two cars, one of them a maintenance vehicle.

"Here," Ray Carlson said and separated himself from the dark shadowy trunk of a tree. "I was watching to see if anything else moved."

"Nothing?" Jasper asked.

"There's some deer over that way," a second voice said, making him turn swiftly. "Relax, Mr. S. I'm with Ray."

"Our driver," Ray said. "Let's get out of here." He ushered Jewel toward the sedan.

In the darkness Jasper couldn't tell what color it was and didn't care. The interior lights were off too, so he fumbled for his seat belt, found it, and reached for his wife's hand.

"What's this?" He heard Jewel ask and he dimly saw a dark semi-flexible shape laid on his wife's lap.

"Extra insurance," Ray said, "and it will keep you warmer. Just keep it there."

"Yes sir." Jewel murmured in a meek tone.

"Let's go." Ray took his own place in the front seat.

The driver slid the car quietly out of its parking spot, its electric engine nearly soundless as he nudged it down the silver ribbon of road. No lights.

Jasper wondered if that was safe but he could see the road. The driver didn't seem to need them as he sped up. Once they reached the main highway, he flipped the lights on and Jasper relaxed.

Jewel turned her pale face toward him and gave him a tentative smile but he could see the nap had done her little good. It hadn't helped him much either. He had started at every imagined sound in the house and was relieved when he could finally get up and wake his wife.

He'd put the belt with the jammers on her, activated the decoy, and grabbed his briefcase and their coats. Jewel had grabbed that damned drum. What was she thinking to bring that noisemaker along? He didn't know.

Outside the car, he could see the last of the city's ventilation towers and orchards give way to the featureless plains of Wyoming with its low hills. The night was eerie without the lights of the city. He could see miles of nothingness and it unsettled him.

How far was that damned airport? Even as he thought it, they topped a rise and he could see the dim lights. He willed it to get larger. It was a small airport by any standard, servicing only a few private planes and an occasional bigger jet. There were four buildings, one of them the passenger terminal, and only two jets. The private planes, if any were there, were in the hangars. All the buildings were dark and they passed them by without stopping, heading straight for the black marked government craft. As they passed the corporate jet, Jewel clutched his arm and pointed.

He stared in disbelief at the corporate jet, seeing the Wilson Chemicals logo. That was Baxter's plane? Was he here? He tapped Carlson's shoulder and pointed it out.

"Do you know how long that jet has been here?" Carlson asked the driver.

"About a week," their driver said. "A big shot from Wilson. I think he's in the city. It looks quiet."

"Pilot on board?" Carlson asked.

"Probably," the driver said. "Probably asleep too."

Jasper hoped that was the case. He didn't want Jewel seen by anyone.

Carlson was talking on his com unit. When he finished, he spoke to Jasper. "Everything's fine. Our pilot has it warmed up. We'll be in Denver before dawn."

Jasper said something in return but it was Jewel that had his attention. She watched the jet, a look of fixed fascination on her face. He had to poke her when the car pulled up to their own.

She clutched the drum tightly when Carlson helped her out and took the lap robe she'd been given. Carlson grabbed another off the seat. Her distraction wasn't lost on him. As soon as they were aboard their plane and she was seated, he quietly asked, "Why does that plane bother you?"

She turned haunted blue eyes toward him and clutched the drum tighter. "I think I was on it."

"On it?" Jasper stared at his wife, his thoughts running amok. They hadn't found her in the city. She'd been brought back to him from outside. Could she really have been stashed on that plane?

"Hold on." Carlson told them and disappeared into the cockpit. A moment later the plane lifted, thrusting upwards. It turned on its axis toward the corporate jet, the whine of its engines audible inside the cabin then thrust upwards again. Its main engines fired and they were away from the airport and speeding south at ever increasing speed.

Carlson returned. "We got the number of that jet and I told our driver to get lost. He won't go straight home. I don't want him getting questioned—or hired—by Wilson Chemicals."

"Not one of yours?" Jasper had almost said ours before remembering Jewel.

"No, he's from a local ranch. He's good but usually a lot more talkative," Carlson said. "Something we didn't need tonight."

Jasper nodded and turned to his wife. She was about done. "Go to sleep, love. I'll wake you when we reach Denver."

For once she didn't resist but made herself comfortable, her arms around that damned drum. He watched until he saw the first tears then abruptly got up. Damn them! Grabbing his briefcase, he moved to the small galley, Carlson following.

"Here," he said and thrust the flasher into his hands. "I got everything in the house recorded except for the first fifteen minutes. The Boss is on there."

Carlson's face lit up. "You're sure?"

"Yes and I know who he is," Jasper fiercely said. "Watch it. We can't talk here. Jewel's not asleep."

Carlson gave a sharp look her direction and pocketed the flasher. "You want us to search that plane? If she was on it and we can prove it..."

"Not yet," Jasper said, shaking his head. "I want him for more than kidnapping. He's done something to her besides a transmitter. I want to know what."

"I'll arrange it," Carlson said. "Get some sleep if you can. You're safe now."

* * *

Denver in 2179 was an interesting mixture of new and old. Twentieth century, even nineteenth century, buildings were scattered in the old downtown with here and there a newer building rising above them. Most were old and a couple were dark abandoned structures slated for demolition, their first floors sealed to prevent squatters. The dome of the old capitol, now a museum, was clearly visible among the rest.

From where he stood in the Justice building, Jasper could also see the newer parts of Denver. Lunarex Tower shone whitely to the west, its ivory perfection set against the Colorado mountains. The new town, the underground, lay to the north beyond the massive train complex that served Denver, southeastern Wyoming, and the front range. As at Plains, the underground was marked off by ventilation towers and trees with here and there a building breaking the surface or a skydome marking a mall or some fancy section of town.

It wasn't as black as when they arrived. The plane had settled on top the building in the predawn darkness and they'd been ushered in with just a cursory inspection. Since then they'd been in this well-appointed doctor's suite waiting for the doctor and nurse to get here.

Damn, he wanted to do something besides wait. Jasper had already discovered his com unit was useless in here. He couldn't access the internet or call David. What he had stored on it was accessible but nothing outside.

He wanted to access Butler and find out whether they'd returned to the house. If anyone had been awake on that corporate jet, they might have seen him and Jewel. Even if they'd been asleep, they would have heard the government plane take off. They probably heard it arrive too because it had been on the ground barely ninety minutes.

The pilot hadn't seen anyone. Arriving after midnight as he had, he was under no requirement to log in until the terminal opened in the morning. Under orders not to reveal what agency had requested the flight, he had remained on the plane and in readiness till Carlson returned. An electronic registration would probably be sent later but Jasper doubted DEA would be tagged as the agency using the Plains airport at that hour. Maybe the stop would be explained away as an internal repair.

Now he could see more detail outside and the first faint rays of the sun were visible on the eastern horizon. Checking the time, he saw it was nearly seven. Sunrises were something he rarely saw but he was in no mood to appreciate it today. Turning back toward the couch, he saw Jewel was sound asleep as she should be, her arms wrapped around that drum. Why the hell had she grabbed that? It was the newest item in the house. Of course, he hadn't given her a chance to see what they were leaving behind. Maybe that was it.

She still looked worn out to him but her face was finally relaxed in sleep. Well, if that doctor was going to persist in being late, at least she'd get a good nap. He wished he had some coffee. Not seeing any hope of getting any, he sat down in a chair to watch the sun rise.

A soft click, click brought him back to wakefulness. Jasper sat upright, his hand groping for the trank gun he no longer wore, before he was fully awake. He blinked and saw there was now a woman at the desk that had been empty before. Glancing swiftly at Jewel, he saw she hadn't moved. There was sunlight streaming in the windows though and he knew he must have slept a good hour. God, he needed coffee.

"Coffee?" he asked and heard Jewel shift. "For sleeping beauty too."

"Yes sir. How would you like it?" the woman asked as if it was no unusual occurrence to find people asleep in her waiting room.

"Black and strong," he said. "She likes it with cream and sugar."

"I'd like it black," Jewel said and struggled to a sitting position, the metal drum hitting the floor with a musical tone.

"What is that?" the nurse asked, her eyes taking in the unusual object. "And will it explode?"

Jewel laughed so suddenly Jasper was startled then a grin curved his lips. God, she'd laughed. Suddenly the long wait for the doctor was worth it.

He nudged the drum with his foot and it rang out again. "It's a lotus drum," Jasper said. "Just a musical instrument."

"Oh." The nurse still looked at it suspiciously and Jasper knew that she'd been serious with her question of whether it would explode. He was reminded where he was and retrieved the drum from the floor. Peering inside, he saw it was clean. His hands rubbed the outside as the nurse pulled an old-fashioned wired telephone out of a drawer and keyed in a number. The drum had taken no hurt. Satisfied Baxter hadn't slipped something into it, he set it down on the table.

"Is the doctor here?" Jasper asked.

"Yes sir. He's reviewing the notes. The exam room is also ready. Which one of you first?" she asked with calm efficiency.

"I think my wife would like to freshen up," he said. "Then she's first."

"Yes sir. Coffee and breakfast has been ordered. It will be along shortly."

Jasper gave her a tired grin. "Best thing I've heard today." Glancing at his wife, he refrained from calling the efficient nurse a treasure. That was reserved for his wife. He couldn't help being impressed though by her calm demeanor as she led his wife down a very short hall.

They had found the bathroom early this morning in a brief inspection of the office but neither had gone further than that. Not knowing how long it would be until someone arrived, they'd waited.

He was irritated by the long wait but he'd had little experience with actual doctors. Unless something like a bullet required he see one, he'd usually just gone to a medical terminal. They were efficient, patient, and rarely made a mistake. It had been a medical terminal, not a doctor, that had diagnosed Carol's condition and sent them to a specialist. Because it had caught the early signs of Hades Syndrome, Carol had lived long enough to see Melody graduate high school.

Damn, he needed coffee. His eyes were burning and he was getting morose. He was not going to lose Jewel. They'd get her fixed up. They had to.

Another door opened and a blue clad figure came out. Jasper straightened as the doctor came into the waiting room. "Agent, I need a moment with you please. A few questions before I see her. I'm Doctor Rogers."

Jasper nodded and followed the doctor to his office. Together they watched the vid file he'd given Carlson and he explained the reference to blister in more detail then the signal coming from his wife and what he thought it was.

"I agree she's probably got a transmitter," the doctor said. "The question is what kind and what we need to do to remove it. There's a few different models out there and from the threat the man made, I'm guessing it can self-destruct."

"Self-destruct?" Jasper repeated but it didn't surprise him. Baxter had been very clear about being able to kill Jewel with a touch of his button.

"Yes," the doctor said. "One of the nastiest weapons that came out of the Islamic Revolution. They'd plant them in women they wanted to use as spies. They could eavesdrop quite effectively and, if the woman revealed she had one, kill her. Their favorite targets were the wives of opponents."

Jasper felt a chill run through him. Kill her? Well, he'd known that. "Can you get it out?"

"We'll see," the doctor said. "Right now I'm concerned with identifying the model–and finding out about this drug he gave her. We'll have to check her for injection spots."

"Professor Nugent had pills," Jasper said. "But I can't see Jewel willingly swallowing a bunch of pills."

"That wouldn't be very effective anyway," the doctor said. "No, I think we'll look for another delivery method. It will take a little time because I'm reluctant to use electronics with that transmitter in her."

Jasper nodded.

"First I think you should both eat breakfast," the doctor said. "It will take me some time to pull up what I can on that drug. If it's in our files, I should be able to find it. Bliss reactives are almost unheard of."

"Almost?" Jasper asked.

"I think I've heard of a couple of cases," he said. "I just have to find them again. Now let's get you back to your wife."

"One thing, doctor," Jasper said as they started to leave. "I'm not an agent. My name is Jasper Stone. I'm also known as Sensor Man."

"Got it," the doctor said. "I thought I recognized you. It is policy though not to remember names here unless it is needed. You understand?"

"Yes sir. Just don't call me agent." Jasper didn't want Jewel picking up on that. It was hard enough to keep secrets from her.

"As you wish," the doctor said with a brief smile. "This then, is courtesy to a former police lieutenant."

"Thank you."

After a brief breakfast, Jasper had to sit and wait again while Jewel was taken off to be examined, the nurse accompanying her. He fretted about not being with her but the nurse had bluntly told him he'd make her more nervous than she already was. Having nothing to do, he thought again about calling David West when the door opened and David walked in with Ray Carlson beside him.

"David," Jasper said, rising to his feet. "They let you in."

"With a bit of help," David replied. "I brought the suitcases and Elinor's love. Where's my niece?"

"They're still checking her out," Jasper said. "She's teary but alive."

"Only natural," David said. "Ray tells me you just walked out the door this morning?"

"Pretty much," Jasper said and told him in more detail about what happened, only withholding Baxter's identity.

"We need to find that bastard," David said. "I think fighting Blissex is going to be my new hobby."

Jasper understood that. He'd made the same decision when his younger brother died of an overdose. Since then he'd seen a lot of other families torn apart because their kid was having fun with blissex—usually without the parents knowing about it. Screwing up with blissex was more deadly than any of the old prohibited drugs because it took just one time exceeding your limit. Kids died or had brain damage from overloading their pleasure centers beyond what the body could handle.

"I've worked most of my adult life to get rid of it," Jasper said. "I thought I was done till they took Jewel," he said for David's benefit. "I won't be blackmailed into helping them."

"Uncle David!" Jewel came dashing out and nothing more could be said until David had hugged her and dried her tears.

Carlson waved Jasper to one side and they stepped into the short hall. "You promised me an ID on the Boss. Who is it?"

"Mark Baxter, Wilson Chemicals. He's a vice president," Jasper spoke quickly, keeping an eye on his wife. "You'll have to do a voice analysis but I'm sure it's him."

"A VP at Wilson?" Carlson asked, incredulous. "How'd you ID him?"

"The eyes and an earring he wears," Jasper said. "I never spoke to him before but I saw plenty of him at the Reach Out event a few days ago. If it's him, Blissex is a bigger problem than we thought."

Carlson nodded but Jasper could see his mind was already working on the implications. Wilson Chemicals had reported a breach of security over twenty years ago when the formula for bliss had been stolen. Two of its top chemists had also disappeared and the investigation had been focused on finding them when blissex first showed up in east coast cities. If Baxter was still connected with Wilson and had ties to blissex smuggling that argued for a continued connection between Wilson and the illegal trade. They had to find out how far it went.

"I have your suitcase," David was saying to his niece.

"That's not my suitcase," Jewel said.

"It is now," David said. "You can't expect me to carry a lavender one."

Jasper grinned. David had been appalled when he saw the matching suitcases in Jewel's storage room then went out and bought a plain brown one. Jasper only owned one himself since he rarely evelled . It was a manly black. They'd spent a lot of the waiting time packing what they would need and David had brought both suitcases back with him to Denver.

"I think the blissex smugglers made a serious error in messing with West," Carlson said in a low voice. "And if there's even a hint they were behind the other murders, they'll have an enemy they can't fight."

"Ed Kucera wasn't part of Wilson though."

"No but this Boss said he wasn't guilty. I think maybe you should take another look at that case," Carlson suggested. "With the assumption he's not."

Jasper frowned. "There are some things that don't hang together," he said. "Yes, I'll look into it."

"I've got new identity cards for both of you. Your legal identities will take a few more days to reprocess but these will get you through. You're not Blitzen. We've kept that back," Carlson said.

"Good," Jasper said. "It looks like they're done."

He rejoined his wife and David as Jewel finished recording a message for the missing Elinor. Slipping into the picture, he wrapped his arm around Jewel.

"I'm ok," Jewel said again. "And Jasper is with me. We'll just go on our honeymoon now and be back when this is all over. Take care." Her smile seemed a little brittle to him but she was smiling.

"That will do it," David said and put his com unit away. "Now I'd better get over to the clinic before she starts fretting."

"You have to go now?" Jewel asked, dismayed.

"The baby's ready," David said. "I know I've done my part but Elinor will blast me if I'm not there when they shove him in. She'll be on bed rest until he settles so I came here first."

Jasper's arm tightened around his wife's waist. Could she have children after this? He knew how badly his wife wanted them. He'd have to ask.

Elinor had stored ova before she started her tours on the moon so she could have a healthy baby. The boy—they'd opted for a boy—was about two weeks along in development and ready to be implanted in his mother. He knew it was an old technique and common practice these days.

"Jewel, there's a new com unit for you in the suitcase. I don't want you calling us direct though. I've set up a relay through the Foundation. The number is there," David said. "Those calls are impossible to trace."

"Yes, uncle," Jewel replied, her hand still clutched tightly in his.

"You'd better get going," Jasper said. "Jewel, you can call when you get settled."

His wife let her uncle go then turned to face him to hide the tears welling up in her eyes. Damn.

"Later," David said with a catch in his throat. He was gone before Jasper could respond.

Chapter 19 - Denver

"This is what we've got," the doctor said. "It is a transmitter using just one frequency so it's easy to block. It's made in the Middle East and is an old design. If it's as old as the design, we might have some good luck. Those used old style batteries too, and they're almost impossible to come by. The thing could be out of power in days or last out the month."

"You aren't going to remove it?" Jasper asked and felt Jewel's hand tighten on his.

"I'm not comfortable doing it," Dr. Rogers said. "The model still has to be identified and that could take hours. Until that's done, I don't think anyone will attempt it–and the preferred option is to take it out after the battery has run down. There's no risk that way."

"I want it out," Jewel said.

"I know you do," Dr. Rogers said. "And I understand which is why I'm going to send you to the best at this procedure. You're going to Chicago next?"

"That was the plan," Jasper said, his lips tight.

"Then you'll want to see Dr. McBride there. She has the most experience with these transmitters and she'll be the one removing it if it's still alive."

Jewel clutched his hand tighter and Jasper saw she was on the verge of tears. He understood. He wouldn't want that damned thing in him either.

The doctor cleared his throat and continued. "The good news is the only implant I found is your birth control implant. That needs to be removed since it doesn't seem–"

"Birth control implant?" Jasper's eyebrow shot up. "Jewel doesn't have one."

"No?" the doctor asked.

"No, I don't," Jewel said. "We're trying to..." She reddened and didn't finish.

"Let me see," the doctor said with a frown. Getting up, he felt Jewel's upper arm and his frown deepened. "I need to see it," he said.

Jewel slipped her arm out of its sleeve, baring it for him. Her other hand held her shirt down in becoming modesty.

The doctor felt her arm again then studied the cut Jasper had noticed in the shower. "This is very recent," he said. "We might have something here. Let's go back to the exam room again."

This time Jasper followed, unwilling to be barred again. The nurse glared at him but he didn't budge.

"We need those shields, Rose," Dr. Rogers said. "I want an x-ray of this."

The nurse produced a lead apron and draped it across Jewel. Jasper retreated a few steps but watched as the doctor captured the image on an electronic x-ray.

"It looks like a birth control implant," he said. "There's nothing odd about it."

"It's not," Jewel said. "I've never had one."

"I believe you," the doctor said. "It's got to come out but I can't give you more than a local."

"She can't have anything with a bliss component," Jasper said. "It could kill her."

"I remember, lieutenant," the doctor said. "The local I have here does not have a bliss component. It's based on a much older local anesthesia. We use it to dig bullets out of stubborn agents."

"I want it out," Jewel said through tight lips. "Now."

Jasper wanted to say no but one look at Jewel's set face and he knew he'd lose. His wife was stronger than most realized and she wanted it done.

"Do it," Jasper said.

The half hour that followed was not as bad as he expected. Jewel bit her lip but didn't cry out even when the doctor had to make a second incision to push the implant out. It wasn't deep, he realized but just under the skin and made up of three rods bound together. Was that what a birth control implant looked like? Carol had had one but he had never wondered about it. "Is that normal?" he asked as the doctor glued Jewel's skin back together and applied a see-through bandage.

"No, it's not," the doctor said. "Wrong color and it's short a rod. I'll have to get these analyzed to see what it is and who made it. What did you call that drug? Blister?"

"That's right but it was in pill form," Jasper said.

"This could be an alternative form," the doctor said as he poked at the implant. "Does anyone have any of those pills? We might need to compare."

"The evidence from the professor's house and autopsy was confiscated and the investigation shut down," Jasper said. "But you might be able to get Ed Kucera's autopsy."

"That might do," the doctor said. "I'll make a note of it and send these over to the lab. In any case, you are still to avoid bliss and bliss products until we have answers, Mrs. Stone. If you need relief, use the old-fashioned method—or chocolate."

"Old fashioned method?" Jasper asked, not understanding.

"Sex, lieutenant," the doctor was blunt. "It won't hurt that transmitter or set it off. If your wife needs it, I recommend you comply."

Jasper's eyes flew to Jewel just as she giggled. He could feel his flush and he swallowed hard. "Right, chocolate."

Jewel's response eased his embarrassment but he wasn't done. "Light or dark?"

"Dark," the doctor said with a tight smile. "Just remember you'll sleep better if you use the other method."

Jasper snorted. He had no doubt of that.

"So we have to wait on the bloody transmitter?" he asked again, ignoring Jewel's muffled giggle.

"Yes," the doctor said. "I noticed you had the lap shields but I think they have something better in special needs. The jammers you have should work fine too–make sure you use two. I think it would be better if you stay in a retro hotel with a minimum of electronic traffic. It's safer."

Easy for him to say, Jasper thought. It was his wife and she had to carry that transmitter around until the battery wore down? How many electronics did the Kowalskis have? Well, they were still going there. If it wasn't suitable, he'd find another place later.

"I think we're done here," Dr. Rogers said. "Mrs. Stone, you can get dressed. Just keep that incision clean and check with a doctor if you develop any redness."

With that he was gone and Jasper found himself alone with his wife. Her arm was still numb so he helped her back into her blouse.

"We'll get through this," he murmured and planted a kiss on her neck.

"I want chocolate," she whispered and he looked at her suspiciously.

"I will buy you a ton of chocolate," he said, "but no games till we're settled."

She nodded, her smile fading and he knew tears weren't far away. The old Jewel would have tempted him just because she could. How he missed her.

* * *

Jasper smoothed the crease of his black trousers with an impatient hand then looked up at his wife's strange face once more.

She'd been transformed into someone totally new, her chopped hair hidden by a purple cap with strands of blonde hair peeping out. Her blue eyes, normally so vivid, were framed by stars in purple, blue and gold which dimmed their color and her lips were duo-toned purple and gold. Even her clothes had been changed by the woman from Special Needs. She'd given up her own black skirt for a heavier quilted one that had the same blocking ability as the lap robe. Something called leg warmers added blue and purple to her black leggings and there were glowing clips on her shoes. The overall effect made her look younger than his daughter and his daughter had never dressed so wild.

He looked no better. Because his locket and penchant for black were getting known, he'd had to don a blue shirt with an ultra-modern vest in purple and black. Only his trousers were left alone and his locket was tucked out of sight.

He'd been given an impossibly thin moustache and his hair, usually so neat, had been gelled with purple streaks clipped in. The gold stars on his face were limited to just three but they were glowers and diverted attention from the strength of his jaw. Wraparound sunglasses completed his look.

He had to send pictures of this to his daughter and agent. An effective disguise, this was also the image he didn't want to portray to the public. On second thought, Mitch might like it. His daughter would find it hilarious.

He didn't know what the others on the government plane thought. Right after meeting with the security officer, they'd taken seats at the back of the plane where few walked past them. They weren't entirely trusted though. Someone on board rated Secret Service protection and one of their agents had settled across the aisle from them. Jasper wondered who they were protecting but knew better than to ask. Unwilling to answer questions himself, he contented himself with Jewel.

Pulling out his new wallet, he looked at his identity card again. He was now Flint Black, an odd name but he sort of liked it. His wife was Jennifer Black. She had already discarded that and insisted he call her Jet Black. His lips twitched at her fancy but dressed as she was, it would fit. It was too bad they hadn't given her black hair instead of blonde.

When he asked about the name, he'd been told it was one of a hundred identities they reserved for federal agents or others who needed to be moved quickly and quietly from one place to another. It was just luck he'd gotten Flint instead of some equally bland name.

He needed to send a picture of their new identities to Ivan. He was to meet them somewhere but they didn't yet know where or when. He did know St. Paul was about six hours from Chicago. How long was it since he'd been in a real bed? Just twelve hours. It felt like it had been a lot longer though and he knew that was because he was so short on sleep. It was likely to be another ten or twelve before he'd see another one.

"We'd better nap," he said to Jewel. "There's another long stretch before us."

"Yes, love," she said then turned his face toward hers and gave him a light kiss. "He's watching," she murmured against his lips, "Mr. Black."

Watching be damned, he thought, and made the kiss real. He could feel the flutter of Jewel's pulse in her neck and smell the clean scent of her skin as he ended the kiss. Picking up her hand, he kissed it lightly and smoothed the place where her engagement ring had been. It was on a chain around her neck now. His distinctive black tungsten and gold wedding ring was in his briefcase and a jeweled band had replaced it. They'd thought of everything.

"Sleep now," he said just as a stewardess came by. She stopped, and smiling warmly, handed them pillows and blankets from an overhead bin.

"Would either of you like a bliss?" she asked. "We have mini-doses to help you sleep."

"No thank you," Jasper said, reminded how easy it was to get bliss. "We'll be fine."

Jewel looked at him with shadowed eyes and he kissed her again before saying, "Just nap. I'll join you since we have our own watchdog."

That brought a quick glance at the agent and a bit of a smile. "Yes, love but I really want to curl up in a bed with you."

"Me too," Jasper said. "The bed would be very, very welcome."

She glared at him with mock anger then covered up with her blanket and closed her eyes.

Jasper didn't find it that easy. The thrum of the airplane was comforting but his thoughts wouldn't quiet. He found himself reliving those moments with Baxter and starting awake. They didn't play out true. Somehow Baxter knew he knew and Jewel, who he knew had been oblivious the entire time, kept waking up and calling his name. Lori was even there. God, he missed her. There had never been a romantic relationship between them but they had been good friends.

He needed to get Slasher too. He clearly worked for Baxter. Would Baxter keep him around all the time? Could he be identified that way? He'd have to mention that to the captain. The entire police force in Plains would like to get that guy. Come to think of it, there was a remote cam at the Plains airport. He should be able to see if that Wilson jet was still there. Making a mental list of all the things he should do, he finally dozed off.

* * *

"I have to agree with my colleague in Denver that letting the transmitter run down is the best course of action. There's no risk to removing it then," Dr. McBride said. "If we nudge it the wrong way right now, it could go off and it would require major surgery to repair the damage—if we didn't lose you. It's simply too risky at this stage."

Jasper felt Jewel's hand tightly clench his and knew she was close to tears. "Have you ever removed a live one, doctor?" Jasper asked.

"Yes, I have," Dr. McBride turned her cool blue eyes toward him. "I've also had one blow up and lost the patient. I don't recommend it, lieutenant. Your wife is young and I understand you're newlyweds. I want you both to have a long and productive married life and that means we need to wait."

Jasper nodded but he hated to put Jewel through it. Doctor, be damned. He put his arm around his wife and let Jewel snuggle into his side.

"We do have better news about that implant," the doctor said. "It was definitely not a birth control implant. We don't have the manufacturer yet but the drug has been identified as X-31652. It's shown up before, usually as an implant but sometimes just in the blood stream with no sign of an implant. It most recently showed up in a detention suicide in Denver. Do you know about the Edward Kucera case?"

Jewel muffled her snort against his shoulder.

Jasper nodded, restraining his own urge to laugh. "Yes, I'm aware of it. I also have a possible name for the drug which might be helpful beyond the number designation."

"A name?" The doctor looked interested.

"Yes," Jasper said. "The man who put the implant in my wife called it blister. He also wanted to know how Edward Kucera got it."

"He was a source and didn't know?" The doctor laid down her old fashioned pen and looked at him, her neat grey hair looking like a helmet in the artificial lights of the office.

"Apparently," Jasper said. "Now how long is it likely to last with the implant gone?"

The doctor studied him then sighed. "New territory, lieutenant. It was a timed release delivery system so it could be out of her system tomorrow or next month. We don't know enough to tell at this point. The only thing I can tell you is it will eventually be gone since the implant has been removed.

Once the transmitter is dead and gone, we'll be able to tell you more. As long as that's in place, it limits us on what we can scan for. The only way to diagnose it without a scan is repeated blood tests."

"Speaking of blood tests, my nurse will be in shortly to draw some blood, Mrs. Stone. After that you'll be free to go."

"Precautions?" Jasper asked.

"Avoid places with heavy electronic traffic," she said. "A retro hotel is best since they have no electronics."

"How likely is this thing to be set off accidently?" Jasper asked.

"Not likely," the doctor firmly said. "It requires a very specific set of audible tones preceded by a long tone of almost three seconds. That's always the same. We tell you to avoid heavy electronic traffic because the signal can be broadcast almost without you knowing it."

"Understood," Jasper said.

"Is your safe house known to anyone outside your family?" the doctor asked. "And have you left your old numbers behind?"

"It's not known outside of her uncle and aunt and the agent who sent us here," Jasper said. "Yes, we left our com units behind and purchased new."

"Then that should be sufficient," she said. "I know you have jammers and you should continue using them with that skirt, Mrs. Stone. If there's any electronics within a hundred feet, you should protect yourself. Do you have a detection paddle?"

"Yes," Jasper said. "They gave me one."

"Good. Check it every morning to see if it's still transmitting. When it stops, call my number and we'll get you right in."

Jasper took the card she handed him.

"This," she said as she handed him a second card, "is the hospital in St. Paul I have a contract with. If there's any problems, go there. They'll have the files."

Jasper took the second card reluctantly, wishing they could just get it over with.

"I'll send in the nurse," she said and left.

"I want it out," Jewel said.

"I know, love," Jasper said. "But we can't make her do it. If she thinks it's too risky, we need to wait." He cradled her head against his shoulder until the nurse entered carrying a tray.

Damn them, he thought. At the same time, he could appreciate why the doctor wanted to wait. If she'd lost a patient removing one, that would be reason enough. He couldn't lose Jewel.

No, they would have to wait.

Chapter 20 - Chicago

"Molly," Jewel said, speeding up as she spotted Mrs. Kowalski. The next minute she was hugging the plump red-headed figure of Sasha's mother. Jasper couldn't help grinning at his wife's greeting but was more reserved as he faced Ivan and a younger man he didn't know.

"It's a good thing you sent us that picture, Sensor Man," Ivan said with a long look at the changes in him. "Jewel would give herself away but you–" he laughed.

Jasper grinned, keenly aware how much this disguise changed him. Who could take him seriously looking like this? He yearned to wash out the gel and take off the damned vest.

"This is Kale Tunis," Ivan said, indicating the well-built Asian looking man. "He's our relief driver this trip and martial arts instructor."

"Martial arts?" Jasper asked as he shook the man's hand.

"I married into the farm," Kale said with a wide grin. "I give a hand here and there and teach the kids discipline."

"That's a good thing to do," Jasper said, wondering if Ivan expected even more trouble than he did.

"Kale has good night vision," Ivan said. "And I thought it might be good for you to get acquainted. Let's get you set. Any other luggage?"

"No, just the two suitcases, my briefcase and Jewel's drum," Jasper said.

"Drum?" Ivan asked. "Shouldn't that be yours?"

"I thought it was," Jasper said. "But she's been clinging to it ever since I got her back."

Ivan hesitated then handed the cloth sack with the drum to Molly. "Better keep that in the cab then."

The vehicle was a sturdy half-truck, half passenger car combination. The back still held some grain sacks but he couldn't tell what in the half-darkness of the parking lot. The cab was fairly spacious and allowed two to sit in the front seat and he thought three could fit in the rear one. Pretty nice but far from new.

"Electric or hydrogen?" Jasper asked.

"It's electric but with extra packs," Ivan said. "Self-generating too. You're up front with me. Molly, Jewel and Kale will take the back for the first hour or two."

"We appreciate this," Jasper said as he took the passenger seat. "We didn't want to go to any of the West relatives right now."

"David filled me in," Ivan said. "And this is best. We've got a guest apartment, plenty of food, and Molly is a physician's assistant. We can even put you to work if you need it."

"With animals?" Jasper asked, his heart sinking.

"No, not you," Ivan said. "We'll find something safer. Kale teaches on our farm and a couple of neighboring ones and Molly doctors. We've got enough people that we can offer a little something for every one."

Jasper nodded in the semi-darkness then said. "I can see that. How many people do you have?" He knew farms these days were never single-family operations but the size varied according to what they produced.

"Thirty-seven adults and forty-five or forty-six kids—I lose track of them. We've also got cows, turkeys, chickens, rabbits, dogs, cats, and what not." Ivan glanced at him then eased the truck on to the highway. Turning on the warn-off, he set the truck on a guide line and put it on auto-pilot. "The pavement's nice and dry. We don't have to strain our eyes tonight."

"What about animals?" Jasper asked, uncomfortable with the exposed road. This wasn't like in Plains because there were trees looming over it. "Aren't there deer in those trees?"

"Probably," Ivan said, "but there's also fences they can't get through all the way up to Madison. After Madison, we'll go on manual. Until then you can fill me in on just what's been happening. David wasn't all that detailed."

"Before he starts talking, let him eat," Molly said from the back seat. "He hasn't had anything since before noon except airport food." A hand thrust a sandwich at him from the darkness and Jasper took it automatically. It was followed by a cup of hot coffee and a container of something he couldn't identify.

"Coffee," Jasper said and heard Jewel snicker. "Jewel, eat." Her wordless reply made him smile. He'd rather have her sassing him than crying.

"You eat," Ivan said. "Molly, give me one of those sandwiches. Might as well keep him company. Coffee too."

"We just packed a lunch," Ivan explained. "It's easier on long trips. There are a couple of rest areas between here and there but the restaurants will mostly be shut down at eight. There's not enough traffic this time of year to keep them open."

Jasper wasn't surprised. There was traffic on this road but it was mostly trucking with a few private vehicles and every one was showing the amber lights of a guided vehicle and maintaining the same speed as they were. Satisfied there would be no accidents, he concentrated on the beef sandwich and coffee then discovered the container held a potato salad of some sort. It wasn't one he'd had before but it was good and filled up the empty spots. He hadn't known how hungry he was and it was a relief to get some real food.

"Molly, you think of everything," he said as she handed him back another cup of coffee. "It's a good thing Ivan married you."

"Thank you," she said with a laugh. "Although Jewel makes good sandwiches too."

Jasper grinned, remembering how he'd thanked Jewel for some sandwiches once. It was only their third kiss but it had been a good one.

He found himself relaxing in their company and losing the tension of the last days. Yes, he'd made the right choice in coming to them.

"Ready to talk now?" Ivan asked. "Or would you rather wait?"

"There's not that much to tell," Jasper said, aware Jewel was listening. "At least not from my side. I do want Jewel to wait until we can get it on record." Quickly he told him about the confession that wasn't a confession and Jewel's abduction, only pausing when they needed to absorb Lori's death. They'd met her at the wedding but didn't know her well.

His voice got tight as he described Jewel's return but he didn't go into detail about the long wait for her to wake up or mention the shower. Their escape was more interesting to Ivan.

"No sensors on that upper door of yours?" Ivan asked. "Or could you turn them off?"

"They disabled them," Jasper said. "I didn't turn them back on. They left stealth cameras on every floor of the house. I threw out the one in our bedroom but didn't mess with the others. I'm sure they would have told me I had to leave them on today."

"Good thing you got out then," Ivan said. "So is this about blissex or about Kucera?"

"I think it's both," Jasper said. "I need to look at the old case again and see what's there. Jake might not have known as much as we thought."

He heard Jewel's sniffle and Molly hushing her. So she was listening.

"How are you going to do that?" Ivan asked.

"I've got my case notes," Jasper said. "And even though I'm locked out of the police net in Plains, I still have contacts there. Now that Jewel is safe, there's no reason I can't contact them through a back door we set up."

"As long as it can't be traced back to us," Ivan said. "New com units?"

"Jewel's is new. I've got a secure one not registered to me," Jasper said. "David got me a third one just in case. There was just enough on it to convince them I was using it. They took it with them." He hesitated. "You weren't in the address book on either one and the two messages we've had from Sasha weren't either."

"Did they get your music?" Jewel asked from the back seat. "Your flashers?"

"They got flashers, love but nothing I wasn't willing to let them have. Mitch has my completed compositions and I have a few others in my briefcase. What they got is very rough."

"I'm glad," Jewel said. "I couldn't stand it if they got your best."

"They never will," Jasper said. "I haven't written it yet." He knew that much was true. Every piece he wrote came closer to perfection but there wasn't any one composition he could say was perfect, not even his requiem.

"You had to leave your equipment behind," Jewel said. "You can't play."

"That's temporary," he said. "And not as important as you."

Silence was the only answer he got and he felt tears sting his eyes. What he'd said was the truth. His equipment could be replaced. She was the important thing. He couldn't replace her.

The silence stretched on in the back seat and Ivan busied himself checking the truck's controls and the map he'd displayed on the control screen. Speaking briefly to Kale about the truck's performance, he finally lapsed into silence too, and Jasper felt his eyelids getting heavy.

What seemed like hours later, he was told to shift to the back seat and Kale took over the controls. Jewel was soundly sleeping, her head on a cushioned pillow and Molly was reading something on a com unit. Jasper took the pillow she offered and, when he found the drum by his feet, put it in his lap, wrapped his arms around it and went to sleep.

He woke from a deep sleep to the sound of dogs, a half dozen or more, barking like mad outside. The sound was so foreign to him that he sat bolt upright, instantly alert then relaxed as he recognized the truck and knew he was safe. The dogs, for they were not figments of his imagination, stopped barking except for one. He heard the sharp command that silenced it.

The truck was rolling past a fence and into a snow-packed drive behind some low buildings. Jasper peered out at the snow and tried to get some idea of the size of the farm but his mind was just too tired to grasp it. Feeling Jewel's hand creep into his, he clasped it reassuringly. It was strange to think about living entirely above ground—or did they have an underground here? He knew some farms did. The summer temperatures at the height of the climate change had forced almost –eryone to go underground to escape the heat. Even now the temperatures were high enough to kill some days.

"Here we are," Ivan said. "The guest house is down below. We'll take you in through ours so we don't disturb anyone." He was out of the truck and lifting the suitcases out of the back before Jasper could move.

"Not disturb anyone?" Jasper asked, remembering the dogs. "They can sleep through dogs?"

Ivan chuckled. "If they shut up, yes. Everyone knew we were coming back late so it's more of a welcome home and nothing to worry about. Let's get you two in before you freeze."

Chapter 21 - Sunday, 14 Nov 2179

Glancing at the time, Jasper knew they'd taken too damned long to get up and moving today. It was nearly eleven and he'd heard farm people were up by six. What must they think of them? Well, Molly and Ivan would excuse it. No doubt they'd slept in too, after that drive last night. He just hated to make a bad impression but they'd both slept sound until after ten.

It worried him that Jewel had slept so much yesterday but maybe it was the aftereffects of the kidnapping. He would have to ask Molly if she didn't get back on a normal schedule in a few days. At least she was looking better today with the last of the dye gone and those stars off her face. His were gone too, and his hair looked normal. That god awful vest was hung in the furthest corner of the closet until he could return it.

Jewel came out of the bathroom and did a twirl for him. "How's this?"

Jasper eyed her critically. Her hair was still choppy but nothing could be done about that in here. The cream colored dress looked to have two layers to the skirt and did, the top one being the blocking fabric Jewel had to wear. She'd covered that flaw up with the scarf she'd brought from Plains so it looked fairly decent. Her shoes were just light slippers and he hoped no one would suggest she wear those outside. "It looks good."

"Should I wear the hat?" she asked and tugged on a strand of hair to cover the gap where he'd cut it.

"No, better to get it over with," Jasper said. "I'm sure they know a hairdresser if they don't have one here."

She looked almost ready to cry again so he held out his arms and asked "Do you approve?" He was back in black with his locket dangling in plain sight, his tailored pants and black shoes more suitable for the city than the farm but he didn't own any others.

"You always look good," Jewel said. "Even when it was those cheap suits you had to wear for the force."

"Thank you," Jasper said, his lips twitching. "So you think I look good in stars?"

She grinned and shook her head.

"Come here, love." He opened his arms again and caught her up. His lips were tender on hers, teasing but her response was half-hearted. Frowning, he pulled back and looked down at her. "What's wrong?"

"I'm just queasy this morning," she said. "I just can't."

"It happens," Jasper said. "And it's been a rough week. Let's get you some food and you'll feel better."

Opening the door, he ushered her out, catching her hand as they saw a young woman in a rocking chair, her arms around a very young baby. Looking to be in her twenties, she was as fair as Sasha had been. Jasper saw her ready smile and relaxed.

"Good morning," she said. "I'm Rachel. Did you have a good sleep?"

"Yes," Jasper replied. "We overdid it."

"Not to worry," Rachel said. "We all know you got in late. Molly just asked me to show you the way when you appeared."

"She's already up?" Jewel tugged on her hair.

"Habits are hard to break," Rachel said. "Just follow me."

Jasper could see they were in a great room longer than a football field with pools of sunlight hitting here and there from skylights above. Mirror strips on the upper walls magnified the light but some of the recesses were still dim. So they did have an underground connecting the houses. That was comforting.

Ivan's house was just a few steps away. They followed their guide in and up some stairs to a living room Jasper abruptly recognized. He'd seen it before from the other side of the vid screen. This time there were no children, no dogs, and no Sasha. He wondered if Jake's young widow had sent any more messages from her ship headed to Mars.

"Here you are," Rachel said and led them into a nice cheery kitchen. It was well appointed with professional-looking appliances and two tables. Windows let in light and showed it to be impeccably clean. Molly was also there clad in jeans and a T-shirt.

Jasper smiled, liking it at once. "Wonderful kitchen," he said.

Molly Kowalski turned toward him and smiled. "I'm glad you like it," she said. "Have a seat. Coffee and breakfast coming up."

"Can I get tea?" Jewel asked. "I'm not too hungry."

"Then tea it is," Molly said. "French Toast or eggs and hashbrowns?" She turned toward her and abruptly changed her mind. "No, I think Jewel should have some nice Texas toast with that tea."

"That sounds wonderful," Jewel said. "I think it's just reaction to the last few days."

"That could be," Molly said. "But you've also got that transmitter irritating you. I'll check you over later."

"More poking," Jasper said.

"You'll get your turn," Molly said as she set a cup of coffee in front of him. "And I'll use the cold stethoscope if you give me any lip."

Jasper's eyebrow shot up and he knew he looked startled when Jewel laughed but he hadn't seen this side of Molly before. "Yes ma'am."

"That's better," Molly said as she turned back to the stove. "I'm the resident medical person—a physician's assistant. I plan to check you both over since I can't just request your medical records right now."

"There's not much to tell with me," Jasper said. "A little undernourished from the last few days but I'm sure you'll fix that now."

"Have you had chicken pox?"

The question was so unexpected, he had to stop and think. "Chicken pox?"

"We have three children down with it," Molly said. "I need to know if you two have had it."

Jasper looked at his wife, guessing she would likely catch it if she could. She was too vulnerable right now. "Jewel?"

"Oh, yeah, I've had it," she said. "I was three or four."

"Sure?" Jasper asked.

"Yes, Amber gave it to me," her voice was low and tinged with tears. "I miss her."

Jasper caught his breath. Amber West had been dead since his wife was six and this was the first time he'd heard Jewel admit she missed her.

Molly had the good sense not to ask her who Amber was. "And you, Jasper? You're the one we don't want catching it."

Jasper shook his head. "I won't catch it. Germ camp, first grade."

Molly started to make a note then stopped. "Are you sure you got it?"

"Yes, I got the damned stuff. They injected me when I wouldn't catch it the normal way."

"Wouldn't?" Molly looked surprised.

"I was stubborn," Jasper said. "Played with everyone who had it but didn't catch it. They made me stay twice as long then decided to induce."

"Did you have it before?" Molly asked.

Jewel was paying attention, half-smiling now.

"No, I was just stubborn. I didn't like camps, hated bugs, and wanted to get out of there. No one told me I had to have it before I could go home so I just didn't get it."

Jewel looked at him with wide blue eyes and an uncertain smile.

"Ok, I'll accept that but I want to draw some blood anyway and confirm your immunity is still up," Molly said.

"I knew you'd say that," Jasper said in a long suffering tone. "They always do."

His wife gave a half-hearted giggle.

Jasper took that as a good sign. God, he'd give anything to have the old Jewel back.

Molly smiled. "If you're stubbornly healthy, you're suspect," she said. "If you did things the way you were supposed to, you wouldn't be."

"Yes, I've been told that too," Jasper said and his wife hid her face to smother another giggle. He grinned and winked at Molly. "I can get you my medical records without an official query. Give me an hour or so."

He was reluctant to leave any traces of where he and Jewel had gone. If Molly Kowalski requested them, they could conceivably find her and then him. He could ask for his own though and copy them to her using a flasher and it wouldn't be traceable. Anyone could request their own medical records at any time. He'd have to show Jewel how to do it.

He hadn't been lying about germ camp. Children regularly got sent off to be exposed to specific diseases that weren't fatal. Part of his first grade year and all the way into his third grade year, he'd spent weeks in such camps. They were always outside and always had bugs and he had hated them. It wasn't even a reprieve from school because their home class teacher went with them and kept up their lessons. There had been nice airy beds in nice airy dorms with little or no privacy and it had been his first experience of having to be in his classmates' company all day and all night. Yeah, he had hated it.

"I think Ivan is going to give you the tour," Molly said. "Jewel isn't dressed for outside so I'll show her around inside and get the poking done. Later we'll go out."

"I had some jeans," Jewel said. "I just have to wear this skirt and it didn't look right."

Molly set tea in front of her. "Skirt?"

"It's supposed to block the transmitter," Jewel said. "I have to wear jammers too."

"That makes sense," Molly said. "Well, we'll figure something out. I'll ask Karen in to cut your hair. They really butchered it."

"I know," Jewel said. "Thanks." Her smile had faded again.

"I only did some of it," Jasper said.

Jewel's smile resurfaced at his confession.

"The worst part," he added.

"You did?" Molly looked aghast. "Oh, the eggs..." She turned back to her stove.

"In the shower," Jasper added in a low voice only Jewel could hear and she choked, having just sipped her tea. "Should I tell her?"

"Don't you dare, Jazz Stone," she whispered fiercely back, her cheeks turning pink.

"I won't," Jasper said. "I want to do it again."

"Not my hair," Jewel said, her voice louder but her blush had deepened. "And not today."

"Not today?" Molly was back with toast and eggs. She took one look at Jewel's color and added. "Either I missed something or you've got a fever, Jewel. Which is it?"

"You missed something," Jasper said but didn't volunteer details.

Molly laughed and said "eat your eggs."

Jasper obeyed.

* * *

Once Molly had taken Jewel off, Jasper returned to his quarters and began work. Tapping into Butler's system, he checked for signs of entry and found them. Around two p.m. yesterday someone had come in through the upper door. Butler had automatically recorded the intrusion so he downloaded the vid.

One look at the big black man who entered the house and Jasper grinned. Lori's killer. Throwing it on to the vid panel so he could see it in more detail, he found himself looking at the blackest man he'd ever seen. His nose was broad and almost flat and his bald pate completely bare of hair. Pure African, he thought, and this time he wasn't wearing tattoos or a mask. He could be identified.

"Music man?" The man asked just once before shoving the bedroom door in and seeing it was empty. The next instant he had a com unit in hand. "They're gone," he said.

"The woman has to be there. I've got her transmitter signal," a voice answered.

"She's not. He must have got the damned thing out last night while you were jerking off." Slasher tossed the covers back but didn't find anything. "No transmitter here."

Jasper grinned at the man's frustration. Unless he checked between the mattress and springs, he wouldn't find the decoy. The tracers he'd left inside a pillowcase.

"She's gone. Ring up that bastard's com unit. I want him back here."

"He could be downstairs," the voice said.

"He could be on the moon too. Ring up his unit," Slasher snarled.

An instant later the buzzing of Jasper's com unit could be heard and Slasher cussed. It was on the table where Tech had left it.

"Ring up hers," Slasher growled and it started chiming from the bedroom dresser. Ten seconds later Slasher was out the door and Butler came to the end of the vid.

Jasper knew he'd crossed the line and, if Slasher found them, he'd have no problem killing them both. It didn't worry him. Since they had waited so long, he doubted they'd seen the government plane leave the airport. Had their pilot even been on board?

He would check the airport vid next. Right now there was something else he wanted to do. Scrolling through the vid, he found a spot where Slasher was looking full face at one of Butler's cameras and clipped the vid. A little quick manipulation and he had the background a featureless grey. No one would be able to tell it was taken inside his house.

That done, he forwarded the picture to Captain Reynolds under his DEA ID. The message was brief. "Intruder. Does he match Slasher's ID? Do not detain at house."

If this helped them get the man out of circulation, it might force someone else out in the open. He had no illusions about what would happen to the man if the police caught him alone. Since he'd already identified the guy's boss, he wasn't going to worry about a cop-killer.

That done he called up the vid for the airport. That required using his DEA ID but the results were worth it. The Wilson jet was gone. Tapping in an official query of airport records, he discovered it had been there from the fifth thru the thirteenth, leaving at nine am that morning. So Baxter had left without confirming he had stayed. Too bad.

He wondered who had that damned button. if Slasher had it, he had probably pushed it already. The man couldn't know Jewel was nowhere in Plains. Would he immediately report them missing to Baxter? If Baxter had it, he might have to return to Plains.

Since they'd used government transport all the way to Chicago, Baxter's people would have to be very lucky to pick up their trail—or spend a hell of a lot of money bribing people. Either way it would take time so they had breathing space.

Requesting his medical records next, he knew he'd have to wait on Jewel's. To get updated records, they'd have to wait until at least Monday. His might not even show up till morning. He'd check later.

Chapter 22 - Amber

"Ready?" Ivan asked as Jasper met him in the kitchen. "No, you're not. Grab that coat on the hook. It's warmer than the one you have on."

Jasper saw there were a number of very warm looking coats hanging on the back porch and picked one he judged to be his size. It was three times as thick as his city coat. "Are we walking?"

"No, I wouldn't do that to you," Ivan said as he led him outside. "I've got the gadabout and it's warmed up. There's not enough snow to bother it."

Jasper eyed the small farm truck dubiously. It would seat two but no more and its back end was all truck. It was smaller than a city maintenance vehicle with just one wheel in front and two wheels behind. "All electric?"

"Yes," Ivan said. "These are good enough for checking the acres but I wouldn't use one on a real road. Too slow."

It didn't feel too slow when it got moving. Ivan drove with one hand and talked with the other, pointing out things they passed.

"We've got sixteen houses and a few odd apartments like the one we put you in. There's also a veterinary clinic right there," he said pointing to a squat building. "The human clinic is in our office building so it's connected to the underground. We have rabbits, poultry and hydroponics too. Those are accessible from the underground so you don't have to go out to see them."

"How many hydroponic buildings?" Jasper asked. Those he understood since Plains depended on them for fresh winter produce and to revitalize the air in the underground.

"Seven so far," Ivan said. "We'll put in an eighth this summer. Two of the buildings though are reserved for our use. We don't buy produce."

"Home grown is best?" Jasper asked.

"Yes," Ivan said and gunned the engine to take them over a small snowdrift. The little truck did its best, only slowing slightly through the thick snow.

"The poultry barns are over there," Ivan pointed to more long structures. "After this week we'll be down to just the laying hens until spring. The turkeys are on their last days."

"Last days?" Jasper repeated.

"Thanksgiving is coming up," Ivan said. "And your timing on getting here was pretty good because we start the processing tomorrow. I'll be tied up the next three days."

"Processing?" Jasper said, feeling like an idiot.

"We kill them, clean them, pluck them, section them, package them, and shove them out into a truck," Ivan said then added when he saw his face. "No, we don't need you. We've got fifteen experienced hands to do the work. Best thing you can do is get Jewel healthy again."

"How many will you process?" Jasper asked with a sense of relief.

"Thirty-two hundred," Ivan said. "Sectioned birds get a higher price so we section them."

Thirty-two hundred? Three thousand two hundred? Jasper found he couldn't get his mind around the number. He'd seen live turkeys once and couldn't fathom that many birds in one place at one time.

"Do you have other birds?" he finally said.

"Just chickens," Ivan replied. "Laying hens. The meat birds have already gone to market and we won't have new chicks for a week or two."

Jasper nodded, trying to look like he knew what Ivan was talking about. He was almost relieved when they pulled up to one of the biggest structures. The bumpy ride was hard to get used to.

"Dairy barn," Ivan said. "We won't stay long. I just need to check out a new calf."

Jasper followed him in and was struck first by the odor of cattle and secondly by the immense size of the barn. Before he could recover, he heard a spate of joyous barking and saw three huge dogs bounding toward them. He froze, unsure what else to do as the dogs surrounded them.

"Just let them sniff you, Jasper," Ivan said. "These three live in this barn. You won't see them up at the house. Their names are Tom, Dick and Hairy."

The dogs wagged their tails at their names then one planted a wet nose in his dangling hand. Jasper didn't move. How did you make friends with dogs? The only ones he'd ever met were trained police dogs and none were this large. He could swear one would be taller than him if he stood it upright.

"Just give him a pat," Ivan said. "That's Hairy. He's Russian Wolfhound and something else."

Jasper forced himself to pat the dog and found he didn't mind it. The big dog butted him for more attention and Jasper smiled. Not half bad. "Something else?"

"Most of our dogs have something else," Ivan said. "True American dogs—all mutt. The cattle dogs are papered but the rest are fixed so we don't drown in puppies."

"That sounds sensible," Jasper said as one of the other dogs horned in for attention. "I thought these guys were fierce."

"Oh, they can be but they know you now. It's people who shouldn't be here that need to fear them."

"Got it," Jasper said. He found himself patting the third dog.

"That's enough, boys. Tom, Dick, patrol. Hairy, heel." Ivan shooed two of the dogs away and the third obediently followed them.

Jasper looked around, seeing a cow's rump in the nearest stall and a man in the next with his shirtsleeves rolled up.

"How's it going, Bob?" Ivan said as he led the way. "Mama doing okay?"

"Yes, she's fine now," Bob answered. "It was a bit rough getting him out. He's on the big side."

Jasper peered into the stall and had to look again. The calf and cow standing in the straw were far from big. The mother stood waist high on the man and her calf was a quarter her size. This was a milk cow?

"This is Jazz Stone," Ivan said. "Sensor Man. Jazz, meet Dr. Bob Fletcher. He's our veterinarian."

"Pleased to meet you, Mr. Stone," the vet said with a smile. "I've got that latest album of yours. It's a nice one to chill with."

"That's what I designed it to do," Jasper said then waved at the small cow. "What is she?"

"This little lady is a mini-Jersey," the vet said. "They've been bred down from that full size Jersey. They give almost two-thirds the milk but eat about half the feed and they're easier to handle than the full-sized ones. The only problem is sometimes the calves come out a bit big–especially the bull calves. We only get three of those each year but they need help getting born."

"This one's going to be okay?" Jasper asked. The mother was already licking her son. She was a nice warm brown color and when she turned her head to look at them, her eyes were soft brown. Beautiful eyes.

"Yes, they'll do fine. I'm glad he finally got here though. He took longer than most to greet the world."

"How many cows are there?" Jasper asked, struggling for some sort of intelligent question.

"Four hundred minis, another fifty Jerseys, and a dozen black Angus in the back pasture," the vet said. "Angus are beef cattle. We don't milk them."

Jasper nodded. "I've actually seen Angus before," he said. "They have them in Wyoming."

"That they do," the vet said. "I'm going to get this calf cleaned up. And fed. Ivan, see you tonight."

"Right," Ivan said. "Thanks for helping with that calf." He turned back to Jasper. "Have you seen enough of cows?"

"Yes but it was interesting. I didn't know about the compact ones."

"Innovation. They needed the small ones for smaller farms–and they sent a pair up to one of the space stations about five years ago. I think it was Highside. There's talk about sending some to Mars but I don't think it will be soon. They still need almost a ton of hay per year."

"They ship hay to Highside?" Jasper asked as they climbed back into the truck. The dog wandered off after a command from Ivan.

"No, I think they feed them leftovers from other plants and seaweed. I don't know how good the milk tastes on that diet but they're still up there." Ivan grinned then gunned the engine again. "Now let me show you the fields and those Angus. We've got a total of six hundred acres. The buildings sit on about fifty of it and we use another hundred for grazing and fifty for forestry. The rest gets planted in crops to support the livestock."

Jasper listened, aware he was really ignorant of what all they did here. He'd known farms were diversified these days but that hadn't meant much to him. Ivan and Molly Kowalski clearly knew what they were doing.

He was only amazed that they hadn't kept Sasha here to help out. They must need every hand they could get to run such an operation.

He was to get Jewel healthy. They didn't expect him to work at killing turkeys or milking cows. Wondering what else he could do to contribute to this farm, he knew he'd have to wait for the answer—and he had to go over his case files. He knew there were things he'd missed, things that hadn't hung together from the first, and he needed to find them and check them out one by one. That and Jewel were his priorities. No, Baxter was too. He wanted that bastard caught.

"And that's the end of the fifty cent tour," Ivan said as he turned the truck back toward the ring of homes. "Everything else is accessible from the underground and you can explore it when you want."

"Why are some buildings three stories?" Jasper asked as they approached them. "I only saw three like that."

"Those are the specials," Ivan said. "One is the school, another is our community center, and the last is offices. From those, we can see all the buildings and most of the acres. There are cameras mounted on each."

"Lookouts? For trouble?" Jasper asked.

"No, we're mostly concerned with wildfires, lightning strikes and tornadoes. Our dogs take care of any two-footed pests."

"Good dogs," Jasper said, relaxing.

"Only the best," Ivan responded. "Time to get in. If you have any questions about things the next three days, Molly will settle them. She'll also see you meet the other managers. I think I told you I'm the livestock manager?"

"Yes, I got that last night." Jasper knew Ivan wasn't the top man but close. "Who is your general manager?"

"Mr. Fletcher," Ivan said.

"The vet?" Jasper asked, surprised.

"No, Bob is his son," Ivan said. "You'll probably meet him tomorrow."

"Got it and thanks again for taking us in."

"It's not a problem," Ivan said. "Just keep Jewel safe. She's like a daughter to us."

Jasper was still musing over that daughter comment when he finally tracked down his wife. He'd been told she was in the community center but finding that building was more of a challenge than he thought. Here there were no maps and few street names. He had found one street marked Rabbit Run but the sign had looked homemade and was probably a joke. He knew where the building was on the topside but it was hard to keep directions under ground. Finally a boy pointed him toward the far end of the underground.

They must all know where everything was and he guessed he'd better learn. He had marked where Ivan's house was since his was beside it. Walking wasn't a problem for him since the design of Plains had always encouraged walking in local areas and train or bicycle use to get further afield. He was just happy he didn't have to walk outside in that cold weather.

Ah, the door was marked. Finding the community center sign comforting, he peered around the dark interior of the first floor then headed upstairs. The second floor was at ground level and seemed to be mostly gym equipment. Going on up to the third he could hear voices before he got there and something that sounded suspiciously familiar.

Pool tables. He knew it. Not just one but three. Well, he knew what Jewel was doing and he wouldn't get in the way of her fun.

The November afternoon sunlight was pretty strong in this room and Jasper had to blink a few times to clear his vision before he could see his wife clearly. Jewel still wore the skirt and jammers but there were black jeans beneath it and sensible black shoes on her feet. Her hair—what they done to it?

"Jazz." Jewel spotted him and met him halfway to the tables, her cue still in one hand.

He fended it off to give her a hug then held her back to look at her hair. It had been curled and trimmed to an even shorter length than before. The semi-bald patch seemed to be gone and he wondered how they'd done that. It was back to its normal chestnut color too. The style was pretty but it made Jewel look like a pixie—far too cute on her. "I like it," he said and she beamed.

Turning, he looked to see who else was here. He nodded to the elderly man playing pool then eyed the two old women. There was a basket between them and he thought they were playing with green beans.

"Come on and meet them," Jewel said. "That's Uncle Harold and this is Aunt Ruby and Aunt Lill. This is my husband, Jasper Stone. He's also Sensor Man."

"Uncles and Aunts?" Jasper asked.

"We're actually the elders," one of them said. "Over seventy. Everyone calls us aunt or uncle. I'm only related to three families here but Ruby can claim more."

"Ah," Jasper said with a smile. "So you're Aunt Lill?"

"That's me. We were just sitting here snapping beans and watching Harold try to teach Jewel about pool. It's been entertaining."

"Jewel?" He looked at his wife suspiciously.

"Just having fun," she said. "And Uncle Harold is a good teacher."

"She's been having me on," the old man said.

Jasper relaxed. Harold wasn't fooled by her. "Then this should be good. I think I'll watch."

Jewel went back to her game and he settled next to the aunts to watch as the old man pointed out an easy shot. Jewel studied it but flubbed it, sending another ball into a pocket. It was her own and she wasn't calling shots so it was legitimate. The old man studied what she'd done then shook his head. "Way too lucky, girl."

"I didn't see that one," Jewel said and one of the aunts laughed at her ingenuous tone.

"Ok, lucky girl, sink that seven if you can."

Jewel made a show of lining it up before hitting it hard and bouncing it around the table. It stopped just short of the corner pocket.

Uncle Harold didn't say a word but took his own shot and missed.

"Get your seven now," he said.

Jasper studied the table and saw the cue ball was now in the perfect position for the seven. Ok, so maybe Harold was having his wife on too. That was a change.

Jewel smiled and sank the seven then took the nine ball out before missing again.

"So how good is she?" Aunt Lill quietly asked. "My husband is a lot better than he's playing."

"She's too good," Jasper said. "I can keep up with her but barely."

"I thought so," Lill said. "That might make an interesting match."

"Against Harold?"

"Oh, no, he's not that good. Someone who thinks he's good."

Jasper wondered what she meant but just then others started coming up the stairs. One young woman went to the small bar and a couple of men set up their own table.

"End of day, lovely lady," Harold said. "Stand back and watch this." He sunk one ball after another ending with the eight.

"Good game," Jewel said. "And I think I'm done." She put her cue back in the rack even as one of the guys offered to let her play. "Not tonight, thank you. I've got a hubby to tease."

That brought laughs from all and Jasper took it in good part. They didn't escape before more introductions were made but then he managed to get his wife away.

Finding more people on the second floor, he took her all the way out to the dim underground where they found a quiet corner.

"Are you feeling better?" he asked.

"Yes," she said. "Molly thinks I'm just worn down and anxious about—" she motioned to her belly. "But I'm also low on Vitamin D and I have to spend three hours in a sunroom every day. She'll probably tell you the same thing."

"Possibly," Jasper said. He knew about Vitamin D deficiencies. Usually he'd just take pills but he didn't have any here. He wondered if those other two towers had sunrooms. He didn't want to watch Jewel do trick shots every day. He had work to do.

"I've given her my medical records," Jasper said. "She said she'd work on me tomorrow morning. Hopefully, I'll find a place to work too."

"That would be nice," Jewel said and snuggled in closer. "Do you really like my hair?"

"It's dangerous," he said. "I'm going to have to fight them off you."

Jewel laughed and he was tempted to spirit her away to their quarters. Knowing dinner was too close, he settled for a kiss. When that threatened to get too hot, he firmly ended it and looked down at his wife.

"I keep hearing there's forty some kids around here but I've only seen three. Where do you think they stashed them?"

"It's Sunday. All the schoolage kids are out and about. They get to play outside when their chores are done and most of them do," Jewel said. "They'll be in when it gets dark."

Jasper just looked at her.

"Really. I saw some take off with a horse and a sled. It looked like fun." Jewel sounded wistful. "I did find out they have a daycare and a school here," Jewel said. "It's only through third grade. The older kids get bussed to another farm and a bigger school. They go to town school from seventh grade on up."

Jasper decided not to ask what a sled was. "So how many little ones? Have you tried to get a job yet?"

"I have one," she said. "Tomorrow I start helping with reading. There's only eighteen actually in school here and half of those come from another farm. I wish there were more."

"Maybe you can tutor some older ones," Jasper said. "Or learn some new recipes."

"Yes," she said but her tone showed she wanted more. "I'm sorry, I just..."

She buried her face in his shoulder and he sighed.

"Maybe you can feed rabbits," he said. "Or skin turkeys or whatever they do to them. Just something to keep busy."

When she didn't move, he gently asked. "Would you rather to go to your Aunt Jessica's?"

"No," she said. "I don't want people fussing over me."

"Then let's make the best of it here. It won't be that long."

"But you hate being outside," Jewel said and looked up at him. "I know you do."

"I'll get used to it," Jasper replied. "I've already been told I can't help with the turkeys. As long as I can duck cows, rabbits, dogs, and horses I'll be fine."

"What about ducks?" Jewel asked, her lips curling upward. "Are you going to duck ducks too?"

"Duck ducks?" he repeated. "Can ducks be ducked?"

She giggled. "You quack me up."

"Come on, witch. Let's see if we can help cook." Jasper pulled her to her feet, satisfied she'd hold it together for a while. He knew it was a fragile calm but he wanted it to last the rest of this day. Tomorrow they might deal with it.

Chapter 23 - Underground

As the last light faded from the skylights, the folk of the farm started gathering in the underground. Lights, powered by solar panels, were turned on to light the biggest single room they possessed and Jasper could finally see the details.

On one side there were actual stores. He noted a clothing store, an import store, and a small grocery store and pointed them out to Jewel.

"Been there," she said. "The hairdresser and salon is over there." She pointed to the far end. "She does barbering too."

"Good," Jasper said but was certain he didn't need a trim yet. He'd had it done before the wedding. "So did you get groceries?"

"Fully stocked. Not your brand of coffee but we can special order that. The import store will accept it so we don't have to give names."

"Good," Jasper said. "I have some in my suitcase though."

"Of course." Jewel smiled and turned back to her task.

The two of them had volunteered to help set the long tables for the Sunday dinner. Apparently the farm had a potluck every Sunday to promote the community feeling. Jasper had been told it was very informal and gave people a chance to mix beyond their specialties and immediate families. He would have preferred a quiet dinner himself but knew he had to face this eventually. He tried not to think of meeting eighty odd people at once, all of them neighbors.

It wouldn't be that bad, he told himself. There had been more than three hundred at the Reach Out event and almost that many at his wedding. He was used to dealing with large numbers, it was just these people were all neighbors and farmers as well. They would be a heck of a lot more friendly than the city folk he knew—he hoped.

"Molly said her brother-in-law is coming," Jewel said. "Sasha's Uncle Uri. She said he was with Minneapolis PD."

"Good," Jasper said as he finished laying out silverware on the last table. "Him I could understand."

Jewel smiled. "Maybe that's why he's coming."

"Maybe," Jasper said. He would appreciate having someone to talk with but this Uncle Uri was probably only going to be here the night.

"That looks good," a woman said as she set out plates of butter and carafes of coffee on their table. "You're the Stones?"

"Yes," Jasper said. "And you?"

"Betty Talbot, Hydroponics Manager," she said. "My husband, Jim, manages field crops."

"Pleased to meet you," Jasper said. "I haven't made it to hydroponics yet."

"Come by any time," she said. "I'll show you where the fresh winter food comes from."

"Thanks," Jasper said. "I've toured hydroponics in Plains and Chicago."

"It's not much different here," she said. "Just the scale. It's the livestock that pays most of our bills. We use hydroponics because we need them."

"Any dirt gardens?" Jewel asked.

"Yes," she answered. "Some herbs and garden crops still do better in full sun and dirt. We just don't get the same yields from dirt farming and there are more pests. Flavor-wise they do better."

"How do you keep them from burning up?" Jasper asked. "I didn't see that many trees."

"Oh, we have trees, just not that many close to the buildings because of the fire danger," she said. "Most are on the other side of the county road. The dirt gardens though have shade fabric. We string that up in July and August to diffuse the sunlight and keep the temperature down."

Jasper nodded and she moved on to get more of her self-imposed chore done. It was nice that managers took on such chores. He hadn't expected it.

By the time people started sitting down, he'd met two other managers and one high school student. The meetings were naturally brief but he started to relax and note the organization of this weekly event. Food was heaped on a sideboard buffet style and everyone was free to pick and choose what they wanted. The only difficulty he had was choice because there was an immense amount of it and it all looked good. The freshly snapped green beans were there and chicken and beef and at least four different potato recipes and he lost track of how many desserts and salads.

"Oh, deviled eggs," Jewel said and snatched two whole eggs from the plate. "You've got to try them."

"Deviled?" Jasper asked.

"Deviled," she said. "A real treat. Grandmother used to make them."

Obediently, he took one. The choices were so mind-boggling that he ended up taking just a little of about a quarter of the dishes and a slice of beef and piece of chicken. He couldn't believe they did this every week. It was a feast.

When he ended up sitting next to Uncle Harold and across from Uri and Ivan Kowalski, he was pleased. Uri Kowalski, like his older brother, looked fit. He had the indefinable air of an experienced police officer and Jasper found himself warming to him at once.

"So how many years did you have on the force?" Uri asked when the formalities were done. "I've got twenty-three myself."

"Sixteen," Jasper said. "The last ten split between vice and homicide."

"That sounds good. I was in homicide most of my career," Uri said. "Now I teach at the academy and write books. Unless there's a stumper, they don't ask me back."

Jasper paused, his fork stopping halfway to his mouth. "Pretty good," he said. "Homicide?"

"Yes. Some of the rookies coming out of the academy didn't know enough on how to treat crime scenes. My job is to teach them right so we don't lose evidence in the shuffle."

"That I can understand," Jasper said. "I've seen it happen too. They ignore the obvious because it is obvious."

"How many years were you a lieutenant?" Uri idly asked after a while.

"Seven," Jasper answered without looking up. "It was as far up as I could go without being stuck in administration. I preferred working cases myself."

"Understandable," Uri said. "Not everyone likes being stuck behind a desk. So was it vice or homicide you preferred?"

"Vice," Jasper answered quickly. "Our biggest drug problem in Plains was blissex and I lost my brother to that. I really wanted to shut that down but all we could get were the local bottom feeders."

"It's the same in Minneapolis-St. Paul," Uri said. "Since we can't get recreational use of bliss stopped, it's almost impossible to stop blissex."

"Is there a problem with it here?" Jasper asked Ivan. "Bliss, not blissex?"

Ivan paused in his eating long enough to gesture toward Uncle Harold who answered for him. "We took a vote about fifteen years ago not to allow recreational bliss use here. It's still available through the pharmacy but Molly has to approve it and she doesn't very often. The youngsters are taught it's a trap—which it is."

"Yes, it is," Jasper said. "My daughter avoids it too. I haven't played with it since my college days—and even then I preferred music." Jewel touched his hand and he smiled at her. "Although my latest distraction is right here."

Uncle Harold chuckled. "I can remember those days," he said with a fond look at Aunt Lill. "I saw a few dawns I recall." His hand got swatted before his elderly wife stoutly ignored him.

Jasper found himself grinning and hoping that he and Jewel could have such a long marriage. "How many years do you two have?"

"Fifty-eight," Harold said. "We got married when we both didn't know any better. Once we did, we found out how lucky we were so we stuck with it."

"Good for you," Jasper said, remembering how young and in love he and Carol had been. He'd had that but knew what he had now was just as good—better in some ways. "I've been blessed twice," he said. "Jewel is my forever love."

His wife looked up at him in surprise, her color heightening at his choice of phrase. Borrowed from a popular movie, it described how he felt. He had loved Carol dearly but he wouldn't trade Jewel for a lifetime with her. Jewel was his and he meant for it to last forever.

"Some people are twice lucky," Uri said, his eyes taking them in. "It gives me hope. Now I'm going to check out those desserts." So saying, he left them.

"That sounds like a great idea," Ivan said and followed his brother.

"Touchy subject?" Jasper asked after they'd departed.

"A little," Harold said. "Uri's been married twice but it didn't stick. It's hard to find a woman who can handle being a cop's wife."

"True," Jasper said. "Even in Plains, there were a lot of broken marriages. It must be worse in above ground cities."

By the time Uri and Ivan returned, the topic had changed to something more neutral. There was no mention of pool but Jewel fetched the drum after dessert and he did an impromptu number on it. That pleased the kids and several clamored for a try on it. Knowing the drum couldn't be hurt by young hands, he left it in Jewel's charge to follow Ivan and his brother.

"Let's get you set up with office space," Ivan said when they were far enough away from the crowd. "I've got it cleared for you to use the conference room until Thursday."

"Sounds good," Jasper said. "Is it sunny?"

"Yes," Ivan said. "Why?"

"Jewel has been sentenced to a sun room and I figure I'll get the same after Molly gets my blood," Jasper said. "I'm just thinking ahead."

Ivan grinned. Uri didn't and Jasper was beginning to wonder exactly what was eating him. It certainly couldn't be his relationship with Jewel. He was a cop.

"Let me grab my files," Jasper said as they passed by his temporary quarters. He had his com unit with him but not the flashers. Alone inside the quarters he considered making a quick check into Uri Kowalski's clearances but rejected it. There was time enough for that later.

"Got them," Jasper said as he rejoined them and this time he caught the unhappy look on Ivan's face. "Ok, what is this about?"

"Do you know there's an APB out on you and your wife?" Uri asked.

"An APB? From who?" Jasper looked as shocked as he felt then he knew. "FBI?"

Ivan was clearly unhappy, his jaw tightening as he looked at his brother.

"Yes," Uri said. "Their agent died and they want answers."

"Died?" Jasper repeated and realized he hadn't even thought of the agent–just Jewel and Lori. "I didn't know."

"I don't have the details," Uri said. "The report said one police officer dead at the scene and the agent died in the hospital. Anyway, I need a real good reason not to take you in. The farm can't afford legal trouble."

Jasper didn't respond at once. Did he have a problem going in? If they found out where Jewel was, yes. She had that damned transmitter in her and couldn't be questioned with either an interrogation room or truth serums. He had to keep her safe until the transmitter was out at the very least.

"I don't have a problem with going in," he finally said, "but not Jewel. There are medical reasons right now she can't be interrogated–and I have to keep her away from electronics."

"Why?" Uri asked.

"Let's take this more private." Ivan broke in. "I don't want everyone knowing about it."

"Some of the answer is in these files," Jasper said, his voice grim. "There's a reason this has gotten big. Ivan knows some of it already." Would he have to blow his cover? Could he trust Uri to keep it quiet if he did?

Following the two brothers across the underground to the wide entrance of another building, he saw it had a freight elevator. Ivan motioned him toward it and took them up to the third floor.

"The conference room is over here," Ivan said and led the way.

Jasper glanced through the windows but could only see night sky. The rest of the room looked as good as he ever got on the force. There was a large vid screen on one wall with a dock for flashers and a light that showed him it was capable of outgoing and incoming calls. The table was large, meant to seat a dozen, and a large coffee maker set on a sideboard. It had everything he needed—even whiteboards.

"Looks great," Jasper said. "I've got it until Thursday when?"

"Morning," Ivan said. "If you need to lock it, the key is on the hook over there by the door."

Jasper was amazed they used non-electronic locks.

"I'm not going to get into this," Ivan said. "Uri, I know Jasper well enough to be sure he's not involved in murder, drugs, or anything more than protecting his wife. That said, I'll leave you two alone. Just let me know later what I need to know."

"Right," Uri said. "I'll do that."

As Ivan left Jasper laid out three flashers by the docking port then turned his com unit on and set it to his secure mode. "I have to record this," he said. "I'm not sure whether or not you should."

That got Uri's attention. He was a veteran cop and Jasper had just told him he wasn't in charge. Jasper knew he was going to have to back that up.

"Can this vid screen be isolated from the rest of the farm's system?" Jasper asked.

"It is," Uri said. "You can call from this one to any other but they aren't tied in to where others can snoop. A net is too expensive a system for a small farm and we don't need it. Are you going to tell me you're a fed?"

For answer Jasper flipped over his locket and scanned the back with his com unit. Pointing the com unit at the vid panel, he threw his credentials up on the screen.

"Jesus!" Uri stared at the screen then back at him. "I was joking."

"I'm not," Jasper said. "You're the fifth person to know. My wife doesn't."

Uri studied the screen, taking a long time to check it out then waved it away. "Okay, that APB is a pain in the ass but I'll listen. I suggest you kill it if you can."

Jasper wiped the vid screen and dumped the credentials from his com unit. "How do you suggest I do it without tipping my hand?"

"Call your superiors," Uri said. "You can't do it. Let them tell the FBI to back off. They should be able to do it without breaking your cover."

"I'll do that. I didn't know about the APB."

"I gathered that. I would like to know what the hell is going on. If the FBI doesn't back off, it could be a problem."

Jasper rubbed a hand through his hair and thought. "Okay, even I don't know what all is going on but I can tell you what I do know. Did Ivan brief you on the West murders?"

"To a point," Uri said. "This ties in to those?"

"Yes. The conclusions we reached may be entirely wrong," Jasper said. "I don't know. I need to re-examine it all again. We thought–I thought–Ed Kucera was the one behind it and Jake even said so in his confession. Since Kucera left a confession too, we thought it was done."

"Jake left a confession?" Uri's grey eyes darkened. "That I wasn't told."

"He did," Jasper said. "And it saved Jewel's life. Since I got shot not ten minutes after viewing it, letting others know might have slipped my mind. Jewel and David have seen it but I didn't think it was necessary for Sasha to see it."

"Probably not," Uri agreed. "Jake is something she has to put behind her. So who all has copies of this confession?"

"Cheyenne PD, Plains PD, and probably Denver PD. The FBI should have it. I know the prosecutor does." Jasper frowned. "Unless it's disappeared out of the system, it's there."

"Disappeared?" Uri asked.

Jasper wondered briefly if it had but Jake was not a mystery like the professor. "We've had other evidence disappear but nothing that's related to Jake. In any case, I have a copy. Do you want to see it?"

"Yes."

Jasper set the right flasher in the drive then used the controls to bring up the right file. It was passworded to keep Jewel from viewing it without his knowledge but that was the only security on it. Once again Jasper found himself looking at a agitated Jake West and he braced himself for what was to come.

"If you're seeing this, I'm dead. Hell, I know I'm dead," Jake wrung his hands in his lap and there were clear signs of grief and fear on his face. "If they catch me before I enter quarantine, I'm dead. He'll kill me for sure."

Jasper saw Uri frown and it deepened as Jake went on. "My only hope is getting into quarantine but I'm pretty sure I won't make it. I know just enough to hurt them. Well, if they're going to kill me, there's no reason to keep quiet about any of it."

"Lieutenant Stone, I admit to killing my grandmother, Elizabeth West. Well, almost. I gave her some poison but it didn't work. She tasted it. I was desperate so I hit her but she was still alive. When Smith got there, I was told to get out. I left by the upper door, took father's car and went back to Denver."

"I didn't do anything to Uncle Mike," he said. "Nothing! I didn't even know that was planned. I guess I was naive. I thought it was just going to be grandmother but... " He took a deep breath. "They wanted me in Denver. They needed me to get Smith into Lunarex Tower and Dad's apartment. That's why I left the funeral but...I... couldn't do it." He rested his head in his hands and didn't look up.

"I didn't plan this. Hell, when I took the sponsorship, I had no idea they'd ask me to do this. Ed said I'd have to do something to prove my loyalty but... damn him! He threatened to pull my sponsorship. I was less than a month away from leaving this fuckin' planet and he talked about killing my only chance. I couldn't let it happen. I couldn't."

"It's Kucera–Edward Kucera," Jake said and Jasper's jaw tightened all over again. "He got me the sponsorship with Centrax. He threatened to pull it if I didn't kill Grandmother. He hired Smith to help. There's a second man too by the name of Jones. Hell, he even gave me the evell for Uncle Mike."

"I dumped all my texts from him on to this flasher. There's no vid. Lieutenant Stone, save Jewel and Dad. I know he wants the damned house but I think there's more to it than that. Tomorrow I'm going to an attorney and getting him locked out of my trust. That's all I can do to help."

"I'm done. I should have gone to Dad when this started but I didn't. I'm as big a fool as Dad thought I was. Worse. I killed Grandmother."

The confession abruptly ended and Jasper remembered his first reaction to it. All he could think about was Jewel and two assassins. He'd barely been in time to save her–and it had cost the life of another good officer. Bleakly he realized three had given their lives for his wife–and he nearly had. Could he keep her safe?

"So he admits to almost killing his grandmother," Uri finally said. "That's all?"

Jasper looked sharply at him then shook himself. "Yes, that's all."

"It sounds to me like he was blackmailed the entire way," Uri said. "I knew he wasn't the strongest man but this–" He waved a hand at the image of Jake still on the screen. "This makes him look pretty weak. The only thing he did right was owning up to it."

"In my initial interview with Jewel she told me Jake never finished anything," Jasper said. "One of the reasons she laughed off him being involved. My impression of him in his interview was different. He was calm and ready enough with his alibi. He even explained why he had to get three degrees to qualify for Mars."

"And the interrogation chair didn't pick up on his lies?" Uri asked.

"He didn't tell any," Jasper said. "We started the interview with him handing over his cash card with transactions that placed him in Denver. He even told me about a movie he'd seen. It was very clean but.... hell, we'd lost the technician for that first part." He thumped the table. "And I never went back and asked him point blank whether he was in Plains after the technician got back. I got played."

"That sounds like it," Uri said. "I've had that happen. How did you lose the technician?"

"A mix-up on how many interviews I had and then he was called to the lab," Jasper said. "He was reassigned after that so that's all I know."

"It's surprising Jake could do that to you," Uri said. "I've seen career criminals do it but not an innocent."

"Me too," Jasper said. "But Jewel said Jake had lots of practice lying to psychiatrists. That came out later. I think Jake was dead by then or shortly after."

"So that's one murder solved," Uri said. "You got Smith?"

"Yes, he's sitting in the Denver detention center," Jasper said. "Jones is dead. Their real names were Samuel and John Starling."

"And he hasn't talked?"

"No."

"That makes me curious as to why the FBI is not demanding that he be questioned," Uri said. "They know for damned sure he's involved."

"Good question," Jasper said. He knew Starling could clear his wife. "I think I'll ask."

"Oh, before we get off on another tangent, I just want to say having viewed your credentials, I find I cannot detain you or your wife without clearer instructions from my superiors. I'll get those Thursday or Friday."

Jasper knew he was being given three days grace.

"You need to get those APBs revoked," Uri said. "And I would be interested in working with you the next few days. If you want a second set of eyes."

"Yes, I think I need that. We've barely scratched the surface."

"It's too late to get much done tonight. It's nearly nine."

"Right. Let me put in a call and then I'll rejoin the party." Jasper took the flasher out of the drive and tinkered with his com unit until Uri left the room then put in his call.

"Stone here. I need to talk to Carlson."

Chapter 24 - Monday, 15 Nov 2179

Jasper lay on his side, his brown eyes taking in the sleeping face of his wife. She looked peaceful now but twice she had cried out in her sleep and he'd had to wake her from nightmares. Unwilling to disturb her sleep now, he let her sleep on.

He was beginning to like those curls, especially the one that persisted in lying on her forehead. It made her look so young. The temptation to kiss those soft lips was strong but he really didn't want to wake her. Not this early.

The clock on the vid panel had come on at six am. It hadn't made any noise but the vid panel had gradually brightened to a daytime intensity, lighting the room as effectively as a window above ground. He hadn't used that effect before but he liked it after months of sleeping in a windowed bedroom. What he needed to go with it was some birdsong giving away to music that gradually got louder. He would like to tease Jewel awake gently, so gently.

Morning Grace would work but he was sure he could do better than that with that drum. It had a whole scale in it and was perfectly tuned. If he lowered the volume and stepped it up gradually, it would slowly intrude into the sleeping mind. He'd start with a repetitious melody first on low drum then a harmony on soft flute. The number could become full blown after five minutes, waking the mind up to a new day. His fingers tapped out a rhythm and he ached to try it but didn't want to wake Jewel yet.

Damn, he didn't have his equipment. Without it, he'd have to stop and write down notes instead of letting the computer catch them and put them on paper. Tedious. The composition itself should be simple—two or three overlapping tracks should do it. Without proper equipment though he would need to write the parts and hire players. He hated doing that.

He couldn't even get his equipment. He had no place to set it up and it was too likely it would be traced to his new location. All it took was one mover taking a bribe. There was no help for it, not right now. He had to solve this case first.

Shifting on to his back, he thought about his call last night to Carlson. Like him, Ray hadn't known there was an APB out for them but he'd confirmed it and promised to do something about it. He would also look up Uri Kowalski and do a background check on him. There wasn't much Jasper could do about breaking cover so he hoped Uri was as good as he thought. He'd certainly recovered quickly from finding out he was a fed.

Maybe it would be a good idea to call David and ask him to set his lawyer on getting Starling questioned. It was very strange the FBI had been so willing to go after Jewel when they had Starling in custody. Could it be they thought Jewel would be more cooperative? Maybe she wouldn't get a top notch lawyer like Starling?

His jaw tightened. Yes, Jewel would have wanted to get it over with. He'd sent her down there with his doubts. He'd let her believe he doubted her. He did for just those few minutes but it was unforgivable. He should have stepped back and looked at it again. His personal feelings for her aside, he knew Jewel had nothing to gain from being the only West and she loved her family.

Jake had been weak enough to almost kill his grandmother but he hadn't touched Mike and hadn't wanted to touch his father. No, he couldn't believe either Jake or Jewel were behind the murders. As soon as Jewel could be questioned, her possible involvement would become a dead issue but he had to protect her until it was safe—and they wouldn't get her again without a hell of a legal fight. They would have to charge her before he gave an inch.

He needed to move. Molly Kowalski would be —ady to poke him then he wanted breakfast. A good strong cup of coffee and some eggs would take the edge off and get him ready for the day. Slipping free of the covers, he half-rolled out of bed to keep from waking Jewel.

Closing the bathroom door behind him, he went about his morning preparations as quietly as he could. Jewel seemed to have unpacked everything for his depilatory cream, his own wedding ring and toothpaste were waiting. He took off the borrowed ring and left it in the medicine cabinet. It was really too garish for his tastes, having too many diamonds and gold in it. His band was black tungsten with white gold. Like him, it wasn't flashy. Jewel's wedding ring didn't match it but she had picked out his ring and insisted it was him. It was her engagement ring that had flash. The paired diamond and ruby stones nestled against each other like two halves of a single heart or—as she put it—two lovers.

He couldn't be thinking of —wel just now.—e was hungry and needed coffee and Molly had been clear he had to have blood drawn before he could have either. It was time to get moving.

He eyed Jewel as he dressed but she hadn't stirred. Watching the rise and fall of her perfect breasts almost undid his resolve but he left her untouched. Later. She'd wake up eventually with that vid panel giving off so much light.

"Here he is," Molly said with a bright smile as he entered her kitchen. "No Jewel?"

"Still sleeping," he said. "She had nightmares last night. Good morning." He eyed the coffee pot then turned to the table where Uri, Ivan, and two of Ivan's boys were enjoying a large breakfast. It looked pretty damned good.

"Come on," Ivan said with an inviting wave. "How bad were they?"

"Bad enough I had to wake her," Jasper said. "She said she was trapped."

The boys paused in their eating but didn't say anything. Mikal was older than Sasha and looked like a younger version of his dad. The youngest, Anton, took after his mother.

"Have a seat, Jasper," Molly said. "I'll just be a minute."

He sat and reached for the coffee pot, filling his cup before he remembered he had to wait. He hated blood draws.

"Shouldn't we do this somewhere else?" he asked as Molly sat down at the table, her small box of medical stuff in hand.

"Are you squeamish?" she asked.

"No but they might be." He nodded to her family.

"What's a little blood?" Mikal grinned and continued eating.

"It takes more than a blood draw to slow them down," Molly said as she poked him. "If you get queasy, don't listen to them talk about the turkeys."

Jasper flexed his fingers once then waited for her to finish.

It was over pretty quick and she pushed his coffee cup toward him. "I'll just go stick this in the machine. Eat your breakfast. After this crowd leaves, we'll have our talk."

Jasper obeyed, thinking how different it was here. He was sure everything was sanitary but he'd never had blood drawn over breakfast before. Everyone just seemed to take it in stride.

"Convenient, huh?" Uri said with a small smile. "No lines, no waiting room, and no waiting for something to eat." He passed him the bacon and eggs. "You better have some juice too."

"Right," Jasper said. "How fast is your analyzer?"

"Fast enough," Ivan said. "Unless there's something unusual, it will spit out the results in ten minutes. The one in the vet barn is even faster."

Glancing at the clock, Ivan rose to his feet. "Mikal, done?"

"Just finished," his son said with his own glance at the clock. "See you tonight, Mr. Stone."

"See you then," Jasper said. They were already shrugging into coats and headed out the door. He hesitated over his own meal but neither Uri nor Anton showed signs of stopping.

"So what's on your schedule today, Anton?" Uri asked his nephew.

"Classes this morning then I'm driving over to the Svensons' to look at their new hydroponics system," the youngest Kowalski said. "Lars promised me a copy of the schematics."

"Nice of him," Uri said. "Don't mention our company."

"Yeah, Dad already said," Anton answered with a grin at Jasper. "You're not here until you're ready to be here. It's the little ones that might blab it but they don't leave our farm."

Jasper nodded and finished the bite he'd just taken before he spoke. "I doubt they have any idea who or what I am. I'm probably just Jewel's husband to them."

"True," Uri said. "All to the good. And your wife is a lot better looking that you are."

"Thanks," Jasper said, not bothering to hide his smile. "Just remember she's a crack shot."

Uri laughed. "Can't forget that."

"Got to go," Anton said and rose from the table. "Have a good day." With that, he was gone.

"And here's Molly back," Uri said and rose to his feet. "I've got a meeting. I'll see you at the conference room?"

"Yes," Jasper responded. "Thanks."

Just like that he was alone with just Molly Kowalski for company. He wasn't sure what to say because she was both the wife of his friend and a medical practitioner. Which hat was she wearing now?

She poured herself a cup of coffee and sat down across from him. "That almost does it for now," she said. "I'll check over your medical file more carefully today and look at the blood report. Did they check you over thoroughly in Denver?"

"Yes," Jasper said. "I wasn't drugged or anything either. Just Jewel."

"Yes, she got the worst of it," Molly said with a nod. "I'll keep an eye on her. Unless I find a reason to prod you, you can relax."

"I do want you in a sunroom for three hours a day though," Molly said. "If you're low on Vitamin D, that's the prescription. If you're not, it still won't hurt. The conference room qualifies."

"Thanks. I expect to be there most of the time," Jasper said. "How is Jewel?"

"Low on Vitamin D and slightly anemic," Molly said. "Her state of mind is affecting her but you know about that. The transmitter is an irritant and I wish they'd been able to take it out but I understand why they didn't."

"Is there anything we can do for the nightmares?" Jasper asked.

"No drugs," Molly answered. "Anything I could prescribe for that would have bliss or something like it. At this point all I can suggest is some physical activity in the afternoon and a warm glass of milk before bed. Being there for her is the best cure though. Letting her talk about it helps too."

"Got it," Jasper said. "With Uri here, I might be able to do an official debriefing. That's something that requires an actual officer and I'm not."

"It would be good to get it done," Molly said. "That way you'll know what she's dreaming about–and how are you holding up? Any dreams of your own?"

"Yes," Jasper said. "I'll get through it though. Once I have the bastard caught, I won't have more problems." The savageness in his tone made Molly study him more closely.

"I wish it hadn't been your partner," she softly said. "She was a nice woman."

Jasper nodded, feeling his eyes burn but refusing to let it show. "She was a good friend. I got an ID on her killer and it's been sent back to Plains. If he's still there, they'll have him soon."

"Good." Molly rose to her feet. "I've got this to clean up. I'll talk to you at lunch about the results. I am mostly concerned about your immunities so stay away from the schoolrooms. If you're ok in that area, no more poking."

"And no cold stethoscopes?" Jasper asked.

"No, not today," Molly said. "But don't go telling Jewel I didn't prod you. She got the works."

"I won't breathe a word," Jasper said. "I like the haircut, by the way. It looks nice."

"Karen will be happy to hear you approve," Molly said with a smile. "Now out of my kitchen. I've got chores to do."

"Yes ma'am."

Stopping at the apartment to get his flashers, he found the bed empty and heard the shower running. The vid screen had been turned off—sensible since she couldn't wear the jammers in the shower—and the overhead lights were on. Tempted to stay and watch her dress, he restrained himself. That could delay him more than an hour.

Poking his head into the bathroom, he just called her name.

"What?" Jewel called back.

"I'm going over to the conference room. Are you eating breakfast here?"

"Yes," she said. "I don't want much."

"Just take care of yourself and don't forget your jammers," he said.

"Of course not." She turned off the shower and stuck her head out of the stall. "But I want my kiss."

"You want to soak me," Jasper said but he came on in and gave her a warm kiss anyway. She smelled good straight from the shower with her curly top just shampooed. With an effort, he ended it. "You're going to make me late," he said.

"Would love to," she said with a wicked smile. "But I have school and I don't plan on being late. You'll just have to wait."

"Minx," Jasper said but he was relieved. "I'll see you tonight."

Convinced she was ok, he picked up his briefcase and headed across the dim underground to the offices. He saw a couple of women with toddlers heading for the school day care center and a number of older kids seemed to be heading for the offices like him.

"What's this?" Jasper asked when a tow-headed boy about ten got close enough he could ask.

"School bus," he said. "Both of them stop outside the office. It's on the main road."

"Makes sense," Jasper said. "And you're?"

"Toby Fletcher," he said. "My dad is Dr. Bob."

"I met him yesterday," Jasper said, remembering the vet. "Have a good day at school."

"Yes sir," the boy said as he and the other students got off the elevator at the first floor.

It was only after they'd gone that Jasper recalled Molly's warning to stay away from the school kids. Well, he knew his immunities were up and none of those kids looked sick. He hadn't even heard a sniffle. They all looked nicely tanned and incredibly healthy. In Plains at this time of year school kids tended to be pale and grumpy in spite of everything the schools did to counteract the lack of sun. He hadn't seen a single sun lamp here.

When he stepped into the conference room, he knew he wouldn't need sun lamps. The wide windows on this floor of the building let in an incredible amount of sun. Walking over to what he judged was the front side of the building, he watched the school buses—two of them—arrive and carry kids off then he began making coffee and considered how to go about his investigation.

By the time Uri joined him, he had one of the white boards evelled Michael West. He would start with him since they already knew who killed Jake's grandmother.

"Michael?" Uri looked at the board. "David's brother?"

"Yes, the second victim," Jasper said. "I only met him once and he was in no shape to be questioned. Before I could get him into an interrogation room, he was dead."

"As near as I could piece it together, Jake drove his dad's car up to Plains and parked it not far from the house. He walked over to the house, knocked on the door, and Mike let him in," Jasper said. "Jake jammed the door using a piece of magnetic metal just the right thickness and size to do the job. He shouldn't have known how to do that which is the first inconsistency."

"But that's Jake, not Michael," Uri pointed out.

"I need another board for Jake," Jasper said and headed a new board with his name. "Jake said he supplied the evell to Mike," Jasper said. "And he got it from Kucera."

"Where does the evell come in?" Uri asked.

"That's why I couldn't question Mike," Jasper said. "He was on evell and in shock too. When Jewel found her grandmother, Mike was sound asleep."

"Ok, I'm lost," Uri said. "Chronologically?"

Jasper nodded and backtracked. "Mike let Jake in and Jake jammed the door. He gave evell to Mike—a blister pack. After that Jake either left until he knew his uncle had taken it or he convinced his uncle to go ahead and take it while he visited with his grandmother. I think he left and came back but that's just assuming Mike would have wanted to visit with him too."

"Sounds reasonable," Uri said. "I would have stayed up."

"So would I," Jasper said. "Especially knowing he'd driven up from Denver and would be leaving for Mars quarantine in a week's time."

"Why was Mike taking evell?" Uri asked. "Why not bliss or a bliss derivative?"

Jasper paused. "Good question. He was taking it for nerve pain following an accident. His doctor had him on narcoset, which didn't seem to be helping. He was even taking it—and the evell—with scotch. It would have made more sense for him to go back and request stronger pain killers through his doctor."

"A lot more sense than accepting illegal evell," Uri said. "You talked with his doctor?"

"Yes," Jasper said. "The doctor said he was unlikely to be returned to work status. They were just trying to control his pain."

"If the doctor was giving him narcoset, he wasn't trying too hard," Uri said. "I've had that and it barely touches really intense pain. They should have given him one of the bliss family. Where was he injured?"

"His back and arm," Jasper said. "An air cleaning unit fell—which is another thing." He wrote that on the board and added the date of the accident then noted inspection system upgrade beside it. "I found out from one of his co-workers that Mike was working on upgraded inspection sensors—a new design. We also weren't sure even at the time of the murders whether he was the target. Elizabeth might have been killed to make Mike more vulnerable."

"Now that's logical," Uri said. "If he was working on inspection systems."

"He was," Jasper said. "The upgrade got shelved after his accident."

Uri stood back and studied the boards then shook his head. "This just got a lot more complicated. We'd better go back to chronological again."

Jasper knew exactly what he meant. He'd been there for the initial investigation and even he was still confused.

"Ok, back at the house Mike took the   evell and laid down. Sometime after that Jake came back in the door—if he left at all—and went downstairs to talk to his grandmother. She made him tea. He dosed hers with cyanide but she smelled it or tasted it and didn't swallow. That we know for fact—autopsy result. After that he clubbed her from behind with a Japanese god figure."

"A god figure?" Uri asked.

"Yes, there was a collection of Japanese gods on the mantle. The one missing was Fukuro-something, the god of longevity. A little more than a foot tall with about half of that head."

"That's fact?"

"Yes, we have one foot that shows the material and Jewel pointed out that figure was missing. The foot was found embedded in Elizabeth's skull." Jasper paused. "Jake admitted to almost killing his grandmother—and the autopsy showed she was still alive when she was thrown from the third floor staircase."

"But Jake didn't do that," Uri said. "Smith did?"

"That's what he said. Jake also said he left by the upper door. I think Smith came in and left through the lower one. It only logged users from the outside, not inside. Once Jake let him in, Smith could come and go as needed."

"So Smith came in and finished Elizabeth. Any proof of that?"

"Two things," Jasper said. "First we have Jake putting him there in his confession but we also have an overheard conversation by a witness."

"Do tell," Uri said.

"Two men in the confessionals at the Catholic Church. One was firmly identified as Smith and told the other the kid was too green and he had to kill the old woman. He was really upset about it. His employer hasn't been identified. We thought it was Kucera but the witness said no. Approximately an hour later I saw Smith at Elizabeth's funeral—and there's another thing," Jasper quickly said. "When Smith murdered Jake, he said 'you made me kill her.'"

Uri stared at him. "You have that too?"

Jasper nodded, not meeting his eyes. "It's not pretty. I haven't let Jewel or David see it."

"Damn, this a mess." Uri exploded. "How the hell did they expect you to come to any conclusion in—how long?"

"Elizabeth's murder happened on Monday, Mike's on Tuesday, Jake's on Friday, and then I got shot the following Tuesday." Jasper hesitated. "The attempt on David was the day before I got shot. Jewel was actually the target when I stopped the bullet."

"Damn."

"Yeah, damn," Jasper agreed. Even he was appalled at how fast things had moved. When did he have time to court Jewel? He didn't. It had just happened. "I didn't even know Jewel when the case began but came out of it with her."

"Didn't know her at all?" Uri was sharp. "That wasn't the impression I got from Ivan and Molly."

"I saw her once before that when I was a rookie cop," Jasper said. "She was fourteen, had big blue eyes, and curlers in her hair. The next time I saw her, she was trying to keep her Uncle Mike from falling apart."

"Back at the house?" Uri asked, his frown deepening. "Ok, let's get back there again. Smith finished Elizabeth. You said she fell from the third floor balcony?"

"She was thrown from there. A fall would have put her in a different spot. We found some bloody maintenance overalls stuck in a cupboard, which suggests Smith came in looking like maintenance then ditched them. Since he left them in the house, we're fairly sure the upper door was properly locked by then and he couldn't open it. The club—that Japanese god—wasn't found in the house."

Jasper thought back. "The front door was left ajar when Smith left. We're not sure why he did that except to muddy the trail. That's all of the actual crime. The upper door was relocked at 2:15 so that's probably when Jake left. Jewel came back to the house at 3:50. She clocked out of her school at 3:40."

"So her alibi was solid?" Uri asked.

"Very solid. Nineteen kids in her class and a co-teacher for part of that time," Jasper said. "She was out walking with her kids around 2:15 and saw David's car leaving. That's what put me on to Jake."

"It couldn't have been David?" Uri asked.

"David's alibi was as solid as Jewel's," Jasper said. "He was on shift at Lunarex operating some mining equipment on the moon. Again too many witnesses and logs for him to be anywhere else. I knew that even before the car itself confirmed Jake was the last person who had driven it and the last trip was to Plains."

"What kind of car?" Uri asked.

"A Ford Javelin."

"Impressive," Uri said. "I didn't know they had logging features."

"They do," Jasper said. "David said it's logged everyone who has driven it clear back to the factory."

"Did you get to drive it?" Uri asked.

Jasper looked at him, startled by the question then relaxed. "No, I didn't. I'm not sure I would have dared drive a car that pricey. All it would take was one deer."

"True," Uri said but he was smiling. "Still it would have tempted me. I've only seen a half dozen in my life."

"You need to visit David sometime and look around the garage at Lunarex Tower. There isn't a single car in there worth less than two hundred grand."

"I might have to do that," Uri said. "So when did Jewel call in her grandmother's death?"

"Immediately," Jasper said. "The call was received before four. I was there before five–they pulled me off another case."

"Got it," Uri said. "So Mike was still half-drugged with evell and Jewel was distracted by him and you spent most of your time going over the scene. Interviews the next day?"

"Yes," Jasper said. "But Mike died that night and Jewel was the only one there when he died. No alibi. Just like Mike was the only one with no alibi at her grandmother's house. Except for his medical condition, he could have done it himself."

"Unable?" Uri said.

"In his doctor's opinion, he was completely unable to carry a hundred pound weight to the third floor and drop it. What we're fairly certain of is Smith didn't know Mike was in that third floor bedroom or he might have killed him then. Since he was a target, there wouldn't have been a better time."

"That suggests Smith wasn't calling the shots," Uri said. "But then you already knew that from the church."

"We thought it was Kucera but I recently found out Ed Kucera was not in Plains that day. He had plenty of witnesses that put him in Denver. My informant that witnessed the confessional meeting also stated quite definitely it was not Ed Kucera he heard. Since he placed Smith with no problem, I have to assume he's right."

"But Kucera left a confession?"

"It wasn't a confession," Jasper said. "We were told it was but it was sealed. Now we have it." Finding the right flasher, he threw it up on the vid screen and let Uri read it. Would he believe it too?

Going back over the events, he knew he should believe it. Jewel was there when Mike died but he also couldn't forget her puzzlement when she heard Mike missed his appointment and her genuine grief when he found Mike dead. The police psychiatrist had also said she wasn't guilty. Did he ever get a copy of that? He didn't know. They would have to get it.

"Jesus," Uri said as he finished reading. "He put it all on Jewel?"

Chapter 25 - Uri

"And you?" Uri demanded, his eyes sharpening. "He did mean you?"

"No, he didn't," Jasper said. "Ed Kucera never met me and he certainly didn't know I was DEA. He meant someone Jewel was engaged to but his information was old and wrong."

"Ok, that one sounds interesting." Uri folded his arms and waited.

Jasper was suddenly thankful there were so many white boards. The third board he evelled Professor Andrew (Drew) Nugent. "Professor Nugent was sixty and a friend of Mike West's. At some point–I'm not sure when–he offered to marry Jewel. Mike and David were both in favor of it until Jewel put her foot down. That happened weeks before she met me," he added. "David couldn't move back to Plains and he worried about her."

"Why? Mike was there. So was her grandmother."

"Elizabeth had applied for euthanasia then changed her mind during the walk. That was two months before and several weeks after Mike's accident. And–" Jasper abruptly remembered the interview at Soma, Incorporated, "Mike had asked about the process for himself."

"He was thinking about it?" Uri frowned. "Are you sure his death was murder?"

"I'm sure," Jasper said. "He was shocky but he had Jewel to think about. He was as close as a father to her. When her parents died, it was his parents and him that raised her."

"I was wondering where her parents were."

"New Wave colony," Jasper said and knew by Uri's expression he didn't need to say more but he went on. "Jewel's parents, her sister, another uncle and his wife and Jake's older brother."

"God." Uri's face registered his shock. "All of them?"

"Yes, Jewel was almost seven."

"Jake couldn't have been much older," Uri said.

"He wasn't." He knew what Uri was thinking. In an age where it was almost unheard of to lose any children, the West family had been decimated. His frown deepened as he realized they'd been hit twice–once by bad design and the second time for greed or drugs. Right now only David and Jewel were Wests. He needed to change that. David had done his part. He was going to help Jewel do hers. Once that transmitter was out, he'd get serious about it.

"Mike was not suicidal," Jasper repeated. "I don't think he would have left before Jewel was settled---and that might be why he was pressing her to marry Drew Nugent," he said. "Now that makes sense."

"You could just ask him," Uri said then stopped at the look on his face. "He's dead too?"

"The day before Jewel was kidnapped," Jasper said. "Now I know who did it." And he finally understood why Drew Nugent had wanted to marry Jewel. He had thought it was the house or her money but the professor had a comfortable house and money of his own. He clearly hadn't been lusting after Jewel. Mike had asked him to marry her. Why the hell had Nugent agreed?

"If you know, put it down," Uri said. "And tell me about it."

"That's tied in to the kidnapping and possibly the whole Blissex operation. I mean to get him for what he did to Jewel and the professor but he could be a much bigger fish."

"Sounds interesting. Who is it?"

The strident buzz of his com unit distracted him and Jasper automatically picked it up then looked carefully at the ID. At first he didn't know why he'd be getting a call from the West Foundation but then he recalled the relay. "It's David."

Throwing the call on to the vid screen, he knew instantly it was good news. David was almost jubilant and it didn't fade when he saw Uri.

"They got Lori's killer," David said, his grin fierce. "Your captain just called me with the news. It took less than four hours for some subbies to turn him in."

"Is he still alive?" Jasper asked.

"Yes," David said. "And he's going to stay that way. There are armed guards on him and a private nurse to make sure no one kills him like they did that FBI agent."

"Killed the FBI agent?" Jasper repeated. "What do you mean?"

David stared at him, then his smile faded. "I guess you didn't hear. The agent was murdered in the hospital. Some nurse with chestnut hair walked right past security and into his room. The FBI tried to get me to identify her as Jewel but I know my niece. This woman was at least fifty pounds heavier and walked wrong. Someone else said it could be and they used that for an APB."

Jasper met Uri's gaze. "Then that's where it came from," he said. "Was the agent recovering?"

"Yes," David said, "he was due to be released."

"And what day was this?" Jasper asked but felt he knew the answer. "And time?"

"Around five pm day before yesterday," David said. "Why?"

"Slasher–Lori's killer–found out Jewel and I were missing from the house around two that day. I think he was turning up the heat."

Uri muttered something under his breath.

"He couldn't have known we were out of the city," Jasper said. "Not for certain. He was probably trying to flush us out by getting the FBI involved."

"That could be," David said. "As soon as he's questioned, they'll clear that up."

Questioned? With a bliss-based drug? Jasper felt a chill. "David, can I use the relay to call Captain Reynolds?"

"Of course," he said. "Just tell the operator the number. Why?"

"I'll call you back." Jasper cut the connection and started punching in numbers.

"What gives?" Uri asked.

"There's a drug that reacts with bliss. They gave it to Jewel and I bet Slasher has it too," Jasper said. "Operator? Yes, this is Jasper Stone. I need you to connect me with 307-555-83928." He hoped the number was not busy. An instant later, he heard the familiar ring and then the captain was there.

"West?"

"No, Stone," Jasper said. "Captain, Nugent was killed with a drug called blister. It's a bliss reactive. Pedro Kruger can test for it. If Lori's killer has it in his system, bliss can kill him–just like the professor and Kucera."

"Got it. I'll pass that on. Are you ok? How's Jewel?"

"Jewel is doing well. I'm fine. There's another thing. The professor had pills with that stuff. What they stuck in Jewel was an implant very like a birth control implant. Upper left arm on her but it could be anywhere on him."

"They did that to her?" Jasper could hear his fury.

"Yes and more. She's got a transmitter in her that can explode given the right signal. Until that's out, we have to stay away from electronics."

His captain fell silent. When he finally spoke again, his words were clipped. "I'll keep that bastard alive. You take care of Jewel." With that he broke the connection.

"That transmitter can explode?" Uri looked grey. "How big a charge?"

"Not big," Jasper said. "But enough to kill her. It was their insurance." Bitterness soured his voice. "And that is why I want Mark Baxter." He wrote the man's name on the professor's board and underlined it. "He told me he killed Nugent then he stood in front of me and told me about his damned insurance. I was chained, Jewel was drugged, and he was laughing in my face. I want him dead."

Uri stared at him then seemed to shake himself. "So we get him. Who is he?"

"He's a vice president of Wilson Chemicals," Jasper said. "And I have to call David back."

"Forget David!" Uri thundered. "What do you mean he's a vice president at Wilson? Why the hell would he be–" His eyes widened and he buried his face in his hands. Indistinguishable curses streamed from him.

Jasper waited, finally certain of Uri's loyalties. Grimly, he considered his options. They had to solve the West murders once and for all but he was betting there would be some tie to Baxter if he could just find it. If not, he could definitely get him for kidnapping. That one charge would be enough to bring him in for questioning but he wanted more. If he was behind blissex, he wanted him shut down forever.

Chapter 26 - Settling In

"Your immunities are fine," Molly said as she gathered up the lunch dishes. "And, according to your records, you're as healthy as horse except for Vitamin D. You'll need to spend some time in our gym though. You can't spend all your time in the conference room."

"Is that a prescription too?" Jasper asked. "Physical exercise? Sunlight? Diet?"

"Don't go sassing me," Molly Kowalski said. "As long as you're here, I'm going to keep you healthy. I know you're working hard right now but you need to take care of yourself too."

"And Jewel?" Jasper asked.

"She can do the treadmill and dancing exercises but she's not to do crunches, sit-ups, or anything that stresses the midsection. I'll let both of you off gym time if you get other physical activity like dancing. That's a good compromise."

"You have a good dance floor?" Jasper asked.

Molly laughed. "Of course. We even have a first-rate music system. It's the second favorite exercise around here."

"And the first?" Jasper asked, struggling not to smile.

"If you don't know that, Jazz Stone, you aren't married." Molly glared at him in mock severity.

Jasper laughed. "Ok, no problems there. Is Jewel allowed?"

Molly nodded, her smile fading. "Yes. It's not going to hurt anything and emotionally she needs it. Just no really twisty positions."

"Twisty positions?" Jasper's eyebrow shot up. "And what do you know about twisty positions?" He watched in fascination as Molly's cheeks reddened and she turned away. Interesting. He knew better than to pursue that but he wondered if Ivan could teach him a thing or two.

"Ok, I'll try to get some time in the gym today," he said. "Or the dance floor. Do you have a piano here?"

Molly smiled, her composure back. "What's the time?" She looked at the clock and said "One fifteen."

"Does that mean you have one?" Jasper asked, mystified.

"Yes, we have one," Molly said. "Second floor of the school. The door isn't locked but there are classes there until two. If you go up, make sure you're out before eleven. The light circuits go off then and you'll find yourself stumbling home in the dark."

"They go off?" Jasper was surprised.

"Energy conservation," Molly said. "Since everyone is in bed by then, the circuits for the offices, school, and community center shut completely down then so the power is available for heating the barns. It gets shunted back at six am. There are night lights in the underground but not enough to actually do anything."

"Right. I'll have to set an alarm then." Jasper knew once he set down at the piano, he would play for hours. He wasn't sure even having no light would stop him but he didn't want to try it. Stumbling around in a strange place with no light was not his idea of fun. "Thanks for warning me."

"I remember how you play," Molly said. "It was wonderful and I am so glad Sasha got to see it. One of the things she'll miss out on now."

Jasper nodded, realizing Molly was missing her only girl. Is that why Ivan made that crack about Jewel being like a daughter? Hopefully, Jewel would not take to farming and doctoring animals like Sasha. He wasn't ready for that.

"Did Sasha play any instruments?" Jasper asked.

"A recorder," Molly said. "Small, light, and easy to pack. She did take some strings as trade items."

"Now that I can see," Jasper said. "Smart. If there's any string players there, they'd need those."

"Exactly," Molly said. "But I need to get this lot cleaned up and Uri is probably waiting for you."

"Yes," Jasper said. "Thanks."

Tomorrow he might actually manage to fix something himself in his tiny kitchen–and spend time with Jewel but he didn't have high hopes for that. He'd expected to see her at lunch but found out the school kids helped with the cooking at the school and the teachers were expected to stay and help. The workers at the turkey barn had had lunch delivered so it had been just him and Molly. Uri had another meeting.

It was curious that Uri had meetings but he wasn't sure if that was because his meals with Molly were medical or because he actually had one. He certainly wasn't meeting with Ivan. Well, he'd probably be back by now so he'd better hurry.

Crossing over to the offices, he said hello to Kale as the martial arts instructor was leaving then headed up to the third floor. As before most of the building was quiet. He supposed there was a secretary or someone on the first floor-the ground level entrance-but he had no reason to stop there. The third-floor conference room was his. He'd explore the rest later.

Stepping off the elevator, he was surprised to see Uri and Uncle Harold in conversation. The elderly man looked stronger today and looked like he'd just come from town. There was something about him, an air of confidence, in the way he turned to smile at Jasper.

"Here you are," Uri said. "I was just telling Mister Fletcher why we need his conference room."

"Mister Fletcher?" Jasper put that together quickly with the man's confident look. "The CEO?"

"General Manager," Uncle Harold corrected with an easy smile. "Yes, that's me but only in this building. Otherwise I prefer Uncle Harold."

"So you were doing more than putting one over on my wife at pool," Jasper said. "Getting to know us first?"

"That's right," he said without letting go of his smile. "I knew your reputation and hers through Ivan and Mr. West but I prefer to judge people myself. Now with what Uri's told me, I'm ready to give you the full cooperation of Amber Farms."

"Amber Farms?" Jasper blinked. "I'm sorry, I never asked Ivan what this place was named."

It was named Amber? He wondered how Jewel would react to that in her present state. Of course, she might already know.

"Understandable," Harold Fletcher said. "Ivan is livestock manager as you know. I'm the general manager until we can finally agree on my successor. Fortunately, there's not so much work in this position that I have to forego a game of pool."

"True," Jasper's mind was racing. Had Uri told him he was DEA? "How much do you know?"

Harold shot a look at Uri then motioned toward the door. "Let's go in."

Jasper obediently unlocked the conference room door, keenly aware that this man should have his own key for it. He might have been wrong to trust Uri so completely.

Harold made no attempt to hide his interest in the boards but sat down at the head of the table. "I'm told you're a federal agent and I should ignore the APB Uri told me about yesterday. I'm also told you're working not only on the West murders but the blissex problem. I don't know details, of course, and I don't need to know them. I also won't get in your way."

Jasper shot a look at Uri then paid attention as Harold spoke again.

"Now that I'm satisfied as to what you're doing, I can tell the others it's legal and won't adversely affect the farm. I'm also the legal counsel, you see."

"I won't be telling them—not even Ivan—that you're DEA. That is between you, me, and Uri. Does your wife know?"

"No," Jasper said.

"I didn't think so," Harold said. "I suspect there will be times when you have to leave us and you'll want to leave Jewel here?"

"Yes sir." Jasper hadn't thought that far ahead but he knew he didn't want to take Jewel along—not with that transmitter in her.

"Then leave her here," Harold said. "I don't like to see women in jeopardy. When you go, I prefer you take Kale. He's a good driver and his martial arts training would be more useful than Ivan's luck. He can reschedule his classes as needed."

Jasper understood now why Kale had just been leaving. "I'll do that."

"This conference room just became your office until this is done," Harold said with a wave at the white boards. "I can put our weekly meeting somewhere else. No one will clean it either."

"Who else has keys?" Jasper asked.

"There are four. Two are master keys for all the doors in the building. I carry one of those and the other is in the key safe. The second key for this specific door I'll give to Uri. You have the other one." Harold studied him. "We have some nosy kids but they usually stay out of the offices since we have a habit of locking them. The adults don't pry."

"Truthfully, I'm more concerned about Jewel poking in than anyone else," Jasper said. "She's as nosy as they get."

"Ah then I'll see she's kept busy," Harold said. "That's the best thing for her."

"Thanks."

"Now tell me," Harold said with a smile on his lips, "how good is she at pool?"

Jasper hesitated, remembering exactly how Jewel played him. The little minx hadn't let him finish a game since he caught on to how good she was. "She can clear the table anytime she likes."

"I thought so." Harold slapped the table. "A shark?"

"With teeth," Jasper said. "I didn't know when her uncle gave us the table."

"Then this should be interesting," Harold said. "It's been a long time since anyone challenged Jim, much less beat him."

"Jim?" Jasper asked.

"Jim Talbot," Uri supplied. "Our resident shark."

"Isn't he one of the managers?" Jasper placed the name even though he didn't think he'd met him.

"That's not important," Harold said, waving that aside. "He's been cock of the walk long enough. I want to see her take him down."

"He could find out about it," Jasper said.

"And that was why I ended our game last night," Harold said. "I'll make sure she isn't playing when his workers are there—or not playing well."

He rose to his feet and Jasper found himself following his lead. "You'll want to get back to work. I just wanted to clear the air and let you know where we stood."

"I do have one question," Jasper said as he turned to go. At his quizzical expression, Jasper ploughed on. "Ivan hasn't mentioned how much that guest house rents for and I'd like to pay it up."

Uri coughed but Harold just smiled. "We've already settled that with Mr. West. It's your honeymoon and he's paid it for two months."

"Two months?" Jasper was stunned.

"Yes," Harold said. "He doesn't want you going back to Plains—at least not with Jewel."

Jasper's jaw tightened but David was right. Jewel shouldn't go back. "Thank you. I have to agree it's not safe for Jewel—and I will think twice before going back."

"Good. I'm already fond of her." Harold smiled. "Just remember I'm Uncle Harold in the pool hall. She's being nice to the old uncle."

Jasper smiled. "I won't blow your cover. You had me completely fooled too." Now he knew why Harold had been sitting by him at dinner last night.

"That's the way I like it," Harold said. Nodding to Uri, he left.

Jasper studied the closing door, both impressed and amused by the man. He had presence and Jasper thought he was exceptionally capable by what he'd just seen but he was also very approachable. "How many years has he been the general manager?" he finally asked.

"At least thirty," Uri replied. "He's had the job as long as I've been around."

"He'd be hard to replace then," Jasper said. "A generation has only known him."

"That's why we won't let him go," Uri said. "We'll have to face it someday though."

Jasper hoped it wouldn't be soon. When someone was that entrenched, change wasn't easy. "We'd better get back to work," he said, putting thoughts of Harold Fletcher off for later. "Any suggestions on how to go about it now that you've had a taste?"

"The way I see it we're going to have to go through this step-by-step and prove or disprove every fact we've got," Uri said. "Back it up with hard data."

Jasper considered it then nodded. "Too many inconsistencies. That might be the best approach."

"I'd like to look at those text messages Jake left," Uri said. "See exactly what they say and whether they actually came from this Ed Kucera. If we can't prove they did, there's room to doubt Jake."

"True," Jasper picked up the flasher and handed it to him. "I have Kucera's whereabouts for that week. I think I want to start with a search on where Smith was—and Baxter."

"A suggestion," Uri said. "Go back to the week before Michael West's accident and go forward. You might catch one or both in Plains."

"Good thought," Jasper said. "I'll make more coffee then let's get to it."

They worked on in silence. It took time for the access reports from Plains to wind their way through DEA channels to him so he sat reviewing what he knew about Mike's accident. Sanders had said the air cleaners normally had three tie-downs and not the single one found on the one that fell. How had that one happened to fail at the right moment? Was it jostled? It was odd they could have timed it that close unless someone had been on the catwalk. Yet if someone had been on the catwalk, they could have charged him with attempted murder. That was something he couldn't turn around and investigate again. The only one that could was Sanders and he wasn't sure the detective was willing to cooperate with him after their last encounter.

He'd had it coming. Jasper's jaw tightened as he recalled that scene. He could have gotten Jewel killed. At the same time, he could see why Sanders had been such an idiot and he needed him now.

Carefully he composed a text. "Want to clear up Michael West's accident? Maybe there was someone on catwalk. Timing. What he was working on factor. Report to Reynolds. Jewel safe." He would have to send it under his name. Damn, he was going to need another com unit—a new one. He didn't want anyone knowing about his secure one that he didn't trust.

"Where's the nearest place I can buy a cheap com unit?" he asked. "Not one of the farm's."

"A throw-away?" Uri frowned. "Even those cost six hundred dollars. That Solstar you carry must have cost three times that much."

"It did," Jasper said. "But it's not a model sold to civilians."

"I gathered that when you used it to scan. Mine can do that but it's police issue."

"So is mine," Jasper said. "I need a throw-away to send messages to people I don't completely trust. It can't be registered to the farm or purchased through farm channels."

"Got it," Uri said. "That means you'll have to go yourself to purchase it and that APB is still out. It could show up on official queries."

"True," Jasper said. "I don't want an agency connection either."

"How about West?" Uri said. "He can get one here in two days."

"Not David," Jasper said. "Ah, hell, I can use Milt. He's a hell of a lot closer." Punching in his agent's contact info, he threw the call on to the vid screen.

"Boards," Uri said before the call connected and Jasper hastily put it back on his unit. The boards were clearly visible to the vid unit's camera.

"Thanks," Jasper said. "Bad habit." He held his com unit out so the secretary who answered could see it was him. His ID was off.

"Mr. Stone!" Mary recognized him at once. "Are you safe? Is your wife ok?"

"Yes and yes, Mary. We have to keep this short. Write down an address for me?"

"Yes sir," Mary already had pen in hand and wrote quickly.

Uri supplied the address from off camera and Jasper noted it was a post office box off site. Good.

"Ok, what I need is two com units, both cheapies. Have the FBI been there yet?"

"Yes sir. They asked questions and want to know if you contact Mr. Anderson," she said.

"Ah then don't tell him I've called until after this is done," he said. "Just buy the com units. Send one to me at that address. I want you to give the other to Milt. Charge them to my account but use a cash card to actually buy them. Can you do that?"

"Yes sir," she said in her cool professional manner.

"Oh and lose the address after mailing the package," Jasper said. "I'll give it to you again if needed."

"Yes sir."

"Mary, good job at the Lantern. I hope you enjoyed that dinner."

"It was excellent," she said, relaxing into a smile. "And fun."

"Good. Must go now. I'll contact you again when I have the new unit."

"Yes sir."

Jasper broke the connection and glanced at the time. Under a minute. Good enough. Even if they had put a tracer on their main line, there wasn't enough time to get a fix. Milt might have agreed to have a recorder put on his phone but it was unlikely they'd asked his secretary. He'd known a few bosses in the past who had pulled that trick. All incoming calls he didn't want authorities to hear stopped at the secretary. They'd also switched offices and used throw-away com units to avoid cooperation—just what he was planning on doing.

"Can you trust her?" Uri asked. "If they're watching her, there could be a tracker in the box or even on the unit."

"Possibly," Jasper said. "But Mary is good. If she knows there's something wrong with it, she'll probably just send it to another address then buy another when they aren't looking and mail it off."

"Is she an agent?" Uri asked, surprised.

"No, just a damned good secretary. Milt is lucky to have her," Jasper said. "I'll probably have that com unit tomorrow." Frowning, he saved the text to Sanders to memory.

"What have you found out?" he asked, looking at Uri. "Is there anything in those texts?"

"Oh, there's plenty," Uri said. "He was being blackmailed alright. The only problem is we can't prove any came from Kucera. We don't have Jake's com unit or the one they were sent from. The headers say either Kucera or Smith but it's all inadmissible."

"Waste of time, huh?" Jasper frowned. "Is there anything?"

"One item," Uri said. "A memo from Centrax that's in photo form. It will have to be verified and examined but they might allow it as proof of Jake's motive."

"Let me see it," Jasper said.

Uri put it on the vid panel and Jasper studied it. The Centrax logo and headers looked real. Seeing it was an internal memo addressed to Edward Kucera, he frowned. "I'm not sure Kucera was part of their company. We'll have to check that."

"Noted," Uri said. "Read on."

Jasper saw Jake's name in the subject line then his frown deepened as he read.

"Concerning his contract with this company, remind him he has obligations to us and time is running out. We didn't enter into that contract lightly and we don't expect him to reject the terms at this late date. If he cannot deliver as promised, we will withdraw our support and terminate."

It was signed by the well-known CEO of Centrax, his trademark signature covered by a corporate seal to prevent forgery.

"Blaine Robbins actually signed that?" Jasper was appalled. If this memo was real, Centrax was obliquely asking for murder. The man was not only CEO of Centrax but owned the Chicago Comets—one of the hottest and most controversial teams in the Team War League.

"It looks like it," Uri said. "You notice he didn't spell out exactly what he wanted Jake to do?"

"Yes, corporate liability," Jasper answered and felt sick. He had thought Kucera had made the corporate withdrawal up or Jake had misunderstood. Why was Centrax involved in drugs? Blaine Robbins was another who detested bliss—publicly. He'd fired two very popular players from his team for using and people still thought he had lost the Comets the championship.

If this memo was real, Blaine Robbins was more than involved. He condoned murder.

"I'm inclined to think this is a fake," Uri said. "And not because I'm a Comets fan. It's sticking his neck out too far. Blaine Robbins isn't a fool."

"It's an internal memo," Jasper said. "Maybe he didn't know Kucera would send a copy to Jake."

"Maybe but I'd want to know what Kucera's connection is to Centrax before I go for a warrant," Uri said. "If this is real, it will get us one."

Jasper nodded but he wasn't too sure he wanted to tackle that. If it had been Wilson Kucera with his drug company, he would have been delighted. Blaine Robbins was different. He wasn't a Team War fan but he had applauded his decision to throw two players off a team for drug abuse.

He would have to be absolutely sure the memo was real before going further in that direction. "Yes, let's make sure it's real," Jasper said. "I wouldn't want to cross Blaine Robbins if it's not."

"Agreed," Uri said.

His com unit buzzed and Jasper looked at it, saw it was Carlson and answered. "Yes sir?"

"Kowalski can see this," Carlson said. "You're alone?"

"Yes, hold on." Jasper threw the call on to the vid screen.

Ray Carlson looked to be in his office this time. He gave Uri a nod and said "Welcome to the team, Mr. Kowalski. I'm Agent Ray Carlson."

"Good to meet you," Uri said. "As you can see, we've been busy." He motioned toward the visible white boards.

"Yes, I see that," Ray said. "This is about that APB."

"What about it?" Jasper asked.

"I'm getting yours released now," Ray said. "It will be out of the system nation-wide at midnight. I couldn't get Jewel's released. Someone ID'd her at the hospital. I told them that wasn't possible because I extracted you from Plains myself but they aren't buying it yet. West told them it wasn't her but some nurse thought it was."

"A nurse?" Jasper frowned. "Jewel hasn't been in the hospital."

"No but she spent quite a lot of time there after you were shot," Carlson said. "Enough time that the nurses remembered her hair."

Jasper nearly groaned then changed his mind. "Her hair? Do they know it got cut? You saw how they butchered it."

Carlson looked surprised then his jaw tightened. "I didn't get pictures of it."

"I have one that's date stamped," Jasper said. "Hold on." He split the vid screen and brought up the picture he'd taken of Jewel holding her sign. "Can you see that?"

"Yes, got it. Let me save that." Carlson smiled fiercely. "That just might do it but I also need a debrief. The FBI has got it into their heads that the kidnapping was her idea after that confession was released. They aren't sure of your involvement now that they know you're an agent but they won't let the notion go without proof."

"Not the vid from the house," Jasper said and saw Carlson shake his head. "Then what?"

"I'm getting the doctor's report to explain why she isn't willing to appear. I also need you to debrief her. Kowalski can do it. Assume they'll analyze everything and keep the background clean. I want you on camera with Jewel but he's to stay off camera."

"We can't use electronics," Jasper said, aware even the most portable equipment used them.

"I know that," Carlson said. "And I will make damned sure they know that. Once that transmitter is out and that drug is definitely out of her system, she'll probably have to do a regular questioning session but I'm going to buy you time."

"And the APB?"

"We'll let them know she's in custody at a secure location. For that to work, she can't be seen away from that farm."

"That's not a problem," Uri said. "We already have it cleared that she stays here. Jasper though is going to need mobility."

"Tomorrow he'll have it. I'd like that debrief tomorrow afternoon. See if you can get it done by then."

"Not a problem," Uri said.

"Jazz, have you discussed what happened while she was missing at all?" Carlson asked.

"No sir. She has said she was trapped and she's had nightmares but I knew this was coming. We've not discussed it."

"And the only thing she said to me was she thought she might have been on that jet. Make sure you cover that thoroughly. If we can prove it was used in the commission of a crime, we can hold it as evidence."

"You'd need a pretty big evidence room," Jasper said.

"The DEA has the largest. It won't be lonely. The last time I looked we had some others—there's one that dates back to the 20th century."

"What kind?" Kowalski asked.

"An old antique Cessna," Carlson said. "That case is in permanent limbo. I couldn't tell you how long we've had it."

"Well, some collector will be happy if it gets released," Uri said. "Ok, so you want to know more about the plane. How about the other kidnappers? West told us they caught the one Jasper has been calling Slasher."

"Yes, that's Chuma Johnson. His street name was Slash and he's from the New York metro plex," Carlson said. "They brought him in pretty well beaten by civilians. He was living in an apartment over in Section 18."

"I warned Captain Reynolds about the blister implants," Jasper said. "It was relayed through the West Foundation."

"Good. I have seen Kucera's autopsy report, by the way. There was no implant there. Let me send it to you." He fingered something off screen and Jasper's com unit acknowledged the incoming file. "The judge ordered it released since it has bearing on Jewel's kidnapping. He is not buying it that Jewel arranged the whole thing. She had less than three hours between the FBI agent arriving and appearing at that train station. During that time she made no calls—the FBI agent testified to that in the hospital. From what I've heard, he was determined to get her back and not because he thought she was guilty."

"What was his name?" Jasper asked. "I don't know if I even heard it."

"Cord McCain," Carlson said. "He had a good rep."

"Was he told she was safe?" Jasper asked, knowing how bad he would feel if he'd lost someone out of his custody.

"I don't know," Carlson said. "I can ask."

"It's not important," Jasper said. "I can find out later."

"It is," Carlson said. "I notified the FBI and Plains PD she'd been recovered once you were on that plane to Chicago. They should have told him immediately."

"Right," Jasper said, thinking back. What time had they got on that plane? Three? Time enough for him to be told. "What killed him?"

"There was an unidentified drug in the IV bottle. They found it after he had a reaction to bliss." Carlson was grim. "My guess is it was blister."

"Damn!" Jasper exploded. "How many ways have they got to deliver that stuff? Pills, implants and now liquid?"

"Considering I'd never even heard of the stuff before this week, I'm starting to get interested." Carlson looked disgruntled. "No one bothered to tell the DEA about Kucera, you know."

"No, I didn't," Jasper said. "If I'd known that, you would have had my report."

"It happens," Carlson said. "And you were in the hospital when it happened. Let's just make sure there are no more cases. We've had enough of that."

"Yes sir. Anything else?"

"No, that will cover it," he said. "How is Jewel faring?"

"She's holding up. They're keeping her busy for me," Jasper said. "The nightmares are the worst."

Carlson nodded. "Well, keep her safe. Kowalski, I'm glad you're there to back him up."

"Thank you," Uri said. "You'll have that debrief tomorrow."

"Good enough," Carlson said and broke the connection.

"We won't do it tonight," Uri said. "It's getting late. Copy me that autopsy?" He held out his com unit and Jasper touched his to it, transferring a copy of the file.

Seeing it was just past four, Jasper considered pressing on but Uri was right. Jewel would need some time with him—and he had to prepare her for tomorrow. She'd need to get time off but that shouldn't be hard. She was, after all, an extra.

Chapter 27 - Blow by Blow

The commons, the local name for the underground, was populated mostly by children and teens when Jasper crossed to his quarters. He didn't see Jewel and wondered if she was playing pool until he opened the door to their apartment and heard music he instantly recognized as his own.

What the hell? BLOW BY BLOW was not a number he liked or had shared with Jewel but that's what it was. God awful stuff. The next instant he saw Jewel–his Jewel–dancing and his protest died on his lips.

Unaware he was there, she was half exercising and half dancing, her graceful movements unconsciously sinuous as she moved to the beat. She still wore that damned skirt and jammers but even those couldn't hide the shape of her lovely ass. Jasper gulped and quickly closed the door behind him. His pulse quickened as he stood back to watch, aware she was really into the beat.

It was escalating, quickening and becoming louder. Jasper had never thought of his tune as being sexual but now. Setting his briefcase down, he moved into the room and relaxed into the beat himself. Moving in time to it, he stepped into Jewel's line of vision and saw her smile. Far from embarrassed at being caught, her movements became more sinuous and he found himself trying to match her and not being able to keep his mind on what he should be doing. When she wiggled, he couldn't think.

There wasn't room enough for a lot of steps but Jewel didn't use much of what there was. With him in front of her, she came closer. The intensity of the music built up and up and her movements got quicker and closer. When she practically climbed on him, he couldn't take it any more. Sweeping her up, he dropped her on the bed so hard she bounced.

Her laughter sparked his as he pinned her to the mattress and then they were both laughing so hard that he didn't care about the damned music. It finally ended but he didn't want to move. Grinning down at her, he rolled, pulling her with him so she was on top.

"Oh, I like this," Jewel said and snuggled into his chest. "Not as much as..."

"Minx," he said. The next instant her lips were on his, smothering any further protests. His pulse raced and he knew he was hard but he resisted the urge to take control. Instead he let her kiss him, part his lips, and let her tease his tongue. She took a long, long time. He ached to take it further but when she sat up on his hips, he knew they should wait.

Damn it, he didn't want to wait. He wanted to feel her around him but it wasn't even five o'clock yet and anyone could stop by. He hadn't even locked the door.

"Jewel," he said and rolled her aside. She looked surprised then locked legs around him. Patting one, he firmly unwrapped it and saw her disappointment. She was so ready. So was he. "Christmas."

"Christmas doesn't come often enough." She pouted and he grinned ruefully down at her. It had become their code phrase for having to wait.

"Oh, I'd love to have you now but... it's five o'clock. Not even farmers go to bed this early."

She giggled and relented, unwinding her other leg before she sighed. "Mustn't shock the farmers."

"I don't think you can but I sure as hell don't want to have to live it down," Jasper said. "And I'm hungry."

"So am I," she said and wiggled.

"Stop that," Jasper growled. "I want food first."

The minx laughed again but Jasper got to his feet. Crossing the room, he threw the deadbolt then headed into the bathroom. God, she was lusty. He grinned, remembering his concern after the kidnapping. Apparently it was unfounded. He hoped so.

He could like that song now. BLOW BY BLOW was one of his early tunes and it was full of rebellion and frustration—or so he thought. It had charted but he had put it down to rebellious teenagers hearing it in the sensa dens. He had never thought of it as sexual. He hadn't even met Carol then. It obviously was but he hadn't known it till now.

Wondering how sound-proofed the apartment was, he had to grin. If their construction followed the usual pattern, there were at least two feet of earth and cement between this apartment and the ones around it. There was no house above it and none below so they should be ok. He hoped so. That music played loud. Maybe they could do something with it later. He had an image of Jewel dancing naked and swiftly shoved that thought away. He didn't need that just now. He needed a cold shower.

It was some time before he left the bathroom. Casting a wary eye toward the little kitchen, he saw Jewel wasn't laying in wait but cooking. So they were staying in. He didn't object but were they expected anywhere? "What's on the menu?"

"Green beans, some of those delicious potatoes Betty Talbot served last night, and hamburgers," Jewel said. "I thought we should go lighter after last night."

"Probably a good idea," Jasper said. "And I love your green beans. What do the others do on Mondays?"

Jewel looked thoughtful, her hand pausing in stirring the beans. "It's a quiet night usually. Karen—she's the hairdresser—said everyone likes to hole up after Sunday. It's more that way today since they've been processing turkeys. There is a movie on the big vid panel out there," she said. "But it's homework for the fourth graders. It's some historical movie called Johnny Tremain."

"Never heard of it," Jasper said. "You?"

"No," Jewel said. "All I know is it's Revolutionary War. They're studying early American history."

"Movies are a good way of doing it," Jasper said then added, "if they're halfway accurate."

"Right," Jewel replied and put the beans in the oven. "The fifth graders have a movie tomorrow night—20th century history—and the sixth graders on

Wednesday for world history. Thursday night is for us old folks and Friday night is a family night."

"What do they expect us old folks to like?" Jasper asked, his lips twitching. "Car chases and special effects or sex?"

"Sex for me," she said with a wicked smile. "I didn't check what was scheduled."

"Doesn't matter," Jasper said. "I'd rather spend it with you." Or that piano, he suddenly thought. "Did you know there's a piano here?"

"Yes," Jewel said. "It's not a grand piano but an electronic one with organ settings too. I peeked."

"And you didn't tell me?" Jasper asked.

"Well, I couldn't. I promised," Jewel said then looked at him suspiciously. "Who did you ask?"

"Molly," he said. The kitchen was too tight for two unless they got very close. "Hand me that hamburger?"

"What time?" Jewel asked. "I want to know if I won."

"Won?" Jasper looked blank.

"The betting pool," she said. "I think Ivan set it up. No one could tell you about the piano. They were betting on when you'd ask."

Jasper suddenly remembered Molly's smile and her asking what time it was. "One fifteen," he said.

"No, I lost," Jewel said. "I thought you'd ask over breakfast. Everyone thought I was crazy."

"No, you know me better," Jasper said. "When did this come up?" He was curious and a little amused to be the subject of betting.

"During the potluck last night Kale told me about it and I got my bet in. You were off with Uri." Jewel looked at him uncertainly. "You aren't mad?"

"No," Jasper said. "That's harmless enough. As long as they aren't betting on which meal we'll miss first."

"They'd lose," Jewel said. "Because I'm going to feed you first." She looked a little cross at him and he laughed.

"I'm hungry," he said and grabbed her waist and pulled her against him.

"Food first, Jazz Stone," she scolded but she didn't pull away.

Damn, he liked being married to her. Kissing her neck, he let her go and turned to the hamburger. Food first.

* * *

They were just finishing dinner when his com unit buzzed again, making Jewel jump. He laughed then checked the ID. "I think it's David," he said and threw it up on the vid screen. Jewel's uncle was looking pleased again.

"Aha, got both of you this time. Jewel, how are you?" he asked.

"Waiting for Christmas," Jewel said with a long-suffering tone and he laughed.

"It's good you're getting back to normal," he said. "And Elinor is here. Hold on." He waved to his wife to join him.

"What's up?" Jasper asked, guessing this was more social as David's petite wife settled on to the couch next to him.

"The baby has made himself at home," Elinor said. "I can get out of bed now."

"That's good," Jewel said, her smile genuine. "I'll keep my fingers crossed."

"So when will he pop back out?" Jasper asked and got a scandalized look from his wife and a punch on the shoulder.

Elinor laughed and David looked pleased as hell.

"Early August," Elinor said. "He's already two weeks along. He could be born on our anniversary."

Jewel's smile got tighter but her voice was bright. "Oh, I hope so. That would be nice."

"Yes, one less date to remember," Jasper added, acutely aware her mood had shifted.

Elinor seemed to sense it too. Her smile was a little less ready. "How are you liking the farm? We loved it there."

"I haven't seen much of it yet," Jasper said. "Jewel found the pool tables right off and there's a plot to pit her against the local shark."

"That will be fun," David said. "Have you talked to Harold yet?"

"Yes, he's been teaching Jewel to play pool," Jasper easily answered. "And Mr. Fletcher has set me up with office space. Thanks for the honeymoon by the way."

Elinor looked a little confused but David caught the double reference. "Teaching Jewel to play pool? Jewel, are you taking advantage of him?"

"Of course not," she said. "I'm just being nice."

"Uh-huh," David said. "You're welcome on the apartment. I know it's not as large as some hotel rooms but we didn't spend a lot of time there. Jasper, if you haven't seen the hydroponics yet, you should. They've got very good yields for the amount of space they've got."

"I'll remember that," Jasper said, wondering when he'd get time. "I did get driven around the out buildings and met Tom, Dick, and Hairy."

David laughed while Jewel just looked questioning at him. "Dogs, Jewel, very big dogs. I wondered how that would go over."

"I'm still in one piece," Jasper said. "Jewel will get out to meet them eventually."

"Jazz, there's dogs like those in all the barns," David said. "If you've only met the one lot, be careful going in. There's a few more in the houses but they don't let them in the underground much. Have you run into any cats yet?"

Jasper thought back. "I've seen a couple but they kept their distance. One was a big white mass."

"That's Cloudy," Jewel said. "He was Sasha's cat before she left."

"Good name for him," Jasper said. "Have you been cozying up to him?" He wondered if he'd end up with a cat before he even petted it. He didn't object to cats. There were areas of Plains where they roamed at night to take care of the mice that found their way in.

"I can't," Jewel said. "I tried but he could hear the jammers or the transmitter or something." Her voice was forlorn then turned wistful. "He is such a gorgeous cat."

"Is that thing bothering you?" David asked. "If it is, I can find someone who will take it out."

"Not really," Jewel said. "I'm queasy in the mornings but it goes away." She shrugged it off. "Molly says it just irritating me. I try not to think of what it can do."

David frowned then looked at Jasper. "If she needs it out, call me. I'll make damned sure she doesn't have to wait."

"It's too risky," Jasper said. "As long as it's quiet, we can wait. It's unlikely they'll find us here—and there's darn few electronics. I've only seen five com units since I got here and none of those robot toys."

"They've got real animals," David said. "Why would they want fake ones?"

"The fake ones turn off," Jasper said, using the same answer his father had given him once when he asked for a live pet. He hadn't known then that live dogs cost thousands to keep in the underground. Naively, he'd assumed they'd use the toilet like everyone else.

"The fake ones are just toys," David said. "But you never had a real one, I take it?"

"No." Jasper's answer was short. "Did you?"

"Yes, we had a dog and a cat both when I was a kid," David said. "Mother had a cat too. It's been dead for years though."

Jewel sniffed. "It was my cat."

Jasper looked at her in surprise, never having heard of this before. "You'll have to tell me about it," he said. "You've been holding out."

Jewel nodded but she didn't smile. There was something there. He'd have to ask David, he thought. Or was she dwelling on that transmitter again?

"It was a good cat," David said. "Inky. Terrible name but a good cat. She would have looked good with you, Sensor Man. When she shed it was always black hairs."

"Cats shed?" Jasper did his best to look and sound confused.

Jewel giggled and even Elinor laughed. David just raised an eyebrow and muttered "no one is that ignorant."

Jasper shrugged. Of course, he knew cats shed. Dogs did too. It was one of the things advertisers pointed out when they tried to sell the robot pets. Well, he wasn't going to let on until Jewel told him something—anything—about the family pet. He hadn't even seen a picture of it and he'd been with her for four months now.

"Oh, I got a call from the FBI again wanting to know if I'd heard from you," David said. "I referred them to my lawyer. Since neither of you have been charged with anything, they can kiss my—" he glanced at Elinor and cleared his throat.

"They should quit asking soon," Jasper said. "I understand they'll be dropping the APB on me tonight and we might get rid of the one on Jewel in a couple of days."

Jewel stared at him and he realized he hadn't told her yet. Damn, he needed to tell her about the debriefing tomorrow. "Uri and I will be getting her report down tomorrow and sending it off through his connections."

"Report?" Jewel said, her voice faint.

"Yes, love. They need to know what happened," Jasper said to her. "It's tomorrow. Molly said it might help your nightmares to get it out."

She looked upset and it was a minute before David broke the silence. "We'd better go. Jasper, if you need anything, just let me know." He hesitated then added. "There is one thing you can do though when you get time."

"What's that?" Jasper asked.

"The Foundation would like that thirty million back," David said. "When you get around to it."

"God, I forgot about that," Jasper said. "It's still sitting in my bank—and I don't have access just now."

"Of course it is," David said. "Just don't go blowing it on fancy clothes. That would take an awful lot of explaining."

"Thirty million?" Jewel asked.

"That's what I figured you were worth, brat," David said. "When you're thirty, we'll double it."

"Thanks," Jewel said, her smile returning. "I love you too."

"I know," David said. "But not as much as that guy next to you. You keep him safe from all those animals."

She smiled as he broke the connection.

Chapter 28 - Drumming

Jasper stirred back to wakefulness in the almost dark room, not sure if he'd heard Jewel or not. No, her breathing was even and she seemed to be sleeping finally. It had been a mistake telling her about the debriefing. Her playful mood had evaporated and she'd spent far too long in the shower. He knew without asking that he wouldn't be welcome.

He had managed to draw her out about the cat, learning her parents had given it to her to ease her disappointment in not going with them. Inky had lived a respectably long life and was now buried in their garden in direct violation of city ordinances. He couldn't care less about that. For a wild second he'd been tempted to offer her another cat but no. Not sure cats even liked him, he couldn't see living with one. Not only did they shed and poop but they were harder than kids to train. He'd rather have children for pets.

Was that setting her off too? She and Elinor had had a bit of a competition going over who would have the first child–the reason Elinor and David had waited until his marriage was official. Now Jewel had definitely lost the race. They'd lose another month, maybe two, to that transmitter. Damn, he wished he could get that out. Jewel was dwelling on it and making herself sick and he hated that. Tonight's little flirtation had eased his worries but now it looked like that was an exception. He should have let her have what she wanted when she wanted it and people be damned.

Damn it, he wanted her. They'd gone to bed far too early and she hadn't been receptive. Unable to release energy in his favorite way, he found himself simply holding her and thinking of the music he wanted to write until he fell asleep. Now she was asleep and he was wide awake.

It was too damned late to go looking for that piano. It must be past midnight. If Jewel was really asleep, he had to be quiet too. The apartment was too small for one to sleep and the other not.

Carefully he eased himself out of bed and dressed then took his com unit and drum. Unable to find the drumsticks in the dim light, he left them behind and walked barefoot into the Commons.

It took a bit for his eyes to adjust to the limited light. He could see patches of light from the nightlights and overhead he could see the gray round circles of the skylights against the blackness of the ceiling. Nothing was stirring. Leaving the door of the apartment slightly ajar, he made his way to the nearest group of furniture.

Now for that melody he couldn't get out of his head. Balancing the drum on his lap, he gave it a few tentative light touches then repositioned it so he could find the right notes in the dark. Keeping his touches light, he could barely hear the resultant tones but it was enough. The composition should start out with music barely heard.

He didn't bother to record it while he tinkered. He had the melody in his head already but it took a bit of experimenting and adjusting to get the drum to do it. One note had to be changed since the drum didn't have it and that required reworking a phrase. Only when he felt he had something close to the finished melody did he reach for his com unit to record it.

What was that? Jasper's pulse leaped then he made out the shape of that damned white cat on the arm of the couch not three feet away. Where had it come from? His lips twitched. How long had it been listening? He relaxed, eyeing the cat not as an animal but another music lover. "So do you approve?"

For answer the cat stretched and walked over to him, brushing against his hand. It was clearly inviting him to pet. Jasper held out his hand for the cat to sniff then gently stroked the furry white back. The cat didn't pull away but leaned into his hand. When it started purring, a low motor sound, he was lost. The purr was soft, almost melodic, and Jasper was surprised at how natural it sounded. Smiling, he stroked the warm fur. It was softer than he thought it would be. The cat arced its back under his hand and he laughed.

"You should be Spook coming out of the dark like that."

The cat flopped on its side against his thigh and he obediently gave it more attention, his music temporarily forgotten.

When the cat grabbed at his hand with both paws, he decided it had had enough and, greatly daring, set it on the floor before reaching for his com unit. It took him a moment to recapture the rhythm of the melody but he found he didn't mind.

Drumming it out softly, he played it through three times to be sure he had it right. Playing it back, he listened with a critical ear then changed a couple of notes and recorded it again.

That was a good start. He also liked working in the dark commons. It didn't have great acoustics like his studio but it gave a feel of openness to the drum number. He could almost imagine he was playing it outside.

Satisfied with his work, he set the drum aside and checked his com unit for messages. Seeing an alert from Butler, he tapped into its system to watch the latest invasion of his home.

This time it was an Asian man, slight of build, and looking to be around thirty. He was moving purposefully through the house, checking cabinets on the upper floor. When he opened the stereo cabinet and poked at Butler's brains, Jasper nearly swore but the man spent just as much time poking at the master stereo system before closing the cabinet. Didn't he know what he'd seen?

The man pulled out his own com unit and looked straight into one of Butler's cameras. "This is X. I need to kill our cameras before I can check this place out otherwise I'll get false readings. Note that for the Boss."

"Got you," a faint voice said.

X? That was the tech. Jasper wondered how he could have missed Butler's electronics. The man went around the room pulling the stealth cameras out of their sockets then proceeded down the stairs. Butler automatically switched views and Jasper saw him pull two more cameras before going to the first floor. There he watched him enter the kitchen and come out again then pull three more from the main room. Eight cameras? That was a lot of tech to waste on one house. Jasper knew even plug-in stealth cameras weren't cheap.

"This is X again. Confirm how many cameras here and tell me if any are still working," he said into his com unit.

"Eight and you got them all. Just hurry it up."

"I will. Look, you might as well get lunch. I'll holler if I need help."

"Ok, I won't be far."

"Suits me. I'm going to start doing the sweep now," X said.

If only he could have killed Butler when this guy entered, Jasper thought. Well, he'd get him out of circulation too. He watched X pinpoint the active camera and grin then the bastard waved at him.

"Hi, Stone. If you're seeing this, don't get any ideas about turning me in. I'm your insurance."

Jasper stared, unable to believe what he'd just heard.

"Yeah, I saw the Butler logo upstairs," he said. "One heck of a system. I suspect you've got it tweaked since I didn't detect it the other night. As much as I'd like to rip out its guts and play with it, I'm not going to. If the Boss finds out I slipped up, he'll have me killed because you got him on vid."

He looked toward the front door and back again. "Look, I want out of this racket. I got in not knowing what it was but they've had me on a short leash ever since. My name is Kin Koasa, federal ID number 18-768-34-9292. You won't find any priors on me. Check it out. I know you've got connections and you're probably using them."

"Now here's what you have to know. Johnson—the slasher—got nabbed after he came in here with no mask. I got sent in to make sure there are no cameras here. The idiot calling the shots here said no mask. If I get nabbed, they'll know this place is bugged and you'll lose a chance to catch them all. They'll also kill my mother and sister. I don't want that to happen." His voice was grim, his face set. "These guys don't play nice. You were smart to get her away when you did."

"Here's what I want. Find my family and get them to safety. My sister teaches at the University of Chicago and her name is Sachiko Koasa. My mother lives with her. You can't warn Sachi in advance because she'll argue with you. Just take her and explain later."

"My com unit is 387-241-5587. Send me a text when Sachiko is safe and I'll get out. Just send one word—Tora. That's T O R A. I know what it means."

"Now what I'm giving you. I'll tell them this house is clean so you can use it one more time. After that they'll probably put it together and I'll be dead. The big shipment is coming through here on the twenty-seventh or twenty-eighth. Get this: *They know what the bliss packaging will be next month and in January.* They don't have to wait. They've never had to wait. They've got an inside man at the top. I probably don't have to tell you it's the Boss but there's someone else he takes orders from too."

"I've been working for them for three years," Kin continued. "I've kept notes that only I can retrieve. You need to get me out of here if you want them. Just rescue my family first. If we have a deal, have someone scrawl the word Sayonara on the South Mall's art wall on Wednesday. I'll see it if it's still there at 4pm. Make it big and at the east end."

"Remember the twenty-seventh or twenty-eighth. My family has to be safe then but not too soon. If word gets here, I'll have to run. Now I'm going to reset our cameras and tell them this house is clean. Don't blow it for me."

Jasper watched, still stunned as the Asian man calmly reset cameras on the first floor and worked his way up in the house. They had an insider? He had to get this to Carlson and the captain. He couldn't trust anyone else on Plains PD with the possible exception of Kruger and Hunter. How the hell did he get so lucky? When the vid ended, he replayed it just to be sure of his facts.

They were going to have to extract his sister and mother and deliver them to a safe house. Too aware of Jewel's vulnerability, he knew it couldn't be the farm. The DEA would have to do it. Damn, he wanted to help but if he were caught on camera, he could be sure of repercussions. Jewel was safe but Mel was still in Plains. They couldn't get David but they sure as hell could strike at Milt and his office staff. No, the people he knew were too vulnerable. Hell, he might have to ask them to kidnap Mel. She'd made it clear she wouldn't leave Plains until her last final was done on the third. After that she would go to David in Denver and he would arrange for her to come to Minnesota later. Corey might come with her.

Well, they might be able to get Baxter before then. If the big shipment was caught, they'd have proof that blissex producers had a connection to Wilson Chemicals. From there it wouldn't be hard to nail Baxter. The only question was whether they could get Wilson Kucera himself.

With quick decisive movements he saved the file and appended it to a message to Carlson then recorded his own conclusions. If Carlson agreed, he'd get the file to Reynolds. Plains PD couldn't do it alone. They would need the DEA–and the DEA would need Plains PD.

That done, he looked at the time. Just after three. If he wanted to get any sleep tonight, he'd better get to it. He hoped Jewel hadn't woke up to find him gone. She didn't need that right now.

Gathering up his drum and com unit, he headed off to bed.

Chapter 29 - Tuesday, 16 Nov 2179

Jasper critically surveyed the corner of the guesthouse they would be using for the interview. He and Uri had shifted the small table to the corner and moved one of the big chairs completely out into the commons. That had freed up more room too, and he didn't want to bring it back in. Now he and Jewel could sit at the table in full view of the camera while Uri would sit off camera in the last big chair. Behind them there was nothing but plain wall. It wouldn't give anyone any clues.

Jewel had gone up to the school to arrange for her absence. At Jasper's suggestion, she was working the first hour but not the rest of the day. Worried about how hard this would be on her, he planned to distract her afterwards. Maybe they would go exploring. Maybe they would stay in. He didn't know.

Looking around the rest of the room, he had to admit it was simply too small for an extended stay. They had closet space and decent dressers and the little kitchen but there was little free floor space. The bed was spacious though. His lips quirked at that. He wondered where they would put visiting kids if this was a typical guest house.

Of course, they only spent evenings here. Unless they spent more time actually here, they didn't need more room. Maybe that was the philosophy.

"Better," Uri said and leaned over to touch the recorder. "Testing." He played it back then moved to check the camera on its stand. "Jazz, sit in the right hand chair please."

He did. "Jewel is about four inches shorter," he said. "Aim on mouth instead of eyes."

"Got it," Uri said. "That takes care of the fussing. It makes you appreciate a regular interrogation room though."

"Right," Jasper said. Since they couldn't use a lot of electronics, they'd gone back to an older less intrusive style with a dedicated camera/recorder backed up by another. Jasper would get a vocal copy on his com unit. No electronics would be touching his wife.

"Now we just have to wait for her to get back," Uri said. "She was going to work an hour?"

"Yes," Jasper said. "I'm hoping it will help relax her. She didn't eat much again this morning—just some crackers and tea."

Uri frowned. "Nerves?"

"Molly thinks that transmitter is irritating her more than anything," Jasper said. "She eats well enough at dinner."

"As long as she's eating," Uri said. "She doesn't have a lot of spare weight."

"I know," Jasper said then set thoughts of that aside. "I have a new development for you." He put last night's vid on the screen and let him watch it through. It was just ending when Jewel walked in.

"What's this?" she asked as the Asian man got busy resetting cameras in the house. "Someone in our house?" There was a flash of anger in her eyes and her mouth set as she watched him plug cameras in. "How?"

"They put an override on the upper door," Jasper said. "This is the second time someone has been in. That's how I identified Johnson for the Plains police. Butler recorded his visit."

"And now you'll get this guy?" Jewel looked a lot happier. "Can we keep nabbing them through the house?"

"Not this one. He knows Butler is there and isn't telling them. He wants out and offered me a deal. I'm waiting to hear back if it's approved," Jasper said. "It's a major break. He's willing to set up the rest if we protect his family and him."

That gave her something to think about.

"Jewel, we'll get them all including their boss." Damn, Uri was there and they had business. He wanted to hold his wife but this wasn't the time. "We need your interview to make that happen."

She nodded then took a deep breath. "I'm ready."

"Then have a seat, Mrs. Stone. Your chair is on the right. Jasper will stay on the left. You'll both be in frame but I won't. You will call me detective and not by my name. That's important since this tape will get analyzed by everyone who can get hold of it."

"It's easier for me to call you lieutenant," Jewel said with a quirk of her lips. "I'm used to that."

Uri hesitated and Jasper wondered what his rank really was. He knew he had to be more than a detective to get an academy post but if he was a lieutenant, that would be too close.

"That's fine," Uri said. "It won't give anything away."

"And when have you ever called me lieutenant?" Jasper asked as they settled into their chairs. "I remember a lot of sirs but not that."

"I hear it all the time," she said. "Even when they don't actually say it, they do. That's why no one believes you've actually left the force—not even me."

Jasper frowned. Was she right? Well, his police friends did forget and gave him his due without thinking. And that doctor in Denver had called him lieutenant. No one here did but they didn't know him that well. That could be a real drawback to his musician image. He'd have to work on that.

"Initial interview of Mrs. Jasper Stone, 16 November 2179. Background: Mrs. Stone, a.k.a. Jewel West was abducted at 2:15 p.m. or 1415 hours on 7 November 2179, from the South Train Terminal, Plains, Wyoming. One officer was killed at that time and another, an FBI agent, was critically injured. Mrs. Stone was recovered at–" he looked at Jasper.

"Approximately eight p.m. 12 November 2179," Jasper finished, slipping back into his old habits. Damn, would he ever lose them?

"Also present for this interview is Mr. Jasper Stone, her husband," Carlson continued. "Mr. Stone, has your wife discussed this with you?"

"No sir." Jasper replied. His hand took hold of Jewel's and he felt her cold fingers press his. He had known this was coming and knew the regulations well. Wanting to get it on official record, he hadn't asked her for any details.

"Sequential interview will follow. Mrs. Stone, tell us what happened at the train station."

"The train station but I-" Jewel looked surprised.

"Sequential, love," Jasper said.

She looked ready to rebel but caught the warning look he gave her and subsided. "Ok, I was at the train station. We'd just checked in and Lori Brown–Detective Brown–was walking with me to the VIP car. The agent was behind us somewhere. A couple of men blocked our way then one of them turned and said something to Lori. I was grabbed from behind and she–Lori–reached for her trank. She turned toward me and there was blood everywhere and–she fought." Her eyes filled with tears and she clasped Jasper's hand hard.

"I heard three shots but didn't see who shot. I cried out but someone sprayed something in my face. I don't remember what happened after that."

"Nothing else at the train station?" Uri asked.

Jewel shook her head, a tear leaving a streak on her cheek. "I woke up in a closet. I was tied up and my com unit was gone."

"What kind of closet?" Uri asked.

"Maintenance," she said. "There was a vacuum and some mops and some tools. There was a cat cage too but it was empty. No smell of cat."

Jasper straightened up. How many maintenance closets housed cats? Cats were rarely confined in such dark places.

"How long were you there?" Uri asked.

"I don't know," Jewel snapped. "It was dark."

"What happened there?" Uri asked.

Jewel glared at him then answered. "They took my picture," she finally said, "then left me alone for hours. When they finally came back a woman told me Lori was dead and I had to record a vid. I did it." Her eyes flew to him and he nodded encouragement. "Did you go?"

"Yes," Jasper said. "I had to."

"Mr. Stone?"

"Jewel told me I had to go to the funeral of Detective Brown and wait for another message. I went. I have a copy of that vid."

"We'll get to that," Uri said. "Mrs. Stone, do you have any idea how long you were in the closet? How many meals you missed? Did you have to pee?"

Jewel frowned, her nose wrinkling as she thought. "I was really hungry and, yes, they made me pee in a bucket." Color rose into her cheeks. "Twice. They didn't feed me but I got water–bottled water."

"Maybe four or five hours?" Jasper said with a look at Uri.

Uri nodded. "How many bottles of water did you drink?"

"Two," Jewel said. "They gave me a third but I couldn't." Her cheeks were really red now.

Jasper almost laughed at her embarrassment but she'd just given them a time frame–a valuable one. "Make it six hours if she didn't drink a third bottle."

"Did you see anyone? At the train station or in the closet?"

"At the train station a big black man–bigger than Jasper. He's the one who killed Lori. The other guy was thin and sort of weasly looking. I didn't see the one behind me. In the closet, I saw the woman and the big black guy."

"What did the woman look like?" Uri asked.

"Like Molly," Jewel said. "But not quite as plump. Black hair and glowers on both cheeks."

"Stop," Jasper said and Uri stopped the camera. "No cuts, right?"

"That's right," Uri said. "This is official. I don't want Molly mentioned though."

"What's wrong?" Jewel asked.

"You gave them a lead to where we are when you mentioned Molly," Jasper said. "We'll have to start over."

"But." Jewel looked ready to cry. "Start over?"

"Start over," Jasper said. "We can't have any cuts or blank anything out. This time find another way to describe that woman."

"But how?" Jewel asked.

"Why did she remind you of Molly?" Uri asked. "Was she plump? Motherly?"

"No, that wasn't it," Jewel said with a frown. She hesitated, looking for the words. "She was no-nonsense like a nurse–professional. Just like Molly when she put on her medical hat."

"That will work," Uri said. "If you can give details about her appearance, even better."

"I'll try," Jewel said. "I'm sorry."

"Not a problem. We caught it early. Don't mention any names except Jasper's."

"What about Lori?" Jewel looked to him.

"It's okay to mention Lori," Jasper said. "No one here or Carlson or Mel or Corey."

"Got it," she said after a moment. "Ok, do it again."

Uri started the camera and did his introduction and they wound their way through it again. This time Jewel was calmer through the train station– a sure sign she'd said it before–but that couldn't be helped. It also wasn't important. They had vid of the train station. When they got to the closet, Uri asked the same questions, finally asking about the woman.

"I think she was about my height but heavier," Jewel said with a frown. "Black hair. She knew what she was doing–like a nurse." She paused. "I think she was a nurse but she had glowers on both cheeks. They were so bright I couldn't even tell what color her eyes were."

"What were the tattoos of?"

"Flowers and butterflies," Jewel said.

"Did they dye your hair in that closet?" Jasper asked.

"No," she said. "They moved me to an apartment–a subby apartment. No kitchen, one room and a bathroom. It was dirty and....a man lived there."

"How do you know that?" Uri asked.

"The laundry," she said. "It was all grey and blue and not neat. I saw underwear too."

Jasper hid a grin. Yes, Jewel would notice that. His wife didn't like laundry on the floor. "Good detail, love."

Jewel flashed him a quick smile.

"So what happened there?" Uri asked. "Did you see any clocks?"

"No," Jewel frowned and shook her head. "I got tied to a chair and they cut and dyed my hair and put butterflies on my face–glowers. Then I had to eat a greasy hamburger–no wrapper–and fries and more water."

"And pee?" Jasper asked.

"Twice," Jewel said. "That was the only time they let me up and the woman was there both times."

"How was she dressed?" Uri asked.

Jewel thought then shook her head. "Not subby clothing. Black pants and a splotchy top with a lot of colors in it." Before they could prompt her, she added. "They made me change to black pants and I had to wear one of those short capes the kids wear."

"Did you sleep there?" Uri asked.

"No." Jewel seemed certain of that. "As soon as I'd changed and my hair was done, they said we were going. I thought I could call for help but they gave me something. After that I could barely walk."

"Do you remember anything else from that day?" Uri asked. "Anything?"

"I remember being outside," Jewel said. "It was raining and I got wet and they were in a hurry. They put me in a car, I think. When I woke up I couldn't see anything."

"Couldn't see?"

"Blindfold," she said. "The woman was there and told me not to take it off if I wanted to live. I didn't. When I felt it, I was bandaged all around my head."

"Hungry?"

"Famished," she said. "And I had to poop." Her cheeks flamed red again. "The bathroom was really small and smelled funny."

"Were your hands free?" Jasper asked.

"Then, yes," she said. "When I was sitting down, no."

"When you escaped the city, you told us you thought you were on a plane. Why?" Uri asked with a warning look at Jasper.

"The bathroom," she said. "I could barely turn around. It was really awkward. And when they made me lie down, I had buckles in my back. It wasn't a bed with sheets either. The fabric had a weave to it."

"Makes sense," Uri said. "Do you know how long you were there?"

Jewel shook her head then said "No." After a moment, she added without looking at him. "They told me they were going to give me truth serum and I would sleep. I don't remember anything of that."

"It was Penseek," Jasper said. "He told me."

"Who told you?" Uri demanded.

"The bastard who returned her," Jasper said. "Not my interview."

Uri looked interested but turned back to Jewel. "Do you remember anything after that?"

"Waking up famished again," Jewel said. "Having to poop again. Same small bathroom. Then they made me sit on a chair and it moved. Then I was outside again. Then a car–and a shot. When I woke up, Jasper was there and we..." she stopped abruptly, her eyes going to him.

Uri cleared his throat. "You said they. Do you have any idea how many were at your plane?"

Jewel thought, her brow wrinkling. "The woman, the big black man–I'm sure I heard him. There was another too but I only heard him once. He told them not to hurt me because I was no good to him dead."

Baxter. Jasper knew who that had to be. That cold-hearted son-of-a-bitch. "Can you recall ever having heard him before? Anywhere?"

Jewel's eyes flew to him and, puzzled, she shook her head.

"End of interview," Uri said. "Jasper, what are you getting at?"

"You'll have to debrief me but not in front of Jewel," Jasper said. "I also have vid on what happened at the house."

"Is it off?" Jewel asked with a wave toward the camera. "Really off?"

"Yes," Uri said.

"Mr. Carlson said he got the number of that private jet," she said. "Will he need proof I was on it?"

"That's what he'll look for, yes." Jasper said then caught her little smile. "What did you do?"

"I was wearing my lucky ring," she said. "The one Uncle Rory gave me. It's engraved and I tucked it into the seat cushions. I thought they'd notice if I left my wedding rings."

Her lucky ring? Jasper smiled then turned to Uri. "It's a pearl with two tiny sapphires and it's engraved."

"You took a hell of a chance, Jewel," Uri said. "But that would be proof. Do you have pictures of it?"

"In my insurance file," Jewel said. "And my love just happened to put it in my suitcase along with Grandmother's box and my little bit of jewelry."

"I didn't even notice that ring wasn't there," Jasper admitted. "I wasn't thinking too clearly when I packed that." Hell, he barely remembered packing anything at all. David had done most of it. He had remembered her grandmother's box because of the insurance file and financial documents. As Jewel had once told him, David didn't know where the box was hidden. He did.

"Ok, another question. How many days was she gone?" Uri asked Jasper. "Five?"

"She was taken the afternoon of the seventh," Jasper said in a flat tone. "And returned about eight p.m. on the twelfth." He clasped Jewel's hand tightly.

"That's what I thought you said," Uri replied with a furrowed brow. "Jewel, how much weight did you lose?"

"Almost ten pounds," she said in a quiet voice.

"Ten pounds?" Jasper stared at her. His wife had always been slender. Losing ten pounds in that short period was nearly impossible unless–"Do you remember any meals?"

"A few," she said with a shrug. "I was too scared to eat–and I don't remember much when I wasn't scared."

"How much have you gained back?" Uri asked.

"Four," she said. "I'm working on it," she said in a defensive tone. "I just can't eat much at a time."

"Uh-huh." Jasper realized he hadn't paid enough attention. Those bastards hadn't even fed her decently. One more reason to take them down.

"Molly said I'm doing ok," she said. "I'm just not supposed to miss any meals." Her eyes went to the clock and Jasper realized it was near lunchtime.

"And you didn't eat much breakfast," Jasper said. "Uri, can we break till after lunch?"

"Sounds good to me," Uri said. "Then I just need you–and I want to see that vid of what happened at the house. We should attach it if we want the FBI off our backs."

"I have to ask Carlson about that," Jasper said. "It's his case." Jewel perked up at that but he was not going to let his nosy wife in. "You can watch it though."

"And I can't," Jewel said.

"You don't want to see me trussed up," he grimly said. "You have enough nightmares now."

Her eyes widened but she didn't argue. Seeing the shine in her eyes, he knew she was close to tears.

"Let's get fed," Jasper said. "When I'm done with my debriefing how about we go find the hydroponic buildings and see what's so exciting about them?"

"Ok. I can do laundry too," she said. "You need more clothes."

On that prosaic remark, they left the apartment with Uri.

Chapter 30 - Debrief

Jasper settled into the right-hand seat this time and waited for Uri to adjust the camera and give him the go ahead. He had already decided his debriefing must take the form of an official report. Uri might question him at the end to clarify things but he'd get it out first–without mentioning his DEA status. He didn't know how much longer he'd be useful to DEA but he didn't want to shorten the time by revealing it now.

When Uri gave the signal, he looked into the camera and began. "I'm Jasper Stone, formerly a police lieutenant of Plains, Wyoming, and this is my official statement which I will re-record later in an interrogation chair. None are available at my current location."

"First off I have the confession of Edward Kucera and would like to state for the record he never met me. I called his office to set up an appointment once and he took the call. Basically he refused to cooperate or set an appointment because I was out of my jurisdiction on the West murders. We never spoke again or met. At the time I was not engaged to Jewel West."

"My wife believes he was referring to Professor Andrew Nugent who she was briefly engaged to. I know for a fact that Professor Nugent was the last visitor to Mr. Kucera and they were acquainted. I've seen the vid of that meeting even though the record and the vid have since been lost. Unfortunately, Professor Nugent died of a bliss reaction on November sixth. I don't know the status of that investigation."

"Kucera's second statement concerning my wife, Jewel West, seems logical and even I had to stop and consider it but it isn't true. If Mr. Kucera had been better acquainted with the West Foundation, he would have known neither Jewel nor Jake would have gained anything by being a sole survivor. Both would have had sixty million made available to them on their thirtieth birthdays but that amount would neither increase nor decrease if other family members died. The West Foundation controls the bulk of the West fortune, which is in the billions. What Jewel will have as her personal fortune will always be sixty million." He noticed Uri's astonished look but didn't let it interrupt his flow. "My wife would give every cent of it up to get her relatives back–especially her Uncle Mike who was the closest thing she had to a father. She values family more than money and always will."

Taking a deep breath, he continued. "I admit I suspected Jake before I knew the truth of their inheritance but that was the same ignorance. I am aware through Jake's confession that he attempted to kill his grandmother. He was being blackmailed but I am no longer certain it was Edward Kucera."

"Jake believed it was Kucera. I am sure Samuel Starling knows who it was but he still hasn't been questioned. I would like to know why, after four months, he's still not been questioned under verifying drugs when he's been seen on vid killing Jake West and was caught with a deadly weapon attempting to kill David West. He's been charged with murder and attempted murder. My wife has not. Until Samuel Starling has been questioned properly, my wife will not agree to any more interrogations. Her cooperation has ended."

He knew that wasn't going to be popular but there was no way in hell he'd let them get away with treating his wife that way even when no charges were pending. Their ill-conceived end run around legal procedure had cost two people their lives and could have cost hers. Deliberately he sipped the coffee he had sitting there and let time run on.

"At the request of the West Foundation, I am re-examining the case evidence from the West murders as a private consultant. If you have problems with that, contact David West."

Another sip of coffee then he refolded his hands and looked at the camera. "Regarding the kidnapping of my wife, I am attaching the vid of my wife and a picture of the instructions I received at the funeral of Detective Lori Brown."

"I was first shown a picture of my wife by David West with a note for the police to back off. That picture and note were copied by Plains PD. That was late on the seventh and I don't remember the time. On the eighth I received the vid. I attended Detective Brown's funeral on the eleventh to receive my other instructions and pay my respects to my partner of eight years." He paused, his breath catching in his throat. To cover his lapse, he took another gulp of coffee and waited till his eyes quit burning. "The note was left in the basket of cards. David West found it and handed it to me."

"After that I returned home and David West returned to Denver. On the evening of the twelfth, they came into the house through the upper door. I let them in." His voice was wooden. "They checked the house for surveillance and chained me up. There were four of them at first. I got first names on three: Joey, Carl, and Rod. The one who muscled me around and threatened me has been identified since as Chuma Johnson—he's the one who killed my partner." His voice was fierce. "He's in custody."

"The fifth one I have no name on," Jasper said. "The sixth was called Boss. The five wore full head masks. The Boss wore a stealth mask. He had icy blue eyes and a plain earring and was white. By his manner of speaking, I have to say he had a college education. So did the fifth guy who was their technician. Chuma Johnson does not. I didn't hear enough of the others to know."

"The Boss and one of the others brought my wife in unconscious and put her where I could touch her with my one free hand. My other hand and feet were chained," Jasper reported in a wooden tone. "Before I was chained, they had me open up the family safe—a Matrix model 3418-3 with palm print ID and finger combination. They removed my flashers, a second com unit I kept in there, two thousand dollars cash and approximately a thousand in cash cards."

"They then proceeded to move stuff through my house into the city and plant cameras. The one I call the Boss wanted to know what I knew about Professor Nugent's death and admitted to killing him by accident, which tallied with what I observed. The professor had a reaction when they injected him with penseek, which has a bliss element in it. The Boss gave me the name of the drug that caused his reaction as being blister and wanted to know why the professor had it. I didn't have that answer."

Uri was writing down notes now, his pen flying across paper.

"He then told me my wife had been injected with it and I had to keep her away from bliss. He wanted me to find the answers about the professor. I haven't done it. He also told me my wife was boobytrapped and he had a button that could kill her. I had some idea what that could be and it was confirmed by medical examination. I'll attach that report." His jaw tightened as he remembered that moment and his fists clenched. Deliberately, he took another gulp of his cooling coffee.

"Before leaving he told me I was to stay in Plains with my wife and have no further contact with the police. He also said the boxes they were moving into the city that night had nothing illegal in them. It was a dry run to see if the police would stay out of the way. They did."

"He left the key for my chains a few feet from me. My wife had been given Sleeper. Some hours after they left, she woke up and managed to release me," Jasper said. "I cut off two tracers they'd planted on her, confirmed she had a transmitter signal, and at three am we left the city when I felt surveillance might be lax."

He finished drinking his evelle then cradled the cup in his hands. "There was a car waiting and a plane. At the airport we saw a private plane, which Jewel felt she had been on. It's number and company were noted by Agent Ray Carlson, DEA. I did not get the number. After that we were taken to Denver where a government doctor examined my wife and found a drug we have tentatively identified as blister in a birth control device. She also has an imbedded transmitter in her womb that could... detonate... and kill her... any time she gets the right signal. That can't be removed until the battery runs down."

His hands clenched on the coffee cup so tightly his knuckles went white. "We are now in a safe house and I intend to keep my wife here until that damned transmitter is out. If you need to contact me, I can be reached only through Agent Carlson."

"End of report," he curtly said and motioned to Uri to cut it off. Without waiting for leave, he walked into the bathroom and bent over the sink, his hands clutching the rim. He fought back the frustration, the anger, the helplessness he'd felt in those moments and tried to concentrate on the present. He had Jewel. She was safe. Those bastards would never touch her again.

Gradually he calmed then splashed water on his face before returning to the main room. Grabbing his coffee cup, he took a moment to refill it. Uri waved his cup at him and he refilled it too.

"I'm glad we did this first before I saw that vid," Uri said, his voice gruff. "That must have been hell."

"It was," Jasper said then drank deep of the barely warm coffee. "I'm not going to give them that tape."

Uri studied him then asked, "Does Carlson have it?"

"Yes."

"Then I'll agree to omit it. If you're right, it's DEA business and not FBI," Uri said with such calm authority that Jasper wondered again what his rank actually was. "I do need to view it."

"I know," Jasper said. "I don't want to be here."

"Understood," Uri said. "You were thorough and I don't think I have questions except about that drug. He called it blister? What do you know about that?"

"Damned little," Jasper said. "The first time it showed up was in Edward Kucera. He finished that damned confession, asked for a bliss tab when he was ready for bed and laid down and died of the reaction so quietly the bed sensors didn't go off until his heart stopped. No one gave him that drug and he'd been in custody for several days before he suicided."

"You know it was suicide and not an accidental reaction?"

"He was ordered to suicide by Professor Nugent," Jasper said. "Another vid you need to see. That was the first real proof we had that Nugent was involved with anything. I suspected him because he was once engaged to Jewel but he passed that interrogation."

"You didn't pull him in?" Uri asked.

"No. We thought it was the blissex organization and waited to see where he would lead us. Instead they tried to question him with penseek and he died of the same bliss reaction during questioning. We found the drug that time in his medicine chest and it was disguised as low dose aspirin—same color and size."

Uri looked thoughtful. "Any analysis?"

"Not of those," Jasper said. "The investigation into his death was shut down and all materials—plus his body—were confiscated. Officially Professor Nugent died while grading papers in his study."

"Who shut it down?" Uri asked, his tone sharp. "Was he a fed?"

"We don't know," Jasper said. "He's not DEA and probably not FBI. CIA would have no business in Plains."

"That doesn't leave much," Uri said. "ATF and the Secret Service were folded into Homeland Security nearly a century ago. If he was, he was probably HSS or CIA. I just don't know why they'd have someone in a small city. What did he do?"

"He was a history professor with a love of books," Jasper said. "He didn't like bliss, much less blissex, and hated scandals. He also recorded his lectures in a series of vid broadcasts for the subby channel—and he was a major donor to Reach Out."

"And he was engaged to Jewel?" Uri said. "A history professor?"

"I don't think it was his idea," Jasper said. "He was a good friend of Mike West's and Mike was checking into euthanasia. Professor Nugent might have agreed to marry Jewel to ease Mike's mind not hers."

"Fate worse than death, I think," Uri said.

"After you see the vid, you'll be sure of that. Jake called him a stuffed shirt." Jasper remembered that description. "And I have to agree."

"Ok, you found this blister in his possession—and you said it was in a birth control implant too? And Carlson said it was found in the FBI agent as a liquid? Or was that Reynolds? I'm starting to get confused."

"One of the two," Jasper said, his lips twitching. "It wasn't David. I'm beginning to wonder if it might be as big a problem as blissex."

"Not if it's just used to kill or suicide," Uri said. "But we need to track it down. First though give me those vids. If you don't mind, I'll watch them here and make copies to append to the interviews-or do we want that?"

"I'm in favor of getting the Kucera one into as many hands as possible," Jasper said. "Not the one from the house."

"Noted. Ok, go find your wife. I'll see to this."

Jasper stepped out into the commons then got his bearings. He knew Jewel was doing laundry and had seen the small laundromat near the stores. He was gradually learning his way around and thought he understood the organization to a point. The buildings that needed road access—the main offices and the stores—were on the side of the commons that faced the main road. The small medical clinic was also over there. Houses lined the other sides with small apartments like his in the underground. They weren't really guest apartments but housing for those adults who hadn't enough income for a house and had no children. Roads led off through the underground in three directions, giving access to the barns and outbuildings. He'd found Rabbit Run, which led to the rabbit and poultry barns. The other two were named Farmer's Row and Milk Lane.

Walking into the small laundromat, Jasper hesitated then spotted his wife taking clothes out of a dryer. Another woman was also there so he resisted the urge to hug his wife and just admired the view. That damned skirt again. He turned to the other woman. "Hello, looks like I'm on time."

"To fold? Yes, you'd better get to it," she said. "You must be Jasper."

"Yes," he said. "And you?"

"Beth," she said. "I'm Kale's wife and an aquaculture specialist. I raise the fish."

"Fish?" Jasper didn't remember hearing about fish.

"Part of the hydroponic operation," she said as Jewel joined them. "We need fish for the plants. I grow them and make sure they stay healthy. We mostly have catfish, trout, and lake bass."

"That must take a lot of water," Jasper said.

"Not something we're short of," she said. "Minnesota, land of ten thousand lakes."

Jasper gave his wife a smile and started folding automatically. "I'm surprised you can even build underground then."

"We can, just not very deep," Beth said as she moved to help. "Twelve feet is the limit and even then we pump some water out and use it in the fish farm. How deep did your city go?"

"We had a total of six levels," Jasper said. "Maybe a hundred feet. They only have water problems near the river and lake. That gets pumped into the city water supply."

"The best way to handle it," she said. "If it persists in being a problem, make it a benefit."

"Right," Jasper said and reached for the last pair of his pants. "Is this all?" He looked at Jewel, half expecting her to say there was another load or two.

"All," she said. "You don't have many clothes you know. They're all black too."

"I've got some blue shirts," he said.

"Yes but you're going to get tired of wearing black dress pants and dark shirts," she said. "And Beth and I are going to fix that."

Jasper eyed her. "Are you trying to change my image?"

Beth laughed as Jewel gave him a stern look. "You stick out like a sore thumb. We're supposed to be in hiding and you don't look like you belong here."

Jasper glanced down at his black pants and city shoes and ruefully had to agree. No one else wore such nice polished shoes. If he was going to have to go outside, he needed others. He wasn't going to leave the farm for just that though.

"I give," he said. "Who do we have to call to open the store?"

"We've already got permission," Jewel said. "Beth can do it."

"Storekeeper too?" Jasper eyed her.

"No, we're too small to have people permanently assigned there," Beth said. "The rule is any senior resident not related to the customers can play storekeeper. The key is kept in here and we log it out and log it in. I got my senior status a year ago."

"Does it take a while to get it?" Jasper asked, curious. She looked to be in her twenties.

"Depends on the person," she said. "We have to have firm ties to the farm, understand the economics of it, and be trustworthy. Uncle Harold said I was ready so I got it. Kale is still waiting."

"Is that unusual?" Jasper asked.

"No," she said but her smile was tighter. "Kale married in and he's still making his place. Minnesota is pretty different from Hawaii and he's still adjusting. Teaching martial arts has helped since no one around here has a teacher. He teaches here three days a week and three days a week over at Sunrise Farms–they're just across the state line in Wisconsin."

"Sounds good," Jasper said as she opened a small safe with a code combination and took out an old-fashioned key. "Will this take long?"

She laughed. "Two customers at once? Not at all."

Over the next hour Jasper found himself waited on by not one but two attentive women. He didn't have much to say because they knew what he needed and what he should wear. He came away with boots, brown loafers, blue jeans and black jeans, a black leather belt, flannel shirts, sweaters, underwear, and a warm hat for outdoor wear. It was a new experience for him because Carol had never attempted to pick out his clothes. Jewel though was having fun and he let her dress him like she would an oversized doll.

It was nice having just the three of them in the store. Beth was kept busy replacing items and ringing up others for them on one of their cash cards. Once Jewel had his size, she found what she wanted him to have.

She had good taste he had to admit. The flannel shirts all had patterns but those she picked had some black running through it. He found he liked the green, black, and white one the best.

"You're going to have a lot more laundry to do after this," Jasper said as they finished up. He looked like a farmer now although he'd opted to wear the brown loafers instead of boots. The jeans were pre-washed and he liked the feel of them.

"I'll do it," she said. "And those won't show white hair on them so bad."

"White hair?" Jasper wondered.

"That white cat must have got into the apartment and laid on the laundry," she said. "I found white hair on your pants."

Remembering his late night session, Jasper smiled. Before he could confess though, Jewel added, "If he won't come to me, I don't want him in there."

"That cat's magic," Beth said. "He hasn't really warmed up to anyone since Sasha left but plays the field–and gets into some really strange places. I caught him terrorizing the fish and Kale says he attends his classes regularly."

"Kung fu cat?" Jasper smiled, remembering an old cartoon.

"Karate kit?" Jewel added.

Beth laughed. "Heard them," she said. "He's strictly an indoor cat with all that hair but he thinks the entire underground is his."

Jasper wondered what the other resident cats thought about that but decided not to ask or confess to Jewel he'd been petting the beast. He'd let her solve that mystery on her own.

"You're going to need another cash card," Beth said. "This one is about played out."

"I'll get another," Jewel said but Jasper stopped her and handed over the one from his wallet. It was for fifty dollars. He frowned at it, suddenly remembering that scene in the apartment. Had he picked that card up? He usually didn't buy cards that were less a hundred. If he had–snapping the card back, he fished out another one worth five hundred.

"I'm not sure that fifty dollar card is good," he said. His hand trembled slightly as he put it back. If that was the card, the serial number could be known to Baxter. He might even have paid to have a tracer put on it although that would cost more than the card was worth. More importantly, Jasper might be able to do a reverse trace to see who had purchased it where. It was a slim hope that Baxter had bought it but something he could have checked out. In any case, he needed to get it away from here before it got used.

Damn, he needed to do something about that thirty million. He couldn't until his bank card was restored or he could get to the Chicago bank. He could possibly do it by com unit but he'd have to talk to one of the upper management. Once he had that throw away com unit, he might do that. What time would someone pick up the farm's mail? Had they been told about the PO box? He couldn't fetch it himself. The PO box wasn't his.

"You're thinking too hard," Jewel said as the last purchase was rung up. "Do we need to go back?"

"To deliver this stuff, yes." He said. "And I need to ask Uri a question. Then we'll explore."

"Right," she said with a too bright smile. "Let's get it done."

"Use the cart," Beth suggested. "Bring it back and park it outside the store later. That will save your back."

"Thanks and thanks for the help. Jewel has got shopping out of her system, I think."

"For today," Jewel said. "I'm keeping this card."

"Good idea," Jasper said. "Order some coffee with it."

Jewel smiled. "That's already been done. With luck, we'll have a big grinder and a fifty pound bag of beans tomorrow."

"Fifty pounds?" Beth paused in locking up the store.

"He drinks a lot of coffee," Jewel responded before he could. "Seriously, the big grinder is a commercial one and it's going into the grocery store. I made a deal with Aunt Lill and she'll price the coffee just high enough that it will pay off the grinder."

"Smart," Beth said. "Fresh ground coffee is the best and I haven't had it since college."

"That's where I got hooked on it too," Jasper said. "You did order Aruba?"

"Of course," Jewel said. "But not from your usual source. I ordered it out of New York just in case anyone was watching."

"Good," Jasper said, a little surprised she'd been that quick. He wasn't worried about Baxter and his crowd being able to trace him that way but the FBI could if they knew enough about his coffee habit. "Let's go exploring."

Tugging the cart with their purchases and laundry behind, they made there way back to their apartment. Uri was still there and his face cracked into a grin when he saw Jasper. Surprised, Jasper looked at him suspiciously. "New development?"

"Nope, I just watched those vids. I assume you didn't cut either one before giving them to Carlson?"

"No, of course not." Jasper frowned.

"Should have," Uri said then tried to quit smiling when Jewel looked at him. "I think I'd better get."

"I have a couple of questions," Jasper said before he could escape. "What time will they pick up from that PO box? Do they even know about it?"

"Yes, they know to check it. We have other stuff come through it. Jim picks up the mail this month and he'll get it all. He should be back by four. Anything else?"

"Yes," Jasper said. "This card was one the Boss gave to me. I don't have any hope of fingerprints but the serial number might be interesting. Can you run it officially when you get back to work?" He held up the fifty-dollar card.

"Will do," Uri said. "Was he wearing gloves?"

"Yes," Jasper said.

"No fingerprints then," Uri said. "Ok, I've got the camera out and collected those files. The one flasher is still in the dock. I queued it up to the interesting part." He was grinning again. "I would love to have seen Carlson's face."

He left and Jasper could hear him chuckling. There was nothing amusing on that vid. Frowning, he turned it on and saw himself. Jewel gasped then burst out laughing.

He reddened as he saw himself in his naked glory, his staff semi-erect and clearly visible. Damn, when had he stood like that? The only thing he had on was his locket.

"Don't you dare delete that," Jewel said and swatted his hand away from the dock. "I want a copy."

"I'm not deleting it," Jasper said. "That vid is too damned important to delete—and Carlson." It finally sunk in that he hadn't told Butler to stop recording until he copied the record. Thank God that metal-assed Butler didn't have eyes in the bedroom!

"Carlson got that?" Now Jewel was blushing too. "And did he get us?"

"No, I told you I wouldn't have Butler looking up my ass," Jasper said. "This is why." Damn he was going to have to live that down. Hopefully Carlson had cut it before entering it into evidence. He should have watched the damned thing after all.

"I won't poke into the rest if you give me that one bit," Jewel said. "I want to see you, all of you, walking bare assed naked through our house."

"Witch," Jasper said. "You'll send it off."

"I won't share it with anyone on Earth," she said, holding up her right hand. "I promise."

Jasper looked at her suspiciously. "Sasha."

Jewel burst out laughing and he felt the heat rise again. "Minx, not even her."

She shook her head and those curls flew everywhere. Grabbing her head to keep it from bobbing, he pulled her closer and pressed his hips against hers. Her eyes widened but she pulled away.

Thinking she wasn't in the mood, Jasper just grinned when she pulled the cart the rest of the way inside and locked the deadbolt. Well, he could explore right here.

Chapter 31 - New Start

It was well past four before Jasper was ready to face the world again. Aware he needed that com unit, he left Jewel putting clothes away and sought out Jim Talbot. Seeing no sign of him, he headed for the small import store next to the grocery. That would be the logical place to pick up packages.

He didn't recognize the woman manning the counter but there were a lot of people he still didn't have names for. She seemed to know who he was because she smiled and reached under the counter for a package. "It's not addressed to Jasper Stone but I figure Mr. J. S. is you?"

"Probably," he said. "Let me see the return address." The package was the right size and it did come from Chicago. He looked at the return address and grinned. "The Merry Lantern," he said. "That must be it."

It was clever of Mary to put that. He'd sent her to have dinner at the Lantern and she knew he'd recognize the reference. It was too bad she hadn't come up with something more creative for his name. Well, maybe she was in a hurry.

"Jim figured you were out about the place somewhere so he left it here," she said. "Anytime you need something else ordered, remember we're here."

"I will," Jasper said. "This just couldn't come straight to a farm address. Did Jewel get coffee ordered?"

"Yes sir," she said. "Lots of it. We should have it Thursday."

"It will be nice to have fresh ground again," Jasper said then extracted himself from the conversation. He needed to check the com unit out and get messages sent.

Stopping at the first group of seats, he snapped open the reusable plastic box and pulled out an older model Galaxy. Perfect. It had a good-sized screen and texting features but not a lot of other options. The keyboard on these was comfortable and not as cramped as newer models, and he was pleased with the choice.

Using the reset options first, he restored the unit to factory defaults and programming then used his cash card to buy time for it. When it asked for his identity, he typed in Jazz Weststone. That was far enough off that an automated search wouldn't turn up the unit. At the same time, people would recognize it as him. That done he started keying in the message for Sanders and sent it off.

Who else? It was nearly five but his bank was in the same time zone now. Before he could think twice, he keyed in the number and waited for a response. He was dealing with the main bank now and they prided themselves on being open all American business hours from East Coast to West. They should still be open. Whether a manager was available would be the key question.

The switchboard answered and Jasper waited for the operator to finish identifying the bank then spoke in a crisp tone. "This is Jasper Stone. I need to speak to a manager."

"Yes sir." The operator was quick and professional. He had to give her marks for that. It took a minute, maybe two, before he was seeing another secretary.

"Can I help you, sir?" she asked.

"Yes, this is Jasper Stone, account number 8231448VAX. I need to speak to a manager."

The secretary's eyes widened slightly and she nodded. "Of course, Mr. Stone. I'll transfer you right away."

Jasper felt a smile on his lips. The next transfer was very quick. It always was when he ran that account number by them. They didn't have so many millionaire clients that they could afford to annoy one and the VAX account designation was limited to them.

"Mr. Stone," the manager said. "Yes, it is you. I'm Ira Fleming and I'll be happy to help you."

"Thanks," Jasper said, eyeing him. "I need a favor. I had to report my account card stolen and the new one hasn't caught up with me yet. Could you please pull up my account?" He repeated the account number for him.

"Of course," the manager said. When he saw the balance, his smile widened.

"Give me the balance, please," Jasper said.

"Thirty two million five thousand and fifty two dollars and thirty cents," the manager said. "A very impressive balance."

"Yes, more impressive than usual," Jasper said. "Now I need you to reverse the deposit of the thirty million and send it back where it came from."

"Mr. Stone?" The manager looked shocked.

"I think you can do that, am I right? Or does your authorization go that high?" Jasper tried to look puzzled. This manager was younger than most and he knew bankers had limits. Let's see what his were.

"I can do it but it's very unusual," the manager said. "Reverse the deposit? Refuse it?"

"It would be more unusual if I told you to open a new transaction," Jasper said. "And you'd be perfectly right in refusing to do so since, as I told you, my account card is in the process of being replaced. Would you like my security information?"

"Yes sir. That would be appropriate."

"The first word is Melody and the second is Requiem. My number code is 9993478," Jasper said and waited for him to check the security codes.

"Yes sir, I can see you're Jasper Stone," he said. "And you simply want the thirty million returned to the depositer?"

"Yes, that's it." Jasper almost relaxed. Not as hard as he thought it would be.

"That's been noted," the manager said. "Now would you like a new account card? We can cut one very quickly at this location."

Jasper considered it then nodded. "Yes but I want it held there. I'll be in Chicago probably Thursday and will pick it up. Since my identity card was also stolen and not yet replaced, I'll have to verify anyway."

"Yes sir. I'll start them on your new account card tomorrow morning. The thirty million will be transferred tonight. Your new account balance is two million five thousand fifty two dollars and thirty cents."

"That sounds right," Jasper said. "Thank you, Mr. Fleming."

The manager beamed, happy that he'd remembered his name, and Jasper cut the connection. Just another thing done. He should try to get an interview with the Centrax CEO but wasn't sure he'd be available this close to five. Besides, he had arrangements to make before he talked to Blaine Robbins. He wanted to be sure he could get in and out of the building and he wanted to make damned sure that corporate seal was real. He'd do that tomorrow.

Uri was probably with his brother's family. Aware that Ivan would be tired after processing birds, he decided to return to Jewel. He could cook tonight and maybe lure her away to where that piano was. It would be good to play again.

"Mary," he said and picked up the com unit. Scrounging in the box, he found a number written on a slip of paper. That would be Milt's new number. Keying it in he was surprised when Mary answered instead.

"Mr. Stone," she said. "Good to see you again."

"Can I ask why?" he asked, knowing there had to be a good reason.

"I asked Mr. Anderson if he wanted to know when you called the office. He said no so I kept this phone. I'll help you any way I can."

"He's still got an FBI tag?" Jasper frowned.

"Yes sir." Mary looked very noncommittal, a sure sign she didn't like it.

"In the morning tell him that APB has been lifted. It was lifted last night but he can't kick them to the curb tonight and make it stick. It might take Brad's legal muscle."

"Yes sir." Mary looked happier. "Now is there anything I can do for you?"

"Yes, there is. Can you tell me how well Milt and Brad know Blaine Robbins?"

She blinked. "I don't think Mr. Anderson knows him at all but Mr. Brad–yes, he'd know him. He's a Comets supporter and being in corporate law, he almost has to know him."

"I may need to meet with Mr. Robbins. I'd like to talk to Brad about it first," Jasper said.

"Would you like his number?" Mary asked.

"Yes, please," Jasper said, smiling. "Milt is damned lucky to have you."

"Thank you," she said and Jasper noted with surprise that her cheeks had gone pink. "Here is the number. His office phone is...." and she rattled it off. "His secretary is Cleo. Ask about her cat and she'll put you right in."

"Her cat?" Jasper was mystified.

"Brad's important clients know to ask about the cat. It's a code," Mary said. "And it keeps reporters out."

"Ah," Jasper said. "Do you have a similar one?"

"Not for you," she said. "As long as I can see you, I know who you are." She looked slightly embarrassed at that admission.

"I will try not to call you when I'm in disguise then," Jasper said. "Mary, forget about that. It actually worked out well. David West heard who I was at the right moment and we've developed a good working relationship from it."

"I'm glad," Mary said. "Here's the home number."

Jasper took it down. "Does he have a com unit number?"

"That one I can't release," she said. "I have it for emergencies only."

Jasper considered it then nodded. "You're right. This isn't an emergency. If I need him that badly, I'll let you relay it. Good enough?"

"Yes sir." She looked more relaxed. "How is your wife?"

"She's happier now that we're away from Plains," Jasper said. "There's enough for her to do and she's getting acquainted."

"And you? I am to ask if you need a new music system," Mary said.

"I've thought about it but the one in Plains is customized," Jasper said. "I'll get it back. In the meantime, I've got a new instrument I'm playing with. It's a century old lotus drum. I'll send you a sample when I'm satisfied with it."

"That would be nice," Mary said. "Tell Jewel I'm thinking about her and I'm glad she's safe."

"I will," Jasper said. "There's nothing else right now. Thanks for the help."

Thursday. If he could arrange to meet Blaine Robbins this Thursday, he could hit his bank as well and maybe stop in and see Milt. No, that was day after tomorrow. It might have to be Friday. He still wanted that corporate seal verified and see what ties Kucera had with Centrax.

Jewel wouldn't be happy if he kept working tonight and, frankly, he needed some play time. It could wait until morning.

* * *

"Are you going to show me where that piano is tonight?" Jasper asked as he pulled the last dish from the drainer and wiped it dry.

"Do I get to listen?" Jewel asked, her smile expectant.

"Yes, witch but bring a book. I don't want you doing some sensuous dance and trying to break my concentration." He'd experienced that before and, even though it led to a lot of fun, tonight he wanted to compose.

"Now would I do that?" Jewel said in an injured tone.

"You have done that," Jasper said. "And you've had your fun already." He scowled at her with mock ferocity.

"But what if I want an encore?" Jewel asked and slipped closer to him, running her hand over his flannel-covered chest. "Just a quick one?" Her hand slipped inside his shirt and stroked his bare chest. "I like this shirt."

"Witch," he said but didn't draw away. Picking her up, he sat her down on the kitchen counter. "We need a bigger kitchen," he observed. "Can't escape." So saying, he slipped by her just as her leg came up to block him. "Missed."

She slid off the counter just as they heard a deep bell sound. Frozen in place, they both listened intently and heard a lighter tone follow it.

"Fire?" Jewel asked.

"I don't think so," Jasper said and ran a quick hand down the apartment door before opening it and stepping out. "The second tone was different and light."

Having spent most of their lives in undergrounds, both knew about warning bells and sirens. They were supposed to be standardized though and that wasn't one they'd learned. The cities were actually built so well with such good fire suppression systems that evacuation rarely spread beyond the house affected and its immediate neighbors above and to the sides. With no one above or below and the usual building gaps on the side, they should be safe enough.

"There's people out here," he said, sticking his head back in. "Come on."

"Assembly?" Jewel ventured a guess. "Weird."

Farmers, children, and others were all gathering near the big vid screen. Molly and Ivan seemed to be leading the excited pack.

"What is it?" Jasper asked as they got closer.

"Mail from Sasha," one of the kids said with a big grin. "For all of us."

Jewel's hand snaked into his and he half-turned to find her smiling. She always liked hearing from Sasha. They'd barely known Jake's wife four months ago but Jewel had developed a long distance friendship with her since. Now the infrequent message bursts from the colony ship allowed Sasha to send messages home. They were always careful to reply, knowing that Sasha was so isolated from the rest of her kin.

"We have the entire message queue," Ivan was saying. "Not many individual ones this time but she has the group message for all of us. Molly will deliver individual messages when she gets them sorted out."

Jewel leaned closer to him. "She doesn't know we're here yet," she said. "Can I tell her we're visiting?"

Jasper considered it. "No harm in telling her. Just remember no dark stuff."

Jewel's smile faded but she nodded.

"Let's watch this," Jasper said as people started claiming seats or standing room where they could see the large vid screen. When everyone was settled, Molly put the flasher in the dock port and called up the general message. The vid screen cleared at once to show Sasha twice as large as life sitting cross-legged on her bunk.

Sasha Kowalski West looked as pretty as ever with her long yellow braid tossed dangling over one shoulder. She was barefoot and wore a halter top and shorts that left little to the imagination. If Jasper hadn't known better, he would have placed her age at about fifteen, not the twenty-six years he knew she had. He already knew the colonists tended to wear just enough for decency since clothing was weighed like everything else. Laundry was also a factor in space. She did look good and when someone let out a wolf whistle, everyone laughed.

"Hi, guys," she said without uncoiling from her bunk. "Another letter from almost Mars." She smiled. "It's the same boring routine. I look after the animals, do my exercises, and eat and sleep. I did have a new litter of bunnies today and one of the chickens finally listened to me and laid an egg. Lucky won't be on the menu tonight."

There was a stir of laughter and Jasper guessed Lucky had been a subject before.

"I finished reading that new book Betty recommended and I'm still trying to get through the god awful veterinary text Dad sent. The only thing that helps is I can skip the chapters on cows and horses because we don't have any. Bob, you need to rewrite that book into English for us poor Martians. If you could just call a spade a spade and a tit a tit, it would help."

"Spades?" Dr. Bob looked confused.

"It's in the chapter on how to play poker while you're waiting for the calf to drop," someone said and there was more laughter. Molly waved them to be quiet.

"Now I got something to show you," Sasha said and reached behind her to pull out a fluffy ball of something. Jasper looked closely but couldn't tell exactly what it was until she held up a long floppy ear. A rabbit?

"Meet Daisy," she said and showed off the plump little white rabbit with her sable nose and ears. "She's a Californian and I'm designating her as a breeder. She's only six weeks old now but she'll be about ten pounds when grown. The others just have numbers but Daisy will be around for a while so I named her." She stroked the bunny with one hand. "It's not quite the same as having a cat but I'll make do. Let me know how Cloudy is, will you? I kind of miss the old cat."

Her expression changed but she didn't quit petting the little rabbit. "I'm doing ok. I'm getting along fine with Krista and we've decided to team up for a while. There's such a shortage of men, it just makes sense." She kept her voice light but there was an edge to it. "I don't know why they do that. We have nineteen women on this ship and only a dozen men. The only unattached ones are on the crew and they don't mix with us Martians. I was told they forfeit their pay for the entire trip and get grounded too, if they do. I don't know if it's true but they sure act like it is."

"Anyway Krista is pretty rad and she plays the dulcimer. I have my flute and Paolo managed to pack along a guitar. I think they used a lot of their weight allowance but it was worth it. Both of them were real happy I had extra strings. Those are going to be worth their weight in gold, I think."

"There's not much else to say this week so I recorded a little song with Krista. Don't tell Jasper I'm trying to copy one of his melodies. His music is really popular here. Lucky started laying when I put it on for her."

There was a spate of laughter and Jasper grinned, embarrassed and surprised his music could get that kind of response then remembering Jewel dancing to *Blow by Blow*, he cast his doubts aside. If Sasha saved a chicken from the pot all to the good.

"We'll have to ask her which tune," Ivan said with a grin at Jasper. "We could increase egg production."

"Be careful," Jewel said. "Some have other effects."

"Oh?" Ivan raised a thick brow and Jewel shook her head and hid her face against Jasper.

"Silly people," Molly said. "Listen or go away."

They settled down again but the rest of the message wasn't memorable. Sasha mentioned someone Jasper didn't know and talked about the ignorance of the guy but that was it. He found himself wondering which tune Sasha had used on the chickens. She'd got his newest album and Jewel had sent her one other. He knew the colonists could still shop for downloads until Mars went behind the sun. It was time consuming with communication speeds but could be done. Twice Sasha had asked Jewel to just buy a couple of things for her and send them with the next message queue from the Colonial Authority since it was easier.

When the message ended, Molly located the music file and people hung around to listen to the little number Sasha and her roommate played. This time there were two very fit young women on the bunk, Krista supporting her dulcimer in her lap. Jasper listened, recognizing the melodic line from Morning Grace. It hadn't been written for those two instruments but they did a fair job of it. He should send Sasha some sheet music files.

That was something he could put in his personal reply to her. He could also show her the drum and what it could do. She couldn't copy the drum out there because metal was still in short supply but she might get some ideas or know someone who could design an instrument like it. He'd seen a clip once of a set of pan pipes made from PVC pipe. It had a totally different tone than wood ones but worked.

"It seems the show is over," he said to Jewel as people started drifting away. "And now you can work on a message to her."

"Yes, I can," Jewel said. "I wonder if her message to us is here or whether it got sorted out and sent on to Plains?"

"Probably here. Go ask Molly. I'm going to go get a flasher," Jasper said. "Then you can show me where that piano is."

"Can you grab my com unit too?" Jewel asked and he nodded. Like his throwaway unit, it didn't have much programming in it but Jewel's was a top of the line model and she just needed to tweak it to her satisfaction and put in her new address book. Her old unit was back in Plains since Jasper was sure they had put tracker software in it. The one they'd left him was either his old unit from when he was on the force or the new throwaway David had given him. The one he needed he'd stashed in his briefcase instead of the safe.

Opening his briefcase, he glanced at the stash of flashers then pulled out the one he'd last used for his music. In doing so he jostled the pink one he hadn't touched in ages. Picking it up, he set it back in its place. There was only one composition on it and he hadn't listened to it in over two years or given it to Milt because he just wasn't ready to share Carol's Requiem with the world. He'd composed it for her, working long hours to get it finished and recorded in time but he'd done it. When Carol slipped away from him, she'd done it with his music filling her ears.

God, he hoped he'd never had to do that again. Thinking of Jewel and that damned transmitter, his gut tightened and his jaw set. She was not going to die. He knew they'd get it out. They just needed to wait until the damned battery ran down. When had he checked it? He had to do it. Hell, it was a waste of time for at least a week. He'd do it tonight.

Snapping the briefcase closed, he grabbed his com units and Jewel's and headed out the door.

Seeing Jewel waiting just outside, he smiled. "Ready?"

"Yes," she said. "And it's right over here." She led him part way down Rabbit Run to the schoolhouse. "The original school was too small so they built a new one. This one is too large but there's room for expansion."

"Got it," Jasper said. "I thought the day care was in the same building."

"No, they're using the old one," she said. "Kindergarten through third grade are here."

She pulled open the door and led him through a dimly lit lobby and up a staircase. There he could see the doors of three large classrooms. Up two more flights of stairs there were two more classrooms and a very large, well appointed general purpose room. When Jewel turned on the lights he could see mats on the floor in half of it so he supposed Kane taught his classes here but the other half contained what he wanted to see. A piano-organ by the wide windows beckoned him.

"Too much light," Jewel said and killed those over the mats. "That's better." She smiled at him. "And since you won't let me send Sasha the vid from our house, I'm going to get some of you playing."

Jasper tried not to feel self-conscious. "Just make sure she knows it's rough. I'm composing tonight, not playing finished pieces."

"Then I'll be quiet," Jewel said. "And I think I'll sit over there on the mats. I want to do some stretches anyway."

Jasper frowned at her. "Are you going to distract me?"

She smiled. "No, I'll wait until you're into your music."

"Just be careful," Jasper said. "No twisty stuff."

"Yes sir," Jewel's smile faded. "Molly has already told me. Now quit stalling and start playing."

Giving her a light kiss and her com unit, he headed for his prize. He hadn't brought his drum along, fairly certain that part of the melody was done. First he'd just find out what this instrument could do.

A Bellmaster piano-organ. He knew that was a good company but didn't have the long credentials of Steinway or Wurlitzer. This particular one looked to be old and the cabinet was pine—one of the cheapest woods—stained a dark color. Cabinets didn't matter though. It was the tone. His hands ran over the keyboard then he eyed the controls. No flute setting. Well, he would make do.

Sitting down he began with the simple melody of Amazing Grace to learn the tones. Playing it first in the normal range, he took it down to bass and smiled at the clear notes. The middle A seemed to be flat and the key was less responsive to his touch. Making a note of that in his mind, he went on to play a more complicated piece that took in the high notes and pedals. Yes, only that middle A needed to be avoided. He could work around that.

Satisfied he knew the quirks of the keyboard, he tested some of controls then looked up to see what his wife was up to. She seemed engrossed in her com unit and he smiled. It doubled as a reader. Maybe she'd bought a book and had given up on the notion of recording him.

Picking up his own com unit, he found the file of his drum tune and played it back, listening till he caught the melody in his mind. Playing it out on the keyboard, he memorized the notes and played them with his left hand. Simple and repetitious, that's what he needed. Uncertain how to begin the harmonic line, he tried the opening phrase of Amazing Grace then modified it, going up three notes to avoid middle A.

No, not Amazing Grace. Closing his eyes, he tried to think the harmony into being, his left hand still playing the drum part. He stroked three or four keys before he found the right one then relaxed. Yes, that was it. He left off playing the drum part and concentrated on the harmony, taking it up into the flute range. It was light and sounded almost like a hymn when he was done but not one he consciously remembered. Once he had his equipment back, he'd do his usual search for identical phrases to be sure.

When he had the harmony set into his fingers, he played both parts over and over, his eyes closed so he could hear every nuance. Yes, a good beginning.

Opening his eyes, he started at the sight of a white whiskered face, big teeth, and blue eyes just inches from his own. His hands came down hard on the keys and the cat freaked at the burst of sound and leapt away. Jasper heard Jewel's laugh and knew she'd caught it on camera.

Irritated as much by his reaction as the cat, he looked around for the beast then glared at his wife. "Did you bring him in?"

She was nearly bent over with mirth, her laughter so wild she could only shake her head.

"Someone let him in," Jasper said, his heart still thumping in reaction but he was finding it hard not to smile. "Cats don't just appear."

Jewel shook her head and thrust her com unit at him, still laughing too hard to speak. He left the piano and played back what she had captured. The screen was too small but he could see himself engrossed in the music. The camera was steady on him so Jewel must have set it down. When it did move, the focus was drawing back and he could see the cat leaping to the top of the piano.

Damn, it had sat there cleaning itself while he played on. His eyes were visibly closed as he concentrated, playing the same notes over and over. The damned cat was licking in time to his tune. His lips relaxed into a smile as he found himself watching that feline head bobbing up and down like it was directing him but the whole pose was ridiculous with one hind leg up in the air and–how did cats do that?

When the music stopped, the cat unwound itself and leaned over to come nose to nose with him. Jewel had shifted the camera position so he saw his eyes widen in startled fright and heard his hands clamp down on the keys. The cat jumped straight up in the air, its fur standing on end, and was gone. After that the camera jerked around and he heard Jewel's gale of laughter and his own demand whether she let the cat in.

He chuckled and handed it back, being careful to hit the save key. Jewel was gasping for air, she'd laughed so hard and that got him going. That set her off again and it was a while before either could speak.

Where had that damned cat got to? Jasper finally managed to get his full-bodied laugh down to a chuckle and started looking. He'd shot toward the mats. Surely he could find a white cat there but there were cubbies in the shelving unit. Before he could reach them, something white and long streaked past him, startling Jewel, and flashed down the stairs.

"And stay down there," Jasper called after the cat and set his wife off again. "Damned cat," he grumbled in mock anger and pulled his wife close. His eyes danced as he kissed her, feeling the force of her laughter against his lips and in his mouth. Her body shook with it and he wondered if she was hysterical but he had the cure for that. His hands slipped underneath her shirt and she gasped as they stroked her ribs. Her eyes widened as he played his tune on her ribs with light touches, ending with his slender hands tweaking her erect nipples.

"Oh, you're wicked," she said, melting into his arms. "You need to make good on that."

"Here? Now?" He smiled at her shock and her glance at the stairs. "Ok, not now. Let me just record that harmony before I lose it."

Reluctantly he returned to the piano and set his com unit on record. Playing the single parts first, he repeated them three times then played them together. This time he didn't close his eyes and wasn't surprised Jewel had recovered herself enough to record him. That damned cat didn't make an appearance. Apparently he'd had enough of music tonight.

When he was done, Jasper smiled at his wife. "You can send that first one to Sasha. Tell her that damned cat is picking on me."

Jewel giggled and nodded. "I'll do that. It was just so priceless."

"I haven't been that scared in years," Jasper said with a wide smile. "Holy hell! Did you know cats have big teeth?"

That set her off again and he just let her laugh. Checking the playback on his com unit, he couldn't hear it well but it was there. Shutting down the power on the Bellmaster, he checked the time. Almost ten. They'd be home in plenty of time before lights out.

"That cat is not coming home," Jasper said when Jewel piped down. That got a giggle but nothing more. Was the cat sleeping up here? Or had it followed them in? He hadn't seen it. In the future, he'd have to be prepared for such shocks since it seemed the cat was a music lover. He'd be damned if he called it Cloudy. Stupid name. Spook or Magic was far more appropriate for a cat of such talents.

Gathering up his wife, he took her home.

Chapter 32 - Wednesday, 17 Nov

Something woke him. Jasper waited, one arm flung across Jewel, and listened. Was she having a nightmare? No but she was too still, her breathing too shallow. His arm tightened as he realized she was wide awake.

Clearing his throat, he asked, "what is it?"

"I can almost hear it," she said in a voice tight with tears. "It's there. I can feel it and–I hate it." As if the words were a release, a sob tore through her body and Jasper's arm tightened. She didn't turn to him but lay there half curled against him and cried.

Damn. What comfort could he give her? He'd hoped she would get a night of good sleep after that laughing jag but it wasn't happening. He couldn't even give her anything to sooth her nerves and help her sleep. All he could do was hold her or–remembering what he'd done for Carol when she woke in pain, he shifted then climbed out of bed. "Stay here."

Seeing it was only four in the morning, he turned on a small light and fished through his flashers. Finding the right one, he queued up the composition he was looking for. Jewel had heard it the night they escaped. *Sleepwalking* was deliberately repetitive but he hadn't told her how to use it then.

Jewel had gotten up and gone into the bathroom. She came back with a wan face and slowly settled back onto the bed, her every move careful.

"Were you sick again?" Jasper asked with a frown. He was starting to worry about that.

"A little," she said, trying to make light of it. Picking up a cracker from a package beside the bed, she nibbled on it. "I'm sorry. I just can't..."

"Don't worry about it," he said. "I've been through worse nights. Now I'm going to put on *Sleepwalking* like I did that last night at the house. This time I want you to listen to it. Let your mind follow the notes and try not to think of anything else. Since you're queasy, I won't give you a back rub with it."

She made a face but continued nibbling her cracker. "I hate this. I don't even like crackers."

Jasper smiled. "Then find something you do like, love. I won't tell on you."

"I'd like a glass of water."

"You got it," he said and fetched one for her. By the time he came back, he could see she was trying to follow the song, her brow furrowed in concentration. When she'd had a sip of water, he helped her slide back down into the bed then grabbed a pillow and pressed it against her skirted abdomen.

He took his own time getting settled, letting the rhythm of the music sooth her. He knew if he listened to it, it would be just as effective. He'd made it deliberately hypnotic. Carol's pain had been severe enough that he'd resorted to back rubs with it, the back being the area least painful for her. Even so he'd had to quit those in her last months.

Setting the timer to turn off the music in an hour, he settled back into bed. Right after breakfast, he was getting back to work. He could call Brad at eight–and he was going to finish tracking Baxter's whereabouts. He still felt he was the key.

April tenth arrived Plains via train station, Jasper noted on the board. *Left April thirteenth, returned April sixteenth. Left the last time in April on the twenty-fourth.* Jasper looked at the list and frowned then wrote down Mike West's accident on April nineteenth. Baxter was in Plains but why had he stayed so long? There was a Reach Out event on the seventeenth but it made no sense that he would have stayed until the twenty-fourth unless he had other business in Plains. He'd stayed far longer than Mike's accident could account for too. Who could he have met? Was it something innocent or not?

He had left the city almost every day for an hour or two but Jasper couldn't be sure that wasn't walks or runs outside for exercise. The weather in April was pretty changeable but that didn't stop some people from going out. He wouldn't but there were die-hards who didn't care about the weather. Baxter just didn't strike him as the type.

Weather reports. Grinning, he keyed in a request for daily weather reports in the months of April, July, and November for Plains, Wyoming. It would take an hour or so to get them but then he would have an idea what the weather was doing and how absurd it was to walk in it.

Where was Starling those days? He brought up the report of Starling's entrances and exits for April 2179. With him he'd had to tie it to his fingerprint ID because he'd been Smith part of the time.

His first recorded entrance into the city was on April sixteenth. He'd left on the nineteenth but returned again on the twenty-first. He'd left the last time in April on the twenty-fourth–the same day as Baxter. Three times he'd left the city and returned within two hours. Those times matched when Baxter was out, although they'd left from different points. They probably had met outside, shared information, and returned. It still wasn't proof the two men knew each other.

He desperately wanted to interrogate Starling. He couldn't do it but he felt the man had the answers to at least this part of the puzzle. It looked to him like Baxter had hired Starling, met him in Denver, and brought him back although they had not been checked in through the same terminals and there would be no train station vid from months ago.

Where Baxter had stayed might also be a clue. A man of such stature should have stayed in one of the five star hotels Plains possessed. Those would include the Grand, the Laramie Peak Hotel, and the Plains North. There were some four star hotels, one of which boasted an incredible virtual adventure ride but those were all touristy. Those who had real money preferred the five stars with their quiet elegance. It would take a court order to obtain guest names at those hotels. Making a note of it, he went on.

Maybe Lowe could shed some light on the timetable they used for those new detection systems. When had the first one been installed? More importantly, he needed to know how many had been installed. Something told him there hadn't been many or he would have heard about it.

He looked up as Uri entered the conference room and smiled a welcome before returning to his thoughts.

"How long have you been here?" Uri asked.

"Since six. Jewel had a bad night and I couldn't get back to sleep," Jasper said. "Coffee's on."

"Right. I sent the interviews to Carlson yesterday," Uri said. "With the files you'd indicated. The house tape was not included." He couldn't quite hide his grin. "Did seeing that help your wife at all?"

Jasper finally turned to him with a smile of his own. "Oh, it was interesting. I had to put my foot down to keep her from sending it to Sasha."

Uri swallowed wrong and sputtered, barely missing his shirt with spilled coffee. Recovering his breath, he looked at Jasper. "Saving that one, I think."

"You bet," Jasper said. "Payback."

"Ok, subject closed."

Jasper nodded, his smile just tipping the corners of his mouth. He was finding these farmers were protective of their daughters. Uri had no children of his own but he was a very close uncle to his brother's kids. The jokes were raunchy and there was plenty of horseplay but there were limits even here.

Frankly, he didn't want naked pictures of him floating around Mars. It wouldn't take long for Sasha to share it and once it was shared, it would be only a matter of time before it got back to Earth. No, he was right to stop Jewel from doing that. The cat vid he didn't care about. It was funny.

"Now where was I?" Jasper said as he turned back to the board. "Oh, yes." He moved over to Michael West's board and wrote down Lowe's name and circled it.

"You still think there's a link?" Uri asked, his blue eyes taking in the new notes.

"I'm fairly sure there is," Jasper said. "Especially since Starling made his first trip to Plains just before Mike West had his accident then he left."

"Why did he leave?" Uri asked.

"Maybe he rigged it and left thinking it was full-proof," Jasper said. "Then came back when it failed, planted the poison in Mike's apartment and left again."

"He was pretty confident it would work then," Uri said. "Too confident."

"Well, if Mike was the target, it did work. It just took killing his mother to get him home where the poison was planted."

"I got that," Uri said. "But it still doesn't explain why they involved Jake."

"I know," Jasper said. "The security on the West house was good but it wasn't unbeatable. I could have gotten in without using either police codes or members of the family. With a little bit of money, Baxter might have been able to get the manufacturer's override codes. The only thing I can figure is they got lucky and found out Jake's vulnerability—or Centrax *was* involved."

"That again?"

"It's something I have to rule out. I know a corporate lawyer in Chicago and sent him a copy of the letter. He's also getting me an appointment tomorrow to meet Blaine Robbins."

"No warrant?" Uri asked, his frown deepening when Jasper didn't answer. "That's awfully risky."

"David reminded me the West Foundation has business with Centrax and suggested I use that to get in," Jasper said. "They've filed a claim against Jake's estate for what the Colonial Authority didn't refund. David knows I'm going and so do two other people Centrax would have a hard time shutting up," Jasper said. "I'll also be with Brad Anderson from Jeffers, Sullivan, and Grant. He may be a junior partner but the firm would take a dim view of something happening to him. Not even Blaine Robbins is above the law."

"True," Uri admitted. "But I suggest you take Kale along anyway. A musician of your stature could have a driver or bodyguard and Kale is both."

"I'm planning on asking him," Jasper said. "Like you, I'd feel a bit better if there was someone outside the meeting looking in."

"Good. I've got to be back in place tomorrow or questions could be asked. I took most of this week off so I could fill in for Thanksgiving. It's hard for the regular officers to get time off for that holiday," Uri said.

"I gathered that," Jasper said. "And being a semi-retired captain doesn't let you off the hook."

Uri looked sharply at him. "I wondered how long it would take you to look that up."

"Too long," Jasper admitted. "I should have done it Sunday night. I knew you weren't a detective and when you didn't flinch at Jewel's suggestion to call you lieutenant, I suspected more."

"I do teach classes," Uri Kowalski said. "Some of the toughest crime puzzles that have ever crossed a cop's desk. Getting into cases like this is just something extra."

Something extra? When he'd finally got Uri Kowalski's records through the DEA, they had been impressive. He was listed as pensioned but he was very active for all that. Besides teaching at the academy, he'd written several books on crime and served on two state investigative boards and one federal one.

"I have to wonder sometimes how I get so lucky," Jasper said. "You're just the kind of partner I need for this case."

"That's how it happens," Uri said. "I tend to luck into the challenging cases. This one isn't the toughest but it's interesting."

"Not the toughest?" Jasper asked.

"No, we have suspects. If your ID on Baxter holds up, we just need to prove his connection and see where it leads. Proving Kucera is innocent is a little harder but I think we'll get it. Did I tell you that Kucera is not employed or retained by Centrax? He shouldn't have received an internal memo."

"That's something," Jasper said but at the same time he felt conflicted. Remembering that conversation with the professor, he was certain he'd put Baxter on to him. Now he wondered if Kucera's arrest had been the reason for his death. Well, that was tied to Jake's confession. He would like to know how Jake had been fooled into thinking he was dealing with Kucera if Kucera wasn't involved.

"There may be a social connection between Robbins and Kucera but nothing professional unless Kucera was a stockholder. Yes, that he could be," Uri mused. "It will take a warrant to uncover that. In any case, the internal memo is questionable even if the seal is real."

"It's good to hear that, I think," Jasper said. "Are you a Mason?" he suddenly asked.

Uri studied him then answered. "No, I dropped out a long time ago. Ivan has kept his up though. Why?"

"Something interesting about the Professor is he was a Mason in good standing but he also wore another ring with an eye on it. I've been told that wasn't Masonic but close. Now I'm wondering if Kucera was Masonic or had one of those eye rings. It could be a related group but not too closely related."

Uri paused to consider it. "If they were both Masons, it could prove a connection between the two but do you have a picture of this eye ring?"

"I do," Jasper said and pulled it up on his com unit.

"Copy to mine," Uri said. "I'm not a Mason but I have enough connections I might get answers. I'll check it out when I get back."

"Thanks," Jasper said.

"Is there anything else curious about the professor's life? We've covered his murder."

"There was a book on Secret Societies that was pretty well marked up—a physical book, not an ebook," Jasper said. "The professor was so careful of his collection, it was odd to find a marked up book. I don't know if it was seized when they took the other evidence. The plan was to copy it and return it last I heard."

"You'll have to follow up on that. If you get it, get me a copy and I'll see if there's a puzzle there," Uri said. "It could simply be that book was too valuable to discard because a previous owner had made notes in it."

"True," Jasper said, "but it was also on his desk."

Uri looked at him. "On his desk? Were there a lot of books on his desk?"

"A half dozen. That was the only one I saw with marks. Most of the books were stored in individual plastic boxes on bookshelves—hundreds of them."

"Ok, that's got me interested," Uri said. "It could be a cypher key."

"Oh, and there's this," Jasper switched to the next photo and showed him the enhanced notepad and the cryptic message. It clearly asked T. S. if all copies of the vid had been destroyed.

"Who is this T. S?" Uri asked. "Or do you know?"

"I don't know of any T. S. but I was told the professor was a good guy and it was strongly suggested I lay off him by Rick Gordon, the Plains city attorney–and he is a Mason," Jasper said.

Uri stared at him then shook his head. "This is not a Masonic plot," he flatly stated. "Not if it's connected with drugs or tearing down society. That's not how they work."

"I know that and I'm not suggesting that," Jasper said. "It might not be connected at all except there is a connection between Kucera and the Professor and between the Professor and Gordon–and now someone with the initials T. S. I don't even know if Kucera was a Mason."

"I'll find out," Uri said. "But this ring is more likely to be the connection. You do know it's called the All-Seeing Eye?"

"Yes, I was told that," Jasper said. "But not the Masonic eye."

"No, it's not. It's been used by other groups but most have fizzled out. They were watchers rather than doers. It's hard to keep an active membership in groups like that."

"I would prefer to think the Professor was a watcher but he was also a very active critic of bliss and a major donor to Reach Out," Jasper said.

"And the other two?" Uri asked.

"I think Gordon lost a child to blissex so he was no fan. Both he and Kucera were also Reach Out donors."

"So there's another connection beside Masons," Uri said. "I've heard of Reach Out, of course. Tell me is Baxter a donor?"

"He is," Jasper said. "So is Jewel and her uncle and grandmother."

"And you?" Uri asked, one eyebrow going up.

"Just recently," Jasper said. "I'm probably not on the list yet."

"It sounds like they court millionaires," Uri said. "If that's the case, it would be an excellent place to make connections."

"True," Jasper said. "And they have quarterly fundraisers to draw them in from other towns. At the auction they just held, I met two from Chicago, several from Denver, and a couple from California."

"Was it a pricey affair?"

"Two hundred a plate. I think the lowest item sold was more than that and the highest item thirty-eight thousand dollars." Jasper recalled the frenzied bidding on the maracas at the end. They had been one of those special items but he hadn't tried to get them. They'd gone for three hundred and ten dollars.

"That's way too rich for my blood but it goes to a good cause."

"The way I felt," Jasper said. "I came away with just my drum and Jewel."

"Good enough," Uri said with a smile. "Now about–" he stopped as Jasper's com unit buzzed.

Jasper checked the number then threw it up on the big screen.

Ray Carlson looked tired but happy. "We have a break on the blister drug," he said. "Its codename is blister and it's manufactured by Wilson Chemicals for--get this--the CIA."

Jasper stared, his mind reeling. "The CIA?"

"It's a spook drug?" Uri frowned. "So they can't be questioned?"

"You've got it," Carlson said. "For the agents on hazardous duty overseas. It's not licensed in the US and it never went through the FDA."

"Which form?" Jasper said. "I can't see even CIA embedding it."

"That's the interesting thing," Carlson said. "I had a heck of a time getting them to acknowledge the drug existed until I told them we had dead and one was FBI. Then they got interested and opened their files. The pill form is the only one they use. They didn't know about the other forms at all."

"So were Kucera and Nugent CIA?" Jasper asked.

"No, definitely not," Carlson said. "They ran their prints and came up empty. Since it's also illegal for CIA to operate inside the USA without disclosing it to other agencies, we ran their prints through FBI too. Another empty. I know they aren't DEA. How they got such a specialized drug has been gnawing at the CIA."

"The FBI is also doing case reviews for bliss-related deaths in custody and they've found more than a hundred nation-wide. Most were small time felons suspected of smuggling blissex but one was a well-respected man brought in by mistake and run through interrogation. He died like the professor. That was in New York City nearly ten years ago and it caused a huge scandal."

"The Jackson von Kliburg case?" Uri asked.

"That's the one," Carlson said. "His death was put down to an unnatural allergic reaction to the truth serum but there were so many violations of procedure in his case that a federal investigation was done and several officers were found guilty of corruption."

"I've studied that one," Uri said. "If Von Kliburg hadn't died in custody, the thing wouldn't have unraveled so quickly but the corruption was there and it was widespread. Before the dust settled more than thirty officers were jailed and so were two elected officials."

"Anyway, these were all isolated incidents before," Carlson said. "Now the DEA is officially interested in who is making blister and who is selling it and who is receiving it. The CIA is also interested but that's because they had to come clean. As far as I can tell they thought they were the only ones who had it."

"Surprise," Jasper muttered and Carlson shot him a look. "Can we find out if Von Kliburg was a Mason?"

Uri frowned at him.

Carlson looked interested. "A link?"

"I'm not sure but Nugent definitely was and I think Kucera might have been. That doesn't mean this is Masonic in origin but it would give a link between them."

"I'll pass that on to the FBI but I don't think it has anything to do with it." Carlson frowned. "It is a possibility though. I knew Nugent was from the

Plains report but I hadn't put it together. Let's not dismiss it yet. I did hear mention of another ring the professor wore but no one seems to have that report. Do you know about it?"

"Yes sir," Jasper answered. "Hold on. I thought that might get lost." He copied the picture of the professor's hand to the vid screen and Carlson had it appear on his. "It's not the Masonic eye."

"No, it's not. I'll see if it turns up in the files," Carlson said. "Starting with Kucera's effects. They've been given back to his widow, of course but there are pictures."

"What are your plans now that the APB is gone?" Carlson asked.

"Chicago tomorrow," Jasper said. "Jewel will stay here but I have an appointment with Blaine Robbins."

"Robbins?" Carlson frowned. "About that memo?" He hesitated. "Well, it does need to be explained. Make sure you have a witness. I can't get you a warrant on what we have."

"No sir," Jasper said. "This will be more social. There's the matter of a quarter million that the Colonial Authority didn't refund to Centrax. I'm bringing that up as the reason for the visit."

"Quarter million?" Carlson frowned. "Oh, that's what they didn't refund?"

"Yes," Jasper said. "David said Centrax had filed a claim against Jake's estate for it and they'd have to pay it but it hasn't been paid yet. That should be sufficient to get me in the door."

"Don't go alone," Carlson said. "And keep me posted."

"Yes sir. Never alone."

With that the connection was broken and Jasper turned to Uri. "It's time I talk to Kale."

Chapter 33 - Chicago

Jasper hesitated at the door of Anderson & Associates, knowing full well what the reaction would be when he walked in. He hadn't been here more than a dozen times over the past twenty years but now everyone on Milt's staff should know who he was. He wasn't just Milt's old college friend stopping by for a visit now but their biggest client.

He smiled at Kale. The younger man was proving to be a good companion as well as bodyguard. "This should be fun."

Walking in, he saw the receptionist glance up from her work then freeze, her eyes widening with recognition. He caught a stammered "Mr. Stone is here" before she rose to her feet. He motioned her back down as he removed his overcoat and handed it to Kale.

"Is Mister Anderson in? I'm Jazz Stone," he said.

"Yes sir, Mr. Stone," she said. "And Mr. Brad too. Do you know the way?"

So she was fairly new. Jasper hadn't been in these offices for almost eighteen months but they hadn't ever changed floor plans. "Yes, I do," he said. "Mr. Tunis will come with me."

"Yes sir," she said with a glance at the Hawaiian then a second glance. He understood that. Kale was handsome enough to rate a second glance even when he was with him. His features were a blend of classic Hawaiian and Japanese and he'd gotten the best of both.

Smiling, he led the way down the hall. The business wasn't huge but it was prosperous. Since Milt was more publisher than agent for his works, it included some production capabilities but most of that was contracted out. Before he went public with his identity, it had been absolutely essential to guard his secret so Milt had started wearing two hats—publisher and agent—for him. It had paid off for both of them. Milt had made enough to set himself up comfortably with his own firm and he hadn't had to worry about leaks. He knew Milt had other clients but he remained the first and most important one and he liked it that way.

Mary was waiting. Jasper smiled at the secretary as she greeted him and eyed Kale and without further ado ushered him into Milt's office. Kale stayed outside and Jasper knew he'd be well taken care of and probably grilled by the efficient secretary.

"Jazz," Milt Anderson said as the door closed behind him. "Good trip?"

"Yes," Jasper said. "How are things here?" He nodded to Brad.

"The FBI is no longer interested in us," Milt said. "Although I'm not sure I believe they've pulled all surveillance yet."

"Persistent, huh?" Jasper knew what that was like. He'd even done it a few times in his career.

"I had one parked in my office for two days," Milt said. "It's a good thing you only talked to Mary. As far as I know, they never tapped the main line."

"They often make that mistake," Jasper said. "Brad, how are you doing?"

"Coping," he said. "I'm not sure how you got that APB lifted but I'm glad you did. How is your precious Jewel?"

"I got her back but she's traumatized and they planted a transmitter in her. We have to wait to get it out."

"Who did?" Brad frowned. "The kidnappers or the FBI?"

"Kidnappers," Jasper said. "As far as I know, the FBI has never used internal transmitters without consent."

"No, they wouldn't," Brad said. "They still work for us even though sometimes I doubt it." Brad Anderson looked the success he was in a tailored suit and a couple of high quality rings. Like Jasper and Milt, he'd had his beard eradicated although he currently had a dark well-trimmed mustache. Corporate law had been as good to him as the music business had been to Milt and Jasper.

"We've got about an hour before meeting Mr. Robbins," he said. "The corporate seal, by the way, is real. I still don't believe the memo is."

"I'm not sure it is either," Jasper admitted, "but Jake thought the memo was real. I'm just here to clear that up and discuss the claim against Jake's estate."

"Fair enough," Brad said. "Blaine Robbins is a client I'd like to have, you know. One of the few men I know who isn't afraid to admit he's wrong."

Jasper nodded but held back his own judgment. He was fairly sure the memo was faked but he had to disprove it. That would lead him closer to Starling and maybe Baxter. He knew he was going to have to make a trip back to Plains too but had carefully not told Jewel about it. That was for the future.

Before they could get further, the door opened and Mary came in with the coffee service, followed by Kale with the coffee pot and a selection of rolls. His bodyguard looked quite at home in the office but carefully followed Mary's lead.

"This is Kale," Jasper said, omitting his last name. "My driver and bodyguard."

"Welcome Kale," Milt said with a smile. "I'm glad Jazz saw sense."

"Thank you," Kale said. "I'm always ready to protect a man of such talent."

Jasper raised an eyebrow, wondering when he'd decided on that line but let it pass. It worked.

"Mary, thank you," he said to the secretary. "I've gained a new appreciation of how good you are these last days."

"Thank you, Mr. Stone," she said. "And it was a pleasure. Will there be anything else, Mr. Anderson?" she asked Milt.

"No, Mary. Just hold my calls until they leave."

"Yes sir." The secretary looked at Kale and he got the message and followed her out again.

"Ok, how did you meet him?" Milt asked once the door was closed. "And training?"

"Martial arts teacher," he said. "And a pretty good driver. He's from the farm. No formal bodyguard training but if I see a reason to keep him, I'll take care of that."

"You would do well to have him trained," Brad said. "Milt's right in that you need a bodyguard these days–or two. He's been going gray worrying about you."

"I'm considering it," Jasper said. "Now let's talk music. I need a new deadline, of course."

"Not a problem," Milt said. "I've already changed the production schedule and moved another artist up. Will next June be enough time?"

Jasper nodded, reaching for a cup of coffee as they discussed his primary career. There wasn't much to go over but it provided a welcome respite from the case. By the time they were done, he'd had a roll and a cup of coffee and the clock was edging closer to his appointment.

"There is one thing," Jasper said as he rose to go. "Charge a bonus for Mary against my account. I think a thousand would be appropriate for the help she's given this last few days."

Milt smiled. "Yes, that would be good. I've already reimbursed her for the com units. At this point I think she's more loyal to you than to me." He grinned. "You spoil her, you know."

"If I weren't married," Jasper said with a grin of his own. "But she is too. You'll just have to keep her."

Both Milt and Brad laughed. Like him, they treasured a top secretary. He'd learned through his own experience how much bonuses were appreciated and he preferred to keep Mary loyal to him too. Loyalty was hard to replace.

Now for Blaine Robbins.

The walk to the Centrax Offices was brief and assisted by a slide walk, something they hadn't yet added to Plains. Having left his coat and suitcase behind in Mary's care, Jasper found it easy to blend into the Chicago underground. He'd actually grown up here and old habits quickly returned once he was back in the mode. Here overt friendliness could get you shocked stares and people shied away from intruding into your personal space. He'd noticed the same tendency in the most populated areas of Plains but it wasn't as noticeable as in the eastern cities. As he stood on the slide walk, he knew he was nearly anonymous since people mostly kept their eyes down or averted. Only once did a couple of teen girls do a double take and they were gone before they could say anything, sliding back into the other direction. Being mobbed didn't concern him on the walks.

"Next section," Brad said as they came to a break and stepped off one walk and on to the next. "On the left."

"Right," Jasper said.

"No, left," Brad answered then caught himself. "Right."

"Left," Jasper replied and Brad finally grinned. "Sorry, kid's game."

"I'm glad you still have a sense of humor," Brad said. "Has she kept hers?"

"When this is done, I've got a vid for you," Jasper replied. "And, yes, she can still laugh."

Recalling the cat vid Jewel had recorded, he smiled. It seemed everyone on the farm had seen it now and enjoyed a good laugh. He'd gone over it with Uri to make sure there wasn't anything that could lead people back to him and decided it was clean enough that it could be officially released. He should have just given it to Milt earlier but it had slipped his mind. His publisher would know how to handle it. The half-done composition was a worry but he wasn't far enough along for people to know how it would be when released. He didn't even have the drum there.

"Here it is," Brad said and slipped off to the left when the slide walk ended. They had to backtrack a few feet to enter the Chicago Transport Tower. They weren't alone since others followed them in past the arched entrance then took escalators or stairs down to the transport hub. The lighter portion of the crowd went on to the food court. There were very few that headed for the elevators for the business offices themselves.

Nearly all the transport companies had offices here but Centrax dominated. As owners of the light rail in Chicago and most of the   evelle and part of the northeast, they had pushed older transportation companies out with their glider trains. The smooth rides, the low noise, and the constant computer updating and control had made the glider trains the leaders in the industry. Centrax owned the patents and most of the trains.

Jasper frowned. Glider trains required less track than any other kind but needed to be sheltered from the elements. How were they going to get around that on Mars? A question he should ask since Jake was supposed to survey for railways on the red planet. That was what his sponsorship was all about.

At the security desk Jasper felt the first misgiving. His new ident card hadn't caught up with him yet and he was still using Flint Black. Well, it wouldn't trigger any alarms since his prints were on it and it was technically legitimate.

Brad had no problem, of course. He slipped his ID into the reader and laid his hand down on the plate and was done. The guard didn't even look at it or the screen that showed the person the ID belonged to but greeted Brad casually.

"This is Jasper Stone," Brad said, indicating him. "Sensor Man."

"Good to meet you, Mr. Stone," the guard said.

"Thank you," Jasper said and casually stuck his card in the reader then laid his hand on the plate. "You listen to sensa?"

The guard's eyes widened then his eyes flew to Brad and back to him. "I didn't realize you were that Sensor Man."

"Yes, I am," Jasper said, keeping one eye on the screen where it showed Flint Black with his spiked hair. "I'm here to have a chat with Blaine Robbins." He just needed to keep the guard's attention for five seconds more then the screen would automatically cycle.

"Yes sir," the guard said. "Would you like me to call upstairs?" He half-turned toward his panel.

"Not necessary," Brad quickly said. "How is traffic today?"

"Not bad," the guard replied. Behind him the screen cleared. "On Thursdays it never gets bad."

"This one is with us too," Brad said as Kale ran his card through the viewer and placed his hand on the glass. "Bodyguard."

"Right." The guard cast a measuring eye over Kale. "Armed?"

"No weapons," Kale said and opened his coat to show him. "Martial arts."

The guard glanced at Brad then at Jasper, before noting something in his log. "You can go up, Mr. Tunis but stay away from Mr. Robbins."

"I plan to," Kale said. "I'm escort for Mr. Stone."

The guard hesitated then passed them through. Jasper thought he might have liked it better if Kale had been armed so he had something to confiscate. Since Kale had declared his skill, he was still legal.

In the elevator Jasper waited for the inevitable question.

"Why are you Flint Black?" Brad shot a look at him. "You know if he checks his log, he's not going to see your name."

"I know," Jasper said. "I should have gone to the federal building first and picked up my new ID. The other got stolen by the bastard who took Jewel."

"So Flint Black is just one you happened to have on hand?" Brad asked. "Convenient."

"It was issued to me," Jasper said. "Jewel got one for a Mrs. Black. I forget the first name since she insisted on being called Jet Black."

"Uh-huh." Brad ran a hand through his hair. "Fake ident cards are not easy to get."

"No, they're not," Jasper said. "But if I want to avoid leaving a trail back to Jewel, I need this one."

Brad frowned then nodded. "Yes, you would. If that guard sends an alert upstairs, I'll smooth it over. Your own ident was stolen."

"That's it," Jasper said. "I should be able to pick up the replacement today and turn this one in."

"Except you won't," Brad said.

"No, I won't," Jasper said. "Until Jewel's kidnappers are caught, it's mine." He wondered if he'd have to tell Brad he was DEA but he didn't want to. He'd known him for quite a few years but only through Milt and if Milt hadn't told him, he wasn't going to. Milt knew he was government. It was necessary to siphon his salary through the business.

Kale didn't know he was government but the martial artist wasn't slow. He knew he was investigating and he'd more or less been told by Harold Fletcher to make himself available. All the hours he'd spent with Uri Kowalski were a significant clue because he was sure Uri's status was well known at the farm. So far though Kale hadn't mentioned it. Their business conversations had been limited to pay rate and duties.

They had no problem reaching Blaine Robbins' office. As before Kale remained in the outer office and the two were ushered in by an efficient secretary. Blaine Robbins himself met them halfway across the office, one hand outstretched to shake his and a wide smile lighting his too handsome face.

"Sensor Man," he said with genuine warmth. "I loved your last album."

Jasper took his hand, a little taken back by his friendliness. "Thank you," he said. "I'm working on a new one."

"I'm glad," Blaine said then turned to Brad Anderson. "Good to see you again, Brad."

Brad returned his greeting with his customary reserve but it didn't seem to put off Blaine Robbins. Turning back to Jasper, his smile faded.

"I know this is about Jake West but first I'd like to know how is your wife? I heard about the kidnapping. Horrible stuff."

Jasper's jaw tightened. Was he reminding him of the continuing threat to Jewel's life? Or was he really concerned and ignorant of that? "She's safe. We're keeping a low profile until the bastards are caught."

"Understandable. You were lucky you got her back. How much did it cost you?" Blaine motioned them to a couch and chairs there in his spacious corporate office, completely missing Jasper's startled reaction.

Cost him? Jasper worked hard not to let his shock show. Money? Did he really think it was about money? Or was he leading him on?

"It wasn't about money," he said in a rough voice. "Blissex smugglers wanted to use the damned house."

Robbins froze, clear shock on his face. It disappeared quickly to be replaced by anger then he nodded. "Yes, they'd do that," he said in a quiet voice, all warmth gone. "Bastards indeed. Murderers too. The government needs to get serious about them."

Jasper didn't say anything, couldn't say anything. He simply wasn't prepared for this support from a man he both suspected and admired. "Jewel is safe but we won't be returning to Plains."

"No one can fault you there," Blaine said. "Find a new place but I don't recommend Chicago. Blissex is a rampant problem here. It was even in my son's school. One of his classmates, a nice kid, died of it. People think I overreacted pulling my son out of there but I won't tolerate bliss or blissex."

"I didn't hear about that," Jasper said.

"Another rich kid dying from blissex never makes the news," Blaine Robbins said. "The conspiracy theorists know about it. Some think it was murder and in retaliation for what I did to the Comets."

"Die hard fans?" Jasper asked.

"Some of the worst," Blaine said. "I can't tell you how much hate mail I got when the Comets lost but I will tell you I got more applauding my decision. They only knew the public story but it was enough. It was a bad business but no one who plays for me will be abusing bliss again."

He stopped as a secretary came in with a tray of coffee and sat it down on the low table. "Thank you, Sara. Will you pour?"

"Yes sir." The secretary looked first to Brad and poured him a full cup of rich, dark coffee. She was good, taking subtle signals to add cream and sugar just the way he wanted then handing over the mug before looking at Jasper.

Jasper debated the wisdom of taking any then threw caution to the winds. He couldn't see Robbins drugging visitors and Kale was in the outer office.

Robbins took his own cup last and sipped it quietly until the secretary had departed. "I suppose we'd better get to the matter at hand," Robbins finally said. "Frankly, I didn't expect the Wests to send you. It was a pleasant surprise when I learned you were coming."

"There were a couple of questions we had," Jasper said and set his cup down. "Did you know Jake claimed Centrax was going to pull out of the sponsorship if he didn't cooperate?"

Robbins looked puzzled. "Why would we do that?"

"Why did you agree to it in the first place?" Jasper asked. "What did Centrax get out of it? Mars isn't ready for a rail line."

"No, it's not and we were reluctant till Ed Kucera made his case," Robbins said. "I'm still shocked over his death. I thought I knew the man."

"There's some doubt he had anything to do with it," Jasper said. "That's why the questions."

Blaine Robbins looked at him then at Brad. "Official or unofficial?"

"Unofficial," Jasper said. "I'm not a cop. This is for the West Foundation."

Robbins hesitated but spoke. "We agreed to the sponsorship because it was a sweet deal for Centrax. Jake got his sponsorship and he agreed to work for us for two Earth years, which was plenty of time to map possible routes for future rail lines and secure the right of ways. At the end of the two years, he would buy himself out. It would cost Centrax one million dollars to send him there and an additional hundred thousand for wages but Jake would reimburse us two million dollars in '81. That was a very hefty profit for us."

"That was all?" Jasper asked. "No other strings?"

"None that I know of," Blaine Robbins answered. "Now what was this about Centrax pulling out? I never heard about it."

"Jake left us some text messages and his confession," Jasper said. "And one picture file with your corporate seal on it. Brad believes the seal is real."

Blaine shifted to look at Brad. "Then let's see it," he said. "And who were the text messages from?"

"The texts can't be verified but they were supposedly from Kucera," Jasper said as he produced a copy of the memo. "Is that your signature and seal?"

Robbins studied it, his brow furrowing as he read. Looking up, he raised his voice. "Sara, bring in the dirt file please."

"Yes sir." A disembodied voice answered.

Jasper wasn't surprised to find the office was monitored but wondered if Kale could also hear what went on in here. Probably not.

Robbins laid the memo down on the low table. "The signature and seal are real," he said. "Most of the body is. The address and subject line are not."

"Not?" Jasper asked.

"Edward Kucera was not an employee," Blaine Robbins said, "and this memo never concerned Jake."

His secretary came in and handed him a thick file.

"The original memo concerned Alan Roberts, one of my star players," Robbins continued. "He was threatening to walk out after I fired Kuchinga and Samson. I should have let him walk but I wrote the original memo to his coach. Here it is."

Jasper took the memo and saw it was much clearer than Jake's copy. Comparing the two, he could see the memo number was the same but the addressee was not and the subject held the name of Alan Roberts. Everything else was the same.

"The memo got leaked by someone who is no longer with the company," Robbins said. "Since then it's turned up all over the internet and it's even been sent back to me for verification a dozen times. I don't even know who most of these people are who think they got a memo from me."

He opened the file and spread several copies out. Each one had the same number and corporate seal but the headings were different. "This is one of my favorites. Apparently a mother used it to convince her son he had to clean his room."

"This one the headings were intact but they changed the wording of the body to include terminate," Robbins said. "Stronger language than I used–and sinister. Your memo also has that variation."

Jasper studied it and had to admit it had been done well. The type blended in and the changes were nearly undetectable. He felt a sense of relief that he could discount the memo.

"Thank you for clearing that up," Jasper said. "So now we know whoever was blackmailing Jake was not connected with Centrax."

"Not connected with me," Blaine Robbins corrected. "I'll make a couple of inquiries but I'm fairly sure my company is clean. I would have preferred Jake fulfill his contract, of course. It would have been more profitable for us and he would have gotten his dream."

"Yes," Jasper said. "I only spoke with Jake three times–one of them an official interview–but I know he was obsessed with getting to Mars. The Wests should have sponsored him and been done with it."

It was the first time he'd aired that opinion. He knew why they hadn't but it had cost the entire family when they put Jake into such a position. A million dollars and the loss of someone who was determined to go anyway would have been a small price compared to what they had paid.

"Hindsight," Blaine said. "Which is easy to have. I agree it would have been better if they had and I wondered why they didn't. Jake just said they were opposed to him going."

"He was the only grandson," Jasper said. "And they'd lost a lot of family in the New Wave collapse. They wanted the family to continue here on Earth."

Blaine and Brad both looked thoughtful. Looking back, Jasper realized how antiquated that stand had been. Jewel's children could bear her name. In fact, Jasper would prefer they did since it would give them more opportunities than the Stone name would. They could also have a hyphenated name but he hated those. No, West or Stone but not both.

"It's a moot point now," he said. "And he wouldn't have been the last West in any case. David and Elinor are expecting and as soon as Jewel is able, she'll do her part."

"With your help I assume," Blaine said, smiling again. "Now if that's cleared up, what do you know about our expense? The Colonial Authority was fairly prompt at refunding three quarters of the sponsorship but one quarter must come from Jake's estate."

"I'll recommend it get paid as soon as possible," Jasper said. "If you don't see it within three months, call me and I'll get it moving. You've been really helpful in resolving this."

"How complicated did his estate get?" Blaine asked. "If I might ask that. I know his widow did go to Mars."

"It shouldn't be," Jasper said. "I understand his will gave his wife a fifty percent share in his trust. Other than that, there's this debt. His actual trust won't be available till his thirtieth birthday but I'm sure the West Foundation will still get this settled."

"Oh, and Jake will have children on Mars," Jasper added. "Sasha knows Jake was involved in the murders but she'll still exercise her right to have his children."

"Good for her," Blaine said. "He'll get that much and the West Foundation will have representatives and money on Mars. That could be very advantageous for them. Even though Mars has been slow starting, it'll grow when the system ferries are completed and transport costs go down. Having someone already there before the crowd arrives might be really good."

"I'm thinking the same thing," Jasper said. "Sasha is very intelligent and she'll have West Foundation backing and at least four years to get herself established before the first system ferry is ready. That could make a significant difference in her success."

"True," Blaine Robbins said then glanced at his clock. "I'm afraid I have another appointment. Mr. Stone, I would like to spend more time with you another day but let's make it social and bring your wife. I'd like to meet the Jewel of the West."

"Jewel of the West?" Jasper repeated, never having heard the phrase before.

Blaine and Brad both chuckled before Blaine said "You really need to watch the news. That's the nickname popping up all over the media and the internet. You're Jazz Stone, of course but she's being called the Jewel of the West."

Jasper smiled. "I like that," he said, "and that would make a great album name."

"Thinking like a musician," Blaine said as a single chime sounded. "My warning bell. It was good to meet you. Brad, stop by again sometime."

They rose to their feet, ready to go, when the secretary's voice came over the office speaker. "Excuse me, Mr. Robbins," she said. "Security is saying there's a problem with Mr. Stone's ID card."

"What kind of problem, Sara?" Blaine asked.

"He's identified as a Mr. Black," she said.

"And it took this long for them to notice?" Blaine asked.

"Yes sir, I was just notified."

"We passed through there over half an hour ago," Jasper said. "But she's correct. I did come through as Flint Black."

"And our security system didn't detect it?" Blaine frowned.

"It's a valid ID," Brad said. "Mr. Stone's legal ID and bank cards were stolen by the kidnappers. This is a legal temporary one."

"Sara, tell security I'll handle it," Blaine Robbins said. "And have them review their procedures and do checks on their equipment. I don't want it happening again."

"Yes sir."

He turned to Jasper, this time not smiling. "I understand why you have one but I would be interested to know how you've managed to get by without a proper ID for five days."

"It can be done with the right kind of help and enough cash cards," Jasper said. "As soon as I knew Jewel was alive, David West and I sat down and went over possibilities. Losing my ident card and bank card was predictable, so we took steps. They wanted us both to stay in that house in Plains and be hostages for drug shipments—also predictable. As soon as Jewel could move on her own, we left. There was a car waiting and a plane and new ident cards in Denver."

"The West Foundation again," Blaine Robbins said as a second bell sounded. "And now it really is time. It's good to meet you. Brad, come again."

"Yes sir." Brad motioned Jasper to the door.

In the outer office Kale stood up, looking alert and ready. Jasper noted two coffee cups on an end table and guessed he hadn't been lonely. Jasper motioned him to follow. He didn't see Robbins next appointment but knew that didn't mean anything. He could just as easily be meeting someone electronically as physically.

Seeing the activity at the security desk, they didn't pause but continued on into the plaza. Brad stopped them at the entrance to the food court.

"Where to now?" he asked.

"The federal building," Jasper said. "My new ID should be ready. I'll stop in to see Milt on the way out of town."

"That sounds good," Brad said. "And I have other appointments. Be careful with that second ID. It's still illegal to have two on you."

"I know," he said. "Don't worry about it."

"Just don't get arrested," Brad said. "I'd have to bail you out and my schedule is full up."

"Noted," Jasper said. "Thanks for giving us a couple of hours."

"Any time," Brad said. "I'll bill you in coffee." Grinning, he walked away.

"Coffee?" Kale asked.

"The medium of exchange," Jasper said. "I got him hooked on premium Aruba and he reminds me from time to time. I'll have to send him a bag or two."

Kale grinned then motioned for him to precede him to the nearest public com panel. While Jasper pulled up the city directory, he kept an eye on the crowd.

"The federal building is in the same place," Jasper said. "And the office I need is there. They'll be expecting me."

"Special appointment?" Kale asked.

"Yes," Jasper said. "Special case."

Kale didn't ask any more questions but followed him on to the slide walk.

At the federal building, they went to the Bureau of Citizenship and Identification. Kale accompanied him to the counter but as soon as Jasper identified himself, the clerk motioned to a second clerk to lead him down a hall. Kale remained behind.

The office Jasper was ushered into looked like any other office but the man behind the desk was not just any clerk. Ray Carlson stood up as he entered and smiled warmly at him.

"Good timing," he said. "What's the report?"

"The memo is a fake," Jasper said. "A leaked memo that's been altered to include Kucera's name and Jake as the subject. I've been shown some other examples from the internet."

"I'll check for those," Carlson said. "So Blaine Robbins isn't under suspicion?"

"No, we can rule him out unless something else comes up," Jasper said. "I didn't think it made sense for Centrax to cancel Jake's contract or even agree to it in the first place. Now I know how Kucera sold them on it."

"Good. Send me a written report," Carlson said. "Time is getting short for me. Here's your new identification card and Jewel's too. How is your bank card situation?"

"I'm getting a new one today," Jasper said. "Do you want the Black card back?"

"Do you have both?" Carlson asked.

"No, Jewel still has hers," Jasper admitted.

"Keep it then," Carlson said. "Just don't go getting searched while you have three in your pocket. Are you still using an agency issued briefcase?"

"Yes."

"Then you'll be okay. Scanners won't identify it." Carlson frowned. "Who do you have with you today?"

"Kale," Jasper said. "So far so good. He's not certified but he's fairly good for all that."

"Good. It's been approved to extract Professor Koasa and her mother when word is given," Carlson said. "And I've arranged for you to be there. Let's just hope it's not on Thanksgiving. It's too hard to get people."

"It shouldn't be," Jasper said. "He was pretty clear it would be the weekend following. Was the interview enough to please the FBI?"

"Hell, no, but the medical evidence was. They don't have nearly the same experience with those dirty bugs as the CIA does but they have enough to know they don't want to risk her life. Oh, and there's a media bounty out on you now. Anyone who can get an interview is guaranteed nationwide viewing and a ten thousand dollar bonus. It seems to be legit so watch yourself."

"Will do." Jasper examined his new ID and compared it to Jewel's then slipped hers and the Black ID into a special pocket in his briefcase. Placed along the bottom hinge, most scanners would miss it anyway but if the briefcase was placed in the right position, it could be detected along with a special symbol that the scanners would read as authorized. If someone insisted on opening the briefcase, he might have to show his DEA ID but they'd have to be very persistent to do that.

"It's damned convenient that a media bounty went out just as the APB was being lifted," Carlson said. "And it's not just you but there's a second one for Jewel for another ten thousand. You might want to control who gets it where."

Jasper paused, looking at him. "You think it's another attempt to find us?"

"I'm sure it is. You are celebrities now and news. They want to know where you are. It didn't help that you were caught on vid at Brown's funeral and the public is really feeling for you."

"I haven't been watching the news," Jasper said. "Nothing."

"I suggest you start," Carlson said. "And watch your step getting out of Chicago. The best thing for you to do would probably be to walk into a media office and have the damned interview."

"I'm not prepared for that today and Jewel is still vulnerable."

"Not her, just you," Carlson said. "Get it over with as soon as possible."

"I will," Jasper said. "Time is a bit pressing today though."

"Right," Carlson said. "For me too. We're done here."

Chapter 34 - Trial

Jasper rejoined Kale, his mind still working on the media problem. He'd promised Jewel he'd be home tonight and it was past one now. They had to go back to Milt's next then to his bank and he'd be done. Meals. Well, they could get something at the food court at the train station. He wasn't hungry yet but Kale might be. Wait, there were fast food stands across from the bank. It was easy enough to get something.

"When we get to the bank," Jasper said to Kale, "there's a food court across from it. I'd like you to pick up something for the train."

"Sounds good," Kale said. "What's your preference?"

"Chinese with plenty of beef and vegetables," Jasper said, picking something he couldn't easily get at the farm. "And I've just been warned there's a media bounty out on me. Keep an eye out for reporters."

"And don't rough them up," Kale said. "Right. Will you talk to them or not?"

"It depends on how much they push," Jasper said. "Don't give your name and stay off camera if you can. You're a more important lead than I am."

"Got it and easy enough to do. They don't usually shoot bodyguards with cameras."

The stop at Milt's was brief. Milt was out but Mary was there ready to hand over the coats and suitcase they'd left behind. Jasper handed her a flasher with the cat vid and told her it could be used then took his leave before she could queue it up. Before they were halfway to the bank, she was calling him.

"Have you adopted a cat?" she asked with a big smile.

"I have not. Damned thing seems to have adopted me," Jasper said.

"What is its name?"

Jasper tossed out Cloudy as being too close thought about Spook then said "Magic. Call it Magic." If Jewel didn't agree, they would change it later.

"Magic it is," Mary said. "He suits you."

"No, he doesn't. He's white."

"So he shows up better against all your black," she said. "You'd better brush him so he doesn't shed on you though."

"No, I'll just paint him black," Jasper said and heard her laugh as she broke the connection.

"The cat?" Kale asked.

"The cat," Jasper said. "I gave her the vid. That might satisfy the media. If not, at least Mary got a good laugh." He couldn't help grinning at that. "And I think I just adopted him and named him Magic."

"Magic works. That cat always shows up where he's not wanted," Kale said. "Oh, and he definitely gravitates toward men. Sasha was the only woman he'd really tolerate and that was because she fed him and brushed him from a kitten."

"I always thought cats preferred women," Jasper said.

"Not that one," Kale responded. "Very strange cat. If he was intact, we'd probably find out he was gay."

Jasper grinned. "Even in animals, huh?"

"Of course. Not often but it happens," Kale said. "Those animals don't willingly procreate. It's been mostly bred out of livestock and pets aren't allowed to do indiscriminate breeding but it happens. Dr. Bob can tell you all about it."

"I'll ask him sometime," Jasper said then saw the bank was coming up. "Here we are," he said and stepped off the slidewalk not far from the wide doors of the Chicago International Finance Center.

The food court lay outside, conveniently located for the hundreds of people who worked in this area but Kale didn't leave him yet. It wasn't until Jasper had identified himself and been escorted to an elevator that he turned back to the food court.

Jasper followed his guide, acutely aware others had noticed him. Would one of them call the media down on him? For that matter, he hadn't been all that discreet anywhere today. If someone wanted him badly enough, the logical place to spot him would have been at his publisher's. Nothing had happened there though. Milt had good people.

"Ah, Mr. Stone." The office he was ushered into belonged to the same bank manager who had assisted his transfer. He hadn't expected to see him again.

"Mr. Fleming." Jasper smiled, his hesitation so brief it went unnoticed. "Did that reverse transfer go all right?"

"Yes, I have an acknowledgment from them," Mr. Fleming said, beaming. "And your bank card is here. I just need to confirm with your identity card and it's yours."

"Right," Jasper said. This was why he'd gone to the federal building first. Fishing it out, he handed it to Fleming. "It's a brand new replacement. Hopefully, it works."

"I'm sure it does," Mr. Fleming assured him and clicked it into the viewer. "Yes, wonderful." He typed something on his screen and handed it back. "Would you be needing cash cards today?"

"You can do that too?" Jasper asked. "No tellers?"

"Not for cash cards," he said. "I have five hundred and thousand dollar denominations here. I assume you prefer those."

"Yes, I like the five hundred dollar ones," Jasper readily admitted. "The golds–two thousand." Those were the most secure against theft. "But I'd also like six thousand in bronze."

Fleming hesitated only a moment. "Yes sir."

The bronzes were fairly secure but didn't require showing an ident card to use them. A numeric pin was the primary level of security.

"What pin for the bronze? Do you want them keyed alike?" Fleming asked.

"Yes," Jasper said. "311807." He'd already given one of his old ones to Kale to cover expenses and train tickets. It was nearly dry though. They'd gotten a stateroom this morning so they could change in private and he planned to get another one for the return trip. While he was on the Plains police force he'd avoided such a luxury but with his new public celebrity and Jewel's security in mind, he'd quickly changed his habit. Staterooms always cost eight times the price of a commuter ticket but he no longer cared about that.

"Here you go," Mr. Fleming said and handed over his new card and the assorted cash cards. "Would you like to change your address of record?"

"Not today," Jasper said. "Officially I still live in Plains. When I'm comfortable changing that, I'll let you know."

"Understood," Fleming said. "Your tax forms go to your publisher?"

"Yes, that's our arrangement," Jasper said. "And he's my contact."

"Well organized." Fleming smiled. "Is there anything else I can do for you today?"

"I think that covers it," Jasper said. "And thank you. It was Ira Fleming, right?"

"Yes," the manager fairly beamed.

"Thank you, Ira," Jasper said and knew he'd practically accepted him as his personal banker but the man had gone the extra mile for him. He was young but he was efficient. "I have another appointment now. Thank you for making this so easy."

"You're very welcome," Ira Fleming said and rose to his feet to shake his hand. "Call me anytime."

"I will," Jasper said and made his exit. Now for the train.

Kale was waiting outside, a sack of Chinese in one hand and the suitcase at his feet. He seemed to be lolling on the bench beside the bank entrance but his smile seemed a shade too alert and widened as Jasper stopped in front of him.

"What's wrong?" Jasper said, recognizing the tension.

"We've picked up a tail, I think," Kale said. "He got interested when you came out."

"Which one?" Jasper asked without looking.

"Maintenance man, grey coveralls, at seven o'clock," Kale said without moving.

"Not a reporter?" Jasper didn't sit down but casually turned the right direction. The man was hefty and definitely working class but his race couldn't be determined. He was simply too American. No, he looked more like a thug than a reporter.

"Not a camera in sight," Kale said. "A couple of reporters might be better company."

"That's a thought," Jasper said. "Not that I want them to find out where I'm going either." He hesitated. "I'll send out a request. Let's see if we can catch the two thirty train."

"Right," Kale said as the man took a few steps toward them. "You'd better carry the food."

"Agreed," Jasper said. "There's nothing breakable inside the suitcase."

"I know," Kale said. "Might be something breakable outside." He flexed his hand on the suitcase handle and swung it slightly. "Yes, it'll do."

Carrying the food and his briefcase in one hand, Jasper got on to his com unit with the other and found the number for Channel 3. It was the only one he kept saved in Chicago and the person he had saved was not some flunky but a vip. It was his secretary who answered.

"This is Jasper Stone aka Sensor Man," he said to the secretary and held out his com unit far enough that she could see him full face. "Recognize me?"

"Yes sir," the secretary said. "Is there a problem, sir?"

"Not this time," Jasper said. "I've heard Channel 3 wants an interview. I'll grant it if you get a news team to the Southeast Train station in the next ten minutes. I'll be there. Stateroom car. They can ride it with me to Laketown."

"Seriously?" She was aghast but smiling. "Why us?"

"You're closest. I won't repeat the offer," Jasper said. "Scramble someone–no more than two."

"Yes sir."

He broke the connection, certain something would happen. To be sure, he sent a text to another network's tip line that he'd been seen heading for the Southeast Train Station. That network was even closer to the station than Channel 3.

"Where is he now?" he asked Kale.

"Holding back for now," Kale said. "Still alone."

"Do you think there will be more?" Jasper glanced back over Kale's shoulder and saw the man carried a common carry-all loaded with tools. Either the wrench or hammer would make a good weapon.

"It doesn't take a genius to figure out where we're going," Kale said. "And he's used a com unit."

"Right," Jasper said. "Let's linger at the ticket counter."

They had time. Using one of his cash cards, Jasper confirmed his reservation for a stateroom on the two-thirty. Confirming it had an outside door, he led the way to the VIP section. Five more minutes before the train would get here. Where were the reporters?

"Three now," Kale said. "Reinforcements. Hold on." He waved to a transit cop and beckoned him over. At the same time, Jasper saw a reporter come dashing down the platform his cameraman following.

The three thugs slowed as the transit cop obeyed the summons of a VIP traveler. The reporters weren't coming fast enough though having been stopped by another transit cop.

"Yes sir," the transit cop said to Kale but his eyes were on Jasper.

"Bodyguard for Jasper Stone," Kale said. "Do you know who he is?"

The transit cop nodded, a smile twitching his mouth before it left.

"Do you know his wife was snatched from a train platform in Plains, Wyoming?" Kale's voice was crisp and authoritative.

"Yes sir."

"The same is going to happen here and now if those three get close enough," Kale said, turning and pointing out the maintenance men who were now just a dozen feet away.

To give him credit, the transit cop reacted swiftly. Blowing his alarm whistle and drawing his trank gun out at the same time, he fired as the first man lunged forward.

Kale swung the suitcase at the two left, knocking one off balance and dropping the other with a quick chop.

Jasper stepped back, dropped the food and brought his briefcase hard across the last man's face as he came within range. The man's arms were reaching but Jasper twisted away. A foot to the man's knee took him down just as the transit cop tranked him.

Jasper looked around for more but if there had been, they were gone now. Two more cops appeared from nowhere and reporters from two stations were filming. His breath was coming fast and he could feel his pulse pounding but it was over.

"Search them," Jasper said in a crisp voice. "I want to know if they have drugs."

The transit cop didn't question it but cuffed the first one and started riffling his pockets. Nothing. The second tranked man yielded a single syringe filled with something. The third man carried an illegal switch knife the cop instantly pocketed. The man was unconscious and Jasper didn't ask how hard Kale had hit him.

Kale himself was ignoring the search to watch the crowd. Jasper realized the young man was a hell of a lot better than just a martial arts instructor. He thought fast and knew his job.

"We're here at the Southeast Train Station with Jasper Stone, otherwise known as Sensor Man, where there's just been an attack. There are three men down and in custody. Thankfully, Mr. Stone is not hurt. As our viewers know, Mr. Stone's wife was kidnapped in a like fashion at the Plains train station and an officer died. This is not a repeat. Chicago transit officers have the situation well in hand."

Jasper straightened and put on a smile as the microphone was thrust into his face. "That's right," Jasper said and half turned to the officer who had assisted. "The fast response of this officer was remarkable. Officer, your name please?"

The officer barely glanced at the reporters, his attention on the suspects. Seeing Jasper's wave, he set his lips and joined them. "Officer Dan Wilson, Chicago Transit Police. Are you okay, sir?"

"Yes," Jasper said. "And I'm impressed with that fast draw. Thank you."

"You're welcome, sir. I will need a statement," he said as the two-thirty train slid into the platform. "Required."

Jasper knew he was going to miss that train. Damn. There was no help for it though. The next express wouldn't be until four and he'd probably miss that one too. He gave a sharp nod and handed the ticket to Kale. Whoever had sent these thugs would have time to regroup. He wasn't going anywhere for hours.

Chapter 35 - Friday, 19 Nov 2179

Jasper closed his eyes, increasingly aware of the ache behind them, as the farm truck carried him homeward. It was well past midnight and Jewel just might kill him for coming home so late. He didn't know because he'd never done it before.

It wasn't the fault of the Chicago transit police. Their interview had been thorough, courteous, and limited to the matter at hand but they'd called the FBI. By the time he'd gotten done filing charges against the three thugs, it had been too late for the four o'clock train but he could still catch the five thirty.

Then the FBI had stepped in and kept him there, demanding answers about Plains that he couldn't give without jeopardizing Jewel or the investigation. It was Brad who put an end to it. When he saw it on the news, he came right down and demanded he be charged or released.

It helped that the reporter from Channel Three hadn't budged. He latched on to Kale and followed them every step of the way, delivering unflattering comments about the FBI to his station. When Jasper was finally released at six thirty, he'd given the damned interview. He had time since the next express didn't leave until nine.

The picture of Jewel with her massacred haircut was going to be all over the news now. The reporter had tried just once to find out where he was staying then shut up when he told him about the transmitter. He hadn't wanted to use that but it had made his point. Jewel still wasn't safe.

He knew his statement about the kidnapping was going to start something. "There was no ransom demand because they didn't want money. What the kidnappers wanted was an easy access for smuggling blissex. If you think blissex is harmless, think again. Two fine people have died and my wife is still in danger. Today was just another example of the lengths drug smugglers will go to in their illegal activities."

He'd just declared war on blissex smugglers and he was going to have to get Baxter now. So long as the man was free, he'd be after him and Jewel. He could even go after David and his wife but getting to them would be a real challenge since the Lunarex Corporation had some of the best security on Earth. They protected their employees and their families to ensure smooth mining operations on the moon. So long as David was one of their top operators, he'd be safe. Elinor was no longer a mechanic but was busy training new mechanics who would go to the moon and maintain the equipment on site.

That was another problem he had with the case. If Mike had been the target all along, why had they tried to get David? They had gotten Elizabeth to get Mike home to his own house and they had killed Jake to cover their tracks but why had David been a target? Now that Centrax had been cleared, he felt it had to focus on Mike.

He was certain that Jewel had not been on their list but John Starling had tried to kill her to give his brother an out. There had been a previous arrest of Samuel–nicknamed Smith–where he had been released after an identical murder occurred while he was in custody. This time though he'd been caught with curare and had actually injected Ivan's prosthetic arm with it. Since he'd used the same method of murder on Jake, there was no doubt he'd done that murder. Mike's was still unprovable but they had him in Plains the same week as his accident.

A whine sounded in his ear and he could hear the dog shifting on the back seat. Opening his eyes, he wasn't surprised to see they were almost at the turn-off for the farm. Straightening up, he glanced into the back seat and saw Kale was awake too and fending off the large dog Ivan had brought along for company. He'd been told this one was Cap. He wasn't as large as Hairy but looked a lot more vicious. The dog had nearly licked him to death when he was introduced.

There was the usual dog chorus pulling into the yard but it was quickly silenced. Cap whined and Jasper could hear his tail beating against the seat. Looking back, he smiled as Kale grabbed the errant tail to keep it out of his face and ordered the dog to sit.

"Useless," Ivan said as he pulled into his driveway. "He's going to wake the whole house too because he's home."

Catapulting out of the car, the dog let out a short series of joyous barks before Ivan's command silenced him. Other dogs answered before they too were silenced.

"It sounds good," Jasper said as he climbed out of the truck. "I never thought I'd say that about dogs."

"It grows on you," Ivan said. "Ah, Molly is up. Get ready for some questions."

"Hopefully, Jewel isn't," Jasper said. "You did say she didn't know when you left?"

"Molly didn't want her worried," Ivan said. "Bad for her. Now that you're home, she can know."

Molly was up but didn't plague him or Kale with questions. After a quick hug for each of them she sent them off to bed then started turning off lights. Cap followed Jasper downstairs then turned into one of the bedrooms. Apparently that was his usual sleeping spot. He just hadn't noticed him before.

At least he knew his way now. The apartment was unlocked and he set his briefcase down on the kitchen counter then checked to see if Jewel was sleeping. Trying to be quiet, he went through his nightly routine and climbed into bed without waking her.

His hand snaked around her and encountered something metal. The drum? She was sleeping with his drum? Amused, he carefully removed it and dropped it on the floor. It reverberated and Jewel started awake.

"I must have dozed off," she said before snuggling into him. "You've got some explaining to do."

"Tomorrow," he said. "Go back to sleep." He waited for her to demand answers but it seemed that was all she was going to say. Her breathing evened out and he knew she hadn't really woke up.

Relaxing into sleep, he thought about that drum. Did she intend for it to wake her up? Or had she slept with it because he wasn't here? He didn't really care so long as she didn't have nightmares.

Hours later he woke from his own nightmare. He was back in the professor's study but the man in the chair was Mike West, his head lolling against the back of the chair and his sightless eyes staring at nothing. Reluctantly, he checked for a pulse—and was grabbed by a cold hand. Mike's eyes were staring at him now and he fought to free himself. When his hand hit something soft, he woke up. Jewel!

God, had he hit her? He fought to free himself of the nightmare and was relieved to find he'd hit a pillow. The vid screen was on full daylight and he was alone in the bed. He hadn't been alone long though since he could still feel his wife's warmth beside him. When he was awake enough to hear the shower, he knew she was there.

Why had he dreamed of Mike? He tried to gather up the scraps of the dream but that was all he could recall—Mike in the professor's chair. He knew they'd been friends but it was odd he'd put him there.

He wished he'd known Mike West better. Older than David, he'd been the second West brother and the one that had inherited the bulk of the responsibility. David had been free to work for Lunarex and raise his surviving son but Mike had stayed in Plains to help raise Jewel and look after his mother when his father died. He'd been a programming engineer and an inventor, the head of Butler Systems, Inc., when he wasn't working for the city. Given the quality of Butler, those inspection systems he'd developed must have been something. They certainly had gotten the attention of Baxter.

He wondered if Mike had left notes on the development. Apparently not enough because the system hadn't been finished and installed throughout the city. He wondered if Lowe had been working with him on the system and knew he needed to talk to him again. If the inspection system was why Mike had been killed, there had to be something there.

It was too bad he didn't have an assistant who could carry on like he Did with Butler. Jewel had worked with him on that and knew the inner workings and programming of Butler better than anyone.

He stopped. Catching his breath, he was suddenly wide awake. Could Jewel have? No, she would have been targeted. Unless no one knew it was her. Rolling out of bed, he stuck his head in the bathroom door to find the shower was already off. His wife was toweling her hair dry, a second towel wrapped around her. The jammers lay on the sink waiting for her.

"A question, love," he said with deliberate calm. "Did you work on the inspection scanners your uncle was developing?"

"The Seeker S-3 series?" She didn't pause in what she was doing.

"Yes, I think so," Jasper said, his anticipation rising. "Did you?"

"No, there was no need to," she said. "Uncle Mike got those already programmed. All he needed to do was set them up."

"He didn't develop them?" Jasper asked, disappointed.

"No, of course not," Jewel said. "They were mostly hardware. The programming was really simple. Uncle David had them designed that way."

"David developed them?" Jasper stared at her in shock.

"No, David had them developed," Jewel said. "One of those little companies he invests in." She finished toweling her hair and looked at him, her expression changing as she saw his. "What is it?"

"That's why Starling had to get David," he said as that piece fell into place. "Not the house but those inspection scanners."

"But..."

He left her standing there and grabbed his com unit. He barely remembered to use the relay this time. What time was it anyway?

Jewel came out of the bathroom in her robe and settled on the edge of the bed. "Clothes," she said.

Jasper glanced down and swore, scooting out of range of the vid screen. He hadn't bothered finding pajamas in the dark.

Jewel tossed him his pants and spoke to the relay operator in a calm professional voice. "Ah, Tracy, would you put me through to my uncle? I know it's early his time but Jasper thinks it's urgent."

"How is he?" Tracy asked.

"He's fine," Jewel said. "And getting dressed. I don't see a scratch on him."

Jasper glared at her, wondering exactly how chummy she was going to get with that operator. Turning his back, he finished getting dressed. At the same time, he wondered why Jewel wasn't upset with him for not calling. She couldn't have known what delayed him but she clearly knew something.

No time. He was back in front of the vid screen when David appeared, still sleepy but not in bed.

"What is it?" David asked. "Do you know it's only six?"

"A break-through," Jasper said. "Jewel just told me that inspection system Mike was working with came from you."

"The Seekers? Not from me," David said. "Well, I did send him the prototypes to test. They were actually made by Sanchez Surveillance."

"But people knew he got them from you," Jasper said. "They took out Mike then tried to get you because of the damned Seekers."

David swore, any sleepiness gone. Jewel, just off camera, was listening her eyes widening as she took in some of the more colorful phrases.

Jasper felt like swearing himself. Why hadn't anyone mentioned that?

"I assume you agree," he finally said when David wore down. "Mike was the target, not your mother."

"Oh, I agree," David said in a tight voice. "Sanchez had a fire just a couple of days after Mike's accident and the most critical part of their factory was destroyed. It was ruled arson. Sanchez himself was thought to be the arsonist but he died in the fire."

"Damn!" Jasper stared at him.

"Yes, damn it all to hell," David said and ran his hand through his thinning hair. "I was worried about Mike and didn't put it together. Later I knew Sanchez was over extended and just wrote it off."

"So there are no more Seekers?" Jasper asked.

"Not right now," David said in a grim tone. "There will be. If they were that worried about them, there's something there. I just got interested in finding it."

"What was the problem in Plains? Besides Mike's accident?" Jasper asked, certain there had to be one.

"There were six prototypes, each calibrated a little differently," David said. "Mike had installed four of them when two just disappeared from supplies. They looked just like the regular inspection scanners so one of his co-workers suggested they got installed by accident but Mike never found out where. Things happened to the ones that were installed: Lenses painted, power feed pulled, and one was just stolen. Mike was pulling the last one when that air cleaner fell on him."

"What was different about these scanners?" Jasper asked.

"They could capture more images, faster, and see in a greater range of frequencies than the old ones. The home computer program could then sort through the images in a smarter fashion," David said. "Mike developed the programming for the home system but not the cameras."

"Does that programming still exist?" Jasper asked.

"Probably," he said. "Plains should have it. Without the cameras though, it's like having the cart without the horse."

"I'll lay you odds Plains doesn't have it any more," Jasper said. "They might have used it with standard cameras too."

David looked thoughtful then nodded. "Mike would have had backups but I don't know if they were at his house or at work. In any case, the cameras will have to be reproduced. If you can find out about the programming, it would help."

"I will," Jasper said. "Everything from Gracee Place is in storage either at Lily Street or in a storage unit. I'm going to have to go back to Plains."

"No," David and Jewel said in unison.

Jasper turned toward his wife but it was David that spoke up.

"It's time to turn this over to Reynolds," David said. "He owes us for those cameras I gave him. He can get his task force busy on locating Mike's program. Jewel, since you're listening, I want you to contact Butler Systems and see if they have it. Even though that was work for the city, Mike might have stored a secure copy with them."

"Yes, uncle," Jewel said, coming into camera range.

"Get dressed first," David said, eyeing her lacy robe. "The robe is fetching but not appropriate."

"Sorry," Jewel said, "but he was wearing less when he started the call."

"I don't doubt it," David said, a smile returning. "But I'm glad you called. Jasper, does this mean we can disregard Kucera's involvement?"

"I'm not sure he was involved any more than the professor. Someone was clearly using his name and Jake bought it but I don't think it was him. Centrax wasn't involved."

"Why the hell did Kucera commit suicide then?" David frowned. "I'd be happy to know I was wrong about him but that bothers me."

"I don't know," Jasper said. "That's linked to the professor. Do you know if it was the professor who introduced Kucera to Jake?"

"It wasn't," Jewel said. "It was Uncle Mike. Kucera was a member of Reach Out and Mike knew him from there. Sometimes he and Drew and Kucera would go off with some others. We used to joke about the men's club."

"Men's club?" Jasper looked at her. "Do you remember anyone else who was in it?"

Jewel shook her head. "Not right now. They were all older men and most were married so I didn't pay much attention."

"Mike and Drew weren't," David said with a frown.

"They might as well have been," Jewel said. "They weren't interested. Uncle Mike was a registered celibate and Drew should have been." Her voice rose on the last words then she stopped and abruptly left, disappearing into the bathroom.

Jasper watched her go, realizing this was the first time she'd ever said why she wasn't interested in Professor Andrew Nugent. He'd figured there was no chemistry but she obviously knew that and just hadn't put it into words.

"It's hard to speak ill of the dead," David said, his voice soft. "But I'm glad I know why she turned him down—and I'm glad she found you. Jewel is far too young to sit on the shelf."

"She's not on the shelf now," Jasper said. "But I expected her to tear into me for last night and she hasn't. I'd like to know why."

"That could be because she spent hours talking to Elinor last night," David said. "Late night. Didn't get any sleep then either."

Jasper grinned as David faked a yawn that turned into a real one. "I'll let you go then. You're right that I should turn over the inspection system investigation to Reynolds. I'll have to use the relay again."

"Go right ahead. The girls can handle it," David said. "Tell your bodyguard he did good."

"I will. Have a good day." Jasper broke the connection then sat back and thought. There were two interesting facts to consider. He hadn't known of David's involvement with the inspection systems but he also hadn't known Kucera, Mike, and Drew were part of a "men's club" inside Reach Out. He wondered who else was involved. Since those three were dead, he was going to have to look elsewhere.

Stifling a yawn of his own, he thumped on the bathroom door. "Don't take all day." God, he'd be glad when he had a bathroom of his own again.

Chapter 36 - Investigation

Jasper studied the boards in the conference room. They hadn't changed much but he'd been able to line out Centrax and put a question mark by Kucera. He needed to explore the links between Kucera, Nugent and Mike but he was sure those weren't connected with the main case. There had to be a link between Kucera and Baxter though. They were both part of Reach Out and Baxter worked for Kucera's older brother. He just had to prove it and a connection between Baxter and Starling.

The confessional. He had vid of baxter speaking at the house. If Frazier could identify him as the second man at the confessional, they'd have enough to arrest him in Elizabeth West's murder and possibly Jake's. Would Frazier cooperate without him there? He didn't know. What was his informant ID? He'd have to look it up. He made a note to send on to Captain Reynolds.

Satisfied that would cover the Starling/Baxter connection, he returned to the more immediate problem of proving a stronger connection between Kucera and Baxter. Would Kucera's widow know? Probably. He wished he could ask her but the woman didn't know him and she'd been warned against talking to Jewel. Was there anyone she wouldn't suspect? Damn it, this was the kind of work Lori was good at and she was gone.

Burying his head in his hands, he waited for his grief to pass. They'd gotten Chuma Johnson. Her killer was caught. There were others in that group but they had the top man. He wanted the others.

There was something else on his list today too. He needed to watch the damned news coverage and know what they were saying. He didn't want to. Jewel had confessed to watching his interview last night. Just as soon as Molly had let her go to bed, she'd turned on the news and watched it all then called Elinor. When she finally did go to sleep, Jewel knew he was safe and that's why he hadn't caught hell. His wife had just been sensible.

He'd better get it done since it was still too early to call Reynolds. He set his com link to bring up a news search for Sensor Man or Stone then poured himself another cup of coffee.

It didn't take long but the resulting queue of reports was daunting. Limiting playback to those of his favorite station in Plains, he settled down to watch. Thirty seconds in, he had to stop. They had the vid from the train station. It had been edited but he'd still seen the horror on Jewel's face as she was hustled away by the kidnappers. Lori's death wasn't shown, thank God.

Turning his back on the vid screen he just listened to the reporter talking about the crime and knew they'd caught his stunned arrival at the train station too. He hadn't known there were reporters there. Were they there when he woke up? Did they know he'd been tranked and propped in a corner. He hoped not.

The first set ended with the note the police received with Jewel's com unit. The second set was Lori's funeral and it was worse. They'd caught him arriving with David and showed that police honor guard. He hadn't asked for that. He hadn't expected it but he'd been grateful not to be mobbed by the well-wishers who stood silently behind the line of blue. Seeing them made his eyes burn. Public tribute for him—for Lori.

They'd caught him at the urn and it looked so damned posed. He had stood there a lot longer than they showed. Gulping coffee, he tried not to give in to the grief he felt tearing at him. Then he'd been scared for Jewel and trying hard to say goodbye to Lori. They'd been partners for so long. If she hadn't been good friends with Carol too, it might have caused problems but Carol understood their relationship.

When they showed him in his lonely splendor at the door of the church, he couldn't watch any more. Pausing the vid on the screen, he gave in to his grief. It was a good while before he could force himself to move on.

The next report was easier but it shouldn't have been. In each report they'd mentioned the FBI agent and reported his condition first as critical then serious and finally stable. When they reported his death, it was a shock. The picture of the agent, Cord McCain, was given and Jasper learned he'd grown up in Texas and had moved to Denver just a year ago. They called it murder too, and had a still shot of the woman entering his room but they didn't identify her as Jewel. Jasper studied the woman, surprised even the FBI could have believed it was his wife. She had a good fifty pounds on Jewel. The only thing that made her look like his wife was the long chestnut hair.

At the end of the report, the journalist said "Police have confirmed that Jewel West has been returned to her husband alive and the Stones have left the city for a safe house. No other details are yet available."

There was a follow up report with the police commissioner answering questions. It was a very tight-lipped interview because he had too little information to string it out. More than once he had to repeat that he didn't know how the Stones had left the city or where they went. In the end he flat told them no one on the force knew how, when or where they'd gone and they should direct their questions to David West.

David would have loved that, Jasper thought even though he appreciated the spot the police commissioner was in. He couldn't have done anything differently but maybe he should have sent them a statement.

Well, he had yesterday. The public now knew about the transmitter and the continued threat to Jewel's life. They didn't know about blister but he wasn't willing to give them that. He hadn't told them the house was under surveillance by both the kidnappers and him and he'd implied his escape was with the help of the West Foundation. He hadn't mentioned Carlson.

The next report was about the APB and the reporters expressed the theory that they'd met with foul play after all and the previous report had been wrong. At the end they asked if anyone knew where the Jewel of the

West was to contact the station's tip line. That was where the nickname came from. He wondered if his Jewel knew she was the Jewel of the West.

The jubilant report of Chuma Johnson's capture was the high point of the next one and Jasper got to see the battered figure of the man taken away on a hospital gurney. He was in much worse condition than he imagined. Someone had smashed his hand before police had been called. Well, he had it coming. The other injuries included a broken nose, broken ribs, and internal damage. They'd done a real number on him and it looked like it was by persons unknown. No one was in custody for the attack.

The reporter was grim when she reported about the agent's funeral. After that there was more speculation as to where he had taken Jewel. Apparently people were calling in from all across the country about seeing him or her but never both. There was one sighting in Chicago that could have been him but he'd been in that godawful disguise and the man they showed on vid looked more like him than he did that day. He was dressed in black and even had a locket on his chest but the chain was gold and thick and his hair was longer than Jasper's own.

There was little else of interest from Plains TV. Reluctantly, he switched to reports from Channel 3. They had been constrained in their reporting–for them–and had stuck to facts. One thing they'd done was interview a guard at Lunarex Tower who stated flatly that neither he nor Jewel had been logged in to the Tower during the past month.

The fracas from yesterday was in more detail and he got to watch what Kale had told him. The reporter had caught the scene at the train station from the time the guys went down and security vid had been inserted to show exactly what happened. After that the reports followed both the reporter and the scene at the station.

The man had really stuck by Kale. He'd delivered minute long protests at the FBI treatment of him, recorded the arrival of Brad Anderson, and Jasper's own exit from police headquarters. Kale's hands, shoulder and partial body could be seen in some shots but the reporter had not gotten his face. Later when he'd done the interview, Kale had carefully stood on guard out of camera range, accompanied by two police officers.

Kale had done far better than any rookie cop. He didn't have any formal bodyguard training but he had told him about playing bodyguard with his martial arts club back in his college days. They'd not only used their own club members for that but hired actors in an attempt to show each other up. It must have been excellent training by what he'd seen yesterday.

He was about done with the journalist reports when his com unit buzzed. Checking, he discovered it was Carlson.

"Next time I tell you to have a blasted interview and get it over with, can you do it in a less spectacular fashion?" Carlson asked without preamble. "Getting almost kidnapped in a Chicago train terminal was not what I had in mind."

"I know but you gave me the idea of calling in the press," Jasper said with a tight smile. "It's obvious now that I'm still in danger and so is Jewel and I laid it at the door of blissex."

"I saw that," Carlson said. "That I liked. Why do you think they tried it?"

"If the drug was a sedative, they wanted to get me back to Plains," he said. "If it turns out to be poison, they wanted to scare Jewel back to Plains. I haven't heard which one it was yet."

Carlson looked grim. "These people never stop. You're going to have to seal that house up and get rid of that upper entrance."

"I'm already considering it," he said. "But I haven't talked to Jewel yet. It's already in her will that the house will be torn down when there's no more family. Oh, we've definitely established Mike was the primary target and David a secondary." Quickly he filled him in.

"So they used Jake then killed him when he rebelled?" Carlson asked.

"They were going to kill him anyway," Jasper said. "They couldn't let him get into space with what he knew. It wasn't much but they couldn't shut him up if he knew more than they guessed."

"But he didn't know more?"

"Apparently he knew less than they thought," Jasper said. "And I have to wonder why the Colonial Authority approved him for Mars. He had education and physical health but his reasoning powers weren't the strongest."

"Pretty harsh," Carlson said. "I have to agree though. He should have seen it coming." He paused. "Well, millions will get just about anyone anywhere. If he'd got to Mars with that money, they could have used it and him."

"My thinking too. They might have known he could be led when they approved him."

"What about his wife?" Carlson asked. "Is she cut of the same cloth?"

"No," Jasper said. "From the reports I've gotten and the vids I've seen, Sasha is a lot stronger. She's young but she knows what she's doing. If they had stayed married, I think she would have been running the household in short order."

"That's good," Carlson said. "Now for the real reason I called. We've been tracking that plane. We've noticed it doesn't sit still a lot. Corporate planes normally don't get used much but this plane has been to five major cities in the past week–and Harrison, Arkansas."

"Harrison? Where's that?" Jasper was puzzled.

"Not far from a town called Jasper," Carlson said with a smile. "Seriously, it is. Both are very small towns with one or two major employers. There's a Wilson Chemical plant there."

"That plant has passed inspection every two years but the same FDA people have been there for twelve to fifteen years. FDA doesn't particularly like that. At our request, they're sending two new people to poke into production–and one of them is DEA. With luck we might have found the blissex plant."

"With luck," Jasper said, baring his teeth in a big smile. "And Baxter? Is he still on that plane?"

"We think he's back in Chicago," Carlson said. "Oh, and we put a word into the IRS. They're giving him special attention. We have no reason to extend that to Wilson Kucera but Baxter is under a microscope now."

"That's good," Jasper said. "How long before we get a report on the plant?"

Carlson frowned. "The earliest we can get the people in there is Monday. The FDA chemist needs that much notice even though she knows this is short term. A new permanent team will be assigned to the plant based on her findings. The DEA agent is more or less her bodyguard."

"You might need more than that," Jasper said.

"There will be more," Carlson said. "We're sending in a construction management team to assess the airport for improvements. It's federally owned and funded and, I understand, it's far below standard. It may surprise them to suddenly have a federal construction team there but they can deal with it. They'll be there on Sunday."

"As soon as everything is set, we'll close in on Baxter. Having Koasa on our side will be essential to the success though." Carlson looked tired. "Getting his sister and mother out will require a lot of luck if they change the date."

"Will we have any advance warning if they do?" Jasper asked. "Once they enter the house, it'll be a little late."

"We're keeping tabs on that plane," Carlson said. "If it files a flight plan for Plains, we'll know. If it files one for Denver then diverts to Plains, we won't. So far that's not the pattern though. Just be prepared to drop everything and bolt when I say the word. Take that bodyguard with you too. You might not need him but I want it established you have one constantly."

"Agreed. When this is all done, I plan to send him to formal training and certification."

"Good plan," Carlson said. "I think that's about it. Try not to make the news again for a few days."

"Right." Jasper smiled as Carlson broke the connection.

Glancing at the time, he called the relay and set up his call to Reynolds. When his captain saw him, he looked grim.

"About time you called," he said. "We lost Johnson."

"Lost him?" Jasper asked. "I hadn't heard."

"That's because I couldn't get a message to you on any channel I trusted," Reynolds said. "He was already dead the last time you called but I hadn't got the word yet—and it was a bliss reaction. He was so beat up the emergency room doctor sedated him with one of the bliss family. I had Kruger do the autopsy and we found an implant. We've kept it quiet and set up a sting to see if we couldn't get that nurse but no bites yet."

"David would have relayed the message," Jasper said.

"I'm not sure he isn't under some sort of surveillance," Reynolds said. "Only six people know and I'm keeping it that way. If the public hears, I don't want to be here."

Remembering the arrest coverage, Jasper understood. Johnson was the visible villain. It wouldn't matter to the public that he was just another pawn.

"We've had a couple of breakthroughs. The city was testing some new inspection scanners when Mike West had his accident. The prototypes were delivered by David West." Quickly, he explained about the Seekers.

"And West is going to get them back into production?" Reynolds asked. "I'll check at this end to see exactly who was assigned to that program. Since all the cameras were fooled with, someone had to be informing."

"I know Rob Lowe was part of the program but not who else. He said they'd lost some people so it got shelved—and a budget cut," Jasper said, recalling that statement then he frowned. "If they were prototypes handed over to Mike, they may not have cost the city anything."

"So we need to question that statement," Reynolds finished. "I'll get on to that. Any word on K?"

Jasper blinked then caught the reference. K for Koasa. "Extraction has been approved," he said.

"Good," Reynolds said. "By the way, I'm adding Kruger to my little team. He's good and he's managed to keep two of those blister pills for us. Right now he's trying to work up a blood test that will detect the stuff."

"Good," Jasper said. "Carlson said the CIA are unhappy someone is using a drug developed for them, by the way."

"CIA?" Reynolds nearly exploded. "They knew?"

"Yes. Contact Carlson and get it from him. You can use Johnson's death to get it."

"I will," Reynolds grimly promised. "And his body isn't going anywhere. He's a cop killer."

Jasper felt the same way. It was one thing for somebody to suppress an investigation into the professor's murder but no one was going to take Johnson's body before he was publicly recognized as a cop killer. Since he was already dead, it was unlikely anyone would choose to defend him.

"There's a couple of other things I need," Jasper said. "A contact number for a Mrs. Rosalyn Krantz is one. She's an important member of Reach Out."

"Questions for her? You want one of ours to do it?" Reynolds asked.

"I don't think so," Jasper said. "She's a little too impressed with me and might tell more than she knows if I call her. I just need some information and she is supposed to be the gossip as well as the social director."

"I'll leave that to you then," Reynolds said. "Hold on." He relayed the request to someone else in the office then turned back to him. "Anything else?"

"Yes." Jasper hesitated. "Willis Frazier. He identified Starling in the Catholic church for me. I'd like to know if he can identify Mark Baxter as the second man in that church."

"Baxter?" His captain frowned. "You're sure that man who returned to Jewel is Mark Baxter?"

"I'm sure," Jasper said. "He was in Plains on or close to all the important dates. I just need to know for sure there's a connection between him and Starling."

"Right," Captain Reynolds said. "Will Frazier be cooperative?"

"I don't know," Jasper said. "He was with me and he was prepared to be with Brown. You might have to offer him relocation to get him to testify."

Reynolds frowned. "I can do that. Does he have a family?"

"Yes," Jasper said. "And he's gone straight. He's going to be needed to place the connection."

"I'll see what I can do. What's his informant ID?" Reynolds asked.

Jasper paused, thinking back to the interview. A date when everything had gone to hell. Five numbers. 1929. The stock market crash. He remembered that now. "It was 19299."

"Got it," Reynolds said without a flicker of recognition. "Is there anything specific you need on those inspection scanners?"

"Yes," Jasper said. "I know there were six cameras. I need to know when they arrived, when they were first shown to the office, and what happened to each one. I also need to know names and current locations of anyone who was involved with those–and who was with Mike when he had his accident."

He hesitated. "I also need to talk to Mike's doctor again but I don't have the right authorizations. Can you get me a temporary one?"

Reynolds tapped his teeth then nodded. "I can make it clear to him you are authorized–quietly. It's better have an appointment though. These doctors get proddy when you take time from their patients."

"I know," Jasper said. "As far as I know, this number is not being tapped. It's the one I got four months ago. Do you need it again?"

"Yes," Reynolds said. "I scrapped it in case the FBI got too nosy around my office. We've come to an understanding now though. Give it again."

Jasper did then quietly asked. "Have you heard anything from Mel?"

"You haven't?" Reynolds frowned. "She's a smart girl, Jasper. Yes, I have heard from her and she's studying for finals. My wife takes most of the calls since I don't want her thinking I've got a girlfriend."

"I appreciate that," Jasper said. "I'll call her soon."

"Do that," Reynolds said. "All I can do is tell her you're safe and so is Jewel. I did have to order her to stay away from the damned house."

"I told her that," Jasper said. "I don't want her identified as my daughter."

"That's what I told her. I had to tell her the kidnappers planted cameras in there and she can't go in without being seen," Reynolds said. "Since then she hasn't mentioned it again."

"As soon as finals are done, I'll get her out of Plains. Corey too." Jasper recalled his daughter's boyfriend and realized he hadn't done anything to ensure his continuing education. He needed to get that done before Corey decided he had to drop out. He didn't know whether the two of them would ever get married but Corey had brains and shouldn't be forced to quit school for lack of funds. It was just another thing to get done.

A uniformed officer came into his captain's office and handed him a scrap of paper. Reynolds glanced at it then took a picture with his com unit. Almost instantly, the paper appeared on Jasper's screen and it was the phone number he needed. He saved it then wrote it down for good measure.

"I think we're done. I'll get a report for you on those inspection systems," Reynolds said. "Oh, and Hunter said to tell you Ed Kucera was not a Mason. I think that theory just blew up."

"Noted," Jasper said. "And I'm relieved to hear it. I'm working on a different angle now but I don't think it's connected to the murders."

"Send me a report when you get time," Reynolds said. "Now I've got an appointment. Keep safe." He broke the connection.

Chapter 37 - Reach Out

It was mid-afternoon before he decided to call Mrs. Krantz. He'd had lunch with Jewel and the second and third graders, getting to meet eleven youngsters from Amber Farms and two neighboring ones. It was pretty different from his remembered experiences. As a parent, he would have been allowed to drop in and observe Melody's classes at that age but not allowed to participate–and it would have required advance notice. Here he'd been warned to confine visits to lunch time but he was welcome.

The class size was also smaller and more intimate than any he'd ever seen. Well, he liked that. During his own early years he'd not received a lot of attention from teachers. It wasn't until he had a good math teacher and an introduction to higher mathematics that he'd found his place. A year or so later he'd been stuck in a music class and had started playing but that hadn't been encouraged.

These kids really did do their cooking in the classroom and he'd been served up a lunch of ramen with mushrooms, carrots, peas, and beef in it. The beef had been pre-cooked but the kids had prepared everything else. There were also thick rolls with home-made peanut butter and jelly to finish filling the kids up. All in all, a good meal. While the children were washing the dishes, he'd taken Jewel aside and asked her about Rosalyn Krantz and the men's club again. She'd been more helpful on Mrs. Krantz.

He'd been invited to come again and bring his drum and probably would since it made a nice break from thinking about murder and drug dealing. Jewel had also been more relaxed in the school setting. She had taught fourth and fifth graders before but told him privately that the third graders she was helping now were more advanced than most of her old students. It helped that there were no subbies in their number. In the cities every public school had a large base of subbies or subsistence children. They received the same education as everyone else but their parents were less engaged. That, combined with the perception that subbies would never succeed in life, led to under performance in all but a few.

He'd been guilty of the same prejudice growing up so it had shaken him to the core when his family had been forced on to subsistence. His father was unemployed after a lifetime of working for the city of Chicago and his mother had never really worked before. They'd gone from a comfortable two bath house to a cramped subby apartment. They hadn't been on the subby list long because his father agreed to transfer to Louisville but it had been too long for him. He'd graduated early from high school and gone immediately to college to escape the apartment. In college he'd still been branded as a subby for his freshman year but he'd left that behind with the release of his first album. By the middle of his sophomore year he had three charted hits and four albums and was arguably the richest self-made student at Columbia University. After his brother's death from blissex, he had quit music and switched to studying criminal justice. He didn't regret those years in law enforcement or his marriage to Carol but music and Jewel were now the center of his life.

These students would never face the subby prejudice. Even though family income depended on employment, no one went hungry or had to rely on the state for basic needs. The farms did their best to make sure everyone was employed and most adults had two or even three roles to fill. He was probably the most useless of the lot right now even though technically he was richer than Jewel for another three years. She would overtake him when she turned thirty and he was sure he'd never catch up. It didn't matter. He knew from experience only the first million mattered. The rest was just frosting on the cake.

Mrs. Krantz. He was back in the conference room and trying to order his thoughts for the upcoming call. It was more difficult today for some reason and he found himself staring morosely out at the blowing snow. It had fallen gently this morning but now it looked to be blizzard conditions and he shivered just looking at it, glad he didn't have to go out there. As soon as this call was done, he'd put a thick sweater on and start looking like a Minnesota farmer. For now he looked like Sensor Man partly because Mrs. Krantz would be impressed and partly because he didn't want to give any clues to her.

He'd photographed the white boards and wiped them for this interview, aware that three of them would show in camera range. Just one of them had a list titled the Men's Club and the names of Mike West, Drew Nugent, and Ed Kucera on it. He wanted that one filled out.

He was wasting time. Calling up the West Foundation, he gave them the number for Rosalyn Krantz and waited, sitting down at the table and arranging notepad and coffee cup to suit him. He could hear the operator talking to Mrs. Krantz before he could see her. Apparently, Mrs. Krantz didn't allow vid on just any call.

"Mrs. Krantz? I have a call here from Jasper Stone also known as Sensor Man. I believe you're acquainted. Will you accept?"

"Mr. Stone? Jazz Stone? Of course," Rosalyn Krantz's voice was nearly breathless. "Is Jewel with him?"

"He requests vid," the operator said before Jasper could.

"Of course," she replied and Jasper had the picture. "Jazz, Mr. Stone, I... Is Jewel ok? Who was that woman?"

"Thank you, Tracy," Jasper said. "I'll take it from here."

"Yes, Mr. Stone," the relay operator said. "Circuit is secure."

"Oh, I didn't realize she was still there," Mrs. Krantz said. "I'm sorry."

"It's not a problem," Jasper said. "For your information, all my calls are being routed through the West Foundation to protect my location. It's necessary."

"Yes, yes, I understand," Mrs. Krantz said. "How is Jewel? I saw your interview last night and it was horrible. I can't imagine drug dealers being so vicious." She shuddered. It was unfortunate because there was rather a lot of Rosalyn Krantz to shudder. It wasn't flesh but the myriad of beads she was wearing just now—more than Jasper had ever seen her wear in public. Had she been trying on necklaces? Cleaning her jewelry box?

Ignoring the necklaces, he focused on her question. "Jewel is doing fine at the moment. She has nightmares and worries about the transmitter but I'm keeping her busy. I know she misses you and other people in Reach Out."

Mrs. Krantz beamed at that admission. "Oh, we miss her too," she gushed. "And her grandmother. They were such a help." Realizing what she'd said, she stopped. "I'm sorry. I shouldn't mention Elizabeth."

"It's all right," Jasper said with a genuine smile. "She would be pleased to know she's still missed. That is, after all, the measure of a good life."

"You're right," Mrs. Krantz said. "And I can never taste her brownies without thinking of her."

"Same here. Now the reason I'm calling is Jewel mentioned her Uncle Mike had some really good friends and I'm not sure all of them know he's gone and Jewel isn't sure she has all their names. Do you remember a group nicknamed the Men's Club?"

She gave him a little frown. "Yes, I remember it. Annoying little thing, really. Sometimes they'd go off alone and leave their wives behind. We never had enough men for the dances as it was."

"Yes, I can see that would be annoying," Jasper said. "Who were the guilty ones?"

"Well, there was Mike West, Professor Nugent–and he really was a good dancer–and Rick Gordon. Those were the ones from Plains. The others we saw a lot of included Trace Stephens, Dan Mushti, and Mr. Kucera." She said that last name reluctantly.

"I know who Dan Mushti is but who is Trace Stephens?" Jasper asked but his mind was focused on Rick Gordon. So Gordon had known both the professor and Mike West well.

"He's a deputy mayor in Denver," Mrs. Krantz said. "A very nice man. So is Dan Mushti. You wouldn't think a football star could be so nice but he is. His wife is wonderful too."

"I see," Jasper said and wrote the names down on his pad. "I'll see they know about Mike. Were there any others?"

"Oh, lots," Mrs. Krantz said. "You could almost pick them out since they were always exceptional men and everyone was married except Mike and Drew. Oh, and there was one woman they let into their little circle. Beth Burroughs from Los Angeles."

"Elizabeth Burroughs? The judge?" Jasper's question was sharper than he intended.

"Yes, that was her. I understand she died not long after her visit here. A real shame."

Died? Jasper couldn't believe Mrs. Krantz didn't know but she obviously didn't. Judge Burroughs had died in a car accident shortly after sentencing a high-ranking official to life in prison for homicide. A second judge had reduced the sentence to just ten years and had outraged the family and citizens alike. There had been an investigation into that judge but if they had found anything, it was never made public.

"Is that all?" Mrs. Krantz asked. "I think Rick Gordon could tell you more."

"Not quite," Jasper said. "Do you remember if Mark Baxter was part of that group?"

She frowned then shook her head, sending her beads to shivering. "No, no, of course not. He just came in from Chicago for the fundraisers. He wasn't friends with any of them. He wasn't a very nice man and they all were."

"Not friends with any?" Jasper asked. "Not even Kucera?"

"Oh, well, he knew the Kuceras," Mrs. Krantz said. "He'd have to since he worked for Wilson. And he talked to Ed, of course. He just wasn't part of that group. I don't think they liked him. I know I didn't but he is a major donor."

"True, he is," Jasper said. "Locally as well as Chicago?"

"Yes, both," Mrs. Krantz said. "More than twenty-five thousand in Plains and he's on the Chicago list as a major donor too. If he was just more pleasant but he isn't."

"No, he isn't," Jasper said, recalling those ice blue eyes. "Thank you, Mrs. Krantz. You've been really helpful."

"Any time," she said. "Let me know when you're coming back to Plains and we'll put together an event. I need a minimum of two weeks to do it properly."

"I'll remember that," Jasper said. "You'll know first."

She smiled her pleasure and gave a little wave as he broke the connection.

She was going to be in for a long wait, Jasper thought. He would have to return to Plains eventually but it wouldn't be to stay. He just wasn't sure where they would move to. The farm was nice but he needed a proper studio to work in—and a house big enough for any children that came along. The little apartment he shared with Jewel was starting to irritate him. He needed more space.

He should have brought his drum up here. There wasn't much more he could do today but he would get his notes down. With that, he began adding the names of the "Men's Club" to the list but found himself stopping at Trace Stephens. T. S. He underlined the initials then dug out the picture of the professor's notepad. Deputy Mayor in Denver? Had he just solved that riddle? Could a deputy mayor make surveillance vid disappear from Denver's system? Or would it take a city attorney like Gordon?

He sat down and stared at the board. Who were these men? Mike had been a programmer and city engineer with lots of money. Rick Gordon was city attorney of Plains—just a couple of steps down from mayor. Professor Nugent was a history professor, again with lots of money.

Now he had a lawyer who was a professional lobbyist and specialized in family law, a deputy mayor of Denver, and—what was Dan Mushti doing these days? Doing a quick public search, he found his profile and stopped. Dan Mushti was on a college board? He still had money too. In his sports days he'd been one of the highest paid athletes. Now it looked like he was in real estate. He was listed as part owner of a large complex in the Denver underground.

Legal, administration, education–and Judge Burroughs too. He couldn't forget her. He wondered if other men's club members were in the same fields. They all looked to have money too. What was really strange is the ones he knew had good reputations. Kucera had been a lobbyist, it was true but he had no idea who he had represented. He should find out.

Frowning at the list he'd just concocted, he took a picture of the board then wiped it clean. He wasn't sure why he did but he really didn't want Jewel nosing into that.

Mike's doctor. He'd nearly forgot about him. Checking the time, he placed another call and hoped the doctor hadn't left early for the weekend. Something Uri had said about painkillers was bugging him. It was true that narcoset was ineffective against intense nerve pain. Carol had been able to use it for only a year before they had to put her on something stronger. Valium had helped for a while but she was on narcopen fairly quickly. Why hadn't Mike been put on it?

He could only think of one reason he wouldn't be but he needed to confirm it. Aware that he couldn't ask a doctor to sit in an interrogation chair, he set his com unit to record the call. He needed to know if his suspicions were true and whether Mike West had even more in common with Kucera and Nugent than they'd previously suspected.

"Doctor Shamen?" Jasper recognized the doctor who finally appeared. "Jasper Stone. Were you told I'd be calling?"

"Yes, Mr. Stone," the doctor said. "And I'm glad to hear you and your wife are safe. How is she?"

"Nightmares mostly," Jasper said, "and worried about the transmitter. We have gotten to a place with few electronics and that helps."

"Yes, it would," Dr. Shamen said. "I wasn't aware those transmitters were being used in the States but we did learn about them in med school. Unfortunately, I'm not an expert."

"I wasn't calling about that," Jasper said. "We have an expert. No, this is about Mike West again. Since he is deceased and I am now a member of the family, can you answer another question for me?"

"Just one?" Dr. Shamen looked surprised. "I would expect more."

"Only one important one," Jasper said. "Did Mike West have an allergy to bliss?"

"Well, yes," Dr. Shamen said. "An unusually virulent one. We had to avoid all drugs with a bliss element. You didn't know?"

"No, I'm not sure my wife even knew." He had to struggle to hide his reaction. Mike West was one of them. He just wished he knew who they were. "Is the bliss allergy common?"

Dr. Shamen frowned. "No, it's very uncommon. I've only seen it in two others."

"Let me guess," Jasper said, "Andrew Nugent and Rick Gordon."

The doctor started then became expressionless. "I can't answer that, lieutenant, and you should not have asked."

"No, you're right," Jasper said. "I will give you one thing you may not know. Drew Nugent died of a bliss reaction after he was injected with Penseek. That is not for public consumption but you might note it in your records that his bliss reaction was fatal. If you have another patient with that allergy, be warned."

The doctor looked torn but finally asked his question. "And Mike West?"

"Mike West was poisoned with an exotic poison made from passion flower. It wasn't a bliss reaction," Jasper said. "According to the police labs, it was actually a combination of evell, scotch, and the poison but the poison probably would have been enough."

Dr. Shamen looked relieved. "I had warned him about mixing evell and scotch but I'll admit I'm relieved it wasn't that. Mr. West was a good man and deserved a better end."

"Yes, he did," Jasper said. "I'm hoping to get his murderer soon. You've given me some valuable help today. Thank you."

Before the doctor could respond, he broke the connection and let his grin show. Mike West and Drew Nugent–plus Rick Gordon. Whatever they were, they were connected and each had felt it necessary to take blister. Rick Gordon was still alive and Trace Stephens had to be the T. S. in the professor's note.

Ed Kucera was also a member of their little group–and Baxter hadn't known it. He had wanted Jasper to find out where Ed got blister. He still didn't know that answer but he was confident Rick Gordon would have it. He was going to have to ask him before this part could come to an end.

He was almost relieved to hear that Baxter hadn't been included in their little club but not terribly surprised. Even with his limited knowledge of Mike West, he was sure he wouldn't have willingly associated with someone like Baxter. He knew Drew Nugent wouldn't. Kucera had known him but did he like or trust him? Trace Stephens and Dan Mushti might be able to shed more light on that but given what happened to the Professor, he wasn't willing to take a chance on contacting them. No, he would ask Rick Gordon but he would wait till Baxter was in custody. He didn't want more deaths at his door.

Did he want to alert Carlson to this? No. If Carlson passed it on to anyone else, they might get interrogated. This would have to be his secret.

Judge Elizabeth Burroughs. That was surprising to him but again it wasn't. He knew Dan Mushti's reputation. Trace Stephens he didn't know at all but if he was half as intent as the others on fighting drugs and corruption, he'd be a good match. Was that little group crime fighters or something else? He wondered how long he'd have to wait to find out. It was too bad Mrs. Krantz hadn't identified any others. Well, he'd look up those he knew about and see if they had anything else in common besides Reach Out and their little men's club. There almost had to be something– some reason they'd met in the first place.

He sat down with his com unit and started his search.

Chapter 38 - Rabbits

"Now this I like," Jewel said and eyed him with such interest Jasper knew what she had in mind. Setting a small sack of groceries down on the counter, she drew her cool hands across his bare chest.

Jasper captured her wayward hands before she could continue the torture. "Cold hands," he said. "What are you going to feed me tonight?"

"Oh, I like that," Jewel said and turned back to the counter. "Hungry man rejects..."

Jasper grabbed her and pulled her hips close to his. "Hungry man needs to keep up his strength to deal with hungry woman." He nipped her neck and she giggled.

He didn't turn her loose but quietly said "I'd really like to go walk around for an hour. You realize we've been here almost a week and I still haven't seen a rabbit?"

She smiled and peeled his hands away. "Then don't tempt me."

While she put groceries away, he finished dressing in black jeans and flannel shirt. Checking to make sure his locket was secure, he buttoned up.

It was just past three and he hoped there would be enough daylight to see something of the outside. He didn't want to go out in the snow but he was beginning to feel cooped up by the Minnesota winter.

He also had plenty of time on his hands since he probably wouldn't see that inspection report until Monday and there was little else he could do between now and then. The one bright point he was saving was another conversation with David and Jewel. If he was right, they knew nothing of Mike's real involvement with the men's club. He just wish he knew what the goals of that club were. A cursory examination of the members he knew hadn't turned up anything illegal but there had to be some reason the members were taking blister.

"Ready?" he asked his wife as she put her com unit on the counter.

"Yes," she said. "No one calls me on that. Molly said it might be better not to carry it with the jammers."

"But you carry it anyway?" Jasper asked.

"Only when I think you might call," Jewel said. "If you're beside me, I don't need it."

"True," Jasper said. "Where should we go first?"

"Rabbit Run," Jewel said with a mischievous grin. "You have got to see the rabbits. The week is almost gone, you know."

"I heard," Jasper said and followed his wife out the door. It was just a short walk to the homemade sign that marked Rabbit Run. "So who made the sign?" He studied it, seeing the letters were burned into a piece of wood in a childish script. The plank had been painted since to make the letters stand out but there'd been no attempt to make a more professional sign.

"Sasha did it when she was about eight," Jewel said. "Before that none of the streets had names. The others got regular signs but they kept this one because it was first and it was Sasha's."

"Who named the other streets?" Jasper asked.

"The children," Jewel said. "A school project. The older children decided how the houses and barns should be numbered."

"You learned a lot," Jasper said. "I thought you were teaching school, not learning it."

Jewel smiled at him but it was a smaller smile than usual. "They gave me a real intensive tour yesterday. That's how I knew something had happened. I was ready to scream by the end."

Jasper studied her and realized they'd been wrong to keep her in the dark. He could have insisted he needed to talk to her but he'd been plagued with those FBI agents. Kale had called home but he'd been afraid to for fear they could trace the call.

"I'll call next time," he said. "And I won't let them hold me again."

"I want Brad's number," Jewel said with a determined look. "No one is going to keep you from me again."

Jasper stared at her, realizing she meant it and knew he'd better find a way to placate her before she called the entire West Foundation down on whoever was holding him. "I don't have Brad's cell number," he said, "but I have Mary's and she will move mountains to help."

Thinking this was the time, he added, "I'm going to have to leave again and this time it will be almost no notice. It can't be helped."

"Why?" Jewel wasn't giving him room to evade. He'd better be honest with her.

"We have that new inside man in the blissex operation in Plains. He's got valuable information about shipments, personnel and how it's all done. His price is that we rescue his sister and mother and take them to a safe house."

She studied him then said, "You're still on the force."

"No, I'm not but I'm working with them," Jasper said. "When they took you I knew that was the only way we were going to be safe in Plains. I'm using Butler to monitor the house. Our new informant spotted Butler and knew what he was. He made the offer instead of telling his bosses the house was wired. It's been approved and sometime in the next week I will have to go back to Chicago to the College of Asian Studies and extract his sister and mother. When they find out the house is wired and he didn't say anything about it, they'll kill his family and him."

"And the family hasn't done anything?" Jewel's eyes were big and starting to shine.

"Not a thing," Jasper said. "And this guy has been looking for a way out. He didn't have to tell me what drugs they'd given you that night but he did. I don't think it was in his orders."

He remembered trading his password for that info but any decent technician could have broken that in minutes. No, he was sure Kin was feeling him out there.

"Ok, you have to go," Jewel said after a long minute. "But I want you to call me when it's over and you're on your way back. I don't want to worry any longer than I have to. Molly says I shouldn't."

"Then I'll call you," Jasper said. "I would never argue with Molly the medic." He opened his arms and Jewel came into them. This time no kisses but he gave her a hug. "I'll stay safe. After yesterday I have every confidence in Kale—and they'll have officers with me. We're cooperating with Chicago police on this one."

Jewel sighed. "I know you're holding back on me, Jazz Stone," she whispered. "But I am going to get it all yet."

"You'll get more tonight," Jasper said. "Right now I want to see rabbits."

Reminded of where they were going, Jewel drew back and led the way down the street. They'd already passed the school but now she pointed out some blank wood faces. "Home sites," she said. "When they did the underground, they put in some basements and some front doors so they could expand later. Mikal is saving up to build a house there." She jabbed her finger at the second one they passed. "He's almost got enough. Kale and Beth just finished one further down. Three bedrooms, two baths, and a huge kitchen." She sounded wistful.

"I miss our kitchen too," Jasper said and held her hand as they walked along. Finally he could see a door at the end of the road.

Jewel saw it too, and quickened her steps. "Rabbits!" She smiled at him and her somber mood lifted. "They really are cute-especially the babies."

Jasper followed her past another door marked Hydro Farm One to stand in a brightly lit room filled with wire cages and the smell of rabbits. There were hundreds of cages, mostly large ones holding several rabbits and others holding one or two. Not sure exactly where to look, Jasper just followed his wife as she led him up some stairs to another level. He noticed the temperature drop first then the wide windows that let sunlight in. The rabbits were quiet things but he could feel the ambiance of having hundreds of animals here and caught a little bit of urine smell. It wasn't bad though.

"Hi," a fresh-faced girl said as she straightened up from a cage. "Here to pet rabbits again?"

Jewel smiled and nodded. Before Jasper could protest, he found himself holding a little one and thought what do you call a baby rabbit?

"These two are Californians," their guide said. "The same kind Sasha took to Mars. They've got beautiful fur and produce some pretty tasty meat."

"Meat?" Jasper repeated and his wife rolled her eyes. These were for the table? He looked at the little bundle of fur in his hands and felt the softness of it and couldn't imagine eating it. "Does it have a name?"

"No, of course not," their guide said. "These aren't breeders. Only breeders get names."

"So how do you tell them apart?" Jasper asked.

"Microchips," she said. "All meat animals have to be microchipped. That's the law." She tried to sound patient but Jasper could tell he was being dense and this girl didn't appreciate it.

"City boy," he said. "And you must have been raised here. "

"Yes, I was. I'm Lily Hanson." She smiled. "It's not bad. I like rabbits a lot better than chickens."

"I can imagine," Jasper said. "They're a lot softer."

"Smarter too," the girl said. "Excuse me. I have to change a run."

Jasper watched as the girl opened a sliding door then herded a dozen rabbits down a grassy ramp toward it. The rabbits hopped along as if they were used to it. When the last one had hopped through the door, she closed it and walked back. Another batch of rabbits came spilling out another door to hop around in the grass run.

The girl bent over and pulled a cloth pad out of the cage then inserted a new one before checking feeders and water bottles. That done, she bundled up the cloth pad and put it in a laundry bin and picked up an electronic notebook. Every move seemed to be long practiced.

"Exercise time," the girl said and made a note on the pad. "Every rabbit over three months old needs to have it. I'll be glad when summer comes though. We can use the outside runs too."

"How old are these?" Jasper said as he stroked the soft ball of fur in his hand. It fit comfortably in one palm. Fortunately, the grown rabbits the girl was herding were not nearly so cute.

"Six weeks," she said. "They've got a long way to go yet. They're cute at this age though. Done?"

"Yes and thanks. How old are you?"

"Fourteen," Lily said. "I've been doing this since fall. It's my after-school job." She grinned but there was pride in it. "It's not hard herding rabbits."

"Are there any adults around?" Jasper asked, surprised.

"Oh, they can see me or I can ask for help," she said. "Mikal is in the other barn today and he's really good—and Connie is around somewhere, Bart too. It takes a lot of us to get it all done before supper."

"Yes, it would," Jasper said. "We won't distract you any more." He handed the little rabbit back and noticed it had dirtied his hand. Before he could worry about it, Jewel was guiding him to a sink where she too washed her hands.

"Animals," she said. "Always a bit messy."

"Yes, I think I prefer plants," he said in a low voice. "Not so soft."

She grinned and motioned him to follow her, only pausing to thank their guide.

Had he ever eaten rabbit? He wasn't sure. He certainly had never held one before. Chickens he'd seen but never handled and he had no affinity for them. The birds were so dumb and so dirty it was a relief not to deal with them when they were alive.

The rabbits were Sasha's field? Had she started that young? Considering how confident Lily was, he was sure she had prior experience too. She probably didn't start at fourteen.

It was so different from the cities. Children there simply couldn't work until they turned twenty or had a high school diploma to show. There were too many legal adults looking for work to allow children who should be going to school to do it. That reform had ensured kids would get that far in their education—and a lot of them graduated early like him and his daughter. He couldn't work and get off the subby list so he'd studied hard to bring up his scores and graduated when he was barely sixteen. Mel had been inspired b—her mother's determination to stay until she graduated. She'd been fifteen when she got her diploma and already in college on her sixteenth birthday.

Jasper remembered that vividly. Mel had known about her mother's decision to go but when the time came she hadn't been there for her. When she found out her mother had gone without her—that he'd let her—she'd enrolled in college and moved into the dorms to get away from him. It had taken a year and a half for them to finally have a civil conversation. He'd paid her bills and just waited. Now they had a relationship again but Mel would never cling to him. She would never forget.

"You're thinking dark thoughts," Jewel said as they left the rabbits behind. "Do we have to go back?"

"No, let's not. I was just thinking about Mel," Jasper said. "And kids working."

"There's nothing unusual about that on a farm," Jewel said. "Even I worked one summer at my cousin's ranch."

"You did?" Jasper looked at her in surprise. "How did you manage that?"

"I learned to ride a horse," Jewel said with a smile. "If you learned, you could ride with me."

"A horse?" He did his best to sound appalled and she laughed.

"Come on, city boy," she said and led him off to hydroponics.

Chapter 39 - David

Jasper understood the hydroponics operation better having toured several in his school days and occasionally visited those in Plains. The fish operation was larger here with massive tanks full of catfish and another species. In Plains they had relied on other more common nutrients for the hydroponics. Other than that, the operation was virtually the same with row after row of PVC pipes and plants sticking out of them. The building he'd toured was dedicated to the needs of the farm so he'd seen more variety than in the commercial operations. The one thing Betty Talbot had stressed was the farm produced more than a hundred tons of tomatoes for Chicago each year along with cucumbers, celery, zucchini, and strawberries. Those numbers had impressed him—that and squash as long as his arm. He didn't care much for squash but he had no idea they could grow that big. The few he'd seen in the grocery stores were much smaller and even those had been cut and cleaned before being put up for sale in packages suitable for small families.

They'd found a place where they could look out at the fading day but it hadn't done them much good. Snow was still falling sideways and they could see it was drifted against the buildings. Nothing was moving in this weather and Jasper found himself appreciating the underground all that much more. With almost everything connected, no one had a reason to fret or stop work. Everyone was home and safe.

"There's going to be a dance tonight," Jewel said as she puttered around their tiny kitchen. "It's family night and with the weather like it is, almost everyone will be in the Commons. It's warmer than the above ground buildings."

"That makes sense to me," Jasper said. "First though I want to call David. He should be off shift now, right?"

Jewel looked at the time. "Yes, he got off about forty-five minutes ago. It takes him about ten minutes to get home after that."

"That's what I thought," Jasper said. "And I've got something new to ask you both about. Let's get him called."

"Both of us?" Jewel asked. "You're letting me in?"

"You helped me find it," Jasper said. "You and something Uri said. I just confirmed it. Now hold on until we get David here too."

He placed the call then settled down in the easy chair to wait. Jewel perched on the arm and he absently wrapped one arm around her waist.

"Hello again," David said. He looked more relaxed too. "Social or business?"

"A bit of both," Jasper said. "I've identified more of that group Mike associated with. Did you know he was pretty well acquainted with Trace Stephens and Dan Mushti?"

"Really?" David looked surprised. "Well, I knew about Dan. Mike sometimes stayed with him when he came to Denver. He wasn't a big football fan but he said Dan had a good head on his shoulders."

"Like the Professor, I think," Jasper said. "And Ed Kucera and Rick Gordon. They were all members of the same group."

David frowned. "Yes, I guess they were. What are you getting at?"

Jasper craned his head to look up at Jewel. "You said Mike introduced Kucera to Jake?"

"Yes," she responded, puzzled. "It wasn't Drew."

"Jewel, he was living with you and your grandmother. Do you know if he was taking aspirin every day? The low dose kind?"

"Yes," she said. "At first it was one in the morning and one at night. Later his doctor told him to just take one. He never forgot them."

"Did he take a bottle back with him to Gracee Place?" Jasper asked.

"I don't remember," Jewel said. "I don't recall seeing any but he went to bed early and I was still up." Her eyes clouded at the memory. "I should have checked on him. He was upset."

"Hindsight, Jewel." David waved that away. "Jasper, what's this about?"

Elinor joined him in camera range, her petit figure small next to David's taller one.

"Did either of you know Mike had a severe allergy to bliss?" Jasper asked and saw their blank looks. "No, I guess you didn't. I confirmed it with his doctor today because of something Uri said. He thought the doctor wasn't trying very hard to control Mike's pain because he wasn't getting any of the bliss based painkillers–just narcoset and   evell–and he was in pretty severe pain. He should have had narcopen."

"I knew he was hurting but..." David ran his hands through his hair. "And he couldn't take bliss? Are you sure?"

"He was taking blister."

Jewel went pale, David's frown deepened, and Elinor looked confused.

"Blister?" she asked.

"I don't believe it," David said, his voice flat. "Mike? He was no criminal."

"None of those men were," Jasper said. "Not Mike, not Drew, not even Ed Kucera. Whatever that men's club is, it's not a criminal organization. They weren't even CIA and that was the group blister was created for. It's a classified drug designed to prevent interrogations. When we found it at the professor's house, it looked like low dose aspirin–and low dose aspirin is taken once a day, not twice." He looked at Jewel. "Blister is meant to be taken once a day by agents who feel they might be interrogated. It stays in the system when enough is built up. I suspect they–ad to have that in case agents were held for a few days before interrogation."

"Carlson told you this?" David demanded. "Is he CIA? I thought he was DEA."

"He's DEA," Jasper said. "And he got it out of the CIA when he told them Ed Kucera died from blister and the professor too. The FBI agent was also killed with it—and Jewel's implant was something they knew nothing about. They're very unhappy right now. I think they might be even more unhappy if they find out a secret society is using it."

"Secret society?" David questioned. "And my brother?" He snorted.

Jewel was quiet—too quiet. Jasper looked at her. "Jewel?"

"I knew there was something," she said. "Not this. The men you mentioned—all of them came to the house to visit him. One night they showed up together and Grandma insisted we had to stay on the first floor." Jewel wasn't smiling now. "I think Grandma knew."

"Old friends visiting? Did they bring their wives? I know Kucera's wife knew Mother," David said.

"No, they came alone," Jewel said. "Elaine Kucera came other times but not that time. This was just them. There were others too but I didn't know them at all. I only got to see them come and go. They spent the entire time upstairs with Mike."

"Coffee? Refreshments?" Jasper asked.

"Grandma sent them up in the dumb waiter. She didn't let me go up to serve." Jewel frowned. "I thought that was strange at the time but Uncle Mike didn't always let me in. It was after that though, that he added me to his shares in Butler."

"And Drew got interested in you?" Jasper suggested.

"No, that happened before," Jewel said, her cheeks turning pink. "This happened after Grandma took the walk. It was in June. Some of them did come before but not together like that."

"Sounds like a meeting," Jasper said. "I would like to know who the others were."

"I still think you're barking up the wrong tree," David said. "Mike wouldn't get involved in anything shady, much less illegal."

"Was he a Mason?" Jasper asked.

"No, of course not," David said. "He got invited, I'm sure. I know I have but neither of us joined. Too busy."

"Kucera wasn't a Mason either," Jasper said. "That threw me off since the Professor and Gordon are. What these men all have in common is reputation and philanthropy and a concern about the future. I haven't found out much but they're all major donors to Reach Out and the Professor, at least, had personally sponsored outstanding students. My daughter's boyfriend is hardly the first he's helped out."

"Mike has done that," David said. "Hell, even I've done that. It's nothing exceptional."

"No, it's not," Jasper said. "I haven't done it yet but I plan to start with Corey. When I was on the force, I had to be more circumspect about spending money."

He frowned, knowing Corey must be fretting about next semester already. He needed to contact him.

"In any case this group is not connected with the blissex case," he said. "Nothing illegal and no connection to Wilson except Ed Kucera's personal relationship to his brother. I just wanted you to know Mike was part of it and taking blister."

"I still find that hard to believe," David said. "Mike usually told me what he was up to. He was older, of course but we tried to stay informed. He was the first person I called after Elinor's accident."

Jasper found himself glancing at the slightly thicker hand David held in his own. It was nearly normal now. She had been on the moon repairing the equipment David operated when her spacesuit glove blew out and David had stuck with her and actually proposed to her on the long drive back to a pressurized base.

"He probably was honest in every other area," Jasper said then realized that probably wasn't true either. "But you know Kucera was ordered to suicide before he could be interrogated—and he took that order even though he was innocent. I wouldn't be surprised if Mike would have taken it too. This group is that serious about secrecy."

"Then what the hell are they doing?" David demanded. "There's got to be something if they're that serious."

"I know," Jasper said. "But I haven't uncovered it. Once the blissex case is done, I'll ask a few questions but not now. I'm satisfied it's not connected."

"There is something else I haven't told you about Mike," Jasper said. "And it could have something to do with that meeting Jewel knew about. Did you know he was thinking of euthanasia for himself?"

Surprisingly, David nodded. It was Jewel who looked shocked this time.

"Yes, he told me that," David said. "Too much pain. He just wanted to see Jewel married first."

Jasper felt Jewel clutch his hand hard and knew she'd figured it out. That was why he'd been in favor of a marriage between her and Drew. He was going to leave.

"Very old-fashioned, I know," David said, "but he quit pushing when Jewel said no."

"He wanted Drew to take care of me because he was leaving?" Jewel's voice rose. "He didn't think I could take care of myself? I was twenty-six!"

"You were also still living at home with a house too big for you," David said. "When he mentioned a marriage between you and Drew, Mother was still planning on the walk and Mike was on nearly total bed rest. He was in a lot of pain so I agreed it might be an idea. When you seemed to be okay with it, I didn't see any reason to oppose it."

"He was in a lot of pain," Jewel said. "And delusional if he thought I'd marry someone his age. No, Drew was even older. And I was perfectly capable of taking care of myself!" Her voice rose on those final words. She pulled loose from Jasper's hand to fold her arms.

"Maybe," David said and got a glare from his wife. "But I'm glad it didn't come to that. Jasper's timing was good even if the situation was not. Yes, I knew Mike was thinking of it. When did you find out?" He looked at Jasper.

"In the early stages of the investigation," Jasper said. "I had to talk to those at Soma and find out about your interviews. Rachel was your caseworker and she recalled Mike asked about euthanasia for himself. That had never happened before so she remembered it."

David frowned. "And you didn't think he had suicided?"

"It crossed my mind," Jasper admitted, "but it didn't fit. Mike had appointments and his affairs weren't wrapped up neatly. He was also concerned about Jewel. Suicides are only concerned with themselves. If it had been a murder-suicide, he would have seen to Jewel as well. He didn't."

"Basic psychology," Elinor said. "I know about that." She was pale now. "Couples leaving together—or families."

Jasper wondered how the hell she knew about that and why it upset her. David seemed to know because he was holding her hand tight.

"If Jake hadn't confessed, there was still Mike's medical condition," Jasper said. "He simply wasn't able to do what was done. I ruled him out quickly."

"I've got a report coming on the inspection scanners, by the way," Jasper added. "And Mike had to be the primary target. They didn't tell Jake though. If they had, Starling would have found and killed Mike the same day. He was in no condition to resist."

"I wondered about that," David said. "But I don't think Jake could be blackmailed into killing Mike. Mother was different. Jake blamed her and Dad for him not being handed the money he needed to go. I stupidly agreed with Dad on that but it looked like Jake was finally getting it together when he got that sponsorship."

"But you two were a hell of a lot more upset about Mike than Elizabeth," Jasper said. "And that took time to figure out. I finally had to compare it with how I would feel if Mel died when I was prepared for Carol to go."

David looked thoughtful. "Yes, I think that was it for me but what really threw me was both in twenty-four hours. Until you told me it was murder, I really thought Mike's heart had given out or he'd accidently overdosed on painkillers. I knew it wasn't suicide but I didn't think it was murder. Mother's death—Mike just told us she fell from the third floor. I didn't talk to Jewel so I didn't know it was murder."

"I gathered that much," Jasper said. "But I'm surprised Jake didn't give himself away."

"He didn't. He had a habit of hiding in his room when he didn't want to talk. He couldn't do that when you told us about Mike though, and I can tell you it hit him like a ton of bricks. He thought, just like I did, that it was accidental."

"It could have been ruled that way," Jasper said. "A combination of evell and scotch. It just never felt that way to me and Pedro Kruger is one heck of a toxicologist. I'd never even heard of passion flower before he identified it."

"Well, you did good," David said with a slight smile. "But why the attempt on Jewel?"

"Starling or the kidnapping?" Jasper asked. "I'm just sorting out the kidnapping."

"Starling first," David said. "Why? You said Mike was the primary target and I was secondary. Why Jewel?"

"The overriding reason, I think, was to give Sam Starling an alibi but it could have been used to lure you out again too. Jewel would never have left you alone if you missed her funeral."

Jewel's obscene protest caused Elinor to give a sharp exclamation before she glared at her husband. David just grinned. Jasper stared at his wife, surprised she'd used one of David's curses and saw she was just as surprised it had come out.

"The bad habits she's been picking up from you," David said. "Such language—its only fit for a spacer."

Jasper caught Elinor's look of consternation and suddenly had a suspicion. David's language was normally very clean and even more so around his wife but some of those phrases he'd used this morning were true dock curses. He'd heard a couple before but the majority were new even to him—and colorful enough not to have been on vids. Elinor didn't look the type to use them but she'd been on space docks and on the moon. Had David learned them from her? Interesting.

Jewel had left him and he realized he didn't have much more to say. The pertinent points had been covered and he didn't want to go into the blissex case. "I think we're done," Jasper said. "Unless you have anything?"

"No, I think we've covered enough," David said. "I think I'm going to go back through some conversations I had with Mike though. I still find it hard to believe he kept anything so important from me."

"Nature of the beast," Jasper said. "I would give you odds that Elaine Kucera doesn't know any more than you do."

"That could be," David said. "It would be interesting to find out."

"Not unless I have some proof of illegal activity," Jasper said. "So far there's nothing."

"Right, well, I have some things to get done," David said with an eye on his wife. "I'll talk to you later."

Jasper grinned as David broke the connection, convinced his new relative was going to have to placate his wife. If Elinor was the source of his curses, she wasn't happy with it. Even if she wasn't, she wasn't happy. Either way, David was going to have to pay for that spacer comment.

Chapter 40 - Rescue

Aware he had the long weekend before him and nothing pressing, Jasper willingly joined the dance others were organizing. He could waltz, two-step, and tango with the best of them but found they also had a repertoire of older dances they used and people willing to show them how. After a breathless Virginia Reel, he was glad enough to settle into a slow dance.

"I think everyone is here," he murmured into his wife's ear, "even the babies." He steered her to where she could see a cradle and two toddlers watching wide-eyed from a mat. The school-aged children were gathered around a refreshment table, uninterested in slow dancing but they'd formed their own group during the Virginia Reel.

"And where else would they be?" she asked. "I like this. This is much better than dancing in the city. It's more fun."

"Yes, we might just have to stay," Jasper said and he found himself thinking about it. In Plains, he would probably have had another quiet night with his wife. They'd be playing pool or watching a vid or chasing each other around the house. It was rare they went out.

He still didn't know that many people by name but he'd learned there were an awful lot of Fletchers, Hansons, and Talbots in the mix. The younger people had more varied names but twice they had identified themselves as a Talbot or Hanson. It was a bit confusing but he supposed those three families were the oldest or the biggest. He'd get it sorted out eventually. Ivan's family and Uri seemed to be the only Kowalskis.

"Let's hit that table after this dance," he said to Jewel. "The kids are cleaning it out."

Jewel giggled. "Kids everywhere do that. Yes, I'm ready for some brownies."

"As long as they're not special ones," Jasper said. "Your grandmother's would be nice. You need to bake me some."

"We'll see. You have to earn those." Jewel pressed a little closer to get her meaning across.

"Christmas," he said. "It's not far away."

"No, I can feel it coming already." Her wicked little grin told him he wasn't going to be there long if she kept it up.

"Minx." He broke off the dance then guided her from the floor to the table. The selection was still good. Besides brownies and cookies, there were also homegrown carrots, mushrooms, celery and little cherry tomatoes. On a meat platter, there were slices of ham and beef and cheese. Tiny slices of bread completed the selection of foods but there were also a couple of fruit punches—one of them   evelled Fruit Bomb and the other labeled Apple Cider. He decided the Apple Cider was safer but took a cup of iced coffee instead.

"Let's sit with Aunt Lill," Jewel said. "She knows everything."

Seeing Harold was out on the dance floor with his daughter-in-law, Jasper agreed. The general manager was still able to tango, the pre-recorded music having changed to that.

"Hello, Aunt Lill," Jewel said as she made herself at home at the table. "Would you like a refill on punch?"

"That would be nice, dear," the elder said. "And another brownie if those scamps have left any."

"Yes ma'am," Jewel said and retreated to the table before Jasper could offer to go. At a loss what to do, he went ahead and sat down and arranged the plates.

"So how are you liking it here?" Aunt Lill asked. "Now that you've had a chance to get nice and bored."

"Bored?" Jasper looked at her in surprise. "With all this going on?"

She laughed at his expression.

"I haven't had time to get bored yet," Jasper said, his lips twitching. "I think I'm going to have to schedule in some special time for that then find a place to hide where Jewel can't find me—or that cat."

"That cat." Lill's eyes wrinkled up into their laugh lines. "I haven't laughed that hard in a long time."

"Neither have I," Jasper admitted. "And I didn't think Jewel would ever catch her breath."

"I heard," Lill said. "So are you allowing that cat to claim you?"

Jasper smiled over her choice of words. "I'm not sure I have a choice. What do you think?"

"We'll have to see. If you stay, you'll probably have him moving in on you. I can't see him going back to your city though."

Jewel rejoined them before Jasper could say his first thought. He couldn't see himself going back to the city at this point. At the same time, he needed a studio and his own space. He couldn't create with anyone— even Jewel—breaking his concentration.

Jewel set down a small plate of brownies and not one but two more cups of punch. "Uncle Harold might be thirsty too," she said. "He's getting a work out."

"That he is," Lill said as they watched him tango around the floor. "But it keeps him young. I just wish I could keep up with him on dances like that." She took one of the brownies. "And I am so glad you gave us this recipe, Jewel. It's a real old-fashioned brownie. I haven't had this kind since I was your age."

Jasper looked suspiciously at his wife. "I think I first had them about thirteen years ago." He took a bite and nodded, recognizing the texture and flavor at once. "Yes, I was about twenty-five."

Lill looked at him in some confusion. "You've known her family that long?"

"No, I was on street patrol then and her grandmother used to feed me brownies when I stopped by to check the house. My favorite memory of those days."

Jewel paused in eating her own to give him an arch look but Jasper wasn't going to admit he'd seen her first then. Then he was married to

Carol and had a five-year-old daughter at home. The brief glimpse he'd gotten of the teenage Jewel had intrigued him but nothing more.

"And then you found Jewel later," Lill said. "Very romantic. It doesn't often work out that way."

"No, it doesn't. I've been trying to figure out who is related to who around here. Can you help me out?" Jasper deftly turned the subject to safer things, unwilling to discuss how he'd met Jewel this time around.

"That is a great way to give yourself a headache," she said. "There's a reason they just started calling us elders aunt or uncle."

"That intermarried?" Jasper asked, his eyebrow shooting up. "Not too close, I hope."

"Close enough that the grandkids mostly have to find mates outside," Lill said. "Give me that napkin and I'll draw it out."

She made quick lines to illustrate it. "There were three founding families," she said. "The Fletchers, Talbots, and Hansons. I'm not one of them by blood. I married Harold. Neither is Ruby but she's the complication."

"There were two Hanson brothers and Ruby was married to Kyle Hanson but he died after giving her two boys. Then she married the younger Talbot brother and had a girl and a third boy." She waited for them to absorb that.

"Now her girl Abby married my Bob—that's Dr. Bob—so we have a Fletcher and Talbot tie. Then her Alan married Susie Talbot for a Hanson and Talbot tie. Finally my daughter married her other Hanson son—that was Richard—for a Fletcher and Hanson tie. They have three children."

"And Ivan's family?" Jasper was starting to understand. "How are they related?"

"They aren't yet," Lill said. "Ivan and Molly came here as newlyweds. Mikal hasn't found anyone yet but their second son Viktor is going to marry Karen Hanson this summer---and Karen is Ruby's granddaughter and my granddaughter too. Got a headache yet?" she asked.

"Not quite," Jasper said, "but I'm glad I'm already married." He smiled at Jewel.

She laughed. "Oh, it will get a little worse. Anton Kowalski and Lily Hanson are pretty close too. They're both way too young but I suspect as soon as she finishes school, there will be wedding bells there too. That will mean a Kowalski and Hanson tie that's also a Fletcher tie."

"Now I have the headache," Jasper said.

"You lasted longer than most," she said. "We keep very good records because we also have kin in the neighboring farms. The grandkids know they have to look further afield for mates. It's also why we're happy when someone marries in or joins us."

"Does this always happen on farms?"

"Not in the old days when single families ran them," Lill said. "But farm girls did tend to marry farm boys further back and it wasn't unusual for siblings to marry siblings in another family. That died off when farms got small and labor got tight and working in the cities started paying better but we've bringing it back with the new corporate farm communities. It's easier to keep people and be more profitable if we diversify like we have."

"It surprises me that Sasha managed to go to Mars," Jasper said. "How did that happen?"

"That took some debate," Lill said. "In the end we decided it was important to show our kids they could have any dream they really wanted if they worked hard enough. Sasha is a symbol to them."

"It wasn't that hard on us financially. She got her first two years of college through the government and found scholarships for the last two. We made sure Sasha knew everything there was to know about rabbits and poultry. Her last year here, she was rabbit manager and assistant poultry manager—and she was good at it."

"We also supplied the breeding stock Sasha took with her and that was profitable. We miss her but as time goes on there will be more kids who choose to leave the farm. We have to keep expanding to keep them home."

"That makes sense," Jasper said. He looked up as Harold joined them, another young girl on his arm.

"No, Amy, I'm going to sit this one out. Be sweet and get me some water please," he said to the teen girl who had him by the arm. He waited till she headed for the refreshment table then pulled out a handkerchief and mopped his brow. "Not as young as I used to be."

"You can't fool me," Lill said. "You saw Jasper flirting with me and had to check it out."

"Flirting in front of his wife?" Harold said and winked at Jasper. "Brave move, son." He took the punch Jewel handed him and almost drained it in one long gulp. "Much better."

"I was trying to explain who was related to Ruby," Lill said. "But it's gotten so complicated, I just told him the Kowalskis weren't."

"And Kale," Harold said. "How is he working out for you?" His eyes were keen when he looked at Jasper.

"He's good," Jasper said. "And I may ask him to get certified if you can spare him for six months."

"We'll talk about that later," Harold said. "If he wants it, probably but there are other things to consider. No, now is not the time."

Jasper nodded, aware Kale was married and his wife was needed here. At the same time, he'd let Harold know he approved of him.

"His classes are very popular," Harold said. "Kale knows what he's doing."

"I haven't been to his class yet," Jasper said. "Maybe I will when things settle down." Suddenly aware his com unit was buzzing against his hip, he pulled it out and checked the number. His blood went cold as he realized it was Carlson then he was flipping it on and looking at the little screen.

"Damn it, they just filed the flight plan ten minutes ago," Carlson said. "And we can't get a plane to you. That storm you're sitting in won't be gone before tomorrow. Jasper, you might have to sit this one out."

"No plane?" Jasper said without thinking then looked at Harold. "Is there any other way to get to Chicago tonight besides plane?"

"Of course there is," Harold said. "We drive you to the rail line and stick you on the next train that stops. It might take an hour to get you that far but after that the trains are sheltered. No delays."

"In this weather?" Jasper found it hard to believe.

"This is nothing," Harold said. "Get your stuff. Let me handle him."

Jasper hesitated only a second before handing the com unit to Uncle Harold. Jewel watched and listened to every word and he was glad he'd warned her he could be sent off any time. Tonight? He couldn't believe they could go anywhere in this storm but Harold seemed confident.

"Harold Fletcher here" he heard the old man say, "General Manager of Amber Farms. We can get him to the rail line tonight but it will be up to you to get a train to stop. It will be the Moose Creek Station and that's a local stop—no expresses. Can you do it?"

By the time he grabbed his cases and returned Kale and Ivan were also there. Kale nodded and walked swiftly away, no doubt to get his own gear.

"Yes, a freight will do," Fletcher was saying. "And it will give us enough time to get him there. They'll need to pick up just two. Our driver will come back. Here he is again."

Jasper took the com unit back and saw a relieved Carlson.

"It's all set," he said. "You'll still be late but not too much since the flight plan is Denver then Plains. Chicago is in that storm too, so you'll need to hit the underground to get to the college. I'll arrange for locals to help you. Just get those two to safety. I'll tell Reynolds what he needs to know."

"Thanks," Jasper said. "We'll be out of here in five."

"I know. Damn it, this wasn't supposed to be for another week." Carlson broke the connection.

"Jewel..." Jasper looked for his wife but she was already following Ivan to his house.

"Better run," Harold said. "You'll have a couple of minutes before Kale catches up to you."

"Right," Jasper said and followed the others.

Jewel was waiting for him in the porch and, by the cold feel of the air, he knew Ivan had just gone out. Damn, he was taking Ivan out in this too.

"Jewel, I..." He searched for the words to say but she wasn't even looking at him. Her hands were prowling through the coats on their hooks.

"This one looks warmest," she said. "Wear it. You'll need boots too. Those loafers are no good in snow." She pulled out some overshoes. "Honestly, you are such a city boy." Her voice caught and he knew she was close to tears.

"I'll come home," he said but he couldn't hold her. Busy with the unfamiliar overshoes, he knew he was fumbling the latches and felt frustrated until she fastened them for him. She pulled his coat close and fastened it too.

"This is a down coat," she said. "Nice and warm. Don't you take it off out there."

"I won't." Jasper felt like a little boy being dressed but he was no boy. Catching her close, he bent his head to catch her warm lips. She kissed him hungrily and he wanted it to go on and on but the blast of a truck horn told him it was time to go.

"Be safe," she said.

Jasper looked up to see Kale watching from the kitchen door, his cold weather clothing already in place and a grin on his face. "Let's go."

Chapter 41 - Saturday

Jasper stood beside the squad car and waited just out of camera range of the house they needed. Professor Koasa's small house was unpretentious, the only oddity about it being the Japanese characters painted on the door to mark it off from its neighbors. According to the fire marshal's registered plan, it was a simple three-bedroom, two bath house with four rooms on the first floor. It was old and still used gas for heat and cooking—something newer homes no longer had.

He wanted to go up to the door himself but the local DEA supervisor had nixed that. Instead he'd picked Kale to make contact. With his Japanese and Hawaiian ancestry and his youthful looks, he wouldn't arouse as much alarm in the professor of Asian studies. All Jasper could do was watch from a distance and listen through Kale's wire.

Kale strolled into camera range and knocked on the lettered door. It seemed a long time before it opened.

Jasper's nerves were strung tight as Kale said "Professor Koasa?"

"Yes?" a woman's voice answered.

The next instant, Kale was spraying knock out gas in the woman's face and catching her before she fell to the ground.

"Now," the DEA supervisor said and two local agents slid past Kale into the house. A third helped him carry the Asian woman back to the squad car and Jasper.

Professor Sachiko Koasa looked to be in her late thirties with her black hair caught up an ornate braid and bun combination. Asleep, she looked like a classic Asian beauty but there was a firmness to her mouth that boded ill for those who would argue with her. It was just as well they had heeded Kin's warning.

"Is she ok?" Jasper asked as a med tech took her vitals then arranged her more comfortably in the car seat.

"She'll be out for about ten minutes," the technician said. "Time enough to get her out of here if we hurry."

Jasper looked up as the Chicago bomb squad headed for the house. Through the long snowy night he'd tried to consider every way Baxter could kill Kin's family and it had come down as most likely a bomb at their house. Finding out it was gas heated had made it even more likely. They still could have blister implants but that possibility was very low for the mother. She was past childbearing years.

Where was the mother? Jasper frowned and headed for the front door of the house but didn't go in. Aware there were probably stealth cameras inside, he didn't try to push past the agent guarding the door. Kale rejoined him.

"Where's the mother?" Jasper asked.

"There's a delay," the agent said. "She insisted on getting her daughter's computer."

"Computer?" Jasper frowned. "Does she know the danger?" Before he could say more, the woman appeared with a suitcase and two purses in her hands. She was followed by one of the agents.

Jasper studied Matsuki Koasa. She looked her sixty odd years but was still handsome. Even at this early hour, she was impeccably dressed in a simple silk dress and she wore a string of pearls around her neck. Like her daughter, her hair was neatly arranged with a couple of ebony sticks through it. She didn't seem at all distressed to be rushed out of her house and that was odd. Had Kin managed to warn her?

"Good morning," she said as she hesitated by him. "Where's my daughter?"

"The first squad car," Jasper said. "You have what you need?"

"All that is important," she said. "Thank you."

Bemused, Jasper watched her proceed to the car, the agent with the small rectangular computer following like a dog at heel.

"A real okaa-san," Kale said with a grin. "Show her respect or she'll eat you for lunch."

"I don't doubt that," Jasper said. "Let's get out of here. If that house blows, I don't want them to see it."

They rejoined the two ladies at the car. Mrs. Koasa had settled in next to her daughter which Jasper didn't like since it only left him the far seat. He wasn't worried Professor Koasa could get out since squad cars had no handles on rear doors but it would be harder to sedate her again if he had to lean over her mother. Kale took the front passenger seat and a uniformed Chicago officer was at the wheel.

As soon as they were all settled in, the officer reported his intention to move and was given clearance. Their next stop would be the federal building.

Jasper fished in his briefcase to find the transmission detector and awkwardly ran it over the two women and their purses as the car sped along. It didn't detect anything and he relaxed slightly.

Mrs. Koasa took it as calmly as if she'd done this everyday, her hands folded in her lap. When her daughter stirred she turned to her and spoke quietly in Japanese.

The professor didn't seem to be listening. Her hands flew first to her jade necklace then she glared at Kale. Finally her eyes settled on Jasper and there was no doubt she was angry. "Take me home."

"No, Professor Koasa," Jasper said. "You're going to a safe house."

"By whose orders? I'm an American citizen and I will not be interred like a war criminal." She snapped out the words in her fury.

"Protective custody of the DEA," Jasper said and handed her his com link with the vid of her brother on it. "Your brother requested it."

Silently she watched the vid but hid any reaction. Her mother was more open, clasping her daughter's hand tightly as they listened to the deal Kin Koasa had offered.

"They changed the date on us," Jasper said when it was done. "So we had to move fast. Kin may already have been arrested with the rest of the gang but is waiting word on whether you're safe. Will you cooperate?"

"Do we have any choice?" Sachiko Koasa said, her tone bitter. "I knew he was up to no good–a criminal."

"Not by his choice," Jasper said. "These men think nothing of killing families to ensure loyalty. I know." His voice was hard as he thought of Jewel. If Baxter had any idea where she was, he'd try to kill her now.

Carlson had called him two hours ago to say the plane was still sitting at the Denver airport. They intended to seize it and the drugs at Plains then Reynolds would scoop up those waiting on the delivery.

"We need a picture," Jasper said and handed his com unit to Kale.

His bodyguard focused it on the two women. The elder one smiled for the camera but Sachiko sat rigid and disapproving.

"You aren't under arrest," Jasper said to ease the tension. "We want to reassure Kin you're safe."

For answer Sachiko gave the finger and Kale took the picture.

"Great," Kale said and handed the unit back to Jasper. "That should reassure him she's not a captive. If she were my sister, I know it would."

Mrs. Koasa was talking rapidly to her daughter in Japanese and Jasper didn't need to ask what she was saying. Her words were blistering even without translation and Sachiko's protests softened under them, getting weaker and weaker as her mother chewed her out.

Jasper wisely decided to let the mother handle the daughter and sent the word "Tora" to Koasa's com unit followed by the picture. He was glad these two would not be his headache. He wasn't even sure he'd see Kin again. He was in Plains, not Chicago.

Kale was listening to the women and plainly understanding them but he didn't break in. His grin widened until he sat back in his seat to hide it. Sachiko Koasa was no match for her mother.

The tirade didn't stop completely until they reached the federal center and the car slipped into a special slot in the underground garage. Bullet proof doors closed behind it then Jasper was being let out by his bodyguard. Kale jumped to assist Mrs. Koasa as well, bowing low to show ages old respect and speaking a phrase in Japanese that brought a smile to her lips and a quick frown from her daughter.

"That elevator is secure," the officer said, pointing it out. "You want their suitcase too?"

"I need to check it for transmitters first," Jasper said and the officer brought the suitcase out of the trunk and casually opened it.

As he had expected, it contained clothing and a few household treasures including a small jade Buddha and a very old book in Japanese. Jasper didn't handle any of it but ran his paddle over the lot to see if anything registered as electronic. Nothing did. Closing it up, he handed it to the elder Koasa with a small bow of his own. She abruptly handed it off to her daughter who took it with no comment.

The computer CPU was a evelle more than a foot across and just four inches high. Getting no signals from it, he handed it to Sachiko. The techs would have to check it for internal transmitters but that wasn't his problem.

The elevator took them straight up to a checkpoint where they registered their entry then proceeded into a comfortable office. A woman came in and served them coffee then sat down in a chair out of the way, leaving the table to them. Jasper knew it was procedure to have a female operative present when women were questioned so didn't comment on it. Kale found himself a spot by the wall and waited.

Jasper studied them, seeing Sachiko was a little more cooperative after her mother's blistering comments. Her mother seemed as serene as ever and that bothered him. She almost had to have known they were coming by the contents of that suitcase but why hadn't her daughter? Or was she just stubborn as Kin had suggested?

"There will be an agent with us in a minute," Jasper said, "but I want to explain how I got involved in this. My name is Jasper Stone. You might also know me as Jazz Stone or Sensor Man." He could see a flicker of recognition in Sachiko's eyes.

"If you saw the news coverage, you know my wife was kidnapped then returned. When I met Kin, I was chained up and my wife was drugged and lying beside me. He didn't say much but he did warn me my wife was booby-trapped and had also been given a drug that would react with bliss or any of the bliss derivatives. Because of him, we found a birth control implant loaded with blister—the bliss reactive. Do either of you have implants of any kind?"

"I do," Sachiko quietly said, her eyes on her hands. "It is a standard birth control implant."

"It might be," Jasper said. "They will probably remove it and give you a fresh one."

"I have one for hormone therapy," Mrs. Koasa said. "They can have it. I do not need a replacement."

"As you wish," Jasper said, a brief smile flicking across his lips. "I think it's more likely your house was booby-trapped but I wanted you to know these villains will stop at nothing to ensure the loyalty of their people. My wife is carrying a transmitter with detonation capability in her womb. If they locate her, they'll kill her. That's what we're hiding from."

Sachiko went pale. "That's barbaric."

"Yes, it is," Jasper calmly replied. "My wife desperately wants to have children. That was the one thing they could do to her that would hurt us the most. They meant it to buy my cooperation and my silence."

"But it did not," Mrs. Koasa said.

"I'll see them in hell first," Jasper said. "And I mean to see them shut down and in jail before another month is out. Kin can help me do it."

"I will help my son," Mrs. Koasa said. "He has shown his true spirit with this and I will show no less."

Her voice held conviction and Jasper knew she'd try hard not to be a problem. He turned to Sachiko and waited.

"I have my classes," she said. "A duty to my students."

"It cannot be met if you are dead," her mother said. "You must live to teach others."

Sachiko looked unconvinced but was no longer hostile.

"Excuse me, sir," the female agent spoke up. "If I may?"

"Go ahead," he said and beckoned her toward the table.

"You are Professor Koasa from the College of Asian Studies?" she asked and waited until the woman nodded. "Professor, could you request a sabbatical for one semester? If they're unwilling, the government can politely request you accept a post somewhere because of your outstanding reputation. The college can hardly say no to that."

"True," Sachiko admitted. "But I would prefer it be a real position."

"That can be arranged," the agent said. "You might be teaching federal agents but I know I would be honored to take a class from such an outstanding expert as yourself."

Jasper hid his surprise at the agent's tact but it brought back memories of Lori Brown. Like this woman, she'd been superb at soothing ruffled feathers and getting cooperation where it was unlikely—and it was working. Sachiko Koasa was looking mollified and her mother was openly approving of the agent. Even Kale was smiling.

"Your name, please?" Sachiko asked.

"Lauren Kurtz, Special Agent, DEA," she said. "If you approve, I can be assigned to assist you."

Assist, not protect, Jasper noted and found it hard not to smile. Yes, she had the same talent as Lori.

"And you?" Sachiko asked but she wasn't looking at him. Her dark brown eyes rested on Kale.

"I'm Mr. Stone's bodyguard and not DEA," Kale said. "Otherwise I would be pleased to serve you and your honored mother. My duty though is to him and his wife."

"Duty must come first," Sachiko replied and gave him a slight nod. "I think I would be pleased to have Agent Kurtz."

Jasper caught the flash of triumph on the agent's face but it quickly disappeared. Well, she'd done a good job.

"In that case, I'm going to leave you with Agent Kurtz," he said. "My wife needs me now that I have fulfilled my duty to your brother." He remembered to bow and was echoed by Kale.

He never imagined he would be bowing oriental fashion to a pair of Japanese ladies but for the elder Mrs. Koasa it just seemed right. He would give the younger one the courtesy to keep her cooperative. Now he just wanted to get home.

It wasn't to be just yet though. Now that the Koasa women were extracted, he had to catch up on what was happening in Plains—and the DEA supervisor here had a vested interest in that now. He'd been told to report to his office before leaving.

Kale followed him out and they walked in silence until they were aboard the elevators then Kale said "I think I'm in love."

Jasper shot him a glance but wasn't sure how to answer that.

"But she's too old for me," Kale said with a sigh and a smile. "We meet too late."

Jasper smiled. "Too late for her or too early for you," he said. "Yes, she has style. What all did she say to her daughter?"

"Most is not translatable," he said. "But she reminded her daughter of her duty to family and called her ungrateful and a shame to her ancestors. Kin is, technically, the head of the family even though he's younger than his sister. They set great store in that."

"She was awfully quick packing that suitcase," Jasper said.

"It was already packed," Kale replied. "Her son might have got word to her or she could just be that way."

"Be that way?" Jasper asked.

Kale grinned. "She's the mother and living with her daughter. Being ready to leave is an old trick. Blackmail."

"Blackmail?" Jasper found that hard to believe but considered the tongue-lashing she'd given her daughter. He would have expected the elder to kick the daughter out instead of threatening to leave herself but he knew nothing about Asian cultures. "It was good you came along. I never expected you to do more than bodyguard."

"It was a privilege to meet her," Kale said as they left the elevator. "Her daughter is too proud but she is true Japanese. I have to thank my mother for insisting I know the language."

"Right." Jasper smiled. "Let's get this over with. I want to get home."

The DEA supervisor, a Mr. Lane, was ready for them. Waving them to seats, he began pulling up vid of the Plains airport.

"The plane landed half an hour ago but there's been no activity. Let's watch." He touched the icon and Jasper watched vid of the plane landing. A number of cameras had been quietly added to the Plains airport since he was last there to improve surveillance and now they were in use.

The plane was in the parking area but there was no sign of anyone meeting it. How long would they have to wait? As he thought that, he spied a black sedan turning into the airport and thought it looked familiar. Was that the same car that had taken him and Jewel to the airport? The driver pulled up at the plane and stepped out of the car and Jasper swore. The same guy. "You know him?" Lane asked.

"Yes," Jasper said. "And he knows me and Jewel—and Carlson. I didn't think he was connected."

The plane's door was opening and steps were folding out then federal agents appeared, some from the hanger and others speeding up in cars. The driver looked confused but quickly put both hands up, showing they were empty. The plane didn't get a chance to button up again. As soon as the steps were down, federal agents in FBI and DEA jackets were pounding up and past the lone stewardess. There was no resistance.

No resistance? Jasper frowned. It didn't feel right. They were obviously waiting for that car but why? "Is there any way to see inside the plane?"

For answer Lane tapped an icon and they were suddenly seeing what one of the DEA agents was seeing. He expanded the window to almost block the view of the plane's exterior and Jasper frowned again. It looked so normal.

He could see the pilot leaning over a bench seat as he was cuffed and another man, a man in a very expensive suit was confronting Carlson. With a shock, Jasper recognized him. Wilson Kucera!

Chapter 42 - Wilson Kucera

"Shit!" Agent Lane burst out, slapping his hand down on the controls to bring up audio.

Jasper just stared. Wilson Kucera delivering blissex? No. With a chill, he realized their investigation had just hit a very big roadblock. He'd lay odds there was no blissex on that plane.

"Go ahead and search," Kucera was saying as he flipped the warrant in his hand. "And you'd better find something, agent. My lawyers will have a field day with this." The CEO of Wilson Chemicals stepped past him and the cameraman turned to show him exiting the plane.

Thinking fast, Jasper looked at the DEA supervisor. "Can I get a message to Carlson?"

"Through the cameraman," Lane said. "Are you sure?"

"Damned sure," Jasper said. "Put him on."

Lane sent the command then motioned him to speak. Jasper hesitated only a second. "This is Agent Wolfgang von Blitzen. Repeat this to Carlson exactly. Blitzen says look for a sapphire and pearl ring in the seat cushions. It's Jewel's. Have you got that?"

"Yes sir." The agent didn't question who he was but tugged on Carlson's sleeve and repeated "Blitzen says look for a sapphire and pearl ring in the seat cushions. It's a jewel."

Damn it! Jasper heard him flub the last part and almost corrected him but Carlson nodded and started giving orders. One agent pointed the handcuffed pilot toward the door but all the others got busy digging into the upholstery.

"Here, sir," an agent quickly declared and held up a tiny object. "A ring with pearls."

"Over here," Carlson said and motioned the cameraman closer. He took the ring and displayed it to the camera. "Blitz, is this it? Hold on." Carlson took the earphone from the cameraman. "Go ahead."

"That's it," Jasper confirmed. "And it's engraved with *For Jewel with all my heart. Rory West.*"

Carlson peered into the band of the ring and Jasper saw him smile. "Stop the search," he said to his agents. "You, call Captain Reynolds and tell him I need a forensics team out here. This plane was used to abduct Jewel West. The rest of you, back out till they get here. Check the cargo bays but no more in the cabin." A chorus of yessirs then agents were exiting. Carlson waved the cameraman to remain.

"Get a close up of this," he said to the cameraman. "Found one engraved ring with a single sapphire and two pearls. It matches the description given by Mrs. Stone. It was in the upholstery of this bench seat on a Wilson Chemicals jet matching the ID number of the one reported here by Agent Carlson the night of November 12th. Entered into evidence on Saturday, November 20, 2179."

Carlson slipped it into an evidence bag and stuck it in his pocket. "Blitz, you just saved us. Where else did she say she was?"

"Bathroom, the cushioned seat and she remembers sitting in a chair that moved," Jasper said.

"Got it. If there's even a single hair of hers here, we'll find it. Black hair, right?"

"That's right."

"We aren't going for the bonanza," Carlson said, "but we aren't going to be sued, either. That's something. Did your part go well?"

"Yes," Jasper replied.

"Good. I have to fill in the locals. Carlson out."

Jasper nodded to Agent Lane and he muted the feed but left the camera on as the cameraman walked out of the plane to show Wilson Kucera talking on his com unit. The man was wasting no time in contacting his lawyers. Well, it would do him no good. They probably couldn't implicate him in Jewel's kidnapping but they could impound the plane and link it to Chuma Johnson and Baxter.

"You're an agent?" Kale asked. "You aren't just working with them?"

"Yes. Harold knows. Jewel doesn't."

"Right," Kale said. "You might be in for it when she finds out." He grinned.

"You will too," Jasper warned. "No deniability now."

Lane studied him and Jasper knew now he was being measured against a different yard stick. Until this point he hadn't been DEA but an interested party. Now his credentials were acknowledged and he had even given his code name. That couldn't be helped though. He couldn't have field men knowing Jasper Stone was that involved.

"Let me see it," Agent Lane said. "Do you carry it with you?"

"Always," Jasper said. Fishing out his locket, he pointed his com unit at the back and handed it to him. Lane studied the credentials and handed it back without a word.

Jasper turned to Kale. "I'm deep cover. You're the sixth to know. My usefulness might be gone after this but we'll see."

"Right," Kale said. "And I'm still your bodyguard. It's just going to be more interesting than I thought." He flexed his hands and grinned. "I was starting to get bored on the farm."

"What next, Mr. Stone?" Agent Lane asked. "It looks like the plane is almost a bust. Don't you have that inside man? You'd better warn him."

"Warn him?" Jasper didn't understand.

"We can't put the women back," Agent Lane said. "If the drugs aren't moving today, he's got his butt in a sling."

Jasper's heart nearly stopped. Damn it, he was right! If they found out that Koasa's family were in protective custody, Koasa would be the target. He'd practically told them he was a snitch. He had to get him out and it had to be done now.

Thumbing his com unit to find Koasa's number, he saw there was an alert from Butler. He threw that on the vid screen then continued looking. It was Koasa's voice that made him look up.

"Yeah, we got a faulty camera here," the Asian was saying into his own com unit. "I'm pulling both of them on this floor. It could be interference from one to the other. Make a note of it."

"Right, Kin," a metallic voice answered. "Just be quick about it. I want to watch the game."

"Go ahead, idjit. I don't care if you do." Kin pulled a stealth camera out of a plug-in then went over to a second position and pulled another one. Next he messed with something on his com unit. "Are you getting any snow now?"

"No, it's all cleared up," the man said. "I can see the other floors just fine. Blind where you are."

"Ok, I'll get it fixed. Hang loose." Kin laid his com unit down and now Jasper could see the tension in him. The Asian walked over to one of Butler's cameras and stared right into it and said in a fierce whisper, "what the hell were you thinking, Stone? I told you the 27th or 28th. It's not even close and my butt is screwed. You've got to get me out and you have to get me out now."

Jasper keyed up Butler's special functions then started typing. The vid screen in the studio came to life, words appearing as he typed. WORKING ON IT. DEA WILL EXTRACT. DON'T LEAVE THE HOUSE.

Kin frowned. "They can override the lock on this upper door. Any of them."

THAT LOCK, YES. SECOND LOCK ABOVE DOOR. EMBEDDED. YOU MISSED IT. Jasper grinned as he typed that.

The Asian strode over to examine the upper door then opened it and looked again. When he closed it, he couldn't open it again because Butler had obeyed his command to lock it.

GLASS IS BULLET-PROOF, Jasper typed. LOWER DOOR IS ALSO LOCKED. SIT TIGHT AND STAY OUT OF SIGHT. SENDING HELP.

That done, he thought of Carlson and realized he'd be too busy. Reynolds? He was probably on his way to the airport. Who did that leave he could trust? Not Sanders. Kruger? No, airport. Maybe Hunter. No, he had to run it by Reynolds or Carlson. He couldn't contact Hunter directly.

Splitting the screen, he tried first to call Carlson. When he didn't acknowledge, he turned to Lane. "Can we get the cameraman back?"

"Yes," Lane said. "I've got him here on my unit. Carlson is being talked to right now."

"Ok, scratch that," Jasper said. This was a hell of a lot easier when he wasn't a thousand miles away. Calling Reynolds' number, he was relieved to get an answer.

"Blitzen," he said. "Koasa is barricaded third floor of my house. He needs DEA custody. Couldn't tell Carlson."

"Got it," Reynolds said. "What went wrong?"

"Wrong day. We thought they moved it up but Wilson Kucera was using the plane."

"Damn," Reynolds said. "How deep are we in?"

"They found Jewel's ring. The plane was used for a kidnapping," Jasper said. "We can't get Kucera but he might give us Baxter to get free of it."

"That would be something. Ok, I'll get Carlson aside. Wish you were here."

"Me too," Jasper said and broke the connection. Going back to the house connection, he typed DEA HAS BEEN NOTIFIED. SIT TIGHT. MINI FRIDGE IN BAR–MAKE YOURSELF AT HOME.

Koasa laughed and visibly relaxed.

Satisfied he'd stay put, Jasper used Butler to check the other floors and outside the front door and even to get a peripheral view outside the house. Nothing yet. He wondered how they could cover up Kin's absence. When he didn't return and they confirmed his family had been moved, they'd know he went over. They would also suspect the house and he needed them to use it.

A call came in from Carlson. "I got your message," he said. "I'm handing the plane over to FBI and the locals so my people are free. We have a government plane arriving in an hour so we've got transport. Is he still at the house?"

"Yes but the house is going to be compromised unless we come up with something. He's already pulled the cameras on the third floor so we can talk. Can you think of another reason he might get arrested?"

"Larceny," Carlson said. "Out of our jurisdiction but we can use some boys in blue."

Jasper smiled. "Yes, that would do it. If you'll arrange a show for the outside, I'll tell him what I want him to steal."

"Done."

Jasper went back to the house scene and found Koasa drinking a bottle of his best imported beer and eating some ice cream nibbles Jewel liked. He was parked where he could see the vid screen with his com unit in one hand.

"No, I'm not hurrying asshole," Koasa was saying. "I'm eating their food and working on these damned cheap cameras. Hell, I might even watch the game while I'm doing it. This is one big screen I'm looking at."

"Dirtbag, how big is it?" The voice said.

"Three meters at least," Kin said and Jasper grinned. He'd sure inflated that number. "Great resolution too. I want it."

"Fuck you," the voice exploded. "I'm coming over."

"No, you're not," Kin said and his voice had bite to it. "You leave surveillance, we're both dead. They'd have our hides."

"Then get those damn cameras fixed so I can take my eyes off these things!"

"Ok, I'll get back to work," Kin said. "And I'll bring you a bottle of O'Malleys Blue Ribbon Ale. Stone didn't live cheap."

"Right. Just get it done."

GOOD IDEA, Jasper typed, GRAB ALL YOU CAN OF THE BEER BUT THERE'S SOMETHING ELSE I WANT YOU TO STEAL. YOU'RE GOING TO GET ARRESTED IN FULL VIEW OF THE CITY CAMERAS FOR ROBBERY.

"What do I steal?" Kin asked and Jasper told him, watching as the Asian's smile widened.

Agent Lane ordered up some sandwiches and more coffee and they settled down to wait while Jasper watched a little anxiously. The Asian knew what he was doing though. Within minutes he had his music system torn apart. Nothing was damaged except some cables he could easily replace but it looked like an amateur job when he was done. Everything had been sufficiently disarranged to cover up the missing component–the heart of his music system.

The Asian was going after other stuff too but that was what he wanted. Given free range, the Asian trotted down to the second floor once and entered Jewel's old room. What he took, Jasper didn't know because neither he nor the kidnappers had planted cameras in the second floor bedrooms. Knowing Jewel had all of her favorite jewelry, he didn't worry about it.

The thievery lasted less than an hour but in that time Kin had piled up a stash of stuff in the studio–more than he could possibly carry. When he picked up that damned black coat and threw it on the pile, Jasper remembered Jewel's com unit. It wasn't in the coat but he'd laid it on the dresser in the bedroom.

KIN, GRAB JEWEL'S COM UNIT ON THE BEDROOM DRESSER. I WANT THAT TO GO TO POLICE. He knew it undoubtedly had been tampered with so it couldn't come to him. He didn't want it laying around the house any longer though. Jewel's old files were still in it.

The Asian obeyed then scooped up Jasper's decoy unit and stuck it in another pocket. In the end the Asian had a lavender suitcase full of booty and Jasper's music system.

"Ok, got her fixed," Koasa said into his com link. "Well, one of them. The other is shot. I'll need a replacement." He plugged in the camera to a new location, which allowed it to see the outside door and the pool table in front of it but not the small dining table where Kin had piled his booty or the big vid screen. "I've got the beer too."

"Good, come on back," his backup said. "Game is in the second half."

Jasper checked the outside view and saw two cops walking casually along one of the paths, their coats buttoned up against the cold weather. They stopped to look at some vegetation.

TIME, he typed.

"Be there soon," Koasa said and picked up the suitcase, music system, and beer. "And you'll just have to see what all I got." He chuckled.

His only answer was stunned silence.

Jasper, Kale, and Agent Lane watched as Kin Koasa left the house, not even getting the door completely closed, and walked almost straight into some surprised police officers. They had him down on the ground and cuffed in seconds. Other officers arrived on scene and they looked suitably outraged that someone had stolen from Jasper Stone. In the confusion that followed Koasa was hustled out of Jasper's camera range. Convinced they'd disappear him now, Jasper shut down his cameras and reset Butler to allow intrusions for the next two hours without reporting them.

"They could clear all those cameras out of that house," Agent Lane said. "Or do they know about them?"

"I'll let Reynolds handle it," Jasper said. "It would be less suspicious if the police remove them rather than leave them. The smugglers can still get in and I can still monitor with Butler."

"True." Lane glanced at him. "What Butler model is that? It seems better than others I've seen."

"Prototype," Jasper said. "My wife is now owner of Butler, Inc., and one of their programmers. I told her what I needed it to do and she set it up. I think it can do everything but wink at me."

"Nice," Lane said.

"And I'll get my music system back," Jasper said with a satisfied smile. "My publisher can ship me replacements for the rest of the components but the CPU was customized over a lot of years. As soon as I find a place to play, I'll be back in business."

He knew that was going to be the hard part. He still hadn't been everywhere at the farm but he hadn't found the right spot. There was a good chance he'd have to look at renting a studio in the nearest town but that meant travel and snow. He didn't want that either. There had to be somewhere.

"When is the next train to Minneapolis?" he asked Kale and his bodyguard grinned.

"Two o'clock for an express to Des Moines then a four-thirty local to our stop," Kale said. "After that we'd have to take an express to Madison and drive or wait until six to get to Des Moines."

"Let's not wait until six," Jasper said. "The two o'clock will do."

"What is your stop?" Lane asked. "No, never mind. I have no need to know."

Jasper was relieved he hadn't pressed it. He was also glad Kale hadn't mentioned Minneapolis or St. Paul. He knew the farm was a bare twenty miles from that city. He wasn't sure where Des Moines was except it wasn't close. Madison was in Wisconsin somewhere. He supposed he'd better learn his way around this area of the country. If he stayed here, he would need to know.

"I'd better call Jewel now and once more from the train," Jasper said. "Will we get home in time for that pool match?" Remembering the long drive from the farm to the train station last night, he wondered. Of course then it had been blizzard conditions. Ivan had told him the drive normally took twenty minutes, not the ninety they'd used last night.

"Yes," Kale said. "Just in time."

Chapter 43 - Robbery

"And now for another chapter in the Sensor Man saga," the news reporter said. "Today someone broke into the West House and tried to make off with a suitcase full of valuables, part of Mr. Stone's music equipment, and a six-pack of imported beer. On leaving the house he walked straight into the arms of two police officers on ground patrol. It's been suggested he made off with more than a six pack because he'd already had plenty."

"That's insulting," her fellow anchor said. "It's bad enough he stole the man's valuables, did he have to take his beer?"

Both anchors smiled but it was brief. "Seriously, folks, everything was recovered except some beer and the thief is in custody. Police will be investigating any more such attempts so thieves be warned!"

"Any word yet on whether Mr. Stone will come back to Plains?" her fellow anchor asked. "I would really like to see them safely at home."

"No word yet," the newswoman said. "And there are still kidnappers at large. When our Jewel of the West was taken, there were four men and only their leader, Chuma Johnson, has been caught. So far he's still in the hospital and only his public defender has seen him. Police say they will be moving him to a secure location in the next couple of days. Where he will be held has not been disclosed."

He'd forgotten about Johnson, Jasper realized. It was a good thing Reynolds hadn't. It looked like he was baiting the trap now. With the bust today fizzling out, they needed to succeed with Johnson.

God, he was tired. He hadn't caught much sleep on the way to Chicago and he'd caught just ninety minutes worth on the express to Des Moines. It had staterooms so it had been safe. Kale seemed to be a lot more alert than he was and even the martial arts teacher was popping energy pills.

Jasper shook another one out of its package and tucked it in his cheek so he could feel the fizz as it delivered stimulants to his tired body. He wasn't in the habit of using them but he needed to have some energy tonight. They were nearly to Moose Creek Station and he could get off this local train and back into a nice warm farm truck. He smiled, realizing he might have to fend off a dog. If he wanted to stretch out in the more comfortable back, he probably would. Hell, he'd do it. He was just that tired.

Actually, this local train wasn't too bad. Apparently most people used the expresses or were in the business class car. Kale had steered him toward the commuter car, which was nearly empty. The seats had a minimum of padding but it was possible to stretch out on the bench seats at the rear of the car. Since they had changed back to their farmer clothes in the express stateroom, no one took any notice of them. The only thing missing was those heavy coats they'd left with Ivan but they wouldn't have fit in the suitcase.

He missed the coat but he'd picked up two wool traveler's capes in Des Moines. They were large hooded blankets and the one he had kept him nice and warm in the chilly car. Kale had the other. At first he thought he'd made a mistake getting them but there were others on the train using such capes since one size fitted all.

"Moose Creek Station coming up," the automated announcer said. "Get ready Moose Creek."

Jasper opened one eye then the other before sitting up straight and reaching for his briefcase. Kale was already on his feet, shifting the suitcase from hand to hand in the limited room. Jasper followed him out, grateful there was unlikely to be trouble at any of these stops.

Four others got off the train with them but Kale nodded to them and they nodded back. Before they could get into a conversation, Ivan was there and handing them the coats they'd left behind. Climbing the steps to ground level, Jasper was surprised to see brilliant stars in a black sky and a parking lot nearly clear of snow.

"Magic," he said when Kale grinned at him. "Where did they put it all?"

"Over there," Ivan said, motioning toward the shadowy form of a mountain of snow at one end of the parking lot. "They've been cleaning up since this morning. Tomorrow all the roads will be clear and that mountain will get shoved onto a drainage field. It'll water a lot of trees when it melts."

"What time is it?" Jasper asked as he climbed into the back seat of the truck and motioned for Kale to take the front.

"Six fifteen," Ivan said. "Our little match up starts when we get back. Did you get whatever done?"

"Yes," Jasper said. "We rescued two Japanese-American ladies and Kale has fallen for one of them."

"Fallen?" Ivan glanced at Kale but his eyes quickly returned to the road. "Something for Beth to worry about?"

"She's in her seventies," Kale said. "And a real okaa-san. When her daughter talked back to us, she put her in her place in the finest Japanese tradition. She was really eloquent and traditional. The daughter meekly accepted her rescue when she was done."

"That must have been something," Ivan said. "I've gotten the rough edge of one's tongue one time. I didn't understand a word of it but just had to stand there and bow and try not to laugh."

"What did you do?" Kale asked.

"It wasn't what I did," Ivan said. "It was Sasha. We were in the Little Tokyo enclave in Chicago—the one where no one speaks much English and normal Americans are the foreigners. You know the one?"

"I've been there," Kale said.

Jasper was leaning back in the corner of the seat, half-listening to the conversation with his eyes shut.

"Sasha was about five and she'd just learned how to whistle," Ivan said. "She let out this wolf whistle and this ancient mama-san rounded on me, chewed me up one side and down the other and spat me out. There were others who knew it had been Sasha but that little twerp was hiding behind me. There was nothing I could do but let that old lady wear down."

Kale laughed. "I would have loved to see that."

"Everyone says that," Ivan said. "And it was funny but I made Sasha promise never to do it again. Real bad habit to make a fool of her old man."

Jasper smiled, thinking that was something a young Jewel would have done. If he wasn't careful, she'd even do it now. "Don't tell Jewel that one or I'll have to keep her away from Little Tokyo."

"True," Ivan said over his shoulder. "There were plenty of them that did speak English and had seen Sasha do it. After I'd been put in my place, they laughed with me. Sasha got a fuss over her and she was given some toy and a jade necklace. Spoiled rotten."

"That sounds like her," Jasper said. "Little girls always get off easy."

"They sure do," Ivan said. "Still it was a good memory. I just wish I know what that woman said. Could have been a recipe for all I know."

Kale laughed.

Jasper managed to ignore the rest of the conversation as Kale trotted out one Japanese phrase after another for Ivan to listen to. Thinking back over the newscast, he realized there'd been no mention of the plane. Well, that figured. Since they'd found something, it wasn't in Kucera's interest to make a big deal out of it. Right now he must be focused on damage control. Wilson Chemicals needed a good public image and getting associated with a high profile kidnaping and murder wouldn't do it. No doubt Kucera was trying to figure out how to hand over Baxter without handing him over.

His eyes popped open and he reached for his com unit. Typing in a quick text, he read it through. BAXTER COULD BE DEAD IN NEXT COUPLE OF DAYS. ESSENTIAL WE LOCATE. -STONE He sent it off to both Reynolds and Carlson. If Kucera was guilty, Baxter would probably turn up dead. If he wasn't, he'd be alive. If he didn't turn up at all, they'd have to find another way to prove he was guilty—him and Kucera both.

What was Wilson Kucera doing flying to Plains anyway? As far as he knew, the CEO of Wilson Chemicals had never bothered with such a small city before. For that matter, if the plane had picked him up in Denver, what was he doing there? Could it be his brother's death? Had he finally started asking questions? That wouldn't bring him to Plains though unless he knew about the professor—and there was only one way he could know about the professor. Baxter had pocketed the flasher with the vid—his flasher.

Damn, he needed to pass that on too. Pulling out his com unit again, he found it hard to come up with the right explanation in text. Giving it up, he keyed in Reynolds' number.

"Got your text. What now?" Reynolds answered without preamble.

"Short and sweet. If Kucera shows you a copy of the professor vid on a flasher, check the flasher. If it's a red cube with a vertical black stripe, it might be mine. Baxter took it."

"It's not that easy," Reynolds said. "He had the vid on his com unit."

"Damn," Jasper said.

"Yes, damn. He doesn't know where Baxter is. The man's on vacation—Thanksgiving vacation. Right now he'd like to hang him by his heels in a deep tank." Reynolds paused. "Kucera passed interrogation. We couldn't ask him about blissex but he knew nothing about Jewel except what was on the news. I had to let him go."

"And the plane?" Jasper asked, his heart sinking.

"We keep it. DNA search is still going on. Since you sent me a photo of that ring and reported it missing, he can't fight that."

"What about the pilot?" Jasper asked. "What does he know?"

"Wrong pilot," Reynolds said. "There's three pilots for that plane and the stewardesses double as co-pilots. This crew came on duty yesterday. The crew on duty last week are also on vacation since they aren't due back on duty for two weeks. Kucera's office is trying to locate them. If they turn up dead, we'll take another look at Kucera."

"Right," Jasper said.

"Look, I want you to take Sunday off," Reynolds said. "Or at least don't call me. We've got enough to work out here. Monday I'll send a forensics team into your house. What do you want done with those blasted cameras? We can't miss them."

"Pull them," Jasper said. "If you can manage to miss one on the third floor, that will be useful. There's only one up there now. I think the one Kin pulled is lying around too. I want the rest of the house clean."

"Got it," Reynolds said. "Have a nice lazy day with Jewel and don't go getting on the news!"

"Yes sir," Jasper said and broke the connection. After a moment he realized the front seat had gotten quiet. "I've been ordered to stay off the news tomorrow and have a nice quiet Sunday."

Ivan snorted. "That's something you're no good at."

"I'll try. I just want to sleep all day." He yawned. "Can't do that either."

They both laughed and the truck lurched as it turned into the farm's utility road. The dog chorus started up and he grinned. "Sounds like home."

Molly was ready for their return, insisting they both eat before going off to the community center and the waiting pool match. Jasper didn't argue but had the best meal of his day with fried chicken, brussel sprouts, and potatoes. He escaped with a full carafe of coffee, feeling much more awake than before.

When he climbed the steps to the poolroom, he could already hear the clack of balls and wondered if he was too late for the break. A quick glance around told him that Jewel and Jim Talbot weren't playing. Uncle Harold was apparently warming up the table with some trick shots but stopped when he saw him arrive.

"Welcome back," Harold said and began pulling out balls for the rack.

"He's back," a youngster said with a quick smile. Jasper couldn't place who he was and didn't care because Jewel had reached him. A quick kiss was all they managed before the table was ready.

"Get them safe?" she asked in a quiet voice.

"Yes," Jasper said. "Sink him."

She smiled and turned to collect her cue. Jasper watched her, thinking it was a damned shame she had to wear that black skirt and jammers. Underneath she wore her black leggings and it just wasn't the same. He liked it when she wore her short shorts.

"Eight ball, tournament rules," Harold said then flipped a coin. "Jewel, call it."

"Tails," she said.

Jasper nearly groaned, knowing exactly why she always called that. Hopefully, Jim didn't know her little game.

"Tails, it is," Harold said. "Break or pass?"

"Break," she said.

Jim didn't look worried by the decision. Of course, most women would choose to go first.

Jewel moved the cue ball to the left, aiming it for the three ball and shot, scattering the balls across the table and sending one into a pocket.

"Stripe," Harold said. "Show us what you can do, girl."

Jewel smiled and sunk two more stripes before she fouled with a solid ball.

"Tough luck," Jim said and sunk three solids in rapid succession. On his fourth shot, he sunk a stripe with his own solid and handed the table back to Jewel.

"So how good is she?" someone asked and Jasper saw it was Betty Talbot. "He's still holding back."

"She's warming up," Jasper said. "You'll know when she gets serious. How many games is this supposed to go?"

"Three out of five," she said. "Since most games are fast, two out of three is way too short. No one feels they get their money's worth."

"Betting wise?" Jasper asked. "I haven't placed any."

"You have ten riding on Jewel and fifteen riding on Jim," she said. "The guys did it. If you want Jewel to win, you'd better fork over more."

Jasper grinned. "Whose the bookie?"

"Dr. Bob," she said. "It was his turn."

Jasper spotted the veterinarian and noted the box he held and the notepad. Pouring himself a cup of coffee, he made his way around to place his bet. Jewel was still goofing off but seemed to get better after he placed his bet. She finished sinking her balls with some quick shots and called the eight ball for the side pocket.

Jasper watched, knowing the eight ball shot was the trickiest of that game. From the look on Talbot's face, he'd noted it too. They were both more serious the second game and Jim won when Jewel had two balls still on the table.

After the third game, again Jewel's, they called a break and Jasper got a couple of minutes with his wife. She was smiling and he knew she still hadn't got serious.

"You'd better watch it this game," he warned. "Something tells me Jim has been nice to this point."

"I think so too," she said. "But so have I. Got your bets in?"

"Yes, fifteen on him and twenty five on you," he said. "They don't go higher than that here."

"Pity," she said. "Pocket change." She gave him a deep kiss and rubbed against him. "I wish it was you."

"Me too," he said. "Loser has to wash the dishes."

"Winner calls the shots," she responded and headed back to the table.

If she won, he'd let her call the shots. He just wished he could get a nice long nap before she did. Some of their most interesting sessions had been after pool games and half of those games went unfinished. His wife was endlessly inventive where it came to pool.

The fourth game. If Jewel won, it was all over and Talbot knew it. He got the break and started sinking his balls one after the other. With one left, he fouled and sunk one of Jewel's. His supporters groaned but didn't look too worried until Jewel sank six of hers in rapid succession, scratching on the last. That left just Jim's seven ball and the eight ball. He finished up the game for another win.

Now Jim had her measure and so did the watchers. There was another pause and a few last minute bets. Jewel disappeared into the ladies' room and Jasper suspected he knew why.

"She's hot," Harold said as he stopped to talk to him. "This should be an interesting game now they're both serious."

"Jewel is just getting serious," Jasper said and nodded toward his wife as she strolled across to him. He grinned and enjoyed the view. Jewel's long legs were visible now beneath that quilted skirt. Unmarred by blemish or hair, they were slender and smooth as silk. His smile widened as she got every male eye in the place on her.

Harold's eyes twinkled as she came closer. "That top should be outlawed."

"Top?" Jasper looked at it and nearly choked on his coffee. Where the hell had she got a tank top that said Ball Breaker? It had pool balls on it but the low cut neck showed way too much cleavage. He'd never seen it before.

"Like it?" Jewel asked as she stopped in front of him. "My new lucky shirt."

"I think I've seen it before somewhere," Harold said with an admiring eye. "Yes, I've seen it before and I recall I ruled it legal then. Do your worst, girl."

"No, I'm going to do my best," she said. "I've got a bet on it." She strolled back to her cue and took a swig of water before chalking up her stick.

Jim Talbot was saying something to his wife but his eyes were on Jewel. Jasper noticed his wife looked more amused than upset at Jewel's tactics. Well, she hadn't seen the worst of it yet and she'd better not. If Jewel pulled half the tricks on Jim that she used on him, there might be a riot.

The next moment there was a ripple of laughter as Jim Talbot stripped off his shirt and handed it to his wife with a kiss. Jasper grinned but ran an appraising glance over the man's physique. He had muscles, well developed ones, under that shirt. His arms were marked by the old style permanent tattoos, one with his wife's name and one of a dragon. His chest and belly sported a fair amount of hair too. Jewel would like that. The one complaint she had about his body is he'd had his chest and back hair eradicated when he had his beard removed. He'd always be smooth. Women were funny that way. Carol had liked smooth skin against hers. Jewel liked hair and Jim had a lot of it everywhere except on the top of his head.

This was going to be interesting.

Jim got the break. He shattered it, scattering the balls around the table but none went in. The room got quiet as Jewel picked off the three ball then sunk the seven and five. She tried a bank shot and the four ball went in but so did the nine. The tension mounted as Jim readied for his shot, one eye on Jewel.

She wasn't even looking at him but talking to a smiling Aunt Ruby as she stretched with arms above her head. Just as Jim drew a bead on the fourteen, she leaned over to touch her toes and that short skirt hiked up just enough to show a glimpse of hot pink. The fourteen didn't move but the one ball skittered across the table.

"Foul!" Male voices shouted but there was laughter from the women. Jewel swiveled around with a what happened look and Jasper struggled not to laugh. He couldn't keep his cheeks from reddening and he knew he was going to rip those panties off her later. Hot pink? Well, it had worked.

"Now fellas these two have both declared war," Harold Fletcher was saying. "Jim is just going to have to use his manly charms to get his shot back."

"Good luck," Jasper muttered into his coffee cup.

"She's flashing," a sandy haired man claimed. "I saw it."

"And what were you doing looking down there, Ben Hanson?" A woman who must had been his wife demanded.

"Simmer down, Laura," Harold said. "He's married, not dead. Now listen here, folks, if Jim wanted to protest that fetching outfit, he should have done it at the beginning of the game. Instead he took off his shirt to level the field. Like it or not, the game is going to be played without either player having to change."

"He should have taken off his pants too," a woman said. "Let us see those manly legs."

Jim grinned and reached for his belt. A glare from his wife put an end to that and everyone laughed.

"Not strip pool," Harold said. "I think you both are showing enough. Let's get this done."

That said, he motioned to Jewel to continue. Jasper watched as Jewel lined up her shots but the only possible one was too tricky even for her. Instead, she took a safety and left Jim with the same problem.

Jasper watched, impressed as Jim jumped the cue ball over one of Jewel's and knocked the twelve to the side. It teetered but didn't go in. There was a groan from the men as they saw Jewel had two available shots.

She studied the table, bending low to examine angles and taking her time. Minx. Jasper watched her and knew every one of those men were ogling her firm breasts or those skirted buns. Damn, he needed to get her home.

"I haven't missed a shot that easy in years," Jim Talbot said almost in his ear. "She knows how to play."

"She knows how to tease too," Jasper said. "Don't let her get hold of you."

"Now that could get her killed," Jim said. "Although I think Betty is in cahoots with her."

"Definitely," Jasper said. "I think it's a battle of the sexes."

"Yes, I get that feeling too. How good are you?" Jim asked. "Or has she ever let you find out?"

Jasper laughed as Jim moved off to chalk his cue. Yes, Jim Talbot had her measure now.

Jewel took her shot, sinking the one ball but that didn't leave her with another possibility. She took another safety. The two and six stood between her and the eight ball. Jim still had everything except the nine. He took his own safety and it looked like the game was going to drag on.

Jewel was checking the table out again. Jasper eyed it too but didn't see how she could do much. The cue ball was simply in the wrong position to send either of hers into a pocket. Another safety, he decided.

Jewel didn't seem to see it that way. Lining up her shot carefully, she sent the cue ball into the end cushion within a hair's breadth of the eleven and it bounced back, knocking her two. The blue ball bumped against the thirteen and changed direction to teeter on the edge of the corner pocket. It didn't fall.

"Good shot," Jim said then studied the table. Finally he had shots and took them, sinking the ten and twelve in one shot then the fourteen. The fifteen fell next leaving him in the right position for the eleven. It followed and it looked almost like Jewel had lost. There was just the thirteen and eight left. Jewel still had the two, six and eight.

Jasper saw the problem though as Jim studied the table. The thirteen was perfectly aligned with the corner pocket and would go straight in but Jewel's two was balanced on the edge. To sink the thirteen in that pocket, he'd have to sink hers and give the table back to Jewel. He couldn't be sure of sinking the thirteen anywhere else.

He tried a bank shot that sent the thirteen down to the other end of the table. It didn't go in. Worse, it left Jewel with one ball perched on a pocket and the other not quite in position.

Jewel smiled then took out the two with a shot that brought the cue ball rolling back. She was almost casual in taking out the six then paused to chalk her cue and study the eight ball.

Now she had to call the pocket. Jasper waited, wondering if she had noted the thirteen's position. Of course, she had. With two other pockets open to her, she just had to choose and not scratch the cue ball.

With great deliberation, she chose the side pocket and sunk it. The cue ball bounced against the cushions but stayed on the table.

"Great game," Jim Talbot said, extending his hand. "Next time I'm going to take your husband's measure."

Jewel smiled. "He's good when I'm not playing." That brought a laugh and the last of the tension eased. The bet winners, not all women Jasper noted, went to collect their winnings.

Jewel came over and started to drape herself around his neck but Jasper captured her hands. "Cover up, love. You can show me what's under that top when we get home."

She made a face and headed for the ladies' room. Jasper grinned and looked around for the coffee. He was going to need his strength.

He saw Aunt Lill with a carafe and headed that way, seeing Jim and Harold had joined her. Both looked to be in a good mood.

"I think we need to set her up with Little Susie," Jim was saying. "She's good enough and her little tricks won't work against her."

"Little Susie?" Jasper asked as Lill obliging refilled his cup.

"She's the only other female shark I know," Jim said. "I had a hard time beating her about three years ago. It would be interesting to see how your wife plays against another woman."

Jasper thought about it then nodded. "Yes, I'd like to see that myself. She has an unfair advantage against us—not that I mind," he added. "Thanks for the entertainment."

Jim chuckled. "You're welcome. I lost the bet I had with Betty though. She can be wicked when she wins."

Jasper decided it was safer not to answer that. "Who gave her that tank top? I know I've never seen it before."

"We have," Harold said. "And unless there's more than one, it gets passed around. I can't tell you who had it last."

Before he could ask more about it, Harold frowned. "Have you actually got a day off tomorrow?"

Jasper started to nod then stopped. "I'm supposed to have one but don't wish me a quiet one. That's when things happen."

"I won't then. Why don't you and Jewel plan on having lunch with me and Lill? We need to get better acquainted."

"I'm being paged," Jim said. "See you tomorrow night at the pot luck." He gave Lill a little bow and went off to rejoin his wife.

"To fill you in?" Jasper asked.

"Hell, no," Harold said. "Just talk. You need to unwind some. A light lunch and a walkabout should help if you're game."

"That sounds good to me," Jasper said. "Yes, I'm ready for a day off."

"Tomorrow then. Have a good night's sleep."

Chapter 44 - Sunday, 21 Nov 2179

Jasper dreamed of music but it was sort of odd and halting. The soft metallic tones of his drum played nearby but it would stop then start again. Sometimes the note fit right and sometimes it was jarring. He wanted to reach for it but he was too damned comfortable spread out on the bed. He frowned. That was wrong.

Twisting onto his side, he reached for Jewel but she wasn't there. He could still hear that damned drum too. It hadn't gone away with his dream. Opening his eyes, he scrubbed his face and stretched. "I'm going to have to teach you how to play that thing," he said and rolled over to look at his wife. "You keep hitting the wrong notes."

His wife was sitting in the easy chair, the drum on her lap as she tapped this note and that. She looked wide awake and way too healthy. How long had she been up?

Seeing she still wore that sexy tank top, he remembered last night but not all of it. He'd been waiting for Jewel to get done in the bathroom and... "I fell asleep?"

"Out like a light," Jewel said. "You owe me."

"So you wake me with a drum," Jasper said.

"You bet." She set the drum aside and stood up. By her smile, he knew exactly what her designs were. Not only did she have that Ball Breaker top but there was probably nothing under that skirt and it wouldn't be long before he found out.

"I'm going to be used?" he asked and twisted out of bed, beating a not too hasty retreat to the bathroom.

Jewel laughed and pounded a couple of times on the door. "I call the shots, remember?"

"I remember," Jasper said. He still took his time in the bathroom, knowing the kind of hijinks she'd want to pull. "How is your stomach today?"

"It's good," she said. "I've been up over an hour. It's just past nine."

"Just past nine? It's Sunday and I'm under orders to sleep," Jasper said as he came out again and stretched out on the bed.

"No, you're under my orders to spend time with me," Jewel responded, crawling on to the bed. "And I..." she half lay on him and Jasper's pulse quickened, "call..." her hand ran down his bare stomach with a light touch, "the..." Jasper gasped and reached for her as she stroked his staff, "shots."

She batted his hand away and touched him again, daring him to move. He was already hard when she leaned over and licked his nipple. She laughed at his response but didn't climb aboard. "You're my prisoner today," she said. "You owe me."

"I owe you," Jasper admitted, knowing exactly how this game would go. He longed to take charge and play her but this was her day and he knew how much she enjoyed pleasuring him. He was thankful her recent experiences hadn't taken that away. "No handcuffs?"

She laughed and began the torture.

It was very close to noon before they presented themselves freshly showered and properly dressed at Harold's front door. Having missed breakfast, Jasper found himself hoping for a substantial lunch even though he knew the potluck that night would be huge. He wasn't sure he could last that long on just the coffee and crackers he'd grabbed. On the other hand, he wouldn't have traded that morning for the best breakfast he'd ever had.

"You look like you could purr," Jewel said as they knocked on the door and heard the familiar come in. "Shameful."

"Uh-huh," Jasper said. "You need to look in the mirror."

She shrugged and walked on in. "I'm a newlywed," she said. "And I won."

Jasper couldn't keep from smiling as he watched her swing her hips. That damned black skirt was a nuisance but at least they didn't have to shower with it. Once that transmitter died, they could get rid of it.

Harold met them at the top of the stairs. "I thought you might be late," he said with a knowing smile. "Well rested now?"

"I slept very well," Jasper said. "Hungry now."

Harold chuckled and waved him toward the kitchen. "We'll throw another cow on the fire. Jewel, you hungry too?"

"Just for food," she said. "Can you make it two?"

Harold laughed. "Have we got enough, Lill? These two are hungry."

"Of course," she said. "Sara, get out that seven bean salad and the rest of Molly's dish."

"Yes, grandma." A blonde girl calmly fetched the salad, found a spoon for it, and added it to the dishes on the counter. "The coffee's ready too."

"Go ahead and pour," Aunt Lill said. "I think we're ready."

"What's this?" Jasper asked with an eye on the girl. "We can help."

"Ah but Sara is learning how to do things properly," Lill said. "Just set yourself down and let her do the serving."

"Great idea," Jewel said. "I'm sure Sara will do great and the food looks so good."

"It's nothing fancy today," Lill said. "Some cold fried chicken and sandwich fixings. Filling but plain."

"It looks great to me," Jasper said. "Do you often teach girls?" He noted the napkin and unfolded it.

"Yes," Lill said. "When I got so old, they decided I needed some help around the house. Since I used to work at some fancy hotels in my youth, I decided to pass on what I know. Two of the girls have already gotten part-time jobs near their colleges—not the little diner places but good restaurants. They pay well."

"Sara will be able to skip training jobs like Lyn and Robin did." She smiled at her student. "And I do appreciate the help."

Her granddaughter smiled back then brought the coffee round the table, taking care to stay on the proper side of each of them. Jasper reined in his impatience as he eyed the plate of cold chicken on the counter.

"That was some game last night," Harold said to Jewel. "Who taught you to shoot?"

"My grandfather," Jewel said. "He liked to have someone to play with and Grandmother wasn't very good. Uncle Mike rarely had the time so Grandfather and I would play. He also took me out target shooting."

"That would be fun," Aunt Lill said. "Any actual hunting?"

"Not with me," Jewel replied. "He'd go with Uncle David and Jake. I knew I could do it but he liked spending time with them."

"Yes, fathers and grandfathers often make that mistake," Aunt Lill said. "But at least he taught you how to shoot. That can come in handy."

Jewel's eyes flew to his and Jasper answered, "It has. She saved my life."

Harold and Lill both looked a little shocked but curious and he knew they hadn't heard about that. Young Sara kept on with what she was doing.

"The hit man who tried to kill Jewel back in July got me when I got in the way," Jasper said. "Jewel grabbed my gun and fired two shots and I've been told she hit him both times and not an inch apart."

"Pretty good shooting," Harold said. "He died?"

"Yes." Jasper's voice was hard and this time he heard something drop and looked up to see an embarrassed Sara picking a spoon up off the floor. He relaxed and clasped Jewel's hand. "He was a killer and he died."

"That was a good end for him then," Harold said. "Jewel, no nightmares about that?"

"No," she firmly said, "he was trying to kill us."

"Right," Harold replied. "Killing in self-defense is not murder. We all know that. I'll just remember you're a good shot before I make you mad."

Jasper smiled. He'd heard that a lot since Jewel's experience. He didn't recall that much himself since he'd been down and barely conscious but he did remember the two shots and the look on Jewel's face as she aimed and fired. He'd never been more surprised or proud of her. His love would do anything for him. Lifting her hand to his lips, he gave it a quick kiss and Jewel's cheeks turned pink.

"What would like on your sandwiches?" Harold asked. "I think I want roast beef, mustard and swiss cheese—with lettuce and onion."

"That sounds good but I've been eyeing that chicken," Jasper said. "It's pretty good."

"Home grown," Harold said with a wide smile. "Are you ready, Sara?"

"Yes sir," she said. "I can fix the sandwich, right?"

"Serve the other dishes first, lass," Harold said. "Then sandwiches. I have a feeling we won't need more than one."

An hour later Jasper left Jewel talking about what they'd take to the pot luck with Aunt Lill while he and Harold went on the mentioned walkabout.

"We'll just take a quick spin," Harold said as he led him to a farm truck and handed him a coat. "I want to show you some areas Ivan didn't."

The main road the farm sat on was perfectly clear of snow but the little truck bucked in protest when Harold sent it over a small snowbank and on to the utility road that ran around the farm. They went around the ring of houses and out toward the low buildings beyond.

"As you know we've got three tall buildings," Harold said. "From them we can see most of the property but not too far over here. This is where the poultry buildings are and the beef cattle are down in the lower pasture beyond." He stopped beside a tall pole with a box perched on top. "Here's the camera for this area. When we get a building up, it'll be higher and we can see more."

"I see what you mean," Jasper said, wondering what he was getting at. "What are you going to put up?"

"We'd like a business of some kind." Harold gunned the engine and headed for the smallest of the barn buildings. "But this is what I wanted to show you. It's been cleaned up now."

Jasper wondered why he was being shown a barn. The first thing he noticed was the natural light coming through the windows and the warmth of it. He expected an unused barn to be cold but it was a lot warmer than outside.

"Nice," he said. "What temperature is it?"

"68 to 72 Fahrenheit," Harold answered. "When it's packed with birds, we take it down to 62 because they generate a lot of heat themselves. The building is straw bale construction so it doesn't take much to heat it. In fact we overdid it and had to put in air conditioners. The newer buildings are better designed."

Jasper walked down to the main floor, avoiding the waist high fences that marked pens. Everything was clean and he couldn't smell birds at all, just the lingering odor of disinfectant.

The building had a good feel and his steps didn't echo, big as it was. He clapped his hands and no echo returned. Interesting.

Turning, he saw Harold was smiling. "Work space for me?"

"If you want it," Harold said. "I know you're itching to get back to your music. We can take down the fences and run some power cables. It'll be temporary until you can decide what you want to do for a permanent place."

Jasper froze, remembering that stop along the way. "Are you offering me room for a studio?"

"West thought you might be interested. We talked about it while he was here." Harold looked a little embarrassed and scratched his gray head. "Frankly, it hadn't crossed my mind but he started pointing out the advantages of giving you a place."

"And they were?" Jasper wasn't surprised David West had been thinking along those lines. What did surprise him was he didn't resent it but he probably would have a week ago. Now he found the farm welcoming and had even started to think of it as home.

"Stupid idea at the time but we'd been drinking. We can't offer you what the city does but now..." Harold stopped, seeming to be at a loss for words.

Jasper studied him, his lips twitching. "David had some really good scotch," Jasper said, "and he started telling you the advantages of having me and Jewel here. How it would help me and help you."

Harold looked at him in consternation. "You know?"

"Not about that conversation but I've had one similar," Jasper said and he couldn't stop the wide smile. "I came out agreeing to marry Jewel."

Harold's jaw dropped then he chuckled. "Well, that was a good thing."

"Very good," Jasper admitted. "And I'm happy we had that talk. I wouldn't have considered marriage without it. I was attracted, of course but I was also on the force."

David had laid out his points well even though they were both nearly legless and Jasper hadn't been able to argue against their logic. Was David truly drunk that night? He knew he was. "What arguments did he use?" Jasper asked.

"Jewel likes teaching but can't teach in that city of yours now," Harold said, holding a finger up. "We can always use another teacher."

"There's room for a good state-of-the-art music studio and you've got the money to build it–and your fans aren't likely to bother you here," Harold said. "One of the reasons most artists leave the cities."

"True enough," Jasper said.

"It's a better place to raise kids. David really stressed that and said when his are school age, he might reconsider staying at Lunarex."

Now that surprised him since Jasper knew David liked his work. After a second thought, it didn't. David was past fifty and he couldn't do it forever.

"That I think I agree with," Jasper said, remembering the gaggle of kids who seemed to be everywhere. They had more energy than he'd ever seen in city kids and they didn't need to be ordered outside to get some sun. He'd had that battle with Mel a lot growing up. That was why the city schools were always above ground too. They had to keep the children exposed to the sun a certain number of hours per day for them to grow healthy.

Remembering Lily and Sara, he also liked the farm mentality of teaching kids how to work while they were still young. Mel couldn't work until she had her high school diploma and he still hadn't pressed her to work while in college. How was she going to do when she had her first job?

"We've also got good security," Harold said. "It doesn't look it because we don't rely on locks. Our dogs know everyone on this place and they can sniff out any strangers."

Remembering the chorus of dogs, he nodded. "Good security."

"And you know we don't allow bliss here," Harold said. "There's some in the medical stuff but there's no recreational use."

"Ok, you've covered the advantages for me," Jasper said. "What do you get out of it?"

Harold looked determined. "College money," he said. "We've got four kids now who can't go because we don't have the money and a couple more who had to stop after the two years the government paid for. If you can help out with that, it'll take a lot of financial worry off the families."

"The government doesn't guarantee two years?" Jasper asked, his brow shooting up. "Or was it the exams?"

"No, no, they've all passed the exams," Harold said. "The government guarantees two years of college for two children from each family. At the same time, farm families are allowed four children before the extra child tax kicks in. We have to pay for the college of the two younger kids and if the two older kids don't find scholarships, they have to stop after two years. That's not enough these days."

"Why the gap?" Jasper asked, appalled. "I've never heard of that."

"Oh, we figured it out a long time ago," Harold said, his expression grim. "They want us to have more kids so there are more farmers. At the same time, they don't want our kids leaving the farms so they deny the two extras an education. It's a trap. We've been fighting it because our kids deserve to have choice but it's Congress."

"Take the Kowalskis," Harold said. "Four children. Mikal didn't even take the exams because he knew Sasha wanted Mars and young Vic was set on being an electronics engineer. Mikal chose to do on-the-job training here and he's done pretty good at it. That leaves Anton. He'd like to study advanced hydroponics engineering but there's no money right now. We need one but we can hire one for less than it would cost to send him through college."

"And all the families have the same problem?" Jasper was starting to get it. Would he be reluctant to invest in education? He'd have to meet the kids first and see how serious they were about wanting it but he probably would. He knew Jewel would back it. She'd set up memorial scholarships for her grandmother, Uncle Mike and Jake.

"All of them," Harold said. "The younger families are stopping at two children simply because they don't want to make a choice between which children can go to college."

"If that's what will help out most, I don't think either of us will have a problem with it," Jasper said. "On a case-by-case basis."

Harold relaxed. "Of course," he said. "You'll think about moving here?"

"I'll think about it," Jasper said. "We won't be living in Plains." He hated to say that but twice Plains had threatened his wife. He wasn't sure he could forgive Lori's death either. He knew it wasn't the city or that damned house but still he didn't feel safe there. He sure as hell didn't want to raise his kids there.

As an ordinary police officer, it had been safe to raise Mel there. She was just another child of another cop. The children Jewel would have would be members of a very rich family and his children too. Public school would be too risky and he didn't like exposing his children to the rich mentality of the private schools. They didn't have that here.

"I don't want to talk to Jewel about it until that transmitter is gone though," Jasper said. "Before we can make any long term plans that has to be done."

"I agree," Harold said. "And it will take time for you to design what you want since it will be more than a house. We'll talk again."

Jasper nodded then cast another appraising eye around the barn. "Is this accessible from the underground?"

"Yes," Harold said. "And it's actually the closest of the four poultry barns. There are laying hens in number two but you won't be able to smell them over here."

"That's good," Jasper said. "This one cleaned up well."

"Yes, it did. By the way, I'm supposed to ask you how well you liked Molly's chicken."

"It's good," Jasper said. "Better than any I've had in years. Did she have some secret herbs or something?" He was puzzled.

"No, it was a four-legged chicken."

"Four-legged?" Jasper repeated, sure that was impossible.

"Rabbit," Harold said. "Best fried chicken ever and always enough legs to go around."

Jasper stared then grinned. "Ok, you got me. Now I can see why you raise rabbits."

"I thought you would," he said. "By the way, that's mostly what they serve in subby cafeterias. Cheaper and what they don't know won't hurt them. Let's head back and I'll show you the underground route."

Chapter 45 - Sales Pitch

By the time they got back to the truck garage, they'd discussed what he would need in the way of power for his equipment and he'd found out there was an apartment closer to the barn with a bigger kitchen and a proper bedroom.

"It's still small," Harold warned him, "but a lot bigger than your postage stamp one. That one was just closer to Ivan's and you couldn't get lost."

"It was good for the first days," Jasper said. "And we didn't spend much time there. David was right in that we wouldn't."

"People don't stay home much here," Harold said. "Although Mondays and Tuesdays tend to be quiet. Lill says there's too much togetherness on the weekends but we like it that way. People catch up on what's happening at the Sunday potluck."

"I can see that. I did have a question though about Friday. If it wasn't that bad out there, why did the kids stay over?" Jasper asked. "Although I know it took us over an hour to get to the train station."

"Oh, that," Harold said with a grin. "It rarely gets so bad we can't get them home. No, it's to get the kids used to staying over some place that's not home. Starting in second grade, we do that. In junior high they start staying in town on bad days. By the time they hit high school, they don't blink an eye at it. It's one of the ways we build self-reliance."

"So the first graders and kinders didn't stay?" Jasper asked.

"No, they didn't come to school Friday," Harold said. "We knew what the weather was going to be and sent our kids out prepared and the little ones from the other farms stayed home. They hate being excluded but we've found most of them just aren't ready for a night away until they're seven. When they do turn seven, they're chomping at the bit to do it."

"I can imagine," Jasper said. "But the ones who live here don't get to do it."

"We'll send them off for New Year's," Harold said. "There's a big party over at Sunrise. They take our younger ones and give them a night with a puppet show, a magic show, and a feast of their own. The kids love it."

"Got it," Jasper said. "And I think I would too."

Leaving the truck in the garage, he followed the older man over to Ivan's. After greeting Molly and leaving their coats behind, they continued on to the underground and Harold directed him toward Farmer's Row. It wasn't long before they came to a plywood section wider than those of the houses.

"This is where that building will go," Harold said. "The basement isn't dug out beyond the first four feet so it can be whatever size needed."

"What do you suggest?" Jasper asked. "I prefer it to be house and studio."

"That sounds good to me," Harold said. "But you want to aim big since you won't be building a second one. If you want, say, offices and storerooms and a second studio for other musicians, it's best to plan it that way from the beginning. You'll notice we've done that with the business offices and the new school. We can double in size before we have to worry about expanding."

"We learned that the hard way," Harold said. "We outgrew the school first. We built another one because we didn't want the town schools getting hold of our kids and messing them up. That's why we got into an agreement with Sunrise. By the time we have to let the towns have our kids, they know their math and have good reading skills. We used to think we short-changed them on history but they actually learn more here than there."

"What about science?" Jasper asked.

"That's mostly hands on biology," Harold said. "Those that want to know about their insides can assist Dr. Bob. Farm kids learn a lot just by being curious."

"True," Jasper said. "But if a kid has a real bent for a science like physics, what do you do?"

"We make sure they get it at town school or an online school," Harold said. "And we encourage experiments. We just don't have the funds for a regular science teacher."

"I can understand that," Jasper said but he was remembering his own interests when he was young. "And not enough hours in the day either. In the Chicago schools they tended to shortchange it too. We had to form a science club to get anywhere."

"Well, that's an idea," Harold said. "We'll have to think on it."

Jasper grinned, knowing he could easily get tied into something like that. "Where's that apartment you wanted me to see?"

It was more than an hour later before he rejoined Jewel and looked at the time. Something good was baking in Lill's oven and there seemed to be a tuna casserole waiting to go in. It was only three but he was already anticipating the potluck that night. He also wanted to think exactly what he would need for his temporary workspace and the more permanent building. If Carlson got his music system to him, he could get Milt to send him the rest of the components. Since he would have room, he wanted a secondary recording system to capture the live music from the drum or any other musician he called in.

Two studios was a darned good idea too. That would allow him to keep his privacy but give him room for other musicians and a storage room for the few unique instruments he'd collected over the years. Until he moved into Lily Street, he couldn't keep many so he'd simply recorded their tones and sold them off again. He wouldn't have to do that now and he knew he was going to keep that drum.

Wandering back to their apartment, he sat down on the bed and started reviewing his messages. There was one from Pedro and he pulled it up without thinking. The pathologist looked jubilant. "DEA gave me a job offer," he said. "I wanted you to be the first to hear because I'm accepting it. They want me to officially work on that drug that keeps popping up. Anyway, I'm to share what I learn with Captain Reynolds and no one else in Plains. I still have to finish out my two weeks notice but my DEA certification is in the works. It's the same kind of work but no one pulling the plug on me."

Jasper grinned, wondering if Kruger had put it together yet. Well, he probably would in time. He was glad the man was getting a promotion into a more challenging job. He'd been useful in Plains but wasted.

"It's too late to get the professor's body," Kruger said. "And the bottle of pills and the rats they confiscated from me were destroyed. They didn't get the ones I stashed."

"Carlson found out that Kucera's body was released to his widow and cremated months ago. The few blood samples they took disappeared from the lab. Whoever is covering up this blister stuff has got some pull and I'm not sure it's drug dealers. They tend to leave tracks."

"The book Reynolds gave me was a cryptology key. We don't have any messages in it so it doesn't tell us much. I did check and there were old defunct groups using the Eye as a symbol including a group called the Guardians but they had it tattooed on. The symbol mostly appears now in men's jewelry. It's odd that the professor wore it though. I'll keep digging. Let me know how the Jewel of the West is doing. I heard she got blister too."

The message ended and Jasper's mouth curled up at the corners. It looked like his wife was going to be stuck with that nickname. He wondered if she'd heard it yet. Like him, she'd mostly been ignoring the news. He doubted she'd heard the report about the house being broke into.

There was another message from Carlson. He pulled it up and saw Carlson, a grinning Kin, and his music equipment in front of them.

"Sending this to both you and the Koasa family so it will be short," Carlson said. "I assume you don't want to press charges for the robbery so I'm helping him drink the beer and will send this to your publisher." He tapped the unit lightly. "And the suitcase. It was a good way to extract him."

He motioned to Kin and the Japanese-American spoke up.

"I fully intend to cooperate with the government," Kin said. "I've hidden notes on the blissex operation in all three cities they've had me work in. This was just the first opportunity I had to really get free."

"Sachiko, I'm sorry about the college. I needed to protect you and mother and this was the only way. Forgive me." He made a little bow to the screen. "I know you hate bliss. Maybe it would please you to know that my information will be valuable in stopping blissex."

When he stopped, Carlson continued. "There will be more later. The Chicago police confirmed there was a controlled detonation system on the house's gas line. It's been disarmed and dismantled now and the gas line cut off. The house won't blow up but it's still being checked for a backup trap. The contents are being moved to a secure storage locker for now."

Jasper frowned. Contents? He realized he could have that done with his furniture in Plains. He didn't want to move everything and he certainly didn't want it before he had a place to put it but he could have a moving company pack it up and store it. He'd want his clothes and Jewel might want some of hers but almost everything else could wait.

If they built a house and studio here, he'd want it to be for generations. He didn't like moving so he'd better be very sure he wanted to stay here first. Jewel might resist losing the house in Plains too but he was going to have that outside entrance bricked up before they stayed there again. He knew that house was a temptation to smugglers from the moment he learned of Elizabeth's death. What he didn't know is why Baxter had continued to target it if his real goal had been to eliminate Mike and David. Was it because it was too convenient?

When Baxter went after the professor, he was after answers. He had questioned Jewel with penseek before boobytrapping her–and insisted they keep her alive. He had questioned him too before insisting he find out about blister. Jasper thought back and realized Baxter hadn't asked him anything about the West murders. No, he'd been focused on Ed Kucera and blister. He should have noticed that before.

Well, he knew now that he'd led Baxter to Drew Nugent and he'd never forget that. The professor had died because he hadn't heeded Gordon's warning to back off. As for Ed Kucera, it was clear that Baxter didn't know as much as he should about him. Maybe that had him worried. Or maybe Wilson Kucera wanted him to find out more.

He knew Ed Kucera had no public ties to Wilson Chemicals other than being related to the current owner. When Wilson Kucera had acquired the company and changed the name to his, Edward Kucera was already in law school. The two brothers had very different careers with Wilson being the more successful. Ed was married though and had two boys. If Wilson Kucera had ever married, it never made news. If he didn't marry and didn't have children otherwise, Edward Kucera would have been his heir.

He was going to have to talk to Elaine Kucera. She was the only one who would know how close the two brothers were and why her husband was taking blister. Remembering the lawyer who was always at her elbow at the Reach Out event, he doubted he'd be allowed to get that close without legal muscle of his own.

Damn, he was supposed to be taking the day off. If Jewel caught him working on the case, she might exact another penalty from him. Remembering that morning, he decided he didn't want to tempt her. He should get back to her but he wasn't inclined to spend time in a kitchen today.

Seeing his drum, he began tapping out the melody he'd already worked on then found himself simply playing it. He liked using his hands on the metal surface and relaxed into an improvisation that was half melody and half rhythm. The range of the drum was limited to one octave but there was a lot he could do with that. He just played on and on.

"There you are." Jewel's voice broke across his concentration and he looked up at her half-scolding tone. "You're late. Aren't you hungry?"

Jasper glanced at the clock and groaned. Almost six o'clock. Where had the time gone? And he was hungry, ravenously so. Before he could move, Jewel scooped the drum off his lap and stepped quickly out the door.

"I found him," she announced in a loud voice and there was a ripple of laughter as he followed. "Playing his drum," she said and flourished it. "More fun than food, I guess."

Jasper strode after her, flushing as he realized everyone was already seated at the tables and those that weren't eating were looking at him. Grinning because he'd been caught, he tried to catch up with Jewel but she dashed away with that blasted drum while people laughed.

Hands caught him and slowed him down. When he got free, Jewel was heading to the buffet table and her hands were empty. He followed but scanned her path, trying to see where she had stashed the drum.

"Eat," Jewel said and handed him a plate. "They were really starting to wonder where you'd got to. Mikal even offered to go count the trucks in the garage."

"Sorry," Jasper said, "I lost track of time."

"I know that," she said. "I've got you figured out. They're still learning how lost you get in music. Now you'll eat a good plateful before you see that drum again."

"Yes ma'am," Jasper said loud enough for those close by to hear. He heard a note from his drum and turned but there was no sign of it.

"It sounds pretty good," someone said. "Wouldn't keep me from food though."

The next hour Jasper spent eating under his wife's eye and hearing notes from the invisible drum. He could tell it was being passed around but he never actually saw anyone do it. Were they passing it with their feet? Amused and knowing the drum couldn't be hurt by such antics, he paid more attention to his food and company. This time Jim Talbot was sitting by him on one side and a Hanson woman was across from him. This one was older and he wondered if she might be Lily's mother.

"Laura is our education administrator," Jim told him as he nursed his cup of coffee. "She coordinates the education stuff with the various schools and approves after school jobs."

"Got it," Jasper said. "So Jewel reports to you?"

"While she's here and wants to teach," Laura Hanson said. "It's a good fit but she's asked not to be paid and I can't have that."

Jewel looked defensive. "I'm on vacation. If you pay me, it's a job and I never know when I'm going to have to be somewhere else."

"It still throws the economy of the farm off," Jim Talbot said. "We aren't a commune. Everyone gets paid for working in one way or another. If you don't want it, take it anyway and spend it on something or buy a share of the farm. That's what I do."

"Shares?" Jasper asked, perking up. "Stock shares?"

"Similar," Jim said. "It's one of the ways we raise money to expand or bring in things we need or send someone for more education. I ran out of things to buy that I actually needed a long time ago so I just put more into shares. It's limited to those who live here though. You might have to officially join us before you can do it."

"Right," Jasper said. "Everyone retains their own assets, I take it?"

"Of course," Jim said. "We wouldn't have it any other way."

Jasper filed that away and continued eating. Harold hadn't explained that but he also hadn't implied there'd be a joining fee of any type or sharing of assets. No, he'd kept it on a business level. He didn't want to join something with a bad business model but Jim had just reassured him. Yes, Harold had said he could build his studio. He hadn't said the farm would. What he'd be getting in return was the fellowship and security of this community. He'd need it to be a little clearer and on paper but right now that looked like a fair trade. He wondered what Jewel would say to dogs in a house of their own.

His ears perked up as he heard the random notes on his drum change to something like a tune. Looking up, he wondered who was doing it but the adults gave no clue. Some were listening and others were talking. It was a couple of kids whispering and looking under the table that told him where the drum was but not who was playing. The tune was ragged but getting firmer as it went along.

"Who's that playing?" Jasper finally asked.

"Probably Lexie," Jim said. "The two kids snickering over there are her brother and one of her friends. She'll get it back to you."

"She's under the table?" Jasper asked. "How old is she?"

"Nine or ten," Jim said. "She's my cousin's girl. Sings too but she likes to play."

"Better than me then," Jasper said. "I can't sing." Now he was curious but he never saw the girl pop up. After a while the drum moved on to another table and his curiosity waned as Sara set a generous piece of blueberry pie in front of him.

"I baked it today," the girl said with a proud smile. "Jewel said you like blueberry pie."

"No, I love it," Jasper said and saw her beam. "Thank you."

"I saved it for you. Enjoy." She ducked away.

Jim eyed the pie critically. "I think you got a fan," he said with a grin. "Forgot the ice cream though."

"I wouldn't have room for it anyway," Jasper said. "So much food."

Jim laughed. "That's why we keep it to Sundays and spend Monday in the gym. You might have to work extra hard this week though. There's another feast on Thursday. Thanksgiving."

"Don't remind me," Jasper said. "Not now." He dug into the blueberry pie and had to admit it was better than any he'd had in Plains. The piece was too large though and he was glad when Jewel took her cue and ate a few bites for him. He wasn't sure how much she'd managed to eat tonight but he hoped she wouldn't want a repeat of this morning. He was going to be too full for much of anything.

His drum made it back to him finally, passed down the table to sit just out of his reach as Laura Hanson removed her dishes. To stave off having to eat any more, he pulled it toward him and began tapping out a light tune. Voices died down as he continued to play but he didn't intend to play long. He just wanted that young drummer to know what it could do.

Seeing a young girl with light olive skin watching the drum intently, he smiled. That one he could remember. When he ended his song, he beckoned to her. "Your turn."

Shyly, the girl repeated his first notes then part of the recurring chorus she'd caught. When she hesitated, he said "There's no wrong way to play it. Have fun."

Her grin of delight brought him back to his own early days learning to play. Yes, she would be fun to have around. At his motion, she took the drum off the table and disappeared with it to one of the seating areas.

"So is there a music teacher here," he asked Jim.

"Not yet," he calmly replied. "Do you think she's got something?"

"She likes to play," Jasper said. "Experiment. If no one tells her she has to play one certain way, she might be something. She'll need to learn the basics but too many teachers try to drum it into heads you need to play this piece this way and no other way. They kill creativity."

He paused. "Oh, and they love singers more than musicians. That's my experience, anyway."

"I could see that," Jim said. "But I'm glad you didn't get your creativity killed. I haven't heard much of what you write but the piece with the cat sounded promising." He grinned. "I especially liked the cat."

Jasper chuckled. "I didn't know he was conducting until I saw the vid. Where is Magic anyway?"

"Magic?" Jewel caught that. "You named him?"

"I couldn't just call him Cat and Cloudy didn't fit him," Jasper said. "If he's going to keep showing up when I play, I had to call him something."

"You could have called him Maestro," Harold said from further down the table and there was laughter.

"I didn't think of that," Jasper called back. "My publisher's secretary asked for his name and that's the one that popped out. Someone said he was like magic."

"Oh, we've all said that," Lill acknowledged. "Magic he is."

Jasper eyed his wife and she gave him a smile of approval. Great. Now the cat was his. He'd better find out what he had to feed it.

"We haven't located Baxter yet," Carlson said. "According to his secretary, he was going to Costa Rica for two weeks but the GPS in his com unit put him in his office. She found his com unit in his desk and said he often leaves it behind when he's on vacation."

"How often does he go on vacation?" Jasper asked.

"About thirty weeks of the year," Carlson said, his tone calm and deadly. "That tells me right there something is up. Kucera is in the office more than he is."

"Any DNA on the plane?" Jasper asked.

"Still no results," Carlson said. "I'd like to get that woman Jewel mentioned in her statement–the nurse. If she killed that FBI agent, she's got murder against her---and accessory to murder in Brown's death."

"We've looked at the flight logs for that plane and it wasn't common practice to note who was aboard. I know Homeland Security is going to take a dim view of that but it's usually just a fine with no teeth. What they did note was how many bodies–no sex–and where they boarded. When they got off, they're just no longer listed on the next leg."

"Does the pilot know who was on board with Kucera?" Jasper asked.

"No one extra," Carlson said. "Someone got off in Denver though and the pilot isn't saying who. Kucera got the flight crew a lawyer and they clammed up."

"We've got an APB out on Baxter in Denver but we know he's not in the underground on his own ident card. Searching above ground is nearly impossible. Four cars have been stolen since Friday so he may not even be in the city now."

"He'll turn up," Jasper said. "What has Kin said about the shipment of drugs? Is there any chance they'll be stupid enough to use the house?"

"He says no," Carlson replied. "But he gave us more outside of Plains that's useful. It seems there's a winery that produces blissex in liquid form and ships it all over the country that way. He didn't know the complete name but he saw a bottle in the trash once in New York City. The interesting thing is they ship the wine in to a specific restaurant and the bottles go upstairs or to a backroom where they make up the cakes for the blissex, cut and package them then get them out on the street."

Jasper stared, stunned by the revelation. "They make them inside the city?"

"Yeah, we've been barking up the wrong tree in a lot of places," Carlson said. "Not in Plains though. Apparently they couldn't get a liquor license there. They've had to bring it in from outside."

"How does Kin know about the others?" Jasper demanded.

"He had to repair the machine in New York City," Carlson said. "That's where he saw the wine bottle. He's worked in Chicago where he was hired, New York City, Nashville, Denver, Seattle, and Tacoma. Baxter was always there. He couldn't say Wilson Kucera ever was but he had the impression Baxter was taking orders as well as giving them. Three weeks ago they came to Denver but it wasn't the usual routine or the usual people."

"So what turned him?" Jasper asked.

"He was there when the professor died," Carlson said. "They had him checking for surveillance cameras there and he didn't find any. Then when they snatched he realized how ugly it was going to get. He'd been keeping notes for years in case he needed an out and a way to protect his family. He figured an ex-cop was his best hope."

"He figured that right," Jasper said. "What kind of deal will he get?"

"Undecided," Carlson said. "If what he tells us holds up, I'll see what I can do. That bit about the wine alone is pretty valuable. We knew some cities had no visible smuggling activity even though there was plenty of blissex. That explains it. Finding the winery—or the factory—might be tricky though. He's giving us the restaurants."

"He's identified six people by name in Plains and they're being watched. He didn't know many because he came in with Baxter. This was his first trip to Plains."

"What about Chuma Johnson? What does he know about him?"

"He's from New York City and came in with him and Baxter. The nurse joined them just before the professor died and he'd never met her before. Her first name is Mary. He never heard the last. He said that was the usual way of doing things. They used first names or what their skills were but never shared last names. Johnson was Slasher, he was X, and they just called the nurse Nurse until she told Jewel to call her Mary." Carlson paused. "Baxter was always the Boss or Mr. B. He knew he was Baxter but most of them didn't know his name."

"Reynolds is wasting his time waiting for an attempt on Johnson. Someone in the crowd beating him was one of theirs and had the opinion he wasn't going to live."

"I wondered about that," Jasper said. "They've had him over a week now."

"Right," Carlson said. "There are other things to tie up but it looks like it's coming together finally. I've sent what Kin took—minus that very good beer—to Chicago. Since I don't want Lane to know your whereabouts, I sent it to your publisher. I assume he can get it to you."

"He can. What all did he have in that suitcase?" Jasper asked.

"Not your usual stuff," Carlson said with a grin. "He grabbed some picture frames and some cheap jewelry, a stuffed toy, and a lot of sexy underwear. The only thing of value in the whole lot was your music system."

"Sexy underwear?" Jasper repeated and his face got hot. "Jewel's?"

"Unless it was yours, yeah," Carlson said and his grin got wider. "Relax. I think he was going for laughs. He didn't ask to keep any."

"Right," Jasper said but he wasn't amused. No one had a right to see that stuff but him. Well, he knew the man hadn't much time to pack that suitcase. He probably just grabbed.

"I've got more calls to make and it should be close to lunchtime your time. Let Jewel know we're thinking about her."

"Yes sir," Jasper responded. "Once this is over we might have time to visit."

"Don't rush it," Carlson said. "Baxter first. He probably wants to kill you both right now."

"I know," Jasper said. "He'll have to find us first."

Carlson nodded and broke the connection.

Jasper hesitated. Mark Baxter knew how he treasured his wife but he had miscalculated how far he could be controlled even with that. If he got another chance to kill Jewel or him, he wouldn't hesitate to take it. Even though the professor's death was an accident, he was sure Baxter had killed others. Those eyes of his were too damned cold for it be otherwise. He'd seen eyes like that before and the person behind them had always been a killer.

He needed to get over to Molly's. They'd been here over a week now and Molly was insistent they have lunch with her. Hopefully, she'd be able to tell him the blister in Jewel's blood was gone. He also wanted to ask her about Jewel's queasiness. If it weren't for that damned transmitter, he'd think she was pregnant.

God, he wished she were but the next moment he discarded that. It was the transmitter. He knew that a foreign object in the womb could sometimes mimic pregnancy symptoms and would definitely prevent pregnancy. He couldn't recall when he'd learned that but it was a long time ago and probably some vid he'd been forced to watch in high school or college.

No, she wasn't pregnant and that was for the best. As long as that transmitter was in her, he didn't want to think that far into the future. Another three weeks and it might be dead and then it could be removed. After that, they'd make up for lost time. His lips quirked and his stomach tightened. As if they'd been waiting. Hastily, he turned his thoughts toward the upcoming meal and away from his randy wife.

Jewel met him outside and, after a chaste kiss, they walked to the Kowalski house together.

"Missed you," she said.

"Already?" Jasper answered with a smile. "Let's see what Molly has planned. Do I hear kids?" His brow furrowed as he listened. "Yes, little ones."

Not so little it turned out. The boy on the couch looked to be about seven and another in a playpen might have been a year old.

"Babysitting?" Jasper asked as Molly came out of the kitchen.

"Sick kids," she said. "Keep your distance from that one." She waved toward the one on the couch. "Some kind of upset. That's Wayne Hanson, Lexie's brother. He might have just ate too much last night but this close to the holidays, I like to make sure. Cora Talbot is just recovering from a cold we don't want spread around the daycare."

"Nice," Jasper said. "Do you ever feel too busy?"

Molly laughed. "I wouldn't trade my life here for a big city hospital job. Ivan rescued me." The smile on her face made her look younger and more vibrant. "I love it here most days. Now these two have had their lunches and Wayne is set with the remote. We'll just take it into the kitchen."

The seven-year-old didn't look sick now, Jasper thought as he followed Molly into the kitchen. There was a movie on the vid screen and, by the looks of it, he'd had more than dry toast and tea.

They'd just sat down to a hearty soup when an odd buzz filled the living room. It went on for several seconds.

"Wayne, what did I tell you about answering the phone?" Molly said, her tone sharp. "Turn it off right now."

The long tone was replaced by several short ones before it was cut off. Jasper's eyes flew to Jewel's and he knew. Damn, had the entire code been received? Did the jammers work? She was wearing the skirt but...

Jewel leapt to her feet and pressed both hands against her belly and he feared the worst but then the fear in her face edged toward puzzlement.

Molly looked at them, not understanding. "That's the fourth time we've gotten that wrong number," she said. "I blocked it after the second time but they must have multiple com units." She frowned at them. "What's wrong?"

"The activation code for the self destruct," Jasper said, his voice terse. "Jewel, did you feel anything?"

"Nothing," she said then she started to cry. "I thought..."

"You thought right," Jasper said. "That damned thing has got to come out now." His voice was rough. "Today. You aren't going to wait."

Molly was pale now. "I'll get Cora's mother over here and call the air ambulance. I didn't know that's what it would sound like."

"How long will it take to get to St. Paul?" Jasper asked.

"Twenty minutes after it gets here," she said. "By car almost an hour. No, the air ambulance is the best option. You two go get packed and meet me at the office building. I'll go with you." She was all business now.

"Right," Jasper said and grabbed Jewel's hand. As soon as they were in the apartment, he stopped and held her then looked into her eyes. "Did you feel anything? Any pain?"

"No, I'm fine," Jewel said but she was clearly scared. "How did they find us?"

"They found the phone number, not us," Jasper said. "And they can't get past the dogs," he added and pulled out his suitcase. He forced himself through the motions even though all he wanted to do was hold Jewel and wait for the knot of fear in his belly to go away.

That transmitter had to come out and it had to come out now. It was only a matter of time before Baxter located the farm. Blocking fabric and jammers wouldn't protect Jewel when he did. No, it couldn't wait.

McBride, he needed to call her. Where was Kale? Should he call David?

Jewel handed him her own items and it wasn't a large selection. Automatically he tucked them in then turned for more.

"Nightgown and robe?" he asked.

"I don't have anything for a hospital," she said. "Way too sexy. You'd have a problem with..." She tried to smile but he could see she was holding back tears.

"Take my robe," Jasper said. "And I'll..." He grabbed his pajamas and laid them in then had to hold her. "You can use my top. They can't see through it," he finally said. "I'll be close."

"I know," Jewel said and her eyes swam through tears. "I want my drum."

Jasper smiled and got it for her. Two minutes later they were out the door with one suitcase, his briefcase, and that fool drum. Passing one of the Talbot women headed to Molly's they expected to arrive before Molly but she was already there.

"The ambulance will be here in five more minutes," Molly said and she was holding a com unit. "Dr. McBride will meet us at Saint Stephens. We'll have to get them to take us there and not the Metro Hospital."

"I can do that," Jasper said.

Harold Fletcher joined them, his face grim. "I'll call Kale for you and I'm sending out word dogs are to be out as soon as the ambulance leaves. Are you okay, Jewel?"

"I don't feel any different," she said. "Just scared."

"You'll come through. Are you taking his drum?" he asked.

"It's mine," she said. "And I'm taking his pajamas too."

"Good idea," Harold said with a grin. "He can't sleep without them. My son will be here soon. He had an idea to help."

Just as he said it, a farm truck pulled up to the office door and Dr. Bob hopped out carrying something big and black. "Got it," he declared as he walked in.

"What is it?" Jasper asked as the vet unrolled what looked to be a heavy sheet.

"A lead shield," Dr. Bob replied. "It's better than that skirt she wears. This is rated pretty high on the scale for blocking radiation and electronic signals. We use it on the cows. When you get on the ambulance, make sure it's both under and over Jewel. They have a lot of electronics."

"Got it," Jasper said and was glad he'd thought of it. "Thanks."

"Anytime," Dr. Bob said. "Keep her safe. I have to move that truck now." He was gone before more could be said.

"This will do," Molly said with an approving eye. "Heavier and bigger than anything the ambulance would have. Now, Jewel, I know this is scary but you don't want to panic. I'm going to stay with you and Jasper will be right there too. Don't go imagining the worst because it's not going to happen."

"Thanks," Jewel said with a smile for her firm tone. Whatever else she might have said was lost as the ambulance suddenly came into view and started settling on the road.

Harold walked out with them as a paramedic dashed out to meet them. He had no trouble identifying Jewel as the patient and hustled her aboard with Molly.

"Take care, Jazz," Harold said as they parted. "Pull whatever strings you have to pull. Now is not the time to worry about secrecy."

"I know," Jasper clasped his hand and walked on out. Setting the suitcase down near the door, he headed straight for the cockpit.

"You can't come in here," the pilot said as Jasper squeezed in. His instrument panels were active, the engines running but they were still on the ground.

"I need you to take us to Saint Stephens," Jasper said. He was already pointing his com unit at the back of his locket. "No place else. This is a special case."

"We can't do that," the pilot said as his co-pilot half rose from his chair. "Orders are Metro."

"New orders," Jasper said and showed him his com unit. "Get it cleared." His voice was hard and commanding, trained by years on the force.

The pilot's eyes widened as he saw the DEA identification but he read it through before reaching for the mike. Waving his co-pilot to sit back down, he keyed his system.

"Control, we have a DEA request to deliver this patient to Saint Stephens, not Metro. Can you give clearance?"

"Get us in the air," Jasper said to the co-pilot. "Hop it."

"Hop it?" The co-pilot looked shocked. "With a patient?"

"Do it," Jasper said.

"I didn't copy you, AA-23. Repeat."

"Hold on," the pilot said. "You talk to them." He thrust the mike at Jasper. "If we're going to hop, it takes two."

Jasper clung with one hand to the back of the chair and braced himself against the bulkhead as the ambulance hopped straight up, paused then hopped again to cruising altitude. The force of the jump pushed him down and he heard startled exclamations from the back. The pilot veered to the left as soon as the second hop was completed then   evelled out.

"This is DEA Agent Wolfgang Von Blitzen, ID number Delta Echo Alpha-Charlie one eight three two Victor Bravo," Jasper said. "I have a priority patient–a witness–to go to Saint Stephens. Authorize it."

The silence stretched on. Pilot and co-pilot looked at each other then the co-pilot picked up a course book and started programming a course.

"Control, are you there?" Jasper said in a hard voice. "Did you copy?"

Still no answer.

"Course for Saint Stephens laid in," the pilot said. "They've got their heads up their asses."

The radio cracked to life. "DEA override approved," Control said. "Notifying Saint Stephens now."

"Thank you," Jasper said and handed the mike back to the pilot. He turned to see Molly standing in the way and knew she'd heard the exchange. Damn. His DEA status was going to be an open secret by the time he got done. He'd be lucky if no one told Baxter–or a reporter.

"Remember I'm Von Blitzen," he said to the pilot and co-pilot. "Escorting Jewel Stone–not West–to Saint Stephens."

"Got it," the pilot said. "Good to meet you. Now we're going to get you there. Buckle in."

Jasper left the cockpit to go back and sit by Jewel, his hand clasping hers as the paramedic continued taking vitals and attaching monitors.

"No more rough ride," Molly said as she started assisting. "There was a truck coming so they took off fast."

The paramedic looked at her in disbelief but kept working.

"I'm glad that's all it was," Jewel said. "I thought I left my stomach on the ground."

"Any pain, dear?" Molly asked. "I'm going to check you just in case. Jasper, look away." She lifted up the lead shield and poked around then laid it down again. "No, no bleeding. I think those jammers worked."

"Jammers?" the paramedic asked.

"Our patient has a self-destructing transmitter in her womb," Molly quietly said. "The destruction code was sent but it either wasn't complete or the jammers she wears stopped it. We have to watch for blood pressure drop and hemorrhage and pelvic pain."

"Got it," the paramedic said then stopped. "A uterine bomb?" His face paled. "Where the hell did they get that? How much force?"

"Designed to kill the woman, not bystanders," Jasper said in a flat tone. "Research it later."

"Yes sir." The paramedic turned on his monitors and began recording readouts. "Everything normal so far. I could put another monitor on her... No, bad idea." He eyed the black blanket. "I'm going to turn these off and use manual monitors."

"That's a great idea," Molly said. She already had the blood pressure cuff in hand. "But we can accept the current read out for a couple of minutes. Jewel, tell us if you feel anything. Did your stomach catch up with you?"

"Yes," she said then eyed her husband suspiciously. "Why do I think you did it?"

"Me?" Jasper kept a straight face. "I can't fly."

"Uh-huh," Jewel closed her eyes. "And you're not a cop either. You are a trial, Jazz Stone."

"And you married me," Jasper answered. "Maybe you shouldn't have chased me so hard." He lost his smile as he thought about that and his jaw set. She wouldn't be in this danger if she hadn't married him. Without him, she might have even listened to her uncle and moved to Denver. They had schools in Lunarex Tower. She could have worked there or gone to the West Foundation complex in Houston.

"You're not going to get out of this," Jewel said with a flash of anger. "And I will chase you again."

"Yes, you will," Molly said with a warning look at Jasper. "Did you send Sasha that cat vid yet? She is going to laugh herself silly when she gets it."

Jewel smiled and her grip on Jasper's hand relaxed. "Yes ma'am. And she is going to think I'm mad for cutting my hair. I showed her what I look like now."

"It's good to get that out of the way," Molly said. "Next thing you know you'll be telling her you've moved to the farm and have taken over her cat. She'd like that."

"I wish we could," Jewel said and her eyes met Jasper's. "I'm starting to make friends—and I like having a mother again."

Molly hesitated, her eyes flying to Jewel's. "I didn't think you'd mind."

Jasper swallowed hard, caught by surprise with that admission. Molly was mothering her? And Jewel wants to move to the farm? Well, he was in favor of that. If they got out of this, they'd do it.

"If you want to give up Plains," Jasper said, "we'll do it. We'll have to build our house though. That's going to take a while."

"Ok," she said, "easier to catch you in that dinky room."

The paramedic snorted and Jasper felt himself smiling. "We'll get through this," he said, "then you can call the shots."

Jewel smiled then clutched his hand harder as the chopper started losing altitude. It wasn't as steep as the hop though and she relaxed again as the paramedic started taking her vitals.

"Sir, coming up on Saint Stephens. ETA is three minutes." The co-pilot said over the intercom. "We need to know if she's stable. The monitors don't seem to be feeding to Control."

"I'll tell them," Molly said. "Stay here." She shed her seat belt and went to the cockpit.

"How long would it take a plane to get from Chicago to St. Paul?" Jasper asked the paramedic. "We have a surgeon coming."

"About forty-five minutes airtime," he said. "Other than that, it depends on schedule."

"No schedule for her," Jasper said. "Jewel, we'll have some wait time but not a lot. Saint Stephens has those shielded rooms too."

"I remember," she said. "But I want to get up. You aren't keeping me in bed alone until I have to."

The paramedic stared at her then shook his head.

"Ok, definitely not shocky now," he said and rolled up the blood pressure cuff. He took her temperature one more time and frowned. "Horny as hell."

That set Jewel off into giggles and Jasper smiled with relief.

"She can get up and walk off as soon as we've landed. Keep that shield around you though. Someone is going to miss it if you lose it," the paramedic said. "And I hope everything goes well for you two. You said that was a transmitter with self-destruct?" he asked Jasper.

"Yes," Jasper's smile disappeared. "From the Islamic Revolution. You'll find information there."

"I'll look it up," the man said. "Dirtiest thing I've heard about."

Jewel was sober now and clutching his hand again. On impulse, Jasper found the drum and put it in her arms. She clutched it to her as the chopper started its real descent to the landing pad at Saint Stephens.

*   *   *

The wait stretched on as they waited for Dr. McBride. Aware they'd barely tasted lunch, Molly went down to get sandwiches and soup from the cafeteria. While she was gone, Jasper opened his briefcase and found the flasher he wanted and music player he kept there.

"What's this?" Jewel said as she studied the pink flasher.

"Something for you," he said. "For later. I want your opinion."

"Not now?" she asked.

"Nope," he said. "No peeking. I want you hear it from start to finish."

"Okay," she said. "You were going to show me how to play that drum. Now that I've got you and it alone..."

"And you can't chase me..." Jasper said with a knowing smile.

His wife stuck her tongue out.

"Minx!" Jasper growled at her to cover his shock. "You do that again and I'll grab it."

She giggled then her smile faded and she ran her hands over the drum. "I want to learn this," she said. "You make it sound so good."

"Ok." Jasper settled down to teaching her the notes, aware she needed distraction. By the time Molly returned she could manage a passable tune. They stopped to eat then Jewel picked up the drum again.

"Do you want me to call David?" Jasper asked.

Jewel shook her head. "He's on shift. It can wait."

"You're sure?" She just looked at him and Jasper knew he shouldn't push it. "Ok, afterward."

For all her show, Jewel was still as scared as he was. Could they get that out without detonating it? Would it be a C-section? That was probably safest. Hell, could she have anesthesia now?

"Molly, I was going to ask," he turned to her, "is that blister out of her system? It's been a week."

"Pretty much," Molly answered. "If there's any left, the level is so low my equipment can't mark it. That was one of the things I was going to tell you."

"Thanks," Jasper said. Before he could ask more, the door opened and Dr. McBride stepped in, her gray hair as neat as ever, and seeming calm. She was followed in by another doctor and a nurse.

"There you are," she said. "How are you feeling at the moment, Mrs. Stone?"

"Okay," Jewel said but her smile was strained. "Playing to keep busy." She rapped a couple of tones on the drum.

"That's a good idea," Dr. McBride said. "Give me a few minutes to confer and I'll be ready for you. You're Molly Kowalski?" She turned to her. "A PA?"

"Yes ma'am," Molly answered. "I've been monitoring all week."

"Good, join us." Dr. McBride gestured toward the examination rooms and Molly obediently followed.

The next notes Jewel played were so discordant Jasper flinched and turned back to her. There was no hiding her tears this time and he found himself blinking back his own as Jewel cried.

"I want this fucking thing out! I can't take it anymore and if they tell me I have to wait one more time, I... I'm going to shoot them!" Her fists clenched and she started crying in earnest.

"They aren't going to make you wait," Jasper said. "And I'll buy the gun." He held her tight, knowing he could lose her if she went in there but knowing too that Jewel had reached her limit. Could he have lasted so long? He didn't know.

"Hush, love," he said. "It'll be over soon. We'll go back to the farm and build the biggest, baddest house they've ever seen. Everything you want in it. You're going to help me design it. What do you want?"

Her sobs lessened but not before he could feel the dampness on his shirt. He smiled down at her and chuckled. Surprised she looked up at him.

"It's been awhile since you soaked my shirt," he said. "I thought flannel might hold up better but..."

She glared at him then tried to rub the dampness away.

"Never mind," he said and forced her chin up so he could see her eyes. They were blurry then he realized it was his own. Afraid she would see, he covered her mouth with his and tasted the salt of her tears. He tried to keep it tender but when she responded with real need, he answered it. He held her close, his arms slipping under her blouse to rest on warm skin. Fighting down his physical response, he just held her after the kiss ended.

"A nursery," Jewel suddenly said and he looked down at her, having forgotten the question. "I want a nursery and I want you to help me fill it, Jazz Stone. I want boys and girls both—as many as I can get—and the government be damned."

"Hang the government," Jasper said. "A huge nursery just off our room. We have to hear the little ones when they cry."

"Yes," Jewel said. "And a studio. And a big kitchen."

"I like that tiny kitchen we have now," Jasper lied. "You can't escape me."

"Hah," she said. "I never tried." She rested in his arms now. "What will we do about Plains?"

"Nothing," he said. "It can wait. That's not today's worry. Only us and our future together."

"I just want it done."

"I know."

Chapter 47 - Removal

"This is what we're going to do," Dr. McBride told them. "I want you to know exactly so your imaginations don't run away with you. Jewel, I'll be giving you an epidural so you won't feel any pain. There's no bliss in it. It's just an old-fashioned spinal block. Then we'll be working on getting the transmitter out which looks like this except it's surgical steel." She held up what looked like an oversized capsule maybe three quarters of an inch thick and two inches long. It had a short wire coming out of one end. "This is not like birthing a baby and it's not huge. We can get it out just fine through the cervix. That's the way it went in and that's the way it's got to come out."

"The danger lies in letting it contact any metal," she said. "I have some specialized instruments which are all sterile plastic. Even the camera has been checked to make sure nothing metal will connect. I'll be pulling that out once I have the thing netted."

"And this is what the net looks like," she said, holding up a fine plastic net. "Once I've teased the thing into the net so the wire is pointed backwards, I can pull it out. Then it will go in an insulated box until the battery runs down. At that time it can be handed over to the courts as evidence. I don't recommend examining it until the battery is dead."

"Can this thing be taken out with a C-section?" Jasper asked. "Would that be less risky?"

"Absolutely not," the doctor said. "It's been tried and it was a lot less successful. These things were designed to go through the cervix just fine but the trauma of a C-section and the metal surgical tools you'd have to use are too great a risk. This is the best way."

"If things go well, I should be done in thirty minutes. You can't be in there because you could cause contractions at the wrong time. I'll allow your P.A. to scrub and stay with her. She knows what she's doing."

"After the procedure, you'll have to stay on bed rest for two days," she said to Jewel. "You'll have tubes so get used to that idea and a monitor or two. There will be no hand holding, no kissing, no petting, no physical contact for those two days. I don't even want you having dirty thoughts. I know you're young and healthy but rein it in. You probably won't feel sexy anyway but I'm warning you to keep it under control."

"After the two days?" Jewel asked and she was holding tight to Jasper's hand.

"We'll see," she said. "Actually, Dr. Parset will make the call since I have to return to Chicago. I expect Molly to keep an eye on you for a couple of weeks after that but then the danger should be over. If everything goes well, you'll be able to resume normal activities after that."

"Two weeks?" Jasper's lips twitched. "I can get a good rest."

Jewel gave him a dirty look.

"Maybe two weeks," the doctor said but she was smiling. "You've been having regular relations?"

"Very regular," Jasper said as Jewel shook her head no. "Often."

"That's good," the doctor said. "Nothing has jarred loose so this will be easier. I'm going to go scrub now. Molly will get you ready. You'll have the waiting room, Mr. Stone. I suggest you get something to eat."

"In a bit," Jasper said. "Can she have earphones in while this is going on?"

The doctor paused. "Let me see them."

Jasper handed her the earphones with the music player. With a slight tremble, he connected the pink flasher he hadn't listened to since Carol died. He knew the doctor was sugar coating the procedure and not telling Jewel what could happen if the damned thing detonated but he'd done his research. It could blow a hole in her womb and cause a hemorrhage almost impossible to stop. It made sense though that non-conductive plastic instruments might be the safest to use. Handing the complete setup to the doctor, he waited for her opinion.

"Not enough metal to be a risk," she said. "I think it might be better though to put it on speaker. If it's not rock, it won't distract me."

"It might," Jasper said. "No, it's not rock."

"What is it?" Jewel asked.

"A piece only Carol has heard," Jasper said. "The best I've written so far."

"Then I want it," Jewel said and her hand clenched on his. Jasper tried hard not to let his own uncertainty be communicated to her. This was going to be hard enough without giving her his fear.

"Earphones," she said. "It's not sensa, is it?"

"No," Jasper said. "No hidden beats. Just music."

"I think I'll wait until it's published," Dr. McBride said. "Now give her a kiss and let Molly get her ready—and don't get her over excited, please."

As the doctor left, Jasper tried to obey but the kiss he gave her was filled with longing and tender. The last thing he did was queue up the requiem and show her how to start it when she was ready.

Returning to the waiting room alone, he found it too empty and too quiet with Jewel gone. God, would she ever be back? Finally he let the fear he'd been hiding surface and he sat down heavily, burying his head in his hands.

He had to trust God wouldn't do this to him again—not to Jewel. The procedure was simple and if that damned thing didn't explode, he would have his love back almost unharmed and they would continue on. Maybe in time the nightmares would fade too.

He'd give it an hour. He would not count Jewel out before it was done. God, he wanted to be in there holding her hand but he understood the doctor's caution. Even when he didn't try, Jewel responded to him and he responded to her. No, the best he could do was give her his requiem.

That was Carol's requiem. It had taken him almost six months to compose it and record it. He'd even hired musicians and vocalists when he didn't think his own playing was good enough. It was the one piece he hadn't been able to do with his own equipment. It was far too intricate.

Carol hadn't heard the complete piece either until it was time and she hadn't lived long enough to hear the crescendo at the end. When she joined him in the death room at Soma and he'd tucked her into bed for the last time and helped her drink the sleeping potion, it had been playing. Then he'd held her hand and stroked her hair as his wife went to sleep, finally heedless of the pain that had tortured her for more than five years.

He'd been acutely aware when the attendant injected her with curare but Carol had been oblivious. Less than a minute later, he had heard her sigh and her hand relaxed in his. Something was gone. Her soul had fled and she was simply no longer there. And the strains of the music had gone on. He hadn't moved until it was done except to cry for his first love. Not even the attendant had moved.

He'd been told over and over by those who knew that the spirit of the dead usually hovered nearby at death. Sometimes they tried to make themselves be known but mostly they just couldn't pull themselves away immediately. That was why he'd worked so damned hard on the requiem and why he made it an hour long. He knew Carol wouldn't live to hear the end but he'd made the end happy, rejoicing, and welcoming for her soul. He'd cried and now he remembered the attendant had cried too. Rachel. That was her name. Later she'd helped him lay his demons to rest but that day he had hated her for taking Carol from him. He had forgotten she cried too.

Carol. She was gone. Sending a silent prayer that Carol would find Jewel and welcome her if he lost her, he gave in to tears. He didn't know how long it was before he suddenly knew he was being foolish. This was Jewel and she wasn't about to leave him. If things went wrong, there were two surgeons in there who would do their best to keep Jewel here. She might be damaged but his wife would fight with her last breath to stay.

Damn, had he made a mistake giving her the requiem? Would she get tied up in it and forget to fight? No, Jewel would never do that. Not even his music could keep her down. His lips quirked as he imagined her clutching that drum to her chest and refusing to let go of it or him. Who knew when he bid on the thing that his wife would claim it? She was no musician but she was trying. At least she understood him and his music—that in itself was a gift he never expected to get again.

Picking the drum up off the floor, he put it on his lap and began to play. Suddenly he wanted to create a new piece, a full symphony, which spoke of Jewel. Yes, the requiem was Carol's. Jewel's symphony would have to capture her life, her energy, and her love—and he knew Jewel would hear it.

He wasn't sure how much longer it was before he noticed Dr. McBride but his hands stilled and he stood up anxiously. The doctor's smile told him it had gone well before he could ask.

"It's out," she said. "And Jewel is resting comfortably. I don't know what was in that music you gave her but she is not interested in moving which suits me just fine. They'll move her to a private room when we're satisfied she's going to stay stable. You can go in but remember what I said. No getting her excited."

"I'll remember," Jasper said. "Thank you."

"You're welcome," she said. "Watch for heavy bleeding. That's the danger now. It's good that you have a PA with Kowalski's experience close by. Otherwise I would insist you stay longer here."

"Molly has been great," Jasper said. "Everyone has. Thank you again."

The doctor nodded and smiled one more time. "I expect a signed copy of your next album."

"You'll have it," Jasper said.

She disappeared into an office and Jasper saw a nurse waiting. Forgetting drum, briefcase and everything, he hurried after her to the small private surgical suite. He paid no attention to the amenities but went straight to the bed where Jewel lay slightly propped up. Her eyes were closed and he could see a tear lying on her lashes but she was smiling. Glancing at the monitors, he saw her pulse was good. The earphones.

Molly was smiling too as she helped the nurse put away equipment. "It went fine," she said. "But you still have her entranced. She hasn't said a word except don't when we tried to take the earphones. Dr. McBride showed her the transmitter but that didn't break your spell."

Jasper grinned then looked around for the damned thing. "Where is it?"

"Here," Molly said. "We can't take it with us but you can look." She handed him a small thick box. "Make sure you don't touch it."

"Right." Jasper opened the box carefully and looked at the stainless steel capsule inside. It wasn't any larger than the plastic one Dr. McBride had showed them but the wire was thinner and longer. His wife had carried that thing around for over ten days. His jaw set as he closed the box. He wanted the bastard responsible for it and that nurse who must have put it in. She had to have known what she was doing just like she knew what she was doing to that FBI agent. He wanted her found.

"Beautiful."

The one word from his wife brought him up short and he turned toward her as she reached out to touch his hand. He completely forgot the doctor's warning and took it.

"It's so beautiful," she said. "I love it. When will you get it published?"

Molly tapped their clasped hands and he hastily set hers on her chest and removed the earphones so she could hear him.

"I hadn't planned on getting it published," he said. "I wrote it for Carol."

When he reached to remove the flasher and player from Jewel's hand she unexpectedly tightened her grip.

"You wrote it for Carol?" she asked and there was fire in her blue eyes. "And you've been sitting on it ever since? You've been hiding it?"

"I wasn't ready to share it," Jasper said. "Only with you." He wondered if she was getting too excited and looked anxiously at Molly.

"I'm keeping it," Jewel said. "You aren't hiding it away again."

"Ok, keep it," Jasper said, unwilling to argue. "Just don't lose it. That's my only copy."

The rude noise she made somewhat reassured him. Hell, if she wanted it that badly, he wasn't going to argue with her. He hadn't been exactly truthful since he had copies of all his completed pieces in a safety deposit box in Plains. Damn, he'd have to retrieve those.

"Let's get you moved, Mrs. Stone," the other nurse said and wheeled in a gurney. "No, stay flat. We'll do all the work. Mr. Stone, out of the way, please."

He stepped back and made room for the transfer then got shooed out the door. Collecting his stuff from the outer office, he followed them down the hall and into an elevator. Jewel bore it bravely but he could tell she was embarrassed to be rolled around and assumed that meant she was feeling ok.

"Our orders are to put her in maternity," Molly quietly said. "Private room. They're better prepared for anything that could happen. Just don't be surprised."

"Right," Jasper said. "She'll be okay?"

"Probably," Molly said. "The next forty-eight will tell. Dr. McBride was serious about keeping her down and calm."

"You can either speak up louder or go away if you're going to talk about me," Jewel said. "I'm not deaf."

"We'll just put the earphones back on," Jasper said. "You'd better take a good long look, love. In nine months or so, you're going to be back here with our baby."

She smiled up at him then frowned. "Can't see a thing. You look."

Jasper saw the nursery windows and a couple of nurses with infants in arms but his attention was on his wife. By the time she was transferred to a bed and made comfortable, she looked worn out. When she closed her eyes, he settled down in the nearest chair to wait.

"You need coffee," Molly said with a critical eye. "You're getting low."

"I think you need it more," Jasper said. "What do I have to watch? You should call home."

Molly hesitated then pointed to the levels on the monitors. "I really think she'll do fine," she said. "And I won't be gone long. Coffee and a sandwich?"

"Just coffee," Jasper said. "I have some calls to make too. I'll do it from here." He waited till Molly had left then called up Milt's number on his com unit. The call to his publisher was brief and to the point. After telling Mary that Jewel was now safe, he asked for the list of components she'd made up and added a couple of extra pieces to it. When that was done, he talked to Milt.

He knew he had to call David next but he really wanted Jewel awake for that call. He would be more reassured if he could talk to her. He should have taken a picture of that damned transmitter. Hell, he'd like to send a picture of that to Baxter to let him know he'd failed---and if he couldn't send it directly to Baxter, he wanted to send it to Wilson Kucera. He wasn't buying the CEO's claim that he had no contact with Baxter.

Carlson and Reynolds. He was still organizing his thoughts when Molly came back with Kale and another woman he didn't know.

"Mr. Fletcher thought ahead," Kale said. "This is Jessie Fallon from Sunrise. She's an RN and here to spell Molly."

Jasper grinned at the young woman, relieved he wouldn't have to rely on hospital nurses. The brunette was young but already had a nurse's no-nonsense attitude. "Thank you for coming," he said.

"I wouldn't miss it for the world," she said in a nice contralto voice. "Once Kale told me who you were, I had to come. We'd been wondering who the mysterious guests were over at Amber. The kids have been talking about drums and cats and a pretty lady."

"Not about me?" Jasper asked, one eyebrow shooting up.

"Not unless you're the man in black," she said and looked him over. "You look like a farmer to me."

Jasper laughed, cutting it off quickly with an eye toward Jewel. "Disguise, miss. I'm glad I don't stick out like a sore thumb anymore." Recalling what he'd worn the first time he met Dr. McBride, his grin widened. She hadn't mentioned it but she had to have noticed the change. Jewel's hair alone should have gotten noticed.

"Jessie, let me brief you," Molly said. "Jasper, go get something to eat. You can leave that drum here."

"Yes ma'am. If you want to keep Jewel happy, give it to her." He started to follow Kale out then stopped aware he hadn't warned them.

"One thing for all of you," Jasper said, his smile gone. "The kidnappers had a nurse with them and she's still at large. Jewel might recognize her but she might not. This woman must have been the one who put the transmitter in Jewel. I know she cut and dyed her hair and took care of her while she was on the plane. You need to watch for her."

"A nurse?" Jessie asked. "We can spot a phony."

"She's not a phony," Jasper said. "Jewel said she has the same don't mess with me attitude Molly uses. She's also guilty of murdering an FBI agent. She walked into the Plains Hospital past security and police officers and into his room. She also walked out again with no alarms being raised. Don't trust anyone here. No one gives Jewel anything—not even food. Have you got that?"

There were no flip comments this time.

"She'll have to eat," Molly said, "but we can get food from the cafeteria. I'll fetch water and meds myself if she needs them. We'll go down after you're back."

"Good," Jasper said. "And I'll see what I can do about getting an officer for extra protection."

"Yes sir," Molly replied and she said it with such respect Jasper knew he'd gotten through to her.

Motioning to Kale to lead, he wondered exactly how far he could push his celebrity status before he had to use his DEA identity.

Chapter 48 - Tuesday

"I'm bored," Jewel declared for the third time in an hour and Jasper tried hard to hide his grin. Molly didn't even bother to look up, having jumped up twice before to see what she could do. Jasper half expected her to give her some homework if she persisted in acting like a kid.

"Play your drum," Jasper said. "Eat your cookies. Call Elinor again." He ticked off the list of what she could do and Jewel glared at him in mock ferocity, looking anything but sick after a full day of bedrest. He knew what he wanted to do to her but that avenue was closed. Besides, Molly was watching.

"I got something else in mind," Jewel said and Molly looked up from her book "You said I could call the shots."

"Not today, you can't," Jasper said. "None of that." He glanced at Molly and saw her slight smile. "I'm not getting near you."

"Spoilsport," Jewel said and Molly bent over her book again. "Molly, if I promise not to chase him, can we have a few minutes? I'll stay right here."

She looked up at that, studied the monitors then nodded. "I think you're fine," she said. "Just no excitement. I think I'll walk down the hall. Call me if you need me." Picking up her reader, she gave Jasper a warning look that told him he'd better.

"Yes ma'am," Jasper replied.

Jewel waited until Molly had closed the door then spoke rapidly in a fierce undertone. "Ok, I'm calling the shots, Jazz Stone, and this is what I want. You'll tell me exactly who you're working for and what's going on."

Jasper stared at her in surprise, having no inkling she'd ambush him like this. "What do you mean?"

She made a rude noise. "Tell me. You've told Kale. Uncle Harold knows. You are darn well going to tell me!"

"How do you know Harold knows?" Jasper asked, stalling for time. How much should he tell her? Counting up the people who actually knew what he was, his heart sank. There were way too many. He hadn't had to tell the hospital to get increased security but in just the last two days he'd told three more–no, four. He was certain Molly had heard at least part of what he told the chopper control. She hadn't questioned him about it though.

"When you got the call from Ray Carlson, Harold took it over. I heard every word. He didn't ask why you needed to go but told Ray it could be done and how it could be done. He knows, damn it, but you haven't told me." She crossed her arms and glared at him. "No more secrets. I want in."

Jasper studied her. "And you won't believe it's because I was a cop or because I married you or that damned house?"

"No."

"But that's part of it," Jasper said. "If I hadn't been a cop, I wouldn't have married you and we wouldn't be living in that damned house."

"Try again," she said. "You already told us that Uncle Mike was the target and it was about inspection systems. I'm not going to buy it was the house. For that matter, I'd like to know how an old buddy like Ray Carlson could scare up a government plane to pick us up. You never explained that."

"And you didn't ask," Jasper said and smiled. "Ok, let me tell you a story."

She looked at him, her brows knit in a fierce expression. "Make it a good one."

Jasper almost laughed at her ferocity but it was the right time. The transmitter was gone and he was sure Jewel was fine even though the doctor wouldn't release her yet. At the same time, she was anchored to that bed and couldn't get physical. Yes, now was the best moment.

He sat down on the bed, careful not to touch his wife, and looked into her earnest eyes. "Truth, love. It started about five months after Carol died. Lori and I had nabbed a blissex dealer then found out he didn't know anything just like the others. We were frustrated and pretty drunk when we started talking about the case and how one of us needed to get inside to take them down. Lori said it and it made sense. A couple of days later we talked about it again only we were sober. We both knew it would have to be me. She was good but she didn't have a good reason to turn. I did."

"And?"

"I took a couple of days and went down to Denver. When I walked into the DEA office, I showed my badge and told them I had questions about an agent." He smiled at the memory. "They thought I meant an existing agent and shoved me into an empty office so fast I didn't see it coming. Then Ray Carlson walked in."

He saw her eyes widen. "Yes, he's DEA. He's not the top man in Denver but he's close. That was how he could get a plane and he did a hell of a lot more than that. The jammers and most of the equipment I've used came straight from him. Plains PD doesn't have any of that."

"You're DEA?" Jewel demanded.

"I'm getting to that," Jasper said. "And it wasn't that easy. I was a police lieutenant and everyone knew it. There was no reason the DEA should have thought I'd make a good agent but I asked Carlson about it. He didn't say no but asked why I thought I could do it. I put down a copy of my top album and tapped it and said that's me."

He remembered that moment vividly and knew he couldn't have done it any better. Carlson had looked from him to the album and back again. There wasn't another word about why he couldn't do it but how he could do it. Before he left, they had a solid plan.

Jewel was smiling now and he wondered how much more she'd need.

"This was all a year before I met you," he said. "I composed and produced a new album to explain why I suddenly had to leave the force and Milt was brought in so we could get everything leaked at the right time. In Plains only Lori and Captain Reynolds knew what was planned. Lori was supposed to be my go-between since she was such an old friend." His mouth tightened and his voice got harsher. "Now it's just Reynolds."

"By the time I met you, I couldn't really change plans and since we had good reason to think the professor would lead up into the organization, I didn't want to. We also knew some tablecloths Reach Out had ordered were used to smuggle in blissex so there was a connection there."

"The red tablecloths? The ones that got stolen?"

"There was blissex in that box. What happened is there was a tip that a box the professor was receiving that day contained blissex instead of a book. We pulled everyone we could to intercept him at the mall. The package got snatched before the professor opened it and our forces were tied up searching for it. While that was going on, the tablecloths arrived but they were short-handed so the boxes got shoved into storage to be checked in the next day. During the night one box was opened and it looked like several tablecloths had been stolen. It was actually blissex."

"Lori was following up on the blissex case since I'd been transferred to yours," Jasper said. "Even she didn't know it was important until another cop brought it to her attention. The operation was smooth and we knew we'd been played." His jaw set at the memory.

"And Drew's package?" Jewel asked.

Jasper shook his head. "Just a kid's book. Some title called Curious George."

Jewel smiled. "I remember that. We had a Reach Out dinner and he was pretty pleased the book was finally coming. He'd worked for months to get it since it's so rare. Oh, he must have been furious."

"He was," Jasper said. "I didn't see it but Lori thought he was crazy to get so riled over a book. Until it was actually found–unharmed–no one thought that was what it was. When I met him the next day though he didn't strike me that way. He refused to press charges and just wanted the whole thing over and done with. No more news about it. I had the impression he was very private."

"Yes, he was." Jewel's smile faded. "But I would have liked to see him riled up. I didn't think he could be."

"I put him down as a victim but he did mention talking about it at the Reach Out event. I knew Reach Out was a pretty big, pretty wealthy charity so I got interested. I wish he'd told me then who he suspected of calling in the tip though. He had someone in mind when he left."

Jasper hesitated, remembering the accusation Drew had flung at Ed Kucera and Ed Kucera's denial. How the hell had that happened? Kucera was a friend and Drew had suspected him? Why hadn't he suspected Baxter? Damn it, he still had something that didn't ring true.

"Then Mike died," he said, "and things happened. The next ten days were so convoluted, I came to a lot of wrong conclusions. I thought Drew proposed to you because he wanted the house but he denied that in an interrogation room and told me I was out of line too. I admit I wanted to know if he loved you." His lips relaxed into a smile and he almost forgot the warning.

"Was that before or after you kissed me?" Jewel asked with a smile of her own.

"Before," Jasper admitted. "After that dinner at the Grand."

Her smile widened and she reached for his hand. Damn it, they weren't supposed to do that. Reluctantly, he pulled his away.

"What did you tell my uncle to get invited there?" Jewel asked. "I know he knew something about you being a subby and he mentioned money."

"Right," Jasper said. "I was on the subby list less than two years but I told Drew to get closer to Reach Out. He mentioned it in front of David and I had no choice but to prove I had investments like I'd told him. David had a talk with my broker and got curious and that led to that dinner at the Grand where a certain someone checked my hand to see if I was married."

"You noticed," she shrieked.

Laughing Jasper shook his finger at her. "Simmer down or Molly will come shooting in here. You bet I noticed. Every time you looked at me I saw those beautiful blue eyes and those kissable lips and..." he stopped, aware he was treading on dangerous ground. "And you cried on my shoulder. I couldn't help but notice you."

She was smiling now, her eyes shining. "You didn't let me know."

"I was a cop," he said. "I didn't consider you a suspect but I should have. My judgment was sadly lacking." He knew he had let his feelings for her get in the way. She'd been vulnerable and he had accepted that as innocence. Stupid mistake. If it had turned out differently, it could have got him killed.

"It was when you mentioned the car I knew Jake was involved," he said. "Before we could recover from that Jake was dead. No, he was already dead by the time we got to Denver. Starling moved fast but Jake got what he needed to get done done. He tried to undo what he did and muddied the waters even more because Kucera wasn't the one."

"You said that before," Jewel said. "So who was it? Starling alone?"

"No." Jasper stopped, realizing that was something he hadn't followed up on. Had Frazier identified Baxter or not? "Hold on."

Shifting to the chair, he picked up his com unit and sent a text to Reynolds. They had to know if Baxter was the man in the confessionals. If they could prove he was, they were closer to getting him.

"A question I need answers to," he said when Jewel looked impatient. "We had a witness who put Starling and another man in Plains but the second man wasn't Ed Kucera. When you were returned to me, I found out who he was—maybe. Everything seems to point to him now."

"Who?" Jewel asked, her voice nearly breathless.

Jasper considered it then thought she might identify him too. Hell, there was no tape of the confessionals. If there had been, Jewel could have confirmed it was him. All he had was the house tape and he wouldn't let her see that.

"The man you heard on the plane—the one that spoke briefly—had you ever heard him before? He was a Reach Out member but not one you knew well."

"A Reach Out member?" Jewel looked shocked then her jaw set. "Who?"

"I can't tell you that," Jasper said. "You'll have to identify him independently. When he brought you back, I recognized him but since I had never heard him actually speak at the event, we're having to do voice print identification."

"You aren't going to tell me?" Jewel glared at him. "You lead me on then won't tell me who killed Lori and kidnapped me and left you helpless in our house? I should scream."

"You do and you won't hear the rest," Jasper said and he was serious. How far did she think she could blackmail him with her current condition? "I've told you why I can't." He reached for the call button but Jewel stopped him.

"Please," she said. "I'll behave."

He studied her for a long moment, aware she'd been playing him and tired of it. He'd spent too many hours on this case and worried too much about her to let it fall apart. He had to get Baxter and it had to be done properly. He shouldn't have even told her this much.

"I think we've had enough of the story for now," he said. "I'm a DEA agent. My deep cover name is Wolfgang von Blitzen. After this case is over, I'll resign."

Her eyes stayed on him and he knew she was close to tears at his rejection but he couldn't help it. Suddenly the hospital room was too much for him. He pressed the call button.

"I want you to get some rest," he said. "You can mull over what I gave you. I need to take a walk."

Molly returned as he said the last and she took over, helping Jewel to a more comfortable position and shooing him out. Jasper scooped up his com unit and left, only stopping at the elevators. No, he shouldn't go out. Damn it, he needed to get away if only for a few minutes.

"The observation deck fifth floor," a nurse said as she walked by. "It's quiet."

Jasper glanced at her but she'd walked on. God, did he look that bad? He'd never snapped at Jewel like that.

Taking the elevator to the fifth floor, he found the enclosed observation deck. There were people there but he found a quiet corner and sat looking out at the city. With some effort he got his calm back but he recognized the edginess for what it was. He wasn't working, he couldn't play, and he'd been stuck in that little room with his wife and couldn't touch her. His three favorite things in the world were closed to him right now and he was behaving as badly as Jewel. He couldn't even work out. Damn, he was bored too.

He laughed but it wasn't funny. He couldn't even handle two days with his wife in that tiny room. At least at the farm there were places to go. He had the conference room, the piano, even the commons and there were still places he hadn't explored. How long were they going to keep Jewel here? How long could he take it? He buried his face in his hands.

He could work on the case up here but he had never felt less like Working and that drum wasn't what he needed. He longed to have a keyboard under his hands–a decent one–and just play. Did this hospital even have a piano?

"Mr. Stone?"

Jasper looked up and quickly straightened to his feet. One swift look at the man's collar and he knew someone–probably Molly–had sent the hospital chaplain to find him.

"Yes, that's me," Jasper said. "I know what's wrong."

"Claustrophobia or stress?" the chaplain asked with a slight smile. "I understand your wife is improving so..."

"Both," Jasper said. "Have you ever been stuck in a room unable to work, play or touch... well, bored is a light term for it."

"Play?" the chaplain asked with a curious look.

"I'm a composer," Jasper said. "Music is my relief."

"Ah," the chaplain said. "I'm Brother William. I may have an answer."

"A piano?" Jasper asked.

"Possibly something better," he said. "Can you leave your wife for a couple of hours?"

"I don't think she'll want me back for at least that long," Jasper said.

"Then let me make a call," he said. "How good are you?"

"I'm Jazz Stone. They call me Sensor Man."

The chaplain just waited and Jasper realized he'd found someone who hadn't seen the news or heard his music.

"I'm good," he finally said. "A professional."

"Ah, then I think I know who to call. Why don't you go tell your wife you'll be back in about three hours. I'll arrange a place for you to play." The chaplain motioned him toward the elevators and followed him. "Do you know the city?"

"No but I have a friend who does," Jasper said and knew he'd have to call Kale. He and Jessie had gone back to the hotel.

"Call him then. I'll make the arrangements. When you're ready, I'll be in the chapel on the first floor. Meet me there."

"Thank you," Jasper said and got off on Jewel's floor. Walking down the hall with a lighter step, he knew he was going to have to apologize to both Jewel and Molly. How soon could Kale get here?

"Here you are," Molly said as he paused outside the room. She looked relieved to see him and he saw Kale was there too. "Jewel was worried. Go in and give her a kiss then I want the two of you out of here for the rest of the afternoon. Go sightseeing."

"You didn't send the chaplain after me?" Jasper asked then caught her other statement and frowned. "Give her a kiss?"

"Give her a kiss," Molly repeated. "A small one. She's upset and that's not good. She's also been making you jump long enough. I've given her a talking to."

"Thanks," Jasper said and walked into the room.

Jewel looked up from the bed and he instantly felt guilty for the wan look and knew she'd been crying. "It's my fault," he said before she could. "I can't take being cooped up with nothing to do."

"I'm just as bad," she said as he came closer. "I was being a brat." She sniffed. "I just can't take not being able to touch..."

He covered her mouth with his and stopped the flow of words. She started to pull back then responded, opening her lips invitingly but he didn't take the invitation. Too aware of the doctor's restrictions, he didn't prolong the kiss.

She clung to him for a moment then pushed him away. "Go away before Molly catches you." She was smiling but resolute. "I want out of this place tomorrow."

"Both of us," Jasper said. "Want the drum?"

"Yes," Jewel replied and he got it for her then left knowing she'd be ok for a while.

Now he'd find out what Brother William had in mind. He wondered what religion he was but didn't care. If he found him something decent to play, he'd bless him anyway.

Chapter 49 - Pipe Organ

Jasper walked into the imposing edifice of Saint Cecilia's and started smiling when he saw the pipe organ in the main church. Brother William definitely knew where to send him. If he remembered right, Saint Cecilia was the patron saint of musicians and that organ beckoned. Would they let him play that one though? Was that what he'd arranged?

"May I help you?" A middle-aged woman in a clerical collar noticed them first.

"Brother William sent me," Jasper said, trying to focus on the woman but his eyes kept sliding back to that organ. "I'm Jazz Stone–Sensor Man."

"Sensor Man?" Her eyes widened slightly and she smiled. "I was told to expect a Jasper Stone who needed to play an organ–not Jazz Stone. It's a pleasure to meet you. I'm Sister Lydia."

"Pleased to meet you," Jasper said. "This is Kale, my bodyguard." He motioned to his companion. "Can I really get a few minutes with that?"

She laughed. "Yes sir. I just need to check a schedule. Give me a couple of minutes." She left and Jasper, not knowing what else to do, walked down to the nave and studied the myriad of pipes rising from the organ. It had four keyboards and a range of controls even he wasn't familiar with. He longed to get closer.

"Are you in love?" Kale asked.

"This is one incredible organ," Jasper said then shook his head. "No, I'm sure Brother William didn't arrange for me to play this. He didn't even know who I was."

"Well, Sister Lydia does," Kale said. "And here she comes."

There were few others in the church and they were intent on their own concerns and praying. Aware he might disturb them, Jasper braced himself for a no.

"The organ is free until seven tonight," Lydia said. "If you don't mind people coming in, you can play this one instead of the one in the choir room."

"Once I start playing, I won't know anyone is here," Jasper said. "I'll have to depend on Kale here to tell me when it's time to go."

"Yes sir," Kale replied as if he'd heard the order a hundred times before. "Six forty-five?"

"Yes," Jasper responded without thinking. "Do you know the control board very well, Sister Lydia?"

"That I do," she said and talked him through the basic controls and indicated which keyboard did what.

Jasper touched controls, stroked keys so lightly there was no sound, and eyed the music left on the electronic stand. Beethoven's Ode to Joy. Yes, that was a good piece to learn this beauty and it suited his mood perfectly. As soon as Lydia was done talking, he took his seat and turned on the exact controls he wanted.

This was going to be good. Stretching his fingers first, he quietly began. No testing notes today but straight into the piece. The notes reverberated and he almost laughed as he lost himself to the music. The knot in his gut melted away as he played and for these moments he was alone with the most wonderful instrument ever created.

The music soared and he soared with it, feeling the joy clear down into his bones. Not for the first time he marveled that such a piece could capture the feeling of joy so accurately. Beethoven was simply a genius and one he could never surpass. The music on the stand scrolled to keep pace with him but he played from memory. When his memory faltered, he inserted his own variation without pausing to think about it. There were no other musicians to cater to, no chorus he had to be careful not to lead astray. It was just him and this magnificent organ.

When he finished the Ode, he swung into a darker piece of his own creation to test the lower limits of the organ. When that was done, he found himself playing Morning Grace, his new favorite composition. He had no thought for time or listeners or even Jewel as he played. He existed only for the music that filled him and this lovely work of art.

He played on and on. It was only when he began to feel the strain in his shoulders, arms, and hands that he slowed down and finally ended the piece—a traditional hymn with his own flourishes—and looked around. Instantly he was aware how thirsty he was and guessed it was time to go.

"Time," Kale said with a wide smile. "And past time. It's nearly nine."

"Nine?" Jasper looked sharply at him. "What happened to six forty-five?"

"The choir decided not to practice," Kale said. "They were too interested in listening. No one wanted to stop you, so I..."

"Jewel is going to wonder what happened to me," Jasper said, his responsibilities returning. Had he worried her?

"She's been listening," Kale said and motioned toward a camera stand a few feet away that hadn't been there when Jasper sat down. "I was able to send it to her through my com unit. She knows where you're at."

Jasper relaxed but knew he'd have to remind Kale to stick to the plan later. Still, it had been so much fun. He forced himself to turn off the controls before he got up and turned to face the nave and saw Uri Kowalski waiting there and beyond him a crowd of people. He bowed at their scattered applause.

"Let's get out of here," Jasper said. "I don't give live performances."

"Yes sir," Kale said and walked before him down the aisle.

Jasper was acutely aware of smiling, admiring faces, and forced himself to smile back and say a word here and there. Damn, he looked like a farmer. Did they know it was actually him? He hoped not. The last thing he needed was for people to know where he was and where Jewel was.

"Side door," Uri said and steered him out a different exit. "I know another less public route. Good to see you, by the way."

"Good to see you too," Jasper said. "Who called you in?"

"Molly, of course. While Kale was watching your back, she decided I'd be needed. I think she was right. There were reporters out front when I came in."

"Reporters?" Jasper's heart sank. Had he given away his location and Jewel's? She couldn't be released yet.

"I spoke to them," Uri said. "They already knew who you were but agreed not to say it is definitely you and they won't mention Jewel's in a hospital here—just speculation as to where she is."

"They'll do that?" Jasper asked.

"They'll get a lot more mileage out of that angle," Uri said. "The networks might pick it up and play with it too. It might be a good idea for you to make another sudden appearance somewhere else though. This is too close to home."

"I know. I'm sorry," Jasper said and he was beginning to regret that session even though he had badly needed it. If Baxter got to Saint Paul, it wouldn't take him that long to start looking for Kowalskis in this area. There couldn't be that many.

"Elevator," Uri said and led the way.

The elevator took them down two more levels to a tram station and they didn't speak until they'd left the tram three stops further down. Jasper noticed a sign that said Metro Hospital but Uri was steering him toward another elevator and they went all the way up to the surface.

"Wait here," Uri said and opened the door with his ident card.

"He's really taking us roundabout," Jasper said as they followed him out into an unheated entry. "When did it start snowing again?"

"Sometime this afternoon, I think. It won't stop us from getting home tomorrow."

"Good," Jasper said. "Next time I give you a time, I'd like you to remember it."

"Yes sir," Kale said. "I was waiting on Uri. My mistake."

Jasper looked at him and knew he'd had good reason not to alert him but that wasn't the point. He hadn't planned to be away from Jewel so long and he'd taken Kale with him. He was feeling stupid now for giving into his need to play. What if something had happened?

"Thanks for calling Jewel," Jasper said. "She won't worry about my being late."

Kale nodded and opened the outside door as a car pulled up with Uri at the wheel.

The cold bit into Jasper and he hurried into the car, aware he had no coat and the only clothing he wore suited for the outdoors were the boots on his feet. The inside of the car was warm enough after a couple of minutes passed and he could pay attention to where they were going.

"Scenic route," Uri said. "I thought you might like to know there's a number of cathedrals here and most of them have organs. You found the best though. St. Mark's Episcopal has one almost as good. St. Paul's has the best carillon."

"Are you suggesting I try them too?" Jasper asked, his sense of humor starting to return.

"Not tonight," Uri said. "But if you can be lured out by music, don't go to the same place twice in a row."

"Right," Jasper said. "Any chance of getting something to drink and a bite to eat?"

"Dry, huh?" Uri shot him a look then pulled into another parking lot. "There's an all-night restaurant across from Saint Stephens and down two levels. Let's try there. Kale, give Molly a call and tell her we got him away. We'll be at the hospital after we've eaten."

"Yes sir," Kale responded.

Jasper eyed the menu in The Brown Cow with some trepidation after seeing the long list of hamburgers and sandwiches and the even longer list of imported and domestic beers. Seeing his favorite beer–the same kind Kin had stolen–listed, he quickly chose that but the sandwiches were hard to decide.

Kale seemed as undecided about which beer to try as he was about the sandwiches. With a laugh, Kale ordered the same beer he'd chosen and Jasper ordered the same sandwich Kale had. It was too late to stress his brain. Uri had fewer problems deciding.

"I've always liked this place," Uri said. "I just can't afford it often. You're buying."

Jasper smiled. "Of course. Thanks again for the rescue."

Uri nodded. "Now there were things I was checking into for you," he said. "We might as well get them covered. Is Kale privy to this?"

"Yes," Jasper said. "He knows. Hell, even Jewel knows now." He scowled, aware that he was going to have to deal with that. "I think this is my first and last case with them."

"That's probably best since you can't keep from being spotted," Uri said. "The media has too much fun following you two."

"Well, it will help sell albums," Jasper said. "But I do miss the old days when I was just a cop."

Uri smiled and glanced at Kale. "So are you going to be permanent? What does Beth think about that?"

"I'd like it to be," Kale said. "It's better income and a lot more interesting. She thinks it's funny that I found a bodyguard job on the farm. I need to get certified though."

"That you do," Uri said.

"Now as to this card," Uri fished the $50 card out and laid it down. "It was bought by Mary Perkins of Baltimore, Maryland. She reported it stolen on November fifteenth and paid for a tracer on it. She was in Denver then. She cancelled the tracer on Friday and she was in Chicago."

"And I was in Chicago last Thursday," Jasper said. "Interesting. Her first name was Mary?"

"Yes," Uri said. "Does that tell you anything?"

"Possibly. That nurse who killed the FBI agent had a first name of Mary. My informant didn't know her last name."

"Informant?" Uri asked. "Is he yours now?"

"Yes," Jasper said. "Kale helped extract his family and Kin is cooperating. He's already been valuable. We should be able to get some major operations shut down with his help."

"Good," Uri said. "You'll have to give me a full briefing when we're more private. Just pass that card on. It bothers me that she seems to be following you. If she were a lackey, that wouldn't be the case."

"She'll be charged with murder," Jasper quietly said. "That's a hell of a good reason to clean up or hide, either one."

"You'd better get yourselves back to the farm soon," Uri said. "There's no chance she'll reach either of you there. I'm on duty tomorrow and, if you can get FBI or DEA to issue an APB on Mary Perkins, I can make sure it gets special attention. See if you can get it done."

"Yes sir," Jasper automatically responded then glanced at Kale. "And I never thought I'd look on a farm as home."

Kale grinned and Uri gave him a questioning look.

"Yes, I think we're staying," Jasper said. "Harold has made the offer and I like it. Jewel doesn't want to go back to Plains."

"You can't blame her," Uri said. "I can't live at the farm but I escape back when I can. It's my real home."

Jasper nodded and briefly wondered why Uri wouldn't choose to live there full time since he was pensioned and had his own income beyond that. Well, maybe he needed the big city connections. Until he'd lived on the farm for a week, Jasper thought he did.

"I had no idea this town had so much culture," Jasper said. "How many cathedrals?"

Uri smiled. "Four. Two of them predate the underground and one was rebuilt to accommodate it. Saint Cecilia's is the only new one. There's also opera, ballet, and a couple of symphony halls and a bunch of theaters. We aren't New York or LA but we've got culture."

"How did that happen?" Jasper asked.

"We've always had culture and a lot of artists got their starts here," Uri said. "It's not unusual for people to come up from Chicago or fly in from other places for some of our shows."

"I'll have to check it out when things get quiet," Jasper said. "But here's our food."

There was little talking after that. Jasper tried not to hurry but he wanted to get back to Jewel. If that nurse had been in Chicago, she could conceivably show up here. Remembering the reporters, he knew he'd taken a foolish risk in playing that grand organ. Still he longed to do it again. It was a great creation.

He wouldn't try to build one like it though. As grand as that organ was, he couldn't reprogram it to create new sounds like his own console. His was state of the art and he could control volume, pitch, and timber on every sound he'd included. For his composing that was a necessity. He wondered how soon he'd have it back. What Kin had helpfully stolen from his house was the guts of his system, which had every sound and every musical note he'd saved for years. Once it was connected to the system

Milt was getting him, he could re-calibrate and be back to playing within an hour or two. He itched to do that. Tonight was fun but his system gave him the freedom to really create at multiple levels—an essential for a sensa artist.

"It must be late," Uri said as he finished his sandwich and sat back with beer in hand. "And I'm glad I'm not driving any more tonight. Kale, what kind of car did you bring?"

"I borrowed a heavy sedan from Sunrise," Kale said. "Along with their nurse. They'll bill us later. I don't think a little snow will mess with it if we leave tomorrow afternoon."

"Not likely," Uri agreed. "If you can get it back to Sunrise at the right time, you can ride the school bus home."

"True," Kale said. "I'll arrange it. Thanks."

"Is that kind of cooperation common?" Jasper asked.

"The rule, actually," Uri said. "The farms rely first on their own people and secondly on neighboring farms. That's one of the reasons we've got close ties with Sunrise and Butterhill. Butterhill is smaller and less able to help right now but it's expanding. They'll get there. Sunrise is slightly larger than we are but Amber Farms out grossed them last year. I don't know where it stands this year though."

"I hadn't paid any attention," Jasper said.

"I only know because Ivan feeds me the figures," Uri said. "It's not really my business either. Are we done? I'd like to get this over with."

"Done," Jasper said and fished out a cash card. Seeing it was the fifty dollar one, he found another. That one was evidence.

They didn't see any reporters at the hospital but Jasper knew he'd been lucky. Ten minutes later he had said goodbye to Uri and Kale, Jessie, and Molly were headed out to the hotel.

Securing the hospital room door, he studied the sleeping form of his wife and began getting ready for bed. Tomorrow night, with any luck, they would be home in their own bed. How the hell was he going to handle that? If they kept the restrictions on them...

No, he'd move into that other apartment. Jewel wouldn't like it but it would work. She could stay closer to Molly or—did Molly have a sick room in that house of hers? He didn't remember.

Finished with his bedtime routine, he pulled on his pajama bottoms and saw his wife was finally wearing the tops. She must be feeling better then. Was she sleeping with that drum again? Leaning over to check her other side, he saw the rounded form of the drum under the covers and smiled then lightly brushed a curl off her cheek.

"Are you going to two time me with every grand instrument that crosses your path?"

Jasper hesitated.

Jewel's eyes opened and her lips parted to show her even white teeth. "It was beautiful."

How? Remembering what Kale said about cameras, he kept his tone light. "I'm glad you saw it. How much?"

"Nearly all," Jewel said and half rolled to look at him. "Gorgeous organ. So you didn't answer–do I have to get jealous?"

"Definitely," Jasper said. "No women, just music. I needed it."

"I know you did," Jewel said. "Help me?"

He helped her sit up then realized something was different. "No tubes?"

"They took them out after you left," she said. "Molly got the okay and I needed that. I can pee on my own."

"Good," Jasper responded. "It's the simple things."

"Yes, you only appreciate it when you can't or aren't allowed to." She sighed. "I miss the farm already. I miss our house too but the farm is so friendly and secure. Were you serious about us moving there?"

"Very serious," Jasper said. "If you don't want to go back to Plains, I think the farm will do just fine. There is a price for our inclusion though since neither of us are farmers."

"I figured," Jewel said. "High rent?"

"No, I don't think so," Jasper was surprised by that question since he hadn't thought to ask. "No, I'll have to build my own studio and our house. I'm fine with that."

"Then what?" Jewel asked.

"Harold said they come up short on college money for all those kids. If we can help with that, he said it would take a huge worry off the farm," Jasper said. "I'm willing to on a case-by-case basis. What do you say?"

"Invest in their future?" Jewel smiled. "That's what the West Foundation does. The future."

Her smile broadened. "I like raising kids a lot better than raising chickens or rabbits."

"Somehow I don't think I'll repeat that exactly that way," Jasper said. "Considering what happens to the chickens and rabbits."

Jewel laughed.

"So you really saw me play that great organ?" Jasper sat down on the chair.

"Yes," Jewel said. "Kale guessed what was going to happen as soon as you walked up to it and called us then set the camera down. He's a lot better than I am at that. It was wonderful. We had a couple of other mothers in here, some of the nurses wandered in, and even that chaplain."

"Brother something?" Jasper asked.

"Yes, he was funny. When he realized it was you playing that big organ, he couldn't take his eyes off the vid screen. He really had no idea who you were and had never heard your music. I had fun."

"We both had fun," Jasper firmly said. "Now if we can just get through tomorrow, we might survive."

"Oh, we will," Jewel said. "I'm scheduled for an ultrasound in the morning. If that comes out ok, we can leave around two. Did Kale bring a big enough car? There's five of us."

"I think so," Jasper said. "Are we allowed to touch now?"

"No patty fingers, whatever that is," she said. "Brotherly kisses. Don't know those either since I never had a brother. And if you try to be fatherly, I'll hit you with this drum."

Jasper laughed. When Jewel looked cross at him, he laughed again. She grabbed the drum and made to throw it at him but he grabbed it, pinning it between her and him and he kissed her. It wasn't a hot kiss but she tried to make it one. Before she could succeed, he drew back. "That's as close to brotherly as I'll ever get."

"Not good enough," she said. "You'd better try again."

He did, planting a kiss on her cheek and the words coming out of her mouth would have shocked Elinor. There was no help for it so he stopped her mouth again with his. This time he let the kiss go on a shade longer but then drew back. "You'll behave," he said. "Or no more drum for you."

She glared at him, realizing then he'd neatly removed her weapon from her grasp. "You'll pay for that later, Jazz Stone."

"I'm looking forward to it. Now I'm sorry I snapped at you and the only reason I can give is the lack of music."

"I was asking for it," Jewel said. "Molly told me I was behaving like a bored brat. She gave me a boring book on baby care to read."

"A textbook?" Jasper wondered if that was what Molly carried with her. He had the impression she liked historical novels.

"No, it's written for women with very low intelligence. I think I know which end to diaper and which end to burp."

"If not, I do. Let me see this book," Jasper said, curious. Why would Molly give her something like that? Did she just have it on hand or was she telling Jewel she'd have no problem having kids? That would be reassuring right now.

Jewel held out her com unit and Jasper looked at the book, seeing a droll cartoon with the baby switched around by a harassed looking mother. The caption read "Head up or clean up the mess."

Switching to a random place in the book, he found another cartoon with the mother sprawled sound asleep on a couch while the baby played with a toy. "Take naps whenever you can."

No matter where he jumped to, there was another wacky cartoon with just a snippet of sound advice under it. Brilliant and funny as hell.

Seeing Jewel's expression, he tried not to smile. "You're right. This is an insult to your intelligence. I'll get you a better book in the morning. I'm sure they have one on the benefits and drawbacks of spanking."

Setting the com unit firmly down, he eased the bed back down before Jewel could protest and helped her lie on her side again. "Want the drum?" Before she could answer, he placed it in her arms then gave her derriere a light swat. "Yup, I like spanking."

Jewel giggled and he turned out the light, half expecting to hear the drum hit the floor but she resisted. It was time to sleep.

Chapter 50 - Wednesday

"Mary Perkins?" Ray Carlson repeated. "Do you have anything else on her?"

"Uri might have more but he didn't give it to me last night. He said Mary Perkins of Baltimore, Maryland. The card is a Seguro card for fifty dollars. She reported it stolen there in Denver on the 15th and paid for a tracer."

"That and the serial number should give me the transaction information," Ray said. "Is it still stolen?"

"No, she cancelled the tracer at a bank in Chicago." Jasper knew that was going to make it more difficult because it wouldn't show up on the current record of stolen cards. "That was on either the 19th or 20th."

"Not very precise this morning, Stone." Ray studied him. "How's Jewel?"

"She had a nightmare again last night," Jasper said. "It took a while to settle her down. I would really like to get her out of here and back where it's safe."

"It might not be safe much longer," Carlson said. "You made the news again."

"I know," Jasper said. "The local stations were cooperative and didn't ID me but the nationals are certain it's me. We need out of here."

He'd glanced at the news this morning, this time with Jewel, and saw the results of his actions last night. They'd caught him playing Morning Grace and that was a plain admission of his identity. It had topped the charts weeks ago but he hadn't authorized a sheet music release yet.

While the local journalists had marveled at the mystery organist in St. Cecilia's and the treat people had been given and wondered if he might possibly be Sensor Man, the nationals had proclaimed a Sensor Man spotting and had wondered why he was dressed in jeans and plaid shirt instead of his customary black. They also wondered where Jewel was and whether she was well. No doubt they would check the hospitals next.

"Let me see the back of that card," Carlson said and Jasper obediently laid it down and brought the com unit in for an image.

"Got it," Carlson said. "We don't have a DEA in that area so I'm going to send one over from Chicago to collect that card. I want you to drop it at the main police station and he'll pick it up there."

"Thanks," Jasper said. "Any word on Baxter?"

"Nothing yet," Carlson replied. "We think he's in Denver but if he is, he's keeping a low profile in the old city. He may have gotten out though. Two of those cars weren't recovered and another one has gone missing since. That's about twice the average for Denver."

"Not kids, huh?"

"Kids can't get them recharged. Baxter could do it. He could have multiple identity cards but we covered that. It's his fingerprint the alert will trigger on, not his name. He can't fly or take the trains now without being identified."

Jasper nodded. That was standard procedure. "Hopefully, he'll turn up soon," he said. "Mary too. I think the others were local muscle and are unlikely to be anywhere but Plains."

"I think you're right. By the way, I cut that vid so it stops five minutes after they leave. I don't think anyone needs to see that show at the end." Carlson tried to look stern but he was grinning. "It livened it up though."

Jasper felt himself redden. "I forgot about that. At least you know it was uncut."

"True," Carlson said. "You took a chance with that transmitter though. I'm glad it turned out well."

"Yes sir," Jasper responded, silently vowing not to parade around in skin again. He knew there was no way he could keep that vow with Jewel around but he'd make darned sure no vid was taken.

"What's next?" Carlson asked.

"We're waiting on word whether she's released," Jasper said. "And I've asked Reynolds for those inspection sensor reports and tapes of some of the male members of Reach Out. I need an audio lineup."

"For Jewel?" Carlson asked. "Make sure there are witnesses or use an interrogation room."

"Yes sir."

"I would prefer you use an interrogation room," Carlson said. "Now that the transmitter is gone, it should be done. Let me know when and where and I'll arrange it."

"Yes sir," Jasper answered again, feeling like he was back on the force. He didn't object to an interrogation room where he could witness the interview and make sure Jewel was treated properly. It would be some place he chose and with people he trusted. Uri came to mind and he wondered if that would be possible. Jewel was comfortable around him.

"That plant in Arkansas was a bust by the way," Carlson said. "When the new FDA inspector showed up, the old ones ran screaming to the CIA. We found the factory that makes blister and we were told to get out."

"Did we?" Jasper asked.

"Nope," Carlson said. "They had to furnish records. They were producing both implants and pills. The pills were going to CIA but the quantity shipped didn't match what CIA received. The implants were going to three foreign governments and we don't have figures yet for them but their numbers will probably be off too. Two of the plant executives are under arrest and a third one was found dead in his office."

"Was Baxter there?"

"Eight days before our agent got there. The shipping office had a computer meltdown the next day and their backup had to be installed on a clean computer. I doubt they'll find anything. CIA is interested though and sending one of their own people. We'll leave it with them. Are we done now?"

"I think so," Jasper said.

"Then stay out of the news if you can," Carlson said. "And let Jewel know I'm thinking of her."

"Yes sir." After Carlson broke the connection, Jasper remembered he hadn't given him a report on his disclosures. He'd better write that up and send it. Discounting Jewel, there were simply too many people who knew he was an agent. Molly, Kale, Harold, and Uri he could trust but he had his doubts about the air crew. Only the pilot had taken a real good look at his credentials but the co-pilot and dispatcher also knew. The only one who didn't when they landed was the paramedic and he'd probably been told. No, too many. He'd had to disclose it in Chicago too. After this case, he might as well resign and be done with it.

The thought didn't bother him as much as he thought it would. Of course, they were achieving a lot between bringing Baxter in and uncovering the wine operation. He hadn't dreamed they'd get that far when he came up with his plan—and he hadn't planned on getting married or getting so serious about the music career. Moving on might be the best thing. There would also be children in his future and he didn't want to be pulled away from them.

He'd have to get Kale to take the card to police headquarters since he didn't want to leave Jewel again. Maybe he and Jessie could go. It could take hours yet for Jewel to get released—if they released her at all.

No, he wouldn't think that. They couldn't stay here. The national reporters were on the hunt and he was sure Baxter and his people wouldn't be far behind. He needed to get Jewel safe at home so he could concentrate.

The door. He'd shut it during his conference. Guessing that the others wouldn't ignore that, he opened it and stepped out into the hall then stopped. Relieved to see he hadn't shut them out, he walked over to the nurses' station and smiled at the nurses.

"Will you be glad to see us gone?" he asked the nearest one.

"Gone? No sir. Less work for us," she responded with a smile. "And that Kale is very nice. Is he married?"

Jasper grinned. "Yes, he is. You'll have to wait in line too." He was starting to be amused by the number of women who noticed Kale more than him. Maybe he should play his bodyguard some time. It would be an interesting way to throw reporters off.

"Darn, missed again," she said and smiled at him. "And you are so taken. That's the problem with the maternity ward. All the men are married."

He laughed. "Yes or they'd better be. Maybe you should try surgical."

"Or maybe she should marry her boyfriend," another nurse chimed in.

"Hush!" The first nurse laughed.

"There's no law against looking unless you get caught—and I'm about to be," Jasper added as the elevator doors opened and he saw Kale step out. Jewel was in a wheelchair behind him and he noted her smile at once. It went well then.

Jewel looked so different now. That curly mop of hair seemed to suit her and brought a not-so-serious pixie look to her oval face. He liked playing with the curls too. Those blue eyes shone and she looked so small in his robe. Suddenly aware where his thoughts were headed, he looked at Molly and caught a smug look. Ok, what were they hiding?

Suspicious, he looked at Kale but saw no hint there. Well, if it went that well, he needed to send Kale off at once. He didn't want to worry about that card on top of everything else.

"Would you have a plain white envelope I could have?" he asked the nurse he'd been talking to. "And a piece of paper?"

"Yes sir," the nurse answered, her eyes shifting from Kale to him. "Here you are."

"Thanks," Jasper said and followed his wife and Molly back to the room. Once the door was closed, he asked the question. "Well?"

Molly was already helping Jewel out of the chair. "Get dressed, dear."

Ah, she was that certain. Jasper caught that hint but waited for a reply. "Well?"

"Well," Molly repeated. "As soon as the doctor gets here, she'll probably be released. We just have to wait."

"Uh-huh," Jasper said, still suspicious. "Kale, I'd like you and Jessie to run a quick errand. We'll wait until you get back."

"Sure," Kale said. "What kind?"

"Delivery," he said and sat down and wrote a quick note on the paper then folded it around the card. Writing another on the envelope with his DEA ident visible, he made sure whoever looked at it would hold it for the courier and not lose track of it. "Tell them this is evidence in the Jasper Stone case and will be picked up in the next 48 hours. Carlson wants it left at main police headquarters. The front desk will do."

"Yes sir," Kale said. "Just that cash card?"

"Yes," Jasper said. "I should have left it with Uri, I guess." He handed the envelope over. "If you see any chocolate stores on the way back, grab about five pounds. Jewel likes caramels and truffles. Let Jessie pick her own and you pick for your wife. Molly, what would you like?"

"Truffles are good," Molly said. "I can't make those at home."

"Got it. Sweeten the women," Kale said with a grin. "We'll be back soon."

Jasper was sure he'd be gone just long enough. They'd been optimistic and checked out of the hotel this morning and moved their things to the car. He still had his briefcase, suitcase and drum but they were no problem. Jewel would probably insist on carrying the drum.

The next two hours dragged by slowly. Jewel packed the suitcase herself and Jasper knew she was glad to be up and moving again. Only once did Molly remind her no bending and he knew not all of the restrictions had been lifted. Well, he would just have to control himself and hope he could control her. Soon he'd have her out of here.

"Any news?" Jewel finally asked.

"Not a lot except I'm in the news again and Ray isn't happy," Jasper said. "I haven't called David because he'll probably chew me out too. It can wait until we're home."

"Maybe," Jewel said with a coquettish look.

"What's that supposed to mean?" Jasper asked, aware again she was holding something back. "Molly, is spanking on the restricted list?"

Molly Kowalski seemed to consider it while Jewel looked at her and shook her head. Jasper wasn't sure if Jewel wanted to be spanked or didn't want to be but it seemed Molly was just as unsure what she was trying to say.

"I think it should be for at least a week," Molly finally said. "After that, we'll see. Until then you'll just have to send her to her room–alone."

"Not that," Jewel said in mock horror. "Ok, I'll behave."

Jasper doubted that very much but didn't say anything as the doctor came in followed by the nurse who had attended Jewel in surgery.

"There you are," he said with a mechanical smile. "Kowalski, your opinion?"

"The ultrasound was fine. Everything has settled down, doctor," Molly said in her most professional manner.

"You'll be able to limit her activities okay?" he asked.

"Yes sir," Molly said with a warning look at Jewel.

"Then I don't see any reason to keep her here and a lot of good reasons to get her out," the doctor said with a look at Jasper. "There's a media circus on the street. You're not to go out that way."

"Right," Jasper said but inwardly he groaned. "We have other plans."

"Good. Now, Miss Jewel, you will take care of yourself and listen to Molly. She's got a lot of experience with this type of thing." He paused then added, "I expect to know how it comes out."

"Yes, doctor," Jewel said and her eyes were suspiciously bright.

"You're very lucky, you know. Dr. McBride wasn't sure going in that she could save him but he is one stubborn cuss."

Jasper caught that and was confused. Save him? Save who? He wasn't stubborn.

"Congratulations, Mr. Stone. It's a boy," the doctor said as he left.

Jasper stood there, trying to take the words in. It's a boy? Jewel was? He looked suspiciously at his wife and saw her bright smile and knew. The morning sickness. The goddamned morning sickness. He'd been right. She was.... God, she was pregnant all that time!

A surge of anger tore through him but almost instantly he felt relief. He was okay. McBride had saved him–or he was just too stubborn to move. That made him smile. He was having a boy.

"How far along?" Jasper asked Molly, his smile still uncertain.

"Six or seven weeks," Molly said. "I don't think he waited for your wedding day."

Jasper opened his arms and let Jewel in. "A boy," he said and his face relaxed. "And he must be stubborn to go through all that. You, love, are going to have a handful in–how long?"

"July," Jewel said. "I'm going to beat Elinor!"

"Brat," Jasper said without heat. "You'd better call her right now."

She didn't need to be told twice.

Jasper watched as she grabbed her com unit and started the call then turned to Molly. "You knew."

"Yes, I did," Molly said. "First day. So did Dr. McBride and that other doctor in Denver. We," she stressed that, "each decided it was better not to tell her until the transmitter was out and things had settled down. There's still a chance she'll miscarry but it's small. The fetus is completely normal for this stage and moving as it should. Sex was determined by blood test."

"Kicking yet?" Jasper asked.

"No, thank god," Molly said. "When he starts kicking, she'll feel it—and I don't think that transmitter would have taken even a light kick. It was time to get that out."

Jasper saw she was totally serious. "Well, I never liked sharing a room either."

Molly laughed. "He's your son."

Jasper grinned. "You bet he is."

When Jewel called him over to share the news with Elinor and David, he relaxed. Their reactions were just like his—shock that Jewel was pregnant, anger from David that she'd been risked like that, and then joy. After the initial news breaking, Jasper realized there was one thing he still had to do and left them to it. He wanted a picture of that transmitter. He was going to make sure Baxter knew the damned thing was out and Jewel was unharmed. One way or another, he was going to have that.

Chapter 51 - Thanksgiving

Jasper sipped his coffee and stared out the window at more falling snow and mused over how this now felt like home. He still missed that gorgeous view of Laramie Peak but he was beginning to appreciate the serenity of this view.

Here he could see the road as it stretched away to the east and down to the front entrance of the business offices. Beyond that the land was flat were there wasn't trees and there were a lot of trees. He supposed the farm had taken advantage of the government grants they got by keeping so many acres in trees. They were essential for the health of the atmosphere and none of the major governments ignored that anymore.

Trees didn't concern him right now. He was still fondly recalling the warm welcome home last night. If he had any doubts that people wanted them to stay, it had been dispelled when Jewel was hugged, kissed, and congratulated on the baby. He'd gotten his own share of attention, mostly from fathers who were willing to give advice on how to handle pregnancy in a young wife and hints about sleepless nights to come. Finally he'd trotted out pictures of his grown daughter to show them that yes, he knew what was coming.

He knew Jewel wasn't out of danger yet but couldn't help rejoicing at the news of his coming son. If Junior had survived that transmitter so well, he wasn't going to give up now. He was ready to believe that but would take extra care of his wife.

It was David who called him Junior and Elinor had laughingly told him he couldn't call both boys Junior. Jasper agreed but what the heck did you call an unborn child? It wasn't like he'd be stuck with it when he came out because Jasper would never consent to naming his son after him. He'd been named after his paternal great-grandfather because it was a traditional Stone family name but he'd had a hard time listening to the comparisons his father made to the long dead astronaut. It wasn't until he was grown that he could appreciate the uncertainty early astronauts lived with—not that Captain Jasper A. Stone had been one of the early ones. He'd been one of the hundred or so who helped build the first really successful space station.

No, he wouldn't name his son Jasper and on the drive home Jewel had nixed other stone and musical names. That left only every other kind. He knew it would be a long drawn-out process to name this child. It wouldn't be as simple as Carol declaring over dinner that her daughter would be Melody. Fortunately Mel herself had insisted on being called Mel instead. It suited her better.

Well, it wasn't today's worry. He'd been warned there would be a board in the community center where people would write down their own suggestions but he was to take none of it seriously. Apparently they did it to all and, as time got closer, there'd be bets on name, weight, and delivery date. Children didn't just appear on the farm. They were celebrated.

He'd have to get used to it. Jasper sipped his coffee and attempted to get his mind back on the case but nothing wanted to stick today. He knew dinner would be in a scant three hours and, since this was the Thanksgiving feast, it would be even grander than the potlucks and more gut busting. The Commons was being set up for the feast and the children were either helping or watching their homework—a vid history of Thanksgiving—on the big screen. Others were getting the farm chores done.

He'd been ordered out of the way but Jewel had—een pressed into helping. There wasn't much he could do today since everyone he knew was celebrating the holiday too.

Lori. In other years he would have called Lori. Last year they'd spent the holiday on duty but together. Lori's ex had predictably not allowed her son to visit and he'd still been missing Carol. Mel was still mad at him too. The two of them had volunteered to walk beats so some of their married fellows could enjoy the day.

Thanksgiving Day tended to be quiet except for the occasional family row. Those could be either tense or entertaining but were rarely serious. Sometimes they just had to take the key irritant out for a walk. He'd once seen a patrolman with four such irritants trailing behind him on patrol. They weren't all that angry as they shared their complaints and offered to just trade families for the day.

His lips quirked as he thought of the close-knit relationships here on the farm. How the hell would they handle the typical Thanksgiving arguments? Would all Ruby's group band together and all of Lill's oppose them and how would those related to both women fare? Now that could be interesting.

Deciding he'd been alone long enough, Jasper rinsed his coffee cup and turned everything off. He was going to participate. If the women wouldn't let him help, he'd just find out where the other excess men were.

On leaving the office building, he was slightly surprised to find young Lexie hurrying to catch up with him. She and one of her friends danced in front of him. "Jewel said to tell you she's with the piano at the school," Lexie said. "She's got a surprise for you."

"Okay, thanks," he said as the kids took off. He wondered how long they'd been waiting for him and why Jewel just hadn't called. Well, that was a good place to meet her. He'd have to ignore that piano though. If he turned up late for dinner again, he'd have a hard time living it down now that Jewel was pregnant and he should be dancing attendance on her.

Crossing the commons, he noted the tables were covered in white linen and set already. A handful of children were playing a skip rope game on the dance floor and there were more parked in front of the big screen. Again no men. Well, it was still early and there might be farm work going on. He was going to have to find Kale or Harold and find out if there was some place he should be.

Pool? A game? Remembering there were supposed to be old time football and war games both on Thanksgiving, he thought that might be it. Football had lost most of its following in the last fifty years but there were still teams and their games were still broadcast. He'd just never bothered. He preferred the more individual sports when he watched any at all.

The school was deserted and quiet till he got to the third-floor room and stopped. Kale was on the mats with his wife and Jewel was watching as Beth Tunis calmly grabbed her husband's arm, twisted, and threw him to the mats in a move so efficient and swift that Jasper barely grasped it.

"Good one," Kale said from the mat. "And here's Jasper. I want to see what he can do."

"What's this?" Jasper asked although he had a sudden suspicion. Jewel was dressed in loose pants and wore a thick martial arts vest over her top. "Jewel, you aren't?"

"She's just dressing the part," Kale said. "The only moves I'm teaching her are basic self-defense. No bending, twisting, or throwing."

Jasper looked at his wife. Before he could ask, she turned red and blurted out, "I won't be a helpless victim again."

He'd better tread carefully here. How could he tell her he'd never let her be a victim again when he knew the danger was still out there? And remembering that vid of the train station—the one he couldn't force himself to watch all the way—he knew Jewel probably would have been killed on the spot if she'd resisted more effectively. And she was pregnant. She shouldn't be learning this but she was also Jewel.

"So what has he taught you?" he asked to buy time.

Jewel looked uncertain but he waved her to the mat. Betty stepped aside to give them room and Jasper watched as Kale put an arm around Jewel's throat to hold her. In the next instant, Jewel had stomped down where his foot had been a moment before and elbowed him in the ribs then twisted out of his weakened grasp. Kale had successfully avoided the foot stomp but hadn't shifted enough to avoid the full impact of the elbow jab and Jewel hurriedly apologized.

"I'm alright," Kale said. "And I've been punched worse." He grinned and rubbed his ribs.

"I'm supposed to wear heels for that," Jewel told her husband. "But that's the most basic move."

"Yes, I've seen that before," Jasper said. "And it works if your attacker doesn't know about it. If he does though, it's no good. It can be countered."

"That's right," Kale said. "But it's a start. Beth and I were just showing her other tricks."

"There's one I want her to know," Jasper said with sudden decision. "It's not usually taught because it leaves the victim on the ground but it can be damned effective. Jewel, can you go limp?"

"Limp?" she asked.

"Limp," Jasper said. "Totally and completely limp. Here, let me try." Stepping on to the mat, he took the attacker's position with his wife facing out. His mouth was next to her ear and he gave her a quick kiss and felt a shiver run through her. "Stop that," he said with a grin. "You're supposed to be afraid. I've got a knife in one hand and I'm going to drag you off to who knows where. Now what I want you to do is go limp. No resistance. Fall."

"I can't," Jewel said.

"I'll catch you," Jasper replied. "Do it."

Her first attempt was half-hearted but she slipped out from under his arm and fell halfway to the mat before he caught her. The second time he let her almost hit the mat.

"Let me try," Beth said and repeated it with Kale. She went totally limp and Kale didn't succeed in catching her, quick as he was.

"Ok, I haven't seen that as a self-defense move," Kale admitted. "Something from police training?"

"Yes," Jasper said. "One thing we're taught is trank the victim if we don't have a clear shot at their attacker. The victim goes limp, the attacker is stuck with letting them go or trying to hold them up. Either way, he's exposed for a clean shot. The victim wakes up and it's all over with."

"Any fatalities that way?" Kale asked.

"I've never seen one but I haven't had to face real killers with that tactic. It's a bad move to use a hostage for a shield and most won't do it. The amateurs don't know better."

"So why teach me to go limp?" Jewel asked then her expression changed. "Oh, Junior."

"Yes, Junior," Jasper said. "It's too risky to trank a pregnant woman or a child under the age of four. Anyone else the rule book says trank the victim. You need to know that can happen if you're caught in a situation."

"At the train station?" Jewel asked, her face pale. "They didn't trank me."

"They were too far away," Jasper said. "The agent was down and Lori was dead. If they'd been closer, they would have just to keep you from being carted away."

He paused, wondering what Johnson would have done in that situation. His orders had been to take her alive but he doubted he would have followed them if he was facing being caught. No, it was good that Jewel had reacted like she did but she didn't always have to react that way.

"So do you object to her learning some tricks?" Kale asked. "It could help."

"No, I guess I don't object but keep them simple until Junior is out," Jasper said. "And I think I'll train with you too. This is temporary though. When this case is done, I'll just be a musician."

"Seriously?" Kale asked, his expression changing.

"I'll still need a bodyguard when I leave here," Jasper said. "And after Christmas there's a class starting up in LA. If Beth can spare you, that's the best one."

"I can," Beth said with surprising firmness. "And he'll go."

"You'll just be a musician?" Jewel caught that. "No more ... police work?" She caught herself in time.

"This is the last case," Jasper said. "We'll both be witnesses and it could drag on for years but I won't be involved in more."

The relief in Jewel's face let him know he'd made the right decision. Yes, he would have to leave the DEA. He had to think about her and the son on the way.

"That's probably for the best," Kale said and walked back to the center of the mats. "Now do you want to show me what you can do?"

"Two out of three?" Jasper asked and followed him. It was a useless question. Kale let him get ready and made a few feints before taking him down. More wary the second time, Jasper tried to hold on to the martial arts teacher but his trip to the mat was short. Only his pride made him try the third time.

"You definitely need a refresher," Kale said as he helped him up and dusted him off. "We'll start Monday if you're free."

"Thanks," Jasper said. "I think I'm ready for dinner." He tried not to think about how sore he'd be later because Kale was right. He'd better relearn unarmed combat techniques. He was less in favor of Jewel learning them but a few wouldn't hurt.

* * *

Mouth-watering aromas filled the feast area by the time they got there and Jasper found himself appreciating the smells even as he nodded to the families gathered around the tables. There were four sliced turkeys on the sideboard, two of them roasted and the others deep-fried, and an array of side dishes competing for attention. With over a hundred people to feed, the farm had gone all out to provide a gut-busting meal that put the weekly potlucks to shame.

The chink of plates and low conversations punctuated by laughter filled the commons as people ate and caught up on news. No one was in a hurry to leave the tables but lingered to visit with friends and family. Jasper found out that some faces he didn't know yet were actually family from other farms or people who lived in town who had come out for the day. No one suggested he play but Jasper suspected the cat vid was being passed around among the newcomers. It was a good thing he'd given it to his publisher because there simply seemed no way to stop it. He hoped Sasha would enjoy it as much.

"So how did you like our turkeys?" Harold asked as he settled down in the chair vacated by Jewel.

"Great," Jasper replied. "What was this one's name?"

"Tom," Harold said without hesitating and smiled. "All male turkeys are Tom. We never call them anything else."

"Right," Jasper said. "Sasha said she named her rabbit?"

"That's different," Harold responded. "As she said, it's a breeder. The ones raised for slaughter are never named. Our dairy cows have names but they're around for quite a long time."

"That makes sense."

"I've got something to show you," Harold said. "The power feeds are in at the barn and some of your equipment is here. Do you want to take a look?"

"Yes sir," Jasper said and rose then started to gather up his plate.

"Never mind that," Harold said. "You'll be back for pie then seconds, and whenever you get hungry. Let's walk some off now."

Jasper followed him, only stopping to tell Jewel where he was going but she grabbed his hand and stepped out with him. Another man he didn't know joined their company as they walked along.

Feeling the hairs on his neck twitch, Jasper knew something was up but no one else was following. He half expected them to because there was suddenly an undercurrent of tension.

"Why do I feel like I'm on a long walk?" Jasper asked and Harold gave him a sharp look. His wife was smiling so she was in on it.

"Well, folks have worked on this," Harold said. "And Fenton here knows what he's doing. We don't have the core of your music system yet but some of the other components are here."

That prepared him or so he thought but the barn they walked into no longer bore much of a resemblance to a barn. The low fences were gone and fabric was draped from the rail separating the barn floor from the raised walkway around it. A braided rug in shades of brown was centered under the assortment of amplifiers and speakers that made up the peripherals and there were two keyboards, not one, on their stands.

The transformation was amazing and Jasper just stared, unsure exactly where to turn until Jewel pushed him toward the keyboards. He saw the power was on and had to fight the urge to sit down.

"Wonderful," Jasper said to Harold. "That's where everyone was earlier?"

"Some of us," Harold said. "After seeing how you played at the cathedral, everyone wanted in on this. Just be aware we added a gallery over there." Harold motioned toward a section of railing. "And Fenton has rigged up a switch you can hit when you're recording so people will know not to peek in."

"That sounds fair," Jasper said then spotted a camera. "And people didn't follow us in because they're watching us right now?"

Jewel smiled. "I told you he'd spot it."

Jasper grinned and waved at the camera. "Well then, I'm going to try it out. I can't do the fancy stuff without the core but I can play."

"Knock yourself out," Harold said. "I'm going back for pie."

Jasper took the chair waiting for him and tinkered briefly with the keys then started playing. This time he wouldn't play long but he needed to thank those who had made it possible. Yes, this barn would do very well till he got his own studio built.

An hour later Jewel pried him out and they walked back for pie. He thanked the folks of Amber Farms for his new studio and Jewel thanked them for his new distraction which led to laughter because she made it clear it was too much distraction from her. Finding Mr. Fenton, Jasper also thanked him for designing the layout and wasn't surprised he worked for Milt.

"The core might be here tomorrow," he said. "If not, look for it Saturday. Special delivery by someone you know."

"Milt?" Jasper asked but rejected that even before Fenton shook his head. Neither Milt nor Brad drove.

"I think it's going to be Mary," Fenton said. "And her husband. She's curious."

"She's also welcome," Jasper said. "If I needed a secretary, I'd be poaching her."

Fenton just grinned. "It's been a trip," he said. "And I'm glad I got to help. Nice folks here."

"Enjoy it," Jasper told him. "We're looking into staying."

Shortly after that he saw the man dancing and turned his attention back to Lill's cherry pie. When Harold joined him at the table, he knew they had things to discuss.

"I love it," he said before Harold could ask. "Can we get the financial details worked out soon? Jewel wants to stay and I want that studio."

"I've got it in my office," Harold said. "Tomorrow afternoon?"

Jasper nodded, his mouth full of pie. When he could speak again, he asked "How much is the building I'm using?"

Harold shook his head. "Tomorrow. I will say it's a relief to have another use for that one. It wasn't the best barn design."

Jasper waited for more.

"I told you it gets too hot," Harold said. "It was the first poultry barn we built and we overdid it. It keeps a steady temperature but when you start adding in hundreds of birds, the temperature just builds. We lost a flock before we figured it out and built other buildings. We could never have more than four hundred birds in that one before the problem recurred. It's been sitting empty most of the time."

"Well, it will be mostly empty with me," Jasper said. "What will you do with it when I'm done using it?" He wasn't sure whether Harold was justifying letting him use it.

"We're still debating," Harold said. "We might just turn it into a proper gym. It's big enough to hold all the exercise equipment in one building. The heat problem might recur but I think we'd have to have more bodies than we have now."

"Ok, now I don't feel like I'm taking away production," Jasper said. "But we have been disrupting things. I get worried every time Ivan has to fetch us."

"Driving is something he enjoys," Harold said. "If he couldn't tear himself away, you'd find someone else volunteering. It's not a problem." Harold hesitated then continued. "In a community this small, it's easy for people to get bored with the same old routine then you start having arguments and fights and you start losing that community feeling."

"Since you two got here, we've had a darn good pool match, some interesting vids, and quite a bit of excitement—not more than we can handle though. Everyone is rallying around you two and it's pulled them together. It will wear off in time and things will settle down again but right now it's nice."

Jasper saw he was serious and smiled. "I thought we were being a bother. I'm glad you set me straight."

"No, no bother. I think we can make this honeymoon last till your little one is born," Harold said. "After that I'll have to come up with some new way to hold them together, which is part of my job as general manager. That will be next summer though and we don't get the edginess until winter. We might have a really good year."

"I'm especially glad you've got Kale working for you," Harold said. "Teaching martial arts wasn't enough for him but we couldn't let Beth go. There was just enough strain there we worried about them."

Jasper thought about his impressions of the young couple and nodded. "Yes, I can see where that could be a problem. I'll try to keep him occupied."

"Good. Have you tried the strawberry-rhubarb pie yet? That's one of my favorites." Harold quickly changed the subject as Jewel rejoined them.

"We could make a meal on just pies and still never get through all of them," Jasper said. "No, I've had the pumpkin and the cherry and I'm going to have to work those off before I can manage another one."

"Don't push it," Harold said. "We'll be eating leftovers tomorrow. I can snag one of those pies for my office and no one will notice."

"That's another reason to get it all done," Jasper said. "Jewel, are you ready to look over official leases and such?"

Jewel looked at him then at Harold. "Not tonight, I'm not. Tomorrow?"

"Tomorrow afternoon," Harold said. "It's not a reason to get up early."

"No but I'll have to get back to work on the case," Jasper said. "Today I was thinking of other things." He smiled at his wife and her cheeks went pink then finished after a long pause. "It's good I've got that studio to play with since someone has taken over my drum."

Harold laughed and Jewel's expression flitted between vexation and laughter. Before she could retort his com unit buzzed and he glanced at the number then walked away from the table.

"Stone here," he said.

"Did I catch you at the table?" Carlson asked.

"No, what's up?" Jasper said, catching the tone in his voice.

"Something I need you to do tomorrow—Monday if Kucera isn't in. We need to rope Kucera into this plot and the sooner the better. This is what I want you to do."

Jasper listened, his frown deepening as Carlson explained his plan but after weighing the options, he grinned. "Damned if he does and damned if he doesn't, huh?"

"That's the idea. Make sure you have witnesses unrelated to you. That general manager would be a good one. He knows what he's doing."

"Yes sir. I'll try to get this done tomorrow."

"There's another thing," Carlson said. "We've got background on Mary Perkins. Until a month ago she worked for Soma in Baltimore. She left that job but they won't confirm if it was termination or leave of absence. That particular shop was on the watch list because Starling had relatives there—and she's one."

"Related? How?" Jasper's mouth went dry. He thought she was a nurse, not an attendant in a euthanasia shop!

"Half-sister," Carlson said. "Different mother. She was raised with them though and might have been out to get revenge–or answers."

"Answers would fit," Jasper said. "If that's the case, she wants me more than Jewel. Has she been to see Starling?"

"No," Carlson said. "No visitors other than his lawyer. Apparently he's been left high and dry. The case will come to trial in January and the FBI is trying to get permission for a deep interrogation. So far it's been blocked. They may not be able to do it until after he's found guilty."

"Thanks for the info," he said. "I'll see what I can do tomorrow."

"Soon enough," Carlson replied. "Tell Jewel to take it easy."

"Yes sir," Jasper said. She would if he had anything to say about it. He'd considered finding another bed for the next two weeks but he didn't want to be gone if she had another nightmare. He didn't like his own and didn't want her to face hers alone.

Putting away his com link, he returned to the table. He'd have to talk to Harold.

* * *

Jasper studied his grown daughter carefully, seeing her ready smile and the way she kept her hand in Corey's. He was looking good too, Jasper admitted. With finals starting Tuesday, neither looked stressed out.

"Are you having a good time with David and Elinor?" he asked as Jewel snuggled into his shoulder.

"The best," Melody said. "Great Uncle David is fun."

"Great Uncle?" Jasper's eyebrow shot up just as David's bellow told him he didn't appreciate the title. Jewel snickered against him.

"Yup, he's a great uncle," Melody said. "A lot more fun than a real one." A hand came in from off camera and smacked the back of her head. "Ouch."

"Beat her for me too," Jasper said to the unseen David. "No respect." At the same time, he realized she was right. David was Jewel's uncle. When he married her, Melody gained a great uncle even though she was just Jewel's stepdaughter. "If you keep calling him great-uncle, I'm going to make sure Junior calls you Sissy every time he sees you."

"And I'll spoil him rotten," Melody said with unusual calm. "And teach him everything you hate."

"And hand him back," David said, sticking his head into view. "Just like I'm doing to my great-niece. I wish I'd gotten her sooner so I could do a good job of it."

"I'm glad you didn't." Jasper grinned at him. "Have you fed her caviar yet?"

Mel made a face and Corey looked startled.

"That's a thought," David said. "One more great-uncle out of her and I'll feed her fish eggs." He tried to look stern but failed. "Seriously, we had a good day and plan to have a good weekend. I'm showing them some of the machines I work with. If they stick around, I'll see they get the aptitude tests."

"Are there any commitments with those?" Jasper asked. He wasn't sure if he wanted his daughter operating mining equipment even though there was no risk to her with the remote equipment.

"No," David said. "Lunarex makes them available to all likely prospects. If they score high enough, they might get an offer but they won't be obligated."

"It can't hurt then," Jasper said. He knew only a few had the necessary talent to operate time-lagged mining equipment. Lunarex was very picky because careless moves could damage or destroy equipment already in place on the moon. Worse, they could endanger the mechanics maintaining the equipment and they <u>were</u> on the moon.

"Other plans? When are you going back?" he asked his daughter.

"Sunday morning," she said. "We have some studying to do and Corey is setting up the professor's exams."

"The professor's?" Jasper looked at Corey. "They kept his classes going?"

"Yes," Corey said. "He had all his lectures taped and it was decided the classes had to go on till the end of the semester since so many needed the credits. Mrs. Price is overseeing the classes and grading papers but I still have a job. They even bumped my salary up."

"Good," Jasper said. "That will take care of next semester?"

"Yes sir," Corey said. "And I've been told the professor left an endowment with scholarships for deserving students. I'm to get one of those."

"I'm glad," Jasper said. Drew Nugent would think of his students, especially one he had singled out for help. "If you need additional help, come to me. I don't want you dropping out."

"No sir," Corey said. "I mean yes sir. I'll ask if I have to. Help seems to be showing up in odd places though. I got tickets for the Orbital Sensations show this weekend. There were some donated to the college and one pair was specified for me."

"Orbital Sensations? They're in Denver?" Jasper knew the group and approved. They weren't sensa artists but blended physics and music together into an impressive show.

"Yes, at the Astradome," Corey said. "We're going by limo."

Jasper looked at David, thinking of the expense and security.

"It's okay," David said. "A dozen people from the Tower have tickets and they'll be using the limos there and back. It wasn't hard to get Corey and Melody in. Those of us who don't have tickets will just stay home and watch a movie."

"That sounds good too," Jasper said. "Ok, have a good time, you two. Don't go broadcasting which train you're taking back to Plains. It's better for others not to know."

"Yes, Dad," Mel answered. "We'll be careful."

"Good," Jasper said. He wasn't that concerned. With that large a group, they should be safe enough. Seeing Orbital Sensations was a real coup for them. He'd managed to do it just once ten years ago and even then the prices were outrageous and tickets were hard to get. It was good that someone had sent some to the college but not too unusual. A lot of performers reserved some tickets for college kids.

"When finals are done, I'd like you both to come out here for Christmas break," he said. "It looks like Jewel and I will be living here from now on and I want you to see this place."

Mel looked shocked. "On a farm? You? With cows?"

"Chickens too," Jewel piped up, "and rabbits and turkeys and dogs and we've got a cat."

"A cat?" Mel repeated and Corey laughed.

"He's got me," Jasper said. "Damned cat likes music. David can show you the vid. Anyway, plan on coming out here for a week at least. You'll like the people here."

Mel looked really doubtful but Corey grinned. "We'll be there," he said. "I like dogs."

After the call ended, Jewel looked up at him and smiled. "I think Mel is going to be in for a shock."

"She'll adapt," Jasper said. "But she's a city girl. I doubt she'll stay here."

"I didn't think you would," Jewel said and laid her head on his chest. "You liked the city so much. All that food you could order in and the shops."

"We get more than enough food here," Jasper said. "And I haven't seen you giving up shopping."

"No, I haven't," Jewel replied. "And I think I can cook Chinese. We'll make do."

Chapter 52 - Friday, 26 Nov 2179

"Wilson Kucera? I'm Jasper Stone." Jasper saw recognition dawn on the man's face with grim satisfaction. It had taken him almost twenty minutes to get past the security and secretaries at Wilson Chemicals. "I have information about your brother and Mark Baxter."

"What information?" Kucera demanded. "If you're going to tell me Ed killed–"

"No sir but you might want to record this call since I am."

Wilson Kucera looked torn between ending the call and continuing. Finally he bowed his head and tapped a control. "Recording. I'm not in the habit of recording personal calls."

"I understand that sir but I'm still tied to the West case and there have been attempts on both me and my wife."

"I heard. I was stunned by that kidnapping. Have they found Baxter yet? I've terminated his employment." Kucera didn't quite rush the words but he definitely wanted him to know where he stood.

I bet you have. "I haven't heard that he's been found," Jasper said, "but he's not where I am."

"Where you are?" Kucera repeated.

"Yes sir. One of the reasons for this call is to let you know exactly where I am which is Amber Farms twenty miles southwest of St. Paul, Minnesota. Come and visit if you like but watch out for the dogs."

"Is this a joke?" Kucera stared at him, shock on his face. "Why the hell would I want to know where you are?"

"Insurance," Jasper said with a grim smile. "I know that you know. If anyone in your employ shows up here uninvited, the FBI will know as well."

"Baxter is not in my employ," Kucera thundered, his calm gone.

"No, he's not," Jasper smoothly said, "but there were others working with him. Kin Koasa is in custody but Mary Perkins is not. Two others have been identified as well."

"I need to call you back," Kucera said. "Your number?"

Jasper gave it to him, acutely aware that Wilson Kucera was shaken. Whether or not he had anything to do with the kidnapping, he'd just lost deniability with this call. If anything, anything at all happened to him and Jewel, he'd be going down.

No doubt he was checking now to see whether Kin or Mary Perkins was on his payroll and their last known locations. He was probably thinking how hard it would be to get them erased from payroll records too and realizing it would do no good since Jasper had recorded their entire conversation.

This morning's talk with Kin had given him that gambit. The informant had confirmed he was a salaried employee paid by direct deposit through Wilson Chemicals. It wasn't even a subsidiary. He'd also received cash bonuses in the thousands. His legitimate work for Wilson had included debugging communications and computer systems—a job he'd done for more than a year before getting special assignments. His regular salary had continued.

"What do you think?' Jasper glanced aside to where Harold Fletcher and Jim Talbot were sitting just out of camera range.

"I think you've got him by the short hairs," Jim Talbot said. "He's caught no matter which way he jumps. The only safe course is to make damned sure no one shows up here."

"Agreed," Harold said. "The only thing that concerns me is that woman will be dead if the FBI doesn't grab her first."

"She may be dead already," Jasper said. "If she isn't, she's bolted. Her trail stopped in Chicago."

"Well, she is a murderer," Harold said, "and the sister of assassins." He looked distinctly uncomfortable. "I would just prefer she be given a chance."

"So long as she stays away from here, I'm willing," Jasper said. "She can join her half-brother in jail." It still surprised him that she wasn't a nurse but a euthanasia specialist. It shouldn't because he'd experienced the steady serene sympathy of Rachel when his wife chose euthanasia and later interviewed her about Elizabeth West's choice to live. He'd meant to talk to her again after that but never had.

His com unit buzzed and he looked at the time. "That was fast."

Wilson Kucera and another man were back on the vid screen. Lawyer, Jasper quickly decided. He looked unhappy.

"I've confirmed Kin Koasa is on my payroll but I've never met the man," Wilson said. "You said he's in custody? Where? Where did they catch him?"

"Kin was robbing my house when he was caught," Jasper said. "A federal agency has him because he's confessed to being involved in the kidnapping—and he knows what happened to Chuma Johnson in Plains. You might also want to check on Johnson."

"I have," Kucera said. "He wasn't known to this company. Mary Perkins is also not in our records. If Baxter was using them, it wasn't through us. I have no way of contacting them."

"What about Baxter?" Jasper asked.

He saw Kucera hesitate and fought the urge to smile. As he thought, not all ties had been severed. Carlson would find that interesting.

"I know his habits and I can leave messages but there's no guarantee he'll get any," Kucera said. "He knows he's wanted. He'd be a fool to be predictable and Mark Baxter is no fool." He rubbed his hand through his hair. "This is one big mess. I told him I wanted to know what my brother was up to and who gave him blister. That was not carte blanche for murder or kidnapping." His voice was savage. "I thought I knew him."

The lawyer was beginning to look very unhappy. "Mr. Kucera..."

"Shut up," Kucera snapped. "I don't give a damn about classified drugs right now—and I bet Stone knows all about it."

"I do now. Before the kidnapping, I only knew your brother had a bliss reaction. Then one of your brother's friends also died of a bliss reaction while Baxter was questioning him. Baxter himself told me it was accidental right after he told me my wife had been treated with the same drug."

"He told you?" Kucera stared at him in disbelief. "He had a classified drug with him? He's gone mad." He abruptly sat down.

Jasper waited but Kucera didn't speak.

"He was there when my wife was returned and I recognized him. We have him on vid in my house with the kidnappers and threatening me. He also told me my wife was booby-trapped and he could kill her any time. This device was removed from her." He pulled up the picture of the transmitter and sent it to him. "That's a terrorist weapon designed to eavesdrop on a woman's partners and explode if she tells anyone it's there. It's out now and my wife is finally safe from it."

The lawyer looked suitably shocked and Kucera looked grim. Did he really not know what Baxter was capable of? Glancing at his listeners, he saw Talbot and Harold were equally grim. They'd known about the transmitter but apparently they hadn't put it all together.

"I see now that Baxter didn't deserve my trust," Wilson Kucera finally said. "And I hope he's found. He's too dangerous to me, my company, and society. I'll cooperate any way I can."

"Thank you," Jasper said. "You'll want to work with the FBI on that. I just don't want him showing up here."

"Understood." Kucera shot a look at his lawyer. "I'll do what I can. Now what can you tell me about my brother? I know Ed couldn't have been involved in murder. He was too honest to cheat at cards."

"He wasn't involved in the West murders," Jasper said. "We think Baxter used his name to blackmail Jake West. He did admit to introducing Samuel Starling to Jake at the request of a friend. That seems to be the limit of his involvement."

"Then how did he get blister?" Kucera demanded. "And why the hell did he take it?" His voice rose and he seemed unaware he'd named the classified drug again. "He didn't even know we made it—and that was strictly for CIA."

"I'm aware of that," Jasper said, confirming Kucera's suspicions. "It took a rash of deaths from it before the CIA came clean. I don't know how Ed Kucera got it—or Professor Nugent—because CIA has confirmed they weren't agents. FBI wasn't aware of blister and neither was DEA but they are now. Again, neither man was an agent. It's a puzzle I haven't solved yet. Since I never met your brother and barely knew Professor Nugent, I'm not sure it can be. I've turned up nothing illegal and, once we have Baxter, we'll probably be able to drop the murder charges against Ed. That is if Baxter can talk."

He threw that in there on the off-chance Baxter wasn't dead already. "If Baxter can't, only Samuel Starling will be able to clear him."

"The assassin?" Kucera looked grim. "I'd forgotten about him."

"I haven't," Jasper said. "He's still in custody and they'll be able to question him eventually."

"Yes," Kucera said. "But I'd like to make it sooner. I'm going to see messages are left for Baxter—and I will make damned sure he doesn't find out from me where you are. Watch your back though. I don't know where he is now or where that Perkins woman is."

So saying, he cut the connection.

Jasper glanced over at Harold and saw he had produced a notepad and was writing things down.

"Jake was being blackmailed?" Jim Talbot asked. "Does that mean he wasn't guilty of murder?"

"The only charge we had against him was attempted murder which was dropped to assault at the family's request," Jasper said. "Jake was a fool for not going to his uncle or father when this started but he was a desperate fool and Baxter knew it."

"Because of Mars and that age restriction?" Talbot asked. "I keep wondering what the Colonial Authority is trying to accomplish with their selections. They're keeping out the most experienced people and skewing the gender ratio with their current practices."

"I know," Jasper said, "and it will have to end when the system ferry is finished but Jake couldn't wait. He'd worked too long to get on the list."

"You know for certain it was blackmail?" Harold asked. "And this Baxter?"

"We know it was blackmail and we've put Baxter on the scene. Edward Kucera apparently was not involved but hiding something else. I had to let that go to concentrate on the case. I didn't know him but two others involved in the same secret were Professor Nugent and Mike West."

"West?" Harold stopped writing. "David's brother?"

"Yes," Jasper said, "and David doesn't know what it was. We did figure out Mike was the primary target because of his work on some new inspection systems. David was also targeted because he was part owner of the company that made them. The maker of the systems died in a fire at his factory so we're pretty certain there's something there to follow up on. David has the West Foundation looking into that."

"That sounds reasonable," Harold said. "Thought you might like to ask someone about this." He handed the paper to Jasper. "Those transmitters should be hard to get and finding out how Baxter got one should be interesting. The best way is try to buy one."

"Good point," Jasper said. "That sounds like something CIA should do."

"Yes," Harold said. "The other question I had is whether Baxter was married. His family might give him help."

"True," Jasper said. "I did check his status when we started this. He's never been married. He could have other relatives though. If one is in Denver, it might explain where he is. Thanks."

"No problem," Harold said. "Hopefully what you did today will protect the farm but just in case, we'll keep the dogs out. That barn you're using, by the way, has locks on the outside doors. If someone manages to get through the lock on the outside, there's another inside. When you decide you want one, we'll see that you get a dog too."

"Thanks," Jasper said. "And thanks for sitting in—both of you." He wasn't sure he wanted a dog demanding attention but he knew they were the best security. Butler was good but he couldn't stop an intruder.

"I'll see you after lunch," Harold said. "Don't forget I have dessert."

Jasper waited till they had gone then put Harold's note where he could see it. When they got done with the formalities, he'd pass that on to Carlson.

The circle was gradually closing. Blister wasn't his concern now that the factory had been located and blissex was less of a concern with Kin Koasa's tips. Once the winery was found, blissex might actually be stopped for a while. He wondered if Baxter owned that or Wilson Kucera. He would like to be able to tie Wilson Kucera into this but was beginning to have doubts. He'd been too cooperative.

So Ed Kucera was too honest to cheat at cards? That fit with other criticisms he'd heard about the man's legal career. He'd been a lawyer but had specialized in lobbying and civil law. He had steered clear of criminal and corporate law. He should have noted that before.

Well, he'd go find Jewel and see what kind of lunch the leftovers would be. This afternoon they had legal matters to settle and tonight he might be able to play.

* * *

There was a dog in the commons now and Jewel had found it. Jasper watched as his wife petted and scratched the dog behind his ears and the dog, eyes closed, seemed to be in heaven. Taking another bite of his turkey sandwich, he could empathize with that dog. It was really hard to ignore Jewel when she was affectionate.

"What's the name of that one?" Jasper asked after washing down the bite.

"That's one of Jim's," Harold said. "Tango. Now that they aren't shying away from that transmitter, you'll see more of the dogs. We kept them out of the commons so they wouldn't get the wrong idea about Jewel."

"Thanks," Jasper said. "I had wondered about that."

"It's not our practice to have them everywhere anyway," Harold said. "They're security first and child minders second. I can't tell you how many times they've kept the toddlers out of trouble."

Jasper doubted that and must have looked it because Harold continued.

"We don't allow them to breed except for two cattle dogs that are worth their weight in gold. The rest are all fixed so they tend to look on our babies as their babies and they're very protective. I'll tell you I will always be thankful to a dog I named Beau for pulling Jim out of an irrigation ditch fifty some years ago. We still have Jim and Beau lived a very long life."

Jasper shot a look at Jim who was nursing a cup of coffee with the remains of his meal in front of him.

"You'll hear that story a lot," Jim said. "But dogs are important here. We tolerate the cats and they tolerate us but the dogs work."

"Where do you get them?" Jasper asked. "Other farms?"

"Some," Jim said. "There's still a lot of dogs in the old towns and there are still shelters. When we need more, we go there. There are usually some fair-sized dogs going begging. Hairy was one of those and so was Tango—cute little puppies that got too big."

"Any little dogs?" Jasper asked.

"Yappers?" Jim grinned. "Just one. We got a poodle mix to help work rabbits but the rabbits beat up on him. Totally useless. Aunt Ruby keeps him. He's got nerve around other dogs and cats but rabbits scare the hell out of him."

"I can't imagine rabbits beating up a dog," Jasper said.

"Believe it," Jim said. "A proddy rabbit can be vicious to anything close to its size. The one that got him was a sow with a litter and she took a chunk out of him. Animal mothers don't hesitate to protect their young."

"Neither do human mothers," Jasper said. "My experience anyway."

"Here too," Jim said. "Especially with first borns. They get over-protective. Molly has had enough kids that as soon as Anton was talking and trotting, she let him start preschool. The kid is that smart."

"I heard," Jasper said. "I haven't really talked to him yet though." He'd noticed Anton more than most of the kids because he seemed confident and serious.

A speaker on the sidebar suddenly crackled to life and Jasper heard the voice of the farm's young secretary. "We have a visitor for Jasper Stone at the business office. She says her name is Mary."

"Mary?" Harold Fletcher reached for a control.

Before Jasper could react, Jim Talbot was on his feet. A piercing whistle left his lips and the dog at Jewel's feet leapt to attention and dashed away toward the business office with his master. Another dog Jasper hadn't even seen appeared from nowhere.

"Mary who?" Harold was asking.

Jasper thought of Mary Perkins but she wouldn't know where they were unless.... "Mary!"

He dashed after Jim, catching up with him at the doors of the business office.

"Wrong Mary," he said with a look at Jim's grim face. The dogs were wary too and the one he'd just seen his wife petting actually growled at him.

"You're sure?" Jim glared at him, not relaxing. "That's my daughter."

"Mary Wood is my publisher's secretary. She was going to bring the core of my music system," Jasper hurriedly explained. "Fenton told me."

Jim took a deep breath and clicked his fingers. "Heel," he said to the dogs and they obeyed with well-ordered precision, not relaxing but obedient.

Jasper hesitated only a moment at the top of the stairs. Seeing the familiar Mary and a man who must be her husband, he came forward. "Mary, I'm glad you could make it."

Her eyes went past him to Jim and the dogs and her smile was a little uneasy. "I think I'm glad you're here," she said. "My husband Jack."

"Hello Jack," Jasper said and tried to hide his relief that it wasn't Mary Perkins and he had managed to stop Jim and the dogs. What would they have done?

"It's a little tense here," Jasper said by way of explanation as Jack's eyes went to the dogs.

"I'll say," Jack responded. "I wanted to thank you for that dinner at the Lantern."

"You're welcome," Jasper said. "This is Jim Talbot, Crops Manager. His daughter is the secretary."

"Hold on," Jim walked over to his daughter's desk and flipped a switch. "Harold, it's ok. Another Mary."

"Another Mary?" Mary's eyes flew to Jasper's and she managed a smile. "Don't tell me you're two-timing me."

A ripple of humor went through the room and the tension eased.

"Never," Jasper said. "The other one was going to get a rude welcome."

"I can imagine," Jack said then thrust his hand out to Jim, "Jack Woodman."

Damn, he didn't even have her last name right, Jasper thought. Well, he'd never called her anything but Mary.

"Jim Talbot," Jim repeated. "This young lady is Jaime Talbot Fletcher." He motioned to his blonde daughter who was watching it all.

"The music system?" Jasper prompted and Mary nodded. He itched to get his hands on it.

"First class delivery," Jack said. "Which of these buildings do you want it in?"

"It's better to take it through this one," Jim said. "And you're in time for an excellent lunch of leftovers and pie."

"That sounds good," Jack said. "Should I leave the car where it is?"

"Yes, it'll be fine. I'll just grab a handcart," Jim said.

"So what's been happening," Mary quietly asked as Jack followed Jim.

"There's still an assassin out there named Mary Perkins," Jasper told her. "We were discussing her less than an hour ago and..." he managed a smile. "Timing. I knew you were coming and failed to mention it. Sorry." He gave her a hug.

"You'd better watch out for Jack," she said when she'd returned it. "He knows you are my absolutely favorite musician. I have to keep mentioning Jewel—I have orders to see her by the way."

"You will," Jasper said. "And she's pregnant."

Mary looked sternly at him but couldn't hide her smile. "You are the most. Not even assassins and deadlines can keep you from..."

"Not cats, either," Jasper added. "Or drums."

Jim wheeled the music system past him and Jasper noted it was packed up tight in a shipping box and marked fragile. It had been opened so Milt had probably had his techs check it out before sending it on. Soon he'd have his complete system up and running again.

The situation hadn't totally eased. Before they went down, Jim told his daughter to use the electronic lock and ordered one of the dogs to stay with her. The rest of them crowded into the freight elevator.

"Pumpkin, cherry, strawberry-rhubarb, apple, pecan, mincemeat, and peanut butter," Jasper quoted from memory as the elevator opened. "Your choice but the peanut butter might be all gone."

"So is the apple," Jim said. "It always goes first no matter how many they bake."

"A la mode?" Mary asked.

"Can be done," Jim said, finally smiling. "I'll go park this in the lane and we'll finish lunch."

Seeing the legal forms got delayed while they ate then delivered the music system to the makeshift studio. After that Jewel and Mary went off someplace and Jasper found himself talking to Jack. The couple were headed up to St. Paul to see some show. Jasper would have liked them to stay but he also wanted to spend the evening with his system. As it was, it was likely to be after dinner before they got to the forms. Since Harold was keeping him and Jack company, that wasn't a problem.

"I'm ready," Mary said as she and Jewel came back. "I have a vid of Jewel to show to Mr. Anderson and I've petted the cat."

"The cat?" Jasper asked.

"We do have a cat," Jewel said. "He was sleeping on your pillow."

"Great. Did you dump him out?"

"No, because I think you want him in your studio. He might as well make himself useful."

"Right," Jasper said then added with a quizzical expression. "What do you feed cats?"

Harold laughed and Jewel tried to look irritated and Mary seemed amused by it all.

"We've got to go," Mary said with a glance at her husband. "It gets dark early this time of year."

"Come back any time," Harold said. "We'll keep a spot for you at the table."

"Thanks," Mary said. "It's been nice. Now where is the way out?"

Jasper grinned and motioned them to follow him. Jewel tagged along and before they'd finished their goodbyes, Harold was there.

"Jaime, let's lock down and then you can go," Harold said. "Those copies are on my desk?"

"Yes sir," Jaime said. "Triplicates as you requested. Would you like me to stay to make changes?"

"No, I can handle that. Have a good evening."

Harold turned to Jasper. "This shouldn't take long. I'm not one for legalese. Slows things down."

"Neither am I," Jasper said with some relief. Following Harold into his office, he settled himself down next to Jewel and took the mercifully thin sheaf of papers Harold handed him.

"Since we're talking a cash deal for the land and rent of the barn and apartment that knocked out a lot of nonsense. Let's see to that first."

Jasper agreed and read through the forms, only hesitating when he saw the land his studio would be built on was a ninety-nine-year lease and not an outright purchase. Reading on, he saw he'd have the option to buy it if the farm fell into financial difficulty or dissolved for some reason. The purchase price as well as the lease price were clearly stated and reasonable. Seeing they couldn't increase the purchase price after the land was improved, he decided he was okay with that. The rental of the barn was a little low in his opinion but Harold had already made it clear the barn was not needed. Rental of the apartment was more in line with what he have paid in Plains. It was still smaller than any he'd ever lived in but the one bedroom, one bath would work till their house was built.

"The scholarships?" Jasper asked as he finished the last page. "There's no mention?"

"That needs to be kept separate," Harold said. "It's very hard to put a dollar figure on something like that so it's not in there. Besides how many students you help each year will depend on you and them and can't be put on paper."

"True," Jasper said. "But let's still have it in writing that I'll help at least one per year. I'll do more if I think they're serious about going. Tuition and books and lodging included for colleges we can agree on. Do you send your kids to community colleges first?"

"We always have," Harold said. "If they need a four-year college, it's more money so they always get the basics at community colleges."

Jasper looked at his wife and saw she seemed to be in agreement. "Then I think I can sign an agreement to that effect. These," he flourished the papers he'd read, "are fine. The ninety-nine-year lease surprised me but it makes sense."

"It's the same agreement on all the houses," Harold said. "If someone moves away, we buy them out of the lease and whoever buys the house pays them for the building. Since it usually happens when someone just wants to build a bigger house, it hasn't come up often. Yours would be more difficult so I suggest you just stay here."

"If it gets built to our design, I plan to," Jasper said. He started signing and handing the pages to Jewel to add her name.

"I'll have the scholarship agreement drawn up Monday," Harold said.

"It's too late in the day to do the transfer of funds," Jasper said. "Tomorrow?"

Harold nodded. "Or Monday. We don't do business of Sunday if we can help it."

Jasper clasped his wife's hand as she finished signing. "It'll be good to get settled. Sometime in the next month I'm going to get people in to remove all but a few pieces of furniture from Lily Street. I want it stored closer to hand."

"The barn is big enough," Harold said. "And now it's yours."

Jewel smiled a little uncertainly but Jasper had no qualms about being here. It felt right. The city was good but with Lori gone he just didn't want to go back. This was home now.

Chapter 53 - Saturday, 27 Nov

Jewel was running from a shadowy figure and he was trying to catch up but there was a long chain holding him back. He fought it, yanking at the chain around his wrist, until his hand bled and it let go. Yelling for Jewel to run toward him, he almost reached her when his com unit buzzed and jarred him out of the dream.

God, he hated those nightmares. Sitting up abruptly, he reached for his com unit. His body was clammy with sweat and his heart pounded. Taking a deep breath, he cleared his throat and answered. "Stone here."

"David," a male voice answered. "You need to come to Denver. Melody is in the hospital."

"Melody?" His voice cracked. "Mel? In the hospital?" He fought off the last vestiges of his dream and felt Jewel stir behind him. "Why?"

"Blissex," David said and Jasper felt his blood run cold. "She's going to make it but you need to be here."

"How did it happen?" Jasper was fully awake now. Mel had taken blissex? No, there had to be some mistake. His daughter didn't even like bliss.

"Some bastards grabbed her and dragged her into a sensa den," David said, his tone almost savage. "They knifed the boy too but not badly. He'll live. Are you awake now?"

"Yeah," Jasper said, the last trace of sleep gone. "How bad is it?"

"They're keeping her in a coma until the last bliss is out of her system--to protect her brain, they said. Security at the sensa den realized something was up and got to her fast. They saved her life."

Saved her life? How much blissex did she get? Blissex was seven times stronger than the legal dose of bliss but still within tolerance range for most people. Those who overdosed on it were usually using more.

"Look, there's an eight o'clock flight from Minneapolis to Denver with seats available," David said. "The next flight doesn't have any and the Foundation can't get a jet there sooner than that eight o'clock. You need to make that one."

"I'll be on it," Jasper said. "What time is it now?"

Jewel was awake now and taking in every word. Damn, it would have been better to let her sleep.

"Five o'clock your time. Can you get to the airport ok? I don't know when people start moving there."

"That doesn't matter," Jasper said. "If I have to drive myself, I'll be on that plane." He was already pulling on clothes. "You're sure she'll make it?"

"That's what they're telling me," David said. "It happened right after the concert got out. There were plenty of people around too. It shouldn't have happened." His voice was savage.

Jasper wasn't sure what to say. He knew Mel should have been safe but the icy fear in his gut kept asking why and he didn't like the answers he was coming up with. "Can you call Jameson, Denver PD? Tell him Mel is my daughter. This... this could be connected."

It was quiet on the other end then David answered. "I'll do that. Corey said he heard someone say 'Melody Stone?' and Mel turned. That's when it happened."

Jasper felt the knife twist in his gut. Melody Stone, not Melody Munson. His daughter used her mother's name. Someone knew she was his daughter and he felt certain it was Baxter. This was why he wanted her out of Plains.

"Call Jameson," he repeated. "I'll call Carlson. Is Elinor with you at the hospital?"

"No, I wouldn't let her come," David said. "She might divorce me over this."

"I'll come alone," Jasper said and heard a protest from Jewel. Turning, he saw she was half-dressed already and frowned. "I have to go. I'll be on that plane."

"Not without me, you won't," Jewel said, her eyes blazing. "Mel is my family too. If you think I'm going to sit back tamely and wait for news, you have another think coming."

"It's not safe," Jasper said. "You have to think of our baby."

"Screw it," she said. "He's not going anywhere. I have to think of his sister and you're wasting time. We have to wake Kale."

She was grabbing her lavender suitcase and packing clothes for both of them. "Call him," she repeated. "I'll pack."

Realizing he couldn't fight her and still get ready, he did as ordered.

* * *

There were no reporters at the Denver hospital when the limo let them out at the emergency room entrance.

David West was waiting, his tired face cracking into a smile as he counted the entourage. Jasper knew it was getting ridiculous but he'd lost the battle to leave Jewel behind so Molly had to come. Kale was necessary but Ivan had insisted on coming as well. He'd pointed out that someone had to spell Kale and he wanted to see Mel safe too.

"Ivan and Molly," David said after hugging his niece. "I think I'd better let Elinor come over now. She probably didn't sleep last night anyway."

"How bad is it?" Jasper asked as they walked down the hall. "And who is with her now?"

"The hospital increased security at Jameson's request and he's with her himself. So is Corey. I requested and got a private nurse," David said. "She's a long time Denverite."

"Good," Jasper said, remembering Mary Perkins. "How bad is it?"

"They think she'll be okay," David said. "Her brain activity is nearly normal now and the blood samples are almost clean. They'll probably let her wake up in a couple more hours."

Jasper hesitated. If this had happened right after the concert, that would have placed it before midnight and they were still keeping her under? Bliss was designed to wear off with no traces after five hours. Keeping her under this long told him it was more than just a normal dose or they had another concern.

"How soon can I talk to the doctor?" he finally asked.

"He'll be back," David said. "You need to talk to the security guy who saved her. He saw the men. There's no vid from inside the sensa den but he went to check the vid of people entering. Corey got stopped at the door–he was bleeding pretty bad–but Mel and those that grabbed her were already in."

"How is Corey?" Jewel asked, her face pale.

"He'll be okay. They slashed his arm. He bled a lot but he wasn't down till after the ambulance got there. As soon as they patched him up, he insisted on being with Mel." David turned to Jasper. "He's pretty torn up about this, Jazz, and thinks it's his fault for using those tickets. Don't give him a hard time. I decided it would be safe for them to go."

"I know," Jasper said. "And I probably would have let them go too. Was anyone else hurt?"

"One of the other Lunarex kids–a girl–got shoved and fell. She's okay except for her pride. There was a knot of them waiting for the limo when it happened. They raised the alarm at once but they were looking at Corey's blood and didn't realize Mel had been taken until Corey fought them off and chased the men down."

Mel–Melody was stretched out on the bed, her head enclosed by a sensor helmet and an IV in one arm. Her eyes were closed and her face relaxed in sleep but she looked too peaceful. A smile lingered on her lips but it seemed frozen, and Jasper didn't like it. He knew what his daughter looked like asleep. He'd seen her frowns, her smiles, and had even heard her talking in her sleep long into adolescence. She wasn't a peaceful sleeper.

He took a deep breath and looked around. Corey met his eyes and looked away. Jasper noted the taped arm and knew he would recover from the physical hurt. The memory wouldn't go away though. They never did.

Nodding to Jameson, he moved to Corey first. "You did good," Jasper said. Giving him a manly hug, he blinked back tears and took the chair Corey vacated for him. Mel's hand was warm but not unnaturally so. She flexed her fingers in his and he found that comforting. Maybe she knew he was there.

Molly was already reading the doctor's report, her lips pursed as she studied it then put the electronic chart back in its place. "It looks good," she said. "I don't know what that much bliss will do but they started treatment within minutes. Keeping her out longer is just a precaution."

"There were two of them," Corey said. "When the younger one said Melody Stone, Mel turned. I grabbed her arm then this," he motioned to his bandaged arm. "I didn't even see the old man until he did it."

"Old man? How old?" Jasper asked.

"He had a white beard," Corey said, "but I think it was fake. No, I know it was. It was too long to be real. That's all I saw of him though."

Jasper knew that tactic and knew he'd have a hard time identifying a bearded man who wasn't normally bearded. "What about the younger man? Was he disguised?"

"He had a sword glower on one cheek and a spray of stars on the other," Corey said.

"What color were his eyes?" Jasper asked. "And skin color? Close your eyes and think about it."

"Brown eyes," Corey said without blinking. "And he was tanned. I think he lived above ground–natural tan. Those glowers are going to make it hard to identify him, aren't they?"

"Yes, they will. He'll be caught though. He won't get another chance at Mel."

"Why do they even allow glowers?" Corey asked, his voice savage. "They..." He broke off to take a ragged breath. "I'm sorry," he said in a voice cracking with misery.

"It's not your fault," Jasper said. "Not David's fault either. It's mine." He knew that wasn't exactly true but he'd been a fool to think Baxter wouldn't find his daughter. Mel had been in his wedding party–and was that how he'd found the Kowalskis? No, he'd had their phone number and that could only have come from Jewel's com unit. They'd had it a little more than two hours before it was found but that was time enough to crack the codes and download her address book.

It had taken Kin less time to crack his codes on the com units he'd examined. He hadn't got more than David's phone number off his though. He'd deleted Mel's and Molly's. Yes, it had to be Jewel's and he should have thought of that–and the wedding.

He couldn't have kept Mel out of his wedding. His jaw clenched as he thought about that. Nothing, absolutely nothing, would keep his daughter safe now. Until Baxter was caught, she would have to go to the farm and the hell with her finals.

"They gave her a second dose of sleeper about three hours ago," Molly said. "That has to wear off naturally. It might two or three more hours since she had another dose in her system so we have time to eat. I'll stay here with the nurse. Jasper, why don't you and David and Corey grab a bite and talk it out with the detective? Ivan, I need some coffee and a sandwich. Jewel and Kale can stay here."

"Yes, Molly," Ivan said. "Jewel, what would you like? Kale?"

Jasper knew better than to argue with Molly when she took charge and he needed to know more. Following Ivan out, he found himself waiting for direction but Jameson wasn't inclined to go far. Taking them to the nearest seating area, he motioned for them to sit.

"I expect that security man to be back shortly," Jameson said. "Along with my partner. People are pretty upset about this already. It isn't often that a rich kid gets abducted off such a public street."

"Have the press identified her?" Jasper asked.

"Only as Melody Munson," Jameson said. "No one knows she's yours yet except for the two men who took her. I take it the Lunarex crowd just knew she was a friend of David's?"

"Yes," David said. "I wasn't broadcasting it and Mel goes by Munson. I'm surprised she even reacted to Stone." He glanced at Jasper.

Jasper was surprised too. And she didn't go by Melody. Why had she betrayed herself that way? After her mother's death, she'd sworn she would never be Melody Stone. It was only in the past five months that she had been willing to talk to him alone and he knew Corey was the reason.

"Did the street cameras pick up anything?" Jasper asked.

"The closest one was painted," Jameson said. "Another one had its feed scrambled. The last one was too far away and at the wrong angle to get much. Sensa dens aren't allowed cameras on their floors so we knew we couldn't get that but I wasn't aware until today that some have cameras in their lobbies. I don't think they make that public."

"Probably not," Jasper said. "But I can see why." Few kids who overdosed on blissex did it outside of a sensa den. Hungry for thrills, they wanted the full effect of the combination of sensa music and blissex. Since the equipment to produce sensa on more than the audible levels was really expensive, few owned private setups.

Cameras were prohibited in sensa dens because of the uninhibited antics of the seekers. Most were only in their twenties but they were likely to grow up to be executives and managers and bankers. The last thing their families wanted was vid cropping up of their beloved children in the throes of a bliss addiction. The sensa dens employed security to keep things under control and shuttle those out of control to private, insulated rooms to settle down. Blissex was a thorn in their side too. Under normal doses of bliss, users didn't lose all control. They danced themselves to a frenzy or sat and cried at the sheer beauty of the music or laughed themselves silly at nothing but they didn't try to have sex in a crowded room or start punching people.

Was that what they were trying to get Mel to do? Women responded sexually to bliss. Men couldn't. No, if they'd forced Mel to take blissex, they must have intended to kill her. It was a message for him and he knew it.

"Do you know how much they fed her?" he asked, his voice harsh. "It couldn't be just one."

Jameson's jaw set. "There were the remnants of two chews in her spew," he said. "They're still being tested but were probably blissex. That's fourteen times the legal dose and about four levels over the maximum. If the lab tests bear that out, they'll be charged with attempted murder as well as assault."

David didn't look surprised but Corey looked sick. Jasper had heard it before. Almost every accidental overdose case he'd ever investigated had similar levels. Always a rich kid and some had no prior history—like Mel. The only difference is she'd been forced not by friends but strangers she didn't know.

"One of the things that saved her was she didn't chew them up. At least half the drug was still trapped in the cake," Jameson said. "The other thing that saved her was the security at the Heaven's Gate. They'd had a couple of deaths there before so their security was well trained and they had a full triage closet. As soon as Snyder saw your daughter knee the young guy in the nuts, he was there. The other guy had her in an arm lock but let go as soon as he was challenged and stepped away. Mel tried to say something, couldn't, and he whisked her away to the closet."

"She kicked him in the nuts?" Corey asked before Jasper could.

"That's what he said," Jameson reported with just a trace of smile. "Any girl who does that is not in the mood but her eyes were dilated and she looked scared. He took care of it."

"Standard treatment?" Jasper asked but he was glad Mel had fought.

"Yes. He induced vomiting, gave her an oral antidote then—here he is." Jameson rose quickly to his feet and waved a sturdy body builder type over. The man carried a folder.

"Lance Snyder," Jameson said by way of introduction. "This is Jazz Stone, the girl's father, and Corey Morales, David West."

"I met West last night," the security guard said. "And saw him," he said with a look at Corey. "So she's your daughter?"

"Yes," Jasper said. "What can you tell me?"

"She wasn't there because she wanted to be," Lance responded. "Look at these." He opened the folder and laid out two large pics on the table. "This young guy had her by the hand going through the gates but she was pulling back. Her arm's too taut. This other guy didn't look like he was pushing but I bet he was."

Jasper caught his breath. No beard but a jaw line swirl of color that extended down to his chin. His smile was wide but didn't reach his light blue eyes. What had caught Jasper's attention was the small round disk in his earlobe. Baxter!

"Corey," he managed to say without giving anything away, "could this be your man with the beard?"

Corey studied the picture but didn't touch it. "I can't say. I didn't get a good look at him. The shirt's the same color but—I just don't know."

"If he was wearing a full beard, it would have covered those glowers," David said. "Disguise on top of disguise."

"It doesn't matter," Jasper said. "I've seen him in a stealth mask too. I have vid of him in my house when he returned Jewel. He bid against me at a Reach Out event too. That's Mark Baxter of Wilson Chemicals and there's an APB out on him already."

Jameson grabbed the picture and studied it. "Baxter? How can you tell?"

"Eyes are the same and this earring." Jasper pointed to it, his voice cold. "He never takes it off and never disguises it. That's how I identified him in the first place but voice print analysis backs it up."

"I can testify he was holding the girl," the security man said. "And she kneed the young guy. He had a cut lip too. She might have bitten him."

"That helps," Jameson said. "And these pictures really help. He will probably lose the glowers but there could be people out there who have seen him with and without. Baxter is the deadly one though. Did Wilson Chemicals turn him loose?"

"Yes," Jasper said. "Officially. They could be after him too."

"Then he won't have a lot to lose. I'm going to stick close to you. If he shows up, I want him alive." Jameson studied the pic of him. "We need some answers. DEA wants him alive, right?"

"Yes," Jasper said and saw a smile tweak the corner of Jameson's mouth. "At least that's what Carlson told me. I've been working mostly with him since this started."

"Right," Jameson said and Jasper knew he wasn't fooled. He also caught the nod toward Synder and caught the hint.

"Mr. Snyder, I appreciate everything you did for Melody," he said, rising and shaking his hand. "And the photos. I know Detective Jameson will ask you to testify if we catch those two. Would you be willing?"

"You bet. This was attempted murder and I don't ever want to see that happen at Heaven's Gate or anywhere else. Kids love their sensa but they shouldn't have to die for it."

"No, they shouldn't," Jasper said. "Keep up the good work." He wanted to offer the man a reward but knew that would compromise the case against Baxter. He'd have to warn David not to until the criminal case was done. If he knew Jewel's uncle, David would be all too willing to reward the man.

When he was gone and David and Corey started back to the room, Jameson held him back. "Let's talk," he said and led him to the men's room. After checking to be sure no one else was there, Jameson turned to him. "Do you know what we have?"

Jasper studied him, unsure what he meant but Jameson barely hesitated. "If we can prove your daughter went in there unwillingly then I've got what I need to re-open a half dozen cases I'm not happy with—rich kids with no prior record of bliss use who suddenly turned up dead in sensa dens and one in a dorm room. I've never been happy telling parents that their son or daughter was an idiot, especially when the parent was a federal judge or senator."

Jasper stared at him. "You think they were forced?" He had two such cases that he could recall. One had been early in his career but the other— was the kid's name Low? Lori had been the primary on that case, not him. Low or Lowe? Damn, had he missed something else?

"There's another in Plains," Jasper said. "Kid named Low. I'll have to ask Captain Reynolds but if his father is who I think he is, he worked with Mike West."

"Another connection?" Jameson asked.

"I'm not sure. It wasn't my case and I'm not even sure of the dates. It was more than two years ago because Carol was still alive." Yes, he could remember Lori talking to Carol about it as much as him. Neither one could understand why someone who was getting top marks in school had suddenly done that. He was underage too, and shouldn't even have been in a sensa den. Damn, he knew several Reach Out members had lost children to blissex. Hadn't Gordon?

"There's another possible connection," he said. "Maybe strange, maybe not. Do you know about the Reach Out charity?"

"Yes," Jameson said. "Weren't West and Kucera both members?"

"Yes, and Nugent too," Jasper said. "But I understand some of the members lost children to Blissex. I'm not sure how many. There's an awful lot of money going through that charity. You might want to take a special look at it–and Baxter is a member."

Jameson's lips pursed. "Should this be federal? Reach Out is big."

"I know," Jasper said. "I've recently become a member too, and Jewel's been one for years. It might be worth checking out. I'll help if I can but I'm leaving DEA after this case."

"I thought you might," Jameson said. "And it's a shame about Brown. I'm sorry I couldn't get there for the funeral."

"Business," Jasper said. "And I really couldn't tell you who was there. I was barely functioning at that point."

"Understandable," Jameson said. "And now this. Baxter is one mean son-of-a-bitch."

Jasper agreed, knowing Jameson didn't know everything and suddenly reluctant to talk about it. He just wanted to get back to Mel. "I've got to get back. I'll make sure you have a contact number for me before we leave town."

Chapter 54 - Melody

Jasper closed his eyes and rested his head against the high-backed couch and tried not to think of everything he could be doing in his new studio. He'd barely started playing last night, most of his time being taken up with calibrating the system and balancing the speakers. Jewel had been with him and he'd played trumpets, bugles, and some of the odder sounds he'd collected over the years. It had been fun but made for a late night and a very early morning.

A slight sound made him look up and he saw that the nurse assigned to Melody was there. What was she doing? He knew from Molly there should be no more injections and the IV bag on its stand should be the last one. Aware that Mary Perkins was still out there somewhere, he watched as the nurse removed the sensor helmet and hung it on a stand then proceeded to remove the IV. Jewel got up and watched her closely, even engaging her in conversation, and he relaxed.

He was discovering a new side to his wife. In the last couple of days she'd gotten maternal on him. Aware she was pregnant now, she had started reading books on what to expect and he'd caught her in conversation with Rachel, the newest mother on the farm. Rachel's little girl had been held, fed, and inspected thoroughly by his interested wife. Now she was being fiercely protective of Melody. Before this, she'd treated Melody more like a sister but that had changed. There was only a nine year difference in their ages–a fact Jasper still found unsettling–but he doubted Jewel would ever forget again that Melody was her stepdaughter. He wondered how Melody would cope with her changed status.

He hoped she could cope. He knew very few adults who had recovered well from a bliss overdose. Those that had were treated like Melody though. First vomiting then an antidote and lastly sedated into deep sleep to protect their brains. She'd gotten treatment much faster than most. What they'd done at the sensa den before the ambulance had got there would probably make the difference between permanent brain damage and a short recovery period.

She fought them. Jasper found himself smiling as he thought of the bitten lip and aching groin of the one attacker. He must have tried to kiss her to keep her from spitting out the bliss. Well, his daughter was a fighter and he'd gotten what he deserved.

Baxter was there. He was definitely here in Denver. He couldn't afford to forget that. Ivan and Molly were off somewhere with David and Elinor but he hadn't let Kale get far and Corey was with him. Damn, Corey needed sleep too. He should get up and insist he get some but he was reluctant to move.

"That will do it," the nurse was saying to Jewel. "She'll wake up in an hour or so. When she does, just press the call button and I'll be back. She'll want water when she does wake up."

"I can get that at the station?" Jewel asked.

"Let me get it for you," the nurse suggested.

"Let's both go," Jewel replied. "I prefer to get it. She's my stepdaughter, you know."

He didn't hear the nurse's low reply as they left the room. Knowing Kale was outside the door, he let his thoughts drift. He could almost hear the quiet of the hospital. There was a hum of equipment and he knew they'd left some of the sensors on. It was monotonous and unchanging, a background noise punctuated by Melody's sigh and even breathing. He thought of a pin drop and it became a tiny bell against the hum of the equipment.

The buzz of his com unit broke the quiet and he slapped at it, abruptly awake. Catching hold of it, he glanced once at the number and frowned. Who had told Milt about the hospital? He hadn't. Answering the call, he tried to keep his voice low. "Yes, Milt?"

"Did I wake you?" Milt asked.

"No, well, dozing," Jasper said. "Mel isn't awake yet."

"Mel?" Milt sounded confused. "Your daughter?"

"Never mind," Jasper said. "I got the equipment and my studio is set up again. I spent last night calibrating it. What's up?"

"Mary called me about a new piece you'd written and she has. She said it's wonderful and we need to get it released but you might have a problem with it. What is it about your requiem?"

"My requiem?" Jasper's thoughts stopped then he put it together. Jewel had dragged Mary off yesterday. She'd given her the requiem? He should be angry but he couldn't seem to find the energy just now.

"That's what she called it. She listened to it last night then again this morning before she called me. Now what's the problem? Is it an original piece? She said it was very polished and quite beautiful."

"I wrote it for Carol," Jasper said. "It was the last thing she heard."

Dead silence but it only lasted a few seconds. "Okay, I'll sit on it. I just want you to know Mary has it and she thinks it should be released. Let me know what you decide."

"Thanks," Jasper said. "I'll get back to you next week. Right now I need to concentrate on my family."

"What's going on?" Milt asked.

"I'll tell you later," Jasper said. "Right now I'm just waiting for Mel to wake up."

"Okay," his college friend said. "Get some sleep. You sound like you've been up all night."

"Not quite," Jasper said and ended the call.

Jewel had gone behind his back and handed the Requiem off to Mary. Was it the original or a copy? He didn't want to lose that flasher. Even though he hadn't bothered to listen to it again, he knew that someday it would have to be published so it wouldn't be lost. He'd poured too much of his soul into that piece to have that happen.

Why wasn't he angry? He should be. It was Carol's Requiem. Jewel had no right to do that. Hell, he couldn't care—not right now. He just wanted Mel to wake up and be all right. He'd think about the Requiem later. Jewel should be spanked though. The thought made his thin lips curve into a smile. She'd like that. Maybe he should send her to her room alone like Molly suggested. Not now though. Jewel was guarding her stepdaughter. She wouldn't think it was funny. Considering his options, he dozed off.

"Dad?" It was Mel's voice that brought him to full alertness. Soft and husky, it cracked of dryness but it was her voice and she–she was looking at him! Sometime in the last hour she'd turned on her side and now she was looking at him, her brown eyes open and aware.

Jasper was by her side instantly, half kneeling beside her bed to put his eyes on a level with her head. He could hear Jewel's murmured exclamation on the other side.

"Mel," he said, trying to keep his voice even. "How are you feeling? Still got all your fingers and toes?"

She smiled and obediently wiggled the fingers on her visible hand. "Still got my parts," she said but her smile wavered and broke. "Dad, I..." She didn't get anything else out before the sobs came. Jasper held her and she clung to him, letting out a torrent of apologies for being dumb and bringing him back in between tears.

Jasper blinked back his own tears, sure this was normal and silently thanking God his daughter didn't have that vacant smile he'd seen in others. He wasn't catching half of what she was saying but she was saying a lot about how dumb she'd been and how sorry she was. Damn, he should record this. He would never get this again.

"You're soaking me," he finally said to stem the flow of tears. "Jewel's here. C'mon, dry those tears. You're safe." When that didn't work, he motioned to Jewel. She had a water cup in her hand with straw.

"Corey's here and we've had to hire a bodyguard to keep him out," Jewel said. "I don't think it'll work much longer. Should I let him in?"

Mel shook her head and buried her face deeper into his shoulder. "I'm a mess," she said but the words were muffled.

Jasper chuckled with relief and Jewel glared at him.

"We have to let him in," Jewel said. "And you need water. And here's Molly and the nurse," she added as the two women came in.

In the next minute Jasper found himself extracted and shoved out the door as the women took charge. All the men were gathered around with Corey anxiously trying to glimpse inside but the door was firmly shut in his face.

"How is she?" Ivan asked, his eyes going from Jasper's shoulder to his face then his own face relaxed. "That good?"

"She's awake, apologizing for being a bother, crying, and wanting to clean up before she sees Corey," Jasper said. "Elinor, you'd better get in there and help out. She's going to want to see you too."

David's wife smiled and slipped in the door. No doubt they'd get his daughter presentable, maybe even with makeup, before anyone else was allowed in. He didn't care. His daughter was ok. It finally hit him that Mel was going to be okay and he sagged with relief. David was there but he wasn't that bad. Straightening up, he wiped his face with the handkerchief David handed him and smiled at Corey.

"It's looking good," he said. "She knew me and she cried. I don't think she's got brain damage. It bothers me though that I got such a long profuse apology. That's not Mel." He couldn't help grinning. "I should have recorded it."

David snorted and Kale laughed. He could see Corey's disbelief then he smiled too. It was a very shaky smile and he knew the kid wouldn't relax until he saw for himself. How long were they going to take in there?

The nurse came out again with a reassuring smile. "I'm off to tell the doctor," she said. "It looks very good. She's weepy but that's a wonderful sign. As soon as they get her presentable, you can go in," she said to Corey. "She doesn't want you to see bed hair and tears."

Corey's soundless word of protest amused Jasper. Somehow he thought Corey had seen those before. They'd been living in the same house, if not the same bedroom, for weeks.

His daughter was vain. Hell, if she hadn't cared what she looked like, that would have worried him. No, Mel was going to be all right. He'd have to let that security man know.

"You need coffee," David said and led the way to a group of waiting chairs. There was an insulated carafe and some real cups there. He took the one David offered and sipped cautiously, his smile widening as he recognized good Aruba coffee. This was no hospital coffee.

"Elinor," David said. "She insisted on bringing it. There's plenty so drink up. Corey, get yourself another cup and take one to Kale."

"Yes sir," Corey looked relieved to be going back.

As soon as he was out of earshot, David's voice got lower so only he and Ivan could hear. "Is she really going to be ok?"

"I think so," Jasper said and took a deep breath. "I've seen damaged bliss patients a few times. They're slow to recognize people and they're..." he groped for the right word, "vacant. It's like they're only half there. Mel recognized me and cried up a storm. She's quite definitely there and reacting."

"Good," David said and took a long drink of coffee. "Now if she'd forget to call me a great uncle."

Jasper laughed. "But you are," he said and grinned at Ivan's blank look. "You're the best uncle she could have. We're damned lucky to be part of your family. Ivan's too."

"Great uncle?" Ivan asked then his face cracked into a smile as he put it together. "Yes, you are."

David glared at him and Ivan subsided but his grin stayed. Jasper realized that there wasn't more than five years difference in their ages with Ivan being the elder so he'd know how much being called a great uncle would rankle David. He wondered how pleased Ivan would be when one of his children made him a grandfather. Delighted, he guessed. Although it looked like it wouldn't be soon. His second son would get married next summer if all went well. He hoped Sasha wouldn't have the first grandchild. Ivan would never get to see that one and neither would David.

That was a sobering thought. With a baby of his own on the way, Jasper was more aware how hard it would be for a father or grandfather not to be able to see the child and spoil them. Sasha had petitioned for the right to have Jake's children on Mars and won, it being completely uncontested by David and Jewel and the West Foundation. There would be grandchildren for both men that they would never have a hope of seeing since the children couldn't adapt to Earth.

He was glad not to have that problem. There was always a chance his grown children would want to immigrate but that wasn't today's worry. Mel wouldn't go and his son was still safely tucked in Jewel's womb.

"They let him in," David said with his eyes on Mel's door. "Should we wait a couple more minutes?"

"Yes," Jasper replied. "I think those two would make a good match."

"I wondered if you approved," Ivan said. "He's a smart one and he's got guts–keeps his head too. Good breeding stock."

"He looks good too," Jasper added then remembered something he'd heard at the dinner table. "Nice conformation, healthy. Good color."

David looked startled but Ivan grinned. "We'll make a farmer out of you yet."

Jasper shrugged. "I'm learning the language at least."

"That's the best we can hope for," Ivan said. "I won't mess with your music and you won't mess with my cattle."

"Deal," Jasper said and smiled again. He had his place on the farm but it wasn't with animals. His produce would be something else again.

How soon would Mel be released? He was going to take her back with him.

"Let's go," Jasper said and set down his cup. "I think that's the doctor." He eyed the man accompanying the nurse and rose to his feet. "I want to be there."

They all crammed into the room, including Kale, and took places along the walls as the doctor continued his examination. He barely glanced at them as he asked Mel to wiggle toes, touch her fingers to her nose and answer a couple of simple math questions.

Mel played along until he asked her to complete a rhyme. "Jack be nimble, Jack be quick. Jack jump over the ...."

"Candlestick," Mel said. "He wasn't. He burnt his britches and ended up in the hospital and that's why you don't play with fire."

The doctor looked at her in surprise then smiled. "I hadn't heard that one."

"It wasn't just his britches that burnt," Melody said with a grin. "Dad didn't tell me that part."

The doctor chuckled then glanced around. "Ok, who are the parents?" He was looking at Molly and Ivan when Jewel stepped forward.

"I'm her stepmother," she said.

Jasper motioned with his hand. "And I remember raising her and teaching her not to play with fire." He hadn't expected Mel to remember that one.

The doctor motioned them out the door and Molly followed.

"Our own resident medic," Jasper said by way of introduction. "P. A. Molly Kowalski."

The doctor hesitated only an instant then handed over Mel's chart for her to look at. "She seems to be fine," he said. "No physical problem noted and her logic and memory seems to be ok. The nurse said she cried?"

"Yes sir," Molly said. "And insisted on cleaning up before seeing the boyfriend."

"That's healthy," the doctor said. "I have no problem releasing her this afternoon but that's contingent on your evaluation. Get her up and dressed then walking the hall. If she wobbles or has trouble in anyway, the release is revoked. Got that, Ms. Kowalski?"

"Yes sir," she said.

"I don't expect trouble," he said to Jasper, "but I also don't like Murphy. She got first class triage and I have to admit I'm impressed with that sensa den and their security. They patched up the young fellow too. I think he's already been released even though he's still here."

"Yes sir," Molly said. "I've seen his records too."

"Good. Well, since you've got capable care, I'll be on my way. It's good to meet you two." And he was gone.

"How do you like that?" Jewel said. "Did he even know who we were?"

"He knows you're the wicked stepmother," Jasper said, relaxing and giving his wife a smile.

"I am not wicked," Jewel protested then color filled her cheeks and she unaccountably frowned at him. "Not now."

Molly wisely ignored them and went back into the room.

"No, not now," Jasper agreed but his smile didn't quite leave. "Not in front of the kids." He went in to hear the official news and to give his daughter a hug before he got shoved out again with all the other men.

Chapter 55 - Gordon

"You're going to need an architect," David said as Corey and Ivan left them to find a vending machine. "The firm that designed the house in Plains is gone but Mother owned those plans and they're stored somewhere. If those won't work, the West Foundation has dug up a few recommendations to pass on to you. Copy it?"

"Sure," Jasper said and touched his com unit to David's. The file transfer complete, he barely glanced at it before saving. "Thanks. Do you always use scotch when persuading?"

"Nope," David said. "I had to convince Elinor without it." His smile faded. "She could have used some scotch just then."

"It's a good thing you're a fast talker. I might need you to back me about taking Melody back to the farm. If she can remember nursery rhymes, she'll want to stay for finals and I'm not going to allow that."

"I'm sure the college will cooperate with remote testing," David said.
"True."

"What about Corey?" David asked. "I understand he's assisting."

"I know," Jasper said. "No, he'll have to make that decision for himself." Jasper could see the length of the hall to the elevators and noticed a man who seemed vaguely familiar. Baxter? His pulse quickened then the man turned and he knew it wasn't Baxter. When he stopped at the nurses' station, he recognized Rick Gordon and wondered what the heck the city attorney of Plains was doing in the Denver hospital.

The man looked good in a fairly expensive suit and his silvered hair was neatly trimmed. It wasn't long before a nurse pointed him down the hall to where Jasper sat.

"What's wrong?" David asked, his eyes going toward the figure. His jaw tensed. "That's not Baxter."

"No, it isn't," Jasper said. "It's someone I need to talk to."

Gordon saw him now and walked past Mel's room. He stopped a few paces away, his keen eyes taking in Kale and sizing him up before turning back to Jasper and David as they rose to their feet.

"Rick Gordon," he identified himself. "Mr. West, I was a friend of your brother's. I'm the city attorney for Plains, Wyoming."

"I didn't expect to see you here," Jasper said. "Business?"

"Yes, I'm here to talk to you since I doubt you'll return to Plains any time soon," Mr. Gordon said. "You had questions and I have answers."

"Yes," Jasper said, "is this too public?"

Gordon looked around before responding. "Far too public and we're reluctant to have it recorded. We have a room."

"Hold on," David said with a deep frown. "He's not going anywhere alone. I don't care if you're the president, it's not going to happen."

Gordon smiled so warmly that David stopped. Reaching into his breast pocket, he explained "As I said, I was a friend of Mike's–a close friend. He left this with me to be delivered at the right time. I judge that to be now." He held out an envelope addressed in big bold letters to David West.

From David's reaction, Jasper knew that had to be Mike's handwriting. David took it but his hand was none too steady. Intensely curious to know what it said, Jasper also knew it was probably private. David would tell him if he wanted him to know.

"Mr. Stone, if you want your answers, come along. You'll be returned safe," Gordon said. "I've made no secret that I'm here."

"Right," Jasper said with quick decision. "How far are we going? Inside this building?"

"Yes," Gordon said. "Your bodyguard can watch the door for us."

Jasper was willing. As Gordon said, he'd made no secret of his presence here. This was probably going to be his one chance to find out exactly what they were up to.

"I'll be back," he said to David. "Business."

David nodded, his hands already unsealing the envelope.

Jasper followed his guide, every nerve alert, as they entered the elevator and Gordon pressed the button for one of the upper floors.

"I had to shut down some inquiries," Gordon said. "You left Detective Sanders asking questions inside Plains and he was bungling it. Reynolds, fortunately, was cooperative once I explained why it should be shut down."

"I'd forgotten about Sanders," Jasper admitted. "He was drunk when I told him to go ask questions somewhere else."

"He did," Gordon said. "He's been reassigned now and Reynolds will keep an eye on him. Now as to the ground rules: I'm being joined by two men from Denver who I believe you know about. Both have impeccable reputations. There will be no refreshments and no touching since your bodyguard would have a problem with that. This meeting won't take long but I hope your curiosity will get satisfied." He paused. "There is a very pricey, very effective jammer in the room. That's something we have to insist on."

"Understood," Jasper said and handed his com unit to Kale. Two others? Dan Mushti and, he forgot the name, the deputy mayor.

"Are you sure this is safe?" Kale asked.

"Yes," Jasper said. "None of these men are connected to the case and, as Mr. Gordon said, they all have good reputations. Mike West was one of them."

Gordon smiled and Jasper knew he hadn't disappointed him. Well, it had taken time and the right questions but he'd uncovered that. Now he was going to find out exactly what he'd uncovered.

When they reached the room, Kale stepped in far enough to look around, nodded to the two men and stepped back out again. Jasper wondered if he'd recognized the athlete. If so, he did right to make no sign he did.

The room was just a small office lounge probably used for doctor and family consultations. It had two doors and a vending machine, otherwise it only boasted a table and chairs. On the table, a high-quality jammer hummed, its chrome sphere gleaming.

"Mr. Mushti," Jasper said, almost offering his hand before remembering. The former athletic star nodded and smiled. "And Mister..."

"Trace Stephens," the second man said. "Not as memorable as Dan, I'm afraid."

"But deputy mayor of Denver," Jasper said.

"Yes," he said with a slight start of surprise. "I think we were right to call this meeting after all. I withdraw my objection, Rick."

"I thought you would," Gordon said. "Mr. Stone was one of our top investigators and I wasn't too surprised to find out he left the force for a federal position. I haven't asked which agency you joined but I'm guessing it was DEA since Agent Carlson has been closely involved with the blissex investigation and the kidnapping."

"Yes sir," Jasper said and knew he shouldn't be confirming that but he would be leaving soon anyway.

Gordon just nodded. "Let's get this over with. Would you like us to explain first or do you have questions?"

Jasper thought rapidly. "One important one. Mike West was in an immense amount of pain. Was he still taking blister?"

The three looked at each other then Gordon spoke, his smile completely gone. "No, we relieved Mike of that responsibility almost two weeks before he died. He wasn't in any danger of being questioned and there was no need. Elizabeth's death might have made it necessary again but we didn't have time to discuss it."

Jasper put that piece into his puzzle and found it fit. That meeting Jewel had mentioned was probably it. So Mike might have been able to take the bliss painkillers when he went back to his doctor and he might have gotten other treatment. They didn't stop him from trying. It had bothered him that Mike was blocked from using the most effective painkillers by these people but now he was able to put that at rest.

"Mike was a valued member of our group and no one wanted to see him in pain," Gordon said. "We agreed it was acceptable risk to relieve him of blister so he could get better treatment. We didn't want to lose him any sooner than we had to."

"So you knew he was checking into euthanasia?" Jasper asked.

"Drew knew he'd asked about it. That was what sparked our meeting," Gordon said. "It wasn't a choice we wanted him to make."

"Thank you," Jasper said. "I wondered how far you'd go to protect your secrets." Jasper eyed the three of them. He'd been left on one side of the table with Gordon taking the end and the other two on the far side.

"We try hard not to ask for death but sometimes it's necessary," Trace Stephens said. "We're watchers but are sometimes called guardians. Either term is correct because we do both. Ed Kucera, Mike West, and Drew Nugent were all members of our group with Drew Nugent being our mentor. Our calling is to watch and protect humanity from itself."

"That seems like a pretty big job for such a small group," Jasper said. "I assume there are cells in other cities? Jackson von Kliburg?"

That got a reaction. All three men looked surprised but it was quickly gone. He filed that away for later.

"Yes, Jackson was one of ours," Trace Stephens replied. "He felt the only way to expose the corruption in New York was to be a target. Every other way had been tried and blocked."

"So you do more than watch?" Jasper asked.

"We block legislation that's harmful in the long run," Gordon said. "We keep an eye on interesting individuals–some dangerous and some brilliant. We make sure that others get the education they need to be useful. Lastly and most importantly, we make sure history doesn't get revised and people know it."

"Professor Nugent?" Jasper asked, surprised by that last inclusion. "It's that important?"

"Yes," Gordon said with a glance at Mushti. "Do you know how many times the government has weakened the required history curriculum? People today know almost nothing about the worst atrocities in history. It doesn't occur to most that the government could control them with drugs and promises of free food. When people sign up for euthanasia, they don't know the controls they complain about are to keep our government from abusing their right to live. Hell, there's not one teenager in a hundred who can identify Adolf Hitler or tell you what he did, much less _how_ he did it."

"They don't know about the prison purges of 2038 either," Dan Mushti added. "Every prisoner sentenced to death or life imprisonment was forced to take euthanasia. Nursing homes and mental hospitals were emptied the same way. It was one hell of a way to balance the federal budget."

Jasper met his eyes and saw he was serious. He'd heard about the purges but he hadn't heard about them in school. Was that because he cut that class or because they didn't teach it?

"So history is important," he slowly said. "Is it absolutely necessary your people take blister? What would happen if people found out about you? Nothing you've mentioned has been illegal."

"It's necessary to keep it private," Trace Stephens was the one who answered. "If we're known, others can block us. It wouldn't be too hard to discredit us with rumors of scandal or pump money that isn't ours into our accounts. It's too easy to shut someone up these days without killing them."

"But blister?" Jasper asked.

"We've lost access to that," Gordon said. "Your doing I think but I'm not sure. Our contact inside the plant alerted us federal agents were there. We've let others in the network know they are to conserve their supplies for when they suspect they'll be threatened. No more daily use."

"The Wilson Chemicals plane stopped there," Jasper explained. "The same plane was implicated in the abduction of my wife."

The three of them exchanged glances then Rick Gordon spoke up, his voice dry. "You're what we call a catalyst, Mr. Stone. Things happen to you and around you with alarming frequency. It may stop or it may not when you leave federal employment for your music career. I hope it does for your wife's sake."

"We considered bringing you in to our group but we can't have a catalyst–or someone who can't give his full loyalty to the cause. You're trying to serve too many masters right now between marriage, music and justice. You're also too damned visible. Mike would have liked you but even he would have voted against bringing you in—and Drew did."

Drew. Jasper shot a look at Gordon. "You know it was my mistake that got him killed? Baxter overhead us." It was a relief to finally admit that but he knew he wouldn't forget it.

"Yes," Gordon said, "my warning wasn't strong enough. We thought we had all copies of his visit to Ed destroyed. Who gave you one?"

"Detective Brown. She's dead." Jasper didn't even consider telling them she got it from Denver. He didn't want the trail leading back to Jameson. "Do you still need them destroyed? Or does it matter now?" He could recall all but the one Baxter had taken.

"It's not important now," Gordon said. "So many people know there was a connection between Ed and Drew that it can't be buried. So long as the rest of us are not connected, we won't be compromised."

"No one has learned it from me," Jasper said. "But I would advise you not to gather so much at Reach Out events. Jewel noticed and Mrs. Krantz gave me your names."

"Rosalyn?" Gordon asked, his expression going from surprise to irritation. "Yes, she would." He looked at his fellows. "And the warning is taken. Did she identify others?"

"Judge Burroughs," Jasper said and saw mostly relief from them. "You let women in too?"

"A few exceptional ones," Gordon said. "But then every watcher is exceptional. Mike West wasn't chosen for his money but his character and intelligence. His money let him help the young people on our list but it was his reputation that mattered to us."

"You mentioned that before," Jasper said. "Is that why Drew was helping Corey Morales? And did one of you send those tickets to him?" His jaw tightened as he thought of how close he'd come to losing Melody.

"What tickets?"

"Never mind," Jasper said. "Do you have any objection to my taking Baxter down? It's going to happen but I want to know what you think."

"Baxter is a cancer," Gordon said. "You do us a favor removing him."

"Did you know he was behind blissex?" Jasper demanded.

"No," Gordon answered. "We knew the blissex problem had many facets and we were in the process of tying it to someone at Wilson Chems but we were looking more at Wilson himself and not finding much. One of his missing executives did turn up dead recently but what he was doing for twenty odd years, we can't say. Since we have no legal investigative authority there, we didn't get far."

"There is one I'll tell you," Gordon said. "And then we'd better end this. One of our protégés has worked with you and is now going on to a new job—again partly due to you. He has no idea, of course, that our group financed his education. He believes a science teacher he impressed is responsible just as Corey Morales will continue to think Drew Nugent is solely responsible for his. Pedro Kruger was simply too good to leave at the mercy of the government system."

Jasper smiled. "And he doesn't know?"

"No, of course not. There are other students, mostly in mathematics and engineering, who were discreetly helped off the subby list. Not all of them took the path they were supposed to take but you've been the most surprising."

"Me?" Jasper's mouth tightened then he shook his head. "That was a government program."

Dan Mushti was grinning.

"That was almost twenty-five years ago," Jasper said, still denying it.

"Welcome to the club, brother," Dan Mushti said. "Get used to it. The watchers have been around a long time and before you judge us remember to look at what was done for you. We're the solution, not the problem."

With that, he bowed to Gordon then to Stephens and they returned his bows. The one he gave Jasper was shallow but he gave it before turning to go. Stephens followed him out, leaving only Gordon behind.

"Yes, I was surprised too," Gordon said, "but you're in the database. If you weren't such a catalyst, you could be useful. Maybe when your children are grown."

With those words, he reached over and turned off the jammer. Still stunned by that last revelation, Jasper left.

They'd helped him? Thinking back he could remember two teachers who had made a difference for him. One had turned him on to math in junior high and recommended him for an accelerated program. Mister Rice. The other had been a Miss Shubert. She had dismissed his previous music instruction and told him to play what was in him. He had gone on to learn a lot of the major compositions by heart but that was only so he could know what was possible. No, he'd found her in college during the first week of classes. It had to have been Rice.

Wanting to thank him for that long ago recommendation, he realized he probably couldn't. That was almost thirty years ago and he was old then. He was probably gone by now.

Following Kale to the elevators, he frowned as he thought. The Watchers were at least that old and he could swear not one of them was younger than forty-five. Trace Stephens looked to be the oldest of those he'd just met but Drew had been their mentor. Did that mean he'd brought them in or was that simply the leadership position? He was curious but knew he couldn't ask more questions. If he brought any of them into the light, it could mean more deaths. No, that was one investigation he had to leave alone. Thank God he hadn't passed that on to Carlson.

The man at the blister plant who had died—no doubt he'd been theirs. Was it the government coming in or Baxter who had spooked him? Baxter must have gone there looking for his own answers. Why the hell had he asked Jasper to find things out if he'd known where the blister plant was? Or maybe that part of the Wilson Chemicals operation hadn't been entrusted to him.

He was getting a headache.

Chapter 56 - Carlson

Mel and Jewel were walking the hall when he returned and he guessed they were just about ready to go. He just wasn't sure where they were going yet. His preference was straight to the airport and home but he doubted it would be that easy. They had to find a flight with seats enough for....seven? Yes, seven. Minneapolis was his choice but they might be able to make Chicago work.

"Your com link, sir," Kale said and handed it to him. "It's buzzing."

"Now what?" Jasper muttered as he took it. "Carlson," he said. "I'm going to duck in there." He motioned to the men's room.

Kale nodded and took up position by the door.

"Jasper here," he said as he checked the two stalls. "Mel is being released."

"That's good," Carlson said, a tired smile on his face. "And I've got good news too. Mary Perkins is no longer a threat."

"No longer a threat?" Jasper repeated.

"Right. Her trail stopped in Chicago because she took euthanasia there," Carlson said. "And, yes, it's been confirmed it was her. She left statements which their police has just picked up."

"How could they approve her?" Jasper asked, trying not to feel relieved. "It takes months."

"She was pre-approved," Carlson said. "A terminal condition. She's dead now and one less thing to worry about. That leaves Baxter."

"Baxter is still in Denver," Jasper said. "He was one of those who attacked Mel last night. I want to get Jewel and Mel out of here as soon as possible." Why had Perkins chosen suicide now? Did she know the police were closing in?

"Understood and we'll see what we can do about getting you on a flight," Carlson said. "But I need both you and Jewel for an hour or two. Reynolds sent me that audio lineup and we have to get that over with. I also need a proper statement from you about how you identified Baxter. The lab boys have confirmed it's him but we still need a statement."

"It can't wait?" Jasper asked but he knew the answer was no. "Never mind. Let me figure out what to do with the others and I'll be over or.... can you send a car? I want Kale to stay with Mel."

"I'll send one. In fact, I'll be driving it. Don't leave with anyone else," Carlson warned. "Wait for me."

"Yes sir." Jasper finished the call then glanced in the mirror. He was beginning to look old, he thought. The last month had put a lot of mileage on him between the wedding, the kidnapping, Lori's death, and now Mel— and his son. He just wanted out. Well, he'd tell Carlson when he gave that statement. This was his last case.

Heading back to Mel's room, he saw they were all there but the atmosphere was tense.

"I told you I have to go back," Corey was saying and Mel, his daughter, was standing in front of him, her jaw stubbornly set. "You need to be safe but I have to go back. I owe it to the professor."

"They could kill you," Mel responded. "I need you."

"No." Corey stood his ground. "After finals. I can't go before."

Jewel looked at him and Mel must have seen because she whirled to face him.

"Dad, tell him he's got to come," she ordered. "He can't stay."

"I don't think so," Jasper responded, recognizing how important it was to Corey to finish his job properly. "If Corey needs to go back, he should. You were the target, not him."

She hesitated, looking betrayed then said "He got the tickets. They have to know about him."

"If you had got them, would you have gone?" Jasper countered. "Would you have asked me whether it was safe to go? Or David?"

"Of course," she said then her eyes shot to Corey. "But they went to him–through the school."

"An anonymous donor," Corey said, his face grim. "They specified two for me and four more for other outstanding students. I'm sorry, sir, I should have seen it was a trap."

"The best traps aren't obvious," Jasper said. "I didn't see it, either. Did you, David?" He turned to wife's uncle.

"No," David said, "but I would have if Mel had got them. Are you sure Corey will be safe if he goes back?"

"The villain is here in Denver and he can't travel except by stolen car," Jasper said. "He can't get into Plains through any legal means. Once Corey is back in Plains, he should be fine. I still want you to come to Minnesota during break," he said with an eye on him. "Until Ba.... until the man is caught, I prefer it."

"Yes sir," Corey said. "I'll try."

"I'll see you get a ticket," Jasper said. "And if you have any problems, even suspicions, in Plains, you're to call Captain Reynolds. Melody, you have his number. Give it to Corey."

He debated telling him Gordon would watch out for him too but decided against it. Gordon should create his own relationship with Corey if he wanted to. He didn't know how closely Watchers watched.

"Dad, I want to go back too," Mel said. "I have finals."

Jasper eyed her then shook his head. "Finals can be taken remotely–and I don't care if you take them at all when your life could be at stake. You're coming home with me. We'll decide later whether you should transfer colleges."

"Dad!"

"Not now," Jasper said and cut her off. "Molly, can they keep her for being unreasonably stubborn?"

Molly studied her for what seemed like a long time then slowly nodded. "The doctor could order her held for psychiatric tests. He'd probably decide in a week or two she was just being a teenager but you never know."

Mel was flushed now. "You wouldn't do that." Her voice was weaker.

"I would be reluctant," Molly said, "but you know you're a target and want to continue on the most dangerous course? Come to think of it, your father really needs his head examined." She shot a look at him. "If he keeps getting in the news, I think I'll do it."

Mel laughed at the turnaround, others joining in, while Jasper frowned. He knew she was very likely to do it.

"I'll try to stay out of the news," he said. "I am resigning from... DEA." He found it hard to say it in such a large crowd. Ivan didn't register any surprise but he saw his daughter's reaction and Corey's and knew he'd at least kept it from them. "This is my last and only case for them."

David and Elinor. Elinor looked surprised but David just nodded. Hell, he must have put it together before. He knew Carlson was DEA.

"Good," Molly said. "You need to stay home for a while."

"Yes, I do. I want to. This is making me old."

Again a ripple of laughter then Jewel was next to him. "Let's all go home—everyone except Corey," Jewel said. "Can we see him off first?"

Damn. Carlson. "There's something we have to do first," he said. "Just me and Jewel. Carlson needs statements from us. Has anyone seen Jameson?"

"Right here," Jameson said and stepped forward. He had a grin on his face and Jasper knew he'd heard as well. "You aren't made for undercover work, Agent Stone. How the hell can you go anywhere without the press getting wind of it?"

"Exactly," Molly said then at Ivan's look she subsided.

"Yeah, that was the plan," Jasper said. "What made it attractive. Because I became a target as well, it didn't work." Their original plan when he was single was for him to be a magnet for the underworld. He was going to be outspoken about the need for bliss—not blissex. That had all changed when he married. "Ok, Jewel and I have to leave for an hour or two. David, can we meet you at the Tower?"

"Sounds good," David said. "I'll start looking at flights back for you."

"I need to borrow Mel and Corey for statements," Jameson said. "Just a formality. I already have statements from two witnesses as to the snatch. No one could identity the men though."

"I can't," Corey said. "I never got a clear look except at the one who called Mel's name. He had glowers on his face."

"You didn't see the older man at all?" Jameson asked.

"No, he must have been behind me," Corey said.

"I can't say much either," Mel said. "Except the young one might still be sore and have a bit lip. That was all I could manage. The other one had my hands pinned and he had a knife."

"A knife?" Jasper picked up on that. "You saw it?"

"No, I felt it," she said.

"Inspection sensors would have picked up on most knives," Jameson said. "He poked you? Where?"

"In my back," she said, looking pale. She turned around and pointed to the place. "About there."

Jasper pulled up her shirt and looked at the unmarked skin. It was smooth with no hint of damage. When Jameson showed him what he held, he nodded. An instant later his daughter jumped as it touched her bare skin.

"Did it feel like that?" Jasper asked.

"Yes, I.... what was that?" Melody twisted to look at them and flushed as she saw the ident card in Jameson's hand. "He used his ident card?" Her voice rose.

"It's a very old trick," Jameson said. "Inspection sensors don't see it as a weapon but the corner feels like a knife blade. You aren't the first to be fooled and you won't be the last." He put his card away. "Did you see his face at all? Even part of it?"

"I caught a glimpse of a white beard," she said. "And when he held me against him, I realized it was gone. I saw one hand but no rings. I don't think that's much use."

"Ok," Jameson said. "Statements won't produce much. One question— were his hands well taken care of?"

"They were just hands," she said. "Clean but hands."

"Look, I still have to get this down," Jameson said. "But I can do it at the Tower. There's not going to be enough to justify taking them downtown. Stone, is that okay with you?"

"I would prefer they go straight to the Tower," Jasper said. "And Kale will go with them. Carlson is coming for the two of us."

"I'll walk out with you," Jameson said. "An extra set of eyes. Kale too. Then we'll come back to escort the rest. Fair?"

"Fair," Jasper said. "And the best arrangement. David, we'll meet up with you at the Tower."

That settled, he simply had to collect Jewel and his briefcase and give her time to hug Mel. He knew it was a waste of time to try to convince Corey to change his mind and, frankly, he didn't want him to. The boy had obligations and would be a better man for standing up to them. It was Mel he needed to protect.

Thirty minutes later he was quietly watching as Jewel listened to the second of the male voices of Reach Out members. Her eyes were closed with a tiny frown between them as she concentrated. The interrogation chair was set to pick up her reactions to the individual voices.

"I know that one," she said. "That's Mr. Lowe."

"Was he on the plane?" Carlson asked.

"No, it wasn't him," Jewel said. "We talked quite a bit with him at the last event and I know his voice. The one on the plane was someone I didn't know."

"Ok, moving on," Carlson said and the technician obediently keyed up the next tape.

"Not that one," Jewel said after a minute. "The pitch is too low. Nice voice though." She glanced at him and Jasper smiled.

"Do you remember any accent?" Carlson asked.

"Not really," Jewel said. "He only said a few words. Are you sure he's a Reach Out member? I know almost all the major donors."

"Let's move on to the next voice," Carlson said without answering.

"Rick Gordon," Jewel said almost immediately. "He came to the house sometimes."

The next voice puzzled her but she knew it wasn't the one from the plane. Jasper recognized it as Captain Reynolds and wondered briefly whether the deep-voiced one was someone from the department.

"23 hours?" Baxter's canned voice said. "What is it supposed to mean other than 23 hours?"

Jasper froze, remembering that conversation. What else had they used?

"You guys were barking up the wrong tree."

Jasper's gaze flew to Jewel just as Carlson said, "you know that voice?"

"It's him," Jewel said, her voice low and shaky. "That's him."

"You be here. You do what you're told," Baxter said in his coldest voice.

"Stop the tape," Carlson said as Jewel buried her face in her hands. "You're sure it's him? Can you put a name to him?"

Jewel shook her head and she was shaking, her face pale. "He... he sounded like that last one."

"Can you put him on the plane?" Carlson asked. "How certain are you?"

"Damn certain," Jewel snapped. "That bastard told them to keep me alive because I was no good to him dead. He was so cold, I...." She shivered.

"Ok, we have him on the plane. Mr. Stone, is this also the man in your house? For the record." Carlson turned to him.

"Yes, he was. The three samples were from the tape I recorded at the house when he returned my wife," Jasper said.

Baxter laughed. "She's all yours, Sensor Man. I've had her long enough." The unexpected line cut through the room and Jasper felt himself freeze up as the technician hurriedly cut it off.

"Sorry, I hit the wrong button."

"That's Mark Baxter!" Jewel's face blazed with anger now. "That laugh. I know—Mark Baxter did this?" Her voice rose to a shriek. "Him? That mother fucking son of a bitch!"

"Jewel!" Jasper cut across her curse.

"Calm her down," Carlson said, his voice rising to be heard above Jewel's.

Jasper tried but Jewel was still cursing, her fists pounding his chest when he pulled her out of the interrogation chair. Capturing them, he held her tight until she dissolved into tears of rage.

"I'll give you a minute," Carlson said. "I think we got our ID." He left the room, closing the door behind him.

"Hush, Jewel," Jasper said. "He's not going to get away with it. We'll catch him."

"That bastard," Jewel said between tears. "I... he tried once.... Mike told him never to touch me again and he laughed. He laughed."

Jasper's blood went cold. He'd made a play for Jewel? How long ago? Why the hell hadn't she mentioned that one? "Ok, now he's dead," Jasper said and his voice was so cold Jewel looked up at him in surprise, her breath catching. "No one touches you."

Whatever she was about to say, he stopped it with his lips. She tasted salty from her tears and wet but he didn't care. Hungry for the feel of her, he let his yearning show in one long kiss. She responded, clinging to him when he would have ended it, and he groaned. The technician. Was he still taping this?

With an effort, he pushed Jewel back on to her own feet. Not surprising, she was no longer crying or mad. Her breath was coming fast and he just knew his son must be stirring. Damn it, he wanted her!

"I'm not going to last two weeks," he said and his wife laughed.

"We'll get Baxter," he said. "And, yes, I know it's him. That damned earring gave him away. He wore it in the house and he wore it again when he snatched Mel. We'll get him."

"I know you will," Jewel said with uncommon certainty but her anger wasn't all gone. "I've always been creeped out by him." She shuddered and Jasper held her tight.

"Calmed down now?" Ray Carlson came back into the room and motioned for them to take their seats again. "One more question for you, Jewel. Please, no more cussing."

"Yes sir," Jewel replied and her eyes shot to her husband's. "Will that be heard in court?"

"Possibly," Carlson said. "It's a very convincing identification but now we'll do a tamer version. Start the vid again please."

"This is Ray Carlson continuing interview of kidnap victim Jewel West Stone after a technical glitch. Mrs. Stone, you recognized the voice of the last subject?"

"Yes," Jewel stated, "he was on the plane and his name is Mark Baxter."

"How do you know Mr. Baxter?" Carlson asked.

"He's a member of Reach Out and attends some events in Plains," Jewel answered with surprising calmness. "I recognized his laugh."

"Did he laugh on the plane?" Carlson asked.

"No, he sounded deadly there, cold," she said. "I've heard him laugh before. It's not funny."

Jasper thought that was an understatement. Everything about the man was cold. He cared for no one, he decided. Maybe no one but himself.

"Thank you, Mrs. Stone. Mr. Stone, do you agree with her identification?"

"Yes sir. I identified Mark Baxter while he was still in my house. There's no doubt in my mind it was him."

"Lab analysis of Baxter's voice confirms Mr. Stone's identification. There's no tape of him at the plane but he was in possession of Mrs. Stone at the house. It is the opinion of this agent that Mrs. Stone is correct. Interview terminated."

"I have to admit you surprised me there," Ray Carlson said, "but I won't ask. Now we're done with interviews and I want to let you know that Reynolds finally got that informant to identify the second man at the confessional as Baxter. I'm not sure it will stand up because he had to promise relocation for him and his family but we'll try. Since the informant ties Baxter and Starling together with that ID, I think it's safe to charge Baxter with the West murders as well."

"He did it?" Jewel asked Jasper. "He killed them?" She didn't lose her calm again but her jaw was set and lips tight. Jasper knew she was holding on to her temper.

"He ordered it done," Jasper said. "Starling met with him the day of the funeral and they discussed it. My informant overheard but there's no vid. I can also place Baxter in Plains during each happening—including Mike's accident."

"And Ed didn't do any of it?" she asked. "Does Elaine know?"

"Elaine?" Jasper repeated.

"Elaine Kucera," Jewel said. "His wife. I tried to talk to her, remember." She looked impatient. "She was a friend of grandmother's."

"The FBI hasn't dropped the charges against Kucera yet," Carlson said. "With this ID, I think we can get it done. There's still the question of why Kucera committed suicide and how he got blister but we don't have that answer yet. Did you find out anything else on that, Stone?"

"As far as I can tell, he had no reason to," Jasper said. "I couldn't find any illegal activity on the part of either Professor Nugent or Edward Kucera. Except for Jake's confession, there's nothing—and I am fairly sure Baxter was posing as Kucera during that period."

"Ok, we'll let it be for now," Carlson said. "The IRS is getting involved now. They want to know everything Baxter owned and every company he had investments in. It's going to take time though."

"Understood," Jasper said. "But I intend to resign when this case is done. I can't be effective with the press chasing me."

"I agree with that," Carlson said in a dry tone. "But until this case is done, you're stuck with it—and I don't mean just Baxter."

Jasper studied him, fully aware what he meant. They needed to get Wilson Kucera if they could and whoever else was involved. No, the case wouldn't be done when Baxter was caught. Hopefully, it would no longer be a danger to his family. Baxter was the real threat.

Chapter 57 - Baxter

"I've found you six seats on the eight pm flight to Minneapolis," David said over the com unit. "Will you make it?"

"We should," Jasper said. "It's not yet six and we're headed back to the Tower now. Jewel identified Baxter."

The elevator stopped at one of the lower floors and two police officers stepped on with a nod to Carlson and a brief glance at him and Jewel.

"Good," David said. "I'll order up dinner."

"What about Corey? Is he leaving tonight?" Jasper asked as the elevator descended.

"No, I'll get him to the express tomorrow," David said. "The early one. He'll be home with plenty of time to prepare for classes. He's still feeling banged up so we'll keep him tonight."

"That sounds good," Jasper said as the doors of the elevator opened in the lobby. "Got to go."

He broke the connection, aware he had to pay attention to his surroundings now. They were still in the Justice building but he knew their most vulnerable points would be in leaving the building for the car and again when they left the car at the Lunarex Tower. Both buildings had exits only above ground, the Justice building being too old and far away from the Denver underground and the Lunarex Tower being deliberately constructed away from it and neighboring buildings for security reasons.

"I'll get the car," Carlson said as they crossed the lobby.

Stepping outside Jasper knew immediately something was wrong. A babble of voices sounded off to the right and he grabbed Jewel's hand and groaned as reporters pushed past a surprised Carlson with cries of "Sensor Man" and "Mr. Stone."

Jasper started to retreat back into the building and found his way blocked. There was no help for it. They'd caught them both but how the hell had they known he was here? Pushing Jewel behind him, he confronted the gaggle of reporters with a forced smile.

"Mr. Stone, can you tell us what's happening? Is Jewel, oh, she's here," one reporter announced triumphantly as Jewel stepped back up to his side. "Mrs. Stone, are you all right? No one has seen you since your kidnapping."

"We're here at the Denver Justice building with Sensor Man and his wife. The Jewel of the West has been found at last, folks. Stay tuned for more," another reporter was saying.

"Is it true, Mrs. Stone, that you're still threatened? What happened?" A third was asking.

Someone jostled Jasper and he half turned, ready to protest, when he felt Jewel pull away from him. Abruptly every voice was silenced and Jasper spun toward his wife, his blood running cold as he saw the knife—a real one this time—at Jewel's throat.

Mark Baxter's cold blue eyes met his as the man backed out of the crowd and placed his back against the stone of the building. The knife wasn't a large one but it looked sharp and Jasper knew it would take just one cut across the jugular to end Jewel's life.

Out of the corner of his eye, he saw Carlson with his trank gun out. "Don't," he shouted. "She's pregnant."

That broke the silence. The reporters were stepping back but now their cameras were up and he could hear whispers of reporting. Damn them.

Baxter grinned, his knife hand flexing. His other arm held an unresisting Jewel close to him. "Pregnant, huh? You managed it anyway. That will make this sweeter, Sensor Man. You have been one huge pain in my ass. Because of you, I'm dead. I'm going to make sure she goes with me."

"You're not dead," Jasper said. "Let Jewel go." He tried to keep his voice level but knew Baxter had nothing to lose. Could he kill him before Baxter killed Jewel? Damn, he wasn't armed. Carlson had a trank but Jewel–she'd lose the baby if he tranked her. Cold realization hit him. He might have to lose his son to save his wife.

"You think I'm an idiot?" Baxter said, his face twisted with hate. "I'm dead. There's no place to hide. You've destroyed my life now I'm going to destroy yours." His hand flexed and moved but Jewel wasn't there. He grabbed for her as she sagged, his knife hand twisting as he tried to catch her, his body exposed as she fell.

Jasper heard the pop of a trank off to his left and another from where he thought Carlson was. Baxter flung himself downward too late, catching one shot at least and landing on top of Jewel.

It wasn't over. Jasper leapt forward as Baxter tried to bring his knife to bear. A bright slash of blood appeared on Jewel's shoulder before Jasper wrestled the knife out of hand and pulled his wife free of the man.

"You, pin him," he shouted at the nearest reporter and the man moved, flinging himself down on Baxter.

Jasper helped Jewel to her feet. "Stay with me," he growled at Jewel. "Stay calm. Don't you dare lose it now." The next instant she was clinging to his neck with one arm, her lips on his. Stunned, he grabbed her close to keep her from falling and she kissed him for all he was worth.

She was wounded. He had to look at it, make sure the blade wasn't poisoned but damn. It was an effort to tear himself away but he did it to find reporters smiling. They were going to make the news again.

They had Baxter. He looked down to see the reporter still on him but an officer was already cuffing the unconscious man. The knife. "Where's the knife?" A reporter shifted and he could see it there on the ground. Jewel.

"Let me see you," he said. "Any dizziness? Numbness?"

"Only from kissing you," she said then the smile left her face at the look on his. "No, no numbness. It hurts." She offered her bleeding shoulder and he tore her blouse away to get a better look. It was bleeding freely but not spurting.

"Here, Mr. Stone," someone said and handed him a white cloth already folded into a pad. He pressed it against her wound. "I need to get her inside," he said. "Did anyone call an ambulance?"

"Yes sir," several voices said.

"Let's give them some room, folks," Carlson said. "Go file your reports. Mr. Stone will give you an interview after his wife has been treated."

"Mr. Stone?"

"Yes," Jasper ground out. "Metro Hospital. Give me two hours." That seemed to satisfy them.

"When we get home," he said to his wife, "we're staying home. No more of this."

"That's my line," she said. "I need to sit down."

He didn't wait but scooped her into his arms and carried her back into the building and away from prying eyes. Damn, he was going to have to call David.

* * *

At eight o'clock he and Jewel were sitting in a roomful of reporters instead of flying back to Minneapolis. He'd convinced the others to go, knowing Ivan had to get back to the farm and wanting Kale to stay with Melody. Jewel hadn't been admitted so they would be going over to Lunarex Tower to spend the night as soon as the interviews were done.

Jewel had taken one hell of a chance going limp with a knife at her throat but it had worked. Jasper shuddered to think what could have happened. If Baxter had reacted faster or she'd done it wrong, that knife would have gotten more than her shoulder. The cut there was stitched now and the doctors had proclaimed it clean. Jewel had told them of her pregnancy and gone through another ultrasound but the baby seemed to be undisturbed.

Could anything rattle his kid? Jasper was beginning to wonder and it worried him. Well, he'd have to wait until Junior started kicking. Then he'd know and relax.

"When is the baby due?" a female reporter asked. "Do you know what it is?"

"He's due in July or August," Jewel said with a smile. "Nope, no clue as to what he is." A spate of laughter followed that and Jasper smiled. His wife knew how to handle reporters. Even injured, she could give them what they wanted.

"That man who attacked you—do you know who he is?" one reporter asked and the room fell silent.

It was Jasper who spoke up. "We're not allowed to announce his name," Jasper said. "Until he's tried and convicted, the man stays anonymous to deny him fame. He is the man who ordered the kidnapping of Jewel and he'll be charged with kidnapping, murder, and attempted murder. The nurse who killed FBI agent Cord McCain is already dead. There are three more thugs—one of them here in Denver—who are wanted but this man was the most dangerous and he's not going anywhere."

"Will there be other charges against him?" the same reporter asked.

"Yes," Jasper said, "but I can't discuss them. Even though I'm no longer a police officer, I still follow the rules. Leave it alone."

There was a brief silence then another reporter asked, "So what's next for you and Jewel? Will you be returning to Plains?"

Jasper hesitated, looking at his wife before he shook his head. "Not right away. Now that we can have some peace, we're taking a nice long honeymoon and I have an album to work on. Maybe after our child is born, we'll return. That remains to be seen."

"So where will the honeymoon be?" one bold reporter asked and others muttered at her. Jasper knew he still had their sympathy but that was one question he had no intention of answering.

"In a nice big bed," Jewel answered with a coquettish look and the reporters laughed. "Hey, I'm pregnant, not dead."

Good ending line, Jasper thought and rose to his feet. "And I want to keep her that way, folks, so I think it's time we end this. Thank you for your help this afternoon. Which one of you sat on the b... villain?"

A man raised his hand. "Sturgis, Channel 2, BBCS."

"Thanks," Jasper said, "I'll remember it." Helping Jewel to her feet, he guided her out of the conference room. It was time to go.

Tomorrow he'd have to sit in on questioning Baxter but he could leave Jewel at the Tower. It would be tomorrow afternoon at least before they could get back to Minneapolis. He could hardly wait.

Chapter 58 - Lunarex Tower

Staying at Lunarex Tower should have been a treat but it seemed every time Jasper was there he was tired or too busy to enjoy it. Tonight wasn't much of an exception but the dinner was good and Jewel less inclined to tease him now that the painkiller was wearing off and her arm ached.

She'd been damned lucky. Elinor and David examined the stitched up cut and told her so then insisted she take it easy. Corey studied it too then compared it to his. Jasper had to admit they looked like they were made by the same weapon. His daughter could have felt a knife, not an ident card in her back. The weapon had been an illegal sheath knife. With the blade retracted into the handle, inspection sensors wouldn't have noticed it. They were programmed to recognize blades, not rectangular objects that could be anything from combs to portable computers. No, it was more likely Baxter had used an ident card since he couldn't have the blade exposed.

He was still mulling it over while he helped wash dishes. Corey had joined him this time and was doing the drying.

"Can I ask you something?" the college student said. "Not to do with Mel, that is."

"Sure," Jasper said. "About college or life?"

Corey grinned. "I guess both. I'm thinking of changing majors but it's a stupid idea. I was in programming, you know."

"Right," Jasper said, noting the was. Did Corey realize he had already put that in past tense? "And where did the cello fit in?"

"Oh, that was just for fun," he said with a shrug. "I'm not good enough to do anything with it. I just play with it."

"There's nothing wrong with that," Jasper said. "Ok, you were in programming. What field do you want to move into?"

"Teaching," Corey said in a rush. "History. I really enjoyed working with the professor and now that he's gone—well, I just want to do something like that."

Jasper tried hard not to stare at him. Teaching history? That was sort of worthless and impossible to make any money. Remembering Dan Mushti's tirade about the lack of history instruction, he knew the watchers would be pleased. He wasn't though. It might be years before Corey made enough money to support his daughter. He'd do better to play the cello.

"Does Mel know about this?" Jasper finally asked as he handed him another plate to dry. "Is she changing her major too?"

"No, she's sticking with robotic programming," Corey said. "She likes the challenge of getting a pile of metal to do what she wants it to do. I do too but history is.... " he struggled for words, "fascinating, I guess. It's not just dry dates but why things happened like they did. The economic stuff, the political climate, and all. Did you know if the Purge hadn't happened, the Reformation wouldn't have either? People were so afraid they'd be next they called for special elections and voted Congress out and put new people in. It wasn't just the climate changes but that's what we were taught in high school. They barely mentioned the Purge."

"I wondered if I had missed that," Jasper said. "History wasn't my favorite subject."

"I didn't get much history in high school but I'm starting to make up for it," Corey said. "The professor got me interested. He had Mel interested too but not that much."

"Then you should probably switch majors," Jasper said. "But you might want to continue with programming too. Find a way to make the two work together."

"Work together?" Corey looked thoughtful. "Program history?" He grinned. "Or history programs?"

Jasper smiled. "I remember hearing Professor Nugent had history programs on the subby channel. With an actual degree in programming, you might be able to take that to another level. It's not hard to create avatars any more. If you can make history come alive, you'll get further than just teaching history."

"Vid tech," Corey said after a moment. "Yeah, that might work. I don't think there's any studios that will back documentaries though."

"Probably not as a rule," Jasper said. "But a good script, a good story, and a good presentation will always get them. You can do more to educate people through vids than you can in a college. I think Nugent knew that."

They finished the dishes in silence and he knew he'd given Corey something to think about. He couldn't see Mel marrying a plain history teacher even if it was Corey. She had her own ambitions and robotics had always been her fascination. Jewel played with it too but she was less interested in making machines do physical work. Butler was more her style.

Butler. He would need to get Butler out of the Plains house. He also wanted to get some contractors in there to brick up the outside exit. Not today. Not even tomorrow. It could wait but until it was done he wouldn't let anyone live there or put the house on the market.

"Follow your own dreams, Corey," he said as they put the last dishes away. "Just try to find a way to make them pay."

"Like you did?" Corey asked.

"Like I did," Jasper said. "Live symphonic music doesn't make much and the overhead is high. Sensa is hard to produce but it pays well and you can do it without help if you know how."

"Yes sir," Corey said.

"Just don't try to make a living by writing," Jasper said. "You'll end up on subsistence with the rest of the poor slobs."

Corey grinned. "Yeah, I know that. Thanks."

Jasper didn't fear he would. It was well known that writers never made money but they were maniac about their craft. They were just about the only group that would willingly go on subsistence if it meant they could write. Since they were law abiding, the government let them do it to keep them quiet and out of politics.

"Jewel is headed to bed," David said, "and I think Corey should be off to bed soon too. Why don't you tuck Jewel in?"

"Just tuck?" Jasper grinned and went to their room. He had no intention of doing anything else. Even though Jewel wouldn't admit it, that cut hurt–and he still had most of that two weeks to go.

Seeing she was still in the bathroom, he opened his briefcase to find a good flasher for her to listen to. His hand paused where his requiem used to be and he frowned. He still had to deal with that too. Milt wouldn't publish it without his permission but he wasn't sure he wanted it back. Jewel shouldn't have handed it over without talking to him though. The piece didn't even have a proper name other than Requiem. His brown eyes darkened as he thought about the stir that would create. He'd had enough of the press and even fans for a while. He wanted to get out of the news and back to composing. The last thing he wanted to do was take the time to present the Requiem properly. Hell, he should make her do it.

Slowly his face relaxed and he smiled. Turning when Jewel came out of the bathroom, he eyed his wife and saw she was wearing a conservative cotton nightie and knew it wasn't hers.

"Elinor?" Jasper asked. "To keep me away?" Giving her a kiss, he proved it didn't work. Jewel returned it but the passion was lacking tonight. Yes, she was hurting and tired.

"In bed, love," Jasper said. "I'm to tuck you in. Did they give you any pain pills?"

"Narcoset," she said. "No bliss in them and they won't harm Junior." She made a face. "I'm taking it with water."

"Good," he said, remembering Mike and his scotch. "Any topical stuff?"

"That's done," she said and pulled her feet under the covers. "Do I get music or a bedtime story?"

"I don't think you need either one," he said. "But I got something for you to think about. Remember my Requiem?"

She hesitated then anxiously looked up at him. "They called you?"

"Of course he did," Jasper said. "Milt is my publisher. He's holding it and waiting for my go-ahead. I'll give it on one condition."

"Yes?" Jewel smiled happily. "It's really too beautiful to sit."

"I know," Jasper said. "And since you're so willing to champion it, it's yours. You name it, you write the album notes, and you make any publicity appearances Milt arranges. I'm going back to composing."

"I name it?" Jewel's voice rose to nearly a shriek as he retreated to the door. "Me? It's yours. I can't do that."

"Sleep well love," Jasper said and turned out the light. He grinned at the muffled sound coming through the door. Served her right. She'd get to sleep but she could just mull that over first.

David studied him but refrained from asking him what was going on. "Elinor is tucking Corey in. He opened his mouth about not having any one and she caught him. We're free to go."

"Go?" Jasper asked.

"It's too early for me and you can't go back in there just now," David said. "I thought we might have us some fish eggs and scotch."

Jasper laughed and followed him out. "What are you going to try to talk me into this time?"

"Not a thing," David claimed. "I'm just glad you joined the family."

The bar David favored was a quiet place with automated serving tables and private booths. Jasper had been there once before but his memory beyond the scotch was hazy. It was where he'd agreed to marry Jewel. His lips curled into a wry grin. He'd agreed to marry her but had he ever actually proposed? He laughed.

"Remembering last time?" David asked as he took two shots of scotch and an order of potato skins off the service tray.

"I remember last time," Jasper said. "It just occurred to me that I never proposed to Jewel."

David's hand stopped and he shot him a look. "Not at all?"

"Not that I can remember," Jasper said. "Unless I did it after I was shot, I didn't do it."

"You'd better not mention that to her," David said. "Ok, so when did she propose?"

Jasper sipped his scotch and thought. "I remember she said I had to marry her after we slept together on the train—in our clothes, of course." Jasper chuckled. "Oh, and she told me in the hospital that she had to marry me because she'd saved my life. I wasn't ready to argue. Later when I found out how good a shot she was, I decided I'd better not."

David let out a bellow of laughter, throwing his head back. Jasper joined in, still amused by his oversight. He knew the real engagement had been made here without Jewel even knowing. David had pointed out the advantages to him, the advantages to Jewel, and how much he didn't want to have to worry about Jewel himself. It was already clear that Jewel wanted him but Jasper was a police lieutenant assigned to the case. Without that talk, he would never have considered marriage with Jewel West even though he had shared one very hot kiss in the elevator—a kiss he thought David knew about when he brought up the subject.

"Roped in," David said when he finally quit laughing. "Roped, tied and branded before the altar. Dad would have loved it."

"Your dad?" Jasper asked.

"Yes," David said and finished his scotch. "He claimed Mother roped him the first time they met. Mother said she caught him trespassing."

"You're kidding," Jasper said but he couldn't keep the grin off his face. He could see Elizabeth West doing that.

"Then Dad would deny being hog-tied by a hundred-pound beauty queen and they'd go on and on. It made for some entertaining evenings because none of us were ever sure how it actually happened and they'd change the story around."

"No witnesses?"

"To their first meeting? Just a horse and a dog. We couldn't get either one to talk." David chuckled. "Oh, it would have been great if you'd been able to hear them. Happiest couple in the world." His grin faded and he reached for a potato skin.

"Well, you and Elinor are doing ok," Jasper said. "Maybe you'll get there too."

"I hope," David said. "You and Jewel too. I think Mike would have liked you even if you can't keep out of trouble."

"Not my fault," Jasper said as new shots of scotch appeared. This time he nursed his. "He was as private in his own way as Drew. All of them are."

"Gordon and the rest?" David asked. "I wondered if you'd tell me anything about that."

"There's not much to tell," Jasper said. "They keep an eye on the government and try to help kids get an education. They're also concerned that people know their history. That's about it."

"And Kucera was one too?" David's scotch sat untouched in front of him and Jasper knew he was being pumped. Ordering black coffee from the server, he set the scotch aside.

"It's not going to work this time," he said to David. "And you've got something to tell too. What was in the envelope?"

David shrugged a little too casually. "A couple of letters from Mike and some old family papers. Mike had decided against euthanasia. He assumed since he didn't get to hand me the letter that he died of too many painkillers and too much scotch."

"Nothing about the inspection systems?" Jasper asked.

"Not a thing," David said with a frown. "He was concerned about Jewel. He worried how I would deal with her and whether I would disown Jake. That was the gist of it. He wants to be added to the memorial garden at the Sullivan Ranch but I've already done that. Jake and Mother are there too."

Jasper nodded and took a potato skin himself. These were fairly crispy with cheese and topped with caviar and sour cream. Like David he couldn't imagine eating them without scotch but they were good.

"So what's next for you?" David asked. "Plains and the farm or just the farm?"

"Just the farm for now," Jasper said. "I've got an album to write music for and a studio to build. Do you want a separate bath for you and Elinor or will you share with squirmy boys?"

"Separate, please," David said but he was grinning. "Boys grow up and get even more messy. And if you have a girl next, she'll be fighting over space before she's a teen."

Jasper hesitated. "A girl? Another girl?" he said in mock horror then grinned. "A miniature Jewel. She's going to be worse than Melody."

"You bet."

When their conversation was done and before they needed help getting home, they returned to the apartment to find Jasper's music playing.

David cocked his head and grinned. "What's this piece? It sounds good."

Jasper didn't have to guess. He hadn't heard it in two years but he recognized the strains of his Requiem and knew it was close to its end. The bedroom doors were open so Corey had been listening to it too, and Elinor. Jewel again. He paused to listen to a particularly moving passage.

"It's Carol's Requiem or a Requiem for Carol or the Parting Requiem," Elinor said as she came out of Jewel's room. "Jewel's asleep finally. Corey didn't make it through. He was tired."

"Three names?" David asked with a quizzical expression.

"I wrote it for Carol," Jasper said. "Jewel gave it to Milt so I put her in charge of naming it. What were those names again?" he asked Elinor.

Elinor repeated them then added "I like the Parting Requiem the best but I can understand if you'd like to have Carol's name on it. It's lovely."

The Parting Requiem. Jasper tried the name out then tried the other two but Elinor's instincts were good. Commercially it would do better under that name. He would just have to make sure it was dedicated to Carol. He hadn't expected Jewel to name it tonight but he knew he'd kept her from going to sleep. Well, maybe she'd think twice before going around him again.

"The Parting Requiem," Jasper said. "She can call Milt on Monday. He doesn't work on Sunday if he can help it."

"No one should work on Sunday," David said. "But I have to this week. Are you going to stay till Monday or leave tomorrow?"

"I'd better stay," Jasper said. "I want to interview Baxter and Starling both but I suspect they'll scream for their lawyers. They probably aren't working tomorrow."

"Then Jewel and I will have time to catch up," Elinor said. "And you can sleep. You look like you need it."

Jasper knew he did. He'd been up since four this morning after a late night. Damn, he meant to be there to help Melody settle in. Well, Molly and Ivan would see to her. Another daughter for them.

"Sounds good. Just point me to a bed and I'll go," he said.

David and Elinor both pointed and he laughed and said good night. Tomorrow he could think about Baxter. Tonight, bed.

Chapter 59 - Monday, 29 Nov 2179

Samuel Starling had changed little in the last four months. He had lost weight making his face more gaunt than before but he was still clean-shaven and his hair had been trimmed by the jail's barber. Jasper took another good look at his face and realized, like him, Samuel Starling had had his beard eradicated. That was an expensive and time-consuming procedure but most upperclass men did it. He shouldn't be surprised that a professional assassin had the money to do it.

What had changed was the look in his eye. When he'd interviewed him before Starling had been defiant and totally uncooperative but that was before his brother John had died. He remembered the vid of the man praying for his brother and knew he felt guilt. How was he going to feel when he told him about his sister?

He glanced at the lawyer who sat at the end of the table. He wasn't a public defender but neither did he seem to have any connection to Baxter or Wilson Kucera. As far as he knew, the lawyer was someone Starling had picked out of the phonebook but the man was good at delaying tactics. He'd successfully kept Starling from being deep questioned for more than four months by citing the Fifth Amendment and various precedents. Well, maybe today would break the deadlock.

"I have two pieces of news for you," Jasper said. "Your half-sister, Mary Perkins, is dead. We've confirmed it and we have statements from her. She assisted in the kidnapping and illegal questioning of my wife and murdered an FBI agent named Cord McCain."

Starling's jaw clenched but he kept his eyes on the table. He wasn't in an interrogation chair either so Jasper had no idea what his true feelings were. Just when he thought Starling wouldn't respond he looked up and asked, "how did she die?" in a surprisingly gentle voice.

"Euthanasia," Jasper said and tried not to let his own anger show. In spite of the statements she'd left, he still wanted to see her brought to trial. It didn't matter to him that she'd been coerced into killing the agent by threats against her son. She'd still done it and she'd been a willing participant in Jewel's kidnapping and questioning. She even admitted to planting the transmitter.

Starling almost smiled but the quick upturn of his lips was so faint Jasper couldn't be sure he saw it.

"I understand she had cancer," Jasper said. "Why didn't she get treatment?"

"You wouldn't understand," Starling said. "This world is temporary. She was ready to leave."

Jasper stared at him. Temporary? He belonged to the Temporal Divinity? He really believed you went on to a higher plane when you left this one? Then why had he been so remorseful for his brother? For that matter, why had she been willing to be coerced if her son would go on?

"She was ready but your brother wasn't?" Jasper hazarded a guess. "Is there some preparation for leaving?"

Sam Starling shot him a startled look then focused his eyes back on the table. The lawyer stirred but this line of questioning was still legal.

"You must be ready," Starling said. "You must be in a state of grace. There are rituals and prayers and you must examine your soul. John wasn't ready. I wasn't after..." He took a deep breath and let it out. "I've spent these months attaining grace again. When they let me go, I'll be ready."

Jasper stared at him, hearing the calm conviction in his voice and having to damp down his anger. This man killed for a living. Besides Elizabeth, Mike and Jake, he had killed at least fifteen others and here he was talking about a state of grace as if none of it mattered. Hell, his death couldn't come soon enough for him.

He wanted to shake him, to force him to remember Elizabeth West but it wasn't allowed. He knew it was Elizabeth's death that had taken him down from his state of grace. What was there about it that made it different? The blood or the violence? Making a note to research the Temporal Divinity and their views, he changed the subject.

"The other bit of news is Mark Baxter has been caught and is down the hall in a cell like yours," Jasper said and was satisfied to see a reaction.

Starling's hands clenched this time and he looked up and smiled. "The man who kidnapped your wife? That's good news. You must be very happy."

"You must be psychic. You know he kidnapped my wife," Jasper said and saw the lawyer look up suspiciously. "Yes, he kidnapped my wife. He was also responsible for the deaths of Professor Andrew Nugent, FBI agent Cord McCain, Detective Lori Brown, Jacob West, Michael West, and Elizabeth West among others. We're still coming up with the list since they weren't all confined to this region. It's suspected he also ordered the abductions and deaths of several young people. My daughter survived the blissex overdose but others didn't. Would you know anything about that?"

Starling looked thoughtful then sat back in his chair. "I'm not surprised." He paused. "No, I have nothing to say. He's no longer my concern."

Jasper's jaw clenched and his eyes bored into Starling's but the man didn't look away. It was his lawyer who broke the deadlock.

"Mr. Stone, this is inappropriate but since you've brought it up, does this mean Mr. Baxter will be charged with the murders of the West family? How does that affect my client?"

Jasper looked at him. "The charges against your client are unchanged," he said. "You can try negotiating though if Mr. Starling is willing. Talk to the prosecutor, not me."

He rose to his feet. "I have to speak to Mr. Baxter. It may be that he'll be willing to tell us what he knows about the murders."

Starling didn't rise to the bait but his lawyer looked worried. Good. He knew Baxter wasn't going to get off no matter what he said but he might be able to get Starling to name him as his employer. That would simplify matters. The identification by Frazier was good but in giving him relocation before the trial, it had gotten tainted. He understood why Reynolds did it though. A dead witness was no good to anyone and Frazier had been scared.

Well, now he just had the interview with Baxter to go. After that he could collect Jewel and head home. It had been a long weekend.

Like Starling's, Baxter's cell was high security. The authorities were aware someone might try to kill him or he might try to kill himself so every effort was being made to keep him alive. The bed shelf was solid molded plastic designed to hold the usual sensors for jail cells and the mattress was thick foam with a tough cover that couldn't be chewed through or sawn into easily. The shower, toilet and sink were all steel and state of the art. Jasper knew through his own training on such cells that even the food arrived prepackaged and sealed and was heated up here in the guardroom. Nothing was left to chance with a high security prisoner.

He didn't think there was much chance that Baxter would commit suicide but if he wasn't the top man in his little organization, someone would try to kill him. He almost wished they would since it would be an end to Baxter and give them what they need to bring Wilson Kucera into it.

Baxter wasn't in his cell. Going on to the interrogation room at the far end of the cell block, he found him and his lawyer sitting at a table with a uniformed officer standing watch. The security extended here too, with Baxter being shielded by plexiglass from actually touching or receiving anything from his attorney. Since it was an attorney consultation, the officer had earphones on to block any chance of eavesdropping. He didn't miss Jasper's entry though and indicated which seat he was to take. The wired interrogation chair on Baxter's side remained empty.

Baxter looked grim and the hard blue eyes he turned on Jasper held no glint of humor. He was caught and he knew it. Jasper knew it too.

"Are the cameras and recorders off?" he asked the lawyer and the man nodded, tapping a lighted remote in front of him on the table. It showed a steady green to show no electronics were on within ten feet of them.

"Zeb Cummins," the lawyer said. "Attorney for Mr. Baxter."

"Jasper Stone," he replied. "Formerly a police lieutenant in Plains, Wyoming. Currently DEA." He saw Baxter's eyes widen at that admission and felt some satisfaction. Let him sweat it.

It didn't seem to mean anything to the lawyer. Good. If he repeated that to Kucera though it would prove a continued link between Baxter and him. He knew they were grasping at straws now but they needed to.

"My wife knew I was still involved with the police in Plains," Jasper said for Baxter's benefit. "She didn't know I was DEA."

Baxter made no response but his mouth was tight and the hand resting on the table was no longer relaxed. He saw Jasper looking at it though and unclenched his fingers and laid them flat on the table. When he turned his head slightly, Jasper could see that damned earring was still in his ear. Odd. They should have confiscated it.

"What do you want, Stone?" Baxter asked. "Come to gloat? You're a little too quick, I think."

"Possibly," Jasper said, "but I'm required to tell you about another piece of evidence against you. Your lawyer will be officially notified, of course."

The lawyer nodded.

"In the past month, I've been able to trace your movements in and out of Plains back to March and it's interesting that you first started staying in Plains for several days in a row about the time Mike West was installing those fancy new inspection scanners. Did you get a chance to examine one?"

"Inspection scanners?" Baxter replied with a forced smile. "I don't know what you're talking about." He paused. "I remember being in Plains in April and again in July and then there was November. There were Reach Out events. By the way, do you still have that drum? It's a pretty thing."

"I lost it to Jewel," Jasper said. Frowning, he remembered that set of Japanese figures. Jewel would not be pleased to know he had them. Did he ever tell her it was Baxter who got them? He didn't remember. "You still have the seven–six–happy gods?"

"No, I gave those away," Baxter said. "A collector I know." Now he smiled and it was as pleasant as a wolf with his prey in sight but he didn't say anything more.

Impatient, Jasper continued, "besides the travel logs, I have a witness that puts you and Starling together. You were discussing the West family."

Baxter's smile disappeared. "Starling?"

"Samuel Starling," Jasper said. "Not John Starling. Starling, by the way, first visited Plains just before Mike's accident. It was interesting that both of you liked to walk outdoors and you both happened to be outside at the same time."

"Coincidence, I'm sure," Baxter said. "I don't recall the man. I'm sure I saw him on the vid news though."

"You might have heard him mentioned," Jasper said. "But you didn't hear his name. It's interesting that you recognized it though. Very interesting."

The lawyer looked suddenly aware of the trap Baxter had fallen into. Before he could say anything, Jasper went on. "I recall Ed Kucera said in his confession that he introduced Starling to Jake at the request of a mutual friend. I think I'll ask his wife if she knows anything about that."

Baxter didn't flinch. "You do that," he said with a faint smile. "Tell her hello from me."

Jasper's gut tightened. He hadn't been able to get hold of Elaine Kucera or her lawyer. He'd tried all day yesterday but his calls hadn't been returned even with a warning to leave her alone.

"One last thing," he said. "Mary Perkins took euthanasia in Chicago. She left behind vid and written statements naming you as her employer and giving a detailed account of her part in the kidnapping and murders."

Baxter didn't react. "That I'd already heard. Give me something I don't know or get out."

Very well. He really wanted to leave. "Belle Fouche Riesling Special Reserve," he said as he rose to his feet. "The winery is closed."

Baxter's reaction was everything he expected and it filled him with satisfaction to see his shock and anger. Was there fear too? He thought so. Again, there was a possibility of trapping Kucera but he didn't know. If Baxter made any phone calls from the jail that weren't to his lawyer, they were admissible as evidence. They couldn't tap the lawyer's phone because he was protected under the law but they did have taps in place now at the winery. If the lawyer called there to confirm it was closed, they could get an exception to the law by implicating him as an after the fact accessory and tap his calls.

Baxter probably knew all this and the smart thing for him to do would be to sit tight. Jasper hoped he wouldn't be that smart because his connection to the winery hadn't been found yet. The FBI was working with the DEA to discover exactly who was behind the dummy corporation that owned the Belle Fouche winery but the winery and its drug lab had been closed.

It wasn't his concern now. He'd done his best to needle Baxter but now he needed to know where Elaine Kucera was and talk to her. It couldn't wait. That smile on Baxter's face was unsettling. Where was her lawyer? He'd need Jameson.

* * *

The Kucera mansion, like many of the old homes, sat in an above ground district of Denver. Too far from the underground to connect and too far apart for them to have their own underground, the homes boasted multi-car garages, deep basements to escape the heat of the day, and half acre yards given over mostly to trees. From the street side, the Kucera house looked fairly modest with only two floors showing but there was no telling how many floors were below ground.

Jameson used his police codes to bypass the security of the front gate and they proceeded inward, leaving the squad car in front of the attached garage. There were no vehicles in sight but Jasper knew that wasn't unusual. The people who lived in these houses didn't advertise their wealth by leaving vehicles out.

"Front door?" Jasper asked.

"Yes," Jameson said, turning his com unit on to wide record. "You're to hang back. Murphy, this is a wellness check. I need a uniform at that door first."

"Yes sir." The uniformed driver of the squad car stepped up to the porch and hesitated only a second before ringing the bell. Nothing happened. They waited the full ten minutes required by law as the police officer rang the doorbell several times and waited.

"Time," Jameson said. He walked over to the officer. "Wellness check failed?"

"Yes sir," the officer said. "There's no answer at the door. Her number was called?"

"It's been called six times in the past twenty four hours," Jasper said, joining them. "Her lawyer's number as well. No answers. It's gone to voice mail each time."

Jameson frowned. "Mrs. Kucera is the widow of Edward Kucera and may be a material witness in an on-going investigation. It's my opinion we need to check on her well being. I'm authorizing a forced entry of 1313 Ridge Road, Highlands Ranch, Denver, at this time. Officer Murphy, go ahead."

Jasper watched as Murphy clamped a police lock breaker on the front door and set it to work to defeat the electronic lock. It took less than thirty seconds but set the audible alarm inside the house shrieking. Ten seconds later they were in and Murphy was shutting down the alarm. Almost instantly the house phone was ringing and Jameson walked over and answered it.

"Detective Jameson, Badge Number 9136542, at the home of Elaine Kucera. We're performing a wellness check on Mrs. Kucera. Did she notify you she would be out of town?"

Jasper knew she hadn't. One whiff of the house air told him she was here and it was strong—and close. He walked into the front parlor and nearly gagged at the smell but the suited figure on the couch wasn't Elaine Kucera. By the clothes and haircut, it was male but he couldn't tell what the features were. The face was bloated beyond recognition and the corneas were milky white. Fighting his rebellious stomach, he backed away.

"Cause of death?" Jameson asked from a safe distance.

"Throat slit," Jasper said. "More than three days ago, maybe longer." He got himself out to the porch and took a deep breath. It had to be her lawyer. He'd only seen the man once but the hair looked the same. Without fishing for a wallet, he couldn't identify him. It had been too long.

If he was dead, Elaine must be too. There was simply no way Baxter would have let her live after doing that. Was he using her house to hide in? Where were her sons? She had two.

"I've called the coroner and the lab," Jameson said. "We still need to find her though."

"I know," Jasper said. "She had two sons too. I hope to god they weren't here." Could Baxter have killed them all? No, he wouldn't think that. The man had worked for Wilson Kucera and he had confirmed Kucera didn't have family. His brother had been his heir, now his sons were. Other than that, all he knew was they were college age.

Jewel. He opened his com unit and put through the call. She would know. Who else? Dan Mushti, Trace Stephens? Yes, they might. He couldn't see them ignoring Ed's widow.

"Jewel? I'm at the Kucera house. Tell me what you can about Elaine's boys." He listened as his wife hesitated then started talking.

"Two boys," she said. "Rex is in pre-med at University of Colorado. Barry is going to law school at UCLA. What's this about?"

"We don't know yet," Jasper said. "I'll give you a report when I get back." He ended the call. "One of the boys goes to UCLA. He might not be here."

"It's still Thanksgiving break," Jameson said. "Where are those forensics people?" He stepped out into the clear air and Jasper followed. Murphy was back at the squad car and Jasper figured he was getting some remedy for the stomach-turning smell.

The blue forensics van came through the gate followed by the coroner's black van. A third car Jasper didn't know, a white sedan, followed them in to the driveway and people spilled out–two men and a woman.

Jasper stared in disbelief then poked Jameson. She was alive! Elaine Kucera was alive!

Looking much younger in windbreaker and jeans, she strode up the sidewalk and glared at them. "What is this? Why are you breaking into my house?" she demanded. "I want to see your warrant."

"Mrs. Kucera?" Jameson looked just as confused as Jasper felt. "We've been trying to reach you. We thought..."

"You thought wrong," she snapped. "When my lawyer hears of this..."

"Your lawyer is dead," Jasper said. "Inside. We thought you were too. Mrs. Kucera, I have never been happier to be wrong."

"You!" She recognized him then his words registered. "Dead? Frank is dead?" She paled and, stepping back, half fell on to a decorative bench. Her sons rushed up behind her and Jasper watched as Jameson hurriedly explained the situation.

Damn it, Baxter had led him to believe she was dead. Why would he do that? He seemed so smug.

"I was up at Jackson with my boys," Elaine was saying. "We left last Saturday."

"Did your lawyer have entry authorization?" Jameson asked.

"Of course," Elaine said. "Frank was watching the house for me. He told me to leave my com unit behind. He'd call Rex if there were any problems. He's dead? You're sure he's dead?"

One of her sons was holding tightly to her hand and the other seemed uncertain what to do. He finally walked back to where the forensics people were unloading their van.

"We're not absolutely certain it's him," Jameson said. "There is a body and we're assuming it's him at this point–unless someone else had access to the house?"

"Our maid does but she won't come back to work until tomorrow," the young man answered. "Why would anyone kill Frank?"

"I was led to believe your mother was the target," Jasper said. "I'm relieved to find all of you alive." Something was nagging at him. Out of the corner of his eye he saw the forensics van pull back out of the drive, leaving the squad car and coroner's van to one side. The garage door started moving just as Elaine's car edged forward.

The explosion caught them all off guard. Flames shot out from the garage, engulfing the squad car and licking the coroner's van. Jasper flung himself to the ground as Jameson bore Elaine and her son down. Debris flew, one large piece actually hitting Elaine's car but her son hadn't lost his wits. The car was speeding backward and out of the danger zone.

"Where's Murphy?" Jameson said as he jumped to his feet. "Is everyone ok?" He jumped away from the Kuceras and headed for the burning squad car.

Elaine was screaming Barry and Jasper realized it was him driving the car. When she saw him climb out of the sedan, the screaming turned to tears and she clung to her older son. The man looked shaken but competent so Jasper joined the others at the wreckage.

The squad car was a total loss. The forensics team were using a fire extinguisher to put out the flames on the coroner's van but it looked like everyone was accounted for. Murphy was sitting up in some bushes with Jameson checking him over.

Baxter's insurance, Jasper realized. He'd gotten the lawyer but Elaine wasn't home. Did he need to the lawyer to get in the house? Was he using the house to hide out in? He'd been untraceable for nearly a week.

"Who did it?" the younger Kucera was suddenly beside him. "Who wanted us dead?"

"Mark Baxter, I think," Jasper said. "He's in custody but apparently he knew your mother could tell us something—maybe you too. You live here?"

"No," the man said. "That's Rex. I'm Barry. You're Jazz Stone?"

"Yes," Jasper said. "I think we just narrowly avoided disaster. You'd better not stay here tonight. Can you convince your mother to stay in a hotel?"

"After this? Yes. My father didn't do it." His voice was quiet and self-assured. "You're an idiot if you think he did."

"I know," Jasper said. "Help your mother. She needs to see you're in one piece."

The young man walked away and Jasper felt an overwhelming sense of relief. They weren't dead. Baxter—Baxter had failed. He wiped his eyes and reached for his com unit. He needed to tell Jewel.

Chapter 60 - Finale

Jasper poured himself another cup of coffee and refilled Carlson's cup before heading back to the desk. The vid screen was on but was still showing Wilson Kucera's secretary as she attempted to field the call.

"This is Ray Carlson, DEA Agent DEA–C1801RC. Please tell Mr. Kucera we have an update for him."

"Mr. Kucera is not in right now," the secretary repeated but she was starting to look uncertain. "I can schedule this call for a later time."

"We have people there, miss, and we know Wilson Kucera is in the building. I suggest you find him and his lawyer. I'll wait on this line."

The secretary stammered an answer and blanked the screen on her end. Carlson muted his and turned to the others in the office. "Thanks Jazz," he said as he took the coffee. "This may take a while."

"Not too long I hope," Jim Naylor of the FBI said. "Washington wants this resolved."

"So do we," Carlson said. "We have enough to warrant an investigation into Wilson Chemicals but Kucera himself still might not be implicated. The money trail doesn't extend to him and no one can say for certain that Baxter took orders from him."

Jasper sipped his coffee and listened. It had been a long day yesterday and looked to be another long day today but they'd been productive. As soon as Elaine Kucera had recovered her wits and assured herself Barry was unharmed, she had begun talking. After denying her husband's complicity, she had named Baxter as a too frequent visitor to the house and had identified Smith aka Starling as another. Jake West had also visited but not since his grandmother's murder.

Rex had cooperated too, telling the police that he'd been there when Smith was introduced to Jake. Baxter had been too. With their testimony, Baxter's tie to Starling and the subsequent tie to Jake was clearly laid out.

Neither one could implicate Wilson Kucera though. The most damaging thing they had against him is he hired Ed's lawyer and had forbidden Elaine to fire him. The man had kept her from cooperating with the police or making any statements. She hadn't even been allowed to talk to old friends at charity events. It wasn't just Jewel she'd been forced to avoid.

Jasper guessed she wouldn't shed many tears for the man but Elaine Kucera was as good in her own way as her husband had been. Her sons, who had been ready to send him packing, weren't quite so generous. Neither one had known till the skiing trip how badly their mother was worn down by his tactics.

He sipped his coffee, found it near empty, and turned to refill it again. Finding Jameson at the coffee pot, he smiled and held out his cup.

"You're going to have to get some sleep some day," Jameson said. "Four hours and coffee isn't going to do it."

"I know," Jasper said. "Jewel is ready to hog tie me and throw me on a plane." Was it Saturday they were going to go home? Here it was Tuesday and he was no closer. Damn he wanted this case done. If he could just get a breather...

Jameson grinned and refilled his cup. "My wife isn't too happy either. Things just bust loose around you, Sensor Man."

"Don't remind me," Jasper said. Was he really a catalyst? He certainly felt like one.

"Here we go," Carlson said. "Places."

Jasper obeyed, moving out of camera range with Jameson as Wilson Kucera and his lawyer finally appeared. He was their ace but it wasn't time to play him. Kucera needed to be handled first.

This time they seemed to be in a different part of Kucera's office suite. From this angle, he could see a shelving unit in the background and the corner of a bar with a coffee pot visible. There was a conference table in front of the two men but neither was sitting yet.

Wilson Kucera didn't look happy and Jasper wondered if he'd got wind of Baxter's arrest. Certainly there had been enough coverage of him and Jewel. If they had shown the standoff though Baxter's face would have been blurred. The law was very strict these days about releasing the name or image of suspects. Until the trial was over, he'd only be referred to by a state-assigned alias.

That earring though. Did they blur it? Jasper knew Baxter could be identified by it because he'd done it. The man still had it too, since removing it would have required amputation of his ear lobe. Baxter had been tagged by a gang when he was a teen and, when he realized what a mistake that was, he'd had a plain gold disk cold-welded to the gang earring. It couldn't be removed.

"What is this?" Kucera asked. "My secretary said..."

"Please record for your reference," Carlson cut in, his face expressionless.

"Is this official?" Kucera demanded.

"Yes sir. Please record."

Kucera reached for a control then snapped "recording. Now what is this about?"

"Agent Ray Carlson, DEA–C1801RC and my associate is FBI Agent Jim Naylor. This is an information meeting with Mr. Wilson Kucera, CEO of Wilson Chemicals and his legal representative, mister?"

"Stanley Masterson," the lawyer supplied. "Information meeting? This is for Mr. Kucera's information only?"

"At this time, yes," Carlson answered. "We wish to inform him that Mark Baxter, late in his employ, is alive and in custody. Charges of murder, solicitation for murder, conspiracy, drug trafficking, money laundering, kidnapping and attempted murder have so far been filed. Tax evasion charges are also pending."

Kucera studied him, his face expressionless. "Quite a list," he said. "I'm glad the man's been caught."

"You should be," Carlson said. "One of my agents foiled an attempt to murder Elaine, Rex, and Barry Kucera yesterday."

"What?" Kucera's shock was clear. "He wouldn't..." Abruptly he shut up.

"He did," Carlson said. "The family is now safe and Elaine Kucera has been most helpful in providing a connection between Sam Starling, professional assassin, and Baxter. We now know Baxter asked her husband–your brother–to introduce Sam Starling to Jake West."

"That's ridiculous," Kucera said. "Baxter would never involve my brother in something so patently illegal."

"But he did," Carlson said. "It's believed he did more. Jake West thought the text messages he received were from your brother. Many were threats that he would lose his sponsorship from Centrax if he didn't do as he was told–and he was told to kill his grandmother."

Kucera glanced at his lawyer then looked back at them. "And he did it?"

"He tried," Carlson said. "He didn't succeed. Starling finished the job. When Jake was asked to do more, he recorded his confession and put his affairs in order. He believed until he died that your brother was behind it."

"Then he didn't know Ed very well," Kucera said. "Only a fool would think my strait-laced brother would be involved in something so shady."

"Agreed," Carlson said, "but Baxter worked him like a pro. We'll want to examine his correspondence and employment records to see if he's done it before."

"Employment records?" Kucera looked blank but it was his lawyer that answered.

"We'll cooperate with any warrants, gentlemen," he said. "So long as it is clearly stated you are investigating Mark Baxter and not the company or other individuals in the company. You understand?"

"Of course," Carlson said. "We're simply interested in Mark Baxter, although he may have done damage to your company that hasn't come to light yet. We know, for instance, that he was working with a former lab chief of yours named Miguel Rodriguez-Gomez."

"Miguel?" Wilson Kucera looked surprised. "He's been missing and presumed dead for over twenty years. Where is he?"

"In custody," Carlson said. "We found him manufacturing blissex inside a winery. You knew nothing about it?"

"Of course not," Wilson snapped. "A winery? That's hardly sanitary. The FDA would be all over us if they knew."

"They know now," Carlson said. "It seems you didn't know what your vice president was doing."

"I knew what he was doing for *me*," Kucera snapped. "What he did on his own time was none of my business–or so I thought." He sat down finally. "Damn him. If he got Ed killed–how the hell did my brother die anyway? He was in police custody."

"Your brother was taking a classified drug called blister that reacts with bliss. He committed suicide by taking bliss. What his reasons were, we don't know but there was no coercion. If his lawyer didn't make that vid available to you, I will," the FBI agent responded.

"I was told about Nugent and I have the vid," Wilson said. "Do you have anything new there?"

"Andrew Nugent was questioned," Carlson said. "Baxter did it and killed him in the process. After that he kidnapped Jewel West and questioned her. He then attempted to blackmail Jasper Stone into digging out the answers for him."

Kucera stared at him for a long moment then leaned forward. "Stone told me some of this but I still don't believe it. Tell Stone I want to talk to him—his wife too. If they know anything more about my brother's death, I want to know it."

"Agreed," Carlson said. "His wife will have to wait but here's Stone."

Jasper moved into camera range at a motion from Carlson. The shock on Kucera's face was classic and Jasper noted it with satisfaction. His eyes slid to the lawyer and he looked just as dumbfounded as he stood in front of a shelving unit of oriental artifacts.

"Good afternoon, Mr. Kucera," Jasper said. "I'm willing to talk to you again. You may recall our previous conversation."

Kucera recovered quickly. "I recall being threatened if I told Baxter your whereabouts. Are you satisfied I didn't?"

"Yes, I'm satisfied," Jasper said, "and I can tell you now that Mary Perkins is dead. We're only concerned with Baxter." He glanced at the shelves, thinking something looked familiar.

"You know Baxter was trying to solve the death of my brother by questioning your wife? How? Did he use force or drugs?" Kucera demanded.

"Drugs. My wife doesn't consciously remember it," Jasper said. "Mary Perkins left a list of the questions Baxter asked and some of her own. His were about blister and what she knew about the blissex smuggling in Plains—and two questions about her uncle and more about me. He didn't ask about the West murders but Perkins did. Apparently she was looking for proof that her brothers murdered for a living. Once she had it, she was done."

"Her brothers?" Kucera demanded. "She was related to assassins?"

"Yes," Jasper said. "She never meant to be one herself but Baxter threatened her son. Once she had him safe, she left Baxter high and dry." He'd read her account and was trying hard not to blame her for what she did. She wasn't involved in Lori's death. "Jewel was questioned using Penseek."

"I gathered that. Why did Baxter think you had answers?" Kucera questioned. "Or your wife."

"I was the lead investigator into the West murders," Jasper said. "He must have feared I'd found something that wasn't made public. I had but didn't know enough to tell him anything. There's enough now to prove he planned it and ordered the murders."

"Yes, yes but what about my brother? How did he get blister and why did he commit suicide? He could have just waited until he was cleared. My brother was a lawyer. He knew the game."

"That I can't tell you," Jasper said. "He had his reasons, I'm sure. His wife and sons are also mystified but relieved his name will be cleared. That's all we can give him."

"Damn it, it's not enough," Kucera said in a burst of anger. "I want to know why!"

Jasper didn't answer. Breaking eye contact, he looked again at the shelves and abruptly recognized the Seven Lucky Gods. Those were Jewel's figurines–the ones Baxter had bought at the auction. They stood among other oriental artifacts but were arranged in almost the same order Jewel's grandmother had kept them in. Baxter had given them to him?

He tore his gaze away from the seven figures and looked again at Kucera. "I can't tell you anything about his motives or how he got blister. CIA is investigating how that happened since that drug was created for them. You should get a report if you still own the factory."

"Of course I own the factory," Kucera said.

"Have you been there in recent years?" Jasper asked, playing for time. There was something about those seven figures.

"Not in a dozen years," Kucera said. "I have vice presidents who check the factories when they need it." He stopped, his jaw setting. "I'm going to have to change that. I should never have detailed that."

"No sir, you shouldn't have," Jasper agreed, his eyes straying to the shelf again. His pulse quickened as he saw it and his mouth went dry. It was there. Damn it, it was there. "Mr. Kucera, I'm willing to talk with you again at a later date but I think we've taken enough of the agents' time. Will you agree to that?"

Kucera frowned then nodded. "Yes but I want to talk to your wife too. I'm not satisfied as to how my brother died."

"I'll arrange it," Jasper said. "Are we done for now?" He sorely wanted to end the call but he didn't want to make Kucera suspicious. It was there in plain sight. Could it be he didn't know?

"I'm done," Kucera said. "I'll wait for the warrants to examine Baxter's doings here. I assume they'll be coming soon?" He looked at Carlson and the FBI agent.

"Very soon," Carlson said. "Expect them."

"Fine," Kucera said and broke the connection.

Jasper severed the connection as well, turning at once to Carlson. "Do you still need a reason to hold him for questioning? It's right there in his office."

"What do you mean?" Carlson asked.

Jasper was already looking through his com unit, desperate to find the one picture he needed–an insurance photo. He found it and threw it up on the screen. The tall-headed figure of Fukurokuju, the god of happiness, looked out at them, his ebony figure serene.

"What's that?" Carlson asked.

"That," Jasper said in a tight voice, "was the club used to kill Elizabeth West and it's sitting there in Wilson Kucera's office. You want a reason to detain him? There it is."

"You've got to be kidding," Naylor said in stunned disbelief. "The murder weapon? How could he get it?"

"Baxter," Jasper said. "He bought the rest of the set at a Reach Out event then gave it to his boss. It wasn't complete but it is now. You've got possession of the murder weapon at least."

"That won't hold up," Jameson said but he was grinning. "Not for long."

"Long enough," Carlson said. "Let's redo those warrants. I want Kucera too."

Jasper knew they were grasping at straws but it was something. Kucera might be cleared but at least they would know once and for all if he was guilty—and blissex would be stopped.

He grinned. He could go home. They would need him later for the trial but he wouldn't be needed here and now. He could take his wife home—home to his music and the future. He was free.

THE END

ABOUT THE AUTHOR

Ellen Anthony ran away from Wyoming in 2020, traveling through ten states and 5400 miles before the pandemic made her stop. Her characters tracked her down and continue to keep her life interesting in an undisclosed location. To find out more about the Jasper Stone series, the Syran series, and Letters Through Time, visit her author pages on Facebook (The Jasper Stone Mysteries). Your thoughts and reviews are deeply appreciated.

OTHER BOOKS BY ELLEN ANTHONY

THE JASPER STONE SERIES

Murder is Bliss (2013) – Police Lieutenant Jasper Stone is called on to solve the most high-profile case of his career when Elizabeth West is murdered. The suspects include her sons, her grandson, her granddaughter and a family friend. When one son is murdered the same day, Jasper finds himself trying to protect Jewel West as he unravels the case. To complicate matters, his secret life as a popular composer of sensa has now come out and he must dodge reporters while he does his job.

To Marry and Suspect (2013) – Former Police Lieutenant Jasper Stone a.k.a. Sensor Man marries his Jewel in a high society wedding. Afterward Jewel is implicated in her family murders then kidnapped. Jasper must cooperate with the kidnappers to get her back and re-investigate the West murders and the blissex drug ring that now seem to be connected.

Coral Crosses (2014) – A date with an orchestra in Coral Ridge, Florida turns into a plot to bomb the underwater resort city. Jasper doesn't believe for one moment the terrorists have a hydrogen bomb but when his bodyguard and another federal agent are ambushed, he's drawn into the investigation wife and all. Why are the terrorists trying to stop the Ogaden/Somaliland conference? And who is that woman stalking him?

Between Heaven and Hell (2014) – A small investigation into Hades Syndrome unexpectedly blows up into kidnappings and murder. Jasper takes his wife and youngest son to Paradise Station to protect them then finds himself on a space-age ranch in Wyoming where they are tracked by one of the villain's lackeys. Meanwhile Kale Tunis is doing his part in rescuing one of Jewel's employees and following clues that lead him to Puerto Rico. When he joins forces with Jasper Stone, they go after a man who might be responsible for thousands of deaths from Hades—including Jasper's first wife.

Shadow Mars (2015) – Dick Mason, space cowboy and Jewel's cousin from Between, goes to Mars with two missions—protect Sasha West and uncover an illegal gold mine. When he is deliberately infected with a flu virus and inadvertently takes it straight to Sasha's boys, he falls under suspicion and now must prove his innocence as well. Sasha West won't have anything to do with a man who thinks he's cock-of-the-walk and God's gift to women but he has his orders. The hard part is not falling for the magnificent widow of Jake West.

Shadow Earth (2015) – When a space plane gets crashed by a virus, Jasper finds himself embroiled in two new investigations this time for the West Foundation. Will he uncover the source of the viruses that have plagued the Mars ships? Can he prove Kale isn't guilty of rape? And what is it with all those balls?

Webs of Deceit (2016) – Kale Tunis is sent to Africa to investigate a possible genocide while Jasper concentrates on finding out the manufacturer of the gas used. Angel Damask returns with conflicting orders. This time the CIA agent is legally investigating the West Foundation and their mission in Africa—and trying not to cross paths with Kale who knows exactly who she is.

Rebel Circuits (2020) "We will get her back." When 15-year-old Anita Spears is abducted from the West Foundation complex in Houston, Jasper Stone makes that promise to his employees and their families. He never dreamed Anita was not alone. As the case balloons, Jasper finds himself embroiled in illegal experimentation, artificial intelligence, and secrets the Foundation has kept for more than a century.

For the Future (2021) An explosion heralds a package from the future and thrusts David Wilson among the leaders of the West Foundation. Can they believe what it says and can they set the Foundation on a path to guard Earth's future? It all rests on Wilson and a child not yet born.

Light & Shadows (2023) When a simple stock manipulation case blows up, Herb Jordan gets embroiled in bribery, illegal arms sales, and a found missile. Who is his mysterious client? Who wants him dead? And how does the West Foundation fit in?

Shipwreck! (pending) Jasper Stone is back! His return trip from Mars turns into a nightmare and he must depend on his sons for rescue.

The Future Comes (pending) Events predicted in 2090 finally happen. Will the West Foundation find a way to save humanity? Or will they lose Earth?

THE SYRAN SERIES

The Manhunter (1999) Eppie Award Finalist. On a world where a woman can hunt a man. Imagine being able to claim any man for three days just to have a child. He could be an Einstein, an athlete, or the guy next door. What woman hasn't had that fantasy? Yet what happens if the man you choose loves you? Can you walk away with just the child? Can he? Synda of Datyl wants to do a Manhunt and Davyd Yorkson is hired to escort her. What they are separated from their ship, Davyd finds he must protect his charge from bees, wild pigs, raiders, and even himself. His greatest challenge comes when Synda chooses him for the Manhunt and he must accept—or lose her forever.

Search for the Sun (2000) 2001 Eppie Award Winner for Best Mystery. The princess is dead, murdered in a crime that rocks Gardon, and only her infant son is left alive. Who did it—the General, the Healer, or the Prime Minister? And why? Donal Yorkson and his veteran partner try to untangle the wicked crime only to find no motive and a preposterous list of suspects. When his partner turns up dead, Donal must defy his father and even his queen to uncover a crime more terrible than murder.

Too Young a King (2001) Eppie Award finalist. The king is dead! Long live the king! But this king is just ten years old and faces assassination attempts and treachery while his prime minister tries to keep him alive. To complicate things, not one but two old foes are suddenly offering alliances. It's known that the Eagle practices slavery but they offer trade. The Dawn is an unknown. Can Edwin of the Wolf survive his turbulent youth? Or does the prophecy speak of the baby brother still at his mother's breast? And who arranged the deaths of his other brothers?

The Blood Circle (originally 2003, new edition 2013) Eppie Award finalist. On planet Syra a circle written in blood and death draws tighter around the city-states of Sefron and Datyl. Assassins who can be anywhere or anyone—even a young flower girl—have the leaders of both cities worried. How can they destroy assassins when they have no clue as to where they come from? When his beloved master and mistress are murdered by the Blood Circle guardsman Mason Baronson vows vengeance on those responsible. He guards Lord Valon Padrason while the Sunlord investigates suspicious deaths in both cities. Valon is forced into the limelight of the court as he investigates. He doesn't know his greatest ally will be one of those the Circle has raised from birth.

THE LETTERS THROUGH TIME SERIES

Lura's Oregon Trail Adventure (2002) Eppie Award finalist 10-year-old Lura Harding is traveling the Oregon Trail in 1850. Read her letters as she tells about her family, her life, and her love for reading. Follow along as the Harding family faces disease, treacherous river crossings, and Indians. Can Lura survive the trail? Will her six-year-old sister get caught stealing candy? And what will they do when her uncle decides to leave the train? These fictional letters are historically accurate and reflect the living conditions, slang, and attitudes of the 1850s.

Jacob's Oregon Trail Adventure (2002) 14-year-old Jacob Harding is traveling the Oregon Trail in 1850. Read his letters as he tells about why they're going, what they hope to find, and what he wants. Follow along as the Harding family faces disease, treacherous river crossings, and Indians. Share Jacob's secrets about his girlfriend, a runaway slave, and his sister's birthday surprise. These fictional letters are historically accurate and reflect the living conditions, slang, and attitudes of the 1850s.

Mr. Harding's Oregon Trail Adventure (2018) The father of Lura and Jacob tells his own version of traveling the Oregon Trail in 1850. Read his letters for the adult side of the story. What did he know that his children never noticed? What did he really think of Jacob's girlfriend or that colored family he befriended? Get a more complete picture with his tale.